A PEOPLE BETRAYED

A People Betrayed

November 1918: A German Revolution

A Novel by

Alfred Döblin

Translated from the German by
John E. Woods

FROMM INTERNATIONAL PUBLISHING CORPORATION
NEW YORK, NEW YORK

Translation copyright © 1983 Fromm International
Publishing Corporation, New York

Originally published as
Verratenes Volk and *Heimkehr der Fronttruppen*
Copyright 1948/49, Verlag Karl Alber, München
Copyright © 1978, Walter Verlag AG, Olten

Printed in the United States of America

First U.S. Edition

Library of Congress Cataloging in Publication Data

Döblin, Alfred, 1858–1957
A people betrayed.
(November 1918)

Translation of Verratenes Volk and Heimkehr der Fronttruppen,
the first 2 parts of the author's trilogy, November 1918.
1. Berlin (Germany)—History—1918–1945—Fiction.
I. Döblin, Alfred, 1858–1957. Heimkehr der Fronttruppen.
English. 1983. II. Title. III. Series: Döblin,
Alfred, 1858–1957. November 1918. English.

PT2607.035V413 1983   833'.912   82-25133
ISBN 0-88064-007-3
ISBN 0-88064-008-1 (pbk.)

GÜNTER GRASS ON
ALFRED DÖBLIN

When people speak of Alfred Döblin nowadays, they normally speak of *Berlin Alexanderplatz*. There are reasons why recognition for a writer—whom I am prepared to compare and contrast with Thomas Mann, to compare and contrast with Bertolt Brecht—should be reduced exclusively to this one book. The work of a Thomas Mann, and even more so the work of a Bertolt Brecht, was consciously adapted to a classical plan shaped by its author and executed to the last detail. Both writers hewed and set stone upon stone on a clearly marked foundation, with obvious references to the classical tradition they sought to continue. And even when Brecht tried to subvert such a concept with a work like *The Punitive Measures,* he gave up soon enough, making things easier for his interpreters when they later tried to smooth over this explosive phase of his work.

The secondary literature dealing with either of these authors bursts bookcases. Soon Brecht, like Kafka, will be interpreted away until he is no longer ours. Döblin was spared such an abduction to Olympian fields. This anticlassicist has never had a devoted cult of followers, not even a cult of enemies. Generations grew up with Thomas Mann, familiar with every quirk of his style. The term "Kafkaesque" rolls off our tongues the moment we have difficulties with bureaucrats. And our Brechtomaniacs are recognizable by the way they toss participles about. Only Alfred Döblin has provided no impetus for symposia; only he has seldom engaged the industry of our Germanists, has seduced few readers.

I would like to be permitted to set Mann, Brecht and Kafka respectfully aside, though fully conscious of their awesome and frequently touted stature, and to express something of the gratitude a pupil feels toward his teacher. For I am greatly indebted to Alfred Döblin; what is more, I could not begin to imagine my own prose without the futuristic component in his work from *Wang-Lun* on through *Wallenstein* and

Mountains, Sea and Giants and *Berlin Alexanderplatz*. In other words: writers do not simply appear out of the blue, they have their forebearers.

I never saw him, but this is how I picture him: small, nervous, volatile, nearsighted and as a result pressed in all too close to reality; a stenographic visionary, who is so overwhelmed by imaginative ideas that he has no time left to construct his prose periods carefully. From book to book he begins anew, contradicting himself and his continually changing theories. Manifestos, essays, books, thoughts dog each others' footsteps.

This much is certain: Döblin knew that a book must be more than its author, that the author is only a means to the goal of a book, and that an author must learn to find hiding places, which he can then leave to speak his manifestos, but which he must first search out in order to have a place to flee from his own book. Döblin proposes: "The subject of a novel is reality unchained, reality that confronts the reader completely independent of some firmly fixed course of events. It is the reader's task to judge, not the author's! To speak of a novel is to speak of layering, of piling in heaps, of wallowing, of pushing and shoving. A drama is about its poor plot, its desperately ever-present plot. In drama it is always 'forward!' But 'forward' is never the slogan of a novel."

He was an emancipated Jew, a Kierkegaardian Catholic, a firmly rooted Berliner who for a long time took his journeys only via a map of the world—until Hitler seized power and set him into motion, into emigration against his will. Döblin has never set quite right. He was too Catholic for the progressive left, too anarchistic for the Catholics; he lacked the firm theses so necessary for moralists. He was too inelegant for cultural television programs, too vulgar for educational radio.

Döblin's net worth has not as yet been fully evaluated. But one of his followers and students has converted a bit of his inheritance into fame, and it is for that reason that I am trying to repay him today with a few small coins. [It is my hope that] this testimonial . . . can at least contribute toward arousing your curiosity, toward enticing you to Döblin so that he may be read. He will unsettle you; he will trouble your dreams; you will have difficulty swallowing him; you will find him unsavory; he is indigestible, gristly. He changes his readers. The self-complacent are hereby cautioned against Döblin.

Contents

Part II — The Troops Return

Part I

A PEOPLE BETRAYED

Book One

November 22nd and 23rd

It is difficult to build a republic from the debris of a demolished monarchy.
It won't work until every stone has been hewn into a new shape, and that takes
time.

George Christoph Lichtenberg

Attack on Police Headquarters

A young man returns from war, finds nothing appealing about living in Berlin and meets others who feel the same. Some overwrought people attack police headquarters and find they can sleep better afterward. It is November 22, 1918.

Berlin was a proliferation of buildings sprawling low and somber across the sand of Mark Brandenburg. A shabby excuse for a stream, the Spree, flowed between them. The little river took on an iridescent black from the sewage emptied into it, buildings turned their backs on it, sheds and coalyards lined its banks. In the Hansa district near the zoo the world surrounding its murky, proletarian waters opened up somewhat, and it caught a glimpse of trees and boats and was glad to leave behind the heaps of stone that were the source of the refuse. But for some distance out onto the plain the poor river was hemmed in again by industry, by complexes as big as cities, where still more men and women toiled inside.

The city of Berlin spread out across sand that long ages before had lain at the bottom of the sea. Where fish once swam, men lived now, and in such numbers and on such poor soil that the majority of them were in want, barely eking out their lives by drudgery. To the north, south and east of the city, in a great circumferential band, stood factories erected to supply distant cities and countries. Many of them had been built during the war—the one that had lasted from 1914 to 1918 and now was lost— and many others had been converted to war production. But the war was over. What was to be done with the factories? Neither their owners nor the city had the money to convert them to peacetime production. There were eager buyers, but none who could pay while trade with the outside world was closed off.

So strikes broke out. The hatred of the workers for their employers exploded. There was an immediate danger that they would occupy the factories.

People returning from the war thronged into the eastern and northern sections of the city, a continuous stream as demobilization continued in full swing. There was a dreadful housing shortage. Whoever wanted a place to live had to put down hundreds of marks—they called it key money.

In the west, where riches and luxury resided, the splendid and exclusive shops were open, of course. But the suits of clothes, the shoes and the hats in these shops were very expensive, and their elegance was deceptive. The suits were made of wartime cloth that frayed quickly, just as the paper used for newspapers and books turned yellow in no time at all.

The streets and squares had lost much of their evening brilliance. In order to save coal only every third streetlamp was lit. An uncertain half-light spread like fear over much of the city, as if in expectation of a bombing attack.

During those November days, when the darkness of defeat and collapse settled down over the teeming city, many of its citizens sensed the oncoming doom, the approaching danger. And just as during the war notices would multiply on village walls and barns reading "Warning! Cholera!" or "Danger! Typhoid Fever!", so now more and more houses and villas boasted signs: "Six-room apartment, eight-room apartment, ten-room apartment, with garden, balcony, fully furnished, unfurnished, available a single unit, can be divided, for rent, for sale." The greasy divinities to which war had given birth had already moved into many of these villas and apartments. These august powers with the heads of vultures fed on the new human miseries—they were the speculators and their hangers-on.

On this Friday, November 22nd, a former lieutenant, Maus by name, wanders listlessly about the streets of Berlin. His father, a legation lawyer of the old school, interrogates him daily about his heroic exploits so he can then boast of them at the office. His mother is no better. For six months he lay in a military hospital in Alsace; his left shoulder is still stiff and not fully healed. He was sent home via Naumburg, and now here he is with no more sense of what to do with himself in the city than the tens of thousands of others still trooping in. Each evening these idle hordes are sucked up like a thin layer of sludge into their houses, where they remain invisible for the night. But in the morning some gigantic hose sprays them back out onto the streets, where they trickle about for hours on end.

With his youthful, rosy-cheeked face, Maus is an unprepossessing, amiable fellow who hasn't accomplished much in life as yet. He has powerful limbs ready to spring into action, his gray-blue eyes have a look of candor. He no longer has his hopes set on a career, he only wants to know whether he is of any use in this world.

In what was once the Café Luna on the Kurfürstendamm, a temporary office has been set up "for discharging members of the military."

Maus ends up there around noon. Someone in the crowd taps him on the back and sticks his head over his shoulder. It is Karl Ding, nicknamed Big Ding, a former pal from his school and university days. A volunteer in the war, Ding doesn't know what to do now either. Like Maus, he is just looking the place over. They shake hands. Maus is thinking, so he's still alive too. Big Ding smiles his winning smile while eyeing him from top to bottom, a gentle kangaroo. But Maus sees nothing to smile about, and the others look downcast as well. It's like a funeral home in here, he thinks, and the man about to be buried left a lot of debts behind. Big Ding steps on Maus's foot and whispers, "If you think you'll find out anything here, you're crazy."

Ding is here only because there is no heat at home. None here either, for that matter, but at least you move about and there are lots of people. The two of them shove their way back out.

Ding slips his hand in under Maus's right arm. He eyes him a bit, then suddenly asks, "What are you doing anyway, Maus? What's happening with you?"

Maus tells him not to bother him with such questions. Ding is surprised but not offended. So now I've got this fellow hanging onto me, Maus thinks. The tall, friendly figure trots along beside him, babbling away about having been a gunner, until they reach Uhlandstrasse. At the streetcar stop, a grave young woman is standing across from them. Not a bad looker, thinks Maus, even though she does wear wirerimmed glasses. She spots Ding and rushes over to him. They embrace and kiss. Maus assumes she is his sister and that he hasn't seen her since he was called up. But his big friend presents the young lady to him—blissfully, as if giving him a present—as Grete Gries, his fiancée, whom he last saw yesterday evening. They cannot seem to contain their joy that the painful separation has come to an end.

Maus tips his hat and starts to leave them. But he has not reckoned with Big Ding, who is so full of happiness that he has to share it. The tall fellow whispers something to his girl, then she carefully links herself onto Maus's injured left arm while Ding takes his right. And so the downcast soldier is escorted off by the young engaged couple. He has to march off with them, although he had planned to wend his gloomy way alone today as always.

They lead him back to his own apartment, in the expectation, admitted with beaming smiles, that it will be heated. Maus takes no offense at that. He has nothing against sitting at home with Big Ding and his heartthrob and killing an hour or so.

There was indeed heat at his place. His mother was sleeping, so they were spared her astonishment and sympathy. The two guests began to take off their coats and look about the apartment. They then proceeded to outdo each other with proofs of their insatiable affection. At last they made themselves comfortable in the two armchairs in Maus's room and there they sat locked in an embrace as if since time began. Maus let them be, growing more and more indifferent. He had to content himself with a simple cane-bottomed chair.

Suddenly they were ready to talk. The young woman chose to inquire about his shoulder and his pension. "How much do you get actually out of having a stiff shoulder?"

He replied, somewhat vaguely, that the case was still pending, pensions were based on the degree of stiffness. She asked whether he had done manual labor before the war. No, he had intended to become an officer, but that of course was impossible now, on account of his arm and everything else.

"And so you're doing the same thing as everybody else," his interrogator concluded. "You walk around in a rotten mood, communicating your rotten mood to others and waiting."

Maus shrugged.

"It's my guess," Big Ding proclaimed, "that you'll be walking around like for some time to come."

"That's my guess too," Fräulein Gries concurred, gravely and with no sign of sympathy. "More and more people keep coming. The whole front-line army is expected the beginning of December."

"Some things will change then," Maus said hopefully.

The girl agreed. "Sure, then the whole army will stand around on the Kurfürstendamm, in Tempelhof, along General Pape–Strasse, and wherever they are they'll all get handed an unemployment card and someone will stamp it nice and pretty for them."

"There's going to be an awful mob of them," Big Ding grumbled. "And how are things going to change, what's going to change them? The rich gentlemen will get themselves in gear and load up their cars with the charming missus and the brats and a satchel of money and drive to Switzerland, where there's not a breeze stirring. Then we'll be left here to ourselves, and can sit around counting our buttons while we wait for somebody to pay war reparations."

The girl added, "They'll be high, too."

Big Ding summed it all up nicely: "There's simply no way out. It can't go on like this. Wherever you look the road is blocked."

Maus looked irritably at them both. They were sitting in *his* room in *his* armchairs. Why had they come here really? Just to sit here with him? He would have been better off alone.

The girl began to speak again, having exchanged glances with Ding. She suddenly adopted another tone. "There is a solution, Herr Maus."

And strangely enough, the moment she began, his anger abated. She and Big Ding were no longer a bothersome pair of lovers. Suddenly he saw the gloomy earnestness that weighed them both down, the same earnestness that all their suffering comrades out there on the street carried about, not knowing where to go or what to do.

He was listening to the voice of someone who had the same troubles as he, the voice of Fräulein Gries, saying, "We can't expect bread and a job to suddenly fall from the sky. No one is going to take care of us. Everybody wants to avoid responsibility. People are grateful to have any job at all. Just try knocking on employment office doors. They don't have any answers, for there's no money. They tell you to go here or go there just to get rid of you. We're going to have to take our affairs into our own hands."

Maus listened, and it seemed to him as if he were hearing it for the first time. He pricked up his ears. "That's easy enough said, but how?"

"How?" the girl repeated with solemn emphasis, placing an elbow on one knee and propping her head up. "You'll have a hard time figuring it out."

She's a smart, serious-minded girl, Maus thought, as he gazed at the smooth blond crown of her head. That's a cheap wool dress she's wearing, maybe it's not even wool.

"How do you think you're ever going to come up with an answer anyway, Herr Maus? I mean you men in general. You didn't have to when we were at peace, and in war you had to obey orders. But as I told Karl, you're back home now, and you don't have any choice but to pull your wits together. Just don't start in with your stories about military heroics. Look at where that's got you. — You must excuse me, Herr Maus, for speaking so frankly."

"You mean because of my shoulder? Nonsense."

But the shoulder really was quite sore, all this running around was not doing it any good.

"All the things Karl was telling me only three months ago about what Germany would be like after you were victorious—and you were bound to be victorious. I believed it. Why lie about it? But I had already noticed the deception before that, Herr Maus. The deception—do you know anything about that?"

Maus had the feeling of being a little boy in school. "What do you mean by deception?"

Fräulein Gries: "Have you ever listened to Liebknecht?"

Maus: "No, thank God. I don't give a damn about the revolution."

He could see before him the wretched band of warriors that tried to approach the hospital train as he was returning from Alsace, honest fellows standing in formation and carrying a red flag. His friend Becker had been standing propped on his canes next to him, both of them amazed that this is what called itself a revolution.

And as the girl continued, Maus heard his friend Becker speaking, in the train, the night they pulled out.

9

"Night. The night's coming, and now there's peace, sweet peace. We'll never let them snatch that away from us."

What dreams and hopes they had had during those days. And ah, how Maus had dreamed of Hilda, too, who had not written, but whom Maus could not wrench from his heart—Hilda, his nurse in the hospital. She hadn't written. So she hadn't forgiven him for that last day as they were leaving and in the turmoil of saying good-bye, when he had grabbed her savagely, just like an animal, and possessed her. She hadn't written, this woman he loved. That was the worst thing. It was enough to make you go crazy. He lay in a deep, black well.

The girl opened her purse and pulled out a small book. She spoke softly. Maus suddenly paid attention because her voice was trembling.

"You must listen to me, Herr Maus. You have to know what it was like for us. How they kept us going through the war. They smothered us in lies. If you did something that made them suspicious, asked a question without stopping to think, you would be watched, as though Germany were enemy territory. And who were they doing it for? For you, for the soldiers out there? No, for the Kaiser and his generals. They wanted their own war, their own victories. And we civilians were to hand over our brothers, husbands and sons, but otherwise hold our peace. They didn't even let us know what was happening out there. They always acted as if it were some sacred rite, some abstract science that we wouldn't understand anything about anyway. They only wanted to make sure no one saw through their game. And then they lost everything. Including us and our future. And that's why we're running around like this."

That's amazing, thought Maus. That simply can't be true. We fought a proper war and we lost it.

The girl held up her little book. "Take a look at this pamphlet. I'm a grade-school teacher. They gave this to us and made us read to the children from it. The little things sat there in their threadbare clothes, with empty bellies, hollow eyes and pale faces, victims of the blockade. But the fat generals, the whole General Staff all covered with medals, were perched on the frail shoulders of those children, and it was from up there that they fought their war. So that the children would hold up the generals, and do it willingly, we had to tell them stories like these. You only have to look at the cover. Look! 'Germans! Demand German products. German cognac; Hindenburg—a German Liqueur. His Excellency, Field Marshal General Hindenburg has given special permission for the use of the name Hindenburg.' And then come the stories: 'Hindenburg in the Life of a Child.' In front of the Victory Column stands a great wooden statue of Hindenburg. An angel descends from heaven and hammers a nail into it. And there's a poem to go along with it. 'From out of heaven's vaulted blue an angel came one summer night, and in his right hand as he flew he bore a starry nail of light.' We had to read that aloud."

"Stop!" shouted Big Ding. "I can't stand it, Grete."

But she went on talking softly, holding up her pamphlet. "German intellectuals had a hand in this beastly trash, Herr Maus. I love the works of German literature as before, but I have lost all trust in our intellectuals."

Something wrenched inside Maus. What is all this? It has nothing to do with me. She's supposed to be telling me where we go from here. The woman's chatter kindled a sullen anger in him, one that swallowed up his memory of Becker sobbing there inside the train car as they rolled along. Peace. Sweet peace. He looked over at Big Ding. "So what are you doing about it, Karl?"

He wrinkled his brow and raised both his fists. "I'm on the side of the revolution."

The girl: "Do you know any other way out? Who is going to mete out punishment, clear away the garbage, set the people straight, put things in order? The government we have now can't do it. Doesn't even want to."

Big Ding had stood up and was flailing his arms. He began quoting: "The Hohenzollerns had hoped to march victoriously through the Brandenburg Gate at war's end; instead, it is the proletariat that is marching. All the thrones of Germany have toppled. The princes, the generals, the petty junkers, the mass murderers have all crept back into their rat holes."

The girl: "Liebknecht said that."

Once more Becker's words sounded in Maus's ears: "Night. The night. Peace is coming now. I'm glad we've lived to see this."

Maus's sullen anger. He whispered, "Those of us at the front did what we could. We're not to blame if other people acted like that back home."

And his shoulder hurt him. He thought of Richard, the pilot who lay dying in the hospital room next to his, and of Hilda, so distant now. Suddenly he had tears in his eyes, for the whole wretched mess, and because everyone in the whole world deserted you.

The young teacher watched his face grow pale, his lips quiver. She came over to him and took his hand. There. She stroked his hand as he let his head sink down onto his chest.

A canary was singing in the next room. That made the pain all the worse for poor Maus. He pulled his hand away.

And then suddenly everything reversed itself inside him. A decision crashed through Maus like lightning: I'm through with this whole rotten business.

And without paying attention to his two guests he rushed over to

11

the bureau behind the armchairs, with the same rapid movements he always made when fetching his belt and holster from their drawer. The mirror cast his image back at him, the grim face, and he said in a hoarse voice as he threw the hair out of his face with a toss of his head. "All right, let's go. What's it to be? I'm at your service. It won't be because I didn't do my part."

While they got ready to leave, he went back to the bureau once more. He bent down, pulled out the bottom drawer and crammed his revolver into its holster. Out on the street beside the two of them, his revolver in its holster in his hand, he felt good. For the first time since he had been back in Berlin he felt good. Actually he had only just now arrived, back from the battlefield. He recognized everything now, the streets, the buildings, the shops. It was Berlin, but dreadfully gone to seed.

Attack on Police Headquarters

Fräulein Gries and Big Ding took the former lieutenant Maus to a strange assembly at Gesundbrunnen. It was evening, raining and windy, as they rode out there.

The hall was packed. Up on the podium several men were sitting next to the chairman and the evening's speaker. They constantly hid their faces with their hands. Word was that the authorities were after them. After all sorts of discussions and tirades about the "intrigues" of Messrs. Ebert and Scheidemann, who claimed to be "Social Democrats," the speaker, who claimed to belong to no party, broke off suddenly in mid speech. The mysterious men who had been hiding their faces disappeared toward the back. The chairman announced that there would have to be a brief pause, and he disappeared as well. After considerable time had passed, the chairman returned along with a simple soldier, and took up a position at the large table where the lonely speaker who had been interrupted was still seated.

In the meantime there had been significant changes inside the hall, as if something of those hushed conversations up on the stage had seeped out into it. People were standing now for the most part. Benches had been shoved together to make more room. People bunched up in front of the stage. There were cries of "Treason!"

The chairman rang his bell from up on stage. He called for quiet, but none ensued. It only grew still when he stopped shouting and the soldier next to him stood up.

Short and to the point, and in an East Prussian accent, the man announced, "There are political prisoners jailed at police headquarters. All the cells were not opened on the 9th and 10th of November. There are still quite a number of old prisoners there—and new ones, too. New political prisoners."

Incredible uproar. Shouts. "To headquarters!" "Free the prisoners!"

In an instant the doors to the hall were thrown open. The crowd surged out. People clambered over benches, shouted, made wild threats.

Everything was possible during that period. The crowd was not mistaken. Just as people were being shot accidentally, so troublesome ones could simply be jailed somewhere or other. One was defenseless against such actions. And since there was no established order one had to create order oneself. And standing there massed together the mob was thrown back into a primal political state; it was both lawmaker and judge.

The rallying cry, "Political prisoners at police headquarters!" was heard in other gatherings as well. Late that evening of November 22nd, closed ranks of men appeared on the streets in the north of the city, this dark, dismal, defeated Berlin, this torso whose vital organs were contracted with spasms, and they moved along Brunnenstrasse, Rosenthaler-Strasse, Münzstrasse in the direction of Alexanderplatz.

Former lieutenant Maus felt quite odd at finding himself in this throng marching along four abreast like a military company. Many, moreover, were carrying weapons. The teacher Fräulein Gries and her fiancé Big Ding had been separated from him. That didn't matter. There were prisoners to be freed. He hadn't the least notion what all this could be about.

They marched without singing. At Alexanderplatz, in front of the Tietz department store, they came to a halt. They waited. Maus was freezing as he turned his little revolver over and over again in his coat pocket. People spoke to him as though they were old pals. Suddenly they all pricked up their ears; there was singing from Landsberger Strasse: "Brothers, onward to sunlight, to freedom." A column with a flag came out onto the square.

Above them rose the red citadel of the police headquarters.

They moved in on it. They were now several hundred men. At the entrance, facing the dark and narrow Kaiserstrasse, they halted once again. The great iron gate of the headquarters was shut, no one was standing guard outside. Apparently the procession had been reported. The demonstrators shouted through the bars. Soldiers appeared inside, shouting back that if they wanted something they should ring the bell marked "Authorized Entry" at the side entrance. Several people were allowed in there, and when they demanded to see the chief of police or his deputy they were led up to see an official on the first floor, who after a while came shuffling up to them in slippers and with disheveled gray hair. He wore a sheepskin coat, and he stared grimly at the deputation standing there in the icy cold corridor. He asked what they wanted. When they mentioned prisoners, he glanced from one to the other—

they were armed—and made a wry face. Which prisoners did they mean? — The ones kept here illegally, the political prisoners. — He knew nothing about that, there weren't any here. He said no, and added, "We don't have any political prisoners." That ended the conversation. Only after the men had gone back downstairs and stepped out onto the street again did it dawn on them that they had been duped. Their comrades outside understood at once: representatives of the people had simply been sent packing by officials accustomed to authority. That was more than enough proof right there.

And while they were still arguing about this in front of the barred main entrance, a truck filled with armed sailors drove out onto Alexanderplatz. Several people shouted to them what was going on. The sailors promptly jumped down, yelled through the grating, and when no one opened up they started firing.

A security commando was stationed in the courtyard. One of the shots strayed into a group that was setting up a machine gun, killing one of the men. At that point the people inside realized that this was serious, and took cover behind columns and doors. Shooting away, they edged toward the gate while several others fired from the side stairway. The crowd outside scattered, but not for long. Some sailors soon broke down the side door, ran through the lighted hallway of the ground floor, chased the soldiers from the stairway, entered the courtyard and opened the massive gate. Now the host streamed in. The security force had not really wanted to fight and was easily disarmed.

They were able to break into the prison wing on the left. The officer on duty stepped out of his office, and they ordered him to open up. They ran through the halls, insisting that all the doors be unlocked; they refused to make any exceptions. Every prisoner they found was given his freedom. With loud threats and hallos they moved back outside again. The guard detail had been relieved of its rifles and machine guns.

The whole thing lasted just short of half an hour. They all dispersed on Alexanderplatz, which was completely empty now, making arrangements to meet the following morning or evening.

Maus had had his revolver knocked out of his hand by a fellow using the butt of a rifle. In a rage he had raced up the stairs after the soldier, who dropped his rifle and escaped in the labyrinth of dark corridors. Maus helped himself to the rifle. As the forces pulled back, he flagged down a hack and rode home.

He was in a magnificent mood. The ache in his hand was part of it. Softly, without turning on a light, he entered his room and stood the rifle in one corner, a good old Prussian model fondly known as a blunderbuss.

I've joined the infantry. Tomorrow we're meeting on Brunnenstrasse to discuss plans.

He ripped off his coat and jacket, as if coming home from a drinking spree, and pulled off his boots. He threw himself down onto his bed.

A Reunion

And in the morning Maus felt so fresh, so much more alert in body and mind, that as he leaped from his bed he said to himself that he had started off just right yesterday—without second thoughts, because they never produced anything anyway—and that he would do exactly the same today and go join his comrades-in-arms. He liked those men. They were simple young people who knew as little as he where they were going, but wanted to breach the world's defenses somehow.

As he dressed he suddenly thought of Friedrich Becker. There in the hospital they had helped each other dress. Becker was a first lieutenant and more seriously wounded than he, shrapnel in his lower spinal column, injury to the spinal cord. Becker's recovery had been very slow, they had shared that room in Alsace for months. Toward the end they had both been in love with their nurse, with that Hilda in Strasbourg whom Maus was so worried about because she hadn't written. Yes, why doesn't she write? Maus asked himself this each morning when he got up. And today, when he was feeling so good, he loved her twice, three times as much. He was awfully grateful to her; the moment anything good came his way, he thought of Hilda and thanked her. If only she would forgive him that last rash hour.

He stood at the mirror and thought. Becker may well have been released already from the auxiliary hospital in Naumburg where he had been transferred after they were brought back from Alsace; he could be here now.

Maus carefully stowed his captured rifle away, locked up and marched off to see Becker without a word to his father or mother. His heart was full.

Even as he turned into the street where Becker lived Maus sensed— he was that alert and relaxed—the Becker was there. He was sure of it as he entered the run-down building. And when an old lady, a handsome woman, opened the door to the apartment (that is his mother, she makes an even stronger impression than I expected), he gave a military salute and his name. Her whole face lighted up. She asked him to come in, then opened a door into a room flooded with sunlight.

And there he was in Becker's room, where his friend sat in his robe at his desk, his canes beside him. He had turned around upon hearing voices at the door. Maus rushed toward him, he couldn't let Becker stand up. They embraced for a long time without saying anything. His mother stood behind them, beaming.

"This is Maus, Mother, my friend and fellow sufferer from the hospital. Maus, I haven't had my coffee yet. I'm under orders to sleep late. You'll have some too. Did you just come from the train?"

"Why?"

"Because you're here so early."

"But I got back to Berlin before you did, you know! How long have you been here? You're looking good."

When his mother had left them alone, Maus said, "I'll let you in on why I came so early I didn't know that you were here, otherwise I would have looked you up before this. I was down in the dumps. That business with Hilda, you know."

"No."

"I haven't heard a word from her in all this time and that's been really rough on me."

"You poor fellow."

"I've been plain crazy. And there I am out wandering about and I go into an office for military discharges on Kurfürstendamm. Who should I meet but Ding, an old school chum of mine, and his fiancée, a teacher. They weighed into me with a lecture, and so I went along with them and we attacked police headquarters last night."

"You're crazy!"

"You'll have to read the papers. We surprised the security commando and forced them to let out all the people hanging about in their prison."

And he gave a childish laugh. "Lord, was it fun, Becker. Most of them were lying in their cells fast asleep, of course. One o'clock in the morning, and they hadn't even been awakened by the shots and carryings-on. And then we flung open the doors and yelled, 'Get up, you guys, everybody out!' They were scared as hell and were absolutely determined not to leave. They kept asking, 'Where are we going to spend the night?' "

Becker rubbed his cheek. "What's the point of all this?"

The tone in Maus's voice changed, his face closed up tight and grew hard. He cast a sidelong glance at Becker. "What's the point of it all? I don't really care. Something has to happen."

At that Becker silently shoved a pack of cigarettes his way, and they each took one. "Okay," Maus asked, "what are you thinking?"

Becker smoked, letting himself be warmed by the sun, the sharp light modeling his emaciated face. He's doing no better than in the hospital, Maus thought. I'm so awfully fond of him, let him go ahead and read me out. Becker laid his head on his left shoulder. Now he would answer.

"Go ahead and join them, Maus. Someone has to shove from some direction or other."

16

Maus was amazed. "You've changed. During the war you even wanted to keep me from reading the newspapers."

"You should accept nothing for a fact, shouldn't even assume there are any. Everything's finished. First we got smashed up by others, and now it's our turn."

"That's what I think, too."

"We should make use of this revolution. We can't be put off by the rhetoric."

Maus: "My father belongs to the newly founded Citizens' Council."

"Smash it to pieces. Unfortunately I can't help much. You could blow me over with one good breath."

Maus gazed at him. "How are you really feeling, Becker? Doing your exercises? Making progress?"

Becker turned his long, pale face toward him. "Just what kind of a conversation do you want to get me involved in?"

"I'm sorry, Becker."

"Doesn't matter. Next time I'll play 'Tristan' for you. I promised you that when we were in the hospital."

He let his arms fall onto this knees. "You spoke with my mother?"

"Only what was said over coffee."

"The problem is falling asleep and waking up. I'm finally lying comfortably in the evening, and assuming that sleep will come and I'll be off. Night. And then—I hear the church bells; it's six o'clock, I think, but it's only one or two. And at the same moment my back starts to hurt, the pain shoots down into my legs, and I'm back looking it square in the face, the old monster that's been torturing me all day. The pain is back again, still living in the same house with me. He announces himself, my roommate, my bedmate, sprawling there beside me. — How it disgusts me!"

Maus didn't dare look over at him. Alas, Becker had not improved since the hospital.

He was quiet now. He whispered, "Don't tell my mother any of this."

The Authorities

The authorities in Berlin have nothing to laugh about these days. But they are careful to keep their hands clean. A little man has crept his way into power, deceiving the world about him. It is November 23, 1918.

The Army Retreats

Like the many-branched roots of a tree clutching deep into the earth, the troops of the mighty German army had to be pulled out of their trenches, tunnels and fortifications following the armistice of November 11th.

Before November 17th they had to be behind the line Antwerp-Dender-monde, and to the south back of the line Longwy-Briey-Metz-Saverne-Sélestat-Basel. From then on they knew no rest. They had to march quickly in order to reach Turnhout and the Hasselt Canal, Diest and the northern border of Luxembourg. Belgium had to be evacuated by November 27th. By December 1st, according to the dictates of the armistice, both the front-line and back-up armies of the German occupying forces were to be out of all areas west of Neuss and Duesseldorf and were not to advance to the west beyond a line Duran-Sedan-Bernkastel-Rhine-Swiss border. After that they were to yield control of the Rhineland and hand over the remaining territory to the west of the Rhine by December 9th. The victorious Allies were then to follow them to the east bank of the Rhine in order to occupy the bridge-heads at Cologne, Coblenz and Mainz to a depth of thirty kilometers. There they were to halt.

And so the soldiers of the German military were marching, riding, flying, driving—a force beneath whose boots whole empires had fallen like card houses, the infantry and the cavalry, the heavy artillery, the field artillery, the foot artillery, the riflemen and cyclists, the engineer and trench-mortar corps, machine gun batteries and communications groups, bomber and fighter squadrons. They moved from place to place with the precision of a clock. For the same iron will, the same icy cold intelligence that had conceived the plans for conquest that had now collapsed, was still in control, the same General Headquarters—located now in Kassel—with the same generals and officers who had sworn an oath of allegiance to the Kaiser.

The roads were sodden, there were flatlands and high mountains to cross. The military dragon, spotted red, white and black, snaked its way through cities, villages, along the highways. The German nation, which had not known war within its borders, now got to see its shadow.

Everywhere the notice issued by the old field marshal was on display: "Up to the final hour we have borne our arms honorably. The army has accomplished great deeds in selfless and faithful fulfillment of its duty. We depart from the battlefield proud and erect."

The red, white and black military dragon wound its way through the countryside. The generals wanted to let it roll on to Berlin, let it shape the destiny of the city.

Cabinet Meeting

On this morning of November 23, 1918, the streets and squares of Berlin, as is their nature, are standing about in peace, immobile, and the gray November sky looks down on them with no interest whatever. One might call these streets and squares lethargic, since one encounters them there in the same spot at every hour of the day or night, always with the same number of windows, the same number of stories and with only the most minor changes in the windows or shutters, and even those changes do not come about by themselves, but are made by others, by the people who live in them. But then one remembers that they are made of lethargic, recalcitrant materials that are difficult to move, made of stone, mortar, clay and concrete, which have more time at their disposal than we. One is always grateful that they do not participate in the general madness of our times, but show us the same face every hour with never a hint of nervous breakdown.

As on every day, cars are driving about today, winding their way from street to street.

We watch one car roll along from Treptow to Berlin, down Köpenicker Strasse, across the Insel Bridge, the Mühlendamm. It turns down Breitestrasse. We watch it ply along bravely, cross the Schlossplatz and enter Unter den Linden. There it is greeted by historical buildings and statues. The taxi, however, takes no notice of them. Its forward momentum has not yet been exhausted; its driver neither wavers nor falters, for he is a man who has fixed on a particular street and house number. They were called out to him in Treptow, and his brain holds fast to them. Now he is in Wilhelmstrasse and he stops.

He stops in front of a building closed in by a high iron fence; soldiers and sailors are milling along its forecourt. Two young men in stiff hats climb out of the car; they doff their hats to keep them from being dented by the car door as they get out. Each holds on tightly, but unlovingly, to a thick portfolio, and one of them pays the driver after first checking the meter. The journey from Treptow has glided past the meter as well. The meter only stared at the ground and counted the yards running by. The meter was concerned with the pure distance of the trip, had focused its interest on an abstract notion, had functioned with philosophical detachment. With a glance at the philosopher, the driver pocketed his money and the tip, and then there would be the trip back past peaceful buildings—for him, and for the car and the meter.

Behind the two young men, a third man climbed out of the car, as though responding to an announcement of the star attraction. He was a short, plump, squat gentleman, who headed straight toward the barred entrance behind the other two. It sprang open at once: open sesame! He was wrapped in a brown winter coat that only added to his bulk, and he had turned up the collar against the cold. On his head sat a stiff round hat. He climbed the steps of the edifice between his two companions, without glancing at the configurations of soldiers and sailors evidently intent on some display of honor.

The men delivered by the taxi and now entering the building were robust, well fed individuals; they had a peaceful night behind them, although a general revolution was in progress, and were now all ready to go to work. Through the course of events, whether war or revolution, they had ended up with this building as the place they did their work in. This was why they moved about here now with complete assurance. And so that no one is left in doubt about where we are, we will note that we are dealing with the so-called Reichs Chancellery, and thus with one of the buildings that former kaisers and kings had had built so they could have their highest civil servants close at hand. They themselves had lived on the Schlossplatz. But now, kaisers and kings having fled, these buildings were left standing all around; it was therefore inevitable that the survivors, those left behind, should give some thought to what could be done with these buildings, and that they attached some very succulent notions of power and glory to them.

We follow the short, fat man and his entourage through the building. As he strides through an anteroom filled with people, one man on either side, a footman who has been here since imperial days runs after him. And suddenly, as if touched by a magic finger, stroked by a breath of the past, the short man undoes his buttons, hands over his hat, and the footman helps him out of his coat—which proves a difficult process. Then the two men present him with their thick portfolios, and he disappears with them into his office.

He is a people's deputy, the well-known Social Democrat Friedrich

Ebert. He is barely inside, standing there alone in a room paneled in white wood, with pedestals holding marble busts of statesmen and generals, before he tosses the portfolios on the desk. One falls to the carpet. He flings himself angrily down onto a chair, a very ordinary one, though trimmed in gold, and puts his hand to his chin. The entrance and the removal of the coat still had not gone smoothly. They still handed him the portfolios instead of having the footman follow him in with them. These wretched comradely habits. As if they were still dealing with a meeting of the Party's executive committee on Lindenstrasse.

He sat down in the immense president's chair, where Prince Bismarck, the Iron Chancellor, had once sat. Our people can't learn anything. But it's my fault, too. I have to learn not to hold my arms like that when they take off my coat. And then there's the way I walk and hold my head.

He rang. "Ferdinand, it seems to me we used to enter by another way, not through the anteroom. Is the side corridor closed?"

"Yes sir, Your Excellency. People's Deputy Haase has the key."

"Why?"

"The corridor does lead to Your Excellency's room, and the Reichs chancellor used that way at one time, but the corridor also adjoins Deputy Haase's office and has to serve as his anteroom."

"Aha. Not enough space."

The footman lowered his head respectfully and smiled.

Ebert: "Sitting on top of each other."

The imperial footman: "The rooms are large, but only one person occupied them before."

Ebert waved for him to go. "Thanks, thanks. — At any rate, in the future you are to take the portfolios and bring them in, and I will remove my coat and hat in here."

The footman bowed and left.

The people's deputy cursed to himself and drew the cigar box toward him. What sort of an impression that must make with people here stepping all over each other. The Party, the Party, and they wanted to govern the same way. He was still angry even after he had put the smoking cigar in his mouth. But suddenly he stood up, taken by a new and more pleasant thought, and began slowly, slowly to stride back and forth across the carpet, his head laid back, the smoking cigar in his mouth. He said to himself, always one step after the other, left — right, left — right, and never change your expression. When you're thinking, never change your expression. He cast his eyes around the room. Naturally, no mirror to check the effect in. He pulled out his silver watch, its lid cast a reflection but a distorted one. I need a pocket mirror. At once he pulled out his notebook and wrote beneath November 22: "Pocket mirror. Pimple." He added "pimple" so that someone next to him who might get a glance into his notebook would at once read the explanation—"pimple." After he had walked pompously back and forth several times, it occurred to him: now I'll have someone come in and we'll try it out at once. He rang.

When his first visitor entered, he was standing at the filing cabinet behind his desk. Deep in thought, he only nodded, letting the man speak first. Then he began to walk up and down as before, his hands at his back, looking serious. He was still upset; it seemed to him that walking in general was bad if one was short. Standing would be better. And suddenly he was so uncertain about it all that he sat back down in his chair and asked himself whom he ought to speak to about this, with his tailor, or perhaps his barber?

Meanwhile the man was speaking. Ebert nodded testily. If he did not soon get beyond this matter of "dignity" a great many things could go wrong. What was this long-bearded fellow rattling on about? Without the speaker's noticing, he pushed a button under the desktop. Soon there came a knock and two men stormed in, shoving the long-bearded man aside to whisper something, pointing at a folder that one of them held open before him. The gentleman was asked to wait outside.

The two men, who normally came in with any empty folder that happened to be handy, really had something in it this time: the list, just arrived, of the names of prisoners freed during the night, including political ones. Ebert roared, "Filthy mess!" and demanded to speak to the chief of police.

"Who was responsible for this foul-up?"

When one of the men answered "Sailors," Ebert roared again. "There are no sailors. There isn't a single sailor left. Next thing I know you'll start telling me it was God."

After this exertion he settled down. The affair, he noticed, had its good side. There were burglars and pickpockets who had been released as well, the mob would be blamed for that. Then he had the long-bearded gentleman come back in again. It turned out that he was an attorney who had been deputized to bring assurance that the Bar Association was committed to the same "peace and order" that Herr Ebert championed with such strength of purpose.

The gentleman had just delivered his message at some length and with considerable energy, but he was not at all offended to be called upon to do so once again.

Ebert asked mistrustfully what the Bar had in mind.

"Everything that serves peace and order, within our own narrow sphere of course. We are in favor of a citizen's militia so that Berlin can once more enjoy the reputation of being a civilized city."

"I beg you, undertake nothing on your own. Such actions could be misunderstood. You will first have to establish contact with the chief of police and the city commandant."

"Naturally, naturally," the lawyer assured him. "Nothing seems more important to us than that the law be upheld, by all parties concerned."

The people's deputy gave a dignified nod. He was doing well with this attorney. He opened his heart. "The gangs and mobs in this city! We are flooded with criminals. People are attempting to discredit our cause. You've most likely heard of the attack perpetrated last night."

The lawyer had heard nothing.

Ebert spoke now from beside his chair, one hand braced firmly on the desk, addressing the entire Bar Association in the person of its worthy ambassador. In conclusion he managed a smooth "When it comes to safety in the streets, we shall not take a back seat to the imperial government that preceded us."

The attorney was firmly convinced. He bowed several times. It was on the tip of his tongue to report how just in case he had had a new steel grating installed on his own office door just yesterday, and if Ebert had continued this display of friendship for one minute more, he would have done so. But then his hand was being shaken. The long-bearded gentleman departed, beaming, the lyrics to "Manly Pride Before the Royal Throne" and "Bathed in the Splendor of the Throne" running through his head.

To his horror the people's deputy saw his Party comrade Wrede sidling into the room just behind the lawyer. He made no effort whatever to steel himself for this visit. "I'm next," the man laughed from the door, and then approached without any further ceremony. Ebert could do nothing to prevent it, and there it was: the whole anteroom arrangement needed to be changed.

He drummed nervously on his desk. "Well? I'm pressed for time." He pulled out his watch. "We have a meeting at noon."

"No offense, comrade, but I've been sitting here waiting for you since nine. There's a stink at police headquarters."

"What does that mean?"

"There were political prisoners there."

"Rubbish. I've heard that already. You're all crazy." His hand jerked again for his watch. Then his Party comrade pulled a sheet of paper from his vest pocket. "Here you have the names and addresses of people who have come by to see us in Lindenstrasse, and who were locked up at police headquarters."

Ebert, red as a turkey-cock with anger, banged on his desk. "I say you're all crazy! Who is supposed to have arrested them? These people are swindlers. Here is a very different list."

And he reached for the paper that had just been brought him. "These are the people they let out, criminals, perfectly ordinary burglars, two habitual pickpockets—that's what they have set free. My congratulations on this augmentation of the revolution."

His comrade, amicably: "Show me the names. I'm not familiar with them. I spoke to those on ours just a while ago myself."

Ebert put his fists to his hips. "Which means? I'll give you your names. At any rate, you'll take care of the matter, won't you? This attack on police headquarters is intolerable, makes Berlin appear utterly foolish in the eyes of the whole Reich."

Wrede: "There were registered Party members among them in any case. You can't suggest any insulting compromises to them. Some people at police headquarters are involved, though not Eichhorn, of course."

The people's deputy grew calmer now and wrote down the names. "I would simply like to know who is supposed to have benefitted from having these people locked up."

His visitor winked at Ebert. "Well, we've all heard of reactionaries and officers, comrade."

As he closed the door, he did not hear how the little people's deputy sitting behind his desk with his head propped in both hands hissed, "Idiots, idiots."

Ebert picked up the telephone, demanded the city commandant's headquarters. The commandant was not there. He exploded to the man on duty: "What kind of a mess was that last night at headquarters?"

"We didn't have enough dependable people assigned to us."

"I don't care about that. Who jailed the politicals?"

At the other end a long clearing of the throat. Someone else came on, introduced himself in a brash military voice as Deputy Officer Barthaupt, or Bartau. "We know nothing about politicals here."

The people's deputy slammed down the receiver and called the chief of police. Not there. A bureaucrat answered. The prisoners had been jailed in a perfectly legal fashion. He asked if he might tender a request, to wit, that the security forces at headquarters be reinforced.

"Done!" laughed Ebert bitterly.

The deliberations of the people's deputies took place in the Lesser Conference Hall. Only very few of the men who entered it took notice of the august character of the room. All the more so Ebert.

Since Ebert assumed that they would not be long in getting to the attack on police headquarters, he headed things off, which was not difficult for him as chairman, even before they began the official agenda. He roundly condemned the nonsense of handing out credentials to all sorts of people claiming to be members of councils, who then recruited any old soldiers directly off the street for their own purposes. For instance, there had in fact been political prisoners among those released last night, and indeed, he had no wish to hide the fact, political prisoners from the

Social Democratic party. He thundered, "Someone's hoping to discredit the revolution."

Who had arrested these people, a skeptical Independent Socialist wanted to know.

Herr Scheidemann, Ebert's friend sitting next to him, remarked that one must differentiate between two questions: who had made the arrests—people with counterfeit documentation, of course—and who had freed the prisoners by force. Concerning this latter point, at least, they had some very clear answers. An enraged mob with Spartacus at its head.

The questioner muttered that dark forces were at work here. Arrests had been made to eliminate individuals someone found disagreeable, and police headquarters had been in on the game. If the people were sufficiently provoked there would be more than just an attack on police headquarters.

Scheidemann shook his head gravely. "Puzzling insinuations. Say what you want to say more clearly."

Since no one could provide exact details, there was nothing to do but accept a resolution stating that for the second time all credentials issued heretofore were declared invalid, except for those bearing the seal of the city commandant's office.

Then came the day's agenda. Two men were commissioned to draft the proclamation to be directed to the returning troops. Pride and admiration were to be the main tenor of it. Recognition of the accomplishments of the troops in the field, an announcement of the foundation of a new, just order ("God willing!" came the threatening cry of an Independent, while the offended Social Democrats stared at him), and finally remarks to the effect that they were not swimming in an abundance of goods, that there was hard work ahead.

"Hard work, hard work!" Ebert worriedly acknowledged. "What we need first of all, of course, is order, no disruption of food supplies. Which brings us to another point." He picked up a piece of paper. "Field Marshal Hindenburg, Wilhelmshöhe Castle near Kassel: . . ." A loud call came from an elderly Independent who was either hard of hearing or pretended to be: "From whom?" — "From Field Marshal Hindenburg, Wilhelmshöhe Castle, comrade." — "Ah, him. What's he doing there?" — "General Headquarters is there." — "Kassel? Fine. That's where Napoleon got stuck, too, when he lost *his* war." (Disapproving silence and smiles. Clearing of throats.) "Hindenburg's telegram reads: 'It is not impossible that the French will attempt to find a legal basis for a resumption of the war. I must explicitly emphasize that the German army is not in a position to resume the battle, both because of the bitter conditions laid down in the armistice agreement and because of the nature of events occurring in our homeland.' "

The deaf Independent (his hand still at his ear) used the dramatic pause to vent his anger. "Grandpa wants to preach a sermon on morals? He should mind his own business. The next thing you know he'll be blaming us for losing his war. All of a sudden the army can't fight anymore just because of the conditions set down in the armistice or because of the revolution. That's really the limit."

The Social Democrat to the chairman's right, the serious, dapper man with the brown beard—Scheidemann that is,—lifted up his oily voice, "We have, at least, no reason to rejoice in the conditions of the armistice."

The deaf man, his head bent forward: "As far as I'm concerned, they can have all the wagons and cannons—and the generals too."

The oily gentleman: "In any case, other people do not find similar cause to rejoice at these impossible conditions of the armistice."

"Nor at the revolution either, right?"

Indignant shaking of heads all around Chairman Ebert: "Comrade, this gets us nowhere. I'll proceed with the reading of Field Marshal Hindenburg's telegram."

The deaf man: "It'd be better if he'd keep his trap shut."

Ebert sighed patiently, his neighbors seemed to despair. Ebert: "I believe we did agree that there was cause for satisfaction in his having placed himself at our disposal."

The deaf man: "If he hadn't placed himself at our disposal he wouldn't be sitting in his pretty Wilhelmshöhe Castle, but in prison in Spandau or Magdeburg with Ludendorff and his pals, and would have to answer for his deeds."

Ebert saw himself confronted by the outrage of his neighbors, who wanted him to take an energetic stand. But he raised his hands: "For what, comrade? Are you accusing Hindenburg of tactical mistakes in his command of the army? What mistakes, if I might ask?"

The deaf man, with bitterness: "You defend him, too? Wilhelm's Hindenburg? What are you sitting here for then?"

Ebert turned to his neighbors with a perplexed smile, as if to beg their forgiveness for such tactlessness.

Before lying back again in his wide chair, the member of the opposition fired one last salvo to help himself swallow his rage. "Then we might as well invite Hindenburg here and let him do everything for us. We seem to be totally superfluous."

Ebert read on in a business-like voice from the paper in his hand: "I consider it my duty to emphasize this fact, because from statements made in the enemy press it is evident that the enemy governments will make peace only with a German government supported by the majority of the people." — "Well," the chairman concluded after he had finished reading, "certainly no one would wish to object to that, whatever his politics."

The deaf man sat in his chair and gnawed on his anger.

But the influential People's Deputy Haase, a clever, cautious man, now gestured by lifting his little yellow pencil, and the chairman nodded obligingly—we're in agreement there, aren't we—but Haase did not return the look. "Naturally no one objects, neither to the idea, nor to the form in which the field marshal chooses to express himself. We are pleased to take notice that the field marshal has been converted to the view that a government requires the consent of the governed. He declares himself a democrat, as is only proper for a functionary of a republic." (Ebert sat there, motionless, his eyes on the paper; the blow had yet to fall.) "But what moved the field marshal to send this telegram? He is well aware that military rule has been over ever since Ludendorff took flight. The public is at present most sensitive to any presumed interference by the military in civil affairs."

Ebert exchanged a few whispered words with his neighbor; Haase glanced up and broke off politely. "Something you wish to say?"

Ebert, equally polite: "Excuse me. I forgot in fact to read the accompanying letter, which has just been called to my attention. In it the field marshal expressly requests that his statement or proclamation be given to the press for publication."

An Independent with a red, youthful face: "I am absolutely against that."

Ebert, resignedly: "May I state my opinion in the matter? What motivated me and my friend"—and he laid his hand familiarly on the back of the hand of his neighbor, who flinched—"to submit the opinions of the old field marshal was the indisputable popularity of the man with large segments of the populace now estranged from us. Naturally we can simply let the telegram sit. But if Hindenburg's eyes have been opened to the fact that only a democracy can be the basis of a government—and he thereby renounces his own entire past, as Comrade Haase has correctly remarked—why then should we not let that news reach others who are perhaps not yet so far. It is to our advantage. When he publicly retracts his old position and supports us—why reject his help? We will be dependent on a great deal of good will in the coming days. The broader our basis of support, the more secure a German democracy will be."

Haase, having exchanged glances with the chairman: "It would be good if other comrades were to express their opinions."

The elegant Social Democrat with the aesthetic beard: "I move the debate be closed, since we are after all agreed that a broad basis is a prerequisite for democracy."

"Who still wishes to say something?"

The disgruntled Independent, from the depths of his chair: "I am against it."

Ebert, unmoved: "Who else?"

The vote is taken. Four for publication, one against. Haase abstains.

Ebert sticks the paper in the portfolio beside him. "Minor differences of opinion, comrades. A matter of taste. If I had my way, I too would much rather be sitting with my comrades in a beer hall, taking my cues from Marx, Engels and Lasalle. But unfortunately one must first educate the people for democracy, particularly in Germany."

The gloomy Independent: "And afterward you'll trim with the times."

Ebert with a benevolent glance across to him, while already reaching for the next sheet of paper. "Let us hope not."

Secret Line 998

It was Ebert's custom to speak each evening with Kassel, with Wilhelmshöhe Castle, on secret line 998, which even during the war years had led directly from the chancellery to General Headquarters.

Groener, the quartermaster general, answered at once.

Ebert: "Nothing special. But I wanted to thank you for being so prompt with the statement from the field marshal that I suggested. It will be most useful to us."

"The thing is in your hands already? Hindenburg signed without a peep. He only gives a cursory glance to such papers, he doesn't take much time reading them, just grumbles, 'If it doesn't compromise my honor.'"

Ebert, gaily: "No, that it most certainly does not. The statement was in all the papers this evening. Again my deepest thanks. — And then . . . ," he hesitated. "Some Spartacists pulled a nasty trick on us here last night. They attacked police headquarters and freed the prisoners."

"Dirty rotten thing to do. I heard about it."

"They came pretty close to capturing the place. We're short on personnel."

"The scrapes you people get yourselves into. Don't tell me you're afraid, Herr Reichs Chancellor. Do you want me to send you troops?"

The answer came very quickly, hastily. "Many thanks, but not at all, no, thanks again."

"But you don't want these fellows to burn down the house around you, do you?"

Forced laughter: "Certainly not, Your Excellency." A brief pause.

The voice from Wilhelmshöhe was as calm and benevolent as before. "In any case I appreciate your informing me. You are experiencing, Herr Reichs Chancellor, the vicissitudes of war, here victory, there defeat. Whoever has the best nerves, wins."

He spoke about the retreat of the army. Everything was proceeding in a most disciplined, orderly fashion. At the beginning of December the regiments from Berlin would be arriving home. Ebert expressed his thanks for the briefing. He hung up, deep in thought. And at the other end the general from Württemberg sat in his armchair and played with a globe that stood beside his telephone. He frowned and crossed his arms.

Was this fellow in Berlin already causing problems?

Concerning Love, Requited
and Unrequited

The scene changes. Several persons, if not to say the heroes of our account, lead us to think of Alsace. Life's pace is less hectic there. Love adds a serious word. The date is somewhere around the 23rd.

In Alsace

Joy ran rampant through Strasbourg, the charming city in Alsace that had now been returned to France. Toward the end it had briefly been visited by the specter of control by German revolutionaries, but now there was no longer a "Central Workers' and Soldiers' Council." In those last few days, there in the Hall of Justice on the embankment, how courageously they had proclaimed their determination, gripping their pencils in both hands, to reject every "infringement of revolutionary authority." They had since joined the shades.

In their stead, however, the jubilant city learned that a vestige of the specter was still making the rounds; that, for example, a large quantity of snowshoes had disappeared from the Island Armory. Whoever had illegally appropriated these snowshoes was requested to turn them in at police headquarters at once. Failing this, they would be easy to sell on the qt. And to dampen excessive jubilation among both the civilian and military populations, as well as to moderate clashes of political differences, all sale of schnapps was forbidden. Use of the telephone was prohibited, so that whoever had something to whisper would have to shout it. The new army high command also expressed the wish that the public neither hesitate nor stint in disposing of all war materials it might possess, because they were sinful products of the past, and anyone hanging on to them was therefore subject to prosecution.

And the appropriate courts and current decrees were put into action and the orderly process of handing down sentences began.

But let us now leave the lovely, hazy city of Strasbourg to its riverbank promenades, its narrow streets, its squares, its flower and vegetable markets and its covered arcades, and proceed to the small village where First Lieutenant Becker and Lieutenant Maus spent their final months in the hospital.

The charming old Alsatian town to which we now come is no less ancient than splendid Strasbourg. At one time there were even Frankish and Saxon emperors here, holding court within these walls and hunting in the dark surrounding forests. Later the town never managed to rise above the mere cultivation of hops. No one knew the reason. In one sense, however, the town was blessed: since it made no effort to capitalize on those ancient privileges and attract the German Kaiser within its walls, it was spared the pain of dethronement and the tumult of a revolution like the one in Berlin.

Jacob and Hanna

On the floor above the pharmacist's shop on the main marketplace of this happy town, however, a little druggist's assistant sat in his over-stuffed chair in a warm room. It was 8:30 P.M.; he had skillfully hung the long cord of the electric lamp on a nail on the wall instead of letting it hang above him as usual, and was reading in his paper the spirited account of the festivities that were to take place in Strasbourg on the 25th. A nickle-plated teapot stood at his side on a heavy wooden tray, plus a large bottle of rum, a small one of white wine, several glasses, a sugar bowl. He had just brought all this up out of the pharmacy. He wanted to go to bed early and get warmed up nicely with tea and rum before-hand. The tea in the pot was still hot, he tapped his finger against the spout, he took one of the cups from the shelf, a saucer and a spoon. He could drink it soon now. And while he sat there in the deathly still house, his arms resting on the brightly lit newspaper, he felt the rum coursing through him, a lovely warm feeling. What could be more pleasant in all the world, he thought, than to lay one's body, be it ugly or beautiful, in the frying pan of alcohol and let it warm there lightly till it was finally ready for the finest thing in the world, sleep. For if the little, aging assistant had anything that made him happy, it was his bed. It provided sleep and cozy dreams and a great deal of entertainment all night long. He retreated into his room as if into a magic palace. He continued drinking, slowly, and with the precision of a druggist pumping the alcohol into himself.

It was during a moment when he had directed his gaze back at the paper that the pharmacy bell rang. He sat up and listened. There was no second ring. He had been mistaken. Then he reached for the teapot in order to be carried off into that state of sadness for which he had so meticulously prepared himself.

And as he drank and enjoyed himself it seemed as if there were something moving in the house. Yes, someone was coming softly up the stairs. He listened. The steps were tentative, now they were on a landing. He laid his hands on the table, whoever it was could come right on in. Then someone was standing outside his door, not moving. The assistant felt very strange. Now a soft knocking. He got up resolutely, shoved the chair to one side with a great deal of noise and stepped heavily over to the door.

Hanna was standing outside. A new love affair announces itself. The war was not lobbing bullets anymore . . . but the love it had set aflame was still burning. Only a year before, Hanna had been the little druggist assistant's fiancée. Then a Lieutenant von Heiberg had appeared at the army post, and she became very fond of him. They both fell in love. Then came the German defeat and the revolution. And on November 10th the lieutenant had shot and killed two soldiers who had assaulted the colonel of the post. The lieutenant was forced to flee. And—it was the little jilted assistant to whom the unfortunate Hanna turned for help in getting the lieutenant secretly to Strasbourg. He had not refused.

She entered before he could utter a word or form a thought, and closed the door behind her. With her back pressed to the door, she gazed steadily at him. He took two awkward steps back, bowed, made another bow and finally made a small inviting gesture with his right arm. "Please forgive the mess. Won't you have a seat?"

She did not know the assistant's apartment, she had never been at his place before; in the past they had always met either at Hanna's apartment or on the street. "I'm disturbing you."

"Have a seat," he pointed at an armchair. "And please forgive the mess."

She took off her black fur cap and laid it on the bureau. And as she began to unbutton and remove her long dark gray coat with the words "It's hot in here," he leaped behind her to help. He trembled for fear, for joy, and grew confused. He did not think about what she might want, she simply was there, which was more than he had ever dreamed of. He was dismayed and so grateful to her. He could have fallen at her feet. She found it warm, while his teeth were chattering so badly he had to force his jaws to clench tight. She asked, with seeming nonchalance, "You want me to sit there? That's your chair."

"I have another to sit on," he said, pulling up a cane-bottomed chair next to the bureau and placing it at a respectful distance from the easy chair. "And permit me to—clear away this mess."

He wanted to move the dishes from the table to the tea tray, but she pushed his arm aside. "Why do that? It's terribly cold outside. If you have another cup or a glass, you can give me some tea; but not if you have to go downstairs for it."

"I have everything here," he smiled, as disconcerted as before, and as soon as he spoke his teeth threatened to chatter. "I have three cups and four glasses, the sugar bowl there, spoons."

"How rich you are," she laughed. She noticed his confusion and she liked that. She had expected it really. Poor guy, the way he lives. He blissfully set to pouring her some hot tea. She promptly drank a second cup with rum. Then she made him sit down.

"You must be crazy. Why are you sitting out in the middle of the room?"

He sat at the narrow end of the table. She propped her head on her left hand and said, after a pause, "I would like to go back to Strasbourg tomorrow."

He nodded with delight. She wanted something from him. She could have everything. Just two days before he had accompanied her to Strasbourg, where she had searched for Lieutenant von Heiberg. She would not give up, although he was long since back in Germany.

Now she shaded her eyes from the glaring light. "Do you have to be on duty tomorrow?"

He made a little bow. "I'm afraid so." A long pause followed.

"What a shame."

This pained him. He stuttered, "No. Why? Maybe." No matter what, things could not end with "what a shame." Here she sat and she dare not leave without leaving unsullied happiness behind her.

She: "I thought it might interest you this time. Everybody in Strasbourg will be out in the streets."

"Certainly. I'm interested very much." He was supposed to accompany her, she wanted him as her companion, but how to arrange it for heaven's sake, how to arrange it?

"And can you manage it?"

Even if I have to run my head through the wall. — "I can. About what time do you think?"

"My train leaves at ten."

"Fine, fine," he said, but in his head everything was whirling. I don't know how I'll manage it, but I'll have to come up with something. "Okay, then I'll be at the station at ten."

She squeezed his hand. "I'm asking the impossible of you, aren't I?"

"Not at all—on the contrary."

"On the contrary?"

He could not answer, but he looked happy as a puppy. She simply had to understand him, and she understood. She let go of his hand. "Can't you put a shade on this light, it's dreadfully bright." Now he set to work on the lightbulb using all sorts of paper, but nothing would hold.

She said. "Use some light cloth, some silk." She searched the top of the bureau.

"I haven't got any, but I'll run down to the shop, we have a green lampshade down there."

She took off her striped scarf and beamed, "This will work."

But when it got singed, he decided to turn off the light. The ceiling lamp was enough for a conversation.

The ice was broken. They drank their tea without speaking, his memory calling up scenes from before, when they had sat and drunk tea in Hanna's apartment, he blissfully happy, she distracted. The war had not destroyed all that.

Now she spoke. "Mother was the one who gave me the idea. Where—did you leave him off that day?"

"Who?"

She was an elegant, slender woman, she had been sitting there comfortably drawn up into herself. Now she sat up straight and gave him a proud, cold look, her black eyes opened wide, eyes that from the beginning had always cast him into the abyss. Pressing her lips together, she gazed at him. Ah, that's who she meant. He trembled inside.

"I told you. On the Broglie."

"And then you lost sight of him?"

"My return train left an hour later."

"You don't know what direction he took?"

"No. In the opposite direction from the streetcar. Toward the theater."

"To the casino maybe?"

"Maybe."

She stared straight ahead. When she turned her head back to one side, there were lines of bitterness about her mouth. He now understood her sense of being deserted, his own sadness, his sympathy, his beggar's happiness. She whispered to keep her voice from betraying her feelings. "Where did you hide him that time?"

"Here."

She looked around in amazement. "He spent the night here?"

She stood up. He got up with her. She stood beside the simple, low bed with its white spread. "He slept here?"

He nodded. She turned her delicate, care-worn face to him. "Jacob, do you think he's still alive?" She had said "Jacob," she wanted his help.

"Everything is topsy-turvy on the other side of the river. He's sure to be safe and sound."

She began to weep. "But why doesn't he write me, not a word, for two weeks now."

"But there's no mail delivery."

"We were going to write each other via Switzerland. I've got two letters back, address unknown. Where is he?"

He fell silent. He thought of nothing. He could not and would not think about the question. She stroked the bedspread lightly with her

34

hand (he thought, my God, it's my bed after all), then she suggested, "Let's sit down again."

When they were seated, her voice changed. "So we're agreed about tomorrow. You're a dear man, Jacob. I will never forget what you've done."

Then he helped her into her coat. When she turned back again to him, it seemed as if she wanted to make her old gesture of farewell—stroking one side of his face with her hand, passing lightly across his lips. But there was only a long handshake and a look that was so puzzling, questioning, promising, that when she had closed the door, he was almost blind from it. He turned out the light, undressed in the darkness, and flung himself into bed along with that look, his one possession. He, the most orderly of men, forgot to clear the table, and to take his robe and slippers out of the closet even though the doorbell might ring, since he was on night duty.

Her mother was waiting for her; she sat reading in the dining room. "So he's going with you, then?" Her mother was glad. She knew more about Hanna's relationship with the vanished officer than Hanna suspected.

Hanna did not stop to talk, but went up to her room on the second floor. And as she slowly undressed, all the tension flowed away from her again. She pulled back the bedcovers. The sheets were white, someone had changed them. Three days before she had sprinkled them with blood she had bought at a butcher shop.

She was pregnant.

Her mother mustn't notice anything. This is what the war had left behind, a love whose flame would not die and a yearning that consumed her. That was why she had gone to the little druggist. He was supposed to be of help to her, but she didn't know how. She was frightened for many other reasons. She would soon begin to look bad. Perhaps, she dreamed as she lay in bed, I'll find some trace of him in Strasbourg, he can't simply have vanished from the earth. Everything was gray, incomprehensible. The same moaning and begging that happened every night before she fell asleep began again now. My darling, where are you, why are you doing this to me, why don't you want to stay here with me. Come back, they can't do anything to you here. I'll hide you from the French, they won't hand you over to the Germans. Be in Strasbourg, I beg you. I'm pregnant, you've got to help me. I can't be humiliated in front of my parents.

And then a lulling memory: he's a good man, Jacob is, I'm glad I have him. Everything will turn out all right, I don't have to die.

And then, like every other living thing, she was borne through the night, and when the earth had completed its turn and brought sunlight again onto the town, Hanna found herself lying in bed, fingering her breasts; they haven't grown any larger, but it feels as if they're harder. And then she went to the train station and rode into the city of Strasbourg with Jacob. It was Saturday.

From the train station on, all the streets and squares had been decorated.

Not speaking a word, the little druggist Jacob and Hanna wandered up Hoher Steg and let themselves be carried along by the crowd. Flags, pennants, strains of music—those would be the various clubs.

People thronged the streets of Strasbourg, its narrow lanes and bridges, people everywhere who had not been seen for years and now had found their way here. And so the auto-maker Mathes appeared, he had served in the French army; and Viktor Soeffler, a crack pilot, he came from Leipzig; and they had many tales to tell. But defying all the changes time brings, "Rhetal," a preparation for the prevention of dandruff and scurf was still being extolled in the window of the Iron Man Pharmacy. It effected its marvelous cure of human scalp ailments in revolution and in the tumult of war and on this festive day as well. Professors, simple doctors and mere pedestrians recognized "Rhetal."

Here then, amid this merriment, amid flags and music, the earnest druggist's assistant Jacob, whose flourishing head cold was visible to everyone, but not his happiness, and Hanna, a pretty picture in her fur-trimmed suit, moved through the crowds along Hoher Steg. She was wearing her high, shiny boots. Hanna stood waiting once again in front of what had once been the officer's casino. Two guards in helmets and bearing bayonets stood in front of it, French sharpshooters. She needn't ask about her boyfriend here, he wasn't here, and no one knew anything about him here. Nevertheless she stood near the entrance for a long time and watched.

They were separated by officers who made their way in. Things inside the casino had got out of hand in the last weeks: posters, house rules, appeals for war bonds, appeals and proclamations from the High Command and from the Soldiers' Council, the prophecies of Madame Thebes and whole sections of wallpaper had been ripped away, while intruders had meanwhile stolen all sorts of things.

They ended up in the crush. They rolled with the crowd across the square, stood in front of the town hall where the Pompier band was playing, ate in the train station. Hanna wanted—just as he had suspected—to ride out to the Kehler Bridge that led to Germany. she looked pleadingly at Jacob. She could find no peace within.

They rode out on the streetcar, along Schwarzwaldstrasse, past the supply depot and the massive complex of the citadel and its esplanade, to the Kehler Gate. A broad expanse opened up, filled with industrial buildings and docks. They drew closer to the Rhine. A lightly rolling plain of dry grass, few trees. Even from a distance one heard screaming and shouting that would then let up periodically.

36

Hanna pushed her way to the banks of the Rhine, Jacob followed. They wandered slowly down the narrow path along the bank. It was filled with people watching the other side, some with binoculars, some without. Over there some refugees were being picked up and led into barracks.

Hanna stood before a bare shrub on the bank, pulled her fur collar tight, and, awakening from a dream, she said to Jacob in a toneless voice, "Let's go."

"Yes," he answered, "it's getting dark."

The streetcar was overflowing, they took a horse-drawn cab. As they rode along between the shadows and light of the first streetlamps, he gathered his courage. "Hanna, do you love him so much?"

She was glad he spoke that way to her, she took his hand. "At last someone has asked me. Thank you."

And she sobbed for a vanished dream that would not return, and in her rage and wretchedness, in her grief and reproach she let him put his arm around her, and just sat there.

They drove down busy streets, sitting hand in hand. Suddenly she thought of the child inside her body and clasped Jacob around the neck. She did not speak, she did not cry. He pressed her head to his chest with his left hand, he did not dare caress her face. He felt her submit to him, she sought his protection. He did not know from what, but it made him strong and calm. So he was not surprised that as they got off at the Old Wine Market—since they were headed for the station—that she placed her arm in his. She was still wearing a little bunch of violets that he had given her that morning. She sniffed at them and looked around her. Along the Staden several shops were still lit, she made for them. There was a bakery. "I'm so hungry," she said with a smile. He waited outside until she came out with a bag, and they ate rolls as they walked. "They're not any too fresh," she asserted. But they ate them as they moved down Kusstrasse, all four of them. Then they stood in the brightly illuminated square at the station, flags all around. She wanted to throw the bag away, but Jacob said, "Not here, please." She laughed. "What a tidy old Swabian you are. The French'll haul you in yet." And then, before they made their way across the dangerous station square teeming with cars and wagons—more soldiers had just arrived and were drawn up in formation in the square—Hanna looked about and said, "It really is a splendid city. How fine it would be to live here."

It was another, very calm Jacob who accompanied her through the slumbering town to her parents' villa, not far from the long Kasernenstrasse that led out to the military hospital. When she was once again sitting alone on her white bed with its turned down covers, and was taking off her hat, slipping off her gloves, an enigmatic sentence crossed her mind: "Settle the war accounts." She had read it in the paper yesterday in an article dealing with the gradual end of rationing for bread and oil. She understood it only after she lay there and thought of her lover so far from her. She begged him, her face buried in her pillow, to forgive her. "You can be sure I'll do nothing hasty. I'll wait patiently."

Yes, she would have the patience.

She threw a tender, fleeting thought toward Jacob.

Conversations between Teachers

A teacher who returned from the war badly wounded visits again for the first time the school where he taught before 1914. The teacher wants information. In a conversation he raises the questions of guilt and responsibility for the war. He is particularly hard on himself. Various people take part in the discussion, some with a shudder. We shall dispense with naming a date for this day.

In the Faculty Room

We are again in Berlin. Imagination claims its right to change location without the use of train tracks or airplanes. Those who read this are happy to be borne so easily, so lightly from hither to yon. First Lieutenant Becker had been granted a half year's leave from his job as a high school teacher. One morning he felt well enough to ride over to his former place of work. He strode proudly and slowly across the courtyard, supported by canes and accompanied by the custodian, sat down in the empty faculty room and waited until a break between classes. The long room, the middle of which was occupied by a table—along one wall was a bookcase and wardrobe, on the other small chests, a plaster bust of Kaiser Wilhelm I above them—filled up with men who threw packages full of notebooks onto the table and chairs, reached for the newspapers lying about, unwrapped their sandwiches and ate. Becker saw new faces, four of his colleagues had fallen in the war. People gathered about him.

They greeted him with a look of surprise that he attributed to his unexpected appearance. But—they simply did not recognize him. They were taken aback at how awful he looked. What did he want here, why had they let him leave his sickroom? After exchanging a few words, people instinctively drew away from him.

Becker soon realized that everything here was going its same old way. The teachers had grown older; they looked wretched, some of them unkempt, their faces were dull and indifferent. They had the gray and pale yellow complexions that go with malnutrition. That was the reason too, probably, that some of them were so twitchy and excitable.

A few of them walked over to him a second time, eyed the two canes on the chair next to him, extended a hand, then retracted it with some anxiety. There was a pretense of sympathy, but basically they were annoyed, they did not want to hear anything about the war. There were cripples enough. He saw how disconnected they all were from one another as they stood about the room. One group was arguing at a window overlooking the noisy courtyard about a measure taken by the Ministry of Education. They laughed about it, told each other jokes; several people pointedly left the room.

"So what's new?" Becker asked the fat science teacher, Krug, who was the only one who managed to go on standing across from him and was still there as the break came to an end and the schoolyard emptied out once again.

Krug, ten years Becker's senior, sat there, a heavy golden watch chain draped at his belly. He had black bristly hair, a flat nose, a heavy dark moustache and very languid, heavily haired hands. In the days before the war, he and Becker had been on a good footing; he had been able to spend the war years as a technician in a laboratory specializing in gas. Gazing at Becker, his cheerful, rollicking chum, the fellow who was always surrounded by doting women, was for him—though he gave no sign of it—the most profound and terrible experience of the war. He would gladly have gone off with the others, but had felt a duty to Becker, and as he sat there across from him things slowly improved, for Becker's voice was still the same as before, also his eyes. And slowly Krug's mood changed, and he could sit quietly and chat. Krug loved music and dancing, as did Becker. Before the war they had gone out on dates with casual girlfriends together for years; they had heard nothing of each other during the second half of the war.

"What do you suppose is new?" exclaimed Krug. Looking at Becker in his deteriorated condition, at that death mask, was a torture to him. "Everyone in the school is edgy and nervous. We keep coming back to our old topic, marriage. The men can barely keep their families above water. All of them in tatters, kids and wives. No one can afford any kind of entertainment anymore, a square meal would be the height of luxury; we intellectuals and civil servants have landed at the level of the most common workers. The rotten food, malnutrition, the constant worry are wearing us down. Who can afford blackmarket prices? You're living with your mother, is that right, Becker? Let her tell you about it. I have my steady supplier. If you like, very discreetly of course, I could send him your way; the director is very satisfied with him. And clothes! Have you seen what kind of boots the faculty wears? Didn't notice? That's how the royal Prussian pedagogues have to walk about. Oh, pardon, *republican* pedagogues."

"And that's why they were arguing about politics at the window?"

"Of course. They want to blow off steam. Some because they never get a word in at home, hen-pecked husbands, they're easy enough to take and can be calmed down quickly. The others, the worse sort, argue at home too, but never win. So they try their luck with politics here. They're our professional trouble-makers. — The most peaceable are we bachelors." He looked up from the tabletop and gazed at the stern, emaciated face. This is the man I used to carouse with; he's been terribly affected by it all, I should change the subject.

"So you still plead the cause of bachelorhood as before, Krug?" asked the lanky man, who sat up unnaturally tall in his chair. How did he get into the room, do you suppose, how did he manage to sit down?

Krug: "As before. The only person who suits my taste is our new director. How do you like him?"

"Fine."

"All sorts of things are said about him. He is very cultivated, a bibliophile, has money. They don't like him. The fellow should have been a university professor. He doesn't fit in our shop." That was the old tone from days past. "I predict a short stay here for him."

The tall man shook his head. "So that's what the place has become."

"No resemblance to what the school was before. Later on when you are in the faculty room more frequently or at one of our conferences—I hope you're up to it soon—you'll think you're sitting among a bunch of mongrels. Don't rat on me, Becker, people don't understand our sort at all. It's the way they've become. And with politics the mongrels have a bone to chew on. To tell you the truth, the workers and the rest of the middle-class are no different. The workers at least have their socialism, and they've got several varieties of it available to do their cursing in, Majority Socialists, Independents, Spartacists. Yes, the shorter the rations, the more party platforms there are. Till finally everyone has his own party, that is man's primal state. We're not far from it now. Did you see our custodian by the way?"

"He carried my pillow for me."

"Oh, that you sit on. I kept wondering why you are so tall in the saddle.—He's the leader of the opposition here."

A questioning glance from Becker.

"It's the custodian or the doorkeeper everywhere now. They say it was the same way in Russia. The fellow is always snooping around. When they try to find him, he's in the director's room 'putting things in order,' or he just 'accidentally' passes by a door. I like to make him carry my apparatus around behind me, then I know I've got him under control. A spy."

"For whom?"

"Take a guess."

"Now that you ask, I'm not certain at all."

"You're thinking the Socialists or maybe the Independents. Way wide of the mark. He's spying for—Wilhelm II. And for the pastor of the local church besides. His son is in the second form. He's a real chip off the old block; everyone is afraid of the kid."

The ice was broken, a conversation under way.

Becker looked astonished. "That doesn't remind me of Russia in the least."

"Don't say that, Becker. I happened to argue the same thing recently with a colleague sitting across from me at a very, very leftist meeting, and he said that it looked just like that in Russia for a period, too, until in fact the real revolution started. And then the doormen and custodians were shot."

"If you had told me that a week ago, I wouldn't have understood."

"What? You've been in Berlin for a week already?"

"Yes, but I didn't feel up to going out."

"You're feeling better now, Becker?"

Krug heaved a sigh of relief, the terror was gone. It was the old Becker sitting there.

Krug: "By the way, the colleague I was talking about said one shouldn't be upset by all the spying going on. We're only at the beginning of the revolution. But he didn't convince me."

"Why not? Excuse me for interrupting."

"Oh, please do. You've just arrived from the North Pole, I've got to initiate you; love your neighbor and so on. I walk around a lot, because these evenings I've been restless and because what's happening on the streets of Berlin is more instructive than the papers, and I usually end up at some meeting. Any one will do. You're welcome everywhere. You're one more believer, they think. Naturally I keep still as a mouse and sing as is necessary either the 'International,' 'Brothers, Onward to Sunlight, to Freedom' or 'Deutschland, Deutschland über Alles.' Don't laugh. They notice if you keep your mouth shut."

"Well?" Becker urged.

"So I see a lot. But I ask myself: has there ever been a revolution in which people talked so peaceably? Meetings, meetings, nothing but convivial gatherings filled with instruction, about democracy, Marxism, socialism. Learned men stand up and make appropriate remarks. I've been to meetings of squatters, renters, parents, teachers, militia. Once I even ended up at a meeting of prostitutes."

"In order to know, my dear Krug, whether or not that's how things happen in a revolution, a man must first participate in one I suppose."

Dr. Krug was unmoved. "It was my impression. The revolution took a long time in Russia, too, is still going on. But there was a struggle, a visible one, the fronts were clear. With us there's only a hodge-podge. Nobody is really angry at anyone. The only ones who are angry are the Majority Socialists—with the Independents and Spartacists. But that is most certainly not a revolution."

Becker growled softly and shook his head. "You never know. Maybe the fault line of the revolution runs right there, between the Majority Socialists and the radicals, and not between the other groups."

Krug looked at him with eyes opened wide. "Strange. I had the same feeling myself already." He bent over the table and held his hand in front of his mouth, but before he spoke he stood up and went to the door, flung it open, looked around and then came back. He winked an eye. "Believe me, I know why I stick with Falk the custodian. He whispers all sorts of things to me. For example: first the troops have to return from the front and then the house will be set in order."

"By whom, Krug?"

"By the troops. And when they hear this bickering and carrying-on, it will be easy as pie for them. You needn't have any doubts. They'll blow it all away like dust."

"Who will do the blowing?"

"I told you, the troops."

Becker, abstractedly: "It's possible. I haven't been at the front for over a year now. It's possible."

He had laid both canes next to him on the table, sat there tall and at an angle atop the heavy pillow he had brought along. He had propped himself on one elbow and now laid his forehead in his hand. He stroked his brow with his middle finger, as if he were trying to pull back a thought that had slipped away. Softly he remarked, "You're right, you know. People should stop concerning themselves with politics."

Krug let out a little laugh. "Tell that to the people."

"Not me."

Becker fell silent again, then he said softly, "I envy you your work at the school. To be able to teach, to be with young people and to talk with them." He struck at air. "During the war I hardly thought about the school. Now—I can sense those boys right through the walls. What a profession teaching is, Krug—despite the things you've been telling me. There are other things you can talk about, true things."

"What sort of things are you thinking of, Becker?"

"Life, human existence, death that ends life and haunts it. Fear, joy, love, honor, dignity, pride."

Fat Krug listened attentively.

Becker: "And then the things you're involved in—the experiments, air, light, clouds, seasons, days—history, poets, musicians and painters, common people, martyrs. There are truths that one has to remember in certain circumstances."

Becker was looking at him with such self-assurance.

They really were interrupted by Falk the custodian now, a man with only one eye and the moustache of a non-com. He stood modestly at the door to say that he wanted to say good-bye to First Lieutenant Becker in case he was planning to stay a bit longer, since he had to go to the District Board on an errand for the director. Then Becker got up slowly with Krug's help. "You've reminded me at the right time, Herr Falk. I really must go."

He invited Krug to drop by, and they said good-bye to one another. Falk went out with him, carrying his pillow. In the courtyard Falk expressed his wish that the first lieutenant should get well quickly.

Becker: "I thought there were too many teachers already."

"Teachers, yes. But true German men?"

At Home

In the afternoon Becker received a note from Krug by pneumatic tube, asking if he might disturb him that evening.

Krug found Becker in his study, which had a strange and disorderly look about it.

"My mother," Becker remarked from the sofa where he lay on one side, "will bring us tea later on. How nice of you to visit me. I'm afraid I won't be much of a substitute for your meetings."

Krug was no longer terrified by Becker the "ghost," he saw other features in the face now. He inquired tentatively whether the custodian had said anything to Becker as he walked him across the schoolyard. "The fellow was eavesdropping toward the end, I'm sure. Because he couldn't understand anything, he interrupted us. I've come, as you may have guessed, so we can continue our conversation in peace."

"By all means, please."

"You don't think I'm a spy, do you, old friend?"

Becker glanced at him in astonishment.

Krug: "Well, you see, I would hardly even venture such a thing with the others. I'd simply be shown courteously to the door."

Becker: "How pathetic. And that's what's become of our school."

His mother appeared with the tea things. They laughed at the stonehard zwieback.

"Mother, what do you think. Dr. Krug asked me if I thought he was a spy."

Becker's mother: "I'm glad you can say that to him so candidly, Dr. Krug. Yes, Friedrich, that's how things are now. Everyone thinks the worst of everyone else."

Becker shook his head, chewing on his zwieback. "What a world."

"Ah, would you please be so kind, Dr. Krug," the mother asked, "not to inspect this study all too closely. I'm the housewife here, but I'm not responsible for this. Don't look at the walls, either. He's taken down every last picture."

"Indeed, Krug, my mother is blameless."

"What was wrong with the pictures, if I may play the spy?"

"They were hung there in the days before the war. A portrait of Goethe. And a youthful portrait of Heinrich von Kleist. I laid it out flat on the floor and piled two dictionaries on top of it; I'm curious whether he'll slough them off. You don't see the bust of Kant anymore, you know the one I mean, I think. He's lying under my sofa, next to a bust of Sophocles that used to hang on that wall there."

"And why all this?"

"On the right there, behind you, that large gray cloth, is the curtain for my bookcase. I nailed the cloth to the ledge all the way around."

His mother looked behind her. "You did that, too, Friedrich?"

"But why, my friend?"

Becker: "Paranoia."

"But why?"

"I have requested those grand gentlemen, who have occupied my study for so long, to make room for me. I based my request on my state of convalescence. They understood completely. The upheaval was accomplished like child's play. Since yesterday there are no voices here except those of my mother and visitors. And then day is here, he comes creeping in, creeps back out, then evening arrives with his table lamp, the noises of evening, a few voices of the night. That's sufficient for me. I'm on an intellectual diet. Why, you ask. — Am I about to unpack a large trunk perhaps that I've brought back from the war? Not that I know of; I brought nothing with me. I simply find it more comfortable if I can move about freely in my room."

"Friedrich, isn't all this talking a strain? He usually is resting already by this time."

"Then I'll be on my way," Krug declared quickly.

"Mother, allow me one more hour. — So then, the explanation. I'm reminded of the final scene in Kleist's 'Penthesilea': 'And now descending deep into my breast, I'll dig for some cold ore down in the pit, for ruinous emotion buried there, and then refine that ore in sorrow's fire to make it steel; now plunge it into poison acid hot, remorse's purging bath. To hope's eternal anvil then I'll bear it, hammer me my dagger sharp and keen. And with that dagger now I touch my breast. Like this, like this—once more. And all is well.' "

His mother: "How dreadful. What's the point of that sort of thing, Friedrich? It was a good idea to take down the Kleist portrait."

Becker lay beneath his large heavy blanket on his stomach with his face in his pillow. He answered after a while. "How quiet it is here. Berlin, my old room, you mother." He turned his face toward her, his brow furrowed. "But that cannot cause me to forget all I've been through, mother. The longer I am here, the more it clings to me. I'm not ungrateful. My comrades, the war, the misery, the dead and maimed, the terrible battles are all in good keeping with me. Don't worry, I am no Job, I'll not complain. But I won't let it be torn from me either. Although all of them, Goethe, Kant, Sophocles, even Kleist, want to argue with me. I'll not forget what was so unutterably naked and indescribable about it. That's why they're lying down there, and will have to wait until their time comes again."

His mother: "But it's been so long, so long that you've had to endure this, more than twelve months in the hospital, and I know well enough that's why you would never let me come to see you. I was afraid even then what you might do to yourself. But, Friedrich, it's enough, it's enough now."

"Get the pictures back out? Hang them up?"

"That too. You had already torn them down lying there in the hospital. Friedrich, I know more about you than you suspect. The senior medical officer wrote me often."

He took her hand and held it for a long time. She hesitated, then said at last. "Did you know, Friedrich, that I even saw you once?"

His eyes grew wide.

"In July, on the day before your birthday. I looked through the crack in the door. I heard you talking."

"And you didn't come in?"

She wiped her eyes. "I saw clearly enough what was wrong with you. How it was working inside you. I know my son, after all. I didn't want to frighten you. You had taken me down from the wall, too."

He said, "Come here, mother," and he pressed his cheek to hers. She helped him sit back up.

As they then quietly drank their tea, Krug suggested, "If it doesn't bother you, Becker, I'd like to continue our conversation from this morning. That's why I came by, you know. We had rather similar views. It seems to me that here in your study I understand you even better."

"Surrounded by empty walls."

"Right. Please, if you would, say it all in greater detail."

"It would hardly be of much use to you, Krug. What suits one person doesn't necessarily suit the other by a long shot."

"But would you like to say it? Please do."

"He's always this way," his mother sighed. "He doesn't want to talk."

Becker: "Because, being his mother's son, he only likes to say things that make others happy. — So then, Krug, at your wish I'll repeat myself. Politics, public affairs, should be avoided. People should beat them off when they come too close. They should arm themselves against them."

"People say, our colleagues say, that particularly in the wake of the war one has to be very concerned about public affairs."

"In order to do what? To stand at the window and argue? To curse and swear out on the street? To go for a walk in a demonstration?"

"No, in order to take part in public life. They will remind you, Becker, that if everyone thought like you—especially those who served at the front—why then God help the country. Then the rats we've already spotted will creep up on deck, swarms of rats, and they'll take over the ship."

Becker stretched out his legs and leaned back. He denied it with a decisive shake of his head. "That is no reply. I won't buy that. Were rats in charge before now? No, we were governed by an ancient noble family, the Hohenzollerns, a firmly established government, carefully selected administrators, a solid corps of civil servants, a Reichstag, a state parliament—and for all of that here we are where we are today. Why? Because we are the way we are."

Krug sat there comfortably. "But Becker! We! Whatever gave you that idea? Don't make things so easy for other people. The government was bad, it wasn't properly controlled. At any rate, here we are in the midst of chaos and must do something about it."

"So that we can have a government again?"

"Yes. What else?"

"Ah, Krug, that's not what scares me. That's not why you and the others should be scared, my dear Krug. Governing is grist to the mill for certain people. A government is like a fat bull that has wandered off into a jungle filled with lions and tigers just waiting to attack. And you can be certain that the lions and tigers will devour him."

Becker smiled, was silent for a bit and then continued. "Our country can't escape a strong, steady government. Our beloved law and order got away from us during the war and is pitifully lost at the moment. It's the blanket they use to pull up over their heads. And they toss and turn and try ever so hard. But it will appear once again, like some blessed daughter descending from heaven. How happy they will be to have it again. Yes, Krug, there is not another nation for whom government is so important, such daily bread, as for the Germans. Other nations can construct a government for shelter, like a roof over their heads, like furniture that they will demolish eventually. The Germans, however, sit rooted in their government like a plant in soil. Without their soil they'll wither and die. That's why the fall of a government is a catastrophe for Germany, while for others it's the impetus for something new."

Krug: "That's how it is, you think? And what sort of order, do you suppose, will carry the day now?"

Becker laughed. "That's fully immaterial, a republic, a soviet system, a monarchy. We'll be governed in any case, and on the heels of our current turmoil, it will be done with the firmest hand. Anyone who insists on it so passionately is bound to have his dreams come true."

His mother had disappeared while he was speaking.

Krug: "You're being ironic. Don't be ironic. You're too pessimistic."

"And what else? You have some other word on the tip of your tongue, Krug, I know."

"Yes, I do. Defeatist."

"Because I don't want order restored? Because this whining for order disgusts me? Because it disgusts me that our 'democrats,' as they call themselves, are only waiting to start groveling again, for a thunderstorm to break loose over their heads? How they long to know that a tiger is finally on top again, spitting and raging. Ah, tell me about our countrymen, Krug. There are several things that would be useful these days. I was out in the field, so go on and ask me, now that everything is over and it's too late, what it is I've finally come to believe is the real evil behind it all. Not the war. War itself—fighting, or simply lying around, the endurance, the tension—that was nothing unusual, difficult or sinister; you were stuck in it, you did your duty, didn't think anything about it. But when we came up for air, then we did notice something. The incomprehensible, incredible thing about war was—we ourselves. We, you and I, coolies, animals, without the vaguest idea, awareness or understanding, aborigines from Papua, doing what we were told and not thinking anything about it. Yet it was our lives that were at stake, and we had been taught even as children that God himself created them and set us humans above all his other creatures. And here we were flinging them aside, our lives, as though they were dead logs, as though we had never learned anything, heard anything, and lying there numb like the semihumans who slaved to build the pyramids. I did it and so did you, educated men, who had been pumped full of Christianity, ancient and modern philosophy, Plato, Spinoza, Descartes, Kant. And in the end they had merely flowed right on through us and left nothing behind, leaving us oafish slaves, brainless creatures, gasping for air, complete troglodytes, semiapes from the stone age. How is that possible, you ask yourself, how? It was a matter of our very existence. Didn't we really believe any of it, didn't we take seriously what they told us, what we learned? Are we like barrels full of holes? Listen to me, Krug. When I gaze at the sun, the moon, the stars, I become curious. I have to know what that is, what this means. Even the primitive demands that much. And I direct my telescope at them, once I have arrived at that stage, begin to calculate and set my brain to work to discover what they're all about—am I dealing with gods perhaps, with matter of a sort I'm already familiar with? Human knowledge begins in that way. You know that as a scientist. We know we can leave nothing lying there in nature without picking it up, measuring it, weighing, calculating.

48

"But then you receive—a mobilization order. An agency, an office that you don't know, writes: go here, go there, go to your death, to your ruin, go, so that you can lose a leg, so that you can get a bullet in your spine. Be careful, my boy, there will be gas, poison gas, mustard gas; swallow some. And you'll soon notice it may cost your head, your leg, your lungs, your life, and no one will ever replace them, since your mother gave all that to you just once. And you've been expecting it for a long time. During peacetime you prepared yourself for it, in the midst of your Kant and Plato. And you—don't question. You don't question, you go, you obey. The agency that issues the orders is more than God. You listen, more than to God. Because we have begun speculating long since about God just as about the sun, and we each have certain notions about him. But here we hold our peace. Why? For heaven's sake, why? We have to experience a catastrophe like this one in order to get some notion of it. Up on top sit little, miserable men, perhaps littler, dumber than you, perhaps tigers, crooks, scoundrels, parasites. They have neglected to do something, they have paid poor attention or none at all, and yet it is a matter that touches you ten times more intimately than the sun, the moon, animals or plants, it is a matter that clings to you like your shirt, no, like a parasite, a burr."

Becker's face had grown slightly flushed. He had spoken softly, gasped for air and finally whispered in a barely audible voice.

When Becker stopped to drink a swallow of tea, Krug searched for something to divert him with, for this was, after all, an abnormal outburst. Krug asserted, "But there you've just admitted what I was saying. The government is the guilty party and ought to be, has to be, changed."

Becker didn't answer. Krug became uneasy and stood up to go fetch Becker's mother.

"Stay, Krug. Stay. It cannot go on like this. You make yourself guilty, you are guilty, too. Whoever joins in is damned and deserves everything that happens to him. Now we let people babble away, get excited, search for the best 'democratic forms,' we let them get anxious because they can't find the old law and order. But no one abandons the project, no one enlightens them, pulls them back to look at the state, shows them what order actually is and what can be achieved by it. What can 'order,' democratic or any other sort you will, accomplish with unconscious animals, with natural objects, rats, pigs, tigers?"

Dr. Krug: "What are you driving at?"

Becker stared straight ahead. He took a swallow from his glass, refilled it. He whispered, "A new attempt has to be made. — And what sort of attempt is something we should know as teachers. You can only deal with the individual man. He is the one who at some point or other becomes the government. Rummaging around in the garbage looking for some form of government doesn't help. You put the magistrates and authorities on a level beneath you. That's a necessary part of it that's easy to arrange; fat men with a sash around their bellies. You make—room for yourself."

He interrupted himself, glanced at the glistening teapot. "But while we sit here talking, our tigers are already pouncing. Believe me, they want to anesthetize us all over again. That is the point behind every change in government. Krug, our hangmen are already at work."

Krug was glad that he finally understood more clearly. He was delighted to agree. "I'm right with you there. Room for us! What one finally wants is some privacy, privacy. Enjoy your life as long as the little lamp still burns. You're just saying the same old thing, Becker, that we've both believed all along."

He virtually beamed at Becker, seeming to want to charm his old friend, whose appearance he had now grown accustomed to. "Do you know, Becker, I am extraordinarily pleased by all you've said. You were always a completely honest man." He whispered, "But be careful that you don't say it everywhere and in front of everyone. People are stupid, especially the ones at our school. The next morning they would be screaming that you're a traitor to your country." He slapped his thigh. "Do you know what the slogan will be when it's all over? You can kiss my ass."

Becker sighed. Then he added. "So I put it well, did I, Krug?"

"Yes indeed. That you did. You're still the same. Thank God. You really blew off steam. But of course. Let people say what they like, and then do whatever you like. We won't be getting a general mobilization order in the very near future I don't suppose."

Becker's mother entered when he rang for her urgently. He asked for more tea for his guest, but she took a look at her son and whispered to Krug, "I don't believe we ought to overtax him."

Afterward, when his mother had led his guest out, Becker said to her, "No, really, he was good for me. I assure you, you're wrong. We talked about old times together. I want to see him more often."

Dr. Krug descended the stairs, unsure of himself. He was so uneasy that he hailed a cab and gave his own address. Under way he was taken by another idea and had the cab stop at a bar, where he phoned the new school director. It was no later than this when the two had sat and talked several nights before. The director was pleased, he was just leafing through an old portfolio of pictures, he would love to have him stop by.

The director's elegant atelier apartment was not far from Krug's own. The director, easy-going, blond, clever and dreamy, opened the door wearing a blue velvet jacket. There was an odor of perfume and cigarettes in his library. "My housekeeper has already retired," the gentleman apologized, "so I cannot offer you anything." But then he managed to produce some chocolates, sweets and candied fruits.

"Finally someone with a genial fancy, Dr. Krug. I've been waiting for over a year for one of my colleagues to bestir himself."

They leafed through the large portfolio that had been placed on a stand, sitting comfortably in front of it. There were etchings, heliographs, exquisite photographs of antiquities. A life-sized Michelangelo's David stood in one corner before a blue curtain.

The director analyzed the fine points of the pictures, Krug sat amazed. This evening was filled with strange events. And suddenly he began to speak, asking the director if he could guess where he had just come from.

"He was a most peculiar fellow." (He didn't say "too.") "Do you know our invalid, Becker."

"Oh, so that's it." The director feigned interest and laid his picture down. "You've just called on him?"

"You see, he is an old—I cannot say 'friend,' but companion of mine. We've known each other at the school since 1912; we were hired at the same time. Later we struck up a friendship, went on excursions together, took walks."

"Imagine that, all sorts of nice things."

"Aren't they though, Herr Director. And now I saw him again this morning for the first time since the war. I assure you I was shattered by the way he looked. Then we chatted for a while. I really didn't know what to make of him."

"Well," the director said encouragingly, "what had happened? The war and such severe wounds can have serious effects on a person."

"True, true. But when I was up at his place just now, I sometimes got the impression—just between us—that his mind had been affected. In all seriousness. All that brooding about war, the responsibility for the war."

"Very much to the left politically?"

"Not in the least, Herr Director. I thought that, too. At first I thought he's still recuperating, he's brooding about the entire unwholesome business. He says, for example, a person should thumb his nose at politics. He didn't like the discussion in the faculty room at all. I was pleased by that and assumed that he was still the same old Becker. For you can't imagine, Herr Director, what a free spirit, what a harum-scarum, what a fine fellow he was, handsome, open, candid, always with pretty girls from good homes. They threw themselves at him."

The director: "There you have it, a real human being."

Krug pointed at the stand with the portfolio. "He had a taste for art like you, classical art. And now when I see him again, with his dreadful, emaciated face, and visit him again, I meet his charming, sensible mother, but he—I can't help what I feel—he's crazy. He's gone off his rocker. He rails against the state, against all forms of government, councils and socialism included. Well then, I say to myself, that's not so bad, the fellow will get well. He had never been interested in politics, and I saw us out knocking around together again. But then . . ."

The director waited. "Well, Dr. Krug, what happened then?"

Krug felt uneasiness take hold again. "I didn't stay long. He got much too excited, he talked on and on, preaching an endless sermon. Then his mother came in, and I left."

"That doesn't tell me much. He preached? He was out to convert you?"

"Something like that. I don't like that sort of excitement. People drag it in with them from off the streets. Becker was a gentleman, a charming fellow, sophisticated. And now he up and takes the pictures down from his walls, nails a curtain around his bookcase. What do you say to that? Half crazy at least, don't you think? Can the war really have done that to a person?"

The director replied thoughtfully, "The soldiers from the front all come back a bit peculiar. They have no use for those of us who belong to pre-war days."

"Things may prove quite delightful once the whole front-line army arrives."

"We should be prepared for most anything. You've had a taste of it. Just look, for example, at what our good custodian Falk handed me before I left the school today. Two new decrees from the Ministry of Education, I don't know whether they came from Haenisch or Hoffmann. They were sealed by the way."

"Falk opens things, Herr Director. You can be certain of that. Do you still have the envelopes?"

"No. I know the man's a spy—working for the pastor, a few parents, some political party or other. I would never be foolish enough to call him on it."

Krug was surprised. The director continued calmly, "But what can you say to such regulations. They are supposed to be brought to the attention of the full faculty. Here. 'All books glorifying war are to be removed from school libraries.' Can you imagine that, just when the front-line army is to be welcomed home? 'All tendentious and false statements concerning the world war and the causes thereof are to be avoided.' "

Krug: "What, not simply 'its causes'?"

Director: "That's the least of it. The whole thing is impossible. I can't possibly present that to the faculty. At best I can only pass it on as a memo, because any discussion of it would be fatal for the ministerial authorities. 'Tendentious, false'—what opinions are the correct ones? At the next faculty meeting I will be asked to provide clarification." He laid the paper aside, a grave look on his face.

"And the second decree?"

"Not exactly cheering. 'Teachers in all disciplines whatever are to refrain from derogatory statements about or misrepresentations of the causes and effects of the revolution or the present government, as these are likely to disparage the good name and achievements of our national liberation in the presence of the students. It is the task of the school administration'—you don't object to my reading further—'of the school administration'—where am I—'it is the task of the school administration and faculty in their contacts with students to avoid anything likely to incite counterrevolution, especially in rural areas, since such conduct at the present moment carries with it the greatest danger of civil war among our citizenry.' And so now, my dear Dr. Krug, you have been given official notification."

"My profoundest thanks."

"And what do you say to it?"

"I'll sign on the dotted line."

"Sure. You teach physics and chemistry. You come off scot free. But think of what happens in German class, in history, even in foreign language courses. When is one saying something that might incite a mood of counterrevolution? It will drive teachers to despair. What are the gentlemen to say to their students? They won't dare say anything at all. They'll grow bitter. The students will get sulky, naturally. They're being given nothing. You have to give a young man something for his emotions. Even if I can't inspire a student, he wants his attention held. Should I praise the revolution? Glorify it? Well? They give us no materials. Just these two sheets of paper. I shall have to handpick the teachers for it."

Krug was silent.

"You'll see how the faculty reacts to this. — I'm not even speaking of what a devastating impression it necessarily makes for the current government, its highest authorities, to forbid anyone to make disparaging remarks about it."

Krug slid his easy chair closer to the director. "You needn't say anything about it at all. Simply let everyone sign it and let each one deal with his own conscience."

The director: "I have no other choice. I support no particular party. The school must be patriotic, but not partisan. That is no longer possible now. In fact, no kind of education whatever is possible now."

"Take heart, Herr Director."

Krug was amazed at his bitterness. Could there be something to the rumors about peculiarities in the director's private life? There were ambiguous reports about it. He often sat with the last form boys of an evening, gave them special help. Which resulted in some embarrassing remarks.

"What you've told me about Dr. Becker interests me, my dear Krug. I didn't know anything about him yet."

Saturday Evening

Eduard Bernstein, a gentle theoretician, wants to talk the people of Berlin out of their revolution. The public is treated to a high-wire balancing act, but doesn't know how to react. Someone standing at the door captures our interest. That evening an actual murder occurs. Saturday, November 23rd.

A public meeting on Bülowplatz

On Saturday, the 23rd, old Bernstein, a one-time Social Democratic member of the Reichstag, now an Independent, gave a speech at Bülowplatz. A gentle theoretician, he had most certainly not been to blame for the upheaval that had overtaken the German people.

In those revolutionary times the peculiar German form of social democracy felt much the same as the virgin with her baby; it didn't know how it had happened. The socialists had bravely resisted revolution up to the last moment, then it happened and now they had to reconcile themselves to it somehow.

They trimmed their little hall grandly with red cloth and busts. It was a roar of red and revolution. And when one took a seat on a bench beneath the menacing, prophetic beard of Karl Marx, one expected that an uncontrollable revolutionary rage, that terror would explode and come sweeping down over one.

But first a young, broad-shouldered man swung himself up onto the podium and with the most resolute words extolled this overthrow of government for having proceeded without letting of blood. His sentences were well-constructed. He aimed a few benevolent volleys at the rupture that was dividing the working-class. Soaring now, he called the independent actions of several workers' groups arbitrary and irresponsible and so arrived at his genial conclusion: it was desirable, in fact, to have a true expert in the field shed light upon the fundamental question as to what socialism really is, and for that reason Comrade Bernstein had been invited this evening.

As the young man seated himself at the head table and crossed his arms, having yielded the floor to Comrade Bernstein, he appeared to feel that he had herewith set the revolution by the right track.

Bernstein was received with respectful applause by the factory delegations. As always he spoke simply and in words easy to understand. He demonstrated that theory follows a straight path, reality a crooked one.

"Socialist theory finds itself in an unexpected situation. You won't find a description of it in either Marx or Engels. What is so peculiar about it? That capitalism did indeed pile riches upon riches, that the monopolies did indeed grow ever larger, but that the states then at a certain stage of development threw themselves at one another, into a war, during which, as you know, they destroyed the largest part of the riches the workers had created. The issue now is not, as some comrades write, to institute socialism as fast as possible. Rather we must first ask ourselves: under conditions that we did not ourselves create, what do we achieve by instituting socialism when the imperialist war has wreaked such havoc that it will first take years, perhaps decades before we have repaired the damage?

"Recently, before another gathering, I said: Socialize, yes—but be cautious. Everything depends on how advanced the means of production are. Another comrade rightly said that we are forced to accept what we have inherited from the Wilhelminian state and capitalism, but we are not about to dump our socialism onto that mountain of debts, we will not compromise our socialism, we shall keep it unsullied and in our own hands."

Bernstein refrained from repeating what he had said privately to some of his students, namely that the militarists had not only destroyed their state, they had robbed the working classes of the possibility of socialism for the next two generations.

He spoke of the desolate condition of the world's economy. All international relations, including those of industry and trade, had been broken. He recalled a phrase from Bebel: "Where there is no profit, there is no smoke from the chimneys."

"Life must be restored to the ruined economies of the world. Old relationships must be restored, new ones created. Production needs a marketplace in which to sell its goods."

Bernstein concluded: "Either we follow a policy of ruthless force or we proceed organically, step by step, to institute socialism. Our hotheads praise the Soviet Union. But how does that situation look to a level-headed observer?" The delegates, elevated to level-headed observers, heard what he read with not a little malicious enjoyment.

"The public revenues in Russia have decreased from 2,900 million rubles in 1917 to 500 million rubles in 1918."

Loud shouts: "What do the Spartacists have to say to that?" "They don't tell that to the workers!"

Proles Among Themselves

The Imkers, father and son, were metalworkers and had been at the meeting. They couldn't stay for the discussion because Imker's second son, who had come home with the Augustan Regiment, was waiting out by the door. He stood peaceably under the arch, smoking. He was surprised when they came out so early.

The father: "We didn't want to keep you waiting."

The young soldier with the Iron Cross, 2nd Class, grumbled good-naturedly as they started to move on. "All kinds of stuff to watch here. And you learn to wait in the army."

They crossed Alexanderplatz, went down Alexanderstrasse, Blumenstrasse to Küstriner Platz. On Lange Strasse they climbed a narrow stair to the fourth floor. A cozily furnished apartment awaited them. On the table a large bouquet of flowers shone brightly in a blue vase in honor of the hero. This was the living room. The red sofa doubled as a bed for one son. In the corridor mattresses had been piled for the returnee. In the darker room next to it there were three beds along the walls and a large screen.

At the sewing machine by the window that looked out on the gray courtyard sat the daughter, the eldest child of the family. She extended her hand to her younger brother, then went on working. During the war all three had made good money and been able to save some. Now only the father worked full time, the daughter worked at home, the mother and the older son were unemployed.

After the midday meal the mother made barley-coffee.

"Minna is working too hard," the soldier asserted. He didn't want to say that she looked different, older than her twenty-five years, or had something happened to her?

They wanted their soldier to tell about the war, but they had to drag the words out of him. He said, there's just mud, rats and not much to eat. And of course, you attack sometimes or get attacked. "Us guys in the artillery didn't talk much, we played cards and smoked. Most of us was hard-of-hearing besides. With me it's the right eardrum."

"I noticed that," his mother said. "If someone asks you something on your right side, you don't answer."

"Left side too, mother," the soldier laughed.

His sister, with whom he was on especially good terms, wanted to know what the political agitation had been like out in the field. "Who worried about that? Doesn't fill your belly. We were just happy to be going home."

His mother: "You're right there, Ed."

He puffed away on his pipe. "From the oldest sergeant down to the newest recruit we'd all had enough. In the spring offensive, when we found the English had canned food, puttees and blankets and real woolens, some guys wanted to go on. You could buy the stuff cheap. But later on, no sir."

Minna repeated: "What about agitation? Didn't they get to your unit at all?"

The soldier: "I told you, no. I haven't the vaguest what they would agitate about. Was completely unnecessary."

The father and the older son did not enter into the conversation. They seemed to agree with the soldier's answers. The mother offered a conciliatory word. "Minna was always earning good money and never worried about politics either. Only since the revolution."

Minna looked at her mother. "Father came and got me at the factory himself, on the 9th, and talked my ears full. And you were happy about it all too, Mother."

The father, to the soldier: "Minna got converted on November 10th. At the Busch Circus. She'd never been a real party member, in the women's auxiliary like her mother. Only after she was at Busch Circus."

The soldier: "What happened there?"

They looked at Minna. Her hands in her lap, she gazed straight ahead, and said nothing at first. She turned her head to her father; even in the house she wore a dark wool scarf on her head (she said it was because there was a draft at the window), and now she shrugged. "I didn't get converted at Busch Circus. Father's always spreading that story. But he knows; I worked in factories for four years."

The father: "I didn't mean no harm, Minnchen."

The soldier: "Come on, let's hear about Busch Circus."

She recounted it calmly. "There was a general meeting. Ebert was there, as acting president. I came for our factory. Ebert said that the quarrel, the quarrel between brothers in the socialist parties, had been laid to rest. Afterward Liebknecht spoke and Captain Beerfelde. Then we formed a workers' and soldiers' council that was to run businesses and everything. We understood that Germany would become a republic, a socialist republic."

Her features tightened, she sat up straight; the soldier could feel her joy. "And they cheered, Ed, cheered and cheered. I—I cried, it was so beautiful. Someone said that no matter what peace may turn out to look like, it's better than going on with mass slaughter. Ed, I can still hear how they shouted and sang for a quarter of an hour, and the meeting couldn't even go on. They stood up on the podium and they could gong their bells as much as they liked."

The soldier had taken his pipe out of his mouth and was listening to the unusual way his sister was talking. Even their father nodded, and the mother's face showed she was touched.

"They wanted to go on with their speeches. But even up at the speaker's table some of the men had laid their heads down on the table.

And the chairman rang and rang his bell, but you could only see how he was shouting and couldn't hear a word. And then they spoke about the war and the government. Ed, we worked like brute beasts for four long years. You didn't dare open your mouth. And heard nothing but military bulletins. Finally you heard the truth. Finally they were all saying it out loud, what you thought but didn't dare say, and it was the truth."

The soldier lit his pipe again.

Her cheeks were glowing. "Do you know what that is like, to hear the truth and to be able to speak up and ask questions—after being lied to for so long? Ed, it was almost like getting something to eat again. To be able to scream out loud what a pack of criminals and scoundrels they were."

The father: "That's a real socialist speaking."

The soldier: "And where do we go from here?"

The sister grew more businesslike. "It's a shame you weren't along yesterday. Last Tuesday we were all there again, father too."

The older son: "I was there, too. You didn't see me."

The sister: "You didn't say anything to me about it. Well, what do you think?"

The older son, who resembled his sister, even in his dry manner, shook his head. "Go ahead and tell it yourself."

The sister: "They were all there, the workers' councils. Müller spoke."

The son: "Which Müller?"

The father shrugged. "Richard, the mortician."

The sister: "Müller started things off. It sounded very different now than on the 10th. I can't even describe what all he said. Things are so bad, all over the country. The best thing would be just to dig a hole and bury ourselves. No raw materials to be had, and so on. And the way things are going, a complete mess."

The soldier: "True enough."

The sister: "We all know that, nobody has to tell us that. We're not the ones to blame for it. And councils are forming all over the place, but nobody knows what for. Next thing you know there'll be landlords' councils and millionaires' councils. All sorts of committees are being formed and declaring themselves to be at the disposal of the government. And then Müller laid it out in very clear terms, and that was good, and Ebert and Molkenbuhr were sitting right there. These wildcat councils, he said, need to be shown the door. But when people start screaming for a constituent assembly and general elections, why we know what they want. They want to grab the power away from the proletariat that made this revolution and hand it over to the bourgeoisie."

The father smiled sympathetically. "They won't succeed, Minna."

"A constituent assembly, Müller said, is the death warrant for the revolution. And they'll have to ride over my dead body to get their constituent assembly."

The soldier: "And then it was all over?"

The sister let her hands fall. "Then the Independent Haase stood up and demanded a constituent assembly, too. And then some fancy gentleman, a lawyer, got up and had the impudence to tell us that the lawyers of Berlin supported the revolution, too, and demanded a constituent assembly. He's a member of some council or other."

The soldier smirked. "A counselor at the bar, I suppose. My doctor used to sit on the Council of Medicine, too."

The sister, pulling closer to the table: "So how do you like them apples?"

The father sat calmly on his sofa. "Those of us in the old guard think different. You're too hotheaded. Socialism needs to be learned. We need the bourgeoisie. If they sabotage what we do, we're lost."

The soldier: "Let them have their election, Minna."

The father: "We'll have a majority, and that's the main thing, sure as two times two is four. They're going to rise up against the whole country? I doubt it."

Minna sighed and gazed over at Ed. He was smoking happily and said nothing. She stood up without another word and disappeared into the next room. You could hear her machine.

After a silence, the father said, "A fine girl. But too impatient."

Ed: "Why's she mixed up in politics, anyway?"

The mother: "Us women have got the vote now, too."

Ed patted her arm. "You've always had the vote, Mother. — But something's wrong with Minna, she's fretting, a love affair?"

The mother clapped her hands together. "Minna. All those years, nothing but work. Hauled coal like a man, worked on streetcars, the factory after that, and always saved her money and didn't waste a cent."

Ed: "Where's the money?"

The mother: "Father put it in a savings account."

Ed: "War loans?"

Ed nods. "You don't have to be ashamed of it. If you hadn't been making grenades, the French and English would have blown us all to bits."

The father took the socialist newspaper *Vorwärts* from the large fruit bowl on the table and pointed to something on page one. He whispered so that Minna couldn't hear. "Here it is: 'The parties on the right are gathering forces so that they can shape the future the way they wish. On our left are groups who oppose our democratic principles.'"

The soldier stretched his legs. "Holy Moses! You make life difficult for yourselves. Since I've been in Berlin, I've heard nothing but nonstop hot air. If they'd just nail all you Berliners' mouths shut, things would go twice as good. We need peace and something on our plates. All the rest is trash."

The father, alarmed because his wife has nodded her agreement: "And what about socialism?"

"Peace and plates of food."

The older son had sat there totally silent, his head propped in both hands. Now he let his hands fall. "Those guys left the country in such a miserable condition. Pumped it dry. Go out to the factories, Ed. We won't be on our feet again soon. We should have busted it up before this."

Ed laughed. "Before the war would have been best."

The older brother lifted his head. "What Bernstein had to say was a lot of damned crap. Before the war the party duped us all with the International, and now they're duping us with their socialism. I don't believe it, father, I'll tell you straight out. Not a word of it. Not one word."

The father: "And who's going to help build a democratic republic?"

The older brother: "All a lot of crap. The industrialists are settling right back in like before. You can smell it ten miles off. And what happens to us? Minna is back treadling her machine. I'm exhausted."

Ed: "And so what would you like to do, Fritz?"

"Emigrate."

The mother: "But Fritz, we've got our savings and two of us are working."

Ed: "Where to?"

"South America."

"Go work on a farm here at home."

"Let *them* make a drudge of me? They're the worst of the lot."

The father tried to clap him on his broad back. But he pulled away. "We'll go right on slaving away for the capitalists, and for the Entente now, besides. No, sir."

The mother: "Fritz always was inclined to be gloomy, Ed."

Ed: "If I was in your shoes, Fritz, I'd go along with Minna and help bust it up. As far as I'm concerned, I'm going to go get the civvies they're handing out on discharge and my fifty marks. And then I'll watch to see what everybody else is doing. At any rate I'm going to stash my rifle here at home."

Robbery and Murder on Friedrich-Karl Strasse

It started normally enough with an appointment and came to a dreadful end on Friedrich-Karl Strasse.

"And I'm counting on you to be there. Don't bring along nothing more than what you can stick in your pocket. Wear your coat, K."

The pneumatic postcard had been shoved under Lutz's door, had been lying there for a couple of hours perhaps, he had slept away the afternoon. He didn't own a watch, but when he stood up in bed and peered out the garret window, he could twist his head around till he could make out the illuminated clock on a church steeple.

In any case it was evening. He fell back down on the bed; awfully cold today. Wonder if Olga is still there? She sold newspapers—and sold herself too, but not systematically, which was why she could never really get ahead. She often told him that if she had a real boyfriend for whom she had to go out on the street she'd do it, but she couldn't find him. And so she went on selling, here a few papers, there some of herself. She was nice and sweet enough, but not really his taste.

Besides—out on the battlefield an officer and another guy had taken a shine to him. Then in March of 1918, he was sent by an officer to deliver a food package to his home, and he had just stayed on in Berlin, illegally like a thousand others, in garden sheds out in the suburbs. A couple of times swells dressed in the nines had picked him up for a few days in first-class hotels, then back to his rags. He had never looked up his family, they lived out in Friedrichsfelde. Why should he look them up, his father drank, mother drank, beat each other up every Saturday night.

Lutz tried to hear if Olga was stirring in the next room. He knocked on the wooden partition, no answer. She was already up and gone, of course. Had she left money so he could eat? He got dressed. From under his straw mattress he pulled out his striped trousers, wrapped in clean paper; he had lain on them, the creases were perfect. Socks had holes, summer socks. He growled with anger as he pulled them on. The shapeless, yellow, nail-studded army shoes. The water in the enamel bowl was frozen. He broke the icy crust, washed with green liquid soap, it too had a layer of ice covering it. He groaned when he saw himself in the brass mirror. "Money for a shave."

When he was finished, had his coat and hat on, he went out, opened the door to Olga's room and hit the light. The room, a garret, was nicely furnished, clean, pictures and postcards on the wall, the bed covered with a clean red quilt with little round figures crocheted on it.

"Money," he groaned, and shivered with cold. He looked on the table among the perfumes and creams. Under the table, covered by a piece of black canvas, lay a pile of unsold newspaper. He tore back the bed, rummaged between the mattress and pillow. He felt paper—two marks fifty. He was satisfied, rearranged the bed, locked up.

About eight o'clock he walked down Bellevuestrasse, across Kemperplatz. Bellevuestrasse was jammed with cars, a few cops were busy directing traffic into Viktorastrasse and in the direction of the zoo. At the

Rheingold there was a doctors' meeting, an elderly man explained, who just like Lutz stood around with nothing to do, hands in his pockets, watching people climb out of their cars. "Nothing but doctors," said the man. "If somebody comes down with something in Berlin tonight, he won't find a doctor."—"Why are they meeting here?" Lutz asked. The elderly man: "It's on account of syphilis. The soldiers didn't bring nothing back home with them except syphilis."

"Bull," another fellow broke in. "Those fine gentlemen would never come here for that, not by a long shot. Whatever they want, it's something to help stuff their wallets. You can bet your shirt on that."

Countless gentlemen, some in military uniform, came walking up the street from the direction of Potsdamer Platz. Many wore fur coats.

The elderly man spat on the ground. "Bastards."

Kemperplatz with its Roland's Well was deserted; the dimly lit Siegesallee led off into the distance. Lutz moved to the right under the treelined walk bordering the street and leading in an arc toward the Brandenburg Gate. The boulevard lay in complete darkness. Lutz's eyes grew accustomed to it. By the dull glow of a streetlamp he could see people moving here and there. But where was Konrad? This was the "Boulevard of Friends"; some men stood in pairs at the railings and whispered, others cruised. Lutz felt an arm laid on his shoulder, a stranger, he shook him off, he was freezing terribly.

Konrad was standing at the monument and came toward him; he was very young, wore a small, heavy stiff hat, snugly fitting, smart-looking coat, and had patent leather shoes on his small feet. He had put makeup on his cheeks, Lutz noticed as they walked out onto the street. A perfumed dress handkerchief hung from the breast pocket of his coat. His narrow eyes wandering restlessly to and fro, Konrad murmured, "What did you put in your pocket?"

And while Lutz watched him in amazement, Konrad balled his fist up under Lutz's nose and shook it in desperation. "That's why I was waiting for you. Don't you at least have a piece of twine?" Lutz was amazed. Konrad didn't say what he intended to do.

They now headed toward Dorotheenstrasse and bought some heavy twine in a stationery store. Next door they went inside a poorly lit entryway, and he had to help Konrad lay the twine together—it was much too long—and knot it up into several thick ropes. Lutz obeyed; they had to do something, after all.

By that time it was nine. They got warm by standing at a bar, where they ate frankfurters and drank a beer and a brandy. Then Konrad said it was time to go and told him about a disgusting old guy, a lousy lottery dealer who lived on Friedrich-Karl Strasse and was expecting him at ten. The guy lived alone, he already knew where he kept his money, and they ought to make a pretty penny off of him. "He's a loan shark, a cutthroat.

If we skin him, we're just paying him back for a hundred others, Lutz."

Lutz wanted to know what he was supposed to do. Konrad gave him his instructions. "We're not going to kill him, that's for sure. But he'll have to be tied up, and a handkerchief put in his mouth to gag him."

Konrad had the house key. They struck matches and climbed the wide staircase, two floors. Konrad rang, Lutz waited in the background on the stairs. Someone opened up, light fell onto the landing, Lutz pulled back, Konrad went in, the door closed. Long, long minutes passed, Lutz grew uneasy out on the stairs, someone might come. Then the door opened softly, very softly; he saw Konrad in the crack, without his hat and coat, elegant, a flower in his buttonhole, a cigarette in his mouth, motioning for him. In a second Lutz was behind him, on tiptoe, thank God the stairs were covered with a runner, and they walked into the entrance hallway and onto a heavy blue carpet. There was a smell of cigarettes, the door stood open leading to the living room.

There was only a dim ceiling fixture in the hallway, but at the far right end of the hallway a broad swath of light fell out from one of the rooms. From inside it came a hoarse, querulous voice: "What are you looking for out there?"

"Just a sec," Konrad answered and went in. Right behind him, Lutz looked from the shadow of the corridor into a messy, luxurious room furnished with lovely armchairs, a palm resting on a high pedestal, an old brown piano. On a divan that stood at an angle to the room, half sitting, half lying, was an old, very pale man with disheveled dark hair. He had laid one hand on a small round table next to him and used it to sit up a bit straighter now. Konrad, who noticed that Lutz was too close behind him, gave a poke for him to stay back, and, taking a drag on his cigarette, pranced nonchalantly into the room and up to the man.

But the man had become suspicious, Konrad was too obvious in his movements. He sat up, his eyes alert, and stared beyond his friend toward the door. Lutz noticed this from outside. He saw how the clumsy, pale man, without worrying about Konrad, stood up and was about to make for the hallway—and so he charged. He leaped into the room as if he were jumping in assault from a trench, five, six running steps; with one throw of his hand he tipped over an easy chair that stood in his way, and literally threw himself in a bound onto the fully terrified man.

Something had to be done. Konrad had made a frightened move to one side when he heard the wild footsteps. The little table with its lamp fell against him; he caught it with both hands, but his cigarette fell from his fingers as he did. And so it happened that while Lutz struggled as if berserk with the man on the sofa—he had rolled over on his belly to escape the hands at his throat—Konrad was kneeling on the floor looking

64

for the cigarette that was singeing the carpet. Only after it was safely in the ashtray beneath the mirror did he run out into the hall and grab out of his coat pocket the rope they had prepared.

The dreadful struggle inside was still going on, though neither Lutz nor the man uttered a word. Both groaned. Now and again it looked as if the man was about to squeeze out a cry of alarm, but then Lutz, who was lying on top of him, would press his head with both hands down into the cushions of the sofa. As Konrad arrived, Lutz gasped, "Handkerchief, handkerchief!" Konrad went back into the hall, pulled the dress handkerchief from his pocket, and balled it up with his own everyday one. Lutz had finally found the best position to hold his victim—he rode him, clasping the man's legs from behind with his own and holding his head down. As soon as he felt Konrad next to him, he reached for the handkerchiefs and let go of the old man's head, who turned it immediately to one side and gasped audibly for air. Then Konrad quickly stuffed the ball of cloth between his teeth.

"The feet, tie his legs!" cursed Lutz. Konrad set to work. He got it done. Now Lutz slid down from the body, bending first one then the other of his victim's arms behind his back. He had Konrad wind the twine tightly around the man's wrists twice, and then with Konrad's help he bound the arms to the man's sides from the rear.

They let the man slide down onto the carpet. There he lay, his eyes open, his head propped against one foot of the divan, following the two with his eyes; they paid no more attention to him.

Konrad knew the apartment inside out. Lutz, however, was incapable of going up to the man and pulling the keys to his safe from his pocket. Konrad had to take care of that. He did it, without letting the fuming, wrinkled brow of his victim upset him. As the gagged man began snorting vigorously through his nose, it occurred to Konrad: "The hall door is still open!" So Lutz went back and closed it. When he came back he found his friend trying out the key.

Konrad asked him at one point, "Why's the fellow always staring at me? Throw something over his face." And there was nothing for it; Lutz had to do it. He went to the adjoining bedroom and came back with a bathrobe; he threw it over the man from one side, without daring a glance at him. Then he rubbed his hands on his pants as if he had laid them in a fire.

When they had found the money and jewelry and laid it out on the floor, they stuffed their pockets with it. They took off their jackets and vests and bound towels filled with the loot around their waists because they didn't dare go out on the street carrying a suitcase.

They had to leave many beautiful things behind. Of course Konrad said, "We'll come back later," but both knew they wouldn't.

Then just as they were buttoning their jackets they heard someone slowly, ponderously mounting the stairs, and, to their horror, stopping at the apartment door and then moving about a bit.

"Who is it?" whispered Konrad, beside himself. They both thought the old man had made an appointment with yet another young man and that this one would have a key, too.

Lutz: "Quiet!"

Ghastly minutes passed before the stranger went away from the door—while they stood there silently, edging toward the door of the living room. They both realized that the stranger might be able to hear the snortings and puffings of the gagged man. The stranger could also see the light shining out under the door to the corridor. But since nothing more happened, he departed.

They made ready to escape. Konrad listened out into the quiet stairwell, then ran back into the room where their victim still lay under his bathrobe. To prevent him from working his tongue free too soon, he shoved the gag further down his throat.

"Bastard," he whispered, as he looked at his wet, bloody fingers. He wiped them off on the bathrobe.

It Grew Colder Toward Evening

The chapter title tells most of it. The Spanish flu remains a curse; because of it, one man lays hands on himself. — We visit a rich lady on Hoher Steg in Strasbourg and attend a large reception. Two of the guests do not know whether they still love each other. It is November 24th.

It got colder toward evening in the city of Strasbourg, while the happy crowds, civilian and military, poured through its streets. The water of the Ill was covered with a thick layer of ice, and children ran off to ice-skate. In the brasseries and cafés people sat shoulder to shoulder, no one wanted to stay at home on this day of celebration.

Nor did the Spanish flu epidemic refrain from making its gloomy rounds today. Millions of people of every nationality had come down with it, it seemed jealous of the prey taken by its precursor, war.

One man walked mournfully to the funeral of his mother, whom the flu had slain. And when he returned home, where his wife and small child lay ill, they were both dead as well, motionless. The man was not drunk. He threw himself onto the bare floor of the living room, still wearing his black coat just as he had come from his mother's funeral. And when the neighbors looked for him the next morning, he lay in the kitchen, his throat slashed.

A Reception at Frau Scharrel's

The dining room and salon at the home of the rich and beautiful Frau Anni Scharrel on Hoher Steg were brilliantly lit. The ranking general Marshal Foch had already been announced, the important men of the military government would soon follow. In the city shops hung pictures for all to see of the faces so admired these days: Poincaré, president of the victorious republic, with his square face, forceful moustache and

67

goatee, and about him the faces of the other men who had helped maintain the nation's will to victory—old George Clemenceau, who was said to be as ferocious as a tiger, a physician from the Département Vendée, bald, with a white, shaggy moustache that hung down melancholically, and with the deep-set eyes of an old man. There was Foreign Minister Pichon; Lebrun, the minister of the blockade; the presidents of the two houses of the legislature, Dubost and Paul Dechanel, an elegant man who would later become president of the republic for seven brief months, then fall from a train, resign his office and die. There was Maurice Barrès, the academician, a severe face, hair full and parted; he had written about blood, lust and death, and he lived on for five years after this victory that was his victory as well. There were two architects of the France to which one was now so devoted: old Victor Hugo, the mortal shell of whose fervent, shining spirit had long lain in the Pantheon, and Leon Gambetta, patriot and orator, who fifty years before had helped his country, deserted by its emperor and ravished by war, to grow into a republic.

And now so many people, gentlemen and ladies, were moving about and laughing and talking in Madame Scharrel's lovely, fashionable apartment, that the blare and thumping of the band in the Westminster Café next door were no more than background music. And when the noise of conversation, the clinking of plates and glasses subsided and the music became more obvious, people felt as if they were simply sitting out a dance at a ball.

Officers came and went, Frau Scharrel had been chosen to quarter them. People talked in groups, standing with teacups in hand or sipping coffee. Some of them were talking about lunch at the town hall. The officers were brought into the conversation, everyone here spoke French, some better, some worse. The curé, Frau Scharrel's confessor, gathered several earnest citizens of Strasbourg about his armchair, they put their heads together and whispered about the more unpleasant incidents of the day—the ripping down of flags from shops was annoying, there had indeed been some shameful misconduct, who could actually be behind such actions, one was not after all in the midst of a revolution. Among those who stood discussing these matters so seriously and impartially were, of course, those who for one reason or another feared that they themselves might fall victim to some such misdeeds.

Frau Anni Scharrel, a widow for many years now, had lost her eldest son in battle in the first years of the war; she was in partial mourning, a kind of transitional mourning. The rich, handsome lace collar covering her narrow shoulders was the only totally black item she wore. She wore her chestnut hair in an extraordinary way, combed up, a part down the middle, heavy curls above her ears, which this evening bore small coral pendant earrings, their red peering enticingly out of the covering darkness. She wore a dark blue dress of shimmering satin with a small train. Her white neck was exposed. One could see her feet as she walked—if one found the time to free one's gaze from her fine dark complexion and escape her exciting eyes—but just the toes fluttering in silver shoes.

Frau Scharrel put down the cake plate at once when Hilda entered the room and smiled at her. They carefully touched their cheeks to each other—both wore powder and lipstick.

Yes, this was Hilda, the former nurse in the small Alsatian military hospital whom Lieutenant Maus was so worried about because she hadn't written a single line, apparently not having forgiven him for his assault on that last day. The daughter of a Strasbourg architect, she had returned to Strasbourg. What was she doing at Frau Scharrel's? She was looking for someone—ah, and such is love, not for Lieutenant Maus.

She had joined in the war effort in order to escape from an unhappy love affair, had become involved with a man, had let him dominate her, and had had the vague feeling that this was no longer love. Once out on the battlefield, it was all over at once. They did not write. She thought of him only seldom, and then with a shudder. Now the war was over and she had returned. She wanted to see him. Where was he? She did not want to avoid him. She wanted to register some effect of the war within her. Frau Scharrel was a relative; the two had met here.

Before Hilda entered the room, she had seen Bernhard's cane out in the umbrella stand; so he was here. Now she stood beside Anni, who fixed her a plate and chatted away, laughing.

Hilda was a tall, slender woman. Her bosom, where once First Lieutenant Becker had buried his face, swelled within a white silk dress. She carried her head, with its curly light blonde hair, her loose falling hair, very high, in fact haughtily and tilted back. Since daybreak, when she had lain in bed and listened to the tootings of an auxiliary band rising from the street, she had experienced a puzzling change of mood, a playful spirit had risen within her. Since returning from the hospital she had regained her delicate complexion; her cheeks, as if they had been waiting for a return to Strasbourg, had filled out wonderfully. She looked lovely as she gazed out across the bright room with its odor of cigarettes. She stood beside elegant Anni, who was so happy to see her in that long silk dress, and so full of good health and good spirits, that as Hilda was about to place a silver spoonful of cake in her mouth, she grabbed Hilda's hand and said, "Give me a piece," and they ate the rest of the cake together, embracing and laughing.

Two young women, twins, Anni's nieces, were just coming out of the salon into the dining room, and at once they rushed up to Anni and told Hilda how delighted they were to see her. They wanted to go to Paris, but not for a week yet because there was such a great celebration and to-do going on here in Strasbourg. The two inseparable, languid

creatures, both in floor-length evening gowns that revealed not a line of
their bodies and carrying heavy blue shawls, gazed attentively at Hilda.
The sisters walked with Hilda through the two rooms. Hilda felt as if
the twins were leading her somewhere, but it did not matter to her, she
was quite happy. As the twins moved away from her in the salon, the
clever curé came over to her, a French officer accompanying him; the officer introduced himself, they spoke a mixture of German and French.
The officer, no longer young, wanted ever so much to hear Alsatian
German spoken. He called her the loveliest inhabitant of the recon-
quered Alsace it had yet been his pleasure to meet—had she not been
standing one evening recently on Rabenplatz as a torchlight procession
passed by.

But in the midst of the conversation—the curé was telling what devoted volunteer service she had done during the whole four years, in the
east, in Rumania, and finally here—she was struck by the fact that a great
many people were standing about and talking with her and looking at
her. But where was Bernhard? The thought that Bernhard might be in
the room distracted her. She took leave of the two gentlemen and
walked back, watching attentively. The twins latched onto her and
asked, "You're not going so soon, are you?" She would not let herself be
held back.

In the dining room people were coming and going. She did not find
him. But—if he is here, then it's probably best if I stick close to Anni,
he'll show up at some point. Anni was sitting in her armchair, in the
middle of a semicircle of gentlemen Hilda did not know. At Anni's invitation Hilda found a spot beside, or more precisely, behind her. A serious conversation was in progress. Hilda immediately recognized one gentleman, a young one, with a full brown beard and a gold watch chain
across his white vest. He was Anni's personal physician. He was on the
medical faculty of the university.

And then as the three of them stood in the window bay with its
heavy, formal curtains and Hilda and the doctor exchanged recollections
of the war (the clinic in Strasbourg and the little hospital had been connected with each other), an elegant, striking man approached, an artist, a
painter or composer to judge by the full, light brown hair falling down
the back of his neck. The curls also fell across his brow, and one large
strand touched the base of his nose. The soft collar of his dazzling white
shirt, its loose cuffs bulging out from under the sleeves of his velvet
jacket, was open and bound by a small, loosely tied cravat of navy blue.
He skipped along in patent leather shoes, their wide bows carefully and
exquisitely placed. The tastefully dressed but flushed gentleman approached the group at the window—everyone in the room was flushed
from the warm drinks and the close quarters. With a ladylike motion of
his balled-up handkerchief he patted the fluffy, light brown beard that

framed both cheeks but left his weak chin exposed. His moustache consisted of a thin extended stroke of hair. He stopped in front of the group as they chatted, appearing to take in the sight of the three of them standing there on the carpet with the delight of an artist: Hilda, pale blonde, a bright Valkyrie, turned toward Anni, who was shorter than she but who in her peculiar way drew all eyes to her, and the dignified doctor with his worried face.

"Ah, but don't you two know one another?" asked Anni with some surprise. "This is my nephew, Bernhard, and this is Hilda, whom I spoke to you about."

Anni smiled at Hilda. "He has been looking for you all over the apartment for the last hour and didn't recognize you. Have you really changed so much in these four years, Hilda? I think not."

Bernhard, the handsome artist, let his right hand slip across his tie to straighten it and then extended it to shake hands with Hilda while making a series of little bows. He took her hand attentively, and when he had greeted her she was unable to retract it. "I have been followed for days by reports of you, Fräulein Hilda," he lied with dreamy, coquettish eyes. "Aunt Anni has spoken to me of you and your father, too, but now when I learn you're here you make yourself invisible."

"What possible reason could Hilda have for hiding from you, Bernhard? You've met her on the street perhaps, or at her father's and have not recognized her."

"Indeed, I confess my guilt," he declared without taking his eyes from her. At last she had pulled her hand away. "You rise up again from the war like—I cannot find the expression."

"Well, like what, Bernhard?" his aunt prodded, watching Hilda with apparent affection. "What does Hilda look like? Do you see her in a painting?"

"A painting? You are a muse, Aunt Anni, Fräulein Hilda, you look like . . . ," and here he spread his arms, pushing Anni and the doctor close together beside Hilda against the curtain, then whispered, "like Germania."

Anni threw her shoulders back sharply. "Bernhard!"

The doctor made an apologetic bow to Hilda. "An artist's compliment."

Hilda accepted a lighted cigarette and felt quite gay. Aunt Anni had to say good-bye to a guest, but came back at once. And in tow behind her she dragged the inseparable twins, the dark-haired young ladies who had been lurking close by for some time, and as they joined the group their glances flew from Bernhard to Hilda and from Bernhard to Anni. They stood arm in arm like statues, exchanging delighted nudges with their elbows. Hilda laughed, the conversation moved at a lively pace. The twins were asked about their trip to Paris. Anni suddenly exclaimed that she was planning a visit to Paris herself because of some legal difficulties.

"But Aunt Anni," Bernhard asked, "you're off to fair Paris and are leaving us behind alone?"

It was Hilda who was first to leave. Bernhard accompanied her into the hall. As the maid laid her winter coat around her shoulders and Bernhard helped her slip into it, Hilda made a careful study of the umbrella stand and gasped in happy surprise. "Ah! There's your cane, I see. You still have it."

He could not find a reply.

He required considerable time to set his tie and hair in order in front of the hallway mirror. He did not want to venture back into the dining room, but he had to. The guests were departing. When his aunt caught sight of him—she was accompanying two elderly ladies to the door—she nodded fleetingly to him. "I thought you were seeing Hilda home."

He managed no more than an "Oh!" and a meaningless smile.

Hilda hurried her steps toward home. After the frost of the morning and midday, it had now grown slushy.

She still bore with her the aura of good cheer, social bustle, animation from the tea, liqueur, cigarettes. But in the core of her breast, clear up into her throat, she felt a stone.

The meeting after the war that she had so feared, that had been it, with him smelling of perfume.

She turned down a narrow side street, came out onto the quiet St. Peter's Platz and walked on past the houses. Two lonely streetlamps burned murkily. She stepped into the entryway of an unlocked house and leaned against the wall. She was so dismayed she had to stop and rest.

She saw and smelled this strange man, an artist, a handsome dandy, he had almost offered to see her home. He had introduced himself as Bernhard. She had danced to that man's whip, she had fled from him.

She was freezing in the entryway; she pulled her coat about her and moved on. Even when she rose from dinner with her father and went to her room, she had lost none of her dismay.

Anni Scharrel was lost in thought, and Bernhard, who had stayed to dine after the reception, was so as well. Several times Bernhard looked pleadingly in her direction, but she did not react. As they drank their coffee he kissed her hand. He begged, "Have I offended you?"

"Not at all, I have some business matters on my mind."

He continued to busy himself with her limp hand as he sat at the small coffee table. She, still preoccupied, stroked the thick hair at the back of his head. He let himself be petted and finally knelt down before her to make her work easier and to lay his head on her knee. He felt the familiar, peaceful and pleasant feeling of being close to Anni. With his skin rubbing on the stiff satin, the image of his blonde Germania came to him again, that striking picture of Hilda. The war was really over; the swallows were returning home. It was sweet to lie here on Anni's knee and to know that Hilda, a young flourishing, beautiful woman, was back again.

As if she had been touched by something in his dreams, Anni stood up. While she offered him her mouth, which she did not open, she looked into his eyes but could discover nothing. At the door to her room he made as if to follow her, but he was not serious. They were both content to separate after they had exchanged an embrace that was weighted down with questions.

He sat for ten minutes in the noisy Aubette, in a corner by himself, and wrote something on a page he had ripped from the notebook he had laid on his knees—he was sharing a small table with other customers.

"Dearest Hilda," — Would the gentleman care to order? — A cup of chocolate, please. — "The war was destructive of goods and men, but let me utter a word of blasphemy: through it you have grown to become the Hilda I met this afternoon, after four long years," — A waiter: Have you ordered? — Indeed I have, ten minutes ago. — I'm sorry. We're very busy. — "and compensate for much of its destruction. There are two mysteries here: this transformation—and your long silence. Do you think it right that that silence should continue, now, when we and our affairs are thrown so closely together?" — Who ordered the cassis? One cassis, one tea.

He had just got an envelope and a stamp at the bar, when the door was flung open and a wave of cold flooded in bearing a band of young men who stormed in like a swarm of birds, tipping over tables. The waiters rescued the drinks that were still left standing, people laughed and shouted, a few of the young men wore masks—Wilhelm with his moustache. "Success is ours!" announced a surly Ludendorff, a Prussian military policeman on a hobbyhorse.

Book Two

November 24th to November 27th

Book Two

November 24th to November 27th

A Private Revolution

Soldiers march, the Academy meets, thieves steal, ration books for travelers find a remarkable use, and everyone does what he can to survive these dreary times. People know that behind their backs they are being sold out. It is November 23 and 24, 1918.

The Retreat of the Defeated Army

Time vomited what was in its belly. It remained to be seen whether that would make it well again.

The allied troops pressed in behind the Germans. The English sent their cavalry in pursuit. They crossed the field of their old victory, Waterloo, and rode on toward the German border. Along the old battle lines they were met by German officers, selected for their knowledge of English, who handed over an immense number of German cannons to the British.

Behind the French cavalry marched the Americans. They occupied the city of Luxembourg.

On the 22nd, the army reached a line extending along Essen-Düsseldorf-Cologne-Mayer-Simmer, and then, to the west, Ludwigstadt-Offenburg-Neustadt-Schorfheim.

While Wermuth, the mayor of Berlin, was calling on the city to receive its troops with ceremony—"shadows lie over the German nation, but above them all shines its eternal glory. Lift up your hearts to greet Germany's sons, bind for them wreaths of honor to deck the railroads, houses and streets, quarter them in your homes"—the British cavalry was marching into Namur and Liège.

Belgian troops moved toward Cologne, French divisions toward Mainz. The vanguard of the English troops was led by General Harbringer. When he entered Charleroi, driving German regiments before him, they had just left the city, blowing up fifty munition cars before their departure. Civilians were killed. As they marched out, the Germans were attacked by a hostile citizenry. Belgian police had to intervene.

On the 22nd, The Augustan Regiment appeared unexpectedly in Berlin. Not even the Berlin Regiment knew they were coming. The troops quietly occupied their barracks on Friesenstrasse. Along the streets, the first of the black, white and red flags of the old Reich, beneath which the army had marched off, were hung from buildings especially in the west of the city, in Wilmersdorf, Steglitz, Charlottenburg. The streetcars joined in as festivities began. Wherever they ran, hosts of people hung from them, stood on the running boards. The cars clanged their bells and raced along, while up front fluttered the banners of Old Germany and Prussia. In Neukölln, a working-class section, people knew what those flags meant; they stopped the streetcars and ripped them down.

The Silesian Station in Berlin, the Friedrichs Station and the Anhalter Station were transformed into army camps. Baggage was piled in giant mountains. And if each piece of baggage had been a child searching for its mother, at the train stations those days you would have heard nothing but the horrible cries of desperate children looking for their desperate mothers.

The Prussian Academy of Sciences

In contrast, learned men gathered quietly and with dignity in the Prussian Academy of Sciences on Unter den Linden to report on their current work and the extent to which they had pushed forward the frontiers of knowledge. For be there peace or war, victory or defeat, the human intellect does not rest. We are set down in darkness, but the mind rises up in the night like a firefly and looks about.

The learned men of the Berlin Academy of Sciences were nevertheless deeply shaken. They were alarmed by events around them. Their secretary was Professor Max Planck, a man entangled in the delicate theories of physics. Deeply troubled, he posed the question—even before they began their exchange of ideas—whether they truly wanted to go on with this, whether it might not be better to suspend their deliberations. He had spoken with the other gentlemen of the secretariat, and they were united in the opinion that they ought not to interrupt their work.

He did not say: we are set down in darkness, the human mind does not rest, cannot rest. He said: "The enemy has deprived us of our weapons and might, he is about to humiliate us. A serious crisis has broken out in the heart of the Reich." The professor swallowed hard and looked straight ahead with an ashen face. "But one thing the enemy has not taken from us: German science and the honor in which it is held. We are not soldiers in the army, but there is one thing we can do: defend German science and its standing in the world, its splendor and its fame, with all the means at our disposal." He concluded: "It is for that purpose above all else that this Academy exists."

While he spoke, two dozen older men and graybeards had stood up. The learned man spoke no further. They sat down once more in silence.

Now came the scientific section. A philosopher spoke about Spinoza's doctrine of attributes. That thinker had long been dead, but his ideas had extended out across time, had been of consequence.

After the philosopher another man stood up, clad in a simple, everyday suit as were all the others. He wore a narrow black tie and spoke softly. Heads were lowered once more. He read the work of a young historian who had fallen in the war, an examination of the financial administration of Egypt during the Hellenistic and Roman periods.

The Patriotic Watchmaker

In Berlin, you "expropriated." This is the deed the Bible naively calls "stealing" and solemnly prohibits. Now the act had donned modern dress, and philosophers and policemen struggled arm in arm to comprehend this sudden and extreme form the phenomenon had taken.

One group of new foes of the Bible had set their sights on a watchmaker on Berlin's east side. His was a large shop with sales on the ground floor, workshop on the second. During the war, a photograph had been displayed in the window, a family photograph. It showed the owner of the shop with his equally robust wife, and below them to the right and left, symmetrically grouped, four sons and two daughters, all full-grown. One of the ladies wore a pince-nez, two of the sons wore glasses; the ladies all had on work clothes, as did father and mother; the sons were in their field grays and wore helmets. The same sons were pictured in individual photographs besides, as watchmakers and goldsmiths. This dynastic display, together with a lot of black, white and red flags, victory dispatches and pictures of generals, had captured the notice of the neighborhood early on. Now revolutionary cadres were concerned with this imperial watchmaker. Although a police station was in the neighborhood, the ground-floor display window was plundered publically one evening. The panes were broken, the people outside were asked to move on, the members of the family held captive in the upper story. Upon coming down, the owner determined the extent of the damages, but did not lose heart. The first thing he did was order the windowpanes repaired. By the very next afternoon it had been done and on the bare shelves stood a goodly number of mournfully empty cases. Among the things the robbers had not taken with them were the photographs of the family. These the owner now tucked away on one side in a long display case that he barred with a grate. On the inside of the pane he pasted a sign that read: "Despite it all, Germany will be rebuilt." One could see how the six well-nourished members of the goldsmith's family were indeed stubbornly busy rebuilding Germany from behind the grate. On the door he hung a sign: "Warning to thieves. First, everything is insured. Second, spring guns have been installed." All this was the work of the owner, his outraged wife and his two daughters, since the sons were still on the march, coming back from the west and the Ukraine.

This did not prevent a large gang from appearing at the house two days later, from breaking the windows again and this time entering the shop itself and taking a great deal with them. The case at the side did not fare well either; it was wrenched loose and the whole thing smashed. The splinters and some additional thrusts of a knife caused extensive damage to the pictures.

What an uproar there was the next morning, the whole next day, in front of the watchmaker's house. On the far side of the street, the groups of people discussing the matter grew larger and larger. "Why haven't the police done anything?" asked some. Others were more reserved in their behavior, they simply watched and seemed not to be upset by the watchmaker's misfortune. As the Bible says: the human heart is unfathomable. But who would have believed it possible that the watchmaker, wife and daughters did not yield even now? It is difficult to say who was responsible for the lion's share of resistance. Numerous considerations might have induced the man to give in and hold his peace while waiting for better weather like the majority of his countrymen. But the woman was hard. They hurriedly had new prints made of the tattered photographs. They boarded up the large shop window, behind which locksmiths were set to work on a massive grating, and finally they painted the challenge directly on the wood: "Despite it all, Germany will be rebuilt."

Travelers' Ration Books

Whoever wanted something to eat or drink in Berlin at the time had to have a lot of money, preferably in foreign currency. But travelers' ration books were also much in favor. There was one fellow who could sing a short, sweet song about those books, though he traveled little and had just enough money himself to cash in his bread ration coupons.

He was a young worker from Berlin, named Hock or Heck, an unskilled man. But one did not have to be a skilled worker to know that there were beautiful things to be bought in Berlin and that all one needed was the money to buy them. He worked on Beuthstrasse, but only since the revolution; before that he had been a recruit and thanked God that he could ride his motorbike straight home from the barracks in

Jüterbog. His parents had given him the bike six months before as a present so he could visit them when he was on leave. He was staying with his parents again, both of whom had done well during the war as workers in a munitions factory in Spandau. But the war had put an end to making munitions was well, and there they sat in Charlottenburg, cursing peace because it had put an end to the war and blessing peace because it had sent their son home from Jüterbog. But neither of these events had provided a new source of income.

Purely by chance, which is responsible for so much human fortune and misfortune, it came about that their son Max found a job in a printing plant, where he was put to doing heavy, unskilled labor. He had to drag bales of paper and man the furnace. Cleaning up the rooms was one of his duties as well. He swore a lot about that part of it, because he thought they should hire a woman to do that job. But then his parents called his attention to the fact that it is always useful to clean up after fine gentlemen have dined and then departed in some disorder. At the time, the press in Beuthstrasse was printing travelers' ration books. At least they were originally intended for travelers. As things developed they proved to be of use for the non-traveler as well, provided he could get his hands on them. In particular the unfavorable course of the submarine war contributed to the non-traveling public's increasing interest in the travelers' ration card. For whoever had them and the money could buy extra bread and so stave off the effects of the hunger blockade. When Max's parents learned that he had to clean up in the printing shop, they knew that this was their great chance. Both of them were revolutionaries, as only befits laid-off munitions workers, and they wanted nothing more than to make shreds of capitalism. Couldn't everyone plainly see how the war profiteers were getting fat, how they were taking the skin right off the backs of the great mass of the people? Their lives of luxury were notorious, and they managed it by making use of a brilliantly organized black-market, with the cooperation of the farmers. And others were supposed to hold back? No, not for a moment. And the bellicose pair advised their son to do his part to help dying, putrid, staggering capitalism to its final collapse. He should look to see if he could get hold of those travelers' ration books. They would take care of the rest. "How?" Max asked. "By selling them." They wanted to supply the black marketeers with them, offering them either to the black marketeers or selling them directly to the rich. They weren't at all troubled by the contradiction inherent in their behavior. It can't hurt, they said slyly, for the parasites to swell up even more, that way they'll finally explode, and their rottenness will stink to high heaven. They would be contributing to the revolution. No sooner said than done.

At the beginning of November the travelers' ration books in Berlin were renumbered. A large quantity of already printed books were to be destroyed. The person commissioned to carry out that destruction at the printing plant was Max, the unskilled worker. Max had thus far made but meager progress in the world, subsisting on his wages and an occasional theft. But the petty thievery was not thievery to him, since in those days, both in theory and practice, the notion of property was very wobbly. There he stood then one evening in the printshop with a giant bundle of paper stuffed into a sack and he obediently dragged it down the stairs into the cellar. The furnace was down there, and he burned such paper as part of the fuel for the central heating.

At the sight of it, weighty thoughts ran through Max's mind. First he carefully shut the furnace door to avoid temptation. Once the paper was burned it would all be over. And so he took a spade, dug a hole in the pile of coal and buried the sackful of paper in it. He wanted to ask his parents' advice. He rode along the Charlottenburg Chausée on his rackety motorbike, and the closer he drew to Schillerstrasse, where he lived and where presumably his parents had just sat down to a wretched piece of herring tail, the clearer things became to him. And when he arrived home and found everything just as he had expected—his parents, the herring tail—and when he had reported what had happened, or better, what had not yet happened, it hit him like a bolt of lightning. How was it possible that he should have to drive the long stretch from Beuthstrasse in Berlin clear out to Schillerstrasse in Charlottenburg to realize that he should have transported that sack home with all due haste. But now it was too late for today. It could not be arranged until tomorrow noon, and then only with difficulty because a porter was always at the printing plant gate and the sack was a very visible object. But the building had a staircase, and the staircase led to the roof, and Max ultimately transported the sack via that old thieves' route.

Otherwise unemployed, Max's parents used the first weeks of the young German revolution to turn their invalid travelers' ration books into money. It was a great success. They came in contact with the finest people, the kindness of the ladies and gentlemen whom they met fascinated them and began to melt their revolutionary horror of the bourgeoisie. They are cultured, the couple said, it makes you downright ashamed of yourself. They went to the theater, bought themselves new coats. Money's what you need, they crowed at home, hugging Max the recruit who had turned out so well. They wanted to ensure him a brilliant future. In the period between the 10th and 22nd of November so many travelers' ration coupons were redeemed in Berlin that it aroused suspicion. At first it was credited to the flood of soldiers. Supplies of grain were strained enormously and the Food Office got upset. They shouted that the soldiers would have to leave Berlin, they could not afford this. Posters to that effect were hurriedly printed, with printer's errors, but readable. Even when the frightening demand did not subside, however, it took a while until a bureaucrat set about to ascertain the real origin of all these damned travelers visiting Berlin, running around and stealing the bread out of the Berliners' mouths. They didn't even read the new printed posters. It was time to let it rain fire and brimstone, to place armed guards at the train stations and not let anyone out of a train who had no good reason to be in Berlin.

In order to find out where these ravenous bread-eaters were coming from, this one lonely bureaucrat—terribly upset—gained entry to the space, located on the premises of the Food Office, where the mountain of redeemed travelers' ration coupons had been brought. This was a shed in the courtyard that had been cleared especially for the purpose. The shed had at one time served as a cow stall for a dairy. It still smelled like one and it was godawful dark besides.

"Isn't there a light in here?" the bureaucrat yelled at his guide.

"What do cows need a light for?" the man replied. In these revolutionary times such a candid tone of voice had become common between superiors and their subordinates.

"Well I need a light!" shouted the bureaucrat. "I'm not a cow."

"Anybody can say that," came the scornful answer, and a search was initiated for a lantern, which would be no easy matter in a Food Office. So like a cow looking for fodder, the bureaucrat had to grab haphazardly into the mountain for a handful of those damned ration coupons that had already been eaten up. He stuffed his pockets full of them, stuffed the pockets of his guide as well, and so they marched back across the courtyard stuffed with paper, after having closed and locked the dark and dreadfully reeking cow stall that now housed Berlin's misfortune.

Naturally on their return to the central building they first had to overcome the grim resistance of the porter, who absolutely refused to let them in—first because of their suspicious girth and second because of the pestilential stench they gave off. It was as if these ration coupons had mingled their own corruption with the putrefaction of the abandoned stall to produce an uncommon odor. Shoving his way hastily into an isolated room, the bureaucrat went to work—gasping in a gas mask—scrutinizing the material.

After ten minutes he knew the whole story. He roared with anger. He flung off the gasmask. It wasn't the soldiers, it wasn't foreigners, they were simply invalid ration coupons belonging to a series that had been ordered destroyed, that should have been destroyed but wasn't; instead they had haunted the famished metropolis of Berlin like so many ghosts, like living corpses that stank in their guts.

At this point the police were called in. Just as in a war the soldier is the most endangered person, so in a revolution it is the policeman. He never knows whom to side with. He is given the function of making arrests. But if he makes arrests for the wrong side he risks his own neck.

Which is why in revolutionary times the reading of newspapers and the use of the telephone belong to the policeman's most important activities, so that from day to day, if need be from hour to hour, he can determine his position in the state. If suspicion is a character trait of the policeman in normal times, then during a revolution such suspicion increases until he questions absolutely everything, rendering him stubbornly immobile as he clings to his deskchair as the one thing in the world that can promise him security. After several calls to the appropriate police division produced no results, Herr Lustig—our bureaucrat— set out himself to lure the police officer from his chair. This was nothing new to him. But separating a policeman from his chair was as difficult as pulling a hippopotamus's tooth. Lustig armed himself by stuffing a list of numbers and a small bundle of reeking ration coupons in his briefcase. But as bait he left some bands of yellow paper hanging out, the wrappers from cigars.

At police headquarters the commissioner was not, of course, available to talk. The man had surrounded himself with a number of elderly people whom he had acquired very cheaply at the closing of an asylum for the feeble-minded. These individuals would have starved without anyone's noticing, like many of their colleagues, had not the commissioner recognized that they might still be of some use during the revolution. He gave them uniforms and set them up in his reception room; they heard nothing, they said nothing, they only sat there smiling and drooling, writing down what they had not heard. At the sight of these hideous, inscrutable creatures one hundred percent of all visitors fled; they would then enter a complaint at some other office that knew nothing of the trick and which itself then became a victim of the revolution. But Lustig knew about these individuals; when he appeared with his briefcase simply overflowing with cigar wrappers they ran to the commissioner in his office, where he was busy charting the curve of his daily security. The feeble-minded made strange gestures, pointing to mouth and nose. He did not understand. Was this something about their sniffles or those of some stranger? About provender? Did they perhaps have some confiscated food in the reception room? At that thought, Commissioner Sorge jumped up.

Cautiously he followed them. In the front room he saw to his great horror the ill-reputed Herr Lustig from the Food Office, a man he knew only too well, for he was forever pestering him to investigate the black-market. But what was that hanging so gaily, so festively from his briefcase? Cigar wrappers. At the same time, however, there was beyond any doubt a stench of cows in the room. The detective concluded that this could be a case of confiscated cigars and butter or of cigars in a cow stall. Lustig saw how Herr Sorge's eyes shone. The trick had worked. They went into Sorge's office, locking the idiots out.

84

Herr Lustig had no cigars. The commissioner's rage knew no bounds. But Herr Lustig frightened him with the information about what was going on. A large gang was apparently at work trying to starve out the city of Berlin. They weren't content just to cut off the gas, power and water, some of them had got control of the official travelers' rationing books in order to deal a death blow to the government and the revolution.

Herr Sorge listened intently. "Who? The government and the revolution?" The case was heaven-sent. It was a matter of both the government and the revolution. Neither the one nor the other could proceed if there was nothing to eat. Arrests, therefore, could be made.

Whereupon Herr Sorge stood up with Herr Lustig, gave a few pats to his imbeciles out front, who were busy taking down statements from the desperate men and women surrounding them. "Quiet!" the commissioner shouted. "Everyone must wait his turn."

They took a car and drove to the printing shop on Beuthstrasse. The owner, an honest man, was standing in the main hall. When Sorge reported the incident, which brought disgrace upon his good name, the printer fell into a faint. He would have ended up in a rotary machine, into which visitors had disappeared on several occasions, had not a worker sprung to his assistance. This machine, designed for bread ration coupons, had thus been rendered useless; it only produced meat and oil coupons now. The owner, grateful for his rescue, gave the name of the unskilled worker Max as the man to whom he had given the coupons to be burned for fuel. And now the commissioner could proceed with his first arrest, namely of the owner who had escaped death but a moment before, because he had not taken the necessary precautions in having the coupons burned.

The owner wailed, "But I know Max's parents."

"Good God," the commissioner muttered, "who knows who nowadays? Do we even know ourselves? In the middle of a revolution?" He thought of his security chart.

They descended into the cellar. Max was there stoking. That was the second arrest.

Herr Lustig rejoiced, Herr Sorge beamed.

They got back in the car, drove to the police station, took two officers along with them and arrived at Schillerstrasse in Charlottenburg, where Max's parents were said to live in a back building. Crimes of this sort are always played out in annexes and back buildings. The mother knew at once what it was all about as she peered from the window. (We can report that other persons were also watching, and that at this point a great deal of hiding of objects occurred in several small apartments.)

Without a single twinge of conscience, a porter showed the officers the stairs that led to Max's parents.

While the officers stomped up the stairs, the porter gazed with interest at what was happening above. The mother gave a sign and a cigar box plopped right in front of him. He picked it up and disappeared.

Several thousand marks were confiscated in the apartment. But the cigar box had been noticed by one of the officers as it flew by. When they questioned the porter as to its whereabouts, he first replied he was not there at the time, then didn't understand what they were talking about, then remembered vaguely, then discovered the cigar box was missing, and then finally in fact found it in a corner under some newspapers—broken open and with three thousand marks missing.

Such was the gnawing hunger for things of value in Berlin at the time.

Several Romances and Detective Stories Continued

One man agonizes over a woman who has forgotten him. A dream makes another man happy. A report on how things were for women during the war; this is news to some people and they are amazed by it. A lottery dealer is found in the condition someone placed him in the evening before. It is November 24th and 25th.

Prefatory Comment

Man, who is said to be the most powerful force in this world, manages to be so only sometimes, hit and miss. Otherwise he is something quite different.

When the war was over, many thought that peace would now follow, that that was the succession of things, and that they had latched onto the happy ending.

But imagine a man who has had hydrochloric acid thrown on him by some madman or criminal. He screams with pain, and at last someone gets a firm hold on him, rinses the wounds out and neutralizes them. But the poison has already destroyed tissue at a greater depth and has passed into the lymph system, and only with that does the dreadful inflammation and suppuration really begin. The same thing had happened to whole nations when the war was over; only then did they first become truly sick from the war, and they suffered greatly.

Hunger had burrowed its way into Germany. Only the rich and the cunning escaped it, but tens of thousands died. And hunger did not relent at war's end. Cripples, incurables, the blind and the mad flooded the land. There was no increase in reason. No one pointed the way and no voice was strong enough to be heard above the wails of pain and bewilderment.

Worry about Hilda

We look about for Becker and Maus. We find them easily.

Maus is sitting in Becker's study.

He had not been there since the attack on police headquarters.

They had been having great fun together. They laughed so much at the news they told one another that Becker's mother came in and joined in their laughter. Maus, so he explained, had again been reconciled with police headquarters. And his old friend Big Ding and his fiancée were crazy about police headquarters these days and thought it Berlin's most beautiful building. Because there was a chief of police in there that they trusted. He had been there before this, it's true, but now they suddenly trusted him.

Becker and Maus laughed.

Then Maus began to tell about his mysterious double life.

Mornings, afternoons and evenings, at every meal, he was a dutiful son sitting at table with his family. On occasion he would even appear as an honored front-line soldier, a wounded veteran, whenever there was a secret meeting of the citizens' guard or the resident militia, where he could become a general on the spot. His career would be assured. And in between—he was off to either police headquarters or the royal stables. "I've rented some digs where I can do a magical change of costume. If the spirit moves you, come visit me."

"You're totally depraved," Becker said when they had stopped laughing.

Maus: "I make a mockery of whatever is holy. I don't know what else to do with myself. I cannot find anything reasonable to do. You can't give me any suggestions either. Fantastic things are going on in Berlin now, by the way. In the royal stables, at headquarters, at the palace, everywhere in the city."

"Someday they'll chase you out of the palace and the stables like chickens."

"I assume so too, Becker. I understand that much about military games still. Because of course one doesn't serve in any serious capacity. And even now I'm not at all clear about what these commando operations are about. But that doesn't matter."

"Do you get paid?"

"But of course. If there's a hitch there, either we go plundering in the city or we use our cannons to get money out of the Reichsbank." Maus suddenly laughed aloud at the thought. "If it really happens someday that they're not paid the wages they demand, then I'll hire the best of them out to the citizens' militia."

"That won't be easy, Maus."

"You know all about it, don't you. Sure, they've got notions in their heads. 'All Power to the Workers' Councils.' 'All Power to the Soldiers' Councils.' You can't budge them from that. — And what about you, Becker?"

"In a few months I'll be back teaching. I'm really worried about you. Don't get too carried away."

Maus, earnest now: "The last time I was here with you, after our attack on headquarters, you said, 'Everything's finished. First the others smashed us up, and now it's our turn.' You said, 'We should use this revolution. It's good that everything's shaking loose.' You used your fist. 'Smash it to smithereens.' "

"I still believe it, Maus. We've got to prevent them from continuing in the same old way. We've come back after a savage drubbing. Our comrades are lying out there. If we have any obligation at all it is to draw the right conclusions. We're lucky that Germany's shaking loose."

"And what of your sweet peace?"

"When we were leaving the hospital, that little town, we knew everything better than we know now."

"These are some times we live in, Becker."

"Hasn't Hilda written you yet?"

"No."

"Forget her. Hold on to the memories—of what they branded into your shoulder and into my back."

Maus, softly: "Give me some advice, please."

"What you're doing now is no good. Promise me you'll sit down and think it through."

"I can't do that, Becker. Things are moving too fast, you know that."

"You're my friend."

Maus stared straight ahead grimly. "She's never forgiven me. I'm a bastard. The best thing I can do is just throw myself away."

Becker: "Nonsense. I'm telling you, you'll see things differently one of these days."

Maus: "You think so?"

And he threw himself like a lifeless mass onto his knees in front of Becker and wept in his lap.

Bells Toll

Becker was improving. He made better progress in Berlin than in the little Alsatian hospital. But this was a coincidence. In Alsace his illness—the paralysis-like weakness of his lower body resulting from shrapnel wounds and spinal compression—had already taken a decisive turn for the better. But only now did what had there begun become apparent.

A combination of treatments he had undergone helped as well: localized treatment of the nerves, massages, radiation, and the strengthening of his general condition.

He no longer dragged himself about like a wretched skeleton with a waxen skull, the first sight of which had caused his mother to sink to the floor in a faint. Aided by canes in both hands, he lifted his legs more quickly and vigorously. He could walk for certain stretches without tiring, and every success spurred him on. He credited it all to Berlin—Antaeus on his home soil.

His study still looked desolate with its naked walls, the pictures and busts stuck behind the desk and under the sofa. The tightly stretched curtain was still fastened across the bookcase and would remain there.

Immediately after Maus left him—it was late afternoon—a recruiter for an officers' organization came by; at last Becker sat down with his mother in the living room and grumbled, "People are badgering me. What for? If I should want anything, I'll know it all on my own. It wasn't like this before the war. You sat in your study, you were at home, and if you wanted something, you went out and took care of it yourself."

She suggested it was the same as with the black marketeers and people trying to sell you things on time, they wanted to whet your appetite. She laughed. "And maybe you are hungry, but you just don't know it."

His eyes stared wide. "No, I'm not hungry. I object. I'll not let myself be pushed." For the first time since his return, she saw him angry. "Mother, maybe I'm still sick and maybe my wounds still have scabs, and some spots don't look so lovely. And maybe I've only covered it all up after a fashion and I have to be careful when I walk that one or another of the many bandages doesn't get blown away. And then someone comes along and says, 'May I look at that spot, good sir? Would you permit me to see what's under your bandages?' "

She laughed. "You talk as if you were a first-aid kit. The world is like that now, Friedrich. They don't leave you in peace. You used to be able to go get bread, rolls, Sunday pastry, meat, just as you liked. Who cared what somebody else ate. And you didn't let anyone take a peek in your purse either. Now—I have to read in the paper when my ration coupons are valid. Then we stand in line and talk, and naturally you're interested in who the baker favors and why the shop on one street has one kind of bread and the one on another some other kind. It isn't very nice, Friedrich. It's a totally different world."

Becker: "So that's how it is. And since when? Since the war began? Since rationing began?"

She lowered her eyes and nodded.

They sat without speaking, facing one another.

The mother: "The old days, Friedrich, are not coming back."

He let himself fall back against the sofa. "I've no longing for them."

"You shouldn't say that, Friedrich. You had it good. You were happy and lively. You were a ray of sunshine for everyone. Just ask the people you were with. Don't be ungrateful. The world stood wide open. Since the war," she shrugged, "everything has closed over, everything is so earnest, so gloomy, so brutal, as if another race of men were taking over."

"And me, Mother?"

She didn't smile. "It has—infected you, too, Friedrich. Yes. You no longer dare to be what you really are."

She sat down next to him. "And why not, Friedrich? Why don't you want to be my dear old Friedrich again? That Friedrich couldn't have been better."

He didn't answer.

She gave him a pat and raised his hand to her face.

He thought: Shall I tell her what I told Maus in the hospital train when we were on the way home, about my second birth? My first birth has gone to its death, that's true. I am another man now. Or—is it not true? Am I only deceiving myself? My mother gave me life, my body. And look, there she sits beside me, and I lay my arm around her shoulder and see and feel how happy that makes her, my mother. She was given her body by someone else, and they were given theirs by others, and we are a chain that is linked by love.

She felt him give her a warm hug.

My existence comes from her? Perhaps—not. I flowed through her. But I'm fond of her. It's a fine thing that she is alive. That she can call out to me.

His mother noticed what was going on inside him, the struggle back and forth.

"You are so proud, Friedrich. I've noticed that everyone who was in the war and has come back is proud. They seem to think they are something better than other people."

"And what do you think about that?"

"Many of them are right, those who had to bear a great deal for example. But many of them proved to be real barbarians out there. They still run around with the same savage look. They still want to fight a war. I am frightened of what will happen to us when the whole army returns. Don't be so proud, Friedrich. Not of that."

"Of—something else?"

"You know perfectly well what I mean without my saying it, Friedrich. You don't want me to flatter you, do you?" She sighed. "Ah, it would have been a great deal if you had brought just one thing back from the war, Friedrich—a knowledge of how little and poor and wretched we humans are. For the war was certainly a calamity."

Her words struck him like a blow. He pulled away from his mother and sat now bent over forward. The pictures and the busts lay along the wall, the bookcase was nailed up. Little and poor and wretched. Where had he heard that? Where had these words struck him before, this cry, this warning—in the war, in the hospital? Where?

His mother pressed a kiss to his brow as always. He took hold of her hand. She left.

But in his sleep, in a dream, the train that had borne him home from the Alsatian hospital was under way.

He heard a voice in the rolling wheels. Someone spoke, a man, an old man, he had heard that voice back then, too. The man emerged out of white moonlight, Johannes Tauler, in medieval garb, the preacher who had flooded Alsace with his light centuries before.

"Do you know me? I called to you as you left my homeland."

"Yes."

"Dear soul, I follow you like a mother follows her child. Friedrich, you wanted to see the sweet countenance of peace. Now you lie here in your room, among your books. Your friend visits you, you speak with one another, and you think you can advise him. But you will not lie here much longer. You will move. It will make no difference whether you walk along the street or sit here in your study."

"Yes."

"You will move—but where to?"

"I don't know."

"The sickness in your body is giving way. What you have suffered was only preparation. It is closing in upon you. You will not escape it."

"I do not wish to."

"It cannot be accomplished with a single decision. Your soul has now been called upon. Your battle begins. I have come to announce this to you."

"Father, teacher, advise me once my struggle has begun. Show me the way."

"There is no way that leads to this spot or that. Friedrich, you are a great mountain, a man of lofty emotions. Your poor lost soul is caught in great tribulation."

"I do not know what I should do."

"The Evil One will whisper to you. You will not recognize him. You will follow him. Take my hand, hold it tight. Reach out for it, always. The struggle will be a difficult one. Do not forget me, my son. The dread, the despair shall not devour you."

"The dread? The despair?"

"The gates bear those names. Be strong. The Lord will come in a soft rush of wind."

The wheels rolled on. The train cars sank into darkness.

Dawn broke as Becker opened his eyes.

Bells were ringing nearby. Night was past, Becker was conscious of nothing.

He lay there expectantly, very calm. A kind of joy filled him.

With each toll of the bells he swung out above gentle green hills.

Women in the War

For the soldier Eduard Imker, discharged now from the Augustan Regiment, the days in Berlin passed peacefully. He had grown used to a lazy life at the front. He slept liberally, determined that there was no work for him in the city, and was glad of money his family had in reserve.

Close by to where he lived, however, ran Königsberger Strasse. Here he would spend long hours of the day in a tavern where idlers like himself sat and stood around from morning till night. Among them were women and children, for apartments were dark and cold, and you could not simply stand around in the streets. Also the area around the Silesian Station was always a bit risky because of tramps and bums, and of late there had been shootings. So you hung around Hildebrand's Bar. The owner allowed you to eat what you brought yourself without ordering anything else. The room was filled with thick smoke, the gramophone played continuously until closing time.

This morning in Hildebrand's Bar, Eduard Imker is talking with acquaintances and strangers alike; some of them for, some against this government; some for, some against a constituent assembly. Everyone has some handbill or other with him.

Around ten o'clock, Ed is joined by a pale young woman from the same building where he lives. He knows her husband and both her children. The woman accepts the glass of beer he buys for her. She is waiting for her husband, who gets his relief money today.

"But he usually doesn't go till about one."

"Right, he's still at home," the woman says, "but I like to get out with people."

Which makes Ed think she might be an easy catch, and that surprises him.

But then she says, "No, not the way you think. I don't do nothing cheap like that. My husband knows that, too. But that don't mean you can't have fun, too."

And she tells him what good wages she earned during the war, and her husband too, but adds that now everything is shot.

Ed suggests wisely that that's how things are.

Then she starts up again, after drinking half her beer. "You're a halfway reasonable man, I can tell, Ed. You ain't got married, and that's good, right there. So you can understand maybe why a woman sometimes would as soon get out of the house as stay there. Coal—."

He nodded. "Coal. That's what I thought. And so the barkeeps make the money. Somebody always profits."

She answers heatedly, "Sure. What are you going to do in a cold apartment. The kids at least are at school."

"Is there heat there?"

"There is at theirs. The kids are all stuck together in one room, several classes, and it's heated, and that's the main thing. Get milk from the Quakers besides."

"I'll be damned," Ed marvels. "The Quakers, what luck."

The woman: "But we just sit up there and crawl back in bed after breakfast to try and keep warm till noon. Sure, and then . . ."

Ed grins. "I can imagine."

"What can you imagine, Ed? That that's so nice and all? Well, it ain't nice, first it's hard on your nerves, and neither one of us is strong, Max ain't and I ain't neither. The army sent him back home because of his lungs, and me, I've already got two kids. What are we supposed to do. You're a respectable fellow, Ed, so I can tell you all this. That's why I'd rather come to the bar."

Ed can give no answer.

The woman: "I've never argued with Max, not once. We haven't argued with each other a single time since we met. But I don't want no more kids, we got no use for them. Two is already too many."

She turns away, puts her handkerchief to her eyes, but then takes a quick pull on her beer.

"Go ahead and drink, Frau Mieren, puts courage in you. I'll stand you a brandy besides, I will, and not another word."

They sip at the glasses Hildebrand junior carefully serves them from a tray, and fall silent and feel how the pleasant warmth spreads through their bellies.

She taps him on the arm. "Ed, you've got it better than Max. He loves me, you know, but when I take off and tell him, Max, it can't go on like this, that just makes him cry. 'Cause what has he got besides his family? They've been working on him at the relief office that he should get mixed up in politics, and every evening he brings home a handbill from some meeting or other."

Ed's response is decisive and calm, but very soft, so that the others can't hear. "I don't hold much with politics either. Ain't nothing in it for people like us. It's like in the war, we don't know what games they're up to, but we're the ones in the trenches when the gas comes, and the gas masks don't fit. That's us every time. Nope, keep out of it. Tell him that for me, but just don't be so hard on him."

She nodded sadly. "I just got out of the Women's Clinic. Who can keep on going like this?"

Then the woman's husband arrived. And soon a strapping civilian about Ed's age walks in, shoves his way to the bar, and when he sees Ed between the two of them, he gives his cap a tug, opens his eyes wide and goes over to him with arms raised, and the two men embrace and pound each other on the back and laugh and shake hands. It is Ed's best friend, the top man in their athletic club; but he was in the war for only a short time because he is a skilled lathe operator, a capable and sought-after man, considered indispensable by every company he works for.

They say good-bye to the young woman and look for an empty corner in the place, which they manage to find next to the gramophone. Erich Prietsch is a hardy, happy, irrepressible fellow. Since Ed last saw him he's grown stouter. He is glad to see Ed. "I've been out looking for fellows just like you, Ed. Been out looking with a lantern. For our old athletic club. We're starting it up new again."

Ed tells how he has returned home with the Augustan Regiment. "And how about you," Ed wants to know. "How are things with you and the other guys from the club?"

"The other guys?" Erich shakes his head. "A lot of things screwed up there. But I can't complain. Let me tell you, Ed—but don't say a word to nobody else—for guys like me it could have gone right on like it was going, and we weren't the only ones, that's for sure. Man, did we ever live high on the hog during the war."

Ed: "You look real good, too."

"Thanks. May be okay to switch to peacetime, but we're short of everything, even the machines are shot. Our factory did like everybody else. Full steam ahead, like a ship in the night, and when another ship comes along and they collide, well, then they collide. And there's been a collision, sure as hell."

Eduard: "Sure has."

"And what about you guys out there? Where were you? Tell me about it."

"Ain't nothing to tell. You sleep, eat, shit; you're ordered to leave the trench and you go on living or get shot. Then you stretch out in your shelter come evening, all peaceful like after playing cards and smoking some tobacco and the next morning you're not there anymore, and it's as if nothing's happened."

"How's that?" Erich asks, running his fingers through his hair.

"Gas. You don't hear nothing, smell nothing, the guards are asleep up front. The grenades don't make no noise, just a little plop that wouldn't wake anybody up. Afterward you're laying there and you're gone. We had that routine a couple of mornings when we went to change guards. If the guards sound the alarm of course nothing happens."

"Why do the guards fall asleep then?"

Ed laughs and slaps Erich on the arm. "Man, when you're just sitting there in the dead of night, not a peep to be heard, just a rocket maybe from time to time, you'd sleep too. And what about you guys, tell me about it?"

"First-class, buddy. For everybody, really, who was working. Ask your father or Max, or Minna—even Minna, your sister. They must have made a pretty bundle. The dames"—he gives his forehead a slap for sheer enthusiasm—"were really something, especially the last year. Man, we felt like we were in a Turkish harem."

"I've heard," Ed puffed.

"Nah, you can't even imagine what it was like. And in two, three years if somebody tells you about it and says that was Berlin, you won't believe it. You simply won't believe it."

"Why not?"

"Why because we had it as easy as you could ever want. Whichever one you wanted, you got her. With a couple of exceptions, of course. But otherwise . . ." He laughed gleefully to himself, and they toasted each other again with their brandy.

Erich went on in a whisper. "First, of course, there were the young widows, what were they going to live on? Then the ones whose husbands had been up front a long time, not all of them, sure, but a girl like that had to be pretty tough and have something in reserve not to go along and do what the others were doing. They need money, you know, don't want to starve, after all."

"Why?" Ed asks. "If she's making money, she don't need to starve."

Erich stroked his moustache in amusement and snapped his fingers. "That's just like with you and the gas. If you weren't out there you'd never think of it. Sure she's got work, stands there at her lathe like a man or makes gunpowder, and gets her pay envelope afterward. But then the question comes up—who's going to fix her machine, her drill and so on? Well now, we did, the master mechanics. But that can be done in several different ways. Maybe you don't have time or maybe you'll be right there. And it's all according to that whether she gets her wages or not, or gets fired."

"It was all piece work?" Eduard asks.

"Piece work, sure. And if she hasn't met her quota or lets her drill run too hot, she can get bawled out or get fired and go looking for another job. So then it's better to get on somebody's good side, with the foreman, with the regulator, or with whoever's there."

Eduard props his head in both hands, saying only "hmm." While Erich whistles a tune with proud delight, Eduard says half to himself, "Nice bastards you guys are."

Erich: "My son, that we know. But that's just the way things were.

96

When guys came back from the front, recalled for work, they were exactly the same."

Eduard: "I thought you were a Party member."

"What's that got to do with it?"

"Well," Eduard said, making a tentative gesture with one hand. Erich: "You're a dope, Eduard."

Eduard waves this off amicably. "Go ahead and call me what you want, Erich. I mean, you know I've never been interested in politics. Nobody could interest me even now. But you'll have to admit that when it's all said and done, that was a lousy thing to do, and you ought to feel sorry for those women and girls."

"I admit it, Ed. But that's how war is."

Ed: "It was the war, I know, I know."

He sauntered slowly home across the barren Küstriner Platz and past the old train station. He had begun to think of Minna, his sister. Before he had left, she was already at her sewing machine. Actually I haven't once had a straight talk with her, and she was so nice to me in the old days, always stuck together, she always put something extra in my pocket.

When he knocked on the door upstairs, the machine came to a halt. Minna opened the front door. She was startled to see her brother, ran across the room, slamming the door behind her. He entered, he had been startled, too. Ever since he had been back, Minna had always worn that little blue kerchief, never took it off, ostensibly because the doctor had forbidden her to do so because of some sticky ointment in her hair. Now—for a few seconds—he had seen her head. She was almost totally bald, as if shaved by some machine.

Unsure of himself, his cap still on his head, he moved about in the unheated living room. The clattering of the machine in the next room had not yet begun again. He knocked timidly. After a short pause, she called out, "Come in." The machine was running again, she sat bent over it, the kerchief bound about her head. The room was heated. He used the fact to ask if she had anything against his staying there. She said curtly, "Take your coat off, though." Which he did, and then watched her as he stood by one wall. "You have a little time, a quarter of an hour, ten minutes, to talk, don't you, Minna?"

"I've got a lot of work, Ed."

"Drop it for a minute."

She obediently turned the machine off.

He: "We haven't talked for the longest time, Minna. You peeved at me?"

"No."

"I didn't think so. Why should you be peeved at me."

After a pause, during which she blushed bright red and played with the bobbin with one finger, she said, "About my hair. You saw, I know. I had mother cut it off—before you came home."

Perplexed, he said nothing.

"Because it was green, from the acid. At the end I was in a gunpowder factory. On the street I could always put on a headscarf. But now that you were coming . . ."

He walked up behind her and pressed his face against her head. She pushed him away. He said tenderly, "Minna."

She said in a husky voice, "Sit down, Ed."

He sat back down.

She said, "Did you want to know anything else?"

"No, Minna, nothing at all. I just wanted to sit here with you a little, we never get to otherwise. And then mother and the others come later on, and you clatter away at that machine. I was over at Hildebrand's, and it's so noisy there and too many people."

"Always at Hildebrand's drinking. What are you doing, Ed? I can't make sense of you."

"It's not so bad at Hildebrand's, Minna. You just stand around, you know, and listen to what's going on. Newspapers ain't for me. Do you know Erich, the guy from my athletic club, do you remember him?"

"Perfectly."

"I saw him again today."

"Now wasn't that a pretty sight."

"Why?"

"Because it was pretty, that's all. Those are the kind of people you meet over at Hildebrand's."

"Others too. The woman who lives up over us; she was waiting for her husband."

Minna, quickly: "No coal."

"And Erich, so you know him too? Did you work with him?"

She sat up straight and looked directly at him. "That's why you want to talk with me?"

"Why no, Minna, wasn't even thinking of that."

"He never tried anything with me. Maybe he was afraid of Dad or of Fritz."

"I didn't even know he was such a womanizer."

"He doesn't need to blow his own trumpet so loud. There were others."

"Then it's true, what he told me."

"Did he name names?"

"For God's sake, Minna."

She turned toward him in her chair and pulled it closer and spoke softly. "Ed, take a good look at him, it will do you good. Those guys are

98

all like that, one's the same as the other. And that's why you can't do nothing with them, and that's why things are bogging down and we'll soon be sitting in the same old rut. What did they care about all during the war? That they wouldn't get drafted, that they'd be kept on permanent home-front duty, that they would earn good money so they could bet it and have a good time. And the women. A couple of months ago a political dispatch was passed on to me, a very important one, and I was supposed to spread the word at the plant, very carefully, of course. This was a Monday, and it was a really big item, about how things were starting to topple at the front. And so I ran all the way. Do you know they almost beat me to death because I came to them with it on a Monday. Because Monday, you see, was their big betting day; they had already placed their bets and were getting the news of the horses from the bookie. They yelled at me to leave them alone with my news. If I came bothering them again with war stuff they'd punch me in the nose, they said, blow the whistle on me. Pergolese was the horse's name, and do you know where the race was being run? In Paris. I swear it. They placed their bets through a Swiss bookie."

Ed nodded grimly, but he did not let her look at his face; when it came to betting he had a bad conscience.

Minna: "But that bunch'd lick anybody's boots to keep from being sent to the front."

"Well," Eduard said, "they'd probably all been on the front once, and if you'd ever been there yourself, you'd understand."

"Sure, you can't believe how they treated us. We were doing piece work. The men were in charge of regulating the machines. Sometimes there would be six lathes to one man. In the meantime you just stand around and time passes and you know you'll get fired. He's happily working away at his girlfriend's lathe. The rest can wait. Ed, I've stood there sometimes so wild with anger. And when they're eating and drinking, what do they talk about if not the horses? Women. They passed the word to each other who was good in bed. They exploited our misery just like the owners. Or Wilhelm and his generals."

Eduard sat hunched over in his chair. If he had been there, ten to one he would have done the same thing.

Minna sat with her legs crossed. Not one of them had dared approach her. Not that she's ugly, though, not Minna.

"I never would've believed, Minna, that you'd ever care so much about politics."

She spoke so softly that he only barely caught it. "I don't. I just care about people."

"Minna, I'm sorry I've bothered you at your work. You shouldn't slave away so crazy at this machine."

"See you later, Ed." She bent down over her work again.

Murder Investigation on Friedrich-Karl Strasse

When the bread sack and milk can were both still standing at the door that Sunday in the building on Friedrich-Karl Strasse where the lottery dealer lived, no one paid any attention. There was no porter, and anyway the lottery dealer did everything for himself. The *Morgenpost* was still peacefully tucked in the crack of the door with reports of all sorts of things for the man who could no longer read it; and tomorrow and the day after—for a whole week, in fact, since no one canceled delivery—it would provide the grisly details of what had taken place behind the door to this apartment in this building that stood there just now so totally quiet.

The cleaning woman did not work for the would-be financier on Sundays; Lutz and Konrad had known that, had accounted for that in their plans. The man should have to lie there as long as possible. Around five o'clock in the afternoon a telegram arrived. It was—believe it or not—a telegram from Lutz. In it he wrote: "Be there at ten. Wire if okay."

The telegraph messenger rang, knocked, rang at the neighbors' on the same floor; they were not at home. He climbed another flight up to find out what the private address might be, since a sign on the door indicated that this was an office.

On the fourth floor lived a well-to-do gentleman who had only recently arrived in Berlin from eastern Germany, from the province of Posen, where attacks by Poles had begun. He had not wished to wait until he was chased out. He was sitting with his wife and four children in his apartment above the lottery dealer's; he was the man who late the evening before had climbed the stairs and listened at his landlord's door. The man went out in fact evening after evening, in order to establish "business connections," as he confided to his wife.

When the telegraph messenger asked about the landlord and showed him the telegram, the gentleman from Posen, who had slept his Sunday away, replied that the landlord did live here, that his business and living quarters were all in one. He was almost certainly at home. And as he said this, he recalled the little nocturnal incident on the stairs. "I heard him myself last night. That man snores so loud you can hear it through the door."

"He may have gone out in the meantime."

"I was just saying to my wife a while ago, we can be glad our bedroom doesn't lie above his."

"Then he has gone out," the messenger declared, balancing the paper uncertainly in his hand. The lady from Posen appeared, dainty and still uncombed, and the man asked, "Do you suppose he's gone out?"

"We have no way of knowing that," she said, and tried to pull her husband away from the door and back into their hallway.

But instead he said, "Wait just a moment, young man. Let me see if I can't be of help to you."

And he went downstairs with the messenger just as he was, in his shirtsleeves and slippers.

Once down there he rang vigorously, rang again, and again, then knocked with even greater vigor.

"He really appears not to be in." He was tempted to remark inanely once again that he had been there last evening. And in a repetition of that nocturnal incident he laid his ear to the door. And soon his face lighted up, then he frowned. "Psst, psst! He's in there after all. Listen!"

They heard a noise not all too distant from them. What was it actually, snoring or what? They stood there looking at each other. The man from Posen was perplexed. "He's in there at any rate."

The young postal employee was also interested now. He could think of nothing to do but knock again violently. And as he reflected that one ought to have something to force the door with, and pushed even harder against it, the door sprang open on its own. Konrad, hoping to avoid noise, had not pulled it completely closed.

A gas light was burning in the hallway from the night before; they had not noticed it from outside because of the bright daylight. The postal messenger stumbled forward two steps as the door gave way.

The man from Posen said, "Well, that's better," while the postal messenger was already stepping back out. The man from Posen was just able to get by him in the doorway.

The lottery dealer lay across the runner in the middle of the hallway, his head to the door. He lay on one side with his legs pulled up, his hands held unnaturally at his back. The rope was noticeable at once, wound around his legs and feet and trailing clear back to the door to the living room. He head was bent back in a ghastly way, so that even from the rear one could see his forehead and nose, blue and swollen. The noise from before had been his strange, soft, slurping breathing.

The man from Posen (got to get out of here): "I'll call the police." And he races up the stairs like a wild man.

The woman, who has stayed upstairs at her door, shouts, "What's wrong, dear, for heaven's sake?"

He storms into the parlor. "Get the children out." He calls the operator in a voice that betrays nothing; the operator promises to contact the police after he gives the address and merely says something about "accident" and "urgent". He has to go back down again. His wife lays a coat over his shoulders, wants to hold him back, but he goes anyway. The telegraph messenger is still standing there, beside him the neighbors from the same floor are already gathered; doors are standing open right and left.

When the riot squad storms up the stairs, six armed men, everyone in the stairwell sighs with relief. It is no longer their affair, the matter has been handed over to the authorities. Whatever happens now, it will be done in an orderly fashion. Four of the officers enter the apartment, two wander through the rooms, two bend down over the man. One can now see that a heavy trail of blood leads out from the dining room; they find the dining room wrecked. An officer calls headquarters from there. Before the homicide detail arrives, the emergency room has already sent over a doctor, who, with a single tug of his hand pulls the gag, the two bloodsoaked handkerchiefs, out of the man's throat. To do so he has rolled the man over on his back. Down below a crowd has assembled.

The homicide detail finds everything more or less as it had actually been. The attack had occurred in the living room, there the victim had been tied up and gagged. Since there are no traces of any anesthetic and the man was robust, they assume that at least two persons were involved in the crime. But this is left undecided, since they learn from the neighbors in the building of the victim's peculiar inclinations. It is possible that he let himself be tied up out of some perverse appetite, and that the criminal then went about his work. Afterward the victim, though his hands and legs were tied and he had a gag in his mouth, had had enough strength at least to loosen the rope around his knees. That had made it possible for him to roll his way out of the dark room and into the hall. He was conscious, wanted to get help, and the man from Posen on the third floor had in fact heard him. Under careful questioning, this witness states that unfortunately he had not paid sufficient attention to the rasping sound. After the interrogation, the man goes back upstairs depressed. He is interrogated once more that evening in his apartment; he has to say exactly—mercifully his wife is not permitted to remain in the room—when and where and with whom he had last been seen the evening before. They have no evil intent in asking this, but only want to determine the exact time.

Typical photographs, all of them of young men and boys, are found in the lottery dealer's desk along with a loaded camera, which they take along in order to develop the film. And then that mysterious telegram. Who sent that?

If they had gone down onto the street at ten o'clock that evening and arrested everyone, they would have had a good chance of catching one of the culprits right there. Lutz, to be precise. He was standing down there listening to it all while people still gathered around, and then he departed, close to tears.

Since morning Lutz had been arguing with Konrad, who was staying with him in Olga's room. She was happy to have such a smart and solvent cavalier. Konrad locked himself in with Olga, and they let Lutz beg and knock as much as he wanted till noon. Lutz in the meantime had gone out on the street, had fearfully bought the *Lokalanzeiger* and was ecstatic to find nothing in it. He did not stop to consider that a report could hardly be printed in the morning edition. Konrad had teased him dreadfully last night when they returned home—yes indeed, the old fart was dead, they had made much too much of a fuss with him.

Around noon Lutz went looking for a public telephone, tried to call the old man and—was not connected. He tried again with the same results in a bar. And he ran back home trembling all over. What had happened? What have they done? Konrad had tricked him.

Finally he gets to talk with Konrad. Olga has just gone to a bar to get something to eat, beer, brandy and cigarettes.

"Why did you run back a second time and shove the gag in so deep? Now he's dead."

Lutz weeps, Konrad shoves him up against the wall. "Go on and turn yourself in."

Lutz is so stupid and bewildered that he admits that he just tried to call the old man. Konrad cannot believe his ears. He cannot speak for several minutes.

Lutz is seized by an entirely new fear, and rightly so, because in fact Konrad intends to get him out of the way. But Olga, all unsuspecting and cheerful, arrives with her food in a big basket—the bar lent it to her for a deposit—and for a few hours this brings everything back to normal. They drink so much that they get the urge to dance, the three of them together. Konrad with Olga, then, no less ardently, Lutz with Konrad, and when Lutz dances with Olga he absolutely will not surrender her to Konrad.

But when Konrad and Olga begin kissing again, Lutz lapses back into his worries. He slips out onto the street. And then he gets the idea: I'll send him a telegram, he'll get that for sure. He doesn't think it through further. And then he goes home at once, his spirits revived now, and sits there waiting for a stroke of good fortune—the old man's answer.

When it isn't there by evening, however, and Konrad and Olga take off for a stroll, he is clever enough to explain his own departure with an appointment he is supposed to have. It is ten o'clock and people are crowding around the building on Friedrich-Karl Strasse, not far from the royal stables, and the homicide squad is upstairs taking pictures and asking questions.

The lottery dealer, however, is lying in Charity Hospital, untied at last and nicely bedded down; he is unconscious, and he dies on Monday morning. The midday papers spread the news.

It was reported that the murderers were being sought in that "special milieu" in which Herr X was accustomed to move.

On Tuesday we find Lutz and Konrad on a train. Lutz is wearing his coarse army uniform, Konrad is in civvies. Konrad is transporting his prey—Lutz, who has completely fallen apart—to Döberitz, where there is a registration office for discharged soldiers who want to sign up again, who knows for what. That goes off smoothly. Lutz only has a few of his military papers, the rest, as often happens, have been lost.

Relieved, Konrad returns to Berlin. He is now in his "female phase," so he says, and he is having fun dabbling with the ladies. Which is why he walks to Olga's, realizing that he has killed two birds with one stone: first, he has got that ass Lutz safely on ice in Döberitz, and second, he can take over Olga. All of the loot, or what is still left of it, he has kept for himself. He has promised Lutz to send him something from time to time, but just small amounts so that no one will notice anything. Lutz, the nincompoop, came very close to turning even that much down.

A Turn to Lighter Things

The usual jumble of important and unimportant events in Berlin.
A certain Herr Motz and his Toni sleep in another fellow's office.
There is a shortage of coal in Berlin. Foxy officials show their stuff.
One chief fox can't hand over the nation fast enough to the generals.
The unwieldy nature of bureaucracy results in a lengthier chapter.
Tuesday, November 26th.

Prefatory Comment

It grieves the writer of these lines that, despite all the possibilities imagination offers, he has to drive his readers out into gloom and rain so they can follow historical events and the personal fates of his characters, only seldom leading them around in nippy, cold weather or through a merry flurry of snow. It is not his fault. He would rather switch altogether to a warm Adriatic setting, or at least, if one must stay in Europe and Germany, be met by spring breezes. But this is Berlin and it is November. A hard month of pouring rain, a month of destruction and tattered leaves, a grinding, ruinous month. And this November is very long, too long (not just for the reader, for the writer as well). But those who lived through it did not find it any shorter themselves. And so an unvarying parade of people passes by in heavy, shapeless winter clothes that protect against the cold, but not against destiny. For which reasons we will ask some of these ladies and gentlemen to lay aside these disfiguring costumes from time to time and to move about more freely. In this way we can better differentiate between them as they sneak about, wicked and sinuous, charming and deceitful, tender and insatiable.

And so, on this Tuesday, the 26th of November, we meet under pleasant circumstances one Herr Motz, a friend of a Herr Brose-Zenk, alias Schröder. The reader knows nothing of this Herr Motz, nor will the name Brose-Zenk alias Schröder mean much to many of you. They are parasites: Brose-Zenk is a speculator and grafter, Motz a parasite on the other parasites. We find ourselves in a metropolis after a war.

As morning light turned to gray on this Tuesday the 26th—while Konrad was transporting his trembling friend Lutz via train to Döberitz—Motz, the parasite on Brose-Zenk, was sleeping soundly and cheerfully at the feet of his dye-jobbed girlfriend Antonia whom the suspicious Brose-Zenk had figured was a spy—which she was. The young lady was the daughter of a house porter and had just recently been released from a detention home. What she was spying for was any opportunity to relieve gentlemen of their wallets.

They both slept, he under the table, she on the couch, in the office of alias Schröder. Neither Motz nor Toni had any money, but they were in love. Yesterday Brose-Zenk had had to slip his friend a small sum, gloomily remarking, "The government is worthless, we can pack our bags," and then had left it up to him whether he wanted to stay in the office overnight, since Motz had been denied entry to his room on account of unpaid debts. Motz and Toni gaily drank up the whole sum sitting in the financier's office. Motz was a wonderful host, an indefatigable lover. He slept in front of the sofa on a rolled-up carpet that Toni had tucked around him; she lay above him beneath all the coats, towels and napkins they had been able to round up in the office.

Morning arrived, she let her legs down. The bald head shone white at the end of the tube of carpet, motionless. She went to work in the kitchen, found matches, but no coffee or milk. So she boiled some water and brought two cups of hot sugar-water back to the room. She had put a vanilla stick in each one. Then she unrolled the carpet. Motz grunted as he felt himself being rolled over, hung on tight, screamed for help, then lay there fully exposed in his wool shirt, underpants and socks. She laughed heartily. He scolded her for such improper behavior, but calmed down as he scrambled up and noticed what an interesting get-up she had on.

Her youthful, slender, well-proportioned body was clad in a pair of long flesh-toned stockings and a narrow belt from which garters hung. That was all. It did not appear that she was freezing. Motz, deciding not to take too great an egotistical delight in her, wrapped his winter coat around her and quickly got dressed himself. Then they sat down to breakfast on the sofa.

"What's that?" he asked with a whine, looking into the clear liquid in his cup.

"Try it." He smelled the stick, tried the drink and was content. It tasted better than coffee. So she strode into the kitchen to produce another batch of sugar-water.

Meanwhile someone unlocked the outside door. Brave Motz straightened up in astonishment. As the door opened with one vigorous swing, there stood a bearded man in a fur coat, inside which Motz easily recognized the owner of the office, his friend Brose-Zenk. In the next moment the door to the kitchen opened and Toni emerged, tea tray in hand, smiling winningly at the new gentleman whom she had never seen before and remarking that she only had two cups. Because of the heat, she had left Motz's coat lying on the stove.

Motz introduced her with some apprehension. "This is Antonia."

The gentleman in the fur coat lifted his hat with two fingers, gaped at her as she put down the cups and disappeared into the kitchen, glancing over her shoulder at him with a smile. Her backside displayed a state of total innocence, with the exception of the dainty straps of her bra.

"Who is Antonia?" Brose wheezed.

"The dye-job."

"Dyed where?"

"Oh, she's blonde again now, last week she was blue, you know what I mean."

Brose, close to a fit of rage, walked up to Motz. "What difference does that make? What's she doing in my office?"

"We spent the night here—you gave your permission."

"To you, not to her. Besides which I gave you money."

"I can't sleep alone. My nerves are bad, I get scared. The money—is gone. Look at the kind of coffee I have to drink."

Brose glanced at the cup. "What is that stick?"

"Vanilla, left over from yesterday's milk soup."

Brose, who had big, mournful cow's eyes, widened them even more. "Get her out of here."

But then she came in with a third cup of sugar-water and said, "Here's some sugar-water for you, with a stick of vanilla."

She was still in her state of innocence. Brose was resolute. "Young lady, you will first get dressed and then go buy me some cigars."

Motz nodded. She complained that her second cup would get cold, but gulped it down rapidly and after a few minutes was back again dressed in a short, fashionable dress that displayed her knees. Brose, without looking at her, pressed a bill into her hand and gave her a cigar from his etui as a sample. She threw them both kisses and was gone.

"What pigs these people are," Brose exploded, while Motz sat freezing on the sofa.

He asked, "When does the woman come who heats this place?"

Brose shouted, "This is not your home, this is my office."

"But Brose," Motz groaned, "you don't want to freeze either."

He mocked, "But Brose, but Motz."

"What has happened, for crying out loud?"

That was a good question. Brose sat down at once, slamming his hat down on the table. "It's all over. We'll have to join up with the Spartacists after all. This government has collapsed."

"You don't say."

Brose shook his head at the prospect of total disaster. "The country is in unbelievable disorder. We need a strong hand. We need the Kaiser. And if not him, then Liebknecht."

"For God's sake!"

"It won't work any other way. The decision must be made. This republic—they call it a republic—has broken down entirely. They've now started to confiscate cigars."

"What?"

"Cigars."

"Yes, but why?"

Brose, resignedly: "I don't know. I don't understand anything anymore. I don't know what cigars ever did to them. Why don't they confiscate meat or eggs or chickens. Things necessary to stay alive. Or oil. How do average people even feed themselves? Just look at him out on the street. But cigars! My cigars! Just when I started selling cigars a week ago."

He suddenly sat up straight, and turning to one side—they were next to each other on the sofa—he cast a piercing glance at Motz. "Who is this dye-job? A spy. Didn't I tell you?"

"Why do you say that?"

Motz was a broken man. What had he done?

Brose, at his ear now: "Didn't I warn you? She denounced me. She betrayed us both. You too."

"But that's impossible, Brose. She doesn't know anything."

"She knows more than you do. It had to be someone. You and your women have got us into this mess."

"Brose," Motz cried, "you lost at gambling last night."

He answered coldly, "Of course I lost at gambling; gambling is gambling, a real gambler doesn't get confused by that. Do you stop loving a woman because she cheats on you? But 50,000 marks? In all, they are supposed to have confiscated 500,000 marks' worth of cigars, 500,000 marks' worth. Several of those warehouses belong to me."

"Who's behind it?" Motz asked, shuddering at the thought. "Those are incredible sums."

"You tell them that. They go right on about their business in secret. The Spartacists are absolutely right. We need to use force to chase them out of office."

He rummaged in his coat pocket, his hand encountered something, he pulled it out—pure Broze-Zenk: crumpled hundred-mark bills, a whole bundle of them. He was surprised, gazed at the bundle, as did Motz with shining eyes. "Well now. I'll pay a visit to the appropriate office. You can always talk to those people. Where'd that dame get to?"

"I can give you a cigar."

"I don't need a cigar. I just want to know what cigars cost today."

"Then I'll get dressed and go myself."

"Would you please."

As Motz put on his coat, he didn't say a word of what he suspected, that Toni would not be coming back at all, since Brose had given her a hundred-mark bill. But Brose attached no importance to it. He gave him one of the cigars and another crumpled hundred.

When he returned little more than five minutes later, he found Toni, wearing a new hat and a pair of elegant gloves and vainly trying in this finery to embrace a fully indifferent Brose.

"Down fifty percent," he cried to Motz from behind her hat, and pushed the young lady aside.

"And how much did you pay?"

Motz gave the figure.

Brose: "Sixty percent then. Plummeting prices. They're throwing my money away on the streets. They say they're doing the same thing in Chemnitz and Hamburg."

He stood up and marched back and forth between the window and the table. "I'll bring this government down. They'll feel the power of this hand. Impoverishment of commerce. Have you heard what they did at the Silesian Station?"

Motz said he hadn't, he was immersed in Toni's new look. She had on a wonderful cloche, the latest thing, and she had also put on makeup while she was out; though perhaps not spotlessly washed, she looked warm and sated. She discreetly slipped Motz a bag of chocolates under the table.

Brose, coldly: "They confiscated whole trainloads of food. Go to the markets or ask the black marketeers, they'll name you prices you won't believe. They halted one train running at full speed, the engineer was an accomplice of course, and stole three million marks in cash. Those are their methods now."

"Whose methods?"

"The government's. And certain interests are behind it. They confiscate things. And therefore I am for Liebknecht, and I'll stick with him. Nothing half-way."

And he sank down into his chair and buried his face helplessly in his hands. "I'm a ruined man."

Whereupon Motz proved a true friend. He whispered with Toni, they both vanished. Ten silent minutes later they appeared, spreading good cheer. It was a first-class breakfast that they hauled upstairs. Eggs, sausage, bread, beer, cake, even candy. And for the next ten minutes they ate and deadened the pain.

"Give this government one more chance," Motz suggested in the middle of breakfast.

Brose, stubbornly: "No. Enough is enough."

Antonia likewise pleaded with him not to let his anger carry him away.

Brose drank beer. "Those Hohenzollerns left this country in an awful state!"

Finally he and Motz each lit one of the new low cost cigars, and the financier gave himself over to meditation. Toni was graciously dismissed with another new bill, and a wild burst of telephoning began. Motz wanted to flee without being noticed, but he didn't dare. He served as Brose's lightning rod.

"How are those lots of yours doing, those gardens out in Friedrichsfelde?" Brose asked his friend between two stormy phone conversations, stroking his beard at an uncannily even tempo, a sign of dangerous agitation. Motz was quick to assure him that though he did not go out walking in nature in winter, the two lots were still his property.

"Fine, fine," Brose said with an eerie tranquility. "Are you still on the farmers' council?"

Fear surged through Motz; he didn't dare say no.

Brose stood there without moving. "Okay, then we'll use that as our basis. If that's what they want, we'll fight, tooth and nail. I shall not surrender. What sort of a flag do you own?"

"A red one, of course. Or a black one."

"The red one," Brose decreed. "I know no black flag."

"For God's sake!" Motz groaned.

Brose, implacable: "All the warehouses are gone. All of them, do you understand. The red flag. We'll stick with it."

They went to the bar downstairs, smoked and grew more tolerant. Brose gazed tenderly out onto the street through the window where sausages hung to one side. He had laid his watch on the shiny scrubbed wooden table. Motz knew that Brose would now count the number of men and women walking along the street for two or three minutes. He held a small silver pencil in his hand and made marks on the wood, men on the left, women on the right. These would provide the numbers for his gambling tonight.

The Reich Confers on Wilhelmstrasse

In the hours following noon that day, one saw beaming faces in the Reichs Chancellery building, where, having received a call to preserve the unity of the nation, representatives from all member states had flocked together. The whole of the empire Bismarck had built was assembled—even more than that. One gentleman had appeared from Austria, and what he had to say was too wonderful to be revealed immediately.

110

The great assembly hall was opened. The splendid carpets were spread up the staircase, the hall itself glittered with lights. This was officialdom, this was authority. This was Germany.

In the office of the Reichs chancellor, a title Ebert had held for one brief day, three people's deputies were walking to and fro. The gentlemen were debating, but in a perfectly friendly fashion. A man had come from Munich at the government's invitation, and the three right-wing socialists were in a rage, wanting to denounce him in open session. For it had become known that he had been carrying on private conversations behind their backs with representatives of Saxony, Baden and Württemberg in an attempt to get them to form an independent confederacy of southern German states as a counterweight to the incompetent and reactionary German states of the North. Kurt Eisner contra Friedrich Ebert. Nothing came of the plan because there were at least some reasonable gentlemen from Baden and the other states, good democrats all, who at once spread the word. But the confrontation was still bound to happen.

And as they excitedly discussed the matter, though all of one mind—Ebert dismissed the matter as not amounting to much; they all knew Eisner, he would get his fingers badly burned—he was called away for a brief meeting with a certain major.

In the next room Ebert extended a warm greeting to this gentleman, one who occasionally provided him with orientation concerning military affairs. The major, a stolid, standoffish man, was completely beside himself.

"But why, my good major?"

The problem was this same Herr Eisner, that wretch from Munich.

"Your Excellency must understand that this is outrageous. He is destroying every possibility of a just peace . . ."

"How is that?"

"These articles he has published about Germany's being to blame for the war. It's high treason."

Ebert gazed straight ahead, considering. "One has to be prepared for most anything with this fellow. He's a visionary, a dreamer."

The major was amazed. "A criminal. And this man dares to appear here today at a conference of the Reich. Make use of your authority; show him the door. We'll take him in hand."

"You will do nothing of the kind, major."

"I beg your pardon, Your Excellency, it was only a suggestion. But the man is a public menace. He is already prime minister of Bavaria, has access to top-secret archives and is plundering them while the Entente laughs at all of us in mockery."

The people's deputy nodded with a friendly gravity. Despite everything, he was enough of a socialist to enjoy seeing the military upset by such revelations. He told him, "You mustn't take him too seriously.

Someone told him that his candor would make a fine impression on the Allies. And now some unfortunate fool, an American, a pacifist just like him, has convinced him—a certain Mr. Herron—that President Wilson above all wants a complete and open confession of guilt from Germany. He rose to the bait."

The major: "Kassel is in an uproar over what he's published."

"They'll calm down again. And, by the by, we're not going to let the mistakes of previous governments be attributed to us."

The major's eyes registered his surprise, then he smiled. "Of course not."

They understood one another.

The Reichs Chancellery stood grave and dignified behind its iron railing. And when the hour came, the doors of various offices were opened and a number of gentlemen climbed the stairs and stepped into the brilliance of the chandeliers. Heavy portfolios were carried in behind them.

The government entered the hall.

To their dismay they were not received as circumstances would normally dictate. True, several gentlemen ran up to them and shook their hands, but the solemnity was missing, with most people remaining seated or simply standing about. They smoked and kept on talking and took no notice of the government's entrance.

Undaunted, the government took the seats reserved for it at the table up front. In fact some gentlemen busy chewing chocolates had first to be shooed away, and instead of excusing themselves they only smiled and said, "We were just warming up the seats for you."

Since the subject of the meeting was not conditions in Germany, but the empire of Prince Bismarck, they began to deliberate on three specific points: first, the preservation of the unity of this "Reich," for which purpose a constituent assembly was desirable (neither the name Bismarck nor any of the three Kaisers he served was mentioned, out of understandable discretion); second, again the "unity of the Reich," and how until the constituent assembly was held the workers' and soldiers' councils, which after all did exist, would represent the will of the people; and third and last, to hasten points one and two, efforts should be made to move toward a prompt, provisional peace settlement. That was the patriotic agenda for the conference, typed in clean copies lying before delegates from all the German states.

After brief words of welcome, a man rose to his feet who had been a part of the last imperial government and who therefore was truly entitled to speak to this matter, an assistant secretary by the name of Solf. The worthy man spoke without guile.

"In our present situation," he declared with a bureaucratic croak, "our only salvation is a policy of pacifism. With such a policy we can attempt a tactical counter to the imperialism of the Allies. Though one must grant that in America the prevailing mood is one of victory." (After this bit of news he paused. Everyone felt how sad he was that the mood of victory prevailed elsewhere.) He spoke of France's "unqualified intentions to annihilate us." "What is the task of this conference? It must resolve that the government, as the central authority, can be subject to no control. Foreign affairs may be conducted only by the government of the Reich. One must find a location for the constituent assembly outside Berlin."

At this point Deputy Erzberger, journalist and erstwhile assistant secretary, rose noisily, and after extending his thanks to the government for having delegated this report to him, demonstrated what injustice had been inflicted upon Germany with the conditions of the armistice and how Germany was suffering under these conditions and that Germany must protest, protest and protest again. He gave certain dates and pounded on the table.

He came from Buttenhausen in Swabia and was the chubby-cheeked head of a delegation of four men, who on Friday morning, November 8th, had arrived as the German negotiators at the headquarters of Marshal Foch, where the Allies presented them with conditions of armistice. At the early age of twenty-eight he had served as a deputy in the Reichstag for the Catholic Center Party. In the Reichstag he had fought against the idea of submarine warfare, had pushed through a peace resolution and had sworn to them that if he could only sit down at a table with Lloyd George or one of their other adversaries it would only be a matter of a few hours before they achieved complete agreement.

As he sat back down, he and the government bowed to one another.

The man who now took the floor was unknown by sight to most of those present. He was the man who had been pounced upon in the deliberations in Ebert's office, the one-time chief editor of the Social Democratic newspaper in Berlin, *Vorwärts*. Kurt Eisner was a small, elderly gentleman with a heavy gray beard and a pince-nez that sat badly on his nose. He wore an unkempt suit, his long disheveled hair fell down the nape of his neck and over his collar. On November 12th, as prime minister of Bavaria, he had sent a statement via the Federal Council in Berne to President Wilson and the governments of France, England, Italy and to the proletarian workers of all countries. The statement read:

"The people of Bavaria, as a result of a tumultuous revolutionary uprising that has been crowned with irrevocable victory, have removed every last person to blame for the world war, either directly or indirectly. This they did under the leadership of men who from the very beginning of the war had led a passionate struggle against the monstrous policies pursued by German governments and princes. Bavaria has proclaimed itself a people's state, and the entire population jubilantly celebrates its liberation. At this very moment, the publication by the Allied Powers of the conditions of armistice has stunned this new Bavaria. The new republic would in a short time be no more than wilderness and chaos. The moment has come when by an act of far-sighted magnanimity the reconciliation of the nations can be inaugurated. The League of Nations can never become a reality if it begins with the eradication of the newest member of democratic civilization. The fate of mankind lies in the hands of men who are now responsible for the implementation of peace and the reordering of shattered nations."

(A telegram sent at almost the same time by the leaders of social democracy in Berlin to neutral friends spoke of "feeding the nations" and took several good cuts at the armistice conditions "dictated by imperialist governments.")

Eisner, bitter beyond measure and holding the trembling of his frail body in check, forced his voice to assume a businesslike tone.

"I would like to remark that neither of the two speeches we have just heard would lead anyone to suspect that a revolution has occurred in this country." The government gazed straight ahead, disconcertedly, embarrassed by its two imperial orators. "We need people who have not been compromised. Herr Erzberger has poisoned world opinion. Solf in fact—only wants to deal with Wilson. Everything these two gentlemen say and do represents nothing but counterrevolution. I would like to give both these orators some advice: the Kaiser, their lord and master, has fled—they should follow him."

This said, he sat down and adjusted his pince-nez with trembling fingers. There were smiles here and there. The ferocious look on several faces betrayed agreement.

Throats were cleared in the government's corner, and People's Deputy Ebert put on his politest expression. He now had something special to communicate. There was a very special guest present among them, yes, a guest here at the session of the German Reich conference. "As you all know, it is the German-Austrian envoy, Herr Hartmann. May I present him now to the assembly." Hartmann rose, general applause. "We are most happy to have you with us." Hartmann expressed his thanks; he felt very much at home.

People were seated once more. Those in charge of the session whispered that Eisner could not have been glossed over any better.

An attorney named Heine, however, thought it necessary to respond in Erzberger's defense, after having briefly consulted with the government. His voice breaking with emotion, he pointed out that it would not do to hear allegations such as had just been made against Herr Erzberger without having someone contradict them immediately. Leaving aside everything else he had done—all of which was so familiar to anyone who had been aware of things during the last years of the war that there was no need to recount his deeds here—that party in particular who had attacked him so crudely, so brutally, so unjustly, might do well to keep in mind what Erzberger had achieved in his front-line battle against military rule, which in itself had not been an insignificant contribution to the revolution.

Heine sat down, Eisner stared coldly in front of him.

Nothing had happened. They had simply crossed swords.

One fellow was named Ulrich, from Hessia, rural Hessia, a peaceable, easy-going soul. When he asked to be recognized everyone knew nothing exciting would come from him, at most perhaps some pithy aphorism. Without leaving his comfortable chair, he suggested, "The nation must endure. But if a dictatorship takes over in Berlin, then I can answer for nothing." He declared this in no particular direction. He was content, and the others were as well.

But then the long expected incident occurred. When the president of the Republic of Braunschweig, Merger, pushed his chair back like some small and oafish miniature cyclops and fumbled for the table, it looked as if he would turn it over. He was badly, dreadfully out of place in these noble halls, and for that matter he obviously believed that much else was out of place here too; he felt as if he had been lured into a trap and wanted to free himself with one powerful stroke. His first utterances and curses must have been in dialect, for he got his wagon rolling with a series of unintelligible oaths. Then he attacked the government head-on with a roar. A single sentence stood out in his bellowing: "This government must be swept away by the wrath of the people."

He still stood at the table for a few breathless seconds, ready for mayhem; then a neighbor touched his sleeve, shoved his chair up under him and he immediately sat down like a robot, very noisily but without taking his eye off the government.

While to his right and left faces turned red, brows frowned, shoulders shrugged, Ebert sat up straight, staring the man straight in the eye and taking on a certain resemblance to him as if by induction. His voice as well, once Merger was seated, had a peasant heaviness to it. It was not some smooth diplomat speaking, but someone hewn from the same stone as he. He took this attack as directed at him personally, and he waited now until the other man was seated. Then he cleared his throat, and people knew that this throat-clearing replaced a dozen curses of the same sort that Merger had let loose. Then in a voice whose volume had been artificially turned down, but with the same violent manner, came the sentence: "This government is supported by the trust of the workers' and soldiers' councils."

The duel was ended.

Someone laid a memo in front of the chairman. The oily gentleman, Scheidemann, his friend in the Party, requested to speak. He sat there bent forward and gazing at the chairman with an appealing look that promised much. He was given the floor, and behold, he turned toward Eisner, and with sincerity and gentleness declared his support for something Eisner had said—though he could not support his words today—to the effect that at a time of havoc one could not pursue socialism. Doubtless Eisner still stood by that sentence, as he had uttered it but a few days before. Eisner could not contradict him. He had risen to speak only to say as much and to underline their unity in this one central point. Quite naturally there were other issues on which they were of differing opinions, but these were in reality of no consequence compared to other things, and it was actually more a matter of temperament whether such peripheral issues—and who did not get provoked nowadays by one thing or another, revolution being such a potpourri—whether one ought not, for reasons of the general welfare, which after all was equally dear to them all, whether one ought not rather hold on to the essentials, the matters of mutual concern. He directed that question in all seriousness, though of course not as a criticism, he having no right to criticize, to his colleague Herr Eisner and to the others here who all wanted but one thing: to preserve the Reich and to prevent its collapse into disorder. And for that reason he, Scheidemann, as bitter as it was for him to do so—and let no one doubt his socialist priniciples, his faith in the revolution—for that reason he must appeal to the conscience of everyone in this hall, from whatever part of Germany he might come: "Do you believe that a class-oriented parliament of workers' and soldiers' councils can serve the Reich, the unity of the Reich, serve to unify the bonds tying all true Germans together?"

A dangerous murmur came from further down the table. Scheidemann sensed that he had gone too far, and demurred at once with arms spread like angelic pinions.

"What we need after this most dreadful of all wars is peace, peace, peace. That need is vast, desperate. Each of you has experienced it in his own way. We dare not complicate matters. Let us place at our vanguard that which unites us: the rule by popular will, democracy, now that the people have finally gained power."

Someone called out: "Where are the people?"

The chairman, lying there in wait despite eyes that were cast down, retorted, "Part of a government supported by the trust of the workers' and soldiers' councils."

There was nothing to say in contradiction. Eisner mockingly proceeded to button up his jacket.

They arose to go have a bite to eat in the next hall, hoping at the same time to have an opportunity to feel out the delegates.

The opposite occurred. Little clumps of delegates gathered and people whispered with one another.

116

Before the gentlemen dispersed, Chairman Ebert expressed his thanks to everyone who, each in his own way, was working for the welfare of the German Reich in these difficult times.

"One thing is certain. If a German republic is to survive, it will require work. We have spoke about socialism, we must continue to debate it in still greater detail, in the presence and with the assistance of all those involved, the experts, the financiers, the union leaders, workers, politicians. But one thing is certain. Socialism is hard work. (Applause. Bravo.) The redress of the evils of war, seeing to it that there is a sufficient, a normal amount of food for the people to eat is our most urgent task. I appeal therefore to the German workers and soldiers not to forget those fifty years during which they learned to be socialists."

Lingering Echoes

A few echoes from the long conference and various other occurrences of the next evening help explain the emotional state of several officers and a politician. "Good-bye, Sweetheart," a young man says and goes off to fight the Poles. This takes place on the 26th and 27th of November.

Cabaret on the Kurfürstendamm

That evening there was an uproar in a cabaret on the Kurfürstendamm. A band was filling the pauses between artistic offerings, songs and dances, with a bit of music. It was a new, small and very elegant nightspot where people ate and drank. Several officers came in. When everyone was in a good mood after the latest hit song had been played and the music was doodling on more softly, the officers called a waiter over and gave him a request for a song.

The asked for "Hail, King with Glory Crowned!" When the band only played on quietly they raised a row and started shouting. The manager appeared and tried to calm the gentlemen. They demanded the old imperial anthem. The truly terrified man tried to mediate between the officers and the band. One officer, the youngest of the five, stood up and went to the podium. "Why won't you play the anthem we've asked for? You play all the other junk the audience wants."

The first violinist, who was directing, didn't answer because he didn't know how to answer. But the cellist on the platform, an older man, did answer after the officer had repeated his question in a still louder voice and with an added "damn it!" "This is not an army barracks. We won't play your Kaiser song." The manager begged the officer to consider that this was an unpolitical club, a bar for everyone.

"Then it's for me, too!" the young officer shouted. The four others applauded.

Then the five musicians consulted among themselves, the manager went up to them on the podium, and all vanished together behind the door to the dressing rooms. The officer stood there waiting. Several ladies and gentlemen in the audience—there were about thirty—applauded him, but he took no notice. Then the manager reappeared alone and announced with embarrassment that the band refused to play the song.

The officer: "And?"

"They have left."

The officer turned around to the audience and his friends and said, "Turned tail and ran."

The manager spread his arms helplessly.

"Then we'll sing 'Hail, King with Glory Crowned!' alone and do without the rest of the crap."

And—while the officers stood up behind him and several other people rose besides, men and women—he set to in a fairly decent voice, the others joining in chorus, and they sang the second verse too. When they had finished and applauded themselves, the young officer went back to his table, but not without first calling to several people on his right who had not made a move, "You need to be taught some manners, my friends!" The officers disappeared rather hastily.

The manager apologized for this incident to those who were still present. One table suggested he bring in another band. He whined, "Everyone is so touchy nowadays. The musicians don't want to play."

"Fire them, they're ruining your business."

"They're good workers."

"I'll bet they're Independent Socialists."

"Not politically involved at all. All of them in the union."

But they were convinced: "Independents."

A Former Lieutenant in the Imperial Army

Another lieutenant, this one in civvies, was strolling the streets at this late hour not far from the Kurfürstendamm on the arm of an elderly gentleman. They wandered down Wilmersdorfer Strasse, keeping to dark streets, the younger man leading.

The lieutenant's name was von Heiberg. He had last been stationed with the garrison in the Alsation town with which we are acquainted—where First Lieutenant Becker and Lieutenant Maus had lain in the military hospital and Hilda had served as their nurse—and where Hanna and her little druggist's assistant both lived. But this is also the Lieutenant Heiberg, her sweetheart, who had had to flee in the first days of the revolution because he had shot two "mutineers." In Berlin, his hometown, in great, sprawling Berlin, on the very first day he had dared set foot in the city, he had by chance run right into his former major.

The major had had to run after him, Heiberg had stood there rigid when his former major addressed him. Heiberg explained that he was staying in Döberitz where troops were being assembled. Until today his only contact with home since the 11th had been by phone. His father had visited him once in Döberitz, but he had then asked him to refrain from further visits.

The major: "And finally today you couldn't resist. And you run right into me. What a hero you are."

"Please don't speak of that, Major, sir. They're after me."

"Who? Who is after you?"

"My father has received telephone calls. For days on end people have been loitering around in front of our house."

"Because of those two fellows?"

"That has to be it. I was warned about it in Döberitz too. I've changed my name. The pack of them is hot on my trail."

"What's your name now?"

"Müller."

"Perfect. A fine, straightforward name." (The younger man did not join in his laughter.)

Heiberg: "I came into town to pick up my mail." He was carrying a small package in his left hand. "This is the first and last time. I want to get away from here."

"Absolutely no reason to leave. You should stay where you're needed."

Heiberg's cheeks were hollow, his eye unsteady. They walked under a railroad bridge toward the Kaiserdamm. The street was virtually empty.

Heiberg: "I'm superfluous here, Major. I can't do anything here. I'm disgusted at the idea of shooting at civilians."

"You're right, it's a disgusting business, but they're nothing but soldiers in disguise. They just want to be able to run away easier afterward."

"I hope to have our unit complete soon and then to move out, to the east. My comrades, Major, think just as I do—get out of Berlin, get out of the Reich."

"Why? Because of the crap?"

"Yes, sir."

The major: "There is an awful lot of crap here. And we have to clean it up. You can't shirk your duty."

The younger man did not answer.

At that moment a taxi drove by, the major hailed it and ordered the younger man to climb in. Once inside they did not speak. At the corner of Fasanenstrasse they got out.

The major: "Our offices are back there. Come along with me and get to know my men. They're starting to lose interest."

The younger man did not answer.

120

A Former Major in the Imperial Army

The major: "Say something."

"You're quite right, Major, sir, the crap has to be cleaned up. I did my duty. When they attacked the colonel I did not flinch. And I stick by what I did. But here in Berlin—no. I won't be a part of it. I'm not basing my argument on facts. But I'll not be a part of the rise of the inferior classes."

"And what would you do here instead?"

But they were already in front of the building. Quickly they ascended the front steps, someone followed right behind them and entered the Fasanenstrasse Casino. In an apartment on the second floor people were working in the front room. The major introduced him casually, switched on the light in the adjoining room, an office furnished with a sofa and a divan left over from former days. "You can spend the night here if you can no longer find a way back."

Heiberg: "My warmest thanks, Major. I'll accept the invitation."

"And so now please tell me what you intend to do if you are not basing your arguments on facts, facts that you and your comrades evidently prefer to scorn. We can't afford to let you get sidetracked, my friend."

The young man was silent once more.

"Why don't you speak up, Lieutenant? Are you ill? Are you not feeling well?"

"I beg your pardon, Major. We all speak very little to one another. We drill our men and don't think much. We don't write letters either, don't read our mail."

"You know, I wouldn't do that. One has to know what the enemy is up to. I can get angry, too. And when it all gets to be too much I go ahead and explode."

The younger man, sitting all hunched over on the divan, his hands on his knees, his little package on the floor in front of him, said: "We'll fight bravely enough when the time comes. The fatherland can depend on us. The fatherland has not gone under. But we no longer have a home. We're going to get out of this swamp, and when we return we'll have to be reckoned with."

"So first it's to Poland to hunt down Bolsheviks."

"Yes. We've got to get back to work. We want to get back to work. Win or lose. It can't end this way."

The major slid his chair up in front of him, pushed the package aside with one foot, and said, "Do many of the younger men, Lieutenant Heiberg, think as you do?"

"Most of them do, sir."

The major: "A generation ready to commit suicide."

The lieutenant sat up straight for a moment. "No, Major. A generation prepared to sacrifice. We are ready to be that sacrifice. The fatherland can depend on us."

The major stroked his chin and regarded the younger man carefully. "This is all something new to me. I'm happy to hear it, of course. There are some surprises still."

By chance his eye wandered to the wall above the divan, where beneath a huge gaudy battle scene, the storming of the trenches at Düppel, typical office memos and announcements were hanging: "All members of the military entering Berlin are to take note: the Executive Council and the Central Information Office are located in the Chamber of Deputies, Prinz-Albrecht Strasse 5."

Next to it: "Comrades, Workers, Soldiers! Whoever can, should leave Berlin. Workers are urgently needed in Upper Silesia, especially machinists and foundry workers. The Executive Council."

In large letters above that: "Central Office for National Service. Without order, there is no bread. Disorder brings famine."

The major tapped the younger man on the shoulder. "Take a look at that one. That's us."

The younger man let his eyes pass over it. "I know."

"We're not so completely useless after all. Not that I blame you. But I have to justify myself, after all. And if we don't work, don't move forward, then all your sacrifice won't help either. You'll be mowed down and that will be that."

"We're fully aware of that."

The major took his leave, announcing that he would visit the camp next week. The rattling of the typewriter in the next room soon stopped.

The pack of letters lay open next to him. Heiberg reached for one of them.

Hanna had written. Longingly.

Hanna—what a blissfully ignorant year that had been in that Alsatian town; love and duty, duty and love, and somewhere out beyond there was a war and Germany was being destroyed. A faraway world. The way she had opened her door to him that last day as he fled. We embraced once again in the maid's room. Then the night in the room of the druggist's assistant above the pharmacy—and the next morning in Strasbourg—and the Kehler Bridge.

She still writes me. She yearns for me.

I don't understand any of it. It has nothing to do with me. A lieutenant and his escapades. My fiancée.

He pushed the whole bundle away from the divan.

I don't have a fiancée. I'm bound to no one. To no one and nothing. We shall save Germany.

When the busy day had come to an end and all the guests had departed the Reichs Chancellery on Wilhelmstrasse, so brilliantly lit just moments before, People's Commissioner Ebert, a few morsels of some food he had grabbed still in his mouth, proudly shut himself in his study with a sigh of relief. He removed a few books from the bookcase to the left of the large desk, pushed at the wallpaper with the flat of his hand; the wallpaper yielded, revealing a small opening with a telephone in it. Still chewing, he picked up the receiver, and was surprised to hear the expected deep slow voice with its southern German accent already on the line.

The voice spoke into his ear (he quickly swallowed the bread): "Bravo. How about that. Just in the nick of time. I was just about to shut up shop."

The people's deputy pulled over a chair he angled with his foot, sat down, and spoke heavily, softly, his mouth close to the receiver. "Happy I caught you, Your Excellency. You must excuse me. It was a long, hot day."

In curt sentences he reported to the quartermaster general how everything had gone more or less smoothly, how they had shown the gentlemen from the provinces, Bavaria and so on, how the wind was blowing and they appeared to have understood. To which Groener offered his congratulations, adding that God knew they needed some good news now and then. The army's retreat was going nicely as before, and if there was no objection from Berlin, Wilhelmshöhe expected the troops would be marching into Berlin the first week of December and that they could then begin with the mopping-up of the capital.

Ebert pretended not to have heard any of this, and asked how the soldier's council at General Headquarters was behaving itself.

"We've got them completely in our pocket," Groener replied. "We proceeded a little too roughly at first, that can happen in any attack. We're rescinding the order forbidding the wearing of red badges and such. If those fellows are so attached to their red rags, what do I care. The main thing is that our congress at Ems planned for all the soldiers' councils on December 1st is going great guns. You'll be getting the agenda by courier, and I'd like to have your opinion of it right away."

Ebert: "I would hope it's not too extreme."

"We will be making maximum demands, my dear Reichs Chancellor. That you will scale them down does not frighten us."

Neither man laughed.

As Ebert was about to hang up, the voice from Wilhelmshöhe suddenly started again. "Say, by the way, what actually are the plans for this fellow Eisner? Is he going to be allowed to just go on like that?"

Ebert pointed to the fine results achieved at the Reich conference. Wilhelmshöhe: "Yes, we've already spoken about that."

They wished one another good night.

Ebert left the darkened Reichs Chancellery. He was not feeling as good as he had just before. In fact, as the tall iron gates of the building closed behind him and the guard detail on patrol saluted him, his mood suddenly turned around completely. A feeling of bitterness overwhelmed him. They won't let me alone, I'm supposed to catch the brunt of it all. Everyone does what he wants, everyone wants to have his way, do what he pleases—and I see and hear and know what Kassel is plotting against you, against us all, myself included, because they will no more spare me than the others—and we can do absolutely nothing to stop them, they'll scatter us all like a brood of hens. But we won't admit it. We are the people, sure, sure, the autonomous people, individualists to a man, and no one obeying anyone else. A heap of sand trying to defend itself against a steamroller.

Ebert stood there terrified at what he caught himself thinking.

He pulled on his cigar. A cab took him home.

Kurt Eisner

The Bavarian prime minister had not waited for Ebert's concluding remarks at the Reichs Chancellery. He left before the breakfast, biting his lips, trying to calm himself, he smiled distractedly at the servant who helped him into his coat. It seemed to him as if the two weeks following November 8th had been a dream.

Actually he ought to have grabbed a cab at once and driven to Weissensee. His mother had died, the funeral would be in an hour. But he wandered down Unter den Linden to Friedrichstrasse, to the Kranz-lerecke. It had been a good idea after all to come to Berlin. Sitting in Munich he wouldn't have believed it possible. His friends in Munich still had a very poor conception of conditions here in Berlin, of what was being planned here—no, of the threat emanating from here. The government allowed men like Solf and Erzberger, monarchists, to speak for it, and didn't even notice what an atrocity it was perpetrating.

The boulevard Unter den Linden revealed no elegant officers as before the war. It now looked gray, triste, destitute, but everything is possible. The old order was still alive, and even worse things would come, for the revenge of the officers would not spare the child in its mother's womb. Ah, this government, these right-wing socialists! Eisner sensed his own anguish. They have all the reins in their hands, these old tacticians, these tricksters, they've teamed up with the officers, they could hand us over to those mass murderers.

124

He hailed a closed cab. They rattled and clattered past the palace, across the Kaiser-Friedrich Bridge. As he rode past the porticoes, he remembered how he had often accompanied his mother here.

We are Jews, Landauer too. But Ebert and the others, are they really more powerful because they're cast from another mold? His mother had said as much many times, warning him, telling him to be careful when he got too actively involved in Party affairs. He had found such notions small-minded, reeking of the ghetto.

He entered the little building at the cemetary. His relatives gazed at him respectfully. As he followed the coffin they whispered behind him.

He sensed it again: Prenzlauer Allee, Schönhauser Allee, ghetto. At the graveside, where they had let down the coffin and where he was expected to toss a handful of dirt after it, he was all contrition and love and begged forgiveness—and was sitting beside her again on the sofa, letting her butter a roll for him.

He let the dirt fall and left. It never ends, never ends.

Eisner lay in the sleeper, on the train between Berlin and Munich. He was not a young man, it was badly heated, he was freezing. Out of Berlin, out, that was the right thing to do. Every minute the train raced on helped calm him.

After those two glorious weeks he never would have thought that this could happen to him again. To be so completely cast down. Ebert, the Reichs Chancellery, Solf, Erzberger—incredible, that that all of that still existed. The trip had been important, but ghastly, depressing.

You can't break through it. They want to strangle the revolution. They have already tightened the rope we are to stumble over. They are prepared to drive me out just as they did when I was editor of *Vorwärts*.

He slept sporadically. Night could not tear him away from his thoughts. And when gray morning dawned and he threw his heavy winter coat over him as he lay there, he suddenly thought of Liebknecht, whom he had half forgotten in his cares about the Reich conference and the funeral in Weissensee. Liebknecht the evening before last. He had spoken with him for two hours, wrestled with him. Liebknecht held rigidly to his position, to Moscow and Radek, to armed force, dictatorship and terrorism. And that was supposed to be the liberation of mankind. There was no reasoning with him. He had suffered much in prison.

At last Munich. The Central Station with its red flags. They meet him there. Crowds, hurrahs. Another world. I was only dreaming.

He drives to the Residenz.

The man who greets him at the door to his private quarters, this large figure, slightly bent, with a heavy beard, long flowing hair and big gentle eyes that look through a rimless pince-nez, is Landauer, his friend. They embrace.

"Land, land!" Eisner cried, while they help him out of his coat.

"The name's Landauer," the big man laughs, taking his hat and briefcase from him.

"No, I mean my land, our land." And Eisner tells him about Berlin. "My impression is that it is pure counterrevolution. But Munich is still here, the people are here, you're here."

Landauer: "I think you should lie down and get some rest now."

"Not for a second. I'm going to work. Our slogan: Free of Berlin."

"Don't do anything because you're angry or excited, Kurt."

"You great big Buddhist, I know that.

And the intense little man strode into his immense, bright study, a splendid room, where chairs and easy chairs, tables and desks were piled with newspapers, portfolios and books. Eisner greeted several secretaries. Two strangers from the press were there. He said to them, "You can go right ahead and inspect it all, gentlemen. Reports, letters. I have no secrets. If you find something of interest, I'm at your disposal."

In front of the window he read some of the incoming mail while people came and went. Suddenly the tall Landauer was standing bent over next to him. He had followed Eisner silently. While the smaller man had read he had made himself inconspicuous. Then, as Eisner dropped a page, Landauer bent down, and the smaller man looked into that uncommonly tranquil face, into the utterly soft and benevolent eyes of his friend, who handed him the page without speaking.

"Did you want something?" the smaller man asked.

The other shook his head and smiled at him.

"You see," Eisner whispered, looking up at him and taking hold of a button on his vest, "now is the time to act, to act, to act. This is the time for us. The time you have been longing for for decades. We dare not stand off in a corner. This is humanity's new era."

And he was gone.

Landauer followed him with long, stealthy strides. Once in his private study, Eisner began dictating letters. He called Landauer over to him. "I am breaking diplomatic relations between Bavaria and Berlin."

The tall man sat on the sofa, the head of flowing hair laid back. Eisner shouted, "I am drawing the line between them and us. That is the outcome of their Reich conference. Enough of their glory and grandeur. They shall not sabotage the German Socialist Republic."

Only after a long pause did the man on the sofa determine what to reply. "At any rate we have to stand by our principles."

Eisner scurried over to him; he balled up his left fist and whispered heavily into his ear, "And do you know what the worst thing is? Leibknecht. He's playing right into their hands. He's tearing the nation apart. He is sinning against the revolution."

Landauer gazed ahead out of those big eyes. "I know. Moscow first."

Book Three

November 28th to December 1st

General Headquarters in Kassel

The basso continuo of these weeks; the marching steps of the army returning home. In Kassel officers recall times past, and consider how they might be able to throw overboard those who are now at the rudder. An aged lady of the neighborhood, a veritable sibyl, is interested in the proposition and provides a needed pep talk.

Across the Rhine

In the North Sea the first sections of the main body of the German fleet were handed into the custody of the commander of the English fleet: 9 battleships, 5 battle cruisers, 7 light cruisers and 50 destroyers. One battleship, one battle cruiser and a light cruiser were missing. They were promised for later. During the trip across the North Sea one light cruiser hit a mine and sank. The ships were brought to the mouth of the Forth, from there they were to be taken to Scapa Flow. These were the ships of the German Navy on which the disturbances among sailors first began and open resistance to the war broke out when orders were given to sail for a final attack. Later the submarines were handed over. The British vice-admiral, Turwhitt, was in charge of the proceedings, which took place in perfectly calm seas three miles off the English coast. Witnesses report that the affair was characterized by strict courtesy on the part of the English and suppressed rage on that of the Germans.

The troops rolled en masse across the Rhine. Day and night, in an unvarying column, troops of all kinds marched through Aachen. They marched to music, defiantly, in impeccable order. Not a single red flag was to be seen among them. The imperial colors, black, white and red, fluttered on the vehicles. The ranks of men were decorated with flowers and they wore black, white and red ribbons, bows and cockades. A strong "border guard" had already started to be formed out of discharged army personnel.

In Cologne, the imperial governor of the city, the district president, Mayor Adenauer, the socialist Sollman and the industrialist Becker met together and passed a resolution to use former army personnel to form a militia of six thousand men. The workers' and soldiers' councils were involved as well. They placed all military supplies of the city at their disposal. They swore to work together until the constituent assembly could meet.

As General Sixt von Arnim marched through the Rhineland with the 4th Army, he allowed his troops to clash with the organs of subversion. There were battles in Cologne, Düsseldorf, Remscheid, and in Aachen as well. Red flags were torn down. When negotiations were necessary to march through a town, they were carried on with the old authorities.

The generals were obeying orders from General Headquarters, the same people who had commanded the war effort. The orders read:

"The Army must be inoculated against the infiltration of radical tendencies. General Headquarters has placed itself at the disposal of the Ebert government, quite independently of its own political views. Soldiers' councils are everywhere to be elected to serve as delegates who can deal with grievances and provide advice in certain questions, thus protecting the troops from infection by radicalism."

The Guard Reserve Division crossed the Rhine at Düsseldorf with a large park of artillery, its units well ordered. The commander, General von Poseck, took the salute at the march-past. It was November 23rd. That afternoon the 21st Infantry Division and parts of the 56th Division followed.

"Ordered Home" was blazoned on black, white and red ribbons the soldiers wore on their caps. The division of Lieutenant General von Erf, the 5th Army, had the ribbons pinned on the left side of their chests. The heavy and light guns, the field artillery and the foot artillery, engineer corps and mortar throwers, transport services and intelligence corps thundered across the pontoon bridge at Koblenz. Banners waved: "We Salute Our Beloved Homeland."

And how were the infantry, the riflemen, the foot-artillery received? The homeland showered them with green to symbolize that they had them back. Their vehicles were decorated with fir boughs, some with brightly colored paper garlands, and like a moving forest they entered cities as bells pealed, tears flowed, crowds cheered. But all the cheers, all the joy of this embrace between army and homeland did not put an end to the tension between the troops and their officers. The bill for the revolution still had to be settled up between them. In Koblenz, as the general reviewed the parade, an old chauffeur sat on an ammunition box smoking. An officer at the general's side came bounding over to him. "Where do you get the impudence, you clod, to smoke while in formation? Throw that cigar away at once."

130

The man obeyed. The hate and embitterment among the enlisted men was great. They had read the posters in the towns.

Braun, the minister of agriculture, warned: "The cry for the dividing up of wealth grows louder. But it cannot be done that easily. One ought to have no illusions. Every sign of support for it will bring discredit upon socialism for decades ahead." Next to this hung an announcement from Field Marshal Hindenburg: "Germany wants to provide a home for its veterans as soon as it can. Hundreds of thousands of positions will be created for farmers, gardners and rural tradesmen on inexpensive land purchased cheaply with public moneys. For urban workers and clerks, houses will be built in landscaped cities and made available to them at low interest. The great task has begun. Have patience."

The rank and file soldier stood in front of these, nudging his neighbor. "Can't be done that easily, Braun says. No, can't be done easily. We're supposed to be patient."

But he still had his weapon, said "Show me!" and carefully inspected the cities, the houses, the shops and the citizenry.

General Headquarters in Kassel

Major Schleicher came out very soon after the arrival of Colonel Haeften from Berlin was reported to him. He offered Quartermaster General Groener's apologies. The chief was in conference again with other railroad experts concerning Rumania and the Ukraine. Schleicher wrung his hands with comic despair and raised his eyes to the ceiling. "The East will kill us, but we'll not speak any further of that."

They were in Wilhelmshöhe Castle near Kassel, at General Headquarters. "And you've just come from Berlin, Colonel? No bad news I hope?" They walked out of the adjutants' room and into the vast hall of the reception room. The colonel handed an orderly who sprang to his side his coat, helmet and saber.

"Nothing of the sort," the broad, easy-going Haeften replied. "Don't begrudge me the chance of getting away from the people's deputies now and again."

"His Excellency will be finished in half an hour, perhaps a little more. We fear the worst for our troops in the Ukraine. That's on the one hand. On the other," Schleicher glanced at Haeften with an ironic smile, "on the other hand we're not going to scramble to get those fellows out down there. Whole units have gone off of late on their own and started living like vagabonds. Throw in their lot with the Bolsheviks."

131

Haeften shrugged. "We've enough of those fellows, God knows, here at home."

"Exactly," Schleicher said testily. "That's precisely what could cross up our plans. How are things going in Berlin?"

"I can give you a demonstration." Haeften unbuttoned his uniform jacket and took several sheets of paper out of his breast pocket. "This— excuse me, I need my glasses—no, this is our plan for the Congress of Soldiers' Councils at Ems. I have gone through it point by point with Ebert. I wanted to have him sign the minutes that were taken down just to be on the safe side. But he didn't want to, said it was superfluous. In any case—he has agreed. It will all come off then in a couple of days."

"December 1st will soon be here. Sunday," von Schleicher said thoughtfully.

"It'll come off with all our stipulations." They were standing at a high window. Haeften read them: "Immediate convocation of the Reichstag, disbandment of the workers' and soldiers' councils and the total restoration of the authority and right of command of officers."

"Ebert swallowed that?"

"He's a reasonable man. He's been out mixing with people for decades and knows what's what."

Schleicher sniffed and replied, "Hm. Curious fellow. Saw him once in Spa with some other Reichstag fogeys who all wanted to get in to have a look at the grand motor-works as it were. Guided tours Mondays from five to six, the management is not responsible for injury in case of accident."

Haeften: "You know him then."

Von Schleicher, a man in his mid-thirties, passed his hand over his bald head, his very lively eyes laughed. "Like the back of my hand. We appear to have made an almost sinfully good catch with him. I'm told two of his sons fell in the war. He's a sly, respectable fellow and he's got the socialists tied up in his sack. The good Lord heard our prayers after all. Lost the war, but won Herr Ebert."

Haeften: "So, to get back to Ems. Civilians to turn in all weapons, the disactivation of all revolutionary units at the depots and in the reserves. The High Command will have the entire operation in its hands."

Schleicher let his monocle fall. "What? He accepted that?"

"He did indeed. But now he's decided he wants"—Schleicher: "Aha"—"Emil Barth, that loud mouth Independent, to come to the Congress as well. I was present at the discussion in the Reichs Chancellery. Naturally I couldn't do any close questioning, that was Ebert's job. To be frank, I thought he didn't show himself to be forceful enough."

Schleicher: "There you have it. The man's playing a double role. What's the point of this whole conference in Ems? Who came up with the idea to begin with?"

132

"Ebert himself."

"Ah-ha, I thought so. He wants to sneak his friends in and we end up the dupes."

"Major, without the socialists' playing along, it won't work at all. Groener himself has given his approval."

"Tell him about this mess now."

"Ebert wants to feather his own nest, of course. He would like to force the Independents out of the government, freeze out the Spartacists, and finally he wants a solid, unified Reich."

"With His Majesty?"

Haeften carefully tucked his papers back in his breast pocket. "Actually I'd say more with Ebert."

Haeften did not succeed in enticing a smile out of Schleicher.

Schleicher clamped his monocle back in and stared at the orderlies who suddenly poured out of several rooms in great numbers and dispersed in various directions. "It appears His Excellency has finished. Permit me to inquire." He came back in a minute. "His Excellency will receive you now."

While Colonel Haeften took back his sword, gloves and helmet in the reception room, the large, robust figure of the quartermaster general, a man in his fifties, appeared at the door. He walked out to meet Haeften. "Leave all that here, my dear Colonel. We shall most likely not need to disturb the Field Marshal, so let us put on our coats. Major Schleicher, would you join us please. We're going for a turn in the park."

Once outside, Groener carried his cap in his hand for a while to cool his brow. His dark, lightly graying hair was parted in the middle; his face lacked sharp features, was broad and full, the lower portion jutting forward, the moustache drawn out to the sides in the customary fashion.

It was wet and chilly, but there was no rain. The paths through the Wilhelmshöhe gardens were well kept. They marched about in the fresh air without a word. Groener turned to Colonel Haeften and said, "Major von Schleicher has probably already told you about the Bolsheviks in the East. That makes things hot for us. What have you brought?"

"Nothing important. I wanted instructions for my negotiations with the government. The Congress in Ems will take place as planned this coming Sunday. It was impossible to prevent People's Deputy Barth, the Independent, from attending as well. The man is hostile to all our plans."

"Why was that impossible?"

"Ebert did not act decisively enough."

The quartermaster general said, "Hmm, hmm," and walked more slowly. He asked, "You intervened?"

"Naturally."

"Cautiously?"

"Yes."

"The same old story. When I report this to the Field Marshal General he'll delightedly bang on his desk and ask, 'Why do you get involved with this Ebert?' "

Haeften: "The Field Marshal General is still against him?"

"That would be putting it too strongly. Hindenburg knows only useful and useless people. He can't deal with mongrels."

They walked on silently.

Groener: "Speak to Ebert again, just the two of you. He has to stick with us. It won't work otherwise."

Schleicher: "There will come a time when we won't need these marionettes, you know."

Groener clucked his tongue reproachfully. "My dear von Schleicher. What do you want after all? A military dictatorship? Won't work. The Field Marshal himself doesn't want that. This is in fact better for negotiating with the Entente."

Schleicher, pleased: "The Field Marshal is supposed to have said, however, that he is no wooden Hindenburg statuette that they can pound nails into."

Groener glanced at Schleicher's face. "You probably started that one yourself. In any case, we need Ebert. I cannot impress that enough on Schleicher and the other gentlemen. We need a civilian. He makes an excellent impression internationally. The Entente can't figure him out. Domestically he may get in over his head. But we're here in that case. Should the Spartacists be successful and pull the socialists with them to the left, we'll have to have got our grip on Ebert in time to set things right again."

Haeften: "In my opinion he holds the key position in the present situation."

Schleicher: "Unfortunately doubts crop up whenever we speak of the man. He's playing a very curious double role, you know. As for instance with this Congress at Ems."

Groener, quite at ease: "He can be used. Don't ask too much. He's a good man in the right spot. When the decisive moment came for His Majesty, he handled himself splendidly. We dare not forget that. I do not think it impossible that history will hold me responsible for all sorts of things for which I am not to blame. I shall carry my own load. I was not given any freedom to act at the end of October, otherwise I would have been able to strike a deal favorable to the monarchy with this Ebert and the people he had in hand, all of them decent sorts. I asked him in the Reichs Chancellery, this was November 6th—His Majesty was still staying at Spa—which way the wind was blowing. He assured me that he hated revolution and I had no reason for doubting him, given his patri-

134

otic behavior up till then. He told me that His Majesty's abdication was necessary to prevent the masses from deserting to the revolutionary cause. He made me a concrete offer: to entrust one of the younger princes, Eitel Friedrich or Oskar, with the regency until the oldest son of the crown prince came of age. Did you know of that, Colonel Haeften?"

Haeften: "Vaguely. And, Your Excellency, you declined?"

"No. Your Excellency did not decline. The imperial family did. There you have another chapter of German history, this time written solely by its ruling house. The situation was favorable for the Hohenzollerns, they had been presented with an honorable offer. The entire affair was painful—but that suggestion represented the best, indeed I still maintain today, the only true solution for the nation. That they did not accept it will cost us a great deal. I did my best in the matter, no one can deny me that. But then the members of the imperial family began to compete to see who could be the most noble-minded. No one wanted to take the Kaiser's place, no one wanted to do that to him. Have you something to say to this, Schleicher?"

"I merely sighed."

"I am describing the situation falsely?"

"Quite correctly, unfortunately."

"All the sons declared themselves solidly behind their father. I had my directions. It would not do to play the Duke of York and begin running things on my own. The crown prince was father to his son and not I. I only wish to say that Ebert and the other socialists who were with him on this stood there just as much in despair as I. They did not want a revolution, they wanted to work with us. It was not possible. My hands were tied. They moved on to revolution."

Haeften: "All new to me."

Groener marched ahead, his brow furrowed in deep thought. "What I've said is in absolute confidence."

Haeften raised his hand to his helmet.

Groener: "In the spring of 1918 I had already seen all sorts of things, although everything still seemed rosy to them. I was with the Eichhorn army unit in the Ukraine, and we were receiving our German prisoners back from the Russian front. They were supposed to be reassigned in an orderly fashion to their regiments. After a proper period of leave, of course. The fellows mutinied. In all seriousness, they demanded the right not to fight any more. We disciplined them. At that point General Hoffmann came to me and bewailed the fact that we had sent Lenin to Russia to infect the Russian army with the communist plague—and now it was spreading to us. I consoled him—you never know for sure when it comes to medical matters. In any case, I saw things more clearly than did the gentlemen in Spa, than General Barttenwerffer or Major Niemann or even Lieutenant General Plessen.

"Hindenburg and I wanted to save the monarchy at any price. I wanted to move the Kaiser to do something along those lines when he gave up the crown. I told Plessen that the Kaiser should show himself in the trenches, that we had to bring about a sudden change of mood, that the war was lost but that the Kaiser must now show himself at one with his subjects. His Majesty should brave enemy fire like every soldier on the front. It was no longer a matter of handing out medals and reviewing parades. Should His Majesty be slain, my very words, it would be the most glorious end possible for him. Should he be wounded it would result in a change of mood in his favor. Nothing could be done. Plessen looked at me as if I were a cannibal and said, 'You wish to put his life in jeopardy?'"

Haeften: "His Majesty heard nothing of this suggestion?"

"At once. Plessen could not keep it to himself for a minute. The Kaiser declared he would have no part of some absurd and melodramatic gesture. Melodramatic—to go to the trenches! I had not expected that. He was for an armistice with the Allies, and then: About face! March! Back into Germany."

Schleicher: "The chances being absolutely zero."

Groener: "Absolutely zero. — At any rate," Groener tapped Schleicher on the arm, "leave Ebert alone for me. The Kaiser did not make our situation in those days any easier, but look at Ebert. It could cost him his head. You know that. He knows, and knows that we know it. On November 9th, at noon, he holds his own people back in their factories, lets Prince Max of Baden hand over the government to him. Vice-chancellor Payer asked him directly, 'Do you wish to take over the government on the basis of the constitution of the Reich or in the name of the workers' and soldiers' councils?' Ebert answered without blinking, 'On the basis of the constitution of the Reich.'"

An orderly came after them. The walk had to be interrupted, the Field Marshal General was in the building. They turned back, von Schleicher led Haeften to his office.

They smoked for a while in silence, then von Schleicher gave free reign to his bitterness. He rejected, he despised Groener's weakness for Ebert. He said no, no and no again.

Haeften let out a puff of smoke. "Groener knows your opinion?"

"For a long time now. He loves to be contradicted. That's why he always has to argue with Hindenburg, too, who doesn't like debates. The Field Marshal General would love to take care of this 'government' through martial law."

"They suspect as much in Berlin."

"The fellows have a bad conscience."

Schleicher walked up and down. "We shall dine later in town. I am to extend an invitation to you from the widow of a regimental comrade of mine, a countess, a very old woman who once was a lady-in-waiting at the court of Wilhelm I. She would love to have you. If you like, I shall tell her you're coming."

"Much obliged, Major. I still have three and a half hours."

Schleicher: "Fine, that's agreed then. And old Hindenburg? He's growling away. He hasn't stopped growling since Groener meddled in His Majesty's abdication. He won't forgive him that till the day he dies. You will meet my friend Lieutenant Colonel von Bock at the old woman's home. We spent the last days of Pompeii together. That was such a tragic time, those days in Spa, that our children and our children's children will still speak of them—if they still have any sense of history and Germany has not vanished from the earth. The methods they used to sacrifice His Majesty to the Entente! Von Bock will tell you all about it, he heard it from Countess Schulenburg."

"Count Schulenburg was present?"

"He came over from Waulsort, from the crown prince's headquarters. The crown prince had told him the scheme that the prince of Baden had hatched and that Groener seconded. The whole perifidious apparatus to soften up the Kaiser, the interrogation of the thirty-nine commanders who were called to Spa, with questions put to them that—how shall I say it—that stank of defeatism to the core. The Kaiser was furious when he learned the results of the whole dishonorable procedure. He accused Groener of a demoralizing attitude, he openly accused him of treason. They had called in the generals early in the morning, before breakfast. I'll leave aside the question whether, as the crown prince declared, 'the generals would have expressed themselves differently after a proper breakfast and a good cigar.' But most certainly the conditions chosen were not conducive to courageous answers. Count Schulenburg was the only one who threw himself into the breach and openly opposed the general—what shall we call it—spirit of self-sacrifice. Count Schulenburg knew what a Hohenzollern is; a Lieutenant General Schulenburg who served under Frederick the Great is among his ancestors."

"And the Field Marshal?"

"Hindenburg was all military business. He was absolutely irreproachable. The Kaiser wanted to do something—you must beg my pardon—absolutely naïve: to ride at the head of his army back to Germany and so restore order. Hindenburg begged the Kaiser not to make any decisions which, after mature consideration, might prove impossible to execute. He spoke only militarily. Whatever else he had to say he kept to himself, as befits a Prussian officer. Groener, however . . ."

Schleicher held his hand to his eyes and groped for the nearest chair. "This is what I simply cannot get over. And when I let such thoughts wander through my mind, I would just as soon throw down my sword and walk out on the street to lose myself in the crowd. I simply choke on it."

Haeften said nothing.

Schleicher, softly: "At that point His Excellency, Herr Groener, said: 'The army no longer stands behind Your Majesty. And—under such circumstances—the oath of loyalty—is only an ideal.' If you ask me, Haeften, what I think of that, I can only say that I have come to my decision. I'll say no more. I shall keep my opinion to myself."

Haeften: "Colonel Heye knows about this, too."

"Which Heye?"

"The one who kept the minutes while the generals were being questioned. He told me that even the king of Württemberg made a remark about that statement. The king said that as his subject General Groener should have let such a thing be said by a Prussian officer."

Schleicher: "Much obliged, but that did not happen. So there you see the wretched state Germany is in. That, too. — The last to stick with the Hohenzollerns were Schulenburg and Adjutant General von Plessen. But it was too late. The princes turned tail, including your tactful king of Württemberg. The confederated princes deserted their Kaiser. Oh lord, how Schulenburg exerted himself. Kept on bucking up the Kaiser who collapsed a little bit more with each hour. He should at least remain king of Prussia. Ostensibly that was not legally possible. Just imagine, Colonel Haeften, in such a situation they were talking about legal impossibilities. It makes you double over with rage."

Haeften: "Hindenburg thinks as you do?"

Von Schleicher nodded. "You must excuse this confession. But it is no secret. Now Groener is in charge. We are proud of the old man, but he has moderated."

Haeften stood up.

Schleicher: "Till dinner then. I shall say you're coming."

The Sibyl True to the Kaiser

They walked into town.

A loosened poster fluttered on a tree trunk. They read it.

"Field Marshal General von Hindenburg belongs to all the German people." Further down, fragmentary: "contrary to the general prohibition, the Field Marshal and his entourage may bear sidearms and epaulettes."

Signed: "Chairman of the Koch and Albert Grzesinski Soldiers' Council of Kassel."

In a single motion von Schleicher ripped the rest down.

Schleicher talked about the sibyl at whose table they would dine. The Field Marshal General also appeared there from time to time. He, Schleicher, was the wrong person to speak of her, since he had a weakness for her. The Field Marshal General had once taken him along to play cards there, and since then the two of them had formed an almost intimate relationship. It was difficult to say how old she might be, eighty-five perhaps. One did not dine with her; she would first appear at dessert and sip at a cup of coffee. Several people gossip that in 1870, after Sedan, Emperor Napoleon sought permission to see her, and she refused him. Apparently a legend, since in 1870 she would have been thirty years old, and she was already an old woman when she became known in Kassel.

The sibyl's apartments were extensive, furnished in a fantastic mixture of styles. Besides lovely antiques, there were pieces from the heyday of plush; tasteless whatnots with artificial flowers and painted vases. A venerable old woman summoned the three of them, Colonel Haeften, von Schleicher and an older officer with a white beard à la Wilhelm I, from the salon—all in rosewood—where they had gathered, into the dining room. A footman served while they ate from French porcelain; a formal, tranquil mood was set by the tapestries on the wall, by the tinkling crystal glasses into which the wines of Rhine and Mosel were poured. The older officer took part in the conversation with nothing but a friendly smile; he was almost deaf.

When the fruit had been served, a side door opened and a dark, tall, bent figure all in black appeared. She walked without a cane, but her neck and head were bent down so far that one saw nothing but the simple, heavy mass of her white hair, whose lovely curls hung down over her temples, ears and cheeks. The lady who had supervised the dinner till now walked toward her; the countess—so she was addressed—motioned as she passed for the gentlemen to remain seated, she smiled at Schleicher. She took her place next to him at the table and with a warm, indeed affectionate, glance she looked up at Colonel Haeften.

Haeften was amazed at the youthful expression retained by the lean face with wrinkles only on the cheeks. Her eyes simply blossomed, their gaze was clear, insistent, responsive. Her very definite chin jutted forward. She spoke asthmatically in short sentences. She began talking quite soon, in front of her a plate of orange slices. She told of the World Exposition in Paris in 1878. She had come across pictures of it today. What a city, Paris. What a wonderful charm it had. She had been there for the last time exactly twenty years before.

She ordered the coffee. They moved to the great, white porcelain stove ornamented with small dots, where a blue velvet armchair with a high back stood. Chairs were gathered about the table in front of it, the deaf old man excused himself, he suffered from sciatica. The countess held his hand, stroking it, for some time. Meanwhile Haeften whispered to Major van Schleicher, "All we need now is for a green-eyed cat to come walking in and I'd imagine myself in some enchanted castle."

Schleicher shook his head, apparently not quite in agreement. He gave a little wave of his hand—wait a bit.

Once the sibyl was seated in her high-backed chair, she could hold her head back nicely, and now one could look at her face. How well this life had stood up to old age. The brown irises of her eyes had not been able to fight off the white rim of age, there were dark shadows under her eyes, her lids were shriveled as they rolled up, and her lips had lost their color and fullness with time, leaving only a single line, a thin border. But in conversation the lips drew together, came to a point, the utterly smooth brow revealed two diagonal lines, the head could still be laid to one side in a charming way. The fine, pointed nose grew softer when she smiled. Her two hands, gloved in black, were laid together—and there one sat, across from an indestructibly youthful creature with the bloom of a young girl still upon her.

The countess suggested to Colonel von Haeften that despite his duties he not ignore the city of Kassel. The narrow streets, and the half-timbered houses of the old town. "You will find there a house bearing a plaque with the names of Jakob and Wilhelm Grimm, who gave our children the tales of Red Riding Hood and Sleeping Beauty. Walk on then to the Old Market and the Renthof. You'll see the loveliest things, and you need that now, coming back from war. You probably have no patience for reading books. And you, Herr von Schleicher? Have you paid Kassel the honor due it? I always send the gentlemen from General Headquarters into town, otherwise they only stay up there at Wilhelmshöhe or travel to Berlin."

Schleicher: "Which cannot be said of me, countess. I have visited the Hessian Monument."

"Alone?"

"With von dem Bussche. The monument, Colonel von Haeften, is a very old one, erected in memory of German patriots who fell in the struggle against foreign domination by the first of the Napoleons. It is a stone column set in a park, with a recumbent lion on top."

The countess: "First there are a few steps to climb, please. They became more and more difficult for me. Now, is that not a lovely symbol, a more suitable monument than the one in your new Berlin?"

Von Schleicher protested loudly, "I'm not to blame for that. Begas was incapable of anything better."

The countess: "Begas is an example of those people to whom fortune has been too kind. When they are kings they endanger their land, as musicians they compose like Richard Wagner, getting ever louder, heavier, longer. As sculptors—but I know the monument to Wilhelm I only from pictures."

Von Haeften: "His Majesty is said to have offered suggestions and made certain decisions regarding it."

The countess: "What of it? A prince is a patron and always has something to say. But that does not excuse the artist."

Schleicher repeated, "Begas was incapable of anything better, countess."

"Oh, but he was, my dear Schleicher. Do not excuse him. He was capable of much. But not a monument to Wilhelm I. I knew the old Kaiser from when I was at the court of Her Majesty Kaiserin Augusta. He was more than simply the "victor" of Herr Begas. He was a simple man. The Field Marshal General is more severe, but he reminds me of him. He was portly. There was something merry about him with his gray and white beard. He was more cheerful than the Kaiserin. He flirted with beautiful women, in Ems and in Gastein."

Von Haeften: "You knew the old Kaiserin, countess?"

"Several years before my marriage, in the sixties. She was from Weimar. Had grown up sitting on Goethe's knee, people used to say; she would have been happy with a Hessian Elector who loved his home, the hunt, his pictures and castles. But she was married off to Prince Wilhelm, a Prussian. It could have worked out well with him, too, for I know how acquiescent she was—in the early years. But there was his passion for Princess Radziwill. No one had whispered a word of this to the little princess from Weimar. She did not know that he had waited for the Polish noblewoman for six long years, hoping that she would be recognized as his equal. What tales were told of those two. The scene at one ball given by Prince Wilhelm—I have this from hearsay—when Princess Radziwill suddenly began to cough blood, in the ballroom, in the Prince's palace. The Kaiserin-to-be ran to her, holding her rival in her arms, suspecting nothing. The Prince had to stand there next to them, without letting his face betray him. A ghastly, a gruesome incident. She died soon thereafter. His relationship with his spouse remained frosty, but correct. He never fully recovered from the blow. And then our Kaiserin Augusta. You would have to have known her, gentlemen. Before and after. It was all over for her, the delicate princess from Weimar, as soon as she understood. She grew hard, and got harder, severer, with everyone. Her face lost the charm of the Weimar days." His hostess looked full at Schleicher. "How did I arrive at this story?"

"Via Begas and the monument to Wilhelm I in Berlin."

The old woman sipped at her coffee, to which her companion had added a few drops of cognac. She turned to Haeften. "You have come from Berlin?"

"I have a military, a political position there, countess. I play the liaison officer between the High Command and the government."

"I wish you good luck. I admire your spirit of sacrifice, Colonel."

"Duty, gracious countess."

"You would accept such a position as well, von Schleicher?"

"With the same reasonings and reservations as Colonel von Haeften."

"Either it's because I'm a woman or I'm too old, but I cannot share your opinion as officers."

She put down the little cup. All that was visible was the snow-white hair stirring at her black breast. Her head shook slightly.

Von Haeften: "If I understand you correctly, countess, you do not approve of our relationship with the government in Berlin."

The countess stayed as she was, her head on her breast. She spoke in a brittle voice. "I don't understand any of it—not even the Field Marshal General."

One could not reply anything to that. One could only wait for her next statement. She gave herself time, and the gentlemen felt uneasy. The housekeeper filled glasses and cups as if nothing had happened.

The countess: "Where do those—gentlemen have their offices in Berlin?"

Von Haeften: "There is no one at the palace except mutinous sailors. The government itself occupies the former Reichs Chancellery."

"Why don't you at least drive the sailors out of the palace?"

Von Schleicher: "At the moment we are busy bringing the army back home from the front."

The countess: "I don't understand that. I don't understand any of it. That you permit such obscenity. The officers are cursed at. Here in Kassel they have been gracious enough to allow the officers to wear swords and epaulettes. Sailors have mutinied, officers have been shot and simply thrown into the water, and they are occupying the palace."

Von Schleicher: "This is a conversation, my dear countess, that has been carried on often at General Headquarters in recent weeks."

The ancient woman now only looked down as she spoke, while her head and hands trembled, though she tried to hold them rigid. "What do you purpose in saying that, von Schleicher? You have sent the Kaiser off to Holland."

Schleicher: "There were thoughts on both sides of that issue as well."

"No. You thought nothing whatever about it."

Schleicher regarded the restless mass of white hair darkly.

The old woman: "I don't even want to know what you thought. You have sent His Majesty off to Holland, and you are still here."

"As is the Field Marshal General."

The housekeeper laid her arm around the old woman. "Countess."

But the old woman had already raised her head, sat up on her own, smiling pleasantly, even sweetly at her companion. "And now you're scolding me, Betty, and justly so." And she turned to the two officers with that same smile, and attempted a slight bow. "You must excuse my letting myself go like that. When you get old you live in your thoughts and try to find nourishment from the people who visit you. And if you do not find it, you complain. Yes, complain. I have met you for the first time this evening, Herr von Haeften. How do you ever manage your superhuman task?" Her eyes were opened wide and moved from Schleicher to Haeften and from Haeften to Schleicher, so that both could gaze into their depths. "Help me to understand it. I see nothing lacking in either of you. Nothing wrong. But just as I enjoy your company and am glad that you are alive and vigorous and have not forgotten an old woman, still I beg you to do me the kindness and explain to me what you feel when dealing with—those people."

Schleicher looked over to Haeften. He seemed to be lost in his thoughts, and Schleicher was the one who had to speak. "May I at least remark that in my relations with revolutionaries I feel exactly the same as you, dear countess. Please be assured, countess, that each of us would much rather meet them with a revolver than with words. Our orders, however, are to negotiate—until that point has arrived when negotiations are no longer necessary."

The countess, looking directly at him: "It were better had you not chosen that formulation. You demean yourself with it. But why have you sent His Majesty off to Holland?"

It was von Haeften's turn. "It was unavoidable. The Reich had to be preserved. We were confronted with an alternative—either the Kaiser or the Reich. The Kaiser's counselors placed the Reich above the Kaiser. He accepted that decision."

At that, the large round eyes of the old woman shone, moving from the one to the other. It seemed for a moment as if she would stand up and manage to force a cheerful smile of farewell. The matronly housekeeper had already stood up. But the old woman remained seated. Finally she found her voice. "What His Majesty himself chooses to do is a separate matter. We have no right to judge him. He did not desert the Reich. He left after they had taken his crown and scepter from him." The red of anger rose in Schleicher's face. "Yes, Herr Schleicher, you shall hear what I have to say, and you may be angry. You have all dealt badly with him. The pain of it all allows me no sleep. The Field Marshal has remained silent. I know that at that moment he died. Because I love you young people and you are attached to me, I tell you all this. But soon you will no longer visit me because you find me unbearable."

Von Schleicher groped for her hand. She held his tight in her two black gloved ones. "Talking wearies me, von Schleicher. But do not believe that the Reich is more important than the Kaiser, and that the Kaiser should perish if only the Reich may endure. The Reich has no life of its own without the Kaiser. The Reich grew with the Kaiser. Do not forget him there in Holland while you dirty your hands dealing with those people. I am afraid for you." —

They helped the old woman stand up. After a few uncertain movements she was up. She stood tall once again, but bent so that one saw the great waves of white hair. A black-gloved hand was stretched out toward von Haeften. "You'll visit the Hessian Monument, colonel? You promise me?"

Out on the street, the two officers walked along silently until Colonel von Haeften said, "She made me completely forget what I was going to say."

Von Schleicher, with biting irony: "One thing for certain—we'll not be able to go on muddling through like this much longer."

The Voice of Liebknecht Over Berlin

Karl Liebknecht warns the sailors about the generals and their accomplices. Nor does he want Wilson's peace, because it would be no peace. This does not sound bad to several officers. The blood of a lottery dealer is not yet avenged. A cute dye-job moves up the ladder. Two members of a soldiers' council get their backs up. And the Spree sighs beneath its bridges at how long a day lasts in Berlin.

Karl Liebknecht before the Naval Committee of Fifty-Three

The voice of Liebknecht over Berlin.

He spoke in the Chamber of Deputies before the Naval Committee of Fifty-three.

"Friends and Comrades!

"No serious socialist was surprised by this war. We had been predicting it for a long time. We sought to prevent it with every ounce of strength we had. The international proletariat hoped to be strong enough for that task.

[The sailors and soldiers in the hall: "We've won, we beat the crooks."]

"How did this war come about? England had learned by experience that naked force and brutality is a two-edged sword. To live in free commerce with free peoples had proven the most useful course—a businessman's point of view. Before the war, England was anxious to provide Germany with greater freedom of movement and had prepared agreements to that effect. The revelations of Lichnovsky have proven that. They have also proven that these agreements came to naught because of Germany's opposition. Why? Because such agreements would have hindered the establishment of German global rule.

[The sailors and soldiers: "The crooks. They've had their teeth bashed in now."]

"After the outbreak of war, it would still have been possible to achieve peace early on. That came to nothing because of Germany's opposition. England put out a feeler for peace in April of 1915, by way of the Dutch undersecretary of state, Dressel Huis. This was rejected for formal reasons as Secretary of State Zimmermann has himself admitted. England was then willing not only to agree to the status quo, but also to make concessions concerning colonies, and even termed possible war indemnities to Germany as open to discussion.

[The sailors and soldiers: "Is that true? Is that true? The bandits."]

"Comrades, friends. We know how those few who stood up against the general madness of those days were slandered. Gradually, however, a portion of the population recognized the validity of our standpoint. The war had its roots in imperialism, and only if these roots are torn out can we achieve a lasting peace.

"What is the nature of the current revolution? For the most part it is a revolt against war and was ignited by the navy's fear that the admirals were about to keep the war going all on their own after the collapse of the front on land. Bourgeois elements joined in as well at the outbreak of the revolution, both within and outside of the army. But today those elements are unreliable and untrustworthy.

[Sailors and soldiers in a storm of voices: "Bravo!"]

"This German revolution is and can remain what it has been till now: a movement for peace and reform on the part of the bourgeoisie.

"Or it can become what it has not yet been: a socialist revolution of the proletariat.

"Even in the first case, it is the working class that must form its most important pillar of support if that movement is not to degenerate into a farce.

"But we cannot let ourselves be content with bourgeois reform. The confrontation between capital and labor, the confrontation crucial to world history has begun.

[How often had they heard it all, it was only a song cranked out on a barrel organ. But the men sitting there below him saw a mouth spread wide, a head thrown back, flashing eyeglasses directed up at the white ceiling, a small human figure dressed in black. Marshaling his energies, he shot the sentences off as if from a bow. They flew like darts from a blowpipe. And they understood as these fragments of the man sprayed the air: it was not just a matter of discussing the question of bourgeois or proletarian revolution, but you also had to decide whether you wanted to go with him, to spit fire with him or not. Now the voice was lowered back down into the hall.]

"Does the proletariat now have the power in its hands? Workers' and soldiers' councils have been formed, but they are not expressions of class consciousness. Feudal officers have been elected to them, members of the ruling class. That is shameful. Only workers and proletarian soldiers belong in the councils, only those men and women who have been

146

legitimated by a life of struggle for the proletariat. That is the one and only clear standpoint for power when confronting the ruling classes. We can use neither cowards who lay down their arms out of fear, nor schemers who are waiting for the first favorable opportunity to attack us from the rear. We can do without people with good intentions.

"It is the Majority Socialists who bear the major blame for the confusion among the masses, having cunningly kept them in the dark right up to the outbreak of revolution. On the morning of November 9th, we issued the call for an armed uprising, using flyers with our signature. In order to frustrate this action, the Majoritists summoned factory workers together for eleven o'clock. But their trick misfired, and when that afternoon the revolution had succeeded, they all tied a red ribbon around their sleeves.

[Scornful murmurs among the men below.]

"I have been asked why I did not join the government. Because I demand all power for the workers' and soldiers' councils. But a great many of the positions of power have remained in the hands of the old class and they are constantly busy snatching away from us those we have already won for ourselves.

"Now the generals are returning home from the front at the head of their mighty armies.

[A general storm of catcalls.]

"They act like caesars at the head of their legions. They forbid the flying of the red flag, disband soldiers' councils. We can expect all sorts of things from them. Do these gentlemen want to try, do you suppose, to raise our spirits once again with the house of Hohenzollern?

[Long laughter.]

"They hope to spread a flood of counterrevolution across the land, that is their sly plan—after they have sown hate against the bloodthirsty Bolsheviks. But whom have we killed? Where have we spilled one drop of blood except when we were attacked? But what we can expect from them, from these commanders of the great offensives, of the grand slaughter of men, that is clear enough.

[They sat there mute, the specter had been conjured up. The voice glowed, burst into flame.]

"The troops are aroused by chauvinistic descriptions of the conditions of the armistice. But we demand that these generals be dismissed at once, relieved of their command, and that all armies be reorganized from the bottom up in a democratic fashion. That cannot be done, so their lies go, because of the difficulties of demobilization. The German soldier, enflamed with the fire of revolutionary enthusiasm, would make child's play of problems portrayed as insoluble. Faith can move mountains. We trust the revolutionary self-discipline of the masses of German soldiers. [Applause.]

"But—is an ordered retreat more important than the revolution in the first place? For the sake of sweet law and order, the deadly enemies of the revolution have been granted powers that threaten the very basis of what has been achieved so far. I warn you. I summon you. Be on your guard.

"We cannot be content with the abolition of the Hohenzollerns. Class rule must be done away with and socialism established. The present 'socialist government' [laughter] has formed a commission to obstruct socialism. Whereas the first energetic steps must be taken now. Major industry is ripe for nationalization. The Reichstag was willing to nationalize the armaments industry as early as 1913. The war economy was a good teacher. It showed how extensively one can interfere with the mechanisms of the economy without causing a disorganization of capitalism.

[The little black figure reached for a glass of water, drank. They drank with him and rested a bit. They waited. He waited. In soft words he tested his way among the sounds and echoes of the hall. He moved on to another topic.]

"The German proletariat cannot conclude a Wilsonian peace, only a socialist one. Because what it wants is the dissolution of capitalism. It is only through socialism that an economy of peace can be built anew, only that can bring us through the difficulties of the next several months. But the eradication of capitalism, the introduction of socialist society is only possible on an international basis. There is doubt whether a revolution can occur in France, England, Italy, America—because, of course, as yet it has not occurred. The German revolution was on November 9th, today is the 27th—how can we expect that in such a few short days the nations of the Entente will follow us. But rest assured, the heady feeling of victory will evaporate quickly, the masses there will recognize that the victory has only strengthened the power of their oppressors and forged their own chains that much stronger.

"And why do they waver so? Did we not leave the Russian revolution waiting for a year? But the German revolution is not yet a socialist one, and we cannot expect to create an upheaval in the western democracies with this insurrection of ours, for they have long since had such bourgeois republics. We will not trigger revolution among them and will not achieve a true peace unless in our own country we advance from the bourgeois reforms of Ebert and Scheidemann to a social revolution.

[Isolated cries of "Bravo, right you are," but they sat there, exhausted now, following only the half of it; he was no longer saying the right things; the white ceiling and the little black figure at the podium were still there, but what had happened?—How was that just a while ago, hadn't his words shot into the air like rockets? You watched that little dark figure, all his energies marshaled, behind him lay detention, prison, hard labor—his sentences had struck fire, almost making you forget who you were. And now he had become just a speaker, and you could look at your neighbors and think about things at home, you wanted new razor blades and knew where you could buy underwear cheap. The voice comes from far away. You don't look up.]

"There are two possibilities for settling the accounts of this war. The first provides a temporary peace that is an affront to human dignity. The second is a permanent peace with prosperity. The first preserves the class structure, the second liberates the people.

[And suddenly the black dove was there again. The whirring bird flew up with a cry toward the ceiling. The voice.]

"The social revolution in Germany must come and from it the world revolution against imperialism, slavery, plundering and murder at home and abroad.

[He shrieked.] "What? What? They accuse us of murdering, of plundering, of anarchy? Us? Us, who want to abolish such things? Those who accuse us of murdering and plundering are the ones whose basic principle is murder and plunder, who instigated this war and have committed crimes a million times over.

[The face still distorted, the dove kept fluttering about, pecking away.]

"Our goal is happiness and prosperity, brotherhood, freedom, peace among nations.

[They saw the speaker seem to grow smaller, standing behind the table there on the stage, his mouth slightly opened, the eyeglasses directed at the tabletop. His left hand was playing with the empty water glass. A soft, melodic voice submerged in itself grew audible now. The voice spoke in elegiac tones to itself.]

"Dark is the sea, stormy and full of treacherous rocks. Shall we fall back, terrified of our tasks because they are difficult ones? We see the shining stars that set our course.

"Shall we forget our goal because of the rocks? Our noble goal?

"We keep our eyes lifted up and we shall arrive at our goal—despite everything."

[At the end he had closed his eyes behind the glasses. He shrieked those last two words "despite everything." The hall thundered with applause.]

Officers and Spartacus

The dark of night still dominated Wilhelmsplatz in Charlottenburg at seven o'clock. The new day arrived, gray, sober, hard; it proved moody and nasty and blew a cold wind.

In the dark hotel room something breathed, evenly and deep, an elderly man for whom as yet there was no street, no square, no Charlottenburg. Morning had brought him a short deep sleep, the loss of consciousness at last. When during the day, swamped with adversity, he stopped to ponder what was left in this life that was still good, enjoyable, some bright spot, what occurred to him was this black hole into which he threw himself after the long and difficult hours of night. There was at least this black abyss. There was still something good left available to him on earth.

In the narrow empty hotel lobby, where an old woman pushed a vacuum sweeper across the gray, frayed carpet, the tall clock between the two windows struck seven. At precisely that moment a small light lit up on the telephone switchboard in front of the porter, who sat dozing at his desk. With a yawn he clapped the hearer to his ear, pushed a button, then hit another button and cranked.

A harsh noise brayed in the dark room, like the direct hit of a grenade. The elderly man in his nightshirt sat upright, as if he had been pulled up in one jerk by a crane; he was still unconscious, but the small eyes were open, the muscles taut, the chest thrust forward as if ready to march off. He did not move. Though seated, he seemed to be at rigid attention. It was dark and silent in the room.

Again the braying sound. Automatically he turned his head to one side. The sound of a bell, the hotel room, the telephone, night, I was sleeping. His hand groped for the apparatus, halfway up the abyss his arm reached for the apparatus, the cord could become a noose at any moment, change into a gallows' beam and, along with the nightstand the apparatus stood on, melt into nothing, taking him, the man himself, with it back into the abyss. But a sound, a call came out of the receiver, a voice spoke and the man swallowed hastily and knew that he was holding the receiver of a telephone. Someone said something, the captain at the office, an answer came: "Yes, of course." He was "major" once more, he had slept, how late was it actually, it was still dark, why were they disturbing him in the middle of the night.

The captain said the same thing twice, three times, finally the major understood it, though at the last moment a sudden burst of anger had prevented him from understanding. The captain informed him that he had several important matters to attend to in the course of the morning, which was why he would like to speak to the major about one particular subject between eight and nine. He was prepared to come by the hotel.

"No," the major growled, "that won't be necessary. I'm awake now as it is. I'll come over."

He turned the light on and dressed grouchily. I'm already an old man, stiff as hell. As a lieutenant, a captain, I could be instantly alert and in my clothes. Growing old makes you nasty, they've robbed me of my sleep.

Before eight he was underway, reluctantly leaving his bundle of morning newspapers with the porter. In the cold air, in the gray light of day, as his head cleared, he promised himself that he would take up the matter of night duty here on the homefront with the captain. The next thing you know we'll be back to the level of some non-com doing K.P., a lot of revolutionary crap.

In the porter's lodge on Fasanenstrasse, the war widow had just taken over from the blind pensioner who worked as night watchman. He was not asleep yet; lying in bed, he told how lively the building had been the night before, how they all went up to the casino. "Sh," the woman said, you shouldn't say nothing, someday you'll speak out of turn. But he said that the officers had kicked up a row too, so loud you could hear it down here, and didn't lock up and leave till three o'clock.

"Psst," the war widow said, "here comes the major."

"You see," the blind man said, pulling the covers up over his face out of habit, though he could see no light, and getting comfortable. "Something's not right. Be surprised if they don't get raided."

The major climbed the stairs. The war widow whispered beside the blind man's bed, "Max, we're just porters here. If we start in making remarks about the tenants or the guests . . ."

"Oh," said the blind man, "don't get upset about that. Things aren't quite the same as they used to be, neither. I can take a good look at folks, you know, and make up my mind about them."

"They're officers, and that's only as it should be for an elegant building like this. And if they make a little noise and you don't like it, why then you just ought not to live in an elegant building."

"That's where we differ," said the blind man from between the covers. "They're supposed to behave themselves proper in elegant buildings too. I've got my own opinion about these gentlemen, let me tell you. Just let them keep up this kind of stuff and you'll see if they don't get collared."

She was glad that he was interested in what went on in the building, because then he'll probably stick with me. So she said, "Every few days my lady says, 'Don't go burning your fingers sticking them where they don't belong in the first place.' "

He said, "The lazy skunk," and rolled over on one side.

Meanwhile the major was sitting in the front room of the offices, cross and with a bitter taste in his mouth that he could not get rid of. The secretaries weren't due in until nine. He thought sullenly of his coffee waiting for him at home, of the slow procedure of getting dressed—he had got used to the ritual in the small Alsatian town, reading the paper in bed or with only his shirt and pants on—and now this flustered captain had to butt in. He sat there in his coat, hands in his pockets, freezing, watching the captain and waiting till he could let loose with a barrage of complaint.

They had sat here till late in the night, discussing things, the short, squat captain announced. He was your perfect heavyweight boxer, with watery blue eyes, blond hair combed back, bearish paws, a slow, steady man, but now he was fidgeting on his office footstool. Someone from the Naval Committee of Fifty-Three had come by, one of their friends, and had told them what had been in Liebknecht's speech, and there had indeed been several remarkable sentences.

"We'll have to wait till the text appears in the papers, my good Captain."

The first drum roll of thunder had made itself heard. The captain, however, was used to care and woe.

The papers were already there, he said and waved a bundle of them. But at the sight of them the major remembered his own papers, the ones he had curtly left lying with the hotel porter. "But you don't mean to say, my good Captain, that you had to drag me from my slumbers so early in the morning so that I could read newspapers with you. Don't you think I would do better to read my papers in peace and quiet, and then, if something strikes me, to get in touch with you?"

"Without a doubt. And I do beg your pardon, but you yourself, major, impressed upon me how important it is in such cases not to be left in the dark for a single moment. We even thought of sounding the alarm for you last night."

Now the major was awake. "What is so urgent? For heaven's sake, tell me, man."

The captain unfolded the paper. "In most papers you will find no notice of it, or only a brief summary. But here I have a somewhat more complete extract, at any rate it includes the statements that are of interest to us. Here he mentions the generals who 'are returning home from the front at the head of their mighty armies,' saying that these generals must be dismissed at once. That is not so important. But here: 'The German proletariat cannot conclude a Wilsonian peace.' And then he said, just a moment, 'Only socialism, created by soldiers' and workers' councils, can solve the difficulties of rebuilding a peace economy; capitalism, the current privately owned economy, is incapable of doing so.' He points to the wartime economy and its organization as a model for what he means."

The major interjected with biting sarcasm, "Although not in the interests of the fatherland."

The captain let the paper fall, propped himself with both arms against the desk, and silently and steadily gazed at the major for some time. "We discussed that point in detail last night. Allow me first to quote some more of what is in the speech. Liebknecht is of the opinion that only a general world revolution can lead the way out of the dreadful danger of shortages of food and raw materials that now threatens Ger-

152

many. Further he believes that one cannot demand that the enemy nations, that is, their working classes, should already have followed Germany's revolutionary example by now. It was a year later before the Germans followed the Russian example."

"Dear God in heaven, what fantasies! The German and Russian brouhahas, I wouldn't call them revolutions, are the result of military defeat, in our case coupled with incredible blunders, with a mood of panic. Which is why they sent the Kaiser off and people put up with the proclamation of a republic. I've told you that ten times now. The French and the English—and revolution. Absurd."

"He calls upon the proletarians of the enemy powers to make common cause with the German proletariat."

"Pardon me, my dear Captain, but I have never heard the word 'proletariat' issue from your mouth as often as this. A few days ago you told me in this very room that you would use the word only with a spittoon handy."

"Here is the other important section: 'The German working class now has the power in its hands or at least the ability to take power. Should it now let that power slip from its hands, shall it bow before Wilson, shall it, at the behest of enemy imperialists, capitulate to the German capitalists, in order to achieve a peace that will only strangle it? Or should it not rather, as we demand, be just as grim in its defiance of foreign imperialism as it is of the domestic kind?' Those are the very words, Major, that our friend spoke and that kept us busy on through the late hours of the night."

The major stood up and took off his coat. "Many thanks. Until the ladies arrive, I take it this chair is unoccupied."

"Liebknecht maintains that if Wilson and his pals were to go so far as to intervene in Germany after a revolutionary government had refused to accept their conditions, the moment would then arrive when the revolution could spread from here to other countries. The current government of Ebert and Scheidemann, however, is incapable of working toward that end. They would be unable to offer opposition to the enemy's conditions. They would respond with peace slogans and so split the masses into several factions."

Now the major stuck a cigar in his mouth and began to smoke. "You discussed the matter? And what were the opinions offered?"

"There were differing views. It appears to be a matter of age. There were six of us. Three wanted absolutely nothing to do with it, and three—were wildly enthusiastic, the younger three."

"What did these young gentlemen say?"

"They do not like Ebert, Scheidemann and friends. The government has no guts. The people who signed the armistice agreement should step down."

"Don't these children know that the soldiers from the front lines cannot be held back, that they want to come home?"

"The idea is not to fight with the same old army, but with a new one that can and will fight." The massive captain bent forward and tapped a newspaper with his finger. "And what they are thinking of is the revolutionary working class."

"Well, what do you know! So it's come to this, my good Captain. That's Bolshevism, pure and simple."

"As far as I'm concerned, I would ask that you not identify me so simply with their ideas. But after all, we are in the midst of a struggle and ought not take offense at mere words. During the war we would not have been able to take certain necessary measures, the evacuation of the civilian population for example, if we had taken offense at the word 'barbarism.' "

"To put it short and sweet: there are men who would join up with Liebknecht? That's quite a turn of events, I must say."

"I took the liberty of waking you so early because in the course of the day I'll be meeting one or other of these gentlemen and would like to prevent them from being carried away by their own enthusiasm and disseminating their views all too rashly before others."

The major grew very serious. "Yes, I really must ask you to do that at least. That would be . . . The gentlemen could compromise us beyond repair."

"That was mentioned as well."

"Well then . . . I will read the text of this speech very carefully. What groups, by the way, are behind Liebknecht?"

"Apparently the most active part of the working class, the so-called People's Naval Division."

"I'll not take a bite out of that apple."

The captain fell silent. He gazed straight ahead, an impassive military look on his face. After a while he said, "We must make sacrifices. That was said yesterday, too."

"My dear friend, we might as well lay down our arms and close up shop. Our motto must remain: 'Resist and Build Anew.' "

"Our methods are not approved of in all quarters. We are too slow. People want to see results. They suggest that in reality we are actually supporting the current government. We are not mobilizing against the coming peace."

The major paced back and forth in a rage. "Damn it all, I wouldn't have thought it in my wildest dreams. Young von Heiberg whispered something of the same thing in my ear. This appears to be a veritable epidemic."

The ladies knocked and entered. While the captain took his leave, the major sat brooding in the back room. Finally he lost his temper, he walked over to the spittoon and spat in it. As he did he spoke the words "proletariat" and "People's Naval Division." He spat them out, and then he could set to work easier in his mind.

The Camp at Döberitz

It was not to be a good day for him. The major had become devilishly superstitious in the last years. He knew that whatever starts off with a jangling telephone in your sleep cannot turn out well.

The train took him to Döberitz—he had decided that much yesterday—so that he could orient himself about what was going on with these units of young men who were supposed to be sent to the east.

A part of the camp was a holding operation, a barracks for troops that still had to be transported before they could be quartered with their own garrisons prior to disbanding. Then, after passing through this hostile crowd that was kept in order only with difficulty, one arrived at the section, strictly separated from the rest, that served as a camp for assembling and drilling troops. Around the barracks and on the drill field one could see young soldiers and a great many officers. With a single glance the major recognized that something was indeed happening here.

He enjoyed the wait after he was told that it would be an hour before Lieutenant von Heiberg returned from a field exercise. He learned from a captain in the staff room that the whole operation had started well, but that the proximity to a major city, especially since it was Berlin, was obviously having unfortunate effects. The infection deriving from rotten ideas, from the "seditious spirit on the home front," was spreading here as well. And things would not settle down again until they had begun to march. The most vicious elements were not the criminals and that lot, who had got a foothold here and did no work and made things more difficult, but rather undercover agitators.

"I train my people to strictest obedience, blind obedience. It can not work without that. You need only take a look around the barracks in Berlin, absolute pigsties, to see if it works any other way. Anyone who does not want to chase the Bolsheviks back to Asia has no business here. I am unyielding in that."

Such people were a tonic to the major.

But when Lieutenant von Heiberg appeared in the staff room to fetch the major, smart and straight, and they had walked among the barracks in the open air, his impression changed.

The major: "You're in excellent shape here, von Heiberg. A superior location. I would like to know where you could find a better in Prussia these days."

The lieutenant nodded.

"My dear von Heiberg, when I see you here, in this truly refreshing atmosphere, what am I supposed to make of your talk the other evening about a generation prepared to sacrifice itself and so on? Please tell me. You have comrades here? I would appreciate your introducing me to them."

"With pleasure, Major."

Soon they were three, the major in the middle, walking up and down the barracks streets. The lieutenant who joined them was smaller than Heiberg, a stocky lad, from a feudal family of country gentry in the Mark Brandenburg. The major knew him, someone had already brought him to his office at one point or other, but he had not stayed around. The major briefly informed him what he wanted—to know whether he shared Heiberg's opinions about sacrifice and so on. This made the officer laugh. That was a specialty of several of the men here. Heiberg wasn't alone. It was all too rarified for him—the main thing still was, they wanted to march east, hunt down Poles and Russians. "We're not going back home."

Which did not displease the major at all.

Suddenly, however, the stocky young man began the attack. "May I be allowed a question, Major? Why do you have that poster hanging in your office that reads 'Leave Berlin'?"

"It's meant to drive people out of Berlin. We have enough already, they're simply wasted there."

"Permit me to remark, sir, that I am not of the same opinion."

"And what are your thoughts on the matter?"

"That I want as many soldiers returning there from the front as possible."

"I see. And what is there for them to see there, Lieutenant? I myself have noticed nothing except a pseudo government of which I prefer not to speak—and women and racketeers. And you?"

"If I may permit myself a personal anecdote, Major—I was forced to spend a few days in Berlin with some distant relatives. I had lost sight of these people for some time. They were, as I recall, only moderately well-off in the past. Now they eat from the finest dishes. They drink Danish schnapps, the ladies are buried in furs, their fingers heavy with diamonds. They took me, the poor country cousin, out to nightclubs, three or four of them a night. One should take our soldiers and officers to such clubs."

"Would you care to provide me with the addresses of a few such clubs, please."

"The major must not get the wrong impression of my distant relations, they are patriotic people, mourn the loss of the Kaiser and curse the revolution. They told me how much money they have given in the struggle against the Reds. No offense intended, Major, when it comes to financing your office, I'm sure that as an officer on active duty you have not played too great a role."

"What is that supposed to mean?" the major roared.

The small, stocky officer laughed nonchalantly. "I would guess that there is money from my relatives in your coffers."

Pulling himself up with a sudden jerk, the major marched on ahead, saying nothing. The two gentlemen had to hurry to keep pace with him. He halted in front of a company of men moving by and then turned to the lieutenant. "At all events, you will provide me with particulars concerning these people of whom you spoke."

The lieutenant took a visiting card from his breast pocket, wrote something on it with a pencil and handed it to the major, who carefully tucked it into his breast pocket. The company had passed by, they strode on.

The major swallowed his anger. "What does all that have to do with our 'Leave Berlin' poster? Are our soldiers supposed to stay in Berlin in order to watch filthy things?"

"Yes indeed, Major. Because then they would lose the urge to defend them."

"Damn it all, who's defending them? I really must say!"

"The major can be confident that the last thing I wish to do is find fault with his organization. Everyone approves of your intentions."

"Very good. That's the main thing."

"But there are not a few of my comrades who think that you and many of our older senior officers do not, in all good faith, see clearly enough what it is that disgusts us."

"We're not blind either, you know."

"None of us wishes to lift a finger on behalf of what is now flaunting itself in Berlin and elsewhere."

Beside himself, the major bellowed, "But no one asks you to. These racketeers and profiteers you're talking about—we'll see that they are eliminated."

The two young officers responded with silence.

The major: "Well then, go on."

Finally von Heiberg got up the courage. "We are back to the subject, Major, that we touched upon recently. We have looked around at home. We have no home, no homeland, anymore. And so to keep from being ruined entirely, we have no choice but to head east."

"That's another matter. I'm happy for you. But," it dawned on him as he remembered his conversation that morning with the captain at his office in the city, "do you mean to say that you could care less what we do, that you don't want to fight our own Reds?"

The short lieutenant answered quite candidly. "We have talked about that; it's our daily bread and it has indeed caused arguments. We have a number of officers at any rate who would love to see the Reds get a good tight hold on the Berliners. We have a strong suspicion, Major, and I'll tell you frankly what it is: that at some point after peace is made the filthy rich are going to sell the fatherland and our national honor to foreign interests."

The major, sarcastically: "Liebknecht is afoot."

The shorter officer, good-naturedly: "There's no Liebknecht afoot here, Major. We are about to march off to fight the Bolsheviks. A Bolshevik does not know what fatherland and national honor are."

The major noted that yesterday's speech had not in fact touched on such things.

The short lieutenant: "The long and short of it is, as long as we have the impression that the government is watching out for the interests of the plutocrats, and that we are supposed to establish their 'law and order' for them, we're not eager about any of it. We demand guarantees that our national honor is not going to be peddled to the Entente. And that is why we are not interested in how this whole revolution of workers and proletarians against their employers and the filthy rich turns out. In no case are we going to let plutocrats use us as bloodhounds against those poor devils."

The major was deeply worried. "Gentlemen, where does that leave us! You say 'we.' I can only hope that there aren't many of you. Hells bells! Who are you rendering aid and comfort to with notions of that sort? Those red rascals, and no one else."

Lieutenant von Heiberg: "We know who it is we serve. We have only one duty."

And the major once again heard words that stung. "To save Germany."

Things got even worse as he entered the canteen barracks, led by the two lieutenants. Officers and enlisted men sat mixed together. Warmth, smoke, noise, military songs. And the lustiest songs sounding from those young throats were ones that had apparently been written only recently, mocking the leaders of the government. They coupled those who ruled with the Jews and the profiteers.

Afterward, of course, the major joined in the laughter and drank his hot grog. This young brood did not mince words, but they might also very well trample and break all the porcelain in the shop.

Till now he had only felt the indignation of a commander when confronted by a ragtag company. Now it dawned on him how great the gulf between him and these people was. Had there been a revolution after all?

And he was so terrified by the thought that he had von Heiberg show him into the next room to meet his captain, who assured him that they would be breaking camp for Courland in the very near future. The men were simply untamed, like young horses.

In the captain's office the major also met several White Russian officers. They shook hands: "Once enemies, now friends." They were robust men in civilian clothes who showed no signs of having been defeated.

Arrest Warrant

The police investigating the murder of the lottery dealer had not yet found a clue pointing toward Döberitz. Nonetheless they had the chief culprit, the real instigator of the crime, and he was locked up in Moabit prison.

The night after the murder, Konrad had aroused suspicion in one of the bars that he had visited with Lutz. He gave a waiter, with whom he had often done similar business, a diamond ring that he wanted fenced. The waiter took him up on it without a second thought.

The ring, however, was inscribed on the inside, and the dead man had conscientiously kept a record of every piece. And two days later a man was arrested in a jewelry store in the south of the city for showing the ring—but he was completely innocent. He delivered supplies to the bar owner, and so they traced it to the bar and the waiter, and unfortunately the waiter knew Konrad's name. The following night they were able to arrest Konrad gambling in another bar.

Konrad was brutal and cunning. But he had a blind spot—he believed he was lucky. That all was lost made him furious at the police and the investigating judge. He held his tongue.

But he would have known that all still wasn't lost if only he could have looked into the mind of the judge. For the preliminary investigation still considered it a possibility that the lottery dealer had let himself be tied up and had let himself be gagged with the handkerchief in some perverse act or other. The criminal could still have wormed his way out by maintaining that it was the fault of the victim that the handkerchief had gone in too far, that there was at least no intention of smothering him. But Konrad kept silent. Out of a desire for revenge he was absolutely silent, even with his guard.

They had searched his dingy room, had found a great many cards and letters and slowly but surely ascertained who had sent them. But they were too late getting to Lutz. Of course they had at once begun the search for the young man who had been seen in bars with Konrad the night of the attack, but they did not find him, which was perhaps an argument for his being an accomplice. There were plenty of young men who only showed up in such nightspots sporadically and were happy to be picked up. Demobilization had flooded the country with so many young men. There was no name in the dead man's notebook that might possibly have connected to this second man. So they sat and waited to see if Konrad would crack. He didn't.

But there was also Lutz's old girlfriend who lived in the adjoining room. She was a newspaper dealer, but she didn't read the papers herself. She was used to Lutz's occasional absences, and he had had money just before he left, but he always showed up at her place when he came back to Berlin.

But when after several days he didn't appear, she was offended that he had forgotten her now that he was in the chips again, and so she set out to visit the woman who rented the room to Lutz's friend Konrad.

The landlady was in a bad mood to receive her. The police had run her ragged about this tenant—who was in the clink now.

The sullen woman was more than a bit astonished when she realized that the young lady asking about Konrad knew nothing about all this. She didn't believe her. She was suspicious.

She pulled her into her parlor, interrogated her. The strange girl talked openly about Lutz and Konrad. And the longer she sat there with her, the more convinced the woman was: this girl has something to do with the murder. She asked the girl to wait there for a moment, ran to a neighbor and gave her the job of getting the police. That took a while. Meantime, the young lady was pleasantly surprised to be offered a cup of coffee. They drank, and the girl was about to leave when a man appeared who closed the door behind him, took her hand from the doorknob as she tried to leave, and addressed her with the words, "You can stay here a little while. I'd like to ask you a few things."

The blood rose in her face. She didn't know the man. But then he lifted the lapel of his jacket and showed his police badge. She gazed at the man, at the woman; the woman suddenly had a strange, brazen expression on her face. The girl who sold newspapers thought, I'm not a whore, or did someone squeal on me? Because soon a second man appeared.

She explained carefully to the men who she was, how she earned her living, who Lutz was, her relationship to him, and that he lived in the room next to her. The officers were amazed to discover that she really knew nothing about the crime. The girl impressed them with her simple and honest manner. They refrained from explaining everything to her and finally asked her to take them to where she lived.

Completely crushed, and casting a bitter look at the nasty woman who had dared offer her coffee, the girl walked down the stairs, an officer on either side. Doors stood ajar everywhere, women and children were watching her. Loud talking began behind her. She thought, and even if I am a whore, what of it? The officers learned in the car that Lutz had had a lot of money the day before he disappeared—but that had happened before sometimes too; she wept—had he stolen something maybe? Then they climbed up to the garrets under the mansard roof.

They found nothing in her room, until they searched her person

160

and found a small gold ladies' watch in her purse. Things swam before her eyes. "But he gave me that as a present."

They took it from her. They found nothing of value in his room, but beside the bed was a small towel, all rolled up and stuck full of safety pins. They took that with them. It bore the murdered man's monogram and was bloodstained. It was only at police headquarters that she learned from the commissioner in charge of the case—the man showed her the towel and her watch—what it was all about. She let herself be led away, having lost all will of her own.

But there was no trace of Lutz. He was training in Döberitz, bellowing and singing in the camp canteen while the major sat there warming himself with the two lieutenants.

What kind of men did Lutz become acquainted with there? You didn't dare show them you were afraid. They didn't give a damn about peace. They could find no work, didn't want to work. The way life had been the last few years out in the field was how they wanted it to go on. It was better than life at home. They were almost all of them young, some of them kids. There was also a small band of men who had failed in life, crabbed and sour men. Now they formed a military unit. But if they had been let loose, they would have formed a gang of thieves. Things were taking too long here already, and some of them were talking about which side they ought to offer their services to, sell themselves to—to whoever offered the most money, naturally.

"When are we leaving? When are we leaving?" is the daily question. They maintain discipline, and only respect the sharpest officers. No one asks anyone else about his past. They watch each other closely, and if there is anyone who gives cause for the least doubt about whether he belongs here, he knows that he had best disappear quickly if he values his life. They become blood brothers.

None of them is interested in what is happening in the world or in Berlin, what the Allies are planning at their peace conference.

Profiteers and Young Ladies

The sweet dye-job is sitting in her room in the Fürstenhof Hotel on Potsdamer Platz having her nails done.

Who would have believed it just a week ago. But she, accustomed as she is to fluctuations in the curve of her daily life, as calm as she is— the poverty in which she grew up as the daughter of a Polish cobbler in Berlin-Marienfelde, to say nothing of her later life in a reformatory, have left her impervious to the buffetings of fate—she could become a statesman she is so cold-blooded.

What is there about this young lady, really? She has dark brown hair and large soft eyes of the same hue. If one tries to describe her lips, the cut of her mouth, now as she sits in a wicker chair with the manicurist hard at work crouching next to her (how very much Toni would have liked to do that kind of work herself, but she had never learned how), then one cannot deny those lips a certain voluptuousness, a splendor. But there is also something common in the line of the mouth. And so Toni, of Slavic blood and Slavic beauty, was discovered in a little dancehall at the south end of Friedrichstrasse by the attentive Herr Motz.

Today Brose-Zenk wants to take her along out in society—Brose-Zenk, not Motz, but Brose-Zenk, the rich man himself. Motz said, "He wants to show off with you." There is a reception on Regentenstrasse, in the elegant part of town near the zoo. Brose, too, has made his discoveries—he in his casino on Fasanenstrasse. He found a prosecuting attorney there, a serious man, whom no one would have suspected of being such a mad gambler, and Brose had helped him out. And in this perfectly natural act of kindness Brose had had a rival, a certain Herr Finger, whose acquaintance would prove to be of great importance to him. For Finger was also a soldier of fortune, but of a different stripe than he. He gambled only occasionally. His finances were not balanced on the rolling ball of Dame Fortune. Finger made "deals."

Reception at the young Herr Finger's in his luxurious chambers on Regentenstrasse. Toni came along because she was beautiful and looked exotic and spoke Polish. She was strictly forbidden to speak so much as one word of her abominable Berlin street jargon. She was allowed to understand questions in German sometimes, and sometimes she was, so Brose orders, merely to grin. For three days, Motz, who lived in the Fürstenhof as well of course, had labored at training her for the occasion.

Toni looked wonderful, wore borrowed diamonds in her ears and around her neck, was discreet, sexy. From all sides Brose was asked to introduce the lady. Which was done very elegantly and mutely; Motz had done an impeccable job. In the spacious rooms with their white paneling ladies and gentlemen stood and sat next to one another, teacups in hand. Several of the gentlemen were stationary, installed with others of their sort in armchairs. Names of governmental ministers were named. Two high-ranking officers stood eating cake with whipped cream.

In the course of his talking, standing and strolling about, Brose had difficulty keeping under control an old gentleman with a moustache, who had an eye for Toni. The gentleman was introduced respectfully by Herr Finger himself, the name sounded foreign, and to Brose's terror the man began to speak Polish with Toni. Brose was forced to use his charm to forbid this; he too wanted to join in the conversation, he said, and so now they spoke of Warsaw, where Toni was supposed to have been born (her father, the cobbler, did really come from there); finally the young, lively and oh-so-helpful Herr Finger arrived to save the day by fetching the old man away. In doing so he addressed him by name. And at the name, Brose had his breath taken away. It was—Wylinski. He would have loved to run after him. Wylinski.

He stood there berating himself for having offended him. "What have I done?" The words crossed his lips. "Have I driven him off?" Toni was instructed to be very affectionate with him now, but not in any crude way, she was even supposed to address him by his first name.

"Why do that, honey?" she whispered. "That old geezer? You didn't do nothing to him."

He gave her the sign to keep still—the woman needed lessons in speaking German. If only Wylinski would come back.

And Wylinski returned, the boss of the important Herr Finger.

And now nothing could hold Brose back, and via a detour through politics—concern for the preservation of the unity of the Reich, for internal security (while that elegant representative of order tingled as he sensed the presence of the onetime reformatory girl between them)—he directed the conversation to a different area: the supply and distribution of food.

"Ah," Wylinski said, "it is not just food, it's also coal and boots. There is even a lack of paper."

"Beyond a doubt," Brose confirmed, shaken by such colossal perspective, "but—but that can't be managed all at once, you know."

His attention attracted by Brose's active interest—Brose-Zenk looked quite respectable with his soft brown beard—Wylinski inquired (and laughed amiably, hoping to cancel any faux pas he might be making), whether Herr von Brose-Zenk was perhaps interested in commercial enterprises as well.

"But of course." Brose raised his arms despairingly.

Wylinski, the gray, broad-shouldered man, silently laid his hand on Toni's naked arm instead of answering. She made the obligatory big-eyes at him. He went on patting her cordially, the elderly gentleman, and since Brose did not object, Toni let him pat. And then Wylinski suggested to Brose, who hung at his lips, "It's a sign of the times. In days past gentlemen of the nobility, especially from the country, the landed gentry, did not consider it good form to concern themselves with commodities and the stock market. Now everything is being democratized."

"One must engage in some useful work, Herr Wylinski, one must earn one's living."

(What was he talking about nobility and landed gentry for? Motz was behind this, him with his garden plots, one minute the harum-scarum is revolutionary, the next an agrarian conservative, he's really got to rein himself in.)

"But in the old days," Herr Wylinski continued—and now, having encountered no resistance, he had indeed laid his arm on Toni's, carried away as he was by the conversation and because they were standing closer together—"in the old days, many a man would have preferred to put a bullet through his head rather than get involved in matters of business. Do you have a training stable as well?"

Brose unhappily admitted that he had had to dispose of it.

Deep in thought, not uttering a word, the gray-bearded gentleman stood there. He had in fact moved in so close on Toni that he could sniff her, and he was engrossed in breathing in the gentle perfume of her shoulders. He was a very robust man, slightly bent, for whom this odor was among life's highest pleasures. Indeed, it strengthened and animated him. He stood between the two as if hypnotized. And Toni, who was more sensitive to what was going on than Brose, let him take his pleasure.

"You must acquire horses again," Wylinski grumbled. "Horses are a beautiful thing."

At that he took his arm away, smiled thoughtlessly and long, first at Toni, then at Brose, and suggested that they would probably run into one another often enough.

"Might I call upon you?" asked Brose.

Wylinski nodded and went on smiling stupidly and fervently. "Finger will give you all the information. My regards."

And he walked off as if he did not know them.

It was a grand afternoon for Brose. Finger, the nimble, dark-complexioned gentleman, nodded familiarly as Brose moved past him with Toni. He had noticed from the door, he said, that they had been talking with Wylinski. They made an appointment for tomorrow. Finger shook both their hands warmly and smiled again with special intimacy.

A delighted Brose sat next to Toni in the car. Brose alias Schröder stopped at the Fürstenhof Hotel and came up just for a moment to give Motz his Toni back, and also to give him the crushing news that he was to teach her German.

"I spoke with Wylinski himself," he remarked to Motz grandly. "The place was teeming with government ministers. Excuse me now, I have things to do."

They sat there for a little while beside one another, as if someone had dumped them on the red silk hotel sofa. Toni placed the borrowed diamonds in their case and put on her own heavy coral earrings. With a few good digs in the ribs Motz made her laugh. They would have to take the jewels back.

That evening they danced at the Old Ballroom.

A Suspicious Incident

At around the same time late that night, two people in regulation gray-green military coats hurried excitedly across the Reichstagsplatz; they went into the zoological gardens with the seeming intention of taking a stroll. They changed their minds, emerged out of the narrow cross street and turned up Dorotheenstrasse.

They marched along at a lively tempo, past the War Academy and the Physiological Institute.

When they got to the market hall they turned abruptly about and moved back down the street again at the same forced pace.

From the direction of the Reichstag, two other men dressed just like them and just as much in a hurry came up. They did not, however, bother with the zoological gardens, but directed their steps without further ado, except to let a tram by, toward Dorotheenstrasse. There they met the first pair, who had just made yet another turnabout, and joined them.

For half an hour they walked up and down the totally dark and still Dorotheenstrasse together, until seven minutes before twelve, when they shook hands, lighted cigarettes and separated.

After that the street was empty. Some noise could be heard coming from the nearby Friedrichstrasse.

We could pass over this whole sequence of events, now that it has transpired, in silence. It is not worth mentioning. We could even add that the four men did not do anything to hurt anyone in the further course of the night. They went home, two of them to Gesundbrunnen, two to Neukölln, and went to bed.

But they had carried on a furious conversation, there on Dorotheenstrasse, especially the first two.

That makes them suspicious. What are they up to?

Monologue of the Spree

"What a long day," the Spree sighed as it flowed under the Wiedendammer Bridge at about the same time. "How long they're able to hold out, these people. And such crowds of them. If only I were out of the city by now. All this scrambling and hubbub. And there's always something new, always something new. There are really too many people here.

"We waves, we flow on into the Havel. We have been told that later we will flow on among pine forests and hills. What a shame that it has to be winter. We have been told that there is a season called summer, when the trees, like birds, are covered with green feathers called leaves.

165

They want to fly. But they can't manage it because they cannot pull their feet out of the earth. Then, in summer, people are said to climb into boats and rock upon our backs. They sing, it is said, men and women and children all together. Maybe it's only a fairy tale. What all haven't we heard on the way here. But it gives you something to dream about during these long hours.

"There stands a tall building with a dome. The word was we are to pass the Reichstag. That's probably it there, standing there all dark. The people inside have all gone to bed."

The waves splashed against another bridge.

"There's the fourth person now who has come down here to us. A woman. She is settling to the bottom right away. She filled her pockets with stones. How right she is not to want to join in all that commotion up there. We couldn't bear it either. Why do they all come to us looking so serious? They lose their minds up there.

"And now we will swim peacefully on out to the tall pines and the gentle hills. We will receive morning, noon and evening, when the sun brings them out to us, and we will enjoy the clouds and all the many stars that the night plays with.

"And the wind.

"And the soft rain.

"And then the Havel. We'll greet one another. What a reception she'll give us."

Everyone Does As He Pleases

The strikes go on. Public and private discontent grows. A deserter proves himself to be a faithful son to his mother. A spy eats kippers.

Herr Pietsch Keeps His Factory

A new day. Little Emil Barth, an Independent and people's deputy, was most certainly a man who had stood his ground during the war. After the collapse of the big metal workers' strike in January, 1918, he had gone on as the leader of the illegal organization "Revolutionary Shop Stewards"—did it, in fact, in opposition to Ebert, who had throttled the strike, in opposition to the oily Scheidemann who had sung a New Year's song to his electorate to this effect: "We want to live through these dreadful times with eyes wide open. We want to frustrate the designs of our enemies, we want to win," and in opposition to Winnig, the East Prussian, who implored the masses not to swim against the imperialist tide, in opposition to the learned Lensch, who begged them to believe that "the German army is carrying out the work of world revolution against English hegemony."

But now, at the end of November, little Emil Barth stood on the podium in the hall of the "Germania" and implored the workers, "You can't simply make threats to the landlords as in Neukölln."

"And why not?" they hooted from below. "You've been protecting the rich ever since you sat down with Ebert on Wilhelmstrasse."

They demanded the eight-hour day for farm workers. Barth waved his hands in the air. "That won't work. Otherwise hundreds of thousands of tons of potatoes and turnips will freeze."

And when he went so far as to declare, "We will have to introduce the four-hour day in industry because we don't have any coal," they raised their fists and threatened him, calling out in chorus: "Expropriate capital."

He answered, "That won't bring any money in."

But his words were lost in the uproar. They cursed him. "Renegade."

On Seestrasse, in the north of Berlin, there was among other things a large hoist-engine factory. One of its owners was named Pietsch. This factory employed seven hundred workers and had a radical workers' council. Today, payday, all the machines suddenly stood still at ten o'clock. The employees had presented demands, and when Herr Pietsch's response proved to be a sour one, they turned the motors off.

Häussler was a twenty-four-year-old foundryman who had been sent to the front during the big strike in January, and had reappeared at the factory a week before. With five other workers he marched into Herr Pietsch's private office at half past ten and declared to him that the factory was no longer under Herr Pietsch's direction from that moment on. And that he, Häussler, would take care of settling matters of pay right that moment. He demanded the keys to the safe.

Herr Pietsch, a courteous and placid man, declared that he would like to make one telephone call in that case. He did not say to whom. As it turned out the central switchboard was busy.

"What happens now?" Häussler asked, as the boss put the receiver back down in disappointment. "If you don't give us the keys, we'll blow up the safe."

And if Häussler, a tall man, had been the only member of the delegation, that is what would have happened. But there were others who were less hot-headed. And as Herr Pietsch made the modest request that they drive him to the Executive Council on Prinz-Albrecht Strasse, they agreed to it. That was their own organization, and they could have no objection to that.

Herr Pietsch went, and once on Prinz-Albrecht Strasse he complained about his workers' council. They had halted operations in order to achieve their demands. That was illegal coercion.

The members of the Executive Council, those of them who happened to be there at the time, shook their heads over this affair. They muttered among themselves something about an unheard-of lack of discipline among the workers and so on, which heartened Pietsch. They, too, took to the telephone. Their switchboard was not busy, and so they were able to delegate a certain Herr Fischer from the municipal commandant's office to drive out in the company of a sailor to Pietsch's hoist-engine factory and attend to things. Fischer jotted all this down on the telephone, found his mission vague, and hesitated. To this the Executive Council replied that Pietsch should once again be entrusted with the management of the factory, and that the union would take care of the workers' demands.

At that Fischer climbed into a car, along with one of the armed sailors who sat smoking in the guard room of the commandant's headquarters, and drove out to Seestrasse, where Herr Pietsch arrived at almost the same time. After the boss had satisfied himself at the factory gates that the two gentlemen were there, he went proudly up to his private office—and flew right back out almost at once, before Fischer and the sailor at his heels could even enter. The people let Fischer and his sailor inside and talked with them, while Herr Pietsch stood on the landing greatly worried and looked down to where his employees were laughing at him.

The people in the office, however, were not satisfied with Fischer's promises. At that, Fischer and his sailor whispered with one another and the sailor suggested, "Then there's nothing we can do. We can just drive right back home then."

For he had forgotten to bring tobacco along and wanted a smoke. They climbed back into their official car and drove back to the Executive Council on Prinz-Albrecht Strasse, where Fischer explained what he had run into out there on Seestrasse, and the sailor confirmed it all before leaving the room and going down to the guardroom for a smoke.

Richard Müller, "mortician" Müller, took part in this conversation as a member of the Executive Council. He was amazed by it all and said that he had known nothing of the whole affair—which was not remarkable, because he had just turned up. Müller wanted to know who had in fact delegated this job to Fischer and his sailor. Then another member of the council intervened to smooth things over, explaining a few things and saying that Fischer should go out there once again, without the sailor, and set things right. But this Fischer refused to do, because there was no dealing with those people and he would only go out there with an armed sailor. At this Richard Müller exploded and declared the whole agreement invalid. Fischer should go back home and someone else should drive out to see Pietsch.

That took place in the afternoon, around four o'clock, because there had been a noon break in the meantime, during which interval the tall fellow, Häussler, found himself very much in the minority at the factory on Seestrasse. The boss, who had stubbornly remained standing on the stairway landing outside his office, was readmitted into the room. And when, after four, the new representative of the Executive Council appeared, the workers declared that they would agree to have the union arbitrate the dispute. At that Pietsch himself pulled out the keys, opened the safe, and the workers finally got their pay.

One flight of steps below, Häussler was mishandled by a number of his colleagues. The workday had been lost. That was the last anyone heard of the union arbitrating the strike.

Imker the Soldier Learns Something

Imker, the discharged soldier, sat at home brooding.

His father tried to talk him into having a look around town, there was sure to be work somewhere, if only something temporary. His son

169

refused, there would be time enough for that. From day to day he grew quieter. His sister still kept her shorn head under the large scarf; it looked like a bandage. Sometimes he would apologize to her. "I'm lazy, Minna. You get lazy in a war."

After once again watching his sister at her sewing machine for a long time, he laid his pipe to one side and began, "The things we did there in the war, Minna."

She looked over at him and made a slight gesture for him to come over to her. Then he brought his chair over and talked to her while she sewed.

"Once we were stationed at a sapping depot. An honest-to-god sapping depot, no way we would be moved out. We had loads of time. New divisions arrived. Supposed to relax. There were horse-guards, rifles, snappy fellows, they had come from the east, had been playing cavalry there. All noblemen, counts and barons. Didn't know anything about trench warfare. Had been trained at the rear. So they arrived, all decked out first-class, new gasmasks. We stood there like bumps on a log and thought, well just wait, you guys. They moved on up. Three days later they were back again. You should have seen them. We laughed ourselves silly. All tuckered out. All they wanted was to get out of there. They kept saying—that isn't war anymore. What it was they didn't say. And then straight for the ambulances and off they went. And of course they got hit with grenades in the ambulances."

He pulled on his cold pipe. He got it going.

"When the Americans came, we knew all we needed to know. They couldn't pull anything over on us anymore. Lord, Minna, you should have seen it. The way they were equipped. Compared to them we were in the buff. Did they ever give us a scare, let me tell you. We took some of them prisoner. They undermined Lehmann's cause worse than a whole lost battle. Snappy coats, trenchcoats they called them. The gentlemen from the Kurfürstendamm had to go into hiding. And we fought over those camel's hair blankets. And the canned goods, the canned goods, what they had you can't even imagine. We were all starved and wolfed the stuff down and got so damn mad. It had been in all the papers. They won't come, they can't swim the ocean. And all of them big strapping fellows. None of us looked like that. And then their airplanes that dove down at our troops and the machine guns. We didn't have anything. A lot of guys who went home on leave just didn't come back again."

He stared straight ahead. He worked on his pipe, which had gone out again. He talked softly, as if to himself. "We didn't put up with any of their guff. We did our work, and no one shirked his duty, not in our unit. But they didn't dare try to pull anything over on us. We had good officers. Classes strictly separated, of course."

She looked up, "What's good about that?"

170

"Let them be by themselves. We didn't want them with us anyhow. If a man's an officer, let him be an officer. We liked it that way. If he was strict and fair, he was admired."

The needle lifted and jabbed into the cloth.

"You shouldn't get upset at that, Minna, that's the way it has to be in war. The real bullying would start back at base camp, and whoever got sent back to the field hospital could run fifty miles with some monkey on his back afterward.

"We had a sergeant once. We were sitting in a tunnel, took eighty steps to get down into it. He wanted to make life difficult for us. He wasn't a fair man. He wasn't fair divvying up work and could be bribed by anybody who had the money, and if you didn't, then you could slave away at two and three times the work. He was a real criminal. He had the death of at least ten men on his conscience. He had them stand guard over the provisions, which wasn't necessary at all, and dangerous besides, because the provisions were always shot up. All of them ended up laying there dead. So we older guys got together and said that it couldn't go on like that and we drew up a complaint. He intercepted it. When there were packages of food from home, he would open them up. All we got were letters, the food was gone. Everybody said, that's the sergeant that steals the packages he's supposed to distribute.

"And then this is what happened, Minna. A guy was supposed to get coffee from home and he was really happy about that. But when the coffee was supposed to come, there's no package. The next day though, the sergeant sends a package home. So we call the orderly over who's supposed to take it with him, and we demanded that he open it up and show us what was in it. He wouldn't do it. But then he saw that we weren't fooling around, and that he had nothing to be afraid of, and he opened up. There was coffee inside. We all stood there quiet like. And that settled that. He was a bastard, a crook, who just liked having power and robbing us. We'd get rid of him."

Minna had sat there motionless for a good while, her brow wrinkled under the scarf, her mouth set hard. She moved her lips. "What did you do?"

He: "Just so you don't think that you were the big heroes back here in Berlin with your demonstrations and that we were the goats. I'll tell you what we did. There was always an evening benediction, the last light barrage of the day, artillery, field guns, everybody used up the daily ammunition ration before hitting the sack. Before it would start up, our cautious sergeant always headed for the tunnel. After the coffee episode, we knew what to do. Only the old hands knew about it. We didn't tell the young guys anything about it. There were a couple of doors you had to open if you wanted to go down into the tunnel. So he comes along as usual. We had hung a bundle of grenades on the inside of a door. And when he gets there he flings it open and boom. That's it. Bull's eye."

"Did—anything happen afterward?"

"Nothing. We sat around down below. The French fired away. The young guys didn't know anything. Everything had gone off smooth."

With both elbows propped on the sewing-machine table, his head between his hands, the discharged soldier slid up closer to Minna. His mouth was twisted, a sneer twitched lightly across his unshaven cheeks. "That was just to show you we didn't take everything laying down."

"Then don't just sit around here, Ed. I don't understand how you can just sit around as if you're of no use to anybody in the world."

"That's not it. I'll earn my keep, don't you worry."

"That's not what I said."

"I'm not supposed to earn it?"

"I'll give you whatever you need. I'm making money."

"And why shouldn't I earn my own money? You must be crazy, girl, I'm no cripple."

"Join us. We could use you. You belong with us. We need good people, revolutionaries. Ed, come with us."

"First I got to know who I'm supposed to revolutionize against. The sergeant was a criminal."

Her eyes, her sad eyes sparkled. "And here at home, everything is fine here?"

"I didn't say that. We've had enough revolution. Nothing to eat, no food for anybody, and no coal. That's got to stop."

"Then put a stop to it, to them."

"Who's them?"

"Ebert, Scheidemann and that whole crowd. Those aren't criminals?"

"You've told me all about that a thousand times, girl. And you still have to prove it to me. They can try whatever they want—the war's lost, and you could turn Wilhelmstrasse over to the pope or God himself and it wouldn't make no difference. When you've fallen on your nose, it ain't no laughing matter."

She raised her hands. "It's a rotten shame the way you talk, Ed. You're supposed to be soldiers. When a sergeant filches a little coffee, you blow him up with hand grenades. And when Berlin is starving, and you can see what's going on, then you just stand there and say: you got to prove it to me."

She threw the roll of cloth onto the machine and stood up. With her hands clutching the edge of the machine, she stared at him not saying a word. He didn't answer.

With a jerk she flung off her headscarf.

It was awful, that narrow, hard girlish face, no not the face of a girl, a hard sexless human face beneath a skull shorn down to short dark stubble, her ears stuck on like thin pale patches of cloth.

"You did your sergeant in. But what about us? Take a good look at us. Frau Brösch, downstairs, who got the infection from the men at the plant. And Frau Losowski, who walked out on her husband because she found somebody else—but what was she supposed to do, take to the streets? None of us are human beings, is that it? Everything can stay just like it is for us, is that what you think? Go over to Wilhelmstrasse, go on, and yell hurrah when fatso comes out. Soldiers? A bunch of sissies."

He wanted to beg her, "Tie the scarf back on, girl," but she did it on her own anyway.

He didn't know his sister. That's what the war had done to her. She picked up the roll of material and sat down across from him. The machine started up, her hands lay to the left and right of the cloth that moved in his direction.

"Something has to happen, Minna."

She: "So you've got that far."

"If only you wouldn't do such stupid things."

"You did everything perfect in the war, right?"

"I'll come, Minna."

"This evening?"

She stood up quickly, came around the end of the machine and to his surprise laid her cheek against the back of his neck.

He heard her say, "You don't have to be disgusted by me, Ed."

Their mother came in from shopping, weary; standing in long lines was exhausting. He put her shopping bag in the kitchen. She sat down in the easy chair.

"I haven't got much for you today."

In the hall he took his coat and cap from the hook. He was strangely happy. Down on Petersburger Strasse, the houses, the little shops, the Küstriner Platz, people with their parcels, everything was beautiful. He helped an old woman climb onto the tram, lifted a child up too, started up a conversation with the street cleaners and with a man in blue overalls and carrying a lantern who was climbing down a sewer drain.

He strolled up Grüner Weg in his coat of field gray. At Andreasstrasse he turned right, stood in front of the market hall, but it was closed. A number of men were milling about. He asked them what they were doing, they looked at him and grinned. "Nothing. How about yourself?"

He figured they were waiting for something. He headed along Weberstrasse. Alexanderplatz was busy and peaceful. At first he was going to turn right again on Münzstrasse, but then he remembered that a lot of no-goods would be bumming around there and then I'll get dragged into some brawl, and so he marched on under the elevated railroad bridge. He treated himself to a small beer at the Prälaten Bar, and it

tasted good. Then it occurred to him that out in the field they had sometimes risked life and limb to get a glass of beer. Here you had it easy.
You pull out your wallet and you've got what you want. It's not bad,
peacetime isn't. Despite everything, I'm a man who likes things ship-
shape. I'd be sorry if it would all be ruined.

Things didn't look so good at the Rathaus. A bunch of men,
women too, were standing there. They occupied the whole square as far
as Spandauer Strasse. The crowd stretched from one side of Königstrasse
clear across to the opposite sidewalk. But for the most part it was just
people watching or examining the display windows of the bookstores, or
pretending they were. He wasn't able to find out what was going on.

He wended his way past the corner of Spandauer Strasse and amused
himself with new neckties and warm underwear, the prices, of course, all
unaffordable. But that had always been the case, besides his were still
good and he had a reserve.

Once he had passed Poststrasse he switched out of old habit to the
other side, to the left side of the street. Because next to a store for souvenirs and postcards was a stamp store. And he stood all of fifteen minutes
at the display window as his old collector's enthusiasm flamed up again
at the sight of stamps from Trinidad and from the North German Con-
federation with their black surcharge. He had made friends out in the
field with a stamp collector from Bautzen; he had had his collection sent
to him at the front. It occurred to him that he must have mentioned the
fellow's address in a letter to his mother at some point, just to make sure
it wouldn't get lost later. He reminded himself to remember that when
he got home.

The Schloss Bridge, and that old codger, the Elector, up on his nag.
He had sat there during the whole war. If you're made of bronze nothing can happen to you. How about it old man! You sent a pretty big
batch of boys to their deaths, too.

And here we are at the royal stables. Where the revolution is.

He wanted to ask some questions of the sailors who were camped
here, in the palace and the stables. But he wasn't exactly sure what he
should ask them. He just wanted to sniff out what they were up to. Because soldiers or sailors were people he felt more comfortable with than
Minna's political types. He would only feel stupid around the political
people, but he could get along easily with soldiers.

There were sailors standing guard there now in front of the stables,
their rifles on their shoulders, marching back and forth with cigarettes in
their mouths. A lot of people went into the stables, civilians as well. I'll
go in, too.

As he tried to get in, though, a sailor asked to see his pass. He said
he just wanted to make a few inquiries. The guard said calmly, "Then go
on into the courtyard."

174

Cars drove by next to him and into the great hall. He had to press himself against the wall. It was plastered with posters.

"By order of the Central Committee of the Workers' and Soldiers' Council: all automobiles in greater Berlin and the Mark Brandenburg must, after February 14th, display a license to be distributed by the Office of Vehicular Traffic and signed by that office's Soldiers' Council. The Central Committee of the W.'s and S.'s Council: von Beerfelde."

A large color poster: a sailor with legs spread wide, the red banner in his hand. Beneath him stood: "Comrades! Attention! Disrupting Traffic Can Cause Famine."

A flyer had been posted right next to Imker on the massive portal with its ornamental imperial eagle. The writing is hard to make out, the glue has seeped through the low-quality wartime paper. But Imker has time because everything in the gateway has been brought to a halt. Two cars have rammed into each other. The flyer reads:

"Proletarians of every nation! Proletarians, men and women of labor! Comrades! Revolution has broken out in Germany. The masses of soldiers who for four long years were driven to slaughter for the sake of capitalist profits, the masses of workers who for four long years were starved, squeezed and bled dry"—well, father had a different tale to tell than that—"have risen up." I don't know of any soldiers who did, just sailors. "Proletarians of every nation, we call upon you to complete the work of socialist liberation and to make a reality of those words with which we so often greeted one another in times past: the International will embrace all mankind." True, that's what we said, and then came the war and they voted for the credits to pay for it in the Reichstag. "Long live the world revolution of the proletariat. Proletarians of every nation, unite!" We said that often, too; if only people would do something about it; we even said it out on the front, and when we brought in the prisoners they were all proletarians, but how were we supposed to be brothers with them, had to turn them over to the camps; it's easy to say "unite," but first you got to stop laughing. "In the name of the Spartacus League: Karl Liebknecht, Rosa Luxemburg, Franz Mehring, Klara Zetkin." Those are the ones Minna's involved with. Be lovely if it was only true.

In the great hall civilians, soldiers and sailors were standing and walking about. Imker spoke to a sailor. But first he asked for a cigarette, which Imker gave him. Then he explained, "There are only sailors here, no one else is allowed in.

"We're here in the stables, and then over in the palace, and then there are some of us at the Reichsbank and at Moabit prison in the exhibition rooms. All sailors. How did you manage to get in?"

"I just wanted to make some inquiries."

"Well, then, now you know. Visiting ain't allowed."

"I can imagine," Imker replied in a friendly tone.

"But if you want to join up, go over to the Reichstag. They're signing people up. At police headquarters, too, I've heard, in Eichhorn's office."

Imker: "What do you do here?"

The sailor growled proudly, "What do we do? You probably think it ought to be spit, polish and drill. None of that with us. Roll call, keep your boots in order, that's it," he laughed easily, "and pick up your pay."

"A lot?"

"Keeps us happy."

"I understand," said Imker.

The sailor: "Then go on over to the Reichstag. They've got a nice life over there, too. I got a friend there. They wear red and black ribbons."

"Where?"

"On the arm. It's their badge of identification. Not supposed to be fed bad neither."

Then Imker thought of Minna and what he really wanted. He stood there undecided, it would soon be noon, he should get home. He started off. It's funny, really (he marched back over the Schloss Bridge and there was the stamp shop again). You go into town and want to do something, but it doesn't work out. If there's nothing else except joining up with the military, I'd say that I've had enough of that already.

And then it struck him (Post Office, corner of Königstrasse, people streaming in and out): Minna was right. No one cares about anything. Everyone does what he wants, whatever's fun. The sailors, too. Just so long as they get their pay and cigarettes. Would be no different at the Reichstag. Red and black armbands wouldn't suit me, like ushers at a funeral. It's a damn mess, a damn mess. No one cares about anything.

There was still an uproar at the Rathaus.

People have a lot of time on their hands. Makes you sick that nobody knows how things are supposed to change for the better.

His tram pulled up. He noticed he was hungry, it was twelve o'clock, and he rode home to eat.

Explanation for a Suspicious Incident

This noon, in a bar in Neukölln, we discover the men we accompanied during their nocturnal walk along Dorotheenstrasse, and they are still spinning away at the thread. They are wearing the same gray-green military coats. The two from Neukölln are the first ones there of course, and the two from Gesundbrunnen arrive a good quarter hour later. By day it isn't all so mysterious, and if we showed a certain reticence about

176

intruding on their conversation by night, we are rid of it now. We can see through their secret and can go right ahead and divulge it. These are four deeply offended people.

There had been a meeting of soldiers' councils at the Reichstag; the four had been a part of it, at least they sat there not harming anyone. None of the four spoke since they weren't sure what their opinion was, and how one was supposed to form an opinion here where one person said one thing another, another. They were not unreasonable men. They dozed next to each other. Two of them were roused from their rest by a speaker who called them by name and really shook them awake. For the suspicion had already been expressed on occasion that they were not true front-line soldiers. But on this issue they had a very clear position. They called themselves stragglers, one even said he was a deserter and they set some store by those titles. They declared all this now in loud voices from where they were sitting, without having asked for the floor. The assembly reacted with an uproar. But both of them were used to such uproars. There was a brief debate, and the upshot was that they were expelled. They were permitted to remain as guests, however, if they wished. They would have none of that. They hurled their threat with powerful voices back into the hall. They defiantly named the regiments from which they had deserted, or straggled off from, as the case might be, and then left.

That was the first pair. The second, front-line soldiers beyond a doubt, followed them out to demonstrate their sympathy. All four of them were of the opinion that the matter couldn't be left at that.

And now they gaze at each other by daylight, deserters and their sympathizers, and are glad to have gathered here under such auspicious circumstances. They rain soft abuse on the soldiers' councils which are accomplishing absolutely nothing and where the non-coms and officers are always doing the talking. The soldiers' council was so patriotic it might as well make tracks for Kassel to join Hindenburg.

The deserter is a healthy, heavyset young man, but a bit of a dolt, one of those who once out on the battlefield had taken his weeping mother's counsel seriously: "Come back all in one piece, stay healthy." In the trenches, however, it was difficult to stay healthy, and there was no great chance that one would come back all in one piece. So one day in the midst of one of the loveliest offensives, one headed toward victory, he beat his own personal retreat and marched off to a safety zone. Never in the following days of waiting did this faithful son of his mother lose his imperturbability, not for a single moment did he regret having said adieu forever to his bellicose career. Once behind the front line he quickly joined others who found themselves in a similiar situation. And when the war was over and they all went home and nothing had been won by it, he compared his behavior with that of the others and proclaimed to all the world how much wiser he and his mother had been.

But that had nasty results. He allowed himself to be elected to a soldiers' council by this crew of stragglers and deserters—who of course had arrived in Berlin before the army itself. What mattered to him was to inform ordinary soldiers just how stupid they had been.

Sure of how indubitably right their cause was, the two of them sat in the bar, the pair of sympathizers beside them. Now they came up with the idea of a giant protest meeting against the soldiers' council. They had already thought of the possibility of such action last night on Dorotheenstrasse. Especially the two indisputable soldiers were attracted to this idea.

One of the two indisputables was a spy, by the way. There were many spies in those days. They were in the pay of whoever could afford to pay. And since by the very nature of things that was not something deserters and stragglers could do, it was something for their enemies. The spy, Moritz, had a plan ready at once. It had been slipped to him, to be sure, by others. It was supposed to provoke all deserters and stragglers to move against the soldiers' councils by taking to the streets. The slogan was to be: Against Counterrevolution, Against the Menace of the Front-line Army. That was precisely the view of doltish August. Because his mother had warned him against the front-line army. She was not fond of his being involved in politics either, but after all he only wanted to tell stupid people the truth.

The meeting of the four in Neukölln lasted two hours. At the conclusion they were agreed. Meetings were to take place that very week: "Against Injustice and Denial of Rights to Stragglers and Deserters by the Berlin Soldiers' Council; Against Counterrevolution."

And then with a hearty shaking of hands they dispersed—doltish August and his friend to mobilize the groups of stragglers and to arrange for flyers, etc., Moritz, the spy, and his friend to provoke several more members of the soldiers' council.

With the money advanced to him as a spy, he bought a pair of used but sturdy boots and some kippers for himself and his wife.

A Surprise in Strasbourg

A love letter arrives, a tête-à-tête proves that two people have not lost touch with each other. Intellectual workers champion the public interest and eat cake.

Hilda Understands Bernhard and Herself

Just as Hilda was carrying the tray with coffee, malt coffee, into the living room, the bell rang. Her father answered. He sat back down at the table and slid the letter across to her. "For you, my girl. From Bernhard."

She took the letter, stuck it into her apron pocket.

Her father, as he drank: "I've got used to the fellow. He has learned better manners, too. But I don't suppose he'll end up my successor. The people in Paris will make other arrangements, I'm sure. I'm sorry."

When she didn't answer, he continued, "If you want to do him a good turn, something I don't seem to be able to do, then get him away from that widow, what's her name, Karrell or something. First of all it's not very proper, and if she doesn't know that, he should."

She read after her father had gone:

"Dearest Hilda, the war was destructive of goods and men, but let me utter a word of blasphemy: through it you have grown to become the Hilda I met this afternoon, after four long years, and compensate for much of its destruction."

He's crazy, she felt a chill; this went far beyond anything she had expected.

"A mystery here, this transformation—and your long silence. Do you think it right," it was unbearable to have to read it, "that that silence should continue, now, when we and our affairs are thrown so closely together?" He dares to write this, it's just like him.

She paced stormily back and forth in her room. There was no way to think away, to excuse this affront, the frivolity and shamelessness of it. What to do? He is her lover and yet he wants me too. He writes this behind her back, the poor woman. I ought to send his letter to her. Ah, that's her fine lover for her.

She sat down in the nearest chair.

Who was it wrote that really? I don't know at all. And she felt anew her amazement from yesterday. Bernhard, a dandy, an artist, and (she groped for the letter) he writes love letters, cheats on his girlfriend, an artist, an aesthete, Bernhard. No, did I dream it all? She read: ". . . you have grown to become the Hilda . . ." Has the war really changed me?

She put the letter in her pocket, stood up. And suddenly she felt a desire to see him at once. At once. She knew his telephone number. He answered, she quickly said, without even saying "hello," that she would like to see him.

The living room was heated. It was a bright, dry morning. He rubbed his hands. She directed him to a spot next to the stove. "But you know the room, don't you. You've often sat beside this stove."

"Yes. It's changed little. Only you."

"Do you think so?"

"Fräulein Hilda."

She sat in her chair diagonally across from him. "When you look about this house you must have pleasant memories of it."

"And you, Fräulein Hilda?"

She looked at her naked arm, which she had laid on the table. "How old was I when you first began to come here to visit me?"

"You mean, when I—"

"Yes, when you visited me."

"You were, I would guess, seventeen or eighteen."

"I was seventeen and a half. And you?"

"Back then—twenty-six."

"Was I pretty?"

He laughed and ran his hand through his hair. "What a question. A wonderful teenager. Very young, but on your way to becoming a woman. That was you, Hilda. A mystery, a magical creature."

"Why?"

He put his hand to his eyes, he wore rings on three fingers. "It came to me again yesterday evening. There is this girl, a teenager, a young lady I follow with flaming eyes whenever I visit her father's house or when I chance to meet her at friends'. With whom finally I exchange a few words off to one side. Who then sweeps down upon me like a cataract."

"Who?"

He took his hand from his eyes. "I am speaking of Hilda as she was in 1912 or 1913. Like a cataract. It was—love of a force such as I had never known before. It stirred me, it shook me. You made me uncertain of everything I thought about matters of art in those days. Yes, you did, Fräulein Hilda. I told you all this, by the way, at the time. It did not interest you, however."

180

"And?" She was profoundly surprised.

He: "What? Why didn't it interest you? I don't know. You were too young for some things, I suppose. It seemed to me that I was your first love, at least your first real one. And you yielded to it—cost what it might. There is no other way to say it."

"You lay all the blame at my doorstep."

He, dumbfounded: "What blame?"

She could not find the words.

He: "Fräulein Hilda, what sort of blame are you talking about? Do you regret it?"

"I know that I gave myself to you. I wanted to. I had had enough of the innocent teenager. Little crushes disgusted me. I was a woman. You are right, I wanted you, and that is why I gave myself to you and I don't regret that. But what did you make out of me? How did you treat me?"

She whispered the words at him. "Where is your cane, huh? Do you think I didn't see it at Frau Scharrel's? It's the same cane you used to beat me with. To make me crawl in front of you, here on this very floor. And what else did you do to me! I was so terrified of you that I thought I would run to the police or tell father, reveal everything. Then, thank God, came the war."

She looked over to him as he sat beside the stove. And while she gazed she once again saw in him the man she had known then. He had sat up straight under the force of her words and his face had assumed a different expression. He said, "And so you ran away from me. I understood. It was what I wanted, Hilda; for you to run away. We had started down a dangerous path. It wouldn't have taken much longer, and I don't know what would have become of us. But I have a better memory than you. I alone was not to blame. It wasn't only me. You don't remember anymore how you were then. You don't even bear much resemblance to what Hilda looked like in those days. I can show you my diary—I leafed through it yesterday evening—where I wrote that you had completely thrown me. Although you were a child and knew nothing about yourself and looked so gentle and unassuming when you were out in public, in my presence you were a demon, a force of nature, something frenzied that I could do nothing to resist. And it is true that I have changed. I remember those two years, they still course in my blood. You unmasked me. I had my demon, too. But you cannot wish to deny, that you—began it all. That you were Eve, the temptress. The spirits that we called forth we could not get rid of again."

Hilda sat there gazing mutely at him, her chin propped in her hand. Will he attack me again now? Did she want him to? She was not afraid of it.

She said, "We'll speak no more of it."

He: "I think not too, Hilda."

She stood up. "But I'm being impolite. Shall I bring you some lemonade?"

"If it's not too much trouble."

When she came back he had changed places and was sitting at the window where her father always sat to read his books. She served him from a simple tray that she set down on a small table. He drank the glass down all at once. He looked straight ahead, serious and tranquil. "It was good, Hilda, for you to bring up those matters. It was good."

She remained at the table. "I think so too."

She sat down, quietly, bent forward. She suddenly searched in her pocket and read his letter aloud. " '. . . You have grown to become the Hilda I met this afternoon.' — Then the war did change me? Then it was the war after all that made me what I am, so that I can sit here across from you like this, Bernhard?"

"Yes. And I across from you."

She realized only now that she had thought of him. He was a constellation of stars, the Minotaur. He sat there, serious and tranquil, a human being. She had seen so many men in the war.

"What happened to you in the war, Bernhard?"

He crossed his arms. "Not a lot. I'm an Alsatian, like you. So I had my own thoughts about the war, even as a German soldier. But that would not have helped me much, since I was shot and almost killed on the eastern front. The bullet is still in my chest. But they brought me back home. And I stayed here."

"And that's when you got to know Anni."

"That was not the only thing I did to keep busy during the war, Hilda. But it's true, I got to know Anni. Which ended up with my getting to know myself better."

"More than when you were with me?"

"No bitterness. Differently from when I was with you."

"Because you called me a temptress."

"Anni was good for me. She was terribly lonely and then came the tragedy with her son. I was surprised when she started to show tenderness to me. She is much older than I, and my aunt, too, after all."

"She wasn't just trifling with you?"

"Anni? Of course she was. Why shouldn't she trifle? I have the feeling even now that she's trifling with me. Why not? These are difficult times, you know, people show affection to one another, they stick by one another, glad that life is more than just murder and war . . ."

"Or than Hilda."

"Must you always be bitter, Hilda?"

She gave a heavy sigh and put her face in her hands. And sat there like that at the table, her back turned to him.

He, in a gentle voice: "What's wrong, Hilda? Tell me."

"That I went through the whole war and knew nothing, nothing about myself, nothing about you, that I didn't know anything at all."

"You were very young, Hilda."

She laid her arms on the table and wept. "That a person can be so rotten inside."

"What do you mean 'rotten,' Hilda?"

She did not answer.

She sat up and wiped her face. That's the way we humans are. That's why we fight wars and do all the other wicked things."

"Didn't you learn all that in church?"

"I never understood it. I thought it had nothing to do with me."

And she began weeping again, openly in front of him. "Which means that I fought the war too, and shot at people and killed them."

He edged closer to her, concerned. "But you mustn't exaggerate."

"But it's the truth. And now I've come back to Strasbourg, and I walk down the street, and I'm glad to be here and that I'm no longer afraid of you, and that the war is over. But then—the war isn't really over. Because it's never really over."

He: "You're exaggerating, Hilda."

After a while she stood up. "Do you want anything more to drink, Bernhard?"

He got up. "No thank you."

"Are you leaving?"

"Yes, I've got work to do. Your father's expecting me. You'll be staying in Strasbourg, won't you?" They stood across from each other, them embraced. They lifted their arms almost simultaneously.

She whispered, "Not on the mouth, not on the mouth."

And after their faces had rested against each other for only a few seconds, she begged him, "Let me go, Bernhard."

And suddenly, while he was still embracing her, she let out a shrill scream, causing him to jerk back in dismay.

She ran to the door, screaming again so shrilly and horribly it was as if she had seen a ghost; and then she ran down the hall. He heard her fling open the door and thunder down the stairs.

Danger

That evening, when the old architect appeared at his atelier, Bernhard, who had been waiting for him, summoned the courage to ask about Hilda.

"You wrote her a letter, didn't you, Bernhard. Didn't she answer it? She's not feeling too well, been lying down. I hope she hasn't brought the flu home with her."

After a half hour of not knowing what to do, Bernhard phoned Frau Scharrel. He was not surprised when he was told that she was not in. He had already expected as much after yesterday's conversation.

But when the next morning he received a friendly, but cool letter in which she told him that those legal difficulties she had spoken of had caused her to leave for Paris, together with her two nieces, on the evening train—for a two to three-weeks' stay in Paris—that he had not expected.

Two, three weeks of being alone in Strasbourg. He was seized with a feeling of anxiety, of danger.

Intellectual Workers at Breakfast

The facades of the houses lining Motzstrasse, and indeed of most of the houses in the area, are elegant, radiating peace, prosperity and security. It is along Motzstrasse that several gentlemen are making their way. They are grave men with wise, expressive faces, strolling slowly down from Nollendorfplatz, members of the "Council of Intellectual Workers."

As they move down the street they seem to be vague figures from the periphery of someone's dreams. But they are alive and kicking, they have eaten and completely satisfied all the pressing wants of daily life. But they are still not sated. (Perhaps their brains simply devour too much.) They set themselves down in a long, narrow Russian restaurant, where in the front room intoxicating cakes and tortes are piled high. They exchange intimate glances with the pastries as they pass by. And when they are seated and their coffee stands steaming before them, they order pastries. Their hands lift them from the plates with polished spoons, their lips kiss and squash them, they indulge themselves in an orgy of pastry as they sit in one corner at their round table.

Only then, cigars and cigarettes in their mouths, have they provided the flesh with what the insatiable flesh demands and reconciled themselves for an hour with the new day that has just dawned. Now they allow the fountain of their thoughts to flow. It springs up easily from the lower depths, their thoughts still colored by gratitude for the meal just eaten. Slowly their facial features lose their redness and puffiness and show their lines, the eyes begin to focus; sitting about the table are three gentlemen from the Political Council of Intellectual Workers. We know them and they know us. Their communal, bestial gorging at the trough is behind them now, they have drawn back from it for a short while, have become individuals.

One of them is a tall, turbulent lyric poet. He believes in "humanity." That is his magical fetish, he, the medicine man.

Also sitting there, but very still and not quite focused yet after such pleasant gormandizing, is a powerful little novelist, a man of debate, a loud voice in any squabble.

Between them reigns an older gentleman here on a visit, a very prestigious man, serious, sober, not given to talking much. He is from Munich and wants to have a look at things here. He has a long, smooth face, wears a golden bracelet on his left wrist, a brightly colored handkerchief hangs from the tight-fitting, buttoned-up jacket—the gentleman, a giant when sitting, tends to corpulence. The gentleman does not laugh; he also wears dentures.

The other two are listening now to what he has to say concerning last evening's meeting. He directs his words to the novelist, who is still not completely with them.

"One does not achieve much with a dictatorship. After a short time one is back to where one began."

Apparently the novelist had demanded a dictatorship yesterday, but he could not recall the fact, he was digesting.

"We are at war," the nimble lyric poet objected. "We have no choice."

The gentleman from Munich regarded him with cold, blue-gray eyes; he had just finished eating. "Where does that get us? We cannot allow ourselves to indulge in tactlessness. We are on the side of the common people, but we must not become common with them." He turned again to the novelist and said, "Dictatorship is dictatorship, whoever initiates it."

The novelist could remember absolutely nothing. He was at one with all the world, he could easily have dissolved into someone's dream.

The unrelenting lyric poet asked, "So you reject dictatorship even when it is exercised on behalf of the people?"

(What do I care about dictatorship, the novelist thought. What do I care about dictatorship, about the people, thought both of the other debaters, the lyric poet and the man from Munich. But they were celebrities and represented public interests.)

The little nickel coffeepot glistened, small electric lamps burned along the ceiling.

The man from Munich had his answer at the ready. "Socialism is not the most radical position. Above it stands radicalism of the intellect. Moral law must be made part of German politics."

His bracelet had come unfastened. The young poet helped him to fasten it again, muttering admiringly as he did so, "That is excellent, excellent, radicalism of the intellect."

The man from Munich accepted these words of appreciation with a princely nod of the head. He added, "There is a quotation from Klopstock: 'Be not all too righteous.' That is the beginning of the end. I demand justice at any price. One should not allow oneself to be bargained out of anything."

They sat there swollen with pride. The man from Munich stiffly took note of his success, then sought to crown it: "I would like to observe that the development over the next few decades in Germany crucially depends upon the position we take. If the intellectuals betray their cause, Germany has no future."

One could not, to be sure, continue in such sublime realms for long. For which reason they rapidly took leave of one another and once outside each took a long, deep breath.

Driven by jealousy, his coat over one arm, the lyric poet trotted off to see his girlfriend, who took voice lessons in the neighborhood. But he did not trust her teacher with his handsome blond beard.

The novelist, after brief deliberation, sidled into a very ordinary bar nearby, where he got resolutely drunk. And because the day had run its course so delightfully he then fell fast asleep at home until ten. Around eleven he drove refreshed to his "Council of Intellectual Workers," and rampaged about, the image of vitality, the homicidal hero.

The master from Munich climbed into his car at the entrance to the restaurant in order to drive to a medical specialist who gave him shots for his impotence.

The Author Takes Stock

If at this point we look back over the sequence of events that has passed before us, inundating us like doom itself, and if, overwhelmed by a sudden inexplicable weariness, we pause to consider what will now be the result of this irresistible onrush of events (and we are only twenty days into the revolution), some things are at least clear by now: the revolution cannot progress in this fashion. Presumably it may even lose ground.

So far no actual revolutionary masses have come into view. This might be considered sufficient reason for reproaching someone who has set out to describe a revolution. But it is not our fault. This is, after all, a German revolution.

And as far as the individuals go whom we have gradually met, we have found some of them to be of good will and courageous, it is true, but a few drops cannot create a brook, let alone a rushing torrent. Most of them appear to have no interest whatver in the events described in their newspapers.

In fact revolution, which in other nations behaved like a fury, setting fires and driving terrified people from their homes, wanders through Germany, across this wide land unravaged by war, grows ever smaller and smaller, becomes a flower girl in a ragged skirt, shivering for cold, fingers turning blue, looking for shelter. And even where the door is not slammed hard in her face by those who are faithful to their convictions, she is only fed with friendly phrases and a bowl of watery gruel. In her bewilderment, revolution, reduced to the status of a little flower girl in Berlin, considers what she has become. Ah, just think how her big sister did in Russia! She will soon leave this country and see if she cannot find a home elsewhere.

We expect a great deal of Ebert and the generals; though perhaps not revolution exactly. Any reasonable man would bet on Ebert and the generals. One can already envisage how they'll get their way, by turns sly or gentle or unyielding. In war, God is with the strongest battalions, and in peace with the shrewdest operators. What a strange god our epoch has got for itself, one could almost mistake him for the king of Prussia.

As far as the others go, the little people, we simply expect them to leave their flanks open to the shrewd and robust, giving them every conceivable opportunity to be gentle, sly and unyielding—at their expense. For there's nothing they can do. And whoever tries anyway will finish taking care of his business in the cemetery.

But we are curious how the generals will deal with Ebert and he with them. Because we are reminded of Odysseus' wanderings, of when that crafty Greek finally meets up with a terrible monster, the Cyclops Polyphemos, son of the sea-god and a nymph. These savage, lawless giants did not plant, nor sew, nor plow the earth, and were therefore a perfect metaphor of our masters of war. Despite which, Odysseus succeeded in getting the Cyclops drunk (after he had eaten two of his traveling companions), then put out his eye with a firebrand and so saved himself, setting out upon the seas, which though they had proved dangerous till then were once again navigable. We wonder whether Ebert-Odysseus will likewise succeed with his generals. Will he outfox these strong men and blind them? We mutter, possibly, possibly. Does he want to do so in the first place? To be honest, what concern is it to us? For all we care, Ebert can eat the generals or vice versa. Maybe some third party will come along and eat them all.

We sink back into a long, ominous silence.

We could close our book right now for lack of interest—on our part. A serious matter when the lack of interest in a book already begins with the author. But we simply must call ourselves to order. That would be going too far. After all, something may come of the mutual cannibalism of Ebert and his generals. It could at least prove interesting and exciting. One would indeed like to know how they go about it, because it most certainly won't be easily done.

It is also possible that quite by chance something very different might happen. For instance, it could be that two men get into a fight, in the course of which a kerosene lamp is knocked over and the house burns down, while in the building next door, which just happens to be a menagerie, the lion caged there escapes and runs loose in the city. So no pretext of philosophy. *Allons,* to work!

Book Four

Up Through December 4th

Defeat at Ems and a New Offensive

A congress meets at Ems, a man from Berlin drops in on it, causing everything to turn out differently from what several people had imagined. The government is greatly impressed. We learn how one man wishes to set military legs under the republic and now takes fright at the prospect, how he continues to swindle Germany and to deprive it of the fruits of its defeat.

The Retreat of the Army

The last serried ranks of the German army crossed the Belgian border during the night of November 27th. Day after day their firm step shook the pontoon bridge at Koblenz. Banners greeted them with "Welcome!"

Ribbons reading "Ordered Home" were worn by the entire Württemberg Division of General von Erff, the Prussian Guard had attached them on the left side of their chests, as did the 5th Army. This 5th Army that now greeted its native soil, what battles did it have behind it? In the battles of August 1914 it had advanced with parts of the 5th and 6th Reserve Corps, with parts of the 13th Army Corps, with the 12th Foot-Artillery Regiment, the 20th Engineers Regiment. At Verdun it had fought in bloody trench warfare from August 1915 until the end of February 1916, at which time it had included the 5th Army Corps, the 5th Reserve Corps, the 6th Army Corps, the 6th Reserve Corps, the 33rd Reserve Division. It fought in the summer of 1916 around Fleury, at the holding action at Thiaumont, all through 1917 at Verdun, ridge 344. At the end it lay caught in the deadly defensive battlefront between Champagne and the Meuse. These were the survivors marching here.

People's Deputy Emil Barth

They did not get their way as easily as they had hoped at the General Congress of Soldiers held on that December 1st at Ems.

General Headquarters wanted to go for broke; its demands (behind the scenes) were: disbandment of the workers' and soldiers' councils, complete restoration of the old authority enjoyed by officers, the immediate convocation of the old Reichstag, which was to write a provisional constitution, the final draft of which could be left to a constituent assembly; further, the surrender of weapons by the civilian population and, as the capstone, the dissolution of all revolutionary units.

But Barth, the radical, the Independent people's deputy, did in fact appear at Ems, where everything was smooth sailing until he arrived. The radicals had been cursed, Ebert's praises sung, and wherever a contradictory voice was raised, it had been promptly and programmatically squelched. And now came Emil Barth.

The ferocious little people's deputy stood up—and an epidemic gnashing of teeth began. This fellow, this metal worker, called a spade a spade.

"You've been totally misinformed. What have they been telling you about Berlin? Murder and mayhem in the streets? Plundering? Who did you get that news from? I live in Berlin, haven't left it for months. All sorts of things are going on, I would presume in Ems and Kassel as well. There are people who continue to provoke the wretched populace, feasting before the eyes of the starving. And if now and then one of them happens to get a good thrashing, you're surely not averse to that. But that shouldn't be made into tales of banditry. Otherwise the masses just might get the notion to take an official and universal stroll through fine and elegant homes, making thorough house searches, as was the case under Lehmann in the palace at Berlin.

"There is order in Berlin. The rich have full troughs and the poor are starving. Whoever doesn't believe me, just go and have a look for yourselves.

"People spread rumors about Berlin, about corruption and Bolshevik rule. People tell fairy tales about the squabbles between the people's deputies and the Executive Council. The Council is said to be dissatisfied with us. Well, among themselves the people's deputies have, as is to be expected, differing opinions about many things. We are Independents and Majority Socialists. But if there is any issue where we both pull together, it is in our opposition to reactionary forces that want to split the workers and soldiers."

He upbraided them concerning the deceptive slogans being tossed to the multitudes. There had been a motion for a vote of no confidence in the Executive Council. Whom did that help? The people's deputies? No. The people's deputies did not wish to unseat the Executive Council, for it was the link to the people. But perhaps the country squirearchy, the capitalists and the military brass had an interest in dividing the people just to make it easier to wring their necks.

He fulminated against counterrevolution, which was growing bolder every day. At the bottom of this no-confidence vote and the campaign against Berlin and the Executive Council were counterrevolutionary intentions. He wanted to bell the cat. "What are they trying to persuade us to do with such schemes, us, the people's deputies here at the General Congress? That we should be pliable instruments in the hands of the high command? These gentlemen still do not comprehend what has happened. They are awfully slow at seeing the light. But we hope to flip the switch shortly. The Ludendorff Regiment still sits there undigested in the gentlemen's stomachs. They haven't forgotten how they gave the axe to one Reichs chancellor after the other. They didn't even give a chance to their great Lehmann, to whom they had sworn an oath. That those lovely days are over doesn't seem to get through to them. And so they want all of us, the people's deputies, the Committee and the whole Congress to dance to their tune, and are impudent enough to seat their representatives here in your midst."

He told them about the General Staff's forbidding the use of red badges, and how they had drawn in their horns three days before. "Now suddenly these grand generals declare that the soldier's councils are the representation of the popular will. Who's laughing? And you trust these people?"

He gave more data and finally invited the soldier's councils to Berlin.

"It was clever, calling this meeting in Ems, so that they could tell you fairy tales."

The anger of the soldiers' councils was fierce. There could be no question of a no-confidence vote against the Executive Council, let alone agreement to the plans of Haeften and the high command.

To make the pill even more bitter, they decided to send a group of soldiers' councillors to Berlin and to expand the powers of the councils.

The bull-necked man with the black "imperial" on his chin, Ebert, the nutcracker, was not happy with the reports coming from Ems.

He had done nothing to prevent Barth from going to Ems. But sending people here to Berlin to have a look at "conditions" was a little much. How was he supposed to stand up against these ultraradicals, these Spartacists, who mistrusted him, who hated him. And rightly so, he thought contentedly; he despised the morons himself. For instance, Liebknecht had just made a speech in Berlin, in some lavish salon in the west of the city (in front of intellectuals of course, workers wouldn't buy his blabberings), in which he called the old Socialists a "gang of gasbags," just as Moscow had ordered, and said that the constituent assembly would be more of the same and the bigwigs should not reckon on the support of the front-line troops now marching home. It might happen that that army would chase them right out of office.

And "bloody Rosa," his comrade, Luxemburg, had raged at the Teachers' Union Building against her friends the Independents (that was a wild creature, a woman who had completely lost her senses); she said one should take up arms against this government. (Says this miserable cripple that one goof puff of wind could blow over.) And then she demands: "Destruction of capitalism, cancellation of all war debts, confiscation of all food supplies."

Ebert was seized with rage as he read that, there in his handsome chamber surrounded by order. He tended toward violent attacks of temper. If such irresponsible people were allowed to rage on like that, then one really should not be surprised if someday certain people lost their patience and took care of them in a way that would make them forget such agitating. He saw red, truly. The letters swam before his eyes.

Scheidemann appeared, in a good mood after a good night's sleep, the born optimist—who wouldn't like to be in his shoes?—and sat down next to him. What did he have in his portfolio? Cheerfully he blew away those "trifling" clouds that had drifted in from Ems.

"We're in luck," he said, "you mustn't make anything out of this Ems affair. Who can they send?"

"And this rabble-rousing of Liebknecht's and Luxemburg's?"

"That upsets you? I'm surprised. Liebknecht and Rosa can call on the heavens to rain stones if they like. I'm not going to get excited about it. Sit down in a hall next to a couple of workers with common sense sometime when they're giving a speech."

Ebert interposed, "But who's got common sense these days?"

"More people than you think. You have to see how people double over laughing when Liebknecht gets rolling. For most of them it's just a circus."

Ebert blinked mistrustfully. "The man's got courage."

"What if he does. No one gives a damn about that. When he starts in screeching and rolling his eyes—people sit there waiting for him to begin foaming at the mouth—they begin to nudge each other and burst with laughter."

Ebert: "Is that really true?"

"You're a pessimist, always will be. But now I want you to tell me whether we're in luck this time or not."

And smiling sweetly, so sure was he of the effect, Scheidemann pulled a sheet of paper out of his portfolio: a telegram.

"For the Council of People's Deputies in Berlin. It was delivered to me. If Haase had arrived one minute ahead of me, it would have been put in his hands."

Ebert frowned. "Addressed to?"

"The Council of People's Deputies, Berlin."

"That's all?"

"Yes." For a moment Scheidemann was surprised. He seems to reproach me for having opened it; I mean, I ought to be allowed to open a telegram.

"Go on, please," said Ebert curtly.

"Yes, we can call it luck that I snapped it up. A staff sergeant at the high command of the 18th Army wires: 'The high commands have received secret instructions from General Headquarters to purge their most useful divisions of uncertain elements, staff them with active officers and hold them in readiness for moving out."

"Once more," Ebert said, "if you please. I'd like to read it myself."

He read it and laid the paper down in front of him. "Who else has read this telegram?"

"Only you and I. I told you, we're in luck. Because," he whispered, bending close to Ebert, "if Haase or Dittmann had got hold of it . . ."

Ebert played with his watch chain and dryly finished the sentence, "There would have been incalculable consequences. You can see what comes from our being so disorganized."

Ebert did not appear to rejoice at their good luck. He pulled out his notebook and wrote something in it, he did not say what; it was for his phone conversation with Kassel today.

When he had tucked the thin book back into his breast pocket, he nodded to Scheidemann. "It was a good thing you intercepted it, at any rate."

And suddenly his voice grew louder. "What are those fellows up to actually? What are they doing in Kassel?" He didn't say they were operating behind his back. But he grew quieter. It was clear to him now what he had before him; that things were going on behind his back, that he was to be tricked by Kassel. His gaze was uneasy, he rubbed his neck and asked with an uncertain voice, "Maybe Dittmann and Haase ought to be shown that telegram."

Scheidemann was startled. Ebert literally hissed at him. "So that that pack in Kassel finally learns not to be so impertinent."

So that was the joyous news that Scheidemann had brought, that was supposed to be good luck.

Ebert could not stand to sit in his chair any longer. He paced excitedly about the room on his short legs.

Scheidemann: "Perhaps you are taking the matter too seriously. If the Spartacists do get the upper hand after all something will have to happen. You always agreed to that."

Ebert: "That is a matter to be negotiated with me. I am to be informed. These are secret orders."

He tugged at his goatee and whispered, "For God's sake, for God's sake." So the Independents were right after all; the generals in Kassel are trying to pull one over on me. They have lured me out onto thin ice.

Liebknecht will be proven right, they'll brush me aside. I'm done for. They've tied my hands.

"What's wrong with you now?" came the sound of Scheidemann's gentle voice. "First, only you and I know, and second, we'll take them down a peg or two, the grand high command—if there's anything at all to this in the first place."

Ebert approached his chair again, to Scheidemann's reassurance, and sat down. He asked Scheidemann, "What's your opinion then?"

"Very simple," the former imperial secretary of state sang out. "We give the high command, in the person of Herr Groener, the word. And we let them know that we are fully informed."

"You think that will get us somewhere."

Scheidemann laughed. "It's a fine thing for them to find out we know something. That those gentlemen would love to try something is a given. I can sympathize with them, too."

Ebert spat it out. "They're traitors." He did not say who it was they were betraying.

Scheidemann clapped his knee. "You're such a clever man and such a gullible child, and that surprises you." And he folded his hands across his stomach and gazed up at the ceiling. "We've known all along that they would like to betray us. By the way, they've sworn no oath of allegiance to us."

Ebert brooded over the desktop. "In the session later, we'll say nothing about this wire. I beg you. And you leave the telegram with me."

Scheidemann's gesture in the direction of the desk was magnanimous. "Please, under no circumstances, reveal the name of the staff sergeant. He can still be of real service to us."

Ebert growled, "Just like all the others. A conniving bunch through and through. The fellow will tell other people about this as well, and make things difficult for us."

The next day the high command issued a warrant for the staff sergeant's arrest for subversive activities.

The triumphant Barth returned from Ems with the demands of the congress in his pocket. He brought an additional piece of sensational news to the session of people's deputies as well: a new secret order of the high command for enlisting volunteers for service in the east, and for those volunteers to pledge duty on the home front as well.

"And there you have," he thundered, "the fruit of your conciliatory policies. General Headquarters is mustering a White army. Against whom? Against us."

The other Independents supported him. Whereupon Barth made a formal motion, demanding nothing less than Groener's arrest for rebellion against decrees and an open trial before a revolutionary court.

But he was no longer at Ems. Here there were no soldiers shouting and smoking. In the softly cushioned conference room with its carved library shelves, calm men sat around a table piled with documents. The words "revolutionary court" sounded quite out of place. They did not share Barth's opinion. Scheidemann remarked that Groener was still one of the surest bulwarks of the government—for Barth, a monstrous statement.

Ebert bent over the table. "Do you really want to have things end in an outbreak of open fighting between troops still in the hands of the generals and the local populace? What do we have to counter them with in case of war?"

Barth: "Arm the masses. In a few days the phantom will have vanished."

Ebert's head turned fiery red. "While the troops are in retreat, while we have obstacles in our way that we cannot move, like famine, disorder, the transportation catastrophe, not to speak of Eisner. And now we're supposed to unleash a bloodbath at home. The example of Russia is quite sufficient for me. Their revolution has been going on for two years. Besides which, the Entente would simply march in and set up their executors."

Barth, grimly: "And where does your little flirt with Groener get us?"

With a growl Barth asked Ebert to make a formal declaration that he would oppose this plot of the high command.

Ebert, without hesitation: "We will institute an inquiry to determine who originated this secret order in Kassel and who countersigned it. And at once. I am afraid that some things have escaped our Groener's notice. There is talk of cliques and factions within General Headquarters. We must call his attention to the fact."

The whole matter—fizzled out.

Secret Line 998

On the telephone Ebert complained bitterly to Groener about these events. Groener knew about the matter, but he also knew the character of the little people's deputy. Ebert was a southern German like himself. The man who towered above those around him when it came to insight and coldbloodedness was being pressed dreadfully hard in Berlin.

He comforted Ebert and encouraged him. Ebert insisted that he be informed about all, absolutely all military measures, dismissals, reorganizations, formations of new units that might be planned. Under no circumstances would he allow himself to be faced with a fait accompli.

The general shook his head at this. Aha, rebelling again. They had proceeded falsely. He calmed the man on the other end of the line. Ebert had absolutely no reason to fear an attempt to reinstate the monarchy. He could not hide the fact that the officers' corps wished to reestablish their former honor and respect, nor had he hidden it prior to this. But in that point their common interests and wishes went hand in hand.

"Or do you wish, my good Reichs Chancellor, for an expansion of the powers of the soldiers' councils like those the congress at Ems wants to present us with?"

Ebert denied this emphatically, but asked that he be spared any reason for feeling insecure. They had formed an alliance on November 9th. And each partner to that alliance had to take into consideration the feelings of the other—which he had dutifully observed on his part.

Groener confirmed this and once more tried to soothe the voice that was so regrettably excited. "You should think very seriously about leaving Berlin at some point. Among all these Barths, Liebknechts and Luxemburgs there you will in time lose all freedom of movement and fray your nerves."

"Your Excellency, I would just as soon leave today as tomorrow."

"And?"

"What would happen in Berlin behind my back?"

"What do you suppose?"

"It is all easy enough to imagine."

"I'm not frightened. The radicals would at once put themselves in power. Correct? Why not? Once they are there, it would be easy pickings to bring them down."

They spoke amiably with one another, even affectionately—and lay in cautious wait for one another. Groener announced that the next morning he would be having a conference with Colonel von Harbou about the results of the meeting at Ems. The Field Marshal General had also requested a situation report.

"The time is coming, my good Reichs Chancellor, when decisions must be made. I shall reserve till tomorrow evening my report on the results of my conversations. I wish you a restful good night."

The Sibyl Demands a Wallenstein

Major von Schleicher telephoned and telephoned. But it was not possible in Kassel to get a clear impression of the situation in Berlin. He was very excited, and inquired whether the countess could receive him for a game of chess. She consented, via her housekeeper, suggesting he come that same evening.

He sat across from the old woman at the little gaming table in her living room, playing chess for a quarter of an hour. A gas flame burned above them in a bell of frosted glass, the large living room lay in darkness.

Now the white mass of the old woman's hair began to tremble, it rose like a cloud, and the delicate old face became visible, her bright eyes examining him. "You are nervous, von Schleicher. You are making foolish mistakes. Your knight is uncovered."

"I'm sorry."

"You may take back the move. Preoccupied?"

She pulled on the rope beside her chair, the housekeeper appeared, the countess asked for tea. "And be careful removing the board from the table. We are only pausing a bit."

The major allowed all this to happen in silence. The countess's presence did not have the calming effect this time that he had hoped for. He felt imprisoned, but he could not now stand up.

The formal ceremony of the pouring of tea and presenting of cigarettes and lighting them was performed. The housekeeper departed, they had exchanged not a single word the whole time.

The countess said angrily, "Now do speak up. I am not a court of inquiry who will do the interrogating."

The tone pleased Schleicher. He spoke, unburdening himself of his anger at the failure at Ems.

The countess pressed her back against the easy chair and sat up very straight, her small, yellowish, wrinkled face raised. "What refreshing news. Were I in charge of arranging world history and had I to make a move at this moment, I would not have dealt with you in any other way."

"We're not to blame for this wretched situation."

Her wrinkled eyelids were raised for a second. "Are you going to start that again? You are sitting here in front of me, you are alive, ergo you are to blame."

"Gracious countess, let us not return to finished business, I beg you."

The old woman raised a skinny arm from which her black shawl hung like a flag of mourning. "You know what mischief you have done. You are being punished for it. And for the same reason we shall all be punished along with you for having supported you and kept silent. The women in every family in Germany should have left the men who did this, left us with this."

"Gracious countess," Schleicher begged.

But she went on. "If things go badly for you, you are angry and do not wish to accept the consequences. Who gave recognition to the Reds? You did. Then you'll just have to stand by that decision. To be sure things have not gone so far, as in Russia, that they are massacring us. Perhaps you expect me to thank you for it."

"I beg you, countess . . ."

"You will give me a guarantee, von Schleicher? Don't do it. B always follows A. What does the Field Marshal General say?"

"He is not pleased with anything anymore. He plays the great obstructionist, to prevent us from slipping down any further."

The cloud of hair sank down, the countess covered her arms with her shawl. She spoke so softly that he could barely hear. "I believed in the resoluteness of the Prussian court and army. You are all courageous in battle, but afterward you're ninnies. At a given point the Reich no longer had a kaiser, the nation had no center, the imperial crown lay out in the street. It could have been picked up—no one was tempted. You are creatures with a herd instinct. Even now it would still be possible. But no, no one bothers."

"You mean?"

"Yes, a Wallenstein. But you have sworn allegiance to your machinery. You're nothing but machines yourselves. It truly is an era of factory workers."

Von Schleicher sat there silent. A Wallenstein, someone who would make a grab for the imperial crown? Hindenburg? A mute paladin, at best a surrogate for someone else.

But the countess could follow his thoughts, and she whispered, "No. You'll find no ambition anywhere. Power is no enticement. Your watchword is subordination. In Russia there is Lenin. Fate should have sent someone like that to bedevil you. — What will you do now, von Schleicher? You have to act. It is demanded of you."

"It has come to that for us all. I do not know how far along General Groener is."

"Stick with Hindenburg. He knows better what the Reich is. A blow must follow. Should it not come from you, it will fall on you. And though the living may curse you, the coming generation will thank you. Major, you cannot let me die like this."

At last Schleicher felt himself unburdened, sure of himself. He reached for the tea, cold now. The old woman unwrapped her hand from the cloth, and before she put her cup to her mouth, she cast a stern glance at Schleicher. It was as if she were drinking to the future.

"You should have no illusions about me, von Schleicher. As if I were enraptured with the kaiser like some old piece of court baggage. I know who he is. I had tried several times to see him, and finally when he came here I received an invitation. I was at the castle, I had to overcome my fear on hearing him speak. No one could get in a word around him. He had a noisy way about him. I was reminded of an enfant terrible. Her Majesty was friendlier, proud of her husband. I have never forgotten that audience. Groener would not have been able to send some other man off like that."

Schleicher stood up. "None of us will play the role of Wallenstein, I'm afraid."

"Grasp it, strike the blow."

She had never spoken so sternly.

A Satyr behind the Curtain

The old woman drank the rest of her tea alone. She sat there erect for a while. Then she rang and had herself be brought to her bedroom, placed in her easy chair, had a small table with a few books moved close to her. The ceiling lamp burned brightly, the housekeeper was dismissed for a half hour.

But the old woman, huddled up in herself, did not read once she was alone. She had not had the shawl removed from her shoulders. She pulled it up over her hair, let it fall down over her face. She sat there tense. Her eyes stared blankly out through the weave of the cloth.

A drama unfolded. Its meaning was not clear. It first began to form in the dark, images started to move. She rubbed her narrow lips together in excitement.

A battle of goats, black against a gray background, now and again a flash of lightning. The animals danced, leaped, shot past one another, collided in midair, locked horns, went at one another with their forelegs waving and rubbed brows together. They bleated and snorted.

The old woman behind her black curtain also panted. Enraptured, she followed it all through the weave. A bluish iridescent halo formed around the fighting animals and devoured them, but then they reappeared. There were three, four of them, sometimes a wildly churning herd.

The old woman's fingers were cramped together.

All of this went on soundlessly, except for the little cries and snorts. The animals did not stamp their feet. Sometimes, to the mute delight of the old woman, they would fight in the air and then sink slowly back down to earth. The battle developed—now on the ground, now in the air—into a savage frenzy, the animals' horns grew with the pace, their black bristly bodies grew smoother. They slapped together like meat when they touched each other. They wallowed on the ground. Many of them lay there motionless. A stream of blood flowed from them.

With great delight the old woman wadded up the cloth before her eyes, which now gave off only a blurred white gleam.

She was very weak, smiled and gazed at the shadowy wall. "Go to sleep now. You have played." Her nostrils were dilated.

She let herself fall limply against the high arm of the easy chair, breathing wearily. When she rang for the housekeeper and let herself be

201

helped up out of the chair, her features were once more those of a delicate, attentive, serious old woman.

A charming smile illumined her face as she trembled there on the arm of her nurse.

In France

At this point people got down to work in Paris, and the senate commissioned thirty-six of its members to study all the plans and suggestions dealing with the two recaptured provinces of Alsace and Lorraine. These elderly and experienced gentlemen went about the honorable and important task with considerable zeal. The commission was headed by Léon Bourgeois, a man who had presided over the senate and served as a minister in the cabinet on several occasions. Messrs. Doumer and Boucher lent praiseworthy assistance.

The city of Strasbourg, relaxed and cheerful as it was in this period of transition, was happy to be the object of official interest, but things were moving slowly when it came to food supplies. For November 29th the Municipal Food Office could supply only dairy outlet numbers 38–44, 46–60, 62, 63, 65–70, 72–78 with exactly 4½ ounces of Muenster cheese per customer, and then (it is frightening just to write it down, the misery of those days weighs on one so) only for those persons holding white-cheese ration cards number 2, 102, 103, 105, 107, 109–113. One must regretfully ask what happened to those holding other numbers. They did not get any Muenster cheese.

Whoever held a card stamped "Igd," received 3½ ounces of "spread." We don't know what that was, but we would guess that neither ordinary butter nor English marmalade were to be found hidden beneath that embarrassed euphemism.

And whoever went and got his "spread" with his "Igd" card on the 29th was informed that the next day, Saturday, he would not receive any milk.

When one reads that in the week of November 25th to December 1st the citizens of Strasbourg received 8½ ounces of meat (inclusive of bony material) and 4 ounces of cold cuts, one assumes that that means a half or a quarter pound of meat and a quarter pound of cold cuts per day. But no, that was for the week.

And coupons 1–8 could be redeemed for only 1 ounce of meat, and coupons 9–10 for 2 ounces of cold cuts. One ounce of meat with bones included: what's left when it's cooked? They probably ate the bone in desperation.

In return, people were given hope that next week they would have access to an egg, a whole egg, redeemable with coupon 49 in the egg ration book, but only if (lord, what a lot of trouble just to get one's weekly egg), only if they had handed in their order coupon by Friday the 29th at the latest. Presumably the hens were notified in the meantime how many eggs were placed on order.

Hilda Is Sick

The old architect had two doctors come see Hilda. She had brought the flu home with her, he lamented. He went about bewailing his fate.

But Hilda, though vexed by a cough, fever and headache, felt fine. A hand from the years of war reached out to grab her, a hand, not a bullet, not shrapnel; and she held tight to it. She did not want to get well quickly. But she did.

Letters arrived daily from Bernhard. Hilda left them unopened in her night table.

By Monday, the first weekday of December—the difficult November was over—she is sitting up, pale and worn, in the living room. She doesn't want to heat her little room. She gathers the rays of the morning sun like a flurry of flower petals falling from a tree in springtime. Bernhard is outside, about to leave another letter for her. She hears him and lets him in.

The nurse leaves the room. Hilda is sitting packed in heavy covers on one corner of the sofa; she looks haggard, with blue rings under her eyes; her hair is bound at the back of her neck in a simple knot. They have not seen each other since that terrible discussion here in this room.

Bernhard—she asks him to have a seat—hasn't the courage to speak the first sentence, to address her in the familiar second-person form, but she does. "Take your coat off, it's warm in here." Then he asks her about her illness, she warns him not to stay too long, he might catch it. He tells her about the funny things happening in town, and in the same easy tone of voice she asks about Frau Scharrel. He looks at her.

She asks, "Has she left already, she was planning a trip, wasn't she?"

"Yes, she's in Paris."

Hilda, not surprised: "Ah, with the two mademoiselles." She wants to know if he has some time to spare. If so, she'd like to have him read to her from her father's newspaper about what's happening in the world.

He reads her news of the city and of France. She requests the news about Germany.

And he reads, whatever he finds, some of it true, some false, about disturbances, soldiers' councils, the food supply, the retreat of the troops.

"They're still marching?"

"Yes, Hilda, there are millions of them."

"And they are all heading for Germany, and they already have such problems with the food supply. Where are you living, Bernhard?"

He gives her the address of his small apartment, the old one that she knows so well, and she says, "That's nice, that you're still there. People are faithful after all."

"Do you do a lot of philosophizing now that you're ill, Hilda?"

She smiles at him. "All sick people do. What are they supposed to do to keep busy? But I don't think bad thoughts about you, Bernhard, nor about us."

She stretches one hand to him, he reaches to take hold of it. But she pulls it back at once. "Mustn't touch, the flu."

He pulls his chair closer. And while he speaks of his work with her father and of his own poor prospects, she bends forward, takes his head in both hands, presses his face down to hers and lays her face against the crown of his head. She strokes his cheeks and his neck. "Ah, that feels good, gives me strength. I'm good for you, Bernhard, I'm good for you."

And while he snatches up her left hand and kisses it without protest from her, she weeps above him in his hair. Then she lets him go, wipes her eyes, and says, "I'm weak, Bernhard."

He leaves, happy, radiantly happy.

The old nurse finds her sobbing clear, resonant sobs. Hilda cannot calm herself, she whimpers, presses her mouth to the pillow. Without understanding any of this, the old woman stands next to her.

"Forgive me," Hilda manages to say, "don't be angry. It's nothing. Just nerves."

She goes on weeping and trembling and sobbing inconsolably. It takes a half hour before it is all over. Then at last she listens to the nurse and lets herself be led into the next room and put to bed. It hardly takes ten minutes before she is asleep.

The old woman, a white cap on the back of her head and clad in a full black dress, folds her hands as she stands beside the bed. She watches how Hilda trembles even in her sleep. "Oh, is she ill."

Her father, who tiptoes into the room at noon, is glad to see how well she looks in her sleep, how peacefully she is sleeping.

Concerning Bugs and Their Habits

In this chapter we meet nothing but bugs, or those who would like to be bugs. The natural history is given in careful detail, revealing that there is a certain curiousness to be found at all heights and depths of the animal kingdom.

Money and Its Role in the Love Life of Man

Brose-Zenk basked in perfect bliss.

His luck had deserted him at gambling, he went seldom now to Fasanenstrasse, and then in a certain sense only to confirm what he already knew. For in his heart of hearts he did not trust his star; it had been his experience that truth was to be found in an endless ebb and flow.

He lived at the lower end of Wilhelmstrasse, his landlady was a fat woman who had a certain respect for him. And among the police as well, one heard whispers about his good connections. The biggest names were named, Brose-Zenk alias Schröder had been introduced into the best society. He "earned" vast sums. A stunning beauty walked at his side.

The dye-job, Motz's girlfriend, had transferred her affections without opposition to Wylinski, devourer of women. The man was an erotic phenomenon. He was a mill that ground women—though no bluebeard. He despised neither the beautiful nor the ugly, neither the black nor the red or the misshapen. He loved, as he candidly admitted, women in general. He worshiped the eternal feminine in each one.

Naturally Brose-Zenk's friend Motz and he would run into one another, and they had heated discussions.

"I must take issue with you there," old Wylinski declared. "You are a specialist. Take botany, for instance. You are presented with dozens, hundreds of forms of plant life. But you declare that you're a mole and always will be. You are attached to one certain root, which for some reason or other attracts you, and you nibble away at it. I have such personal preferences as well. But when another woman chances to meet my eye— not during business hours—then I am sure to say: she's not beautiful, she limps. But is that her fault? Does that make her any less a woman?

Shall I always think only in the coarsest sexual terms? No, I decide. I shall never, never be content with that. I desire the female, total femininity. I am enthralled by the sexuality bound up inside it and how a woman deals with it, develops it, hides it, presents it, serves it up. It is what every woman possesses in her special charming way, in every instance."

Motz defended himself. "You mustn't think I'm a monomaniac, a Dante crazed by his Beatrice. I was always of the opinion that to know and love only one single woman amounted to a kind of asceticism. I consider marriage a kind of asceticism, a secular form of monasticism. And there is simply no reason for it. Because of their upbringing, family and so on, people for the most part become pious creatures who place their piety above all else. That's why they enter into marriage with one woman. But that is not every man's cup of tea, not mine at any rate—while at the same time I do not intend any denigration of marriage. Whenever I have come to know and love a woman who was married, I have always approached her with a sense of guilt, with the feeling of violating a biblical commandment. But of course that is precisely what makes it all so exciting."

"I've no use for that," said crass Herr Wylinski. "I cut and run in the face of all such adventures of the soul. I wish to be spared all such family matters. I do not wish to hear about Herr Soandso (especially when it may be I've turned some money his way), what he thinks about the fact that his wife is spending time with me. Should the husband's name be mentioned, particularly if I know the name, the lady is taken off my list at once."

Motz: "I only said that in passing. I wanted to defend myself against the accusation that I only run on one track. I do not like being reproached for being ignorant of that great garden of feminine beauty and affection."

"Not a word has been said about beauty. What is 'beautiful' anyway? I prefer: charming, amiable."

Motz: "Attractive."

"Exactly."

Motz: "We are of the same opinion." Ah, he knew they weren't, but he did not dare present his views to this great man, this pasha. "But one must surely be allowed a choice—be allowed to omit a few, I mean, not on principle or out of contempt, but for lack of time, and, frankly, because of preference for a certain type."

"What a shame, Motz. There you have the point that separates us. I would contest that one has the right to any such preference."

"Herr Wylinski, one doesn't eat everything either."

"Almost everything. You don't know me very well. There were times in my long life when I had to eat some barbarous things. My stomach survived. You are constantly searching for excuses for your rejection of this woman or that. And I'm telling you: each one has her charm. It sometimes requires some effort to discover that charm. But I assure you, just as in every human heart there burns both hate and a spark of divinity, so in every woman there burns the feminine."

The subject intrigued Motz. He felt himself beaten; he could not answer. He suggested uncertainly. "But there are limits. Whores for instance."

Old Wylinski shook his head thoughtfully and let out long puffs of air. "I have concerned myself with this matter rather intensively, my young friend. It is impossible to sum it up in one brief sentence. At any rate, since you are still a young man, I would hope that you will continue to gain experience and be chary of rigorous judgments. Why should whores represent a limit? As you are well aware, they cannot be that sharply differentiated from other women, from true ladies. But why should the fact that a woman takes money in exchange for love—because she has nothing else to sell—hinder her from doing a good job of presenting her love? And that is the crucial point. We are always and everywhere, in wedlock and out, involved with money. Money plays some sort of role in all love affairs, with the exception of young teenagers—who are elemental, feline, instinctive, but dumb as well. There one senses a purely organic excitement and satisfies it. Later, everything takes place within a social context, takes on an intellectual dimension, becomes amusing. Even when nude, two people confront one another in a social context. I have money, I give presents. It's only natural that that makes an impression, influences people, changes love's hue. Money is a means to power. I rise in status when I spend it. It makes the woman who receives it from me happy and she is obligated to me. With money I give her sun, light, nourishment. Pleasure. My money envelops her. That does not demean her—on the contrary, it makes it possible for her to find and develop her sense of love."

Motz fretted, "But you've really got to let the money flow in that case."

"Indeed you do. Parsimony is love's archenemy. Women are quite right to despise thrifty people. Parsimony means the death of every genuine human form of cohabitation."

Motz: "I agree with you, Herr Wylinski. But that means you have to have the money in the first place."

But Wylinski grandly waved this aside. "We all come from the same parents, Adam and Eve. No one is at a disadvantage. We all have arms and legs and eyes and ears and can have a look around to see what can be got hold of. The earth was not divided up equally in times past, and it still isn't today. It lies, in my humble opinion, open to every man even now. So no whining, please."

Motz's face showed his respect. "It is splendid that that's how socialists think nowadays."

Wylinski: "And that's what I am and what I'll stay. I've been this way since I was a toddler, so to speak, and no one can change me. Socialism is the crown, the peak of human progress. It is not a gift of nature; on the contrary, it is the result, the goal of man's rule over nature. However, that rule doesn't just drop from heaven. Socialism justifies neither stupidity nor laziness."

Motz: "I am in total agreement with that view. I'm quite satisfied. At last I can honestly say, I too am a socialist. Granted, only theoretically, in comparison with yourself."

Wylinski: "You would achieve much more and acquire a great deal more money if you only knew how good it is to earn money and how good it makes one feel to do something with it. You become free, you gain freedom through money. As a socialist I advocate the liberation of mankind and therefore wish every man to be free. But that is only possible with money, my dear friend."

And with patent tenderness he turned to Motz, who sat next to him in an armchair in Wylinski's office.

Yes, Motz had managed to gain access to Wylinski's office, and because of the very same qualities that endeared him to Brose-Zenk several years before: his amicability, his boundless insouciance, his incompetence—which he bore without a trace of regret—and the innocence with which he offered himself to all worthy and propertied persons as a fellow consumer.

During this industrious period there were always gentlemen and ladies vying with one another to do him some service, to give him things. There was something of paradise lost about him. Old Wylinski, the bee who found every nectared flower, had discovered Motz as a matter of course. With eyes moist from some emotion or other, he said to Motz, "In these last few weeks I've met with yet another example of what it means to rule by virtue of money; perhaps it will interest you. You know Antonia, Brose-Zenk's old girlfriend. I call her Mocha."

Motz stared straight ahead. This was Toni, his dye-job, and his sweetheart as before. For he did not love *en gros* when he happened to find the right woman.

"I know her," Motz confessed. "But why do you call her Mocha?"

Wylinski: "A matter of taste. First, it's the color of her hair."

Motz, dismayed: "Mocha? Since when?"

Wylinski, gently: "It is her natural hair color. For Brose-Zenk she had it painted green or red, I believe."

Motz was beside himself. He had not seen her for three days. "And now she's a brunette."

"No, mocha, a special brunette tone that she's gone back to at my wish. But that's not why I call her that. By the way, she sings your praises. She's seen you many times at Brose-Zenk's, but you've always given her the cold shoulder. Why, if I might ask? Not to your taste?"

"No, she doesn't do anything for me," Motz confirmed with energetic indignation.

"You see where your choosiness gets you. Brose has obligingly ceded her to me, though, of course, she can go back to him whenever she likes, and take all my presents with her. I assured her at once that she has complete freedom, and that made a big impression on her."

"I see," Motz grumbled.

"But she stays on. The reason: my money and me. I don't put myself first on that list, by no means. I know—it's the money. But it comes from me. And she has developed in a way that . . ."

"But why Mocha?" Motz asked, exasperated with Wylinski.

"I can give you the reasons in detail. Every woman is a unique individual. Nature expresses itself differently in each."

Motz raised his hands, pleading. "Now you're philosophizing. Why Mocha, I asked."

"Go drink a cup of real mocha, which is possible at the moment in Berlin only at the risk of one's life, one might add, and then you'll know. She does not intoxicate, but has something about her that is endlessly exciting, a strong pleasant bitterness."

"I'm amazed," said Motz honestly.

"You haven't noticed it? As I said, money liberates people. Besides which, one cannot tell about a person just passing them on the street. Which is why one must love someone, love them a great deal, as I said a moment ago. Mocha is a perfect example of what I'm saying. Even Brose doesn't know her in that way."

"So you'd say, a pleasant, strong bitterness?" Motz asked and made a mental note of the words. Inside him there was a raging thunderstorm of anger and threats.

Wylinski: "An aromatic, bitter perfume. She loves to change her clothes in my private quarters about five o'clock, after the office closes, and then this creature, whom I'm sure you know as rather reserved, a brier rose as it were, walks in here in such a state—one is tempted to say there's something crafty about her. But I am proud of her, happy that she has developed such craft. She wears a short silk jacket, an evening coat, and under it . . ."

"Nothing," Motz suggested. He knew his Toni.

"No," Wylinski corrected him to his amazement. "I have bought her all sorts of things and she wears them, though against her naked skin I'll grant you. Pearls around her neck, a very delicate silver belt with a large, bright, jeweled buckle around her waist, just below her navel. She colors her navel a dark color, and she has completely shaved her body."

"Impossible," Motz groaned. "Her whole body?"

"Then there are two wide garters just above her knees, and her toe-nails are painted red. And not a trace of perfume. She's the first woman I've ever met in Berlin without perfume. I don't know how she came up with the idea. It's a stroke of genius."

Motz did not dare say that he had forbidden her to wear perfume because she didn't know how to use it properly. He had enough of "Mocha" now. He pleaded a headache and left.

Out on the street he vomited over and over, one could follow the trail he was so sick. "Mocha, Mocha!" he moaned. "I'll never be able to drink coffee again."

Ferrymen on the River of Death

"Grand old" Wylinski's motto was: "Live and let live." He had be-queathed it to a whole tribe of Wylinskis that grew up all around him. To what genus of plant or animal this tribe, including its progenitor, belonged was the source of varied opinions among friends, detectives and public prosecutors.

All Wylinskis were conspicuous by their connections, connections to important, high-placed, the highest-placed people. Moreover, they all had offices, apartments and friends, lovers, several cars and a great deal of money. They had at their disposal princely castles, powder mills, cannon factories, mines, right on down to small country places and food. Every-thing flowed to them. But in reality it only flowed through them, rushed on past them. It was the function of Wylinskis to set a mighty machine in motion, to bring about a transformation of all values.

And just as in the fiery transformation of coal into ashes only a por-tion of the fuel releases usable heat while the rest is dispersed to no effect in empty space, so it was with the more gentle transformation of values. Whoever owned something and found himself caught up in the ma-chine along with his castle, house, factory or mine inevitably—lost. But what got lost did not dissolve into empty space; it ended up in the pockets of the Wylinskis.

There were, so nature willed it, many Wylinskis. For just as in war-time no solitary ferryman named Charon can suffice in the underworld of Hades for the masses of people arriving to be transported over the tran-quil river, and the god of death needs a whole host of oarsmen for the job (a mass flight from the world above that has gone mad), so in a post-war period one single Wylinski does not suffice to shape a new disposi-tion of wealth upon the face of the ravaged earth.

And they directed the flow and metamorphosis of wealth. They governed its transformation. They expedited it.

They plundered the passengers on the journey across and enriched themselves. And out of the misery of one man (cruel transformation of energy!) arose the pleasure of another.

One example of the species, one of that swollen, almost bursting host of dung-beetles was an inconspicuous fellow named Finsterl.

He had grown up as a young apprentice in Wylinski's shadow, and it would be difficult to imagine a quieter, more modest creature, submissive, dependable and correct. There was none of the brutality or gargantuan lust for life that characterized his master.

Finsterl crept about on padded soles. He was incredibly alert. Though always vigilant and concerned for others, the man was so inconspicuous that he was overlooked everywhere. He himself often told of how he could walk right into a restaurant or barbershop and sit there comfortably as long as he liked without anyone ever giving him a glance. He considered it an advantage. When he would order something in a bar, the waiter was sure to forget it, not out of disdain for Finsterl, but simply because Finsterl had not made any impression at all. He looked inconceivably ordinary, with full, pale cheeks, friendly and respectful eyes, from which everyone would turn away for lack of interest. Doubtless he also cast no shadow. Few people ever saw him eating or drinking. And when he did, it was most assuredly only to prevent life's most essential physical properties from withering and dying.

This Finsterl, this shadow of Wylinski, set up several offices in major German cities, together with adjoining apartments, in order "to receive guests." Toward the end of November, he moved into the empty fourth floor of an elegant building of our acquaintance on Fasanenstrasse in Berlin. The second floor of the building was occupied by a secret military recruitment center, the third by a gambling club, and its crowning glory was Finsterl. The hostess of the club where we have seen Brose-Zenk and many politicians coming and going recognized him as a dependable man. She understood what it was that attracted him to set up shop in just this building. He could guide the gentlemen whom he had just met on the third floor at the gambling tables one story higher, and if they wished it put them up for the night, breakfast with them, or otherwise do them a good turn.

On the evening of December 2nd, we see three sedate gentlemen slowly walking up Fasanenstrasse, climbing the steps to the door and entering the building. The window of the porter's lodge opens, but they do not look in its direction. Neither does the person who opens it look in theirs. For it is the blind war veteran who follows their steps with sharp ears. He recognizes that there are three of them and that they are serious gentlemen. From the third story on, their steps are no longer audible. He waits to hear whether the bell rings. When nothing happens, he bends his head forward expectantly. Throats are cleared up there, a bell rings, on the fourth floor. As the door opens the blind veteran closes his window and says to the woman lying in bed knitting, "Three men visiting Finsterl." A military report.

Finsterl had furnished his large apartment on the fourth floor in grand style, with carpets, paintings and furniture from a castle he had just purchased in the Mark Brandenburg.

The three earnest gentlemen we saw arriving sat drinking beer in the trophy room; they were served by a husky Bavarian in a short peasant's jacket and green puttees. Gambling had already begun one floor beneath them, here one only drank. They arose and let the servant lead them through the luxurious rooms, gossiping about the former owner of the castle that had been auctioned off.

One of the gentlemen, with a great blond beard, a massive, somewhat hunched figure, seemed perplexed by what he saw. He was a sawmill owner, a jovial fellow who had come along out of curiosity (just as had his friend the brewery owner). They had been enticed by hints dropped by their guide, a business associate of Finsterl, to the effect that Finsterl might possibly give them some important "tips."

After their tour they sat down again and exchanged impressions. The bearded sawmill owner smiled, totally baffled. "I have known Finsterl for four years now. Splendid what he's accomplished. My highest respects, gentlemen. It's enough to make your heart stand still."

They laughed. That had not been the intent of his remark.

The bearded man: "Who knows."

The broad-shouldered brewer across from him: "You fear the sweep of the scythe yourself, perhaps? Then it's not such a bad idea to take a tour of the mortuary. Yes indeed, here is where we'll be buried, friend. Here we can drink one melancholy glass of beer and then another—to the health of our successor."

"There's not much he'll inherit from me. For sure no furniture like this. We've just bought new, and got it for a good price, too."

"I hope we'll all get a chance to see it soon."

The man with the flowing beard used his long arm for a deprecatory gesture. "All normal earnings. Suddenly you have too much money, and you feel uncomfortable with it. My wife said, 'Profits of war, get rid of it!' Her brother died in battle."

"And so now you're buying furniture, is that it?"

"She gives to the Salvation Army. Besides, what's a person supposed to do with so much so-called money?"

The third man, a leather manufacturer, looked very weary. He drank a lot, and between beers would pour himself a kümmel from a bottle set in front of him. At each glass he would make a little bow and say, for absolutely no reason, "Pardon me." He now joined in the conversation. "You should take me on as a partner. I'll associate with anyone who's

212

luck is running." (The man, as they all knew, gambled downstairs and was ruining himself.) "Perhaps you will do me the honor of introducing me to your wife. She can exercise her charity on me."

"Not for gambling," the brewer growled. "You bet too high."

"What does high or low mean in gambling. You either win or lose. If that's not what you want, then don't even start in."

He took another drink, but the brewer pulled the bottle away. "Committing suicide in public is in bad taste. —You're on the right track sticking with Finsterl. It's the secret longing of the criminal for the hangman."

The pale man: "The way everything's going to smash nowadays, it's just like with mother nature. When the plants sprout and the leaves start turning green, right away the worms and beetles appear to devour them. Whatever gets too lush gets eaten up."

The brewer growled in his direction. "And whatever isn't too lush grows. Why don't you invest in boots. People wear boots, even in a republic."

The pale man stood up and paced back and forth (perhaps he had some designs on a distant bottle of cognac). "It's all nonsense, pure stupidity, what they're doing. I have two hundred workers, till last month twice that, and then the part-time help and the salaried employees. I know my people, from the senior foreman down to the greenest office boy. You mention my gambling. Well, I keep my factory in tip-top shape. Every man has his weaknesses. But what's all this nonsense about a revolution? It's a blatant swindle. Don't laugh, gentlemen, I'm fully convinced of it. There's not a penny's worth of truth to the whole thing. The war would have ended much the same anyway. Nobody needed to go out of his way to help. Ludendorff had sold us down the river as it was. So why a revolution? When you ask a worker about it, he babbles some empty phrases and doesn't know what it's all about either. There were some who got together with some co-workers and dressed me down with colossal speeches, all learned by rote. Acted as if they were going to chew my head off right there. And if you meet one of them out on the street by himself, with wife and kids along, you ought to see how reasonable he is."

The man with the long beard, the owner of the sawmill, nodded. "No news to me. Propaganda."

To their surprise the pale man sat down next to the bottle and poured himself a glass without further ado. "Pardon me."

His friend, the brewer: "And that's the last glass. — So what conclusions do you draw from this?"

The pale leather manufacturer stretched out his legs. "That this is no revolution. We learned in school that the French Revolution was started in 1789 by the third estate because the first two had mismanaged things and the whole country was bankrupt from top to bottom. That's what a real revolution looks like. But that's not what we're talking about now. Not even according to what the workers themselves think. Our workers want to move up, to have legal protections, a universal and secret ballot. And that's all they want. Those are reforms they should have been granted long ago. Who do they hurt?"

The brewer regarded him attentively from one side. "You've had trouble at the factory?"

The leather manufacturer had very deep-set eyes, his health was now better, now worse; at the moment he looked sick again, was on the decline. "Nothing new. How do you deal with the workers' council?"

The brewer: "We have some peaceable folk who support us. We see that they get a little something for their trouble."

"They accept it?"

"Of course they do. A man never works without pay."

The leather manufacturer considered. "Then you have a different sort of worker than I. My whole plant is quiet. Only the four they elected raise a ruckus. I can't stand them."

"You haven't offered them anything yet?"

"Bribes? I hadn't even thought of that."

The brewer laughed out loud. The bearded man laughed with him.

The brewer: "You live up in the clouds somewhere, my dear Max."

The bearded man suggested sympathetically, "You shouldn't let yourself get upset. These people aren't so bad. You have to talk to them individually. Maybe things are bad at home with the family. Ask them about it. Of course it's not the pleasantest thing to do. But it's not the worst either."

Though they were expecting Finsterl, he did not arrive. The pale man grew restless. He looked at his watch. The brewer took hold of him by the arm. "Look at this man. He's like a horse wanting to get back to the stall once he gets a whiff of oats. But he doesn't want to eat something—just to gamble his money away."

"I'm not going to gamble, Max. I've got an appointment with someone."

"With the goddess of fortune, I expect."

"With a certain Brose-Zenk and some other gentlemen."

The brewer laughed out loud again. "You know him too? Brose-Zenk? He was introduced to me as Schröder. Then when I met him later he had forgotten about that."

"Schröder is the name of the firm he has taken over."

The brewer: "From heav'n above to earth she comes. My dear old friend, what are you getting yourself into? You're thinking perhaps of shaking the fruit off someone else's plum tree? You're not talented enough for that. Otherwise we wouldn't have had to give you the hint on how to deal with your workers' council."

The pale man was confused, his uneasiness grew, the brewer would not leave him alone. "We shall stick together today, right here in the castle of the late Count von X."

So the three gentlemen sat and chatted in Herr Finsterl's splendid apartment.

As they made to leave, an inconspicuous man stood next to the servant in the peasant's costume and bowed to them while helping them into their coats. He tugged and patted the coats into place. The pale leather manufacturer had vanished for a moment into the next room. When he returned and the gentlemen were standing at the open door, the leather manufacturer and the helpful gentleman greeted one another cordially. It was Finsterl, who had been there the whole time but hadn't wanted to disturb them. He begged them to stay, he did not want to drive them off for heaven's sake. He whispered something to the leather manufacturer and shook hands with them all at the door as if truly grateful. They left with a favorable impression of him.

They were weary from a long day, however, and let their thoughts and desires wander off into reveries. And so they strolled home through the night. Before he got to the Kaiserdamm, the bearded man found an empty taxi, in which he now sat. It was no longer empty, he remarked to himself. Suddenly he was no longer thinking of the ostentation he had just encountered, but of the fact that he was bouncing homeward in a taxi. He shoved his black hat down into his face to keep the light from the swiftly passing streetlamps from hitting him in the eye. He thought of absolutely nothing now. He had already thought enough. He would let the world take care of itself. He snored. The driver would wake him.

The owner of the brewery believed it his Christian duty to accompany his friend, the nervous leather manufacturer, Finsterl's friend, at least partway. He did so until he also saw an empty taxi approaching. At which point his moral scruples waned. For form's sake he asked his friend whether he might not offer him a ride part of the way. But happily enough the offer was declined. And so the brewer too sank down in the cushion of the car, stretched out his legs. And for him too, night arrived, the great creeping darkness, the warm pouch of the kangaroo.

But like a puppy that has broken from its leash, the pale leather manufacturer ran off, ran back the whole distance his friend had so carefully taken him. His excitement grew the closer he came to his goal, the point of departure, the large elegant building on Fasanenstrasse. At the end he was trembling so that he almost stumbled on the stone steps leading up to it.

He rang. The blind veteran opened up. He was amazed as he heard someone storm past him. Up the stairs.

"Where are you going?" Third floor.

My, is he in a hurry. They can't lose their money fast enough.

After Ems

Generals, city commandants, people's deputies, the movers of war march by. They cannot come to any kind of agreement. Afterward six men come by and put up posters.

The Generals Want to Take Berlin by Surprise

General Headquarters picked up the glove that the soldiers' councils at Ems had thrown down.

With growing insistence old Hindenburg advocated the position that the high command represented the sole legitimate power in Germany, which power had passed from the Kaiser to him, Hindenburg, and not to Ebert.

In a conversation with Schleicher, Groener concurred with this interpretation, but felt it better, given the actual constellation of forces, to go on making use of Ebert.

When Schleicher, as always, broached the subject of Ebert's ambiguous position, Groener replied: "We are all in an ambiguous position, my dear von Schleicher. God, what I wouldn't do if I were in Ebert's shoes and had a troop like us there in front of me just melting away. Actually the man could have it all, really all of it, if he were just a bit clever. He could reach out and take every arsenal, then take all the useful people he had shaken loose and put them in his cadres."

Schleicher: "But who would shake loose?"

Groener: "Now there you've asked the right question. It's enough to give one absolutely incredible respect for the Reich—posthumously at least. Except for a few madmen, there is not one high-ranking officer, not one, who has sincerely gone over to Ebert's side."

Schleicher: "That pleases me greatly."

Groener: "And me, too."

Schleicher: "So then what you said about the troop of us melting away isn't true."

Groener sighed. "We're not melting, not you and not I. But the rank and file, my dear Schleicher. We read it in our manuals and we learned by experience in the war: officers need soldiers. How are you going to remedy this evil then? Shall we divide the world: we get the officers and they get the rank and file?"

They decided to take the bull by the horns. From December 5th on, divisions from the east, west, and south of Berlin would begin their move, inconspicuously infiltrating the city, and from the 18th on they would disarm the civilian population. At the same time, to counterbalance democratization, they would begin to recruit a volunteer militia.

Once again the question arose as to how Ebert would react. Groener was confident. "Ebert wants a proud, patriotic officers' corps; he honestly mourns the German defeat, the man is bound to our cause by the blood of his two sons. He is against the revolution."

Schleicher gave this intensive thought, then declared, "It's true, he's against the revolution. But when we move into action he will recognize what Your Excellency says, that we are using him as civilian leverage. And he won't be a party to that. He would not dare, not in front of his own fellow Party members, to call us into action against the revolution."

Groener: "Go on, please."

"I am, as before, completely against his participation."

Groener shook his head vigorously. "Cast him aside then? The Kaiser's old plan of November 7th and 8th? Out of the question. You think too much in terms of domestic politics. The Entente does not want us, and we are in fact incapable of dealing with them. I flatly refuse, given the state in which we find ourselves, to negotiate with the enemy. If Ebert does that for us, we only have reason to be grateful. No, dear Schleicher, I would rather negotiate with Ebert, and subordinate myself to a man who respects me, than to the Entente. They can't find any filthy bog deep enough to drag the German military through. Our motto . . . ," Groener, growing excited, added after a pause, "our motto must be: Act, but avoid everything that looks like action."

Harbou: "What do you think, sir, about Wilson?"

"My good man! What have I done to deserve this? What do we care about that piece of window-dressing? To whatever extent we can, we must deny our enemies the legitimation to deal harshly with us. I do not wish, by the way, to go down in German history as the man who could not for one single moment renounce the interests of his social class, not even when Germany demanded it."

Von Harbou jotted down some notes. "So the orders will be issued to the various army commands?"

Groener: "They still have to be formulated."

Schleicher stepped up to the general. "May I allow myself one remark. Ebert will not accept our decision, and von Harbou will have made this trip in vain. But his trip will have one effect: we will have betrayed our own plans."

Groener lighted a cigar. "One can't win without taking risks. In 1914, when we had won Lorraine, the French under Joffre managed to regroup their retreat, which was more like flight, and turn it into an attack, into the trap that ended up being the beginning of the mess we landed in."

"What trap do you have in mind now, sir?"

"At the start of their retreat, the French did not know either that they could turn it into a trap for Kluck. They did what was necessary and paid close attention to what was happening."

Von Harbou received his traveling orders.

In Berlin the next morning, Ebert looked as terrified as the men at Wilhelmshöhe expected he would. In fact, toward the end of the discussion, during which Ebert constantly emphasized that he wished to avoid bloodshed at all costs, he became curt and unfriendly.

The major departed with a bad impression of the discussion. Ebert appeared to feel pressed by Kassel and to be playing with ideas he did not reveal.

Following a short telephoned report, Harbou is recalled to Kassel.

Ebert Resists Nevertheless

Ebert was seething as the polite and glib major left him. Immediately after Harbou's departure, Scheidemann looked in. Ebert said grumpily, "Ems offended General Headquarters."

"They shouldn't get themselves upset over Barth," Scheidemann said with a smile.

He provoked Ebert. "But they do get upset, and with every right. Because he is part of this government after all, and it is evident what's wrong with this government. Harbou was here and demanded that we take action."

Scheidemann lost his smile. "You'll have to explain that to me."

This was more to Ebert's taste. So Scheidemann was afraid, the fellow who had so bravely proclaimed a republic on November 9th.

"There's nothing to explain. We are supposed to reject the demands made at Ems. We are supposed to interfere. They won't take this lying down. The front-line army is advancing. They demand that something happen."

"Do they set any terms?"

"They're not that far yet. They are upset. And they're right. If things go on like this we'll have the rug pulled out from under us. The agitation must stop."

"The strikes, too."

"Correct."

The corpulent man sniffed. His bulging eyes stared in a frightening, pop-eyed way. Scheidemann thought the man, his friend, looked dreadful.

Ebert: "And meanwhile we're fast asleep. Yes, I mean it, we're fast asleep. What are we doing, I ask you? Why must I have to be told these things by Kassel? Whose side is the citizen's militia on? Who's paying them?"

"We have the National Guard at the Reichstag."

Ebert: "You can have them as a present. And the Republican Armed Forces. A mixed lot of men who couldn't accomplish a thing against regular troops."

Scheidemann: "Well, we haven't anything better at the moment. Do we have something to fear?"

"They will present us with a fait accompli. And you can count the days on your five fingers. Before the troops are disbanded. Perhaps they are already putting a couple of divisions they can trust in reserve."

Scheidemann: "I think that's a possibility. It's what they would like to do. The telegram that I showed you was clear enough. And so now the gentlemen are admitting it. Then we'll swing on around. We'll tell the Independents the naked truth."

Ebert: "Impossible." (The man's crazy.)

The muscles of Ebert's jaw worked. He drummed his desk with his pencil. "You've some trick in mind, some sly maneuver. I don't like the idea. I cannot see all the consequences."

Scheidemann: "But that doesn't mean putting ourselves in their hands."

Ebert snapped his fingers and threw down the pencil. "You always have a tendency to ally yourself with someone. They're just waiting to crush us." He balled his fist. "We have to be strong. People have to be afraid of us. I refused Harbou. I don't want bloodshed, we'd be done for the next day. If we hand the wheel over to the Independents we're lost as well. What I want," he was talking off to one side, his face invisible, but Scheidemann was paying attention and understood what his friend was saying, "is for the army to be disbanded without any resistance and for Kassel to hold its peace. That is all, and I can demand that much. That's what we have protected them for, seeing to it that the masses didn't massacre them."

Scheidemann, softly: "But you can clearly see what they want."

Ebert: "Give the devil your little finger and he'll take the whole hand. The officers' corps will have to help. But don't let them come in here intending to restore the monarchy."

Ebert propped his head up and considered. In a changed, businesslike voice he remarked, reaching for something among his papers, "See to it that something is done by our side. Wels is the city commandant. Lovely title, isn't it? What does he do? Here are letters of support, proclamations. Who is the Action Committee for Heavy Industry? A mass meeting on our behalf by the Reserve Guard Infantry Regiment 93, the Guard Rifles, Guard Service Corps, the 2nd Guard lancers, the Franz Regiment and so on. Who are they? Liebknecht did spadework there, and still they protest against him."

"How many of them are there? What kind of people are they? They write us that someone should see to it they're looked after. Why doesn't anything come of it? Our people are asleep at the switch. 'Alliance of Active Noncommissioned Officers'—sounds promising."

Scheidemann: "Someone will have to look into it."

Ebert: "Well get a move on, dear friend."

When Scheidemann had gone, Ebert stared toward the door, his head propped on his hands. "There he goes and he'll look into it. He knows exactly what a fix he's got us into. Proclaimed a republic when I had given my word that nothing would happen to the monarchy and we had every chance of working amicably with these same officers who have now put the knife to our throats. But he, Phillip Scheidemann, had to be ever so clever, even though we had talked it over a good ten times, had to run to the window and proclaim the republic in order to get the jump on that pawn Karl Liebknecht. A race against Spartacus, Phillip Scheidemann."

And he banged his forehead with his fist. The same monarchy that we could have easily had in any form that suited us is going to be forced upon us one of these days with fire and sword. And they are ruthless. And then I'd like to see what is still left of us, of the entire working class and of social democracy—not to speak of Spartacus.

He brooded. From another dark corner of his mind came the thought that in the final analysis you can't blame them if they're upset with the whole affair and don't want to have to look at this pigsty any longer. What crime did they commit anyway? Liebknecht's stupid battle hymns about how the soldiers were mistreated. I'd like to see the fellow get his German socialist republic, one with a real army, and then have him visit a barracks to see if his officers wear kid gloves. But he is so stupid that he doesn't even notice what's going on in his beloved Russia.

Then he spoke with City Commandant Wels, his fellow Party member, an honest fellow who appeared now at just the right moment to tell him about difficulties they were having with the People's Naval Division at the palace. Ebert nodded without interest.

As Wels was about to proceed with more of the same, however, Ebert interrupted him and let him have a taste of his bitterness and suspicion. "Your position is of primary importance, you know that. Our very existence depends on you. There may come a day when I shall be forced to go to Hindenburg and announce our bankruptcy because we won't be able to make it without him, and need him to provide us with soldiers. A pretty mess, wouldn't you say?"

Wels stammered in dismay, "What has happened now? I've heard nothing."

Ebert gave him a nasty glance. What a good thing it is I don't depend on him. "When the troops march into the city, when the Guards are stationed in Charlottenburg, who do you think will be around to oppose them? How many men do you have all together?"

"The Guards are coming, you say?"

"Yes. And some other time it may be Spartacus. Who can you hold your own with? Aren't you frightened even for a moment? At the least you ought to be afraid of the Spartacists it seems to me. They alone would be more than a match for us."

Wels was still bewildered. "But I know nothing about this."

Ebert cleared his throat. "That's bad. But you are aware, I take it, that the front-line army is on the march. That the officers aren't fond of us either. That the soldiers' council at Ems was so incredibly impudent and stupid as to get the officers angry; that you know, too. what do you suppose will happen if Groener threatens us? How are you going to counter him?" He bent forward but kept his hand in front of his mouth. "Don't you see that this whole glorious enterprise is built on sand? Kassel only needs to make one move and we will have vanished from the scene. The generals have held back till not only because of the Allies. But get them the least bit upset and they'll strike the blow. And what do we have to put up against them?"

Wels: "I really must contradict you there. You see things too blackly. They have the whole nation against them."

"You all can't get beyond the stage of counting heads. How many soldiers, I asked you? It's ridiculous. And most of them are on Liebknecht's side."

Wels: "That will soon come to an end."

Ebert, without listening to him: "They can run right over us."

Wels had had the breath kicked out of him, he did not understand. He helplessly suggested: "Everyone who's for law and order will stick with us."

Ebert: "That's what you think."

Pause.

Wels: "Well then, what am I supposed to do?"

"You're the city commandant. See to it that they shut their mouths. Spoil their fun. We should not have permitted them their insolence at Ems."

"That was Barth's fault, and he's one of us."

"Barth is counting on the sailors here in the city and the rest of that whole gang who are leading us down the road to ruin. Don't you see that if General Headquarters had had to think up a way to get their hands on the rudder again they would have had to invent the Spartacists?"

Wels: "My opinion exactly. So we'll just have to use a stronger hand." He shrugged weakly. "Unfortunately we really have very few men."

Ebert gave a scornful snort. "The whole nation is behind us, but unfortunately we have only a few men."

Wels left, troubled.

After which Ebert studied newspaper clippings. They soothed him. The *Miesbacher Anzeiger* claimed that Kurt Eisner's real name was Salomon Kusnovsky. Other papers reported that this was false; in fact he was the son of a man named Emanuel Eisner who owned a shop specializing in military goods. (The people's deputy grunted merrily to himself. Military goods; the father suited up soldiers and the son was a pacifist.) Eisner, the report went on, had attended secondary school in Berlin, with German as his major, had then embarked on a career as a journalist, etc. Now isn't that a pretty kettle of fish, comrade Eisner, anti-Semitism. Just keep it up.

And he scribbled a few notes for a speech on elections for a constituent assembly: "A warning not to fall back into the parochialism of petty German states—Socialism? Socialism certainly, our whole lives have been devoted to it, but socialism is not an end in itself, but a means. At the least it excludes arbitrary acts of terror. Socialism is an advanced form of order." God, is this boring—a month ago I wouldn't have let such stuff pass my lips.

He exchanged a few words with the veteran Party member who entered his office and wordlessly put the portfolios and newspapers in order. "We've got ourselves into the soup with our socialism, Gustav. We made our speeches and thought we were speaking to reasonable people. Did they think socialism was going to come dropping down from heaven? Some chance. And now they come screaming at us to hand them their socialism. Take a look, Gustav, I've got socialism here in this drawer."

He pulled out a couple of drawers. "You can see for yourself, Gustav, whether I have it here or not. Next thing you know, they'll storm the Reichs Chancellery to look for it."

Two sandwiches were lying on the desk. Gustav asked whether Ebert wanted a beer. "No thanks." Then the man left.

Ebert ate from the waxed paper while walking slowly up and down beneath the portraits along the wall. He was feeling good again. It tasted good, real German sausage; afterward I'll treat myself to that beer. He stood in front of the portrait of Bismarck, chewing. A great man. When you're on the outside it's easy to squawk, but to have managed all that under the old Kaiser and two wars besides, an enormous achievement. You only realize it once you're here.

The waxed paper fell to the floor, he picked it up, amazed. I'm here.

And suddenly he was struck by Wels's statement that the whole nation is behind us. That's true. Everyone who wants law and order is behind us. I'll not let anyone upset me. He went on chewing gravely.

A Suspicious Incident Moving Right Along

Early that morning six men made their way to the north of Berlin and began to paste up posters. With glue pots and large brushes in hand, they manned their posts in front of hoardings and walls and papered them red.

Among these six we notice that four are the men in military coats we first met on the night of November 30th near the Reichstag and on Dorotheenstrasse, where they discussed matters at length without arriving at a decision. That decision, as we have determined, had been made in the meantime on Kaiser-Friedrich Platz in Neukölln, and we are now witnessing its execution.

One of the two new members was a spy, that is, someone who passed on everything he heard to an opposition party, in this case the Majority Socialists or City Commandant Wels. That did not prevent the spy from joining zealously and wholeheartedly in the work of distributing flyers and pasting up posters. For he was not a spy because he was a believer, but because he was paid, and the amount was too paltry to shake him in his real beliefs, which he was fuzzy about anyway.

Both flyers and posters read:

"The proletariat of Berlin, all men and women of the working class, will assemble on December 6th at three mass meetings called by the Council of Stragglers and Deserters. The working class protests the recent reactionary blow struck against stragglers and deserters by the Greater Berlin Soldiers' Council, depriving them of their rights. The intrigues of officers are behind this. Proletarians, be on your guard!"

Talk of that sort was a matter of good form in those days. It did not, however, prove prejudicial to peaceful and reasonable conduct.

Although these six were in part acting out of private interests and in part upholding their rights, they were also contributing to the deterioration of the state of affairs in the city of Berlin. For things were in a state of ferment as the city filled up with more and more discharged soldiers. And more and more civilians from elsewhere were arriving as well, not knowing where else to go.

Along the main streets they would sit down on corners, with or without a dog, with or without children, the victims of war, amputees, spastics and twitchers, mutely displaying their misery. Beyond its borders the bewildered metropolis was a source of fear and suspicion. The farmers had no trust in currency and withheld food even more than they had during the war. And day in, day out, an unbroken column of wretched city-dwellers—whole families on foot and in wagons, men without work, discharged soldiers—moved out into the countryside, toward Bernau or Oraniengburg or wherever, filling the trams, next to them their gunnysacks and baskets.

In the evening many of them would stand in front of the taverns and large restaurants and cafés in the center of the city, to the west, along the Kurfürstendamm, stand there ragged and freezing, staring through the windows and doors into the brilliantly lit room. It was a scene that boded catastrophe, these people in front of places of amusement.

One could see what they were thinking: Spartacus has the answer. It is time to plunder and destroy.

At the Pharmacy and in a Film Studio

Love at the pharmacy. A lusty old man invests his money in mar-
malade. He is a gay old blade who can be chased off with politics.

Hanna Accepts Consolation

At noon, shortly after lunch, Hanna changed her dress and walked
slowly down the broad, winding main street of the small Alsatian town.
She came to the town hall and lowered her eyes at the sight of the tri-
color. She entered the café on Paradeplatz, which was now named Place
des Armes, and sat down on the red sofa along one wall where she had
often sat with Lieutenant Heiberg. She could see across to Bürgerplatz,
where wounded Germans still lay after having been transferred from the
military hospital. While the dainty, elegant, luscious creature drank her
chocolate from a spoon and ate her cake she considered her fate. She had
the place all to herself.

Soldiers walked by outside, in blue, helmeted, French. Now and
then an officer rode by and gazed in the shop window. She knew this
scene. But everything had changed, everything had grown peaceful, they
were living in the country of the victors, she was reading a French newspaper that lay there, people were adjusting. Could she adjust?

Heiberg was silent. That was the monstrous fact to which she could
not resign herself. As a test she had sent two letters to another address
she knew in Germany by the same route via Switzerland. The letters had
been answered promptly. So the mail was being delivered. And now she
was sitting here with her worries.

At two, the customary time now, she went over to the pharmacy
where she would watch Jacob work in his laboratory. The owner kept to
his private rooms upstairs at that hour.

The short assistant had the laboratory all to himself for several
hours. Hanna would sit down there with him while Jacob worked in his
white coat, silent for the most part. He had cursed the war that had
brought Lieutenant Heiberg with it. Now he was grateful for the way

225

things had turned out. He knew all about Hanna. She came to him every day to pour out her heart to him.

Now she was sitting in the darkest corner of the lab, sullen and weeping—because she longed for Heiberg, because she felt deserted by him and, the bitterest emotion of all, rejected. The whole affair, lasting for months, had only been a wartime adventure for Heiberg—but not for her; no, no, and no again, not for her—and she laid claim to him, demanded him.

She sat there crying, demanding him to come back or—at least to write.

Calm, apparently indifferent, Jacob stood in front of the large glass retort, watching the flame and the liquid slowly being distilled drop by drop into the smaller retort. He glanced at the thermometer. The temperature was constant. He could not leave the apparatus at the moment and talk to her. But he knew everything. These tears were the confirmation of his own happiness. He dreaded the day when she would enter with a radiant face—the one he had known in the long months of his humiliation—to embrace him wildly, thank him and say, "He's answered my letter."

The answer did not come. He knew why. That single hour on the morning of November 11th on the road to Broglieplatz in Strasbourg had told him everything. This silent, shaking officer dressed in civilian clothes was a beautiful child, a boy, who had let himself fall in love; but even as they rode along, the thoughts of the cold, immature man were somewhere else entirely, leaving his happiness behind in the small town. He was only thinking about how to save his own hide. He thought only of himself. When Hanna's hands could no longer hold his he would no longer remember her.

Jacob worked with his apparatus, gloomy, blissfully happy, worried, his eyes always on the tall thermometer in the cork of the large retort. He lowered the flame on the Bunsen burner, following the laboratory rule: "It can do no more than boil."

And because the god of love could find nothing to do out in the cold of November, beneath the trees or on the street or out in the hop fields, he found his sport on the ground floor of the pharmacy. He let Hanna weep for a distant love—in the presence of one that was very near.

The present is powerful, and Jacob counted on that. The distant love was handsome, but not present.

When Hanna had dried her tears, she finished with her customary ritual. She took her mirror from her purse, powdered her nose and sat quietly looking at herself for a bit.

Then she walked over to Jacob, with whom she had exchanged hardly a word, came up next to him and laid her arm around him, her head on his left shoulder—the picture of someone seeking refuge. To pat her head he had to make a very awkward gesture with his left arm. At the same time he wrenched his own head around so as to cast a touching glance at her unbound and fragrant hair and in order to let his hand meander along her neck, making him shudder with an ardor that was half criminal.

She permitted him then to turn cautiously to her, while her head found its way into his left hand. Then, breast to breast, she raised her head at last and with moist eyes begged his pardon for disturbing him at his work. He asked her how she felt.

That was the question about her condition, about her pregnancy.

At that she became tender and intense and thanked him.

She had come to him only once, by the way, to ask him to give her "something" for her condition. For several weeks now, especially after the first hint of things two weeks ago, a strange wave of sympathy and rapture had risen up in him. She had perceived it with amazement. She had been prepared for him to be frightened off and had rehearsed a dozen times the scene of desperation she would then have to play in order to wangle that "something" out of him. Instead there had been this reaction, the decision that had come like a shot—to have the baby, to accept it as his own and marry her. The peculiar thing that had happened, something beyond her comprehension, was that as soon as she had told him, he had regarded the baby as his own, taken control of it for her. Not one more word was said regarding the incontrovertible fact that it was Heiberg's. She had departed from the experience in a state of bewilderment, but came again often to visit Jacob in the pharmacy, to let him embrace her and ask about the baby, in order to convince herself.

He's just being sly, he's pretending—she mulled it over in her mind while they embraced in front of the cooling retort—can you imagine a man treating his rival that way? But it must be so. I don't understand men. Maybe for him this is his one great love.

With this very real feeling, that she was Jacob's one great love, the object of such unusual, even miraculous behavior, she left the pharmacy at peace with herself.

As she returned home today, she came to the point of making a decision. She wanted her parents to invite Jacob over, her former fiancé.

She thought happily of what eyes her parents would make, to see me come back again with him. And then when the baby comes two or three months too early, I'll say it's his, Jacob's. They never would have dreamed of that. If only I don't get too big beforehand. In that case I'll go somewhere. But where, all alone?

227

The Author Has Second Thoughts Once Again

A great many forms and colors lie dormant in every human being, ready to be awakened at the appropriate moment.

Many people only come to know themselves in one or two ways, in one or two forms. They curse themselves for their own relentless stupidity at being only one single person. They strut about before others, proud of their straightforward, firmly grounded personalities, while ceaselessly, desperately biting down on the chewing gum of their pride.

Others are willing to accept the pain of change and inconstancy. They know that they are not as strong and mighty as those admired personalities, but they roll on through life, broad and colorful as a meadow, as a luxurious tapestry on which new and surprising scenes constantly flash into view.

No one would guess that these remarks are meant to introduce the account of an elderly general, the stiff senior officer of the garrison in our little Alsatian town.

The town has presented us with many gifts—the voluptuous Hilda, the pensive, metaphysical Becker, the melancholy young Lieutenant Maus. We met Lieutenant von Heiberg there, and a major whom the changing times have left unaffected.

And now there appears this stiff-legged senior officer of the garrison, a general formerly adorned with medals. One asks in astonishment: How can this be, why this pillaging of Alsatian towns? Is Berlin underpopulated?

No.

But why, then, prefer Berlin just because it is heavily populated?

We found ourselves in that small Alsatian town purely by accident. There we discovered a few people who, so it appeared to us, were worth saying a few words about. We followed them to Strasbourg. We will travel with others to Paris. We observe that their lives are much the same as other people's.

We will sit with them in their parlors, drink aperitifs with them in cafés and bars. We will try to hold our peace while they do battle with their consciences and ultimately, whether we want to or not, we will be swept along in their wrestlings with Satan, in their strivings after God.

It is all the same whether in trying to reassure ourselves we use the mirror of a large city or a small town.

A General among Movie Extras

Popping up before us here in Berlin, then, is this general, the senior officer from the garrison in that small Alsatian town. And where do we meet him? In Grunewald near Berlin, but not in one of the villas there, nor in the midst of a conspiracy, but—in a film studio where exterior shots are being made.

The mishap that had struck the German army was not a unique event in Europe. Lightning had struck previously in Russia. And there a real revolution had developed following the military defeat, causing hundreds of thousands of Russians to leave their country, voluntarily and involuntarily. Masses of them poured out to the East, West and South. They flooded Europe. Their mournful flight bore them to Constantinople, Vienna, Berlin, Paris, London.

But the battle went on in Russia. The revolutionary end of the war gave birth to new wars. The revolution had lurched forward in two thrusts, in July and in October of 1917. Disturbances then flared up in all parts of the giant nation. One conspiracy after another, one new front after another was formed to counter the revolutionary state just beginning to gain a foothold. Foreign powers intervened, the revolution had to defend itself with sixteen armies in victory, defeat, attack and retreat. The refugees brought grisly accounts with them to the West. Their tales excited people's imaginations.

These were exploited on the one hand by politicians—for their own purposes; on the other by film producers. Because horror stories are much sought after and pay well.

Our general had returned from the war, which, because of his age, he had directed from behind the lines. He was stranded high and dry.

There was no military use for him anymore; he could no longer wear his beloved uniform. He was alone in his hometown of Küstrin. He was obsessed by thoughts of death. There in his fortress he received a visitor from Berlin, his considerably more lively major, who was constantly on the look-out for helpers. The major was troubled by the old man's desolate state. So he asked his former boss to come to Berlin, there at least he could wear his uniform in private and serve some useful purpose. The presence of a dependable person of high rank was important for the major's office. The old man did not turn him down.

He tried sitting in the office that the major showed him on Fasanenstrasse. And he did not like it. He didn't want to play along anymore. The war had been lost, there was no imperial house anymore. There was no reason for him to be a part of the semipolitical, semimilitary "botch," as he termed it, of these people here.

"I'd rather be a wine salesman and go door to door with my calling card."

"As you please," the major replied coldly.

One day someone came into the office, a former captain, who in the course of conversation admitted to the old man that he was planning to go into business for himself—making patriotic calendars for the rural population. When the old man failed to show any interest—because he had had it with politics—the captain began to tell about the food shortage, and suggested that together (since if they pooled their money they were sure to have sufficient capital) they produce a new brand of marmalade. There was space available in a deserted factory that had once been used for making gas masks. He already had the patent for his special marmalade, that is his wife did. So far she had been unable to do much with it for want of capital and because of wartime regulations. But now one could get one's hands on the imported raw materials for such fancy marmalade. It was possible now to arrange for the necessary import licenses.

At the invitation of the erstwhile captain, the general made a tour with him of the rooms in the erstwhile gas mask factory. They were located in the southern part of Berlin, in a pitch-dark X-shaped building, but they were spacious and wired for electricity. The captain worked on him all that day, then set him down to eat at his home where his wife, too, displayed her enthusiasm for the project, one where they could "finally do something that made some sense." She was a spry, agile woman and made a favorable impression on the old senior officer, as did the captain by the way, who reminded him of himself as a young man.

"All right, then, man the guns!" he said finally, and signed the contract.

After he had invested about ten thousand marks in this fruitful (it was after all marmalade) project, he continued to sit in the major's office, still with nothing to do, pondering how he should occupy his time there. This playing at soldier with neither a kaiser nor fatherland was really nonsense.

One day a first lieutenant dropped in. And as the general proceeded to put to him the questions needed for the files, he learned that this man also had a job on the side, as a walk-on in films and on the stage. The first lieutenant wanted, above all else, to have a military job—what a curious world this is!—and was willing to take one wherever it offered itself.

"What?" the general asked crossly, because he absolutely disliked military urges of this sort. "What is the sense of that?"

The first lieutenant fell into amazed silence, since the general's job was to encourage such things. The old man wanted now to know what sort of work it was he had done in the theater, he had been an extra, was that it?

"Yes," replied the man. "They were all just temporary jobs. Part-time things, just so I wasn't standing around on the street. And then the film work, where you have to sit around for hours unless you happen to be needed. The pay isn't bad."

"I see," the old man growled. He wanted to argue with the man, but the idea did intrigue him. And he began to draw the applicant out, trying to find out what he knew and making his own personal notes.

And what he did that same afternoon was something we would not have expected of this retired, though spritely general and senior officer of marmalade fame. He boarded a tram and set out to visit the film studios. He doggedly asked his way about until he finally ended up—in a troop of soldiers, amid hostile forces, the Russian army. Since he had also served on the eastern front, he knew how such an army should look and was dumbfounded to find real soldiers here, officers too, high-ranking ones. They were lounging about in a large hall, from which a corridor led to a restaurant.

In the restaurant there were still more of them, sitting with glasses of tea at ordinary wooden tables. Beside them were wonderfully, splendidly dressed women, all Russians, some of them dazzlingly beautiful. There were both younger and older officers, many of them beribboned.

Whan an elderly officer, apparently suffering from a wound, came down the corridor on a cane, our general, enchanted by all this, raised his hat to him and spoke to him, giving a curt military bow.

The Russian saluted. He understood him, answering in broken German. He gave his name. He was truly a czarist colonel, a nobleman.

They sat down. The general had him explain what went on here. The Russian described it all in a melancholy fashion and stared at him. With a thin smile he inquired whether the German gentleman might also like to join them. The old man demurred at once. This fellow was a defeated man like himself, but at least things had not come to such a pass that one had to flee for one's life.

The Russian told him that it was impossible for German officers to join up here anyway, since it was authenticity they were after. And how were things going for German officers? He had heard that many of them had reported to work as walk-ons in other films. He went on smiling his melancholy smile and was very polite.

The old man replied (he did not wish to speak with this man about Germany's affairs), "If German officers have come here for work, they have to be reservists, civilians who have donned their uniforms again."

"Oh, no," the Russian said, "there are active officers too. Things are gradually getting to be for them like they were for us. We have all been through a great deal already, everyone you see here. I didn't get this knee wound in the war on the Austrian front, but in Petersburg. Nothing helped, and so here we are now and take whatever is offered us." He pointed out into the great hall and to a few neighboring tables. "Look at that, sir. Several of the ladies are wearing truly luxurious gowns—their own, though they no longer belong to them. They have borrowed them from the shops. Many of the diamonds are genuine. The gentlemen, myself included, are wearing their old uniforms. And sitting here in our uniforms, in full dress, you see is very bitter. Very few of us enjoy it. Those that do think they are showing the whole world the beauty and majesty of Russia as it flourished in the past; they think this is the way to make propaganda for the real Russia. Maybe so. I find it depressing to sit here like this. Like in some menagerie. Making a show of one's misery. Have you ever seen a film being shot before?"

The old man replied he hadn't.

"Don't miss it. You can go right on in if you like. Only don't smoke, because everything is built of very flimsy materials. There are a lot of people there whom I don't know. You can go to where they're shooting another film if you like. But it's better inside than out here. You stand in your spot, smile, smile wrong, raise your arm, salute with your sword, move in closer to the camera. The arc lamps above you are very bright and you sweat. It's all foolish play-acting, but nevertheless, you have work and you do it. You earn some money and can pay the rent and have something for your family to eat for a few days."

"You have no pension? No fortune of your own?"

"No," the colonel replied smiling, "neither pension nor fortune. — Ah, what misery it is to sit here and wait for them to begin shooting, it takes forever—they repeat it ten times at least—and all the while we're looking at ourselves in our uniforms. But one must persevere. One must keep up one's strength for the day of revenge.

At least things aren't that bad for us, the general thought. I have made a good investment with my money.

They went on talking over tea.

The colonel asked, "I actually still do not know—and I hope I'm not being indiscreet—what it was brought you out here. Are things already so bad for the Germans that their officers have to sell themselves to film producers?"

And when the general raised his hands in horror at the notion, the Russian gave him a confidential glance. "Don't gloat too soon. One should not make prophecies. The mob can be terrible when it strikes. It all depends on what leaders it finds. One ought to join forces."

"Who ought?"

"Why, you and we. We are both in somewhat the same situation. Just wait until your army runs off. Then you'll be in the same fix we are."

The general could hardly catch his breath. "You mean, here too— that bad? That they'll go through the houses?"

"And plunder and murder as they please. We talk about it often. How long it will be before things have come to that here. Our friends from the other side, the Radeks and the like, are already working here and no one is stopping them."

The general stared at him helplessly.

"Yes," the Russian said, and nodded, "we've been through it. We're ahead of you by several furlongs. If you have any sense you'll listen to us."

"What should we do?"

"Consider everyone who comes from Russia as part of an auxiliary force, as your most dependable source of aid, general. It is not a crime that we are sitting here, hundreds of capable men, ready for battle, and having to play-act for some financier, a mere film maker? To surrender our women?"

After a pause he added: "We need to join forces. You can help us, just as we can help you."

This was politics again. The old man shook himself and stood up, as did the colonel. The Russian colonel: "I've been boring you, haven't I? May I present my daughter to you?"

A delicate young woman, all in black with artificial flowers in her hand, had approached the table. The general bowed. Together they walked in the direction of the hall.

The daughter was very gay despite her mourning. The old man was so pleased with her that he accepted the colonel's invitation to join him the following evening for a glass of beer, a game of cards and a cigar. The old man was a born ladies' man, but he was out of practice from the dull days of garrison duty. Perhaps he might find some delightful company at the home of this Russian colonel who talked on and on in the same boring way as the major. This film business pleased him no end, he would have loved to change places with the Russian then and there.

At the recruiting office on Fasanenstrasse they waited for the droll old man for several days. But he had broken his leash.

High Strategy and Low Tactics

Someone comes up with the idea of having Hindenburg write a letter. A general in Kassel would like to make a threat, too, but wants to sleep on the idea first.

Tactics at Wilhelmshöhe

Quartermaster General Groener, successor to the ever so decisive Ludendorff, sat in his office, still talking with Major von Harbou, and he could not believe it. The major must have been impolitic in his approach. Ebert had rebuffed him.

Groener stuffed his hands into the pockets of his jacket and stretched out his legs. "So you and Schleicher have your triumph. The result being that we have to proceed without him."

Harbou: "We need have no worries in military terms, our plans had presumed that much."

Groener was silent. "Have you spoken with Schleicher?"

"No, Your Excellency."

"What a shame. — I'm not convinced that our plans have provided for every contingency. We still have had no experience in street fighting, thank God."

Harbou guessed that there would be no serious resistance.

Groener: "I'm not convinced of that."

Some gentlemen entered bearing portfolios concerning the eastern front. Harbou was dismissed until later. He climbed up to the second floor, to Schleicher's office, who with a glance at Harbou's face as he extended his hand said, "Ebert refused."

"Correct," said Harbou, taking a seat.

Schleicher: "Good. That means we have to hurry. Groener, of course, concedes nothing."

"He says our plans are inadequate for street fighting."

"Do we have information about the forces on the other side?"

"Nothing new."

234

"Why are our plans suddenly so inadequate then?"

"That's his opinion."

Schleicher stood up. "He still doesn't want it. That's hard, very hard. How did he take leave of you?"

"The portfolios from the East came in, the conversation was interrupted."

"Did he make a definite appointment with you?"

"No."

At that Schleicher sat back down again and began to consider.

First move: "Ebert can go with the news to the radicals, call out his own party, mobilize. Wrong. He won't dare. We'd blow the whistle on him. That will give him something to think about. That threat can be ignored. — But he could pretend that he had only been playing us along. He has that out. He might go with the radicals after all."

Second move: "We attack as planned, cost what it will. Ebert reveals our 'monarchist conspiracy' and gets the masses to go along with him. The danger arises of our troops being infected by the revolutionary masses. The consequence: we need very dependable troops and a portion of the citizenry that supports us. That means it would be better not to offend Ebert until the moment when we have dependable troops at our disposal."

Third move: "We go along with Ebert and strike our blow together with him. Who is the victor? Can it be our wish to put him in the saddle? Only, of course, if we still have him in our control. Once in the saddle he could replace us with others. The consequence: strike our blow together with him, even if he then appears to be the victor, but let him know that in reality he is not. How? By the force of our troops. We must therefore prevent him from disbanding them. How? We can prove ourselves indispensible on the eastern front and in any disturbances."

Important orders: "The revolutionaries should be allowed to compromise themselves by their excesses, incompetence. We must not be afraid to amplify their excesses, to provoke them, in order to play the role of keepers of public order. There is a very good chance that these orders would prove effective. To that extent, time is on our side. At the moment, however, it's against us. Ebert can gather his forces and disband our troops."

Conclusion: "Quickly assemble reliable troops, underscore the danger inherent in disturbances, possibly provoke some, put Ebert under pressure, first butter him up and then quickly let the blow fall."

Groener did not receive the gentlemen that morning, proof enough that he was still very much preoccupied with the affair, letting them first cool their heels. After lunch, von Harbou asked about the old countess. She had made a great impression on him, too, one that had grown even stronger in the meantime. Von Schleicher asked whether he would like to see her again. Von Harbou replied it would be a pleasure if he were sure they would not be annoying her.

They took tea with her; the quartermaster general had asked to see them at six. Harbou watched with amazement and respect as the countess was led in again on the arm of her companion. A slender, black-cloaked stem on which drooped a large white blossom. The flower lifted again at the tea table. The fullness of her friendly, indeed benevolent, gaze was directed at Harbou. They smiled at one another engagingly.

Harbou was in Kassel again. And had he had that look around? What was new in Berlin? A peculiar phenomenon—a political officer. It made her feel quite old. That would have been impossible under Bismarck.

Harbou: At the moment there was no Bismarck in sight.

"Not for a long, long time now," she said, waving a mournful hand. "Since I saw the Kaiser, I've known. The Kaiser has the failing that he does not allow others to rise. He lacks the princely confidence that was second nature to the old Wilhelm. The English practice of allowing ministers to have their way and even permitting Parliament to determine who the ministers are is much more proper, more royal than the German practice. A mistress of a palace does not concern herself with everything in the household. Even in my suite here, I have a companion with whom I converse merely to find out who it is I'm dealing with. I'm told, by the way, that in the last months of the Reich they wanted to establish another constitution. Why so late? Why should they let the entire blame for a lost war fall on the crown? Why did the chief officers of the high command inform the Kaiser so late? They should not have changed the form of government at the very last moment."

Schleicher: "It was only since August that we saw the situation as serious, very serious. The people on the left who could have stepped in were completely unsure of themselves."

"And why did you give them the reins now?"

Schleicher raised his hand. "That's not what we've done. We've let it happen."

"Who forces you to?"

"Circumstances. The Allies would either refuse to negotiate with anyone else or set even more difficult conditions."

"The 'anyone else' would be the Kaiser and his family?"

"Or us."

The flower dropped to her breast. "We are a defeated, badly led nation."

Schleicher responded after a long pause. "If I might return to a topic you touched upon, countess—Bismarck and the old Kaiser Wilhelm. The imperial throne has been left unguarded since then. The period immediately behind us is much like that in Prussia after Frederick

236

the Great. After him came peace, indolence, a resting on laurels, uncontrolled pride and finally Napoleon I and the battles of Jena and Austerlitz. But that was followed by a period of arming in secret, a home militia, volunteer corps, Lützov, Yorck and Field Marshal Blücher."

The old woman beamed. "I'll not live to see it. But it sounds good."

Harbou: "And to answer your gentle reproach—it is for that reason that we must mix ourselves in politics. General Yorck's shadow precedes him."

She nodded happily. "If only someone were chosen to cast one for us. I am glad you think that way. What comfort in these days. — What is read to me from the newspapers is something quite different."

Schleicher made a roguish face. "We are reluctant to let our work be seen in public. We are happy the newspapers write as they do. What would happen if they truly informed people. Traitors are hanged. But you will nevertheless find one true bit of news in yours these days. Our front-line troops are moving into Berlin and will begin their mopping up operations."

The countess's small, delicate face took on a fantastic beauty. "I'm hearing only good things today. I see that the old officers' corps will form the backbone of the nation. The Kaiser and his Reich."

Von Harbou: "While I sit here and the only news I bring back from Berlin is considerably less comforting."

The countess: "How easily you are dispirited. Do not let yourself be overwhelmed by some small detail or other. Do what your heart tells you to do in these painful weeks: preserve the Reich and the imperial aegis over the Reich. Do not let yourself be troubled by people from the broad masses. They know nothing. The common folk are a rough-and-tumble sort, they must always be reigned in; they have a powerful instinct for license, for turmoil. Believe me, they are afraid of themselves. You must protect them. Otherwise they fall into the hands of the most dissolute adventurers, and these average people," the countess giggled, "—I'll use an expression of my housekeeper's in Berlin—will get their drawers wet."

As Schleicher and Harbou walked back to Wilhelmshöhe, Harbou suggested, "It's remarkable. We are actually in a very vexing situation, but from up there things looked splendid."

Schleicher: "If someone were to see us marching along like this, he would indeed think we were doing fine. You can't deny that."

Groener received them in a good mood. They were seized with apprehension. He told them he had made a report to old Hindenburg. Hindenburg had just been reading the weekly review provided by Count Westarp, and he had handed him the paper and asked him to read it. It appeared that the field marshal concurred, for the most part, with the views of Count Westarp.

"Here, read it yourselves, gentlemen."

While he smoked his pipe and busied himself with documents, Schleicher and Harbou withdrew to the window, to a small reading desk with a lamp, and read together.

Count Westarp wrote:

"No words can suffice to express the feeling of pain, of paralyzing horror which overwhelms us at the total collapse, both at home and abroad, of our German fatherland and of all those things which made it precious and dear to us, which gave us a sense of complete confidence. But this is not merely a bad dream that now torments us. We are confronted with a bitter reality, further dreadful dangers are imminent. We must attempt to take full account for ourselves of what the present situation is and what we must do about it."

(Amazing, to be given something like this to read. Like something from another world.)

"The new government lacks any legal basis whatever. Only because it possesses weapons delivered to it by a few troops and because the state and the social order that preceded it have offered no resistance is it able to rule."

(Schleicher pointed to this sentence with his finger and whispered, "Excellent. I'll make a note of that." And he scribbled it down hastily in his notebook.)

"By legal right the monarchy still exists today in Prussia and in the German Reich. If the king is truly no longer king and kaiser because he has abdicated, then his eldest son is, with Prince Eitel Friedrich as regent. Scheidemann's declaration from the steps of the Reichstag that Germany is henceforth a republic does not change that legal status in the least. Just as the rights of the Bundesrat and the Reichstag have not ceased to exist because they have been passed over in silence."

(Absolutely divine, the old blockhead.)

"The new government has neither the support of the people nor even of a majority of the people. Two delegations to the Reichstag, representing one third of the voters in 1912," (Harbou: "I just read it, I swear, a third of the voters." Schleicher patted him appreciatively on the back.) "have assumed the reins of government in Berlin with the aid of irregular groups of sailors, soldiers and workers. The workers' and soldiers' councils, on which this government is based and which they want to consolidate into a single corporate body based in Berlin, is, to the extent that it was formed on the basis of an organized election, representative of nothing more than the working men and women of the industries in major cities and of some individual troops in the military. This government is not a popular government, but one ruled by a single class."

(True enough, but how does that help us?)

"The new government bases its right to political existence on the

238

fact that it defends law and order, individuals and their property. The two social democratic parties, having united to form the new government of Ebert and Haase, who rule together as consuls, have first used their power not to check the Right, but the Spartacists under Liebknecht and to prevent eventual further disorders. They have succeeded thus far. The army, which in disordered retreat is flooding the land . . ."

(The two officers looked at one another. Schleicher raised his finger. "Here is where he starts to be reasonable. The sentence is priceless. No contradiction, please.")

"The imminent breakdown of transportation and food supply gives reason to fear not only that this government will be placed in great danger, but also all civil order, all life and property. That is the reason why the whole of bourgeois society has come to the aid of this government.

"Hindenburg himself has acted as a model for his officers in this regard in order to bring the army under his command back home in an ordered fashion. The civil service, though much scorned, and deprived of all influence, has shown a prodigious measure of self-control by doing the work of these upstart gentlemen, without which they would not be in a position to wield the tools of government."

(Schleicher: "Read that sentence once again. What do you say? He really gives it to them. But he's quite right. The bureaucracy must be better mobilized. They need to be organized. We must proceed on two tracks at once—army and civil service." Harbou: "All sorts of things are happening there already. Spend more time in Berlin. The civil service bears it all patiently and is flexible. A prodigious measure of self-control. Well, they know only too well why and for what purpose.")

"The assistance of the bourgeoisie, however, places a heavy responsibility on the men who govern, a serious duty, which we must demand be fulfilled. Should in fact a disciplined transition to tolerably ordered conditions succeed, such a development brings with it the great danger at some more distant time in the future—and no one dare close his eyes to this—that the tyranny of the Social Democrats may be permanently consolidated in the institutions they will have created in the meantime and with the approval of the populace. One must see clearly what that would mean."

(*"Voilà!"* said Schleicher, "our own thoughts on the matter. That is the sore point. The man has grasped it.")

They read the article to its end, where it finally veered off into the international political situation; they then stood up again. The general looked over to them at once and asked them to return and take a seat.

Groener: "So you've finished it. I would merely like to call your attention to a small—error on the part of Count Westarp. He speaks at one point about the steps of the Reichstag from which the deputy Herr Scheidemann, now People's Deputy Scheidemann, is said to have proclaimed the republic. — This has now grown into such a legend that one reads it constantly. In fact there was no flight of stairs. Someone had told Scheidemann in the Reichstag that Liebknecht was about to proclaim the republic from the balcony of the Berlin palace. So Scheidemann said, 'We can do whatever they can.' Then he went to the window. The Reichstag was surrounded by people, primarily industrial workers, and Scheidemann was afraid his people might desert to the Spartacists. So he climbed up onto the window sill, the Danish deputy Hans Peter Hansen from Flensburg holding him from behind by the hem of his jacket so that he couldn't fall out. And then Scheidemann proclaimed the republic. Fantastic scene, isn't it, with the jacket hem and a Dane helping out. Ebert in the meantime was sitting in a restaurant down below. And when they told him about this bit of derring-do, he banged his fist on the table. There you have Ebert in a nutshell, the story is true. Scheidemann wanted to make him see how necessary it had been, but Ebert will have none of his masquerade. He spits right back, 'You have no right to proclaim a republic. What Germany becomes, a republic or whatever, is to be decided by a constituent assembly.' And then, as Seyfritz tells it, a southern German labor union man who was present, Ebert roars, 'You have made a perjuror of me.' "

Schleicher: "Is that reliable? It does put Ebert in a good light, I must say."

"Absolutely reliable. But that's only incidental. I think you have noted what a courageous article that is. If we had a soviet republic with a Lenin at the top, it would not have been possible. The Field Marshal General naturally values those sections in which it is explained that the new government has no legal basis whatever. What have you to say to it?"

Von Harbou: "The fact that the article is possible at all, together with your interesting report of the proclamation of the republic and Ebert's reaction, can only be regarded with some satisfaction. One can, then, expect Ebert to yield in the end."

Content, Groener let his right hand fall to the desk. "At last a clear view of the matter. We have to understand the man. He is in great difficulty. We are too, I grant. It is all a matter of time and nothing must be done too hastily. That is what he castigates us for, what he rejects. Though I admit he could be somewhat more forceful."

Schleicher: "When things have progressed that far, certain decisions should be taken out of his hands. We are entering Berlin. He will acquiesce if we spare his people."

Groener: "That is my opinion as well, to be honest. He must be helped to get through these difficult times. I intend to appeal to his feelings of patriotism and by that I mean in a form he cannot resist. Since we cannot get mixed up with these parliamentarians, I would like to ask the Field Marshal General to write him a letter describing the situation. A general appeal, with details left for a later conversation."

Schleicher: "A *coup de theatre.*"

Groener: "What do you think of the idea?"

Schleicher: "I'm agreed, so long as the letter confines itself to absolute generalities and tries to strengthen Ebert's sense of patriotic duty. For the rest, one ought to leave Hindenburg out of the ongoing debate."

Groener sighed and gave a melancholy smile. "My dear friend, that will not be possible forever. I hardly want to approach Hindenburg with this, not after he has just given me the Westarp article, which as he puts it, is very near to his heart, with its assertion that the present government lacks all legal basis whatever. Without any further comment, he also directed my attention to the paragraph that begins, 'Should in fact a transition succeed, such a development brings with it the great danger at some more distant time in the future—and no one dare close his eyes to this—that the tyranny of the Social Democrats may be permanently consolidated in the institutions they will have created in the meantime and with the approval of the populace.' Hindenburg sees that as the great question mark to be set behind our efforts. And," he shrugged, "not without justification."

Schleicher, very calmly and gravely: "We must take care then that the development that Westarp forewarns us of does not happen. As far as I'm concerned—if I may be allowed a personal remark—I have taken note of our external military defeat, and I accept it as temporary, as a passing phase. But under no circumstances will I accept the internal, political defeat. A republic is out of the question for Germany. Monarchy is the historical form of government for Germans. It need not be exactly the monarchy of the prewar period. But under no circumstances shall we allow an unnatural, Social Democratic tyranny to establish itself."

Groener: "And to prevent that?"

"The mopping up of Berlin."

Groener, with a light gesture of his hand: "One is always pleased by such rosy colors. So then, Hindenburg's letter to strengthen Ebert's resolve. I have to deal with him every single evening. I think Hindenburg's appeal will have its effect."

Schleicher and Harbou urged all possible speed. The danger was great that Ebert, vexed at Harbou's announcement, would initiate negotiations with the radicals.

It was a favorable omen that General Maerker was announced, having come to visit the high command for a personal exchange of views. This proven and decisive officer, onetime commander of the 214th Infantry Division, explained that he wanted to recruit a corps of volunteers in Westphalia made up of reliable officers and enlisted men and to present a special plan containing the principles on which this volunteer corps was based. They gladly listened to him, it was encouraging news. As soon as Schleicher and Harbou had closed the door behind them, Groener began sketching out the first sentences of Hindenburg's letter.

An Ideal in the Uniform of a General

Late in the afternoon, the broad-shouldered officer from Württemberg, General Groener, climbed the stairs to the second floor of Wilhelmshöhe Castle; cap in hand, he was followed by an adjutant. While still in the corridor he took the closed portfolio from the adjutant, who clicked his heels and at once turned and walked away.

In the room, sitting up very straight, was an old, massive Prussian officer with heavy bags under his eyes. His white moustache swept out in broad curves, his short white hair stood on end. In a deep, rough voice he asked the man from Württemberg to come in and have a seat at one side of the desk.

The old Prussian officer, now seventy, had entered the military academy at Wahlstatt at age twelve, and then had attended the central military school on Neue Friedrichstrasse in Berlin. As he declared later as field marshal, "Becoming a soldier was not a matter of choice for me, it was a matter of course."

In 1863 his father had retired with the rank of major and moved to his estate in Neudeck. He had served with the 1st Posen Infantry Regiment Nr. 18. At the time he retired, the mother of the lad who would later become a general, herself the daughter of an army doctor named Schwickart, was also still alive.

Now a stiff old man with the fixed features of age, he had at nineteen—the year was 1866—joined the 3rd Foot Guard Regiment in Danzig and marched smartly off that same year with the 2nd Prussian Army to Bohemia, where on July 3rd, the day of the battle of Königgrätz, he had advanced with the 1st Guard Division of Horenowes just at the moment that an Austrian battery to the west of Nedelischt released a volley of grape at the Prussians. The young lieutenant was hit. One piece of grapeshot penetrated the eagle of his helmet and threw him unconscious to the ground. But he was able to pull himself together and find his grenadiers, and together with them he took five cannons of the Austrian battery.

For this, as the troops marched into Berlin on September 20, 1866, he bore the Order of the Red Eagle, 4th Class, with swords.

The War of 1870. He marched off in July. In the deadly frontal attack near St. Privat his regiment lost seventeen officers and 304 men. This time he was spared by the bullets.

He was present when Emperor Napoleon III's army was encircled at Sedan and was his regiment's representative at the ceremony in the Hall of Mirrors at Versailles when King Wilhelm I was proclaimed the German Kaiser.

Then came the long, long years of peace. He joined the War Academy in Berlin. His contemporaries were Karl von Bülow, Hermann von Eichhorn, Friedrich von Bernhardi, all later generals themselves. The dashing young lieutenant from Könnigrätz became an earnest older man who enjoyed hunting.

He was promoted to captain in 1878, and transferred to the General Staff; advanced to the rank of major, old Moltke was his superior officer and immediately above him was Colonel von Schleiffen. He was instructor for tactics at the War Academy, the author of regulations for field engineers and taught the use of heavy artillery in the field.

Lieutenant colonel, colonel, brigadier general, major general, lieutenant general. He is now fifty-three years old and commander of the 28th Division in Karlsruhe. There are still several steps further up the ladder. Finally, according to regulations, he is retired in 1911.

His king bestows upon him the high Order of the Black Eagle. He remains a part of his 3rd Foot Guard Regiment. His career has come to an end. He retires to Hannover.

Then the old worthies of the military are startled into action by a third war, 1914.

The Russians have invaded East Prussia. The Nyemen Army of General Rennenkamp and the Narev Army of General Samnsonov threaten the nation. The leadership of the German 8th Army proves inadequate, wanting to join battle only after the Weichsel has been crossed.

And so the sixty-seven-year-old retired general Paul von Beneckendorf und von Hindenburg is called from his place of retirement in Hannover.

As chief of staff he is aided by a man who last distinguished himself at Liège. The two of them win the battles at Tannenberg and on the Masur. And that is the end of his entire military career.

He is, without having lifted a hand, removed to a sphere into which not even his imperial master can follow him. What they have done with him, a living man, is normally only done with men lost to the distant past, with the dead: he is turned into an ideal.

He is the paladin of the German nation, the invincible hero on the snow-white steed. He chases his enemies into swamps. The Russians are sprites, frogs, who leap into the water. These Russians, how pitiful, how ridiculous, the way they plunge into the morass with their long cannons.

The former general, now conqueror of Satan, directs the entire German war effort, and the nation feels secure. The fatherland can rest easy. Enemies may come—as many as they like—we stand under Hindenburg's patriarchal care. His army wins many battles. He has a clever aide, General Ludendorff.

And who this former general really is only becomes fully apparent as defeat nears. Because he is there—they can deal with whatever happens. Ludendorff can depart, the Kaiser can abdicate, a terrible armistice can follow—there is no defeat. The newspapers write the word defeat, the enemy rejoices; but Hindenburg lives, and so it cannot be true.

The truth is rather that sinister powers in possession of monstrous resources have allied themselves against this shining hero and the invincible German people, that they have surrounded the nation, seeking to crush it.

But the faithful Eckhardt wakes and watches. And the people keep faith with their faithful hero. They make the sacrifices he demands. The base enemy will be destroyed.

The old soldier had undergone this metamorphosis in silence. Even as Field Marshal General he remains a Prussian country gentleman. As he said farewell, the Kaiser had urged upon him his concern for the army and the nation. The old man knew his duty.

He now sits in Kassel across from the man from Württemberg, Ludendorff's successor, the real commander of the lost war. This man from Württemberg is the high-ranking officer who, in the hour of decision and in the presence of the Kaiser had called the oath of allegiance "only an ideal" that under certain circumstances meant nothing. He was the man who history would say had the abdication of the Kaiser on his conscience.

Groener is cautious in his dealing with the old man; he knows, despite all his cool rationalism, that across the desk from him sits a man who, with those gray features already frozen to granite while he still lives, is more than just his superior officer.

The old marshal hears out the report and asks questions.

Lequis has been chosen to be Commander General for Berlin. He is to mop up the Reich's capital city, free it of the radicals who are tyrannizing the population. People's Deputy Ebert is causing difficulties. Groener suggests, despite the slow pace, that the planned mopping up be done step by step, and if it all possible with Ebert's approval.

That idea is a long way from being agreeable to the old country squire, who loathes the notion of Social Democrats occupying the residence of the legitimate imperial government in Berlin. Groener urges him to write a letter to People's Deputy Ebert. The marshal rumbles at such presumption.

He gazes at Groener's rough draft, reads some of it.

He mutters, "I see it this way: I am to call the man to order."

Groener agrees.

The marshal places the paper under his hand. He wants to sleep on the matter.

244

Book Five

To December 7th

Among German Revolutionaries

A man of good will sits in the chambers of the Executive Council. It occurs to him that it would be child's play to arrest the whole revolutionary government—which possibility terrifies him. The Russian Radek encounters in his friend Karl Liebknecht that peculiar German form of irresolution. Rosa Luxemburg has nothing to say.

Private Imker Sees the Point

Private Imker walked down Prinz-Albrecht Strasse in his ragged field-gray togs to where the so-called Executive Council was meeting. This was a revolutionary body, ranking above the Council of People's Deputies and had managed to get into a fight with the People's Deputies about the extent of its powers.

Imker saw cars standing in front of the building and a great many people going and coming. There was virtually no security. You were simply asked where you were going and were shown the way. Imker was amazed at this.

After a while he entered the spacious building that had once housed the Prussian Landtag; surrounded by courts and gardens, it extended from Prinz-Albrecht Strasse as far as the noisy Leipziger Strasse. He found himself in endless corridors. Commissions had had their offices in all these rooms and halls, each of them numbered. For once in his life, Imker too found himself at the seat of real power, at one of those places from which orders were issued, orders sending you here or there at will.

Average people like himself wandered up and down over the stone floor and the dirty runners. Many of them seemed like himself just here for a stroll. Some were looking for something, asked questions, carried briefcases. In a larger, hall-like space, a man sat at a desk with a small telephone in front of him. There were slips of paper on the desk. People crowded around him.

Just as Imker took a seat on the bench in the room illuminated by a skylight, two people sitting there edged closer to one another and began whispering. Imker could imagine what great secrets they could have. Why can't they just speak up loud and clear? He was annoyed by the thought that here in this building belonging to the people, where the high and mighty have no more business, there were people who whisper and had secrets. He began to grow angry when they kept on whispering. They had not been called over to the desk by the man with the telephone and apparently had as little business here as he did. Both of them were in civilian clothes.

Beside him was a column, and two men, both in uniform, both smoking, now moved over to it. They had just met accidently at the desk where they greeted one another in loud voices and shook hands. They continued their conversation, a loud one, next to Imker.

They were on the front together, and now they talked about how it was meeting their families again, they told jokes, lowered their voices and giggled. Imker looked up and realized that although the one was not wearing epaulets, his coat was an officer's coat. He needed a shave, had savage little black eyes and an unkempt brown moustache. They went on talking more softly now, but Imker could understand every word. The officer was amused by all the new commissions, agencies and so on, and pointed them out to his comrade.

At this point a solitary gentleman slowly emerged from one of the rooms along one side of the hall, greeted the man with the telephone, and took off down the wide corridor toward Leipziger Strasse; the officer shut up and laid his index finger to his mouth. Then he whispered a well-known name, that of a member of the highest revolutionary council. Imker was perplexed to hear this. He would have taken the man with glasses, a good winter coat and a stiff black hat for a salesman, wholesale groceries perhaps. That was the famous Herr X? The idea depressed him. He no longer concerned himself with the two idiots on the bench who were still whispering away.

The scruffily bearded officer with the savage Turkish eyes turned to his pal and asked him how he liked things here at the Executive Council.

"How do you mean?"

"How do I mean? Why, you saw the fellow with the glasses. So just imagine someone who doesn't think much of all this. He watches the fellow with the glasses walking along peacefully enough, sees him come out into the garden on the Leipziger Strasse side."

"So what?"

"So what?" The officer laughed right in his face, rather insultingly. "Why there you have him in the garden. And the whole Executive Council with him."

"Just take a look around here." He was whispering now. "People walk in and out as they please. I guarantee you that with a small brigade I could arrest the whole Council, clear the building and throw them all in jail." The other man stared at him in amazement.

Imker had stuck his head out now a bit too obviously. The officer noticed that he was being overheard. He turned abruptly on his heels. They quickly wandered off.

The two men were still whispering next to Imker. He was so angry that he slid down toward them, finally catching some of what they said. To his surprise they were arguing over a girl. One of them had a letter in his hand.

Imker had had enough. He stood up to smoke a cigarette beside the column himself. The two of them had stood there. Here you have this entire immense building with all our top people in it, the ones who are supposed to hold onto what the revolution has accomplished, and— what does the famous Herr X with the glasses look like? A little homebody. I don't like him. A silly nincompoop.

Imker marched on angrily. If I get hold of those two I'll floor them both. And suddenly, as he came out into the garden, where so many people were coming and going, as he looked at the broad, formal expanse of the building, he was seized with the horror of it all. He thought of the war, of friends killed, of Minna and the misery here in Berlin— and here sit these commissions and the famous Herr X is a lazy huckster, who you can bet is enjoying a brandy in a restaurant right now. And that officer with the little black eyes is dead right—if you wanted to you could flush out the whole bunch of them like a pack of thieves.

He stood there as if struck by lightning, staring at the building where at the first floor windows people stood calmly chewing on sandwiches still partially wrapped in waxed paper.

It was Wednesday, December 4th, a date that marked a change of thinking for Imker, the discharged soldier.

We're so alone, so—lost and alone, he felt. The whole world has deserted us. These fellows here set up shop, eat, go for a walk—while there are others already lying in ambush to murder us.

He was cool and calm again now, just like in the war, although there was a difference. In the war you let everything come at you; that wouldn't work now, the threat was here.

He went on home. His sister Minna had an easy time of it with him. But he did not join her group of agitators.

Everything was much too simple for there to be any need for long discussions.

How they had all scattered from that little hub of a world that had once centered in a small military hospital in Alsace.

Two soldiers had been shot by Lieutenant Heiberg when they tried to attack his colonel. Revolutionary soldiers had sworn revenge and the lieutenant had had to hide from their rage. His sweetheart, Hanna, had kept him that evening at her place, then brought him to her former fiancé, the druggist's assistant, who drove with him early the next morning to Strasbourg and let him off at Broglieplatz. Now only thin wisps of all that still swirl about.

Hanna longs for Heiberg—but she already is linked arm in arm with the druggist, he has assumed a new place in her life. And there is no trace in Alsace now of the lieutenant, except for the child she carries.

The group of people—the wounded, the doctors, the nurses, the aides—who had made up the military hospital was like a swarm of bees that loses its queen and is dispersed in all directions.

Bottrowski was the name of a German soldier who had first come in contact with the German revolution in Strasbourg. He was much like Imker—solid, independent, skeptical, gregarious. They both loved to act, to settle things. Bottrowski, however, had come back from the war with a tendency to drink too much, and it could make him irascible.

His wife ran a wood and coal cellar on a street in Neukölln, and from time to time she would deal in potatoes and vegetables, too. It was in this cellar, with its two rooms and a kitchen that opened out onto a bright back courtyard, that Bottrowski lived again after the war. Besides his wife, there was also the wife's doddering old father and a young daughter.

On his return he found his child in bad health. There was immediately an argument about it between him and his wife, but the problem was one of food. Bottrowski could see for himself that the other children playing in the courtyard were no healthier.

He made up small loads of wood and coal for delivery and found his old ramshackle wagon out in the shed. The sideboards had been removed. He had a lot of trouble finding new ones; he rode out to a sawmill and a war buddy he knew there helped him get some planks cheap, and for days he sawed and bored and painted. The wheels were a problem too, and the axle needed to be replaced; heavy loads would be hard to manage with that old crate. But he was content.

The worst problem was the old nag. He had always borrowed the horse from a former coachman who later owned a carriage service on a street nearby. But the man had been killed in the war, and his wife and son ran the business now. That the creature was still alive and kicking was in itself astonishing, but she demanded a hefty sum for rental. Bottrowski was forced to comply with her terms; he could understand, too, that the woman demanded something in return for the use of the old nag, the animal was ready for slaughter and each bit of effort brought it just that much closer to its end. Out on the battlefield, Bottrowski's dream had been to buy a horse—he wrote his wife all about it—enlarge the shed in the courtyard with the help of a friend or even alone and build a stall for the horse. Then he could undertake larger deliveries, move people and so on, and she could give up the wood and coal cellar.

Imker was sitting with the couple in Bottrowski's little living room; the two had met in a Neukölln barracks. The man from Neukölln was in a cheerful, patient mood. He gave his wife what for because she was trying to light a fire under him.

The wife: "Max, the wagon. And the horse!"

"Well, it ain't no coach, and no furniture van neither, not by a long shot. But I can still get to market with it for a good while yet. And if that woman would be a little more reasonable, we could take little Micki for a drive on Sundays with it."

When he was alone with Imker, Bottrowski grew more quiet and serious.

They sat in silence, smoking.

Bottrowski was the first to speak. "I was always a Social Democrat. I still am today. Whatever happens has to happen in an orderly way. You start smashing things and everything will be ruined."

Imker: "You know me, Bottrowski. I'm not saying let's start smashing things. But when nothing at all happens, what then?"

The man from Neukölln was silent, he smoked. Then he said, "You're right there. That's the hell of it."

They were of the same opinion, then, but it didn't help matters. They heard footsteps on the stairs that led out to the courtyard. Frau Bottrowski, who was in the kitchen doing the wash, led a slim man, a gentleman no less, into the room.

He wore a nickel pince-nez, had long gray hair combed straight back; his collar was white, his cuffs too. This was the chairman of a Berlin Party district who was visiting Bottrowski to gather information about certain events going on in the uneasy section of Neukölln.

Noticing the gloomy mood of both Bottrowski and Imker, the latter apparently a discharged solider and therefore worth influencing, he went off into lengthy theoretical observations.

Theory was important, he said, especially now that they hoped to realize things they had only planned before. But that meant, of course, that you needed to know exactly what had been planned and what you intended the revolution to be and what you wanted to do and how you ought to go about it.

And he explained, "The main thing is no sabotage. Disunity will endanger everything. And the ones who'll suffer will be the proletariat. And you can imagine who is going to profit. That's something particularly the people of Neukölln need to hear."

Imker of course then replied with his question about what ought to be happening. The clever guest seemed quite surprised and wanted to know how long Imker had been in Berlin, and if he didn't read the papers, *Vorwärts* in particular, whether he didn't know that there was no longer a Kaiser at the top but people's deputies instead, Ebert and Scheidemann, reliable men who came from the working-class themselves?

Everything had already begun, things were underway. Elections for the constituent assembly were being prepared, the date would be announced soon. Germany would become a democratic republic. But there'd be none of your Russian-style dictatorship.

"Not if I can help it," said Bottrowski backing him up. "I'd like to see someone try and give me orders. I'll do my griping all on my own."

"That's democracy."

Imker was still unsure. "And what then? When the troops are back from the front line, what happens then? They can skin us alive. What are you doing to prevent that?"

And he told what he had heard in the old Landtag building, where the Executive Council was now.

The visitor clapped his hands together in amazement at Imker's gullibility. "What all don't people say? You're not going to fall for a lot of empty phrases, are you?"

Imker was not about to be put off that easily. "Comrade, I know the ropes. I know a little something about that sort of thing. If I check out a building, and at the front and rear are two guards with no machine guns and not another soul in the place is armed and you can go through any door you want anywhere in the building, then you can take whoever you want out of there, easy as pie."

"But no one is going to," shouted the visitor, beside himself with laughter. "It's all in your imagination. That's what Liebknecht and his *Rote Fahne* use to terrify people with. Don't fall for that stuff. And besides," he grew more serious, "give your fellow citizens the benefit of the doubt. Because that would mean we can't do anything. That we're not in business, that our own people are sloppy and lazy."

Bottrowski suggested that you had to be ready for most anything. Something could happen after all.

The visitor stroked his hand over his long hair; he was annoyed. "Liebknecht's influence is much too strong here in Neukölln, you let him have his way, you let him bully you."

He ended up raging at the wild socialists, especially here in Neukölln. He again grew very learned and would allow no contradictions. He talked about Marx and *Das Kapital* and what all had been clearly proven—they should not act precipitously. Socialism was absolutely assured, the workers had the state in their hands and everything was preceeding "scientifically."

"Greenhorns can spoil everything. They want the socialist state by tomorrow morning. Fortunately, we have Social Democrats, disciplined workers, union members. The development in the direction of socialism is a scientific necessity. Basically all that is necessary is not to disturb that development. Our worst enemy is called 'putschism'—from whatever quarter the putsch may come. The entire matter is scientific, scientific."

He departed, leaving two men behind in a sullen mood. They sat

there for a long time, till midnight, smoking, depressed, speaking little—till Frau Bottrowski roused them and pointed out how late it was.

So Imker got up and Bottrowski accompanied him out to the courtyard, where they had another admiring look at the little shed that would
one day be a stall.

They shook hands firmly, dismissing for good the incredible hogwash of the district nabob. Imker reminded his friend in a whisper of the
mass meetings this coming Friday, the 6th.

Bottrowski replied, "See you there."

It was a biting, clear, frosty night.

Radek and Liebknecht

Several brawny men were patrolling the front of the building near
the Anhalter Station; some others stood in the entryway.

This was where the *Rote Fahne* was printed, the Spartacist newspaper. In the editorial room quite a few men and women were typing,
telephoning, speaking in low voices with one another, when two freezing men entered the building, one wearing a simple cap, the other a hat
and a pince-nez. They were both glancing at a manuscript that had been
handed to them by a small gray-haired woman—she went on typing.
After a short whispered conversation with the woman—it was Rosa
Luxemburg—they left. She had said she would not be free for at least an
hour. It was evening.

The two men entered a very dreary room at the end of the corridor.
Bales of paper and stacks of brochures were stored here. There was neither a table nor a chair. People moved constantly up and down the corridor, doors slammed, the phone kept clanging. But there was light here,
and you could sit on the bales of paper. They kept their coats on.

The smaller, younger man, the one wearing the billed cap, never
took his cigarette from his mouth, even to talk. He was Radek, a Russian, a journalist. He looked very pale. He sat on a bale, his back to the
wall, puffing away and paying careful attention that his ashes did not fall
on the paper.

The other man, larger, had a middle-class, intellectual look about
him; he seemed to be about frozen through. He tried in vain to march
around in the cluttered room, snaking his way a few times up the narrow
passage. Then he confined himself to the five paces left free so that the
door could be opened, measuring them quickly back and forth. Finally
he just stood and stomped in place. He was the chief of the Spartacists,
Liebknecht.

They were continuing a conversation that had begun over tea in
Liebknecht's apartment.

Liebknecht was passionate and outspoken. But the last weeks had not made him surer of himself. He vacillated on several issues: whether to participate in the constituent assembly or no, whether there should be an early proletarian attack or a slow consolidation of forces. That most dreadful of words, "putsch,"—one cast in his teeth by socialists and the bourgeoisie—tormented him.

He remonstrated with Radek that it was theoretically difficult to determine when an insurrection was merely a putsch and when it was more than that. Everything depended on how one sized up the present situation.

Then the Russian, the emissary of the Bolsheviks, began to describe in exact detail an example from the course of the revolution in his own country.

"We too discussed the question of the place of a revolutionary insurrection or putsch within the larger revolution—I won't say it was exactly the same as here, but similar. Let us put to one side the objections of the basically passive bourgeoisie and of imperial socialists. Let us speak only of the discussion within the circle of active revolutionaries, that is, the Bolshevist groups.

"At the end of September, 1917, we were faced with the following situation: Kerenski was in charge, the army was locked in battle with Germany, the revolution had arrived at about the point where you find yourselves now. The middle class and Social Democrats officially have power, the old nobility and military is openly or clandestinely allied with them and will strike back any moment."

Liebknecht stood there deep in thought.

Radek asked, "You agree with that?"

"One difference. The war. Kerenski was still fighting a war. Ebert—isn't having to fight one."

"Correct. That makes your situation more difficult—but in another way easier. Within one or two weeks you will have all the troops that are against the war in your hands. The generals are leading them right to you."

Liebknecht, without answering, began to stride his five steps again.

Radek continued from atop his bale. "At that point, in September of 1917—no, end of August—Stalin, who was editor of our paper, printed an article by Zinoviev titled "What Should We Not Do?" What he meant was insurrection. There was one sentence in the article that I can still recall exactly: One must look the facts in the face, and there are conditions present in the current situation in Petrograd that could encourage the same sort of development found in the insurrection during the Paris Commune of 1871. The upshot being a malicious defamation of any uprising whatever."

Liebknecht: "Why malicious? A comparison to the Commune cannot be a defamation."

Radek: "Yes and no. Lenin picked up on the matter a few days later. You are of course correct in a general sense, but we are not talking generalities. Lenin called the comparison of our situation with that of the Commune superficial. You ask why? Why? Because we could offer the people something right then, did offer it to them, something the Commune was in no position to do. We gave the peasants land and made immediate overtures for peace. Furthermore, in political terms, in confrontation with our enemies, foreign and domestic, we did not refrain from attacking our Versailles of 1870, by which I mean our own Petrograd and its bandits, nor from confiscating the bourgeois banks.

"Next came the question of mass insurrection: what answer should we give to that in the Central Committee? First, however, at the end of September, came a resolution from the Moscow District Bureau directed against the Central Committee and demanding a clear line on the issue of insurrection. After a two-day discussion, then, the Central Committee came out against the provisional parliament. Lenin and the masses led, you see, and the committee followed.

"But the discussion continued, mass insurrection had not yet taken place. It had to be organized, the way paved. The Central Committee met once again, on the 10th of October, in Suchanova's apartment. Lenin appeared, still wearing glasses and a wig but without his beard—a sign that he was daring more and more to show himself. We debated for ten hours. Both reports and rumors were in complete agreement: our agents in the Army of the North warned us that units of troops had some deep, dark plans for their retreat. The same reports from Minsk. The word was that the front-line troops were against Kerenski. Lenin's summary of the situation is unambiguous. 'First, the masses are tired of our resolutions. Second, an agrarian uprising is already occurring. And third, for understandable reasons the government refuses to recognize this agrarian uprising or perhaps even hopes to stifle it. We must therefore attack at once.' After that the vote was ten to two in favor of armed insurrection. The two were Zinoviev and Kamenev. That was a bitter pill for Lenin. Rykov as well, by the way. But he was not present.

"There is something else that should interest you, something instructive just in general. Our 'military section' rejected across the board the notion of 'armed insurrection' advanced by the allegedly unwitting dilettante civilian named Lenin, and they rejected it for 'technical-military' reasons. You may want to draw some conclusions from that as regards your own military advisors.

"But they were still not done talking, a date had not yet been set, and so the discussion kept going on, broadened out, took on new dimensions that were dangerous for the party itself. Lenin's opponents were prepared to disrupt party unity. Zinoviev and Kamenev issued an appeal to the Party in which they declared their ideals: they had something entirely new in mind, a combined solution, an amalgam of constituent assembly and soviets. They consoled the workers and peasants, who wanted land and peace, with promises for the day after tomorrow. You know that song yourself. They sing it every day in *Vorwärts*. What the slyboots are up to is clear: they want to wear down the workers and peasants. You cannot conserve a given situation, its élan—tomorrow is no longer today."

Liebknecht: "I agree with you completely there."

Radek: "And tomorrow you don't have the same people in your control that you have today. At the same time it is a question of whether you, who can speak your piece today, will be able to do so tomorrow. You cannot be too clear about that. We had to pay dreadfully for the failure to attend to certain details, for mistakes in planning.

"At any rate, our opposition formulated their idea this way—our catchword of 'now or never' was wrong. One could, indeed one must, 'grow' first. The program of the proletariat first had to be made clear to the broad masses. Only then could one get to the stage of uniting fire and water, of creating this fabled monster that united a constituent assembly and the soviets. And just to make the similarity more cogent, these appeasers attacked us directly by maintaining that in the name of the history of the proletariat we had no right to stake its entire future on an armed insurrection. They preferred to enter parliament as the opposition, the loyal opposition of the bourgeoisie."

Liebknecht: "It really was an enormous risk on Lenin's part."

Radek smiled proudly. "Lenin, the spirit of the revolution, our teacher, the perfect Marxist. He led with absolute assurance right on past all mere observation and pseudo-objectivity. And if there is a snare for Marxists, then it is the delusion that in some way one can be 'objective,' that somehow one can stand outside the situation. That's where Lenin was absolutely sure of himself. He had broken through this error of objectivity on a psychological level as well, saw it as a screen thrown up by bourgeois, academic irresolution. Zinoviev, Rykov and so on were terrified when he stated flat out: no, no long development, conditions were ripe. Success would depend on two or three days of struggle. To them that sounded like the hurrah! of a mad attack, they were aghast."

The Russian knew how deeply each of these remarks struck his German comrade, given as he was to musings, weighing everything, torn back and forth by his scruples.

Liebknecht had, like Rosa, already spoken in favor of a constituent assembly, though not in public. These Germans were terrible gnawers of their own guts. A thousand situations were simultaneously alive in them, every moment was capped with a hesitation and occurred as the result of a single thrust and twenty counters and parries. How had such a people given birth to Karl Marx, Radek asked himself.

And he began to speak again to this other man, the beloved leader of the radical masses, who at one point, fresh out of prison, had come to him and said yes to everything he suggested, like some young starry-eyed socialist, but who now, true German that he was, was crammed full of doubts and knew nothing any more, and might even like to take his seat as the opposition at a constituent assembly—ah, the unswerving pacifist, anything was better than to do battle, to join the armed and bloody mass insurrection.

This man's brother, thought Radek, would not have been hanged by a czar as was Lenin's. This man had not had to live half his life in exile as had Lenin, surrounded by danger. He had been a lawyer and a member of the Reichstag.

The Russian was capable of telling—without irony in either his tone or a glance at the German—of how Rykov had wandered through Moscow one day with a comrade. " 'Do you see these imposing stone buildings,' said Rykov, 'the expensive shops, the teeming shoppers. And here we come along, we, and what are we here? Pygmies who want to move a mountain.' That's the kind of respect Rykov had for the institutions of bourgeois society. But the masses of peasants and workers who had been slaughtered in the war and misused in peacetime, who suffered, they were not on his mind at that moment. He was, to use Lenin's words, superficial, stupid."

Liebknecht made a note of all this, his back to the door, his hands stuffed in his coat pockets, his eyes to the floor. He changed topics by speaking of the mass meetings planned for December 6th. That was actually why they had come here.

Radek understood the maneuver. His suggestion was that the Spartacus League take no public part in the affair, but use it only in terms of general tactics. To use for oneself every revolutionary fire wherever it appeared.

Liebknecht gave a sigh of relief and said that here at least they agreed. He was pleased, by the way, with the manner in which these meetings had been prepared. Deserters, real conscientious objectors and revolutionary pacifists had risen in their own defense because they had not been recognized by a soldiers' council saturated with officers. He hoped they would expose the backwardness of the council, that they would brand it as a breeding place for reactionaries.

"And then into the streets," Radek said. "After the meeting, out with the red flags and sound the alarm against reactionaries."

Liebknecht nodded eagerly. "I have hopes for this particular action. We have to gather more glowing coals to heap on the heads of the reactionaries. We'll find out whether the masses are ripe for an attack, and if so to what extent."

The Russian smiled. "You expect that kind of evidence, do you?"

Steps outside. A male voice. "They're in here."

Radek jumped up.

The gray-haired woman who had been writing in the office entered. She searched the faces of both as she gave them her hand. "Well?"

Radek and Frau Luxemburg began speaking Russian to one another and left the room.

The other man followed slowly, his eyes directed to the floor.

In a Glass Darkly

Here a day begins splendidly, nothing but good signs appear, then an accident occurs, but even that cannot diminish the splendor of the day. There is news of pogroms in L'vov and we meet Jews from the East who have escaped. They want to go to America.

The day began splendidly for First Lieutenant Becker.

He awoke refreshed. In the morning he rode to the military hospital at Friedrichshain for a surgical examination. The air blew cold and wintery. He sat in the coach humming to himself and left the hospital around eleven, still humming. He was confident and his mind filled with cheerful images.

Even as he left the hospital he took one such image with him. He had been examined in a spacious ward, and then had his wound redressed. On each side of the bright, white-tiled room twenty patients lay in their white beds. They were all warmly wrapped in their covers. Some lay in traction. Some wore enormous bandages about their heads and necks. But they all lay there very still while people swarmed about them—doctors, nurses, aides, all doing this and that for them. They laid them out, they wrapped them up, they fed them. They washed and dried them. The patients lay there in their warm shawls and waited, and would have to wait still longer for their wounds to heal, for their flesh and bones to mend. That happened slowly. And meanwhile they were constantly being swathed by the nurses and aides while the doctors looked in on them and they were fed.

It was an ant colony. The teeming masses of little creatures took care of their larva inside parchment wrappings, fussed over them, set them out in the warm sun.

And as Becker slowly strolled down Friedenstrasse on his two canes, he saw to his right and left many things that fit his mood, things touching and pleasant. Women were washing windows. An old woman walked past with a pram. Two men were taking a rest on a bench. The tram rang its bell merrily as it passed.

People had built all of this by working together. They had sat down together and drawn up a plan and tried it out, and now it works and they live in these houses and ride in these cars along tracks.

And then the huge red brewery on the corner, how they work away inside there by the hundreds, standing by vats, watching the fermentation. Out in the courtyard some are rolling barrels, standing at the main gate checking the wagons, while others simply look about on the street.

Becker walked, step by step. He was making the first major attempt today, the specialist had encouraged him to try. He moved along boldly, armed with one cane in his right hand, one in his left. A quadruped.

He walked along a couple of quiet streets, and now he thought—behind the back of fate as it were, fate having already planned so many things for him—he would wend his way to Schönhauser Allee and climb into a taxi there in celebration of his victory.

He crept along without incident to the end of Friedenstrasse and let himself be led across the open plaza at Königstor by a policeman. He was about to climb the Prenzlauer hill when the whole thing became too much for him after all and he halted. That's enough, he told himself, to have come this far, to have made it to Neue Königstrasse. And with this in mind he cautiously crossed the street, tap, tap, all the while enjoying the warm sunshine. Then suddenly the cane in his right hand unexpectedly slipped away and without knowing how it happened he found himself lying on the cobblestones, the cane in his left hand aimed up as if in preparation for a journey to heaven.

Two people came to his aid and lifted him up. He smiled in surprise and confusion and begged their pardon. One of these persons was a baker's boy who had just propped his bike against the curb. He had let his bike coast at full tilt from the top of the hill just as Becker had started to move so implausibly slowly across the pavement. The boy had wanted to pull past him, but caught Becker's right cane instead.

The baker's boy was terrified, tried to explain, pleaded, he was close to tears. Becker was happy just to be on his feet again and said nothing. And then—the little malefactor was already whizzing away.

The second person who had helped Becker up was still standing beside him, a serious young man dressed in black with a black round beard. He offered to give him a hand, but Becker thanked him and said he had only a few steps to go to Neue Königstrasse. Yet as he walked to the corner he felt dizzy, and had to reach for the man's arm, for he was still walking beside him. How sad, it occurred to him, that I'll not be able to report a victory this time around.

He sat down with the man in a large restaurant on the corner, in a heated room, and his head grew clear again after a glass of tea. He examined his neighbor, then suddenly recalled the scene from earlier, the hospital where the ant larva were being swathed. And he realized: this accident happened to me only so that I could see it all again and verify its truth. And he regarded his neighbor attentively, thankful for this one example of the many forms of help people offer to one another when they live peaceably together. For they form circles, rings and chains, great rounds of dancers, as if listening to music.

Meanwhile the man who had helped him, a Jew from the East, told him about L'vov, his hometown. He had been in Berlin only a few weeks. The man wanted to go when he saw that Becker was himself again, but Becker held him back, wanting to know more about him.

In a long tale of woe, told with much stumbling and faltering, Becker learned about the battles in the Ukraine and in Poland, around and in L'vov. And how the Jewish ghetto near the marketplace had been set on fire.

Becker: "When?"

"Three weeks ago. Didn't you read about it in the paper? The papers were full of it. And then came the plundering and the pogrom."

Becker: "Who was behind the pogrom? Were people killed?"

"Were people killed? Hundreds. Whole streets were burned down behind the theater, and the police would allow no one to extinguish the fire."

Becker: "Who was responsible?"

"Who? It doesn't matter who it was. The Ukrainians or the Poles. Both of them, naturally. It makes no difference."

The man sat there gloomily. Another man, like himself, happened into the restaurant. They stared at each other, recognized each other. The new man approached, they whispered something. Becker did not object to the other man's sitting down with them.

Yes, their people were being hunted down; the first one explained. He shook his head. "We have to suffer wherever we go."

The other man: "We're not staying in Berlin. We're going to America."

Becker: "And will things go well there?"

The first one, imperturbably: "Well? Things don't go well anywhere. But we will live."

"That's how it is," the second one confirmed.

They helped Becker into a taxi. He had the first man give him his address. He wanted to thank him later for his help.

The Fate of the Jews

At home his mother was worried when he arrived so late. But he was in a good mood and told her right away, almost laughing over it, about his little accident. It had not been a total victory, only half a one. His mother noticed how calm and self-assured Friedrich looked. The sap was flowing in him again; his eyes were so affectionate, oh my blessed child, she thought—and felt profoundly happy.

Fate, which had led him through this day with such a kindly hand, wanted to show him still further favors today.

In the afternoon who should come by but easy-going Krug, and the conversation soon turned to the accident and partial victory of the morning. Becker was especially concerned with the two men with whom he had sat in the restaurant. He described them both.

"There are a lot of that sort in that part of town," Krug said. "Though actually more in the center of the city."

Becker related how fatalistic they had seemed to him. "Friendly, helpful people. But then the story he told about L'vov. It leaves you with a terrible feeling when people who have suffered so horribly don't complain. They said they are moving on, to America—but that things won't go well for them there either."

"They're right, when all is said and done," said Krug, who was not all that interested. "They're stoics, the true philosophers. They have learned to be thick-skinned out of necessity."

Becker: "That's how Jews are, I suppose. I know Jews from two sources. The one is but a trickle—my own experience of them. The other is a mightier stream, their book, the Bible. And when I compare the two, what I know about them from my own life and from the Bible, they don't match. In their book they are cantankerous farmers who go off to themselves, pray to their one God, and would rather be massacred than forsake him. You could say that they were like martyrs. But you can see it another way too. It reminds me vaguely of Molière's miser. He doesn't spend his money, he buries it. He won't use it, but almost dies when they want to take it away from him. He defends it tooth and nail, with his last ounce of passion. In any case, hard-nosed people. — And in comparison then there are the Jews I know from my own life. Now there's a race of people who are deft, hard-working, businesslike. They don't even allow themselves to rest now and then. They don't hoard their money like Molière's miser, they use it; they know their business and let money work for them. They are bankers, tradesmen, or they take positions in industry, like Ballin the shipbuilder or the Rathenaus with AEG. But they don't really enjoy what they have. Do you understand me, Krug? I mean, they never slow down, they never take life easy, are never sated. It's probably because no one lets them. Despite their status of legal equality they've never really been accepted among us, you know. But that's how they are. And then there's the fellow who saved my life this morning.

"There was something strange about them both, something that bothers me. The first one helped me, you see, dusted me off and gave me his arm to lean on and stuck with me. But it would be an exaggeration to say that either he or the other one was sociable. I noticed quite clearly: he's helping me, it's true, because I've fallen, and one helps when one can; but as for the rest—how can I say it—I'm no more than thin air to him, and he goes his way. I'm neither a Ukrainian nor a Pole carrying out pogroms in L'vov, but he lumps me in the same category. 'Things are bad for us everywhere, and it won't be any better in America.' He holds me responsible as well for the misfortune that he and his family have experienced."

Krug: "Pride. World history centers about them. Although one would like to know what they are so proud of. Since when all is said and done they don't have their monotheism, or their Bible for that matter, all to themselves anymore."

Becker laughed. "That's the worst part about it. Not only has their land been taken away from them, but even their God. At the very least, to put it in business terms, a competitor has opened up shop and left them straggling far behind."

Krug said, "Bosh! They could have joined the new firm anytime."

"He had without doubt been subjected to the most ghastly misfortunes, to things that could drive a man crazy, crush him. You could come to hate the whole world. But is the man crushed? Does he hate? No. Pay attention now, Krug, this is important. That man felt I wasn't worth his getting upset over. It wasn't worth it to hate me. He has hammered out his own theory of things: he accepts injustice and brutality as a kind of gift, accepts them with great pleasure even, as a kind of distinction, all in secret of course. That's the point, and something in me is revolted by that. Now he has the proof, he thinks, now it's absolutely certain what miserable wretches other people are.

"You've seen the same thing teaching, Krug. I've always noticed in the classroom that it is a very serious matter to do a young person an injustice; things become really ugly if by some chance it happens again and the lad begins to think you have something against him. He doesn't say anything. But everything goes cockeyed inside him. The boy becomes obstinate and disagreeable. Finally he begins to get conceited. You see, that's the worst part, that in the end he grows conceited. Because either intentionally or accidentally he has been treated unfairly, he exalts himself above the others."

Krug: "I know the type. But it all evens out in time."

"Sometimes. Sometimes not. And not with the Jews. All sorts of things have been done to them, that's evident. First, as you noted, their religion was taken away from them, and Christianity looks to them like a kind of good-for-nothing child who drives his parents to utter misery. And secondly, there's the constant sorrow they must bear in exile. But it seems to me that they hang on to their perpetual exile now as a way of constantly proving how unjust we are."

Krug: "Your impression is that they provoke their own misfortune?"

"That must be it, Krug, because they must have seen through their fate by now. They must have conformed it to their own will; it has some kind of meaning for their own sense of superiority—and for our malice." He stared blankly ahead at his empty desk. "I'm reminded again of Molière's *L'Avare*. They make their misfortune their personal property and will not let it be taken from them. With each act of injustice they outstrip us who have done this to them. The whole thing has lost its political and psychological character; it has taken on a metaphysical, a mysterious tinge."

Krug: "That sort of thing occurs frequently in nature. Organisms, no longer able to live in their accustomed fashion when temperature or moisture change, accommodate themselves to fit the new environment, adapt themselves. Sometimes they resemble a new species. Ultimately the Jews have no other choice. How else are they supposed to escape their 'environment,' all those Poles and Ukrainians who block their path?"

Becker looked up. "By being unjust themselves. Why not? Everyone else does it. After all, if you add it all up, they have the right to help themselves to a healthy dose of injustice, to acts of violence. Besides which, people who have been caught for so long in the rut of justice and injustice ought finally to have enough of it. They could say: it can't go on like this—let's tackle the problem another way. But they don't. They grow hard and rigid instead of getting nasty, for all I care, and making themselves some elbow room. But they sit there like those fellows at the Königstor who've just had their relatives massacred and declare that that's life and we're going to America, but it won't be any better there. And then—they pray. They 'pray,' Krug, what is the point of that? Under such circumstances, to 'pray.' What do they intend by it? Isn't that the height of naiveté, of absurdity, to approach God in such an instance? It's a kind of burlesque, really, to take off one's shoes and approach God, and at the same time be so disordered inside, to appear before Him with such pride and rigidity, so buttoned-up and cramped. And with every intention of staying that way."

Becker shook himself. Krug gazed at him, surprised at the vehemence with which he had become immersed in the matter. He knew Becker's tendency to get hung up in trivialities. Well, he would be on his way soon he hoped.

Becker continued in a kind of monologue. "Nietzsche spoke of the Jews' subterranean thirst for revenge. I see nothing of that. They only attack themselves. They can't get outside of themselves. They only appear to cling to their god; they don't even have him anymore. Because they no longer pray before the celestial throne: 'Give me *me*, give me back my divine soul.' "

Krug could see no way to get him away from this boring topic. He yawned and said, "There you see what fine folks we Germans are. How did we act in the war? Not like sulking children. We all, Germans, English, French, Americans and so on, fought a righteous war, as if there were neither Christians nor Jews."

Becker was startled. "What a thing to say. What a thing to say, Krug."

"You'll have to admit it. Once in gear, mass slaughter like that has its own legitimation, is carried out resolutely, robustly, with artillery, planes, mines. It won't let anyone rob it of its specific gravity." And so they had finally managed to find another topic.

Becker: "You're tremendous, Krug. The way you put things."

Krug: "Like a scientist."

Becker stared at him in amazement. "The way you do it so offhandedly! You're completely right. You've hit the bull's-eye. — We fought our war righteously, as if there were neither Christians nor Jews. And how did we do it, Krug? As heathens?"

Krug smirked. "Why not? If you like. At any rate absolutely without theology. And that's how it was and ever shall be, *in saecula saeculorum.*"

Becker could not take his eyes off him, as if he were a specter of some sort. "You speak today, Krug, as if inspired. And what do you think of 'prayer'? What happens when you do it, what do you achieve? What effect do prayers have, Krug?"

He laughed. "There you've really got the wrong man, Becker. But now I must beg you to stop this. You're woolgathering. It's all mist and vapors, and you'll be blown away with them."

Becker: "There are things that fascinate a person, and you want to know why. Like a face that simply seems to glow, and you look and look for the source of the light."

But at that, the easy-going, patient Krug got up, walked about the room and began, like an exorcist, to soliloquize. He began talking about whatever occurred to him—about politics, meetings, the school, all sorts of intrigues. He gave his own opinion about the gossip that was going on behind the director's back and could not be squelched. What was behind it all? The ancient hate of the plebians for a rich man of culture living all to himself.

Becker followed inattentively. What sort of gossip?

"The older lads tell all sorts of tales. He has his favorites. That is imprudent. Others are jealous, they gossip."

Becker became inattentive. He asked Krug to encourage the director to visit him. He would be glad of the visit.

Krug: "He'd like to come. But be careful. He knows nothing about the gossip. That he's its chief victim."

Krug was gone, his mother was out.

But Becker was enthralled by the light that came from the two Jews. Why? Because they were trapped, could not break free from the mesh of their own net? Ah, those mysterious faces, what a magic they had. And the more Becker involved himself with that magic, basking in its radiance, the more it seemed to him that he would dissolve into it. Ah, they have introduced me to my own image—a mirror has been held up to me.

How meaningful life is, how transparent things become, how heavy with fruit everything is. It looks as if people were strange, unfamiliar, indifferent human beings, bakers' boys, bike-riders, Galician Jews. But they appear before me, are led before me. I almost feel as if they had emerged out of my own self. I am one in spirit with them, we are spirits playing together, angels—some of those who sank down to earth, grew heavy, took on shadow, color and wickedness.

So I, too, am clothed in black, cramped, hardened. Someone comes, tells me this, shows it to me.

Look, a finger, that shows it to me.

As if someone wanted to help me.

Help. But why? How? Am I getting worse? I can't see it. I feel healthier, things are going better for me.

Why have they shown me these black clothes?

And while Becker sat there on into the late, shadowed afternoon, his mother returned home and was surprised to find him sitting in the dark.

She embraced him and drew him to the window to look into his face. She laughed. "Pleasant, increasing sunshine—for me. Otherwise mostly cloudy."

He said that Krug had left some time before. He had just been sitting there daydreaming. But now he wanted to get a little exercise, march about, but being a clever man he'd do it in the apartment. His mother drew the curtains, turned on the light. He walked holding onto her arm. In the middle of the room he stopped and pointed to the bookcase that had been nailed shut.

"What do you say, Mother? Why do I do such things? I tacked that curtain across it."

"That's what I keep telling you. It's what you want, Friedrich."

"As if I were afraid of them."

"Shall we open it up again?"

"Of course."

She was happy. He was getting better.

And when they passed the door on their way out into the corridor, he looked back into the room once again.

"There's my bed, where I lie like the pupa of an ant and let myself be fed. And underneath the sofa there, the pictures."

His mother: "And behind it the busts. And those ugly marks on the wallpaper."

Becker: "Hang the pictures back up. But wait till tomorrow when the therapist comes; he can do it."

His vitality, his fine seriousness, his wonderful candid eyes pleased her immensely. The way he was coming to himself now, the way he had changed. He had been eclipsed somehow.

Becker knew, even as he lay down, that he was entering upon a dream-filled night. And soon the voice he had been expecting came to him.

"You are lying here oddly today, my child. So strange, so distant."

"I've been waiting for you."

"But why so strange, so distant. The day was filled with hope."

"I've been waiting for you, my father. I am afraid."

"You're afraid? You have been called and you have begun to move."

"Didn't I respond?"

"Oh certainly, my child, certainly. But still you falter. You always want to turn back. You always want to plug your ears. The pupa in its cocoon, the thin skin rips open. How long still, until the skin rips open and you must leave the cocoon."

"Why? What happens then? Another existence?"

"You are thinking it's some magic show, some new theater. But it is much simpler and more wearisome. It is more of your life."

"What kind of life?"

"A freer one, a richer one. More pain, more joy. A new birth: you are the mother and the child. Rejoice in the birth. Do not be anxious about the torments that have already begun. I will help you, Friedrich, trust me, you will not be without help."

"Tell me where I am going."

"What is within you, your self, your soul will speak. It will sing. You will not understand its song, not at first."

The words clung to him for some time. "It will be a chorus of many voices, an antiphonal song."

He wanted to hold onto other words, too, but they drifted off. What remained was a twittering and a humming.

Paris, Fears and Sins

Here we discourse at length about love, nothing but love. A woman is in love and cannot forgive herself for loving. Another woman wanders through Paris and laps up adventure. A third woman becomes an amalgam of lust and innocence.

At the Bottom of the Abyss

Bernhard stood at the window in Hilda's room, it was morning. She had recuperated entirely. She felt, standing close to him, "I could experience all of it, all of it; once more with you."

She sensed the pressure of his arm on her shoulder.

"All of it?" he replied, not uttering a word.

She: "Yes."

She kissed him on the neck and said without speaking, "I could part with everything in the world, even my own self, for your sake."

They stood immobile beside each other. She whispered at his neck, "Kiss me, Bernhard. Everything will be just like before."

"What are you trying to get me to do, Hilda?"

"Everything just like before, Bernhard."

As he was leaving she stood at the door. "I will always love you." She threw herself on the bed, an empty husk of herself.

She dared to speak with her confessor. He advised her to avoid Bernhard. She saw Bernhard every day. She yielded to the temptation, like someone plummeting downward ever faster. She threw herself into the temptation, wanting to reach the bottom of the abyss quickly, oh so quickly. Bernhard tried to calm her. He was tender to her. But the madness, the bruising madness that emerged from her could not be stopped. —

Then came their last meetings.

Bernhard felt the fear rise up in him. He suspected something—but not that their separation had already occurred.

Many thoughts were running through Hilda's mind in those weeks.

They were all wound up with the war years. On the day she had torn herself away from Bernhard screaming she had run to the minister. And as her lips began to form the prayer there in front of an altar, the vision of Friedrich Becker had come to her.

Their farewell in the hospital. She felt a calmness come over her. Later the vision vanished, then reemerged. It's meant to help me, it's been sent to me. Like Bernhard, she felt fate beating its wings. She thought Bernhard would stay away from her. But he clung to her. He loved her, he suffered because of her.

She despaired when she realized this. She dreaded it. She did not want to hurt him, but she no longer could find the will to prevent what had been ordained for her. "End it," it said, it demanded of her. Do not even try to pick up where you left off before the war. Let that be the end of it, Hilda.

And it grew dark within her. She became hard.

She did not know what she should do, what she wanted to do. She spoke with her father, telling him she was going to Karlsruhe for a few weeks to visit relatives.

"Do that, my dear," said the old man. "That will comfort them, tell them not to give up. And when will you be coming back?"

She promised to spend Christmas with him.

While she packed, she thought: I packed and left like this once before, in 1914, trying to escape myself and my past, chancing war and death. Now—I don't want to escape. No, it's not that. I cannot live if I don't begin something new with my life. I must begin anew, even if that means that I must really die.

She was flooded with memories of the war. The stricken nation for which she had worked, the endless dying on the eastern front, scenes from hospitals. Like some black sailboat gliding through the fog—the memory of Becker, of a dying pilot named Richard, of the childish Maus.

Before she departed, she sent word of her intentions to Frau Scharrel in Paris.

Strange, really, that she has to leave Strasbourg. Her bit of luggage is already at the station, but, as if to cover her tracks and mislead some pursuer, she walks, or better strolls, through the sunlit city and stops for a surprise visit with her Aunt Erhardt. They drink chocolate in a café, smoke a cigarette. She saunters across Gutenbergplatz, across Kleberplatz, and now she is standing on Broglieplatz. The French flag waves above the town hall. Her old hometown has taken on a new look, one her father still has not got used to. In front of the town hall they will soon raise up a monument. Three steps will lead up to figures caught in violent motion. A soldier of stone will stand there with legs spread wide. Enraged, he pulls a saber from its scabbard, his disheveled hair falls across his brow, beside him another man carries a flag. It is the flag of revolution. On the pedestal it will read: *"Allons enfants de la patrie."* It will be the monument honoring the Marseillaise and Rouget de Lisle. Hilda thinks of the war and of those many men who died out there and here at home beside her. Suddenly she finds that she is in the eastern part of the city near the barracks. She hails a taxi. She is just in time for her train.

Parisian Amusement

The stay in Paris was doing Frau Anni Scharrel good.

She found herself in a new element, but one that suited her. She had an old, ineradicable affinity for vice. Without the tingle of temptation, without the feeling of sliding close to it, she could not exist. The proximity of sin enlivened her the way the thunder of cannons does the warrior. "I think, therefore I am," said Descartes. "I sin, therefore I am," reasoned Anni. Without the glow of adventure, without the whisper of seduction, the day was lost to her, dark, mute. Only in the anticipation of it could she rise in the morning, make herself ready. She ate and drank for it.

Anni had acquaintances in Paris, and they took her about, girlfriends of the same sort as she. She got her money's worth in Paris. How? Simply by strolling about in this city quivering with excitement. For Anni belonged to that sort of people for whom lust and sensuality and desire are a matter of course, so that merely by moving through such a charged atmosphere they are filled with bliss. She only needed to change her costume, repowder her nose, and she began tingling with delight. Sometimes she felt this so violently that she said to herself: My God, I'm growing worse and worse—am I getting old? She enjoyed what she called her "personal freedom."

Her nieces, the sisters, were staying in the same hotel, on the same floor. The excitement had no less an effect on them, but their upbringing put obstacles in their way; the girls were a bit nervous, and though they wanted to enjoy everything, experience everything, they preferred to do it vicariously.

So they walked along, sticking close together wherever they went, like Siamese twins who could only be separated by surgery. They wore their dark hair parted down the middle and laid back in waves over both ears. The older sister was a bit larger than the other. Both had a tinge of pink to their bright round faces. The large, dark-brown eyes gazed attentively out from under thick brows that reminded one of caterpillars. The girls had long, nicely chiseled noses, small mouths.

And so here they sit in a dark, murky corner of a bar. The table in front of them is laden with a wine cooler, bottles and three glasses.

A younger gentleman, a cigar in his mouth, lies dreaming on the sofa. The two young women are wearing bright, colorful clothes and heavy makeup, they wear long dark gloves. They are both very young, and they point their lips into a smile and listen to the muted violin music from the next room.

It is an hour later, and the gentleman has separated the younger one from her sister, taken her to his room.

She is an utter child, a perverse child. She has a tan complexion, a very slim, firm body without a bit of fat, powerful arms. And atop her slender neck sits a saucy, pretty little sparrow face, that shows not a trace of shame now as she walks naked across the carpet toward the mirror. A mass of brown hair falls loosely down around her neck and ears. She has puckered up her mouth like a cherry that has burst, showing its meaty interior. She squints one eye up a bit. She clamps a monocle into place.

When he returns to the room later to remind her that it is time to go, she does not respond, he finds her fast asleep on the bed.

She has thrown her long blue evening cloak over her. It has loosened completely at the top, slipped off, and now lies crumpled beneath her. Her head, her face puffed slightly from sleep, hangs down over the right edge of the bed. Her right arm has slipped down and her hand touches the carpet.

The gentleman stands there for a long time, already wearing his coat and tophat, engrossed in the curves of her hips and her knees. He has particular trouble tearing his eyes from her knees. They are white, chiseled works of art, and yet so touching, childish. They innocently bear that body wherever it wishes to go. Her left foot still has a shoe on it, but no stocking. She has put on her right shoe as well, but it dangles from her toes. Although her body is completely bare, the sleeping girl seems infinitely chaste and sweet.

But when she sits up, then stands there pertly and steps into her flimsy black dress while she prattles and laughs, pulling it up from her feet like a sheath—her slim body still sticking out naked on top—and as the gentleman bends down to kiss her arm, she very obviously becomes a creature from two different worlds: the aroma of cigarettes, the perfumes of the bar and the ballroom cling to the flimsy black dress caught about her hips. But higher up, her delicate, sharp face smiles and watches the gentleman. And it is this part with its small, budlike breasts, the easy curves of the still naked body, the dip of her navel and the thin arms—this is the other world, for this is a naked, nameless animal, a dragonfly that plays, has played, and wants to flutter on its way.

271

A Conclusion

And once again, love. And death, its old adversary.

At her hotel Frau Scharrel found a letter from Strasbourg written in a hand she did not recognize. She turned pale as she saw Hilda's signature.

First generalities, then came the message that it "might interest" Anni that she was leaving Strasbourg for a while. "My feelings for B. are those of friendship. We spoke often, but I realized that there was no point in cultivating the friendship. You will understand that and also understand when I ask you to look after him if he seems upset during the coming weeks. But perhaps I am wrong in this. I have been mistaken about people so many times before, but this sentimental Gretchen at least does not enjoy watching people suffer. He is very fond of you, I know that. I have only happened to cross for a few short weeks the common path you two tread, perhaps I have upset things. Forgive me, Anni."

Anni did not depart at once. Since she had been in Paris, and now especially after this incident, after their simple farewell, Bernhard had lost some of his value to her. But then her memories of him grew stronger, and after three enjoyable days she departed for Strasbourg, totally calm, even indifferent, as if because some distant relative had taken ill. The two sisters hesitated. They begged. They had been chaperoned by Anni, but they were allowed to stay a few more days.

Anni's indescribable coldness when faced with the devastated man.

One look at him when he appeared on the afternoon of her arrival told her everything. The man was unmasked. He was the soul of misery, of suffering, he was broken. What can you do with that? It had nothing to do with her. He was an embarrassment to her.

It was evening. He tossed about on the sofa in her living room as if he had been poisoned, his eyes closed tight. She watched him and thought: I shall write Hilda and thank her for this dramatic spectacle she's left me with.

He was much too busy with himself to notice her reaction. She offered him some lemonade, as if he were ill. First he refused, then took it and drank it down greedily.

"What's to become of me, Anni? I can find no rest. I take sleeping pills. I can't sleep."

The mocking words of Heinrich Heine tingled on her tongue: "When you've lost one woman, then instantly find yourself another." What a despicable impression he made, this man, this rejected little man. He came toward her, embraced her, clung to her, even demanded she give herself to him. But he disgusted her. She pushed him back onto the sofa. "Pull yourself together, Bernhard. What do you take me for?"

Again he raised his arms to her. "Anni, if you would show me some mercy, if you would be good to me, things would be different."

As a way of fulfilling her Christian duty, she yielded, letting him lay his head on her breast. She thought: "And I loved you? Oh, you men, what odd creatures. You work for us, go to war for us, get yourselves shot. You think you're the crown of creation. But look what's here at my breast, this crown of creation."

While he moaned and she gazed down at him, the idea came to her: Is it possible the man is going to commit suicide? I have the feeling he's planning to. He feels compelled to do it. But he wearies me so. If only he doesn't get too insistent again. He thinks of me as a sleeping pill."

And then she said to him, "I think, Bernhard, that you need a woman. I cannot be the one. Spare me telling you the reasons. But there is definitely someone or other waiting for you. If she could see you like this and you asked her what's to become of you, she would be there for you in a moment and would believe she could be your next love. And perhaps she would, too."

"Then you don't want me anymore?" He had stretched himself out fully.

She stood up coldly beside the sofa. "My dear Bernhard, there are limits to everything. You allow yourself liberties."

He muttered, "I beg your pardon." But he did not move from the sofa.

She thought: What more can he want really? How long is he going to stay? And suddenly she was filled with dread. He wants to kill himself here, in my apartment. She struggled to pull herself together; sitting at the table, she considered a plan. She shook him. "I have a suggestion, Bernhard. Let's go eat somewhere together. We'll go wherever you like. My cook isn't in today anyway."

"Eat, Anni?"

"Yes, eat. I'll go with you."

"You'll come with me?"

"Yes."

Then he sat up, calmly, ruined. She asked, "Are you coming?"

He nodded. She whisked across to the entry, then returned with her coat and hat. He stood up. "Let's eat at my place."

She winced. There he goes again. "But why there? You don't have anyone who cooks for you."

"There'll be enough for us, Anni."

But I don't want to go with him. She pulled herself together. First she had to get him out of the house.

They walked, it was not far, he held her tight, she had to go with him. He sat down in his living room, she ran to the kitchen, made tea and sandwiches. He drank the tea and wanted her to eat. He watched what she did, what she was intending to do. She realized this. Fear makes one inventive; she pretended weariness. He pulled her down next to him on the sofa. For God's sake, what can he really want from me, I can't spend the night here with him.

"And now I shall have to say good night!" She reached for her coat that hung over a chair. "I thought I might find you a doctor, Bernhard, you're ill."

"Don't go," he begged. "Anni, don't go."

She got angry, threw her teaspoon down on the table. "Well I'm not going to allow you to force me to do anything. You are compromising me."

And in her anger, something she had stored up in herself for a long time, the same anger that had often made her scream at her husband in the past—for she was not the elegant lady who had sat in bars in Paris, the two sisters following her blissfully about—she said, "I have had enough, do you understand?"

"But, Anni, why are you so upset. You can't leave me here alone. That is the only thing I ask of you. I don't want anything from you now."

"I would hope not. But I must go. I don't have time."

"You have to stay here, Anni."

She locked herself in at home, barred and bolted the whole apartment. The maid was given instructions to let no one in, absolutely no one. She took the telephone off the hook. She paced back and forth. She had escaped. Her faced glowed with indignation. This was Hilda's fault. In her rage she broke an expensive tortoiseshell dagger that lay on the mantel.

When she awoke the next morning around ten she was curious, and she rang him up.

No answer.

Finally a woman answered, a common voice. She did not understand what Anni wanted. There was a great deal of noise in the room. Then someone took the receiver away from the woman and a male voice asked who she was and what she wanted. She gave her name, surprised and terrified; she wanted to speak with her nephew, was he not up yet?

There followed some coughs and whispers, then: "The gentleman is ill. We are just about to transport him to the hospital."

At her urgent questioning there followed more whispers and murmurs. Then came the answer that she should get her information from the doctor at the hospital.

At the hospital the receiving physician said, "The gentleman has been dead for two, three hours now."

They led her to a bench in the reception room where she sat down. So he did do it. Shame, shame on him to do that. She felt nauseous and dizzy. They let her stretch out on a chaise longue and had her sniff ammonia. As quickly as possible she found her way out of the hospital.

At noon she was visited by the two sisters who had just arrived that morning and knew nothing of this misfortune. For Frau Anni it was a great relief that they had come. They were both horrified. The incident went beyond their powers of comprehension.

Anni wept. He had been dead for six hours now. Now she remembered everything that had happened yesterday and her emotions ran away with her. Without any pretences she spoke to the sisters, who listened breathlessly.

"That wretched woman, Hilda, turned his head. You saw what he was like when she showed up here again. It was as if she had bewitched him. Then she runs off and leaves him in the lurch. She wrote me a letter. But what could I do, can I help heal his broken heart? We were so good together, Bernhard and I. I lost him as a friend. Now I have lost him altogether."

All their lusts and vices were knocked out of them. They were all three everyday people who needed to weep away their sorrow. When they had calmed down again and had begged for mercy and forgiveness from the dead Bernhard, they each stood up, one after the other, and they embraced. Then first the two sisters went upstairs, then Frau Anni, to wash their faces and put their makeup and hair in order. Then they sat back down together again. Anni ordered tea. She invited the sisters to spend the next few days with her. She begged them to.

But the sisters were afraid in her apartment and said that they had to go on to Metz. So Frau Scharrel had the housemaid sleep in her room with her.

Ovations for Friedrich Ebert

Noncommissioned officers give People's Deputy Ebert an ovation. The Signal Corps is not outdone. This storm of sympathy for Ebert even stirs several gentlemen in the Foreign Office, but they soon make off. December 5th looks rosy.

In a city like Berlin there were of course some noncommissioned officers as well.

There is a type of narrator or story writer who swears by logic, and logic alone. For them one thing follows another in this world, and they see their task as one of demonstrating this fact and so develop one thing out of the other as their theory dictates. For each event in their story they invent another out of which the first arises. The second event has simply no choice but to develop out of the first, like a chick from the egg.

We are not given to such strict logic. We consider nature much more frivolous than do these aforesaid writers of stories and history.

We are nearing the middle of the first week of December, 1918, and unexpectedly we bump into noncoms. We notice them while out for a casual stroll. If we were serious philosophers, from which fate God has spared us, we would wring our hands and beg these noncoms to quit the field. Because everything has been made ready for December 6th, which is near at hand now, and we have absolutely no use for any more material on that date. All causes have been established two and three times over, the effect cannot be long in coming. And now, at the last moment, noncoms.

So there they are. We cannot write them away. No, we shall take them along. They can only make December 6th more exciting.

In those days, when all of Germany was in an uproar, countless unidentified persons stepped up and tried, either alone or in groups, to turn the wheel of history. Let it be said that originally the noncoms did not have things bad. But they had not felt good about Wilhelm's and the

Hohenzollerns' marching off like that. What should they do with themselves now? What was the point of the entire army anymore? No matter how you twisted the revolution around, there wasn't much in it for noncoms. They belonged neither to the masters nor to the commonfolk. Which was why they could be slandered from right and left. They bullied the soldiers, but were actually soldiers themselves. They stood side by side with the officers, but were not their equals. Where and how could they live now? Moreover, to a man they had assumed that they would one day be pensioned off.

Sentimentality is not usual among noncoms. Whatever tender feelings may stir in their breasts, they know how to conceal them under a rough exterior. But they had wives and children and no secure position; they were not to be trifled with.

They held their meetings, drank, smoked, and talked. The noncoms were joined by vice-sergeant majors, sergeants, cavalry sergeants, paymasters, homeless barrack dwellers and all bemoaning Germany's fate. They asserted that they would also be willing to stand on friendly terms with the new government to the extent that it would understand the concerns of the noncoms, vice-sergeant majors, sergeants, etc. But where were they to find such a government? So they founded an organization, the Alliance of Active Noncommissioned Officers. And in December they felt they had to go public. They had heard that on December 6th attacks against the government by revolutionary groups were expected. On that same date one ought to march to demonstrate loyalty to the government. Alliances are quick to demonstrate loyalty.

They were encouraged to do so from several sides, especially by people to whom they were accustomed to listen, their officers. What a fine thing such a demonstration would be, not just for its own sake but for the state, for Germany, yes, for the world. A vigorous corps of noncoms, the seedbed of a healthy nation on the side of the government—what more could one ask for!

And so the noncoms decided to take action on December 5th, one day before the menace of the 6th. They gathered, twelve hundred strong, on Thursday the 6th, at Busch Circus, which had been the site of many a revolutionary scene before this, but where now the voice of order was also to be raised. That voice emerged from gruff throats. Till now they had only commanded order, and that in the form of "attention, parade rest, forward march, right face march!"

The noncoms' spokesman, Suppe, proclaimed, "Our future is at stake. We will fight every insurrection, whatever its source. We must turn our words into deeds. Otherwise the Entente will occupy Berlin."

At that, the twelve hundred men formed smart, closed ranks, as is only proper for noncoms, with a military band at their head, and marched off to Wilhelmstrasse to give three cheers for Friedrich Ebert.

At the Reichs Chancellery sixty sailors were standing guard. And as they heard the menacing boom of the band and saw all those noncoms, sergeants, vice–sergeant majors and paymasters, they thought the counterrevolution was on the march, and so they put their machine guns in place. But then they learned that this was a matter of peaceable, worried men, serious fathers of families whose hearts were burdened with care. So they opened the iron gates to them and let Suppe in to see Ebert.

Shortly afterward Ebert himself came out, aware now of what was happening, and thanked them for their vote of confidence, and then he cried: "Three cheers for the German people and for Germany!" This pulled the corks from their throats, and they shouted "Three cheers" and "Hurrah" till you could hear it all the way down Wilhelmstrasse as far as Leipziger Strasse, and the ladies eating pastry in the cafés put down their spoons and said in anxious voices, "They're fighting again." But they were not fighting, they were shaking hands.

The huzzahing men soon moved down Leipziger Strasse, smartly in step and with drums beating, on past the Reichstag, to Dorotheenstrasse, where the Alliance had its office. On Dorotheenstrasse they met another procession, one less disciplined. There were the Signal Corps, who, two thousand strong, had marched off from Treptow with red, black and gold flags waving and were just arriving in Wilhelmstrasse. Ebert set them to crying "Hurrah" as well, this time for the young republic and the German people. He said that he was happy that the Signal Corps had found its way to him. (Later on, to be sure, the signal corpsmen proved to be rather shady figures, since from Wilhelmstrasse they marched directly to the revolutionary Executive Council on Prinz-Albrecht Strasse to present it with a document expressing their full support.)

And there were still more people who wished to place themselves at the disposal of the government. It was amazing how suddenly this sympathy for the government had arisen overnight. Even in the Foreign Office, normally hermetically sealed, a breeze of sympathy was felt and several noblemen breathed it in and winked at one another and said, "A whiff of spring." The names of these gentlemen became known two days later, but those who bore them had already absconded. Their names were Count Matuschka and Herr von Rheinhaben. A commoner, Herr Marten, joined them as well, plus a certain Lieutenant Fischer. They were all filled with goodwill for the government and threatened to display that emotion on December 6th.

A certain Captain Kohler was also present. When he heard about the preparations for December 6th he searched his conscience and was overcome with strong, single-minded passion. "Something must be done," the phrase struck deep within him. He wandered restlessly back and forth between the Reichstag, where the Greater Berlin Workers' and

Soldiers' Council sat, and the Franz Regiment barracks on Blücher-strasse. His first contact was with a Committee of Seven and a Committee of Fifteen, which were supposed to act as the soldiers' council's liaisons to the government and the army. On the 5th he presented himself to the Franz Regiment as a spokesman for the government, aghast at the dreadful state of things in the capital of the Reich. He confided to his horrified listeners that there was an Executive Council on Prinz-Albrecht Strasse here in Berlin and that what he had found there was (and here he raised his voice till it cracked) "a pigsty."

Once that crude word was out, he did not hesitate to document his rage with numbers. No less than two and a half million marks had been embezzled by the Executive Council. The eyes of the members of the Franz Regiment popped out of their heads. (Upon discharge, they had each received fifty marks and not even a suit of civilian clothes.)

"If I am not telling you the truth," screamed the governmental spokesman with the name of Kohler, who claimed to be a captain, "then get your weapons and shoot me."

The regiment refrained from doing so. Whereupon he took command of them. Since it was the regiment's opinion that something must be done, he ordered them to appear for duty at the barracks the next day, December 6th, at 3:00 P.M., with bayonets fixed, ready to move out in the direction of the Brandenburg Gate. They would give Reichs Chancellor Ebert an ovation.

The officers' representative, Fellechner, whom they knew to be a member of the Greater Berlin Soldiers' Council, was standing next to him.

The 6th of December

December 6th weighs anchor and sails forth majestically. On board we find the government in Berlin, the Alliance of Active Noncommissioned Officers, the Signal Corps, the Fusilier Guards, the Alliance of Stragglers and Deserters and several obscure personages. When the ship arrives in port that evening a number of people have lost their lives.

Just as in spring a swarm of bees will attack a tree in full bloom from all sides, so the people of Berlin pressed in upon the 6th of December. Why this date?

It was first discovered by the deserters and stragglers, whom we saw out walking along Dorotheenstrasse late one night at the end of November. They had been driven out of their dubious paradise in the Reichstag with fire and sword and they were not about to take it lying down. We were present when later they busily pasted up their posters—a peaceable sort of work that disturbed no one. There were a great many posters being pasted up in Berlin in those days, usually one on top of the other. And anyone who saw people doing such work merely thought: So, another meeting.

But a devil was sitting there on that sheet of paper.

He crouched there invisible among the black letters on the fiery red paper. When the date arrived, the demon would become restless. He would rip at the letters with his paws and talons and tear himself away from them. He would throw himself croaking and screaming at people, driving them to their public demonstrations, directing them here and there along the streets.

The government in Berlin, keeping alive as best it could, took up the gauntlet of the date the deserters and their adherents had thrown down. It owed that much to a number of people who had doubts whether the government existed or not. It felt, like the homunculus in "Faust," that it had not yet achieved a real existence. There were so many people who wanted to blow out its little flame of life: the army of the generals, Kurt Eisner in Bavaria, the Rhenish folk in Cologne, Karl Liebknecht and Bloody Rosa. And heavy industry, too, which maneuvered back and forth between the high command and France.

December 6th sailed in majestically, just as it came from the practiced hand of nature: spanking new, built for dependability. It had a sunrise and would have a sunset and other standard astronomy. Whatever happens on the trip, it will bear it all into port. And trusting in that fact, people greeted the arrival of the great ship and took their places on it.

The first to show itself on board was the government in Berlin. More than all the others its fear was the greatest, and at the same time it felt responsible for the whole grand passage. Hardly on board, the government reached for the telephone and was connected with the chief of police, whose name was Eichhorn, which is German for "squirrel," though he had long ago put off all the qualities of that darling creature of the forest. Then the government ordered the city commandant, whom we have met, to appear before it. His name was Wels, German for "catfish," and he proudly acknowledged himself a member of this mighty fish genus, from which at one point had diverged the electric catfish and the electric eel, both capable of paralyzing animals and men. We recall that other heroes of this battle bore characteristic names, for instance the leader of the anxious noncoms, Suppe, or "soup." We shall soon encounter an obscure personage whose name is Krebs, or "cancer" and whose effect was similar. And was not the grave people's deputy himself, the squat, shortnecked Ebert, really like the "Eber" or "boar" he was named after? Though of course fate had hung on a "t" at the end, perhaps by way of warning, perhaps as a question mark, for he wasn't really such a savage creature after all.

And so Wels—without fins now—the city commandant, appeared before the government when summoned by phone and described the measures he had taken to protect it. The government demonstrated for him yet again how shaky it was and how the slightest push could throw it off balance. Wels asked the government to remain seated and not to get excited before it was necessary. He showed it his strong muscles and rolled his eyes. The governmental authority, streaked already with white and yellow, breathed a sigh of relief, if only a provisional one.

Later on the deserters and their adherents, men on leave and conscientious objectors, etc., found their way on board, took their places. They began, as planned, to protest.

The protest was however no longer the private matter of two or three people. It represented an altogether different grievance than the one on Dorotheenstrasse. In the meetings, which took place in large public halls, the conveners were first allowed to take the floor. Then one voice after another broke in, and soon the chorus swelled: "The government has failed, the government is to blame, something must be done."

These people were hard-pressed by misfortune. They sought yet once more an opportunity to find happiness. A Private Schulz spoke up: One must prevent, if necessary with armed force, the replacement of a socialist republic by a democratic one. Someone demanded that all members of the army born prior to 1900 be dismissed and so speed up the disbandment of the imperial army. A resolution was read aloud:

"The protest meeting of the stragglers, frontline soldiers, men on leave and deserters objects to the suppression of their interests by the Greater Berlin Workers' and Soldiers' Council."

Wild shouts were directed against Ebert. "Hang him from a streetlamp." In this bedlam Social Democrats desperately tried to offer resistance. One of them yelled, "If you keep this up, you'll get a peace that will destroy us." Mocking laughter. The day dragged on, and then the incident occurred that brought the shouting to an end.

A representative of the deserters stormed into the meeting in the halls of the "Germania," shoved his way through the mob and ran up onto the stage. No one had given him the floor, but he seemed so weighed down with destiny that the people up front made room for him.

"Friends, the Executive Council has been arrested. Ebert has been proclaimed President of the Reich. When you go back out on the streets you'll get the shock of your life. Soldiers with bayonets."

This then was the putsch, the counterrevolution. The meeting erupted in tumult: "To the Executive Council! To the Reichs Chancellery! Storm the Reichs Chancellery."

They had become a seething, elemental force, thirsty for revenge, a people demanding its rights set now into motion.

In the meantime the Franz Regiment had made its appearance on the day's stage. The Franzers, noncoms and supporters, marched as ordered out of their barracks on Blücherstrasse and waited by the Brandenburg Gate at 3:30. There they unexpectedly met up with a group of young civilians, who looked well educated and declared that they were the Berlin Student Militia. Some sailors also appeared, a small group led by their commandant, Count Wolf-Metternich. Plus a deputation from the Committee of Ninety-Three. And once they decided their numbers were complete, away they marched, a hurrah for Ebert in their throats. They moved in closed ranks, weapons on their shoulders, with pipe and drum down Unter den Linden toward Wilhelmstrasse.

In the courtyard of the Reichs Chancellery, where they were allowed to enter, a Private Spiro emerged from the formation and began to speak. He said all sorts of things, some of which people already knew, some of which they didn't, some of which they did not reject, and to all of which they were totally indifferent. For they were there only to shout hurrah. Spiro accused the revolutionary Executive Council of "clumsily interfering with the government." After considerable hemming and hawing he finally came up with a cheer: "Long live Comrade Ebert!" whom he herewith proclaimed President of the Republic, conscious as he was of speaking in the name of the whole nation. The drums rolled. Three cheers were raised.

At this point People's Deputy Ebert came out of the building and could be seen on the lower stairs, a small, stout man. He was greeted with cheers. He smiled. His speech was as follows:

"We stand confronted by immense difficulties. The economy, the very foundation of our life, is threatened by arbitrary measures. Our destiny must be governed by a unified will. Be patient until the constituent assembly and until your comrades from the battlefield are here. What I request is total discipline."

As might be expected, matters could not end with that. A student came forward and promised the government the complete support of the "intellectual workers." But it was Private Spiro who first took the bull by the horns. He stepped forward again and cried:

"I now have a simple question. Herr Ebert has been proclaimed President of the Reich. Do you accept that call or not?"

The people's deputy, pressed to answer, glanced at the ground. In one sense this whole affair pleased him as a countermove to the demonstrations of the radicals, in another it looked as if someone might be setting a trap for him. Who was behind these people? He looked up, raised his voice and said very guardedly: "Friends and comrades! This call that has been extended to me is one I cannot, will not, accept without first having spoken with my friends in the government. It is a matter of primary importance, the ultimate decision for which lies in the hands of the people's deputies."

So there was nothing more to say. Once more cheers, then pipe and drum and the cracking sound of feet marching off in step. The iron gates of the Reichs Chancellery were closed.

A second procession of soldiers had been formed, however, but one that set no store by speeches or ovations. While his troops had been milling about indecisively at the Brandenburg Gate, Captain Kohler had driven ahead in his car with a representative of the officers. He gave an elite unit the orders to build a special detachment and to arrest the revolutionary Executive Council. A Lieutenant Fischer took a hundred men, advanced with them to the Prussian-Landtag building and surrounded it. They had flame throwers. A sergeant major entered the building with thirty men and declared that the Executive Council was under arrest.

People's Deputy Emil Barth, who chanced to be in the building, declared however that he knew nothing about this matter, which took the sergeant major aback and convinced him to go personally to the Reichs Chancellery together with a couple of his men. There he found out that in point of fact no warrant for the arrest of the Executive Council existed. Whereupon Lieutenant Fischer, who had come with him, was himself arrested.

The Landtag building was meanwhile still being held by the soldiers of several different divisions, including the Franz Regiment and the Guard Engineers. Then more than a thousand sailors stormed out of the royal stables, drove the soldiers off and liberated the Executive Council.

It was the rumor of these curious events that found its way into the mass meetings. The crowd that streamed out of the halls of the "Germania," once given the cue, thrust its way down the Chausseestrasse with the intent of reaching Unter den Linden by way of the Oranienburg Gate and Friedrichstrasse. It had been evident since morning that should the crowd take to the streets this was the path it would follow. How it happened, however, that the Fusilier Guards likewise appeared on this same path has remained unclear ever since. It has remained a secret just who gave the Fusilier Guards the order to station themselves with rifles and machine guns on the corner of Chausseestrasse and Invalidenstrasse and thus, by whatever means necessary, to block the way to the Reichs Chancellery. All that could be determined later was that the order came from the army corps command, and more precisely from the mouth of a member of the soldiers' council named Krebs. But nothing more could be learned about this Krebs.

For the Fusilier Guards themselves, the situation in the dark Chausseestrasse was infinitely simple. They intended to take military action against civilians, an action that would present no difficulties whatever.

With songs and cheers and boos, the meeting emerged from the halls of the "Germania." The crowd backed up at the corner of Invalidenstrasse. Those at its head noticed soldiers. There was a shouted military command: "Close ranks! Make ready!" The leaders of the procession saw themselves confronted by a regulation firing line. They were absolutely dumbfounded.

Why didn't those who had attended the meeting pull back at the moment when they realized that, unarmed and exposed as they were, right in front of them stood Fusilier Guards ensconsed behind machine guns? Because when the word of alarm reached them they had been promoted from their former status as participants at a meeting, and, though unarmed, felt it to be a duty incumbent upon them by natural right to confront these soldiers, the rotten element within their society.

Among those advancing were the two offended fellows who had initiated these meetings out of anger at being excluded from the soldiers' council.

Among the marchers, moreover, were Eduard Imker, the discharged soldier, Bottrowski from Neukölln, Big Ding and his fiancée Grete Gries, plus former Lieutenant Maus. Former First Lieutenant Becker was not on hand. His legs could not have managed it; he was being held in reserve for other, no less difficult battles.

The crowd pushed and shoved against those at the front. They sang the International and swung their red flags. The band of soldiers let them come, driving them at bayonet point to the west side of Invalidenstrasse. The procession, angered now, advanced once again and in increased numbers.

For the rumor about the arrest of the Executive Council had reached the meeting in the halls of the "Sophie" as well, and these people had sprung up and marched via the Hackischer Markt and Oranienburg Strasse to the Chausseestrasse, in order to join the others, move on to the Landtag building and free the Executive Council.

And out of the great procession, swelling as it moved, sounded incessant cries of: "Long live Liebknecht! Long live Rosa! Down with the government!" The masses moved toward the barrier thrown up by the Fusilier Guards.

When the bullets started flying and people fell to the ground, the crowd burst into a thousand individuals, each one a splinter of horror, anger and hate.

Terror drove them into the buildings along Invalidenstrasse and Chausseestrasse, harried them up stairways, told them to ring at strangers' doors, tossed them into dark courtyards. After a few minutes the streets were empty, and only the dead and wounded lay there. Women, stumbling over the bodies where they lay, fell sobbing to the ground; men penned up in entryways looked about them. "We should never have handed in our weapons. The workers of Berlin are being murdered. Scheidemann and his cohorts have begun the great counterrevolution."

Imker and Bottrowski stood beside one another in an entryway. Bottrowski nodded to his friend. Both faces bore no expression. And that night made a revolutionary of Lieutenant Maus, whose friend Big Ding had been shot as he trotted full of excitement beside him. He had been unable to use his pistol there in the scramble.

Close by Stettin Station, in the darkness in front of the depot for suburban trains, a crowd of fugitives assembled. One of them, who appeared to have gone mad, a wounded war veteran, raved and shrieked: "Give me a revolver. I'll die gladly."

There were sixteen corpses on the pavement of Chausseestrasse. On the corner of Invalidenstrasse, in front of a department store, twenty wounded lay moaning, unable to move. The wounded were brought to emergency rooms on Eichendorffstrasse and in the university clinic on Ziegelstrasse. A number of people were bleeding profusely from cuts received from the splintered glass windows of Fabisch's department store. One car of the No. 32 tram drove unsuspectingly right into the line of fire. A young female apprentice on the front platform was shot dead.

Private Spiro was not content with having proclaimed the wary Ebert President of the Reich. With two hundred men he marched off at once to Königgrätzer Strasse, to the offices of the *Rote Fahne*. With twenty men from the Franz Regiment he entered the editorial room and declared that he had orders from Ebert to occupy the place in the name of the Soldiers' Council of the Guards. He immediately demanded the key to the safe, but was not given it. After an hour and a half the occupation was lifted.

The guard at the Reichs Chancellery was reinforced toward evening as the news began to arrive. The offices were brightly illuminated well into the night. Telephones rang continually: the Party leadership, the navy. With People's Deputy Ebert sat his friends from the Party, members of the government, the city commandant, the chief of police, all of them perplexed. According to the information supplied by the army command, a member of the soldiers' council named Krebs had ordered the Fusilier Guards to Chausseestrasse. They had fired five hundred shots. As far as the arrest of the Executive Council went, that trail was obscure. The Lieutenant Fischer who was arrested had received his orders from a certain Marten and two officials in the Foreign Office, Matuschka and Rheinhaben. Without any doubt, the troops themselves were under the control of the city commandant, but had been given their orders over his head. Wels, who had offered himself that morning to the government as an old bastion of strength, knew nothing about all this and understood nothing either. He walked about with his tail between his legs and was not very talkative.

With the very first dispatches, a cold dread fell upon the Reichs Chancellery. They had triumphantly witnessed the day as it had developed, had received the faithful delegation of noncommissioned officers, groups of upright citizens who had come to cheer rather than howling revolutionaries. They had thought they would soon be able to show the generals just who they were. But then everything fell apart. Instead of a putsch from the left there was one from the right, and the events had a curious shimmer about them, something phosphorescent, like many objects in nature, an effect that does have a certain beauty about it. But at the moment the men in the Reichs Chancellery in Berlin had no feeling for the magic of nature.

"Bandits," Ebert cursed. In order to compromise him they had arranged a whole conspiracy.

"Bandits," cursed the city commandant.

Who was this Spiro? Ebert stared in despair at his comrades-in-arms. Was this Spiro an ass or a rascal? Who was Krebs at army command? What sort of figures were these who had emerged here in the very center of events, in the very spot where they themselves had stood till now.

Ebert alternated between loud curses and embittered rage. His anger was directed against his friends in the party, against Kassel and Spartacus. This is the counterrevolution. And they want to harness me to it. They are creating chaos so that they can have a reason to march in. They'll be here tomorrow. That was what he thought; but what he said was directed against Liebknecht.

"That madman. He could be on our side. By rights he ought to be. He ought to have alarmed the young workers and armed them, instead of that . . ."

Ebert's friends tried to keep him to the subject: Spartacus and their everlasting rabble-rousing was to blame for everything. But Ebert sat there silently in his chair, pommeled by dark fists. He heard the furies of guilt screaming. For a long time he could not even open his mouth.

When he finally did stand up and start wandering aimlessly about, he muttered, "The fancy gentlemen at Wilhelmshöhe. They're going to find they're badly mistaken. They're provoking the masses. They'll provoke them till blood flows. But I promise one thing: the next time the masses go for their throats, I'll not save them."

For he was smarting from the fact that someone had reckoned with his vanity when they proclaimed him Reichs President. That's how base they are. They dare to mock me.

It was two in the morning. He made for home.

But this eventful Friday—a foretaste of what was yet to come, a larval stage for events that would soon bring horrible convulsions to the streets of Berlin—should not be allowed to sink into the past without first having contributed in yet another powerful way to preparing for those events.

On that same Friday, far from Berlin and the Mark Brandenburg, in Paderborn, on Westphalian soil, there gathered the ranking officers and the General Staff of the Sixt von Arnim army group for a discussion. It took place in the episcopal palace.

The officers conferred—while the troops were still marching home—about the tempo of demobilization, conditions within the Reich, the danger in the East. They debated about the extent to which the troops were crumbling. On this point the leader of the 214th Division, General Maercker, expressed himself very precisely.

He was an old and unusually energetic soldier, having served thirty-four years in the service of the Guard at home and in the colonies. He had participated in five wars under three kaisers. Atop his rather short but sturdy body the general had a roundish head with a weather-beaten, inconspicuous face, out of which deep set eyes looked coldly and searchingly. You could tell by looking at him that it was better not to get on his wrong side.

In the course of the retreat he had continually been at odds with the soldiers' councils. He was not shy in sharing with everyone around him his indignation at seventeen- and eighteen-year-old brats presuming to represent the army. As they marched through Eupen he had completely lost his temper. Together with the commandant of the 18th Army Corps, von Etzel, he had tried hard to get his units onto the right road—while at the other end of town a mere boy in a sailor's uniform, a member of a soldier's council, had created hopeless confusion with his own orders, revealing nothing so much as his profound ignorance.

Maercker said in Paderborn: "We have to put a stop to these soldiers' councils. They presume the right to issue orders, appropriate commissary stores, distribute army property to their pals, to malingerers, even to enemy civilians. They condemn our own divisions to a lack of provisions and disrupt the passing on of orders. They openly encourage desertion by issuing discharge papers to the rank and file."

Maercker placed both his fists next to each other on the heavy oak table around which they sat, and laughed. "Do you know what these fellows remind me of? Of some stupid clown in a circus. Especially when they're zealous. In the Eifel region a mother came running up to me begging me to tan her sixteen-year-old's hide. She couldn't do it anymore; the kid had become a member of a soldier's council."

While they amused themselves at this, he came forward with his plan, the basic features of which they already knew: not to wait until the army had been completely disbanded, no longer to stand by and watch the destruction of the army by revolutionaries, but quickly to assemble the sound elements of the army and make a volunteer corps of them. And what reasons were to be given the government? Danger in the East, domestic disruptions.

This time all the influential officers were at the same table. They found the idea "not half bad." But it hadn't much chance, one suggested. It was too close to the last minute. Even from his own division one infantry regiment and the field artillery had marched off to be demobilized.

These answers proved sufficient for General Maercker, and without further ado he picked up the events of December 6th right where the Fusilier Guards had left them lying on Chausseestrasse. He ordered his troops and staff officers to report to his office, where he informed them as follows:

"I have come to a decision. From the 24th Infantry Division, to the extent that it still exists, we will build a volunteer corps. I will place it at the disposal of the present government. I cannot simply play the role of Yorck and declare war on the Entente—by which I do not mean to say that this will assure us a better future either. But at least we can hold off the corrosive disintegration of our position both at home and abroad. That is what we shall try to begin to do at once, utilizing our experiences from the front line and giving due consideration to present circumstances, by which I mean a certain reorganization of the relationship between officers and the rank and file, though of course absolutely excluding any soldiers' councils."

The general could be certain of the approval of his staff and the troop officers.

Night had not yet laid its cover over that demonic Friday before they had already begun discussing the first steps to be taken.

The men and women killed in the shooting were laid out in St. Lazaus hospital. They were driven to the small yellow building on Hessische Strasse, the morgue. Until late that night people streamed into it, the families of missing persons. The police took down the information provided by relatives.

The morgue personnel, who had to listen to the laments of these relatives, spoke among themselves. "It was no different in the war either. People were even shot in their sleep or when they were sitting down to eat. Civilians too. Nobody got excited about it then."

"Civilians in general have the wrong conception of war. Now they're screaming: He wasn't even a part of it. As if you have to be a part of it. He didn't even have a gun. All of it total nonsense."

"Have you seen the three big guys with the red armbands? They've all been looking at them. They want to give them a grand funeral. That'll mean new corpses."

"What else?"

A man who had his grown daughter beside him comes down the stairs into the icy cellar of the morgue, his face rigid. They hold handkerchiefs to their noses for there is a ghastly sweet odor down here. They shot and killed his wife as she stood next to him.

The daughter: "She didn't want to come along in the first place."

"But she came along anyway, didn't she. Girl, don't keep repeating the same thing."

The daughter weeps. "Mother."

The father: "Things ain't over yet."

She continues weeping out on the dark street.

The street is full of people as far as Oranienburg Gate, police patrols have been reinforced.

The father: "Now stop your bawling. Do you understand, girl?"

"Why shouldn't I cry, Father, with Mother dead? She was our mother, wasn't she? And your wife."

"Just be quiet. That doesn't get you anywhere. We'll go to my bar and ask around."

"Ask what, Father?"

"What they're going to do. And then I'm going to go home and get my gun."

"Are you going to join them, Father? They'll shoot you too."

"You're coming along too. You're old enough."

"I'll come. I'll come, Father. After the funeral. — Oh don't go, Father. Then I'll be all alone."

From the brightly moonlit roofs of the buildings before which the shots had rung out, shadows plummet into the dark, totally peaceful Chausseestrasse. The shadows of roof ridges, shadows of chimneys.

They touch the puddles of blood on the pavement, on the sidewalk. And one would like to believe that blood is blood and will soon dry and be wiped away, that shadow is shadow and plummets black from roofs.

But if all things were merely what our scales and yardsticks make of them, then life would not be life, people not be people, and there would have been no shooting on Chausseestrasse.

The blood that congealed and coagulated on the pavement had borne human souls within it, who likewise did not know much about themselves and who assumed they were simply mechanics or soldiers or people out of a job and that was that. And if they could still go on thinking now, they would swear it was the absolute truth when they told you that they had left the halls of "Germania," excited but peaceable, had sung songs, and were now dead, and that their heavy corpses lay not far from here in the morgue on Hessische Strasse.

But for the shadows these puddles of blood were more than that. All around them came the soft breath of the gray of morning and evening twilight, sunrise and sunset.

Although torn away from the large body that had served as a warm house for it, the blood knew about the path of stars, the sparkle of moonlight, about pastures and alpine meadows, about mountains across whose glaciers hikers trudge, about blue lakes, about dance bands.

And the shadows understood too, although they were only fleeting visions created beneath moonlight, to which one could hardly attribute an existence as compared to the massive chimneys about which they lay, or to the solid ridge of roof from which they plummeted. But they lead a life here no different from that of the roof, the chimney or the clanking cannon or the horse plodding heavily by.

They grasped the yearnings, the pain, the happiness of the people whose blood lay there, and were ignited by it all. They were amazed at the miracle of the great wide world they had never had a chance to see, and they did not want to hear the complaints sighed by the blood— about the brevity of life, the suddenness of death. Their life was briefer still.

The shadows stretched out across the roof, along the pavement next to the shadows of the streetlamps and wrestled with them. They struggled until heavy wagons came rolling down the street and men appeared with brooms to clean the street and the sidewalk, finally pouring water over the pavement.

Then the blood of the slain swirled along the gutters, with twine, scraps of paper, dog shit and apple cores. It fell into the drains to join the waste and sewage.

The journey through the bodies of walking, loving and heaven-crazed men was over.

They had been mere wisps, like the shadows of roofs and street-lamps dissolving now in the dawn.

The Next Day

A people's deputy has spent his reserves of anger. Those around him are still jittery and filled with gloomy visions. Spartacus organizes street demonstrations. Two radicals discuss the inexhaustible topic: When is an uprising a revolution and when is it merely a putsch?

Ebert Is Well Rested

The next day, Saturday, December 7th, the First People's Deputy returned to Wilhelmstrasse, but not too early. He had gotten a good rest and had fully regained his poise. Since yesterday evening the street was under special military security.

The nervous lights of the night before had been extinguished in the Reichs Chancellery. The old building stood there calm, cold and secure. Its corridors teemed with upset friends of the Party; yesterday's mysterious attack weighed upon them. Ebert himself, having spent his reserves of anger, was feeling quite at home again in his bull-like body.

He heard the reports that had come in; as he read and made his notes he secretly regretted having let himself be driven into a corner yesterday and not having responded as he usually did by calmly telephoning General Groener.

On the contrary, he should have called him and sworn at him so that they would know it wasn't that easy to put one over on him.

His gray-bearded undersecretary, an old Party comrade, asked him worriedly what they must be thinking of Berlin in Kassel now. This was grist for their mill.

Ebert growled amid his paperwork. "Naturally. Your typical Berlin mess. But those fine gentlemen are mistaken. The ones who made asses of themselves in yesterday's events were the men in Kassel. If the confusions of yesterday are a sample of their counterrevolution, why just let them keep it up."

He spoke of the noble ringleaders of the putsch who had been found out, the gentlemen from the Foreign Office, Matuschka, Rheinhaben. They had courageously run away. Ebert was furious when it was reported to him in a whisper that a Herr von Stumm, from a family of industrialists, was also involved in the affair.

"Let them just keep it up."

Then came Secretary Schmidt with the latest newspapers. The radical Left was seething. They went at the government with all their cannons booming.

The *Rote Fahne* wrote: "Workers! Join the general strike! We must act. This bloody crime must be punished, the conspiracy of Wels, Ebert and Scheidemann must be smashed with an iron fist, the revolution must be saved.

"Down with Wels, Ebert and Scheidemann! All power to the workers' and soldiers' councils. To work, to the ramparts, to battle!"

Ebert handed one paper after another to the secretary. "Spartacus is ready for the madhouse."

Schmidt, the type one would expect to be teaching public school, serious, wearing wire-rimmed glasses, in his late twenties, carefully stacked the newspapers. "Chausseestrasse won't be the end of it."

Ebert nodded. "There's no helping these people."

The further results of the investigation that came in during the morning did not interest Ebert much. The little man had a soothing effect on everyone. When it was reported that there were new connections discovered between the Foreign Office and Vice–Sergeant Major Fischer, who had wanted to arrest the Executive Council, he assumed an ironic smile and asked his young secretary, "Since when, actually, is everyone so concerned about the Executive Council? Are our comrades so afraid for those fussbudgets? Really? Not me." And he looked into the young man's eyes. "If Liebknecht wants a brouhaha, he'll get it."

With this much information in, about an hour later Ebert's two secretaries sat down to a modest lunch on Dorotheenstrasse, then drank some watery beer in a small bar on Friedrichstrasse. The two were Schmidt and Neumann—Schmidt, with the wire-rimmed glasses; Neumann, younger, with a soft, blond moustache and blond hair cut somewhat long. They had both spoken to friends, it was said the whole city was in an uproar, that Spartacus had called for a general strike and had had flyers distributed, reading: "General Strike! To the ramparts!" New mass meetings were set for today, and in the ill-starred halls of the "Germania" too.

Schmidt said, "Everyone at our place who can get away is going to go to Wilhelmstrasse and stay there as long as they can stand the cold. But we don't have many weapons."

Neumann played the optimist. "Who's going to respond to this crazy call for a general strike? It's always the same ones and a few fellow travelers. But they go right on working peacefully at Löwe and at

Schwartzkopff. Those who come will be from Knorr Brakes and then a couple of hundred from AEG, and German Arms."

The conversation was stuck.

Schmidt: "Would you like to be in Ebert's shoes now at the cabinet meeting? Another incident like last evening's and the Independents will have no choice but to resign, and then the government will fall."

"And we're rid of the Independents."

Schmidt: "And what about us? Who do we work with then? Liebknecht is towing us up the creek."

"Then our people will just have to work a little harder."

"Our people, our people. What are our people going to look like afterward, when everything has been taken away from them and they've been expected to swallow God knows what without ever once being able to let loose?"

"What do you want then, Schmidt?"

"Me? I don't want anything. But all this soft-pedaling. This soft-pedaling. They take everything we have to give. And no one knows what's what anymore. Lord, Neumann, we ought to be able to show we're good for something. Wouldn't you like to have just a little taste of revolution sometime? We're the working class, aren't we? Let's not deceive ourselves, we made mistakes during the war. But now the opportunity is here to make amends, and we could give the Party a fresh look. When I tell this to Ebert, first he's glad to hear it and then afterward he says that I'm an intellectual and that it's not so easy to pull off."

Neumann: "What do you want then? To go with the Independents or with Spartacus? Won't work."

Schmidt, vehemently: "We need unity in the working class the same way we need daily bread. Ebert should show some courage. We'll go with him. He's too afraid of the officers and the front-line army. What a lot of crap we take from them. We showed them our fist on November 9th. And we'll do it again on December 9th. I tell you there's not a dog that'll stick with them, and we have the workers together and can do what we like against anyone. The Spartacists, they're nothing more than ten little men making noise for ten thousand, and without Russia they're nothing at all—and against the Entente too. Of course Eisner is right: we can't carry off anything really big with men like Solf."

Neumann: "But I still don't know what you want."

Schmidt pulls a copy of *Vorwärts* from his breast pocket. "What are we doing? That the incident yesterday didn't turn out any worse is nothing we can take credit for. How do we react? Like the Independents—a little indignation, a little threat; we just run in place. We announce officially that there are good signs that the bread supply will improve: 'As a result of the frost-free weather the potato and beet harvests have been completed sooner than expected,' and that releases workers and makes more grain available. The bread supply is assured until February, 1919."

Neumann: "What do you have against that? Not bad, not bad. It's a solid piece of achievement."

Schmidt, grimly: "And in this way piece by piece we are taken away from our real tasks. They're simply throwing sand in the workers' eyes."

"Nothing will work if there's not a crust of bread around. Whoever provides that has a great argument on his side."

Schmidt: "Sand in their eyes. We act as if nothing were going on in the country. We're feeding our enemies with that bread too. We've got to strike out, I tell you, establish the unity of the working class. People are hungry for it. We're falling behind. We're already retreating. Ebert has put us on the defensive. It's not enough to be sitting on Wilhelmstrasse. We haven't assumed any real power, although we could. In the final analysis we're only a screen for the bourgeoisie."

Neumann: "We need a man for a defensive position, I tell you. Nothing could be more important at the moment."

Through his half-empty glass, however, Schmidt gloomily watched as the earth opened up beneath him. And breathing heavily, he saw workers, men and women, wandering the streets, being shot down by soldiers with rifles. And before the Reichs Chancellery on Wilhelmstrasse the old regiments came marching from Unter den Linden, music blaring, the old flags at the fore. The masses were driven back to Leipziger Strasse, Ebert was brought out and led away captive in a closed car. A general strode into the Reichs Chancellery with his staff, military dictatorship is here.

The Spartacists' Demonstrations

At two that afternoon—the rain had just let up—three thousand people gathered on the Sieges Allee in the Zoological Garden.

Liebknecht spoke. "The masses must realize by now where the policies of these imperial socialists are leading. The putsch yesterday was staged by the government."

The procession began to move, with two hundred armed men from the Red Soldiers' League at its head. A large car with machine guns led the way. At the National Library on Unter den Linden soldiers with machine guns blocked their path. While panic set in at the rear, up front two knots of people formed, and it looked as if a battle would develop.

Then a military car came hurtling across Schloss Bridge. Two people stood up inside and shouted, "Halt! Don't shoot!"

At that, the soldiers pulled back into the National Library. The men of the Red Soldiers' League seized their machine guns.

Now they were in front of the city commandant's headquarters. Liebknecht spoke from the car.

"We are at that spot where the first initiative for yesterday's blood-bath came from. We demand that the present government and Herr Wels be chased from office. Until these tyrants are deposed the revolution is in danger."

After him a man named Ruck from Stuttgart spoke. "Arm yourselves! We want an economic revolution and expropriation of property. Bear arms when you go to your factories and out on the street."

A woman: "Things went badly enough for you during the war, but you'll have to go on being hungry for a long time yet. We must throw down this government, then things will get better. Karl Liebknecht will be our president."

Across the street, next to the armory, among a grove of chestnut trees stood the ancient temple of the city watch. The soldiers inside watched through the gate. They cursed these madmen. "The French will soon be here."

The procession halted at the desolate Lustgarten. There people were told that the commandant of the People's Navy, Count Wolf-Metternich, who had participated in yesterday's putsch, had been removed from office and been replaced by Radtke.

At four o'clock it was over. Cars raced along Unter den Linden and Friedrichstrasse strewing handbills that read: "Workers, soldiers, comrades! The revolution is in great danger. Come to the mass protest demonstration. Sunday, two o'clock, in Treptow Park. The Spartacus League."

Toward evening ten thousand handbills were distributed through the city: "Kill the Jews. Kill Liebknecht!"

At Spartacus Headquarters

That evening people thronged about the dark Schloss Platz in front of the royal stables, the headquarters of the People's Navy. Many of them then moved across the Schloss Bridge through Königsstrasse toward police headquarters, others turned back, and most of them stood around doing nothing, discussing and listening, with spies of all parties on hand.

The Russian Radek shoved his way into the building. He wanted to see which of the leaders he could find to learn something of the situation.

In the noisy offices he learned that Liebknecht was in the building. Radek chatted with several sailors who were in the best of moods and eager for battle. When he opened a window in the stuffy, hot room, Liebknecht's voice rang out from the courtyard—hoarse, as it had been for several days now. He was speaking to the sailors. It heartened Radek, though he could not understand a word.

After a quarter of an hour there was the sound of soldiers' steps tramping up the stairs. Amid the armed men who surrounded him like bodyguards—they were only partly clad in real uniforms, some wore military caps and coats over civilian clothes, there were also simply civilians with rifles—amid them appeared Liebknecht, sweating so that his hair was plastered to his head. He held his cap in his hand.

His face was flushed. He was excited, overwrought. They immediately gathered about him; he wanted something to drink, someone wrapped a scarf around his throat. From a distance, without pressing forward himself, Radek saw him shoving his way among the tables. What an enthusiastic, impassioned, genuine man. How everything in him pulsed. How relaxed the bitter hardness of the features was. Someone was giving him a briefing. People were looking about the room, Radek heard his own name mentioned, Liebknecht was already moving toward him. A quote from Ibsen occurred to Radek: "With grape leaves in his hair." They shook hands. The German smiled abstractedly (the slightest bit crazy, Radek thought. It was how he had looked when he came out of prison and still had not got his bearings).

Someone opened a door for them, they entered the adjoining smoke-filled room that several sailors vacated after a few whispers.

Liebknecht took off his coat and threw it over the table among the empty beer bottles and ashtrays, and sighing deeply he fell exhausted into a chair. He laid his head on his coat.

Radek said, "It was a hot afternoon."

The German did not stir. He seemed to be sleeping. When he lifted his head from the table, he removed the pince-nez; he looked burned out, tired and strange. He cleared his throat. Despite which he still did not have his voice back when he said, "Things are moving."

Radek thought: how different Lenin looked at this point. They have got the hoarse voice in common, but otherwise . . . The one was a mind, all intelligence, ten sources of energy, while this one—a sputtering flame, flickering, now high, now low.

Radek: "Tomorrow then, in the afternoon. The mass meeting in Treptow. You have to be ready for anything. The others will have their people together too. There could be clashes."

Liebknecht: "This time they won't shoot us down."

He ceremoniously wiped his face and neck, poured some water from a carafe and drank it slowly. This brought him out of his reverie and it was his everyday face that he showed now, overtired and bitter with suffering.

Radek: "Then you are aware now that everything is pressing toward an armed uprising, and within the next few days."

"My dear Radek, that's exactly how things are. You have expressed it perfectly. Everything is pressing toward an armed uprising, and within the next few days. I would like to meet the man who could prevent the uprising that has started to develop. Neither you nor I could do it. It would pass right over us. When I spoke today it all seemed quite strange to me. The people, the masses, this hot rage of the masses really did not allow for any personal opinion. I cannot formulate my thoughts at all, make any point of my own. I can only say onward and onward and ever onward. Always just that one thing. They take my sense of self from me. It's as if my own ego had been extinguished."

Out there he had said: "Officers and junkers, generals and admirals as members of the soldiers' councils, princes as their guardians. In Westphalia and elsewhere there are secret meetings of these 'council members' with other officers under the direction of the high command. Hindenburg issues political proclamations just as in Wilhelm's days. Lieutenant General von Winterfeld has marched into Aachen and Cologne with his 2nd Division in order to put down the revolution. And at the head of this mighty army with its black, white and red flag and exemplary discipline and a spurious hate that they have whipped up against us, the Bolsheviks, march the generals, the men to blame for the war. Co-conspirators of the Hohenzollerns advancing from the West into the heart of Germany. The impudence of the military counterrevolution has been growing ever greater. And now they have let the mask fall, on this bloody December 6th, which we shall not forget. Tolerated by the Ebert-Scheidemann-Wels government, sponsored by them, pampered by them . . ."

Radek: "You said what you had to say."

Liebknecht: "You've always been in agreement with that, haven't you?"

Radek: "Completely. If only you don't exhaust yourself. You expose yourself an awful lot, by the way. I saw you speaking later on. I was amazed at your carelessness, or better, at the negligence of your comrades. Someone could pick you off like nothing. In Russia we've always known what a mistake can mean." He smiled archly. "Those of our opponents, too."

Liebknecht: "A bodyguard? You're funny. So then you are in agreement?"

Aha, the doubts rise up again. Holy Lenin, pray for me. The clear, candid eyes of the German are directed at him.

"Of course. You heard me say so."

Liebknecht: "You have to give me more precise reasons, more details, please. With what are you in agreement?"

"You said it yourself, Karl, that things are moving."

"Right. Things are moving."

"Well?"

"And what do you have to say to that? Should one let them move?

You told me recently about how your opponents in the Central Committee wrote an article titled 'What Should We Not Do?' just before the October Revolution."

"Which Lenin refuted. The one with the reference to the French Commune."

"Yes. He called it superficial." Liebknecht brooded; he mechanically stroked the black lining of his coat with his left hand. "What interests me is where the ideas in the article came from. Those ideas surfaced among you as well. Kamenev suggested that you hold out for a while, not give in too hastily, that conditions were not yet right."

Radek, very animated, offended: "He was proven wrong within a week, two weeks. We struck the blow. You're well aware of the results."

Liebknecht pondered and nodded. "Of course you're still fighting too, by the way. You'll win, I don't doubt that. But it may take a while."

Radek shrugged. "Years maybe. You have to stamp out the fire wherever it flares up."

"Of course. Of course. You have an immense country. You can wreck a little bit here, a little bit there. That's difficult for us. We live packed more tightly together."

He faltered and stared at the black coat lining, pinching a fold of it together between two fingers, pulling it up to form a mountain, letting it back down slowly. "We cannot allow ourselves such a grand scale of things."

Radek: "What are you suggesting then?" He acted as if he were engaged in some purely academic debate. He nonchalantly rubbed his brow and nose, hiding his mouth with the same gesture in order not to show his anger.

Liebknecht: "I'm not suggesting anything. After a hot day like this, when I never got to speak my own thoughts, I ought to be able to express myself at long last. Yes, things are moving forward . . ."

Radek: "Toward our goal."

"We have excellent people, splendid young fellows. We're responsible for them."

"Ask them what they want."

"I know what they want. That's why I'm still responsible for them. — I want peace. I've always wanted it. Real and total peace. Plus the disarming of the military, disarmament at home and abroad, socialism, the overthrow of capitalism."

"You can't have it without weapons."

"But if I strike too soon I'm a 'putschist,' a Blanquist, and I ruin everything."

"My dear Karl, the auspicious moment, the inauspicious moment. You come up here. You're beaming. You know yourself you've said

299

what's in the heart of the masses. What you're experiencing now are the doubts, the fears that assail a man when he is alone."

Liebknecht hung on his lips, both his hands placed flat on the table. "Is that true?"

"Our task is immense, our goal the most prodigious one a man may set for himself. You feel you are alone, one solitary person, small and helpless. But when you stand in front of the masses, then everything is clear to you."

"That's it," nodded Liebknecht.

Radek struck while the iron was hot. "To be in accord with the popular will does not make one a Blanquist or a putschist. The outrage over the behavior of Ebert and Wels reaches into bourgeois circles. Read the papers, how they're squirming trying to make the Ebert-Wels slogans plausible for their readers, holding Spartacus to blame.

"The call for a general strike has been given. You'll see the result. On the whole, when I stop to consider it rightly, I can only see the course things have taken as favorable to us. The monarchists thought they would pave the way for the putsch they have planned for next Tuesday when the troops march in. Instead—it's our move."

"They may also have been maneuvering so that we have to make our move, my dear friend."

Radek pulled his chair, which was on the other side of the table, directly across from Liebknecht and shoved the beer bottles between them to one side. The German had recovered. He sat erect, stroking and smoothing his moustache.

The Russian said in a friendly tone, "I can understand your wavering. Of course there is responsibility involved. But only opportunists dodge responsibility by declaring they're waiting for the momentum of the revolution. Opportunists always believe in 'momentum' when it comes time to strike the blow. And so of course they don't strike it at all. Their view of a revolution is that it should run its course without human interference. It's the idiocy of the Majority Socialists. Lenin declared very succinctly, after analyzing the situation, 'The revolt is ripe.' And then added something you should take to heart. 'The revolt is ripe. One must deal with it as one would deal with an art form.' "

The German's eyes widened with joy. "Those are noble words."

Radek, content. 'That's how you begin a revolution. He called the organizations of workers and soldiers to prepare for armed insurrection and moved against Kamenev and Zinoviev. Kamenev declared he wanted to resign. His resignation was accepted by a vote of five to three."

"Five to three? That's a weak majority I'd say. And why only eight votes?"

"We were at war, more couldn't come. — But you should probably join your people. I think they're waiting for you."

Radek was not pleased with this conversation.

The German: "They're patient. They don't need me at the moment."

Radek was still the antagonist. Just to keep things going," he said. "At least you know how things went from there, the garrison, the 'Aurora' on the Neva and so on."

"It sounds like some heroic song now."

Radek: "That's true. But the principles of Marxism are valid everywhere. Lenin's words are irrefutable in all times and places: that opportunists always wait for momentum, and that one must deal with a revolt that is ripe with an active will and mind like an artist with his art."

"Fine. But now permit me, since you've raised no objection thus far, to remind you of a difference between the Russian and German situations, one you've pointed out yourself. Kerensky still had a war on his borders and a front-line army locked in battle. Ebert already has peace. And if, as he spouts daily, what he wants is to secure peace and domestic tranquillity, then he's only meeting broadly-based wishes. The trump card for the revolution that Lenin had, the card of peace, we don't have. On the contrary, we appear to be the destroyers of peace. And consider besides what our thesis, to be precise Rosa's thesis, may mean, namely that a true revolution has not even occurred, that everything, apart from a few personalities, has remained as it was. That's true, but that makes no difference to them. They want peace."

"Just as with us. You've drawn the right conclusions from Rosa's thesis, the ones I have underlined."

"But you're still fighting a civil war, and you can afford to. What would that mean for us? Radek, we have to win fast here in Germany. Fast, fast. For us the question of time is decisive. We stand or fall with it. Or we will be pushed onto the path of a long, slow process of change. — Yes, why not say it. That would mean, for example, that we must regard the constituent assembly differently."

Radek, cold: "Shelve the revolution. Counterrevolution. You cannot conserve a revolutionary situation. The only things you can conserve are revolutionary phrases."

Karl: "We have to keep our eyes on the German situation." Radek's impression now, as the German sat calmly across from him, was no longer that of a sputtering flame, flickering now high, now low, but of an adversary in full possession of his powers. "We must avoid any false move. We have to prevent the return of the Hohenzollerns, to do battle with the generals and their establishment and with a military dictatorship, and under certain conditions we must do so with arms. And we can depend on the entire united proletariat, and others as well. Which of course does not mean that we may have to set the avalanche of a revolution in motion, perhaps we may not need it at all."

Radek: "Quite right."

The German: "And so I'm asking you what you think."

"That at the beginning of October, Kamenev and Zinoviev issued a call to the entire Party, saying that we Bolsheviks did not have the right, not in the name of the history of the Russian proletariat, not in the name of the history of the Russian revolution, to stake the whole future on an armed insurrection. They therefore declared that they wished to join the constituent assembly as the opposition. They were for a union of constitutionalism and socialism. They considered our slogan "Now or never" to be wrong. The party of the proletariat would and must grow, its program must slowly be made clear to the broad masses. Following this declaration," Radek raised both arms, "Lenin gave the signal—for the Russian revolution."

The German: "And you are still fighting a civil war, Radek! But socialism doesn't want to destroy things, it wants them to take a higher course of development."

Radek, savagely: "Served to it on a platter."

"But in fact the Kamenevs and Zinovievs may have shown bourgeois cowardice, been superficial and stupid for the Russian situation, while for us in Germany . . . My God, I'm torturing you, Radek."

Radek: "Go on."

Liebknecht picked up his coat from the table and slowly stood up. He was serious and friendly. "The window's wide open. I'm freezing. We'll talk more tomorrow. Come and eat with me."

Radek helped him into his coat, and while doing so he said, "I hear everything you are saying, all the while recognizing the fact that you've been giving speeches the whole day today. You need to have your revenge for that. The suppressed ego. Rosa has moods like that too."

"We worry you, don't we? I think the problem is that we are nearing some very difficult and decisive matters. From a distance they look very different than from up close."

"Of course," Radek was quick to say.

Liebknecht linked his left arm under Radek's. They started to walk. "Come see our lads, our men. You're pleased with them, aren't you? They are certainly as brave as yours in Russia. That's why I'll not allow myself to do anything rash, not even if they want it. Blood is a very special fluid. They're too dear to me to be used as cannon fodder. We didn't take them out of the hands of the Prussian generals for that. We shall strike our blow for a free, socialist Germany when the time comes. Radek, you need not worry about that."

They opened the door. Liebknecht let go of the Russian. They entered the large, overcrowded room.

Radek was amazed as he watched his friend, how he mixed among the sailors with such enjoyment. He talked with them like a father, affectionately, and like a comrade.

He had changed a great deal in the last few weeks. For the better? He lacks hardness, distance, the Russian thought. A German idealist. Makes me shudder. But he's mistaken. The masses will move right on past him. The revolution will soar right on over his head.

Part II

THE TROOPS RETURN

Book One

Around December 8, 1918

Earth has a place in the order of justice.

Woodrow Wilson

The "Goethe League" and the last president of the Reichstag rise up from their place of residence, the garbage can. The "Council of Intellectuals" meets and poets sing. But from across the ocean Woodrow Wilson comes sailing to put an end to Europe's chaos.

Current Affairs

Time was set down over the world like an incubator, forcing it to distend and yield up what it had within it.

The world, howling with realities, sweating facts in a thousand places at once, would not have been the world had it not produced a jumble of figures—mock-heroic ones, tragic ones, unsullied ones.

At the beginning of December, 1918, the last president of the imperial Reichstag, a man by the name of Fehrenbach, came toddling gravely along and suggested that the most immediate method for remedying the evil of the day was to convoke the old Reichstag once more. It was his opinion; he offered it.

His discontent spread to the so-called "Goethe League," which in the days of imperial Germany had done battle against censorship in the theater. Mildewed, turning a greenish white, the "League" pulled itself together, left its residence, a garbage dump, and hobbled out into the harsh light of day. After pleading to be excused for the odor it exuded as a result of present difficulties, it croaked that the League, though opposed to all chauvinism, could not help but feel that, given the current situation, it was an indignity for a Berlin theater to place on its program a French play "lacking all justification from the standpoint of higher cultural values."

Whereupon the "League" retreated once again to its residence.

A large public meeting was organized by the "Council of Intellectual Workers" in the "Grand Halls of the West." Six people spoke on the topic "The Spirit of Revolution." When it was over they all, speakers and public alike, went home downcast. Nothing had really happened.

But the poets sang.

Meidner, the painter, sang: "Poets and balladeers of the taverns and county fairs, of bars, cabarets and gin-mills;

"And you writers of religious tracts, poets of the Salvation Army, Moravians, Quakers, Adventists, Zionists, and you crackerjack authors of socialist broadsides, rabble-rousers and anarchists whose poems are shoved beneath the parlor doors of the poor as morning dawns;

"You who pen your Communist Manifestos, Marseillaises and Internationales and at least for half an hour shatter the stupor of dark hosts with joyous bolts of lightning—and, finally, you loathers of these times, you true poets and men, you contemporary wrestlers with God, lonely, driven and enthralled. — To all you men of good faith I send my fraternal greeting."

The poet Hasenclever: "From the firmaments the new poet descends to perform great, even greater deeds. / No more the poet dreams in shady groves, / But sees bright squadrons riding forth and dazed / He treads on corpses of the wicked, roves / With nations, peoples, masses, head upraised. / He will be their leader, / He will prophesy, / His flaming word become their music. / And he will bind the nations in one great league, / Secure the rights of men / Found the republic."

Johannes R. Becher: "Storm, storm on, Azure. Ho, bombs and barricades and fire. Storm now. Crash, donnybrooks and drums. Lightning spewed from nostrils, barrels. Spread out, move. Swelling on, unending, sparks rise seething ebbing, citadels. Man the doer. Praise him. Immortality."

Thomas Woodrow Wilson and the Principles of America

But President Woodrow Wilson, a man of sixty-two years, was already underway from America. He was sailing on the *George Washington,* accompanied by the cruiser *Pennsylvania* and five destroyers. He was expected in Brest on December 13th, where nine American dreadnoughts and thirty destroyers were to sail out to meet him.

America was nearing the chaotic, convulsed and ailing motherland.

Woodrow Wilson was of Scotch-Irish descent. His grandfather had come from England at the beginning of the 19th century and had rooted himself in the young democracy that proclaimed every man had within him the power to comprehend all divine law and to recognize the larger order of which he was a part. President Wilson's grandfather, residing in Philadelphia and Pittsburgh, was named a judge. He owned a print shop and newspaper. His son became a clergyman, and his son was Woodrow, who as a student wrote an essay on William Pitt, the Englishman who had organized resistance to Napoleon, the greatest tyrant of modern times and squanderer of the energies of his nation. Wilson became president of Princeton University; he preferred to leave that post rather than accept the twelve million dollars he was offered to drop his plan for educational reform. As governor of the state of New Jersey he proved strict in his cleansing of political morals. He was elected president of the republic.

At the dedication of a building at the naval academy at Annapolis on June 5, 1914, he said to the young men: "When I look at our flag, it seems to me as if the white stripes were strips of parchment upon which are written the rights of men, and the red stripes the streams of blood by which those rights have been made good. Then in the little blue firmament in the corner have swung out the stars of the states of the American Union. So it is, as it were, a sort of floating charter that has come down to us from Runnymede, when men said, 'We will not have masters; we will be a people, and we will seek our own liberty.' "

The nation was swept into the European war of 1914–1918. The Germans had developed a new weapon, the submarine, and they sank whatever crossed their path.

They ran up against the United States.

In Baltimore Wilson raised his voice to say: "There is only one response to Germany's challenge: force, force to the utmost, force without stint or limit, the righteous and triumphant force which will make right the law of the world and cast every selfish domination down in the dust.

"Can a military power or a group of nations determine the fate of peoples over which they have no other right than force? Shall mighty nations be allowed to subjugate weak ones? Shall peoples have to continue to be subjected to the will of others and not be able to make their own voices heard? Will a common ideal for all peoples be realized, or will the mighty continue to act as they choose and torment the weak with impunity? Can the demand for justice be arbitrarily pushed aside or shall there be treaties that enjoin a common duty for justice?"

On Independence Day, 1918, the president made a pilgrimage to the grave of Washington at Mount Vernon—on the battlefields of France tens of thousands of Americans already lay dead. "We fight for the destruction of every arbitrary power. We will not accept any halfway decisions."

That same morning the American visitors of Cantigag marched past Washington's monument on the Place de Jena in Paris. With a jaunty step they moved on to the Place de la Concorde and greeted the statue of Strasbourg.

The war came to an end. The goal was achieved, the Central Powers were defeated. The heirs of the Pilgrim fathers had done their job in breaking tyranny in Europe. Now the president was sailing aboard the

George Washington, the ship bore back to Europe the strength of these, her sons.

There was to be an end to the corruption of the old continent. Europe lay exhausted and mangled. The messenger of justice approached, the messenger of conscience, the representative of the country that was "not a geographical fact, but a moral one."

Woodrow Wilson was aware of the magnitude of his task.

He was a lonely, solitary man. He felt God had laid a heavy burden upon him. He was determined to bear it.

On board ship he spoke to his companions: "If we do not carefully use the powers mankind has given us we will deservedly stand in world history as the worst of failures, by our own fault and before all men's eyes."

The year 1620 lived in his soul, the year the proud Pilgrim fathers had pushed off from Europe, and three hundred years of unbroken and free growth of American humanity lived there too, as did the principles of Jefferson and Lincoln and his nation's dead, the men he had had to cast into the maw of the Moloch that was Europe.

The left half of his face had developed a nervous tic. His eyes lay haunted and deep behind his glasses.

Wilson did not know what awaited him in Europe.

Private Affairs

Brief tales and a love song without words.

Berlin Interiors

An elderly woman in Berlin-Gesundbrunnen is sitting in her parlor at the window—it has grown dark—writing a letter to her father, dead now for a long time. For some years now, since her health began to fail, the woman has been used to chatting in her thoughts with her father. And at last she began to write him in secret, carefully putting the letters in a special drawer in her dresser.

She writes, and weeps once in a while, then she lays her pencil on the window sill and wipes her eyes.

"I have had a falling-out with my sister Emma. My sister you see has a daughter, whom you don't know. She's twenty now and tells me everything. She's been seeing a factory owner and he wants to give us all a job. She used to go with a lawyer who had a four-room apartment, and Emma allowed that. Now she wants to keep her daughter at home, my husband was floored. I've always stuck by my sister, but I've always thought a lot of the girl too. My husband lost his job because there is no work, he gets unemployment allotments, but when he goes out to collect them and stays five minutes too long my nerves are shot. The girl's been running around with nobody but rich folks for two years now, the factory owner lives at her place in Sanssouci, and he wants to give us all a job. The girl's not lying, that's for sure. The man will maybe hear from other people all the bad things Emma says about him, and that'll drive him off. The girl isn't doing anything out of the way, is she? But Emma is driving us all crazy."

A man was a teacher in a private school. He had two children. He and his wife were no longer young, the school wasn't doing well, his salary was cut, the family could not live on what he earned. One day there was a position available with the city welfare department; he read about it in the municipal report and he gave it to his wife to read. She said she could not do it, she hadn't the education, they would turn her down. Then he said that if she refused, he would do it himself. And so she gave him everything he wanted, a dress, her coat and a hat, and she put the powder on his face herself and helped him dress so that the clothes looked right. He had a young, delicate face, had never worn a moustache and when he wanted to could talk like a woman. He'd often made a joke of it.

When he arrived at the mayor's office, smartly dressed, clean and modest, there were already several others there, but he was called in too and he submitted his wife's papers. They talked for some time about the fact that he had no other papers, recommendations from other jobs and so on. He stood there, boldly supplying information. He argued with them, thinking I can do whatever a woman can.

But then another official came in, a supervisor apparently, looked at the papers, looked carefully at the woman. She had such big shoes. Because his wife's shoes had not fit him, he had worn his own. The two municipal officials whispered between themselves and asked the lady to have a seat and remove her hat.

But she could not do that, would not do it. She did not yield, and then he asked them what his hairdo had to do with it. The officials became even more suspicious, they insisted, and when the woman grabbed her papers and left they sent a policeman after her. He pulled her hat off while she was still in the building, whereupon the "woman" confessed to everything.

The man went home. They notified him that they were going to sue for fraud. He wanted to throw himself in the river because now he would lose his position at the private school as well.

But without telling him his wife went to the school director and confessed the whole story, and he was allowed to stay on. Perhaps, that amiable gentleman said, they would cover up the whole affair at the welfare office once they understood the circumstances.

Hilda in Berlin

Hilda pretended as if she were only going across the bridge to visit friends in Kehl. There was a guard posted at the bridge; they let her walk across, suitcase in hand.

And then she rode through the welter of Germany, inundated by the tide of returning soldiers; its cities stood untouched and peaceful, while in the houses people froze and starved and now and then took to the streets with flags and songs.

Hilda wept quietly in the corner of her train compartment. As at the beginning of the war, she was sitting riding in a train. Was there no end to her journey?

A vision of Bernhard rose up in her, turned toward her, reached out to her, flickered like a flame and went out. She shook herself and bit her lips.

In Berlin she settled into a small hotel near Anhalter Station.

She was a stranger to the gigantic, gray and dreary city. She did not know what might happen now.

She immediately had an attack of nerves that first evening. The tension lasted all night and all the next day and only receded after a difficult night during which she slept as if paralyzed.

She did not know that on that first evening Bernhard had begged for help in Frau Scharrel's apartment and died during the night.

For two days she was pursued by the gloom cast over her by that distant event, by the poor tortured soul who reached out for her—until she found herself in front of St. Hedwig's church. She thought of it as an unexpected chance to see a historic piece of architecture. She went in, prayed, supplicated. She cleansed herself, calmed herself. Berlin's museums and avenues were splendid, but what did they mean next to this small sacred building in which she knelt as a lost human being, first in front of the crucifix and then for a long time in front of a painting of Mary. The liturgy, proclaiming its eternal truths, murmured on. The hymn pealed forth: "Holy God we praise thy name."

It was the evening of December 6th, at the same hour when crowds from the Germania and Sophia halls were jammed into Chausseestrasse and Invalidenstrasse and five hundred shots were fired into them—while she walked down the peaceful Königgrätzer Strasse toward her hotel, entered the dark room, at once sensing that it would soon become hers.

Because now she would take off her coat and hat, take paper from her stationery box and write a man whose address she had had with her, written on a sheet from a prescription pad in a military hospital.

She wrote. And while she wrote, everything that had brought her to this city and led her through it lent its support.

The next morning she walked through a changed Berlin. She went her way with a soft, sure step.

Becker was returning from the hospital, moving at a leisurely pace down the street with the help of his cane.

He wore his green military coat. She recognized him from the rear. Tears streamed from her eyes.

When she had regained control of herself, she caught up with him and touched him on the right arm. Then she took hold of him. He staggered as if she were a phantom. Her letter had not yet arrived.

315

She took his cane from him. They did not talk until they reached his place.

She led him, still not saying a word, up the stairs. He was about to ring at the door with the little metal plaque that read "Becker" when she held him back, embraced him and kissed him on both cheeks. His smile was rigid. She ran down the steps.

He stood at the door of the apartment.

He opened it. His mother was working in the kitchen. He could slip into his room. There he sat, just as he was.

His mother found him still wearing his coat and cap. She clapped her hands in dismay. He talked while she helped him out of his coat.

His mother: "And you're not glad about it, Friedrich?"

"Strange. You're right. It ought to make me happy, shouldn't it. But why doesn't it?"

"That's you all over, Friedrich. You just let her go like that."

While they ate—he ate slowly, his head was in a fog—the postman came with Hilda's letter. His mother read it to him.

But Friedrich was already floating. The "demon", his "demon" as he called it, was approaching. He soon got up from the table under the pretense of being tired. His face felt very stiff already, the things he could see behind the fog he could still recognize, but he had to hurry to get through the door to his study so that his mother would not notice what was happening to him.

And as he sat down on his bed and his mother helped him lie back he was already in the demon's embrace.

Becker felt his body, the bed under him, saw the ceiling. But he had been touched by the demon's wand, was under its spell. He lay there fearfully tense. All his thoughts had been taken from him, he could not get close to anything. The lamp was not a lamp, the book not a book, his mother not a mother.

He lay there helpless. He could barely breathe, and sometimes, not too often, he blinked, swallowed. He made little grappling motions, trying to come out of his rigid state. The gorgon head stared at him.

His mother sat anxiously beside him. He wanted to tell her to leave him alone, but his lips would not open. His torment, his dread grew. At any moment the room could burst wide open with a clap of thunder.

Finally—it subsided. The demon turned away, Becker's eyelids grew heavy, his face soft, the back of his head warm again.

Exhaustion came on. While all the objects approached him again and began to speak to him, darkness sank down upon him. His eyes closed.

His mother was sitting beside him when he awoke. He was alert at once and everything was over.

316

"While you slept you had such a happy face, Friedrich, like a child on Christmas Eve."

"Did I, mother?"

"Hilda will be visiting you a bit later. Her letter says around four if that is all right with you. I should let her in, shouldn't I?"

"Certainly."

"Who is she actually? Did I see her when I was there in July?"

"It's possible, you might have seen her."

"And did she take good care of you? Did she look after you?"

"After me, after Maus, after all of us. She wasn't a ward nurse, but a dressing nurse. She came to replace our dressings, to rinse out the wounds and other little things that hurt like hades."

He sat up. "You should know, Mother, how it was in the military hospital, probably it's that way in every hospital. Anyone lying there sick has a twofold reason for feeling good. First because he has lost his name, his privacy, his personality. You lie there in bed and you are a sickness. You are a skull fracture, an abdominal bullet wound, a pelvic fracture. That feels good. The young doctors at the hospital told me that modern medicine is again attaching importance to treating the whole man. I don't think there's anything won by that. They should leave my whole man alone. You lie there, only a number among comrades who are no better off than you. And they treat you impersonally. The senior medical officer glances at you now and then. You know he knows how your illness is progressing. You are ranked with the others in that general progression of illness that applies to everyone and that he knows so well."

"That doesn't sound nice to me."

"The second thing is—something quite different. You lie there in bed and the healthy people move around. They are not just medical personnel, as they call themselves. They are simply the healthy ones, the bearers of health, enviable creatures. Sometimes it is only just a cat that creeps along from the kitchen and lies beneath the window in the sun or beside the stove. Or a fresh bouquet of flowers. But especially it's the people. If they are doctors or nurses, you lie there in wait for a piece of health, of the energy that they are meant to supply you with. You become a vampire. You worship them, envy them, you love them. There is a constant breath of life and energy emanating from them."

"And Hilda was like that?"

"What I've just told you is a strange chapter from the story of my existence as a sick man. People think they are playing the role of invalid, doctor, nurse. But a secret spiritual bond entwines us all. A lot of doctors and nurses sense it at once when they enter the wards. That's what makes them go into medicine actually, I think. Most of them don't notice it until they begin to move about among the beds of the sick. Their remedies are only of secondary value. Doctors sell us a little corner of their brains, their knowledge, but we need more, and we take more."

"Tell me about her."

"She's in her early twenties, I'd say. Her father, she says, is an official with the Cathedral Building Commission in Strasbourg. She comes from Strasbourg."

"And what else?"

Becker shook his head violently. "Nothing else. She'll be working here perhaps. I don't know."

Gioconda

The three of them sat in the living room. Hilda had taken off her dark blue coat; she wore a linen dress with blue and white stripes, a white apron over that, a high white collar that closed at the front with a round brooch. The little cap atop her parted hair was more an ornament than a head covering.

Hilda said she was thinking of working at a reserve hospital. "But first I wanted to see the first lieutenant when I arrived in Berlin. You were such a source of care and joy for us in those days. And now you can move around without anyone's help."

They spoke of Hilda's father.

"Aren't you afraid to leave your father alone?"

"Oh, he's strong, a lot stronger than most people I know."

She laid her hands in her lap and sat there with lowered eyes. When she first met Bernhard before the war, a whole person had risen up within her—another person rose up when she had worked on the front and in the hospitals—but now she sank back into her loam, into maidenly gentleness.

"She is so sweet," said his mother after she had gone. "What a smile, Gioconda, Mona Lisa."

"False like Gioconda?"

His mother: "Gioconda isn't false, she's only as false—as a woman naturally is."

They laughed heartily together.

"I call that a confession, Mother. And you say it so easily and so candidly. Gioconda—she is mercilessly cruel for the sake of being cruel, she's smiling at her victims. But you're not that way, Mother, are you?"

"Mothers are not false."

Becker stroked his chin. "But while she was here I was struck, too, by something mysterious, impersonal about her."

He no longer thought of the phantom that had accompanied him from the street and up the stairs, but of the sweet Hilda, of sunshine casting itself on him in the hospital.

His mother watched him. "You told me she took care of you both, you and Maus. What was Maus like around her? Was he jealous of you because of her?"

Becker: "He loved her. I thought she loved him too. He's such a straightforward, energetic fellow. Then she came to me, the day before the hospital was disbanded. I still lay there helpless."

"She came to you."

"I never told Maus about it. He wouldn't understand. He loves her so intensely. And I don't think that she meant anything serious with me—I don't know what she's really all about."

His mother folded her arms and looked out the window. "You'll always be the same dear old Friedrich. You turn the girls' heads and don't actually care so very much about them. And here she is coming to you again. Maybe she came from Alsace on your account."

"I hope not."

"Have you—any feelings for her?"

"Not like Maus does. No. She represents an energy for me, a certain influence that changes something inside me. I shall ask Krug sometime if that sort of thing can't be construed as a matter of physics. He once told me about changes in climate on earth that result from some distant astronomical influences or other. I'm reminded of something like that when she approaches me. I register the changes of atmosphere inside myself—as 'feelings.' Maybe she will cause new plants and animals to spring up inside me, too."

"This is dreadful, Friedrich. You can never be serious."

Friedrich's face was still terribly small and drawn. The thought crosssed his mother's mind: how strange the attachment of this fresh young girl to him.

Becker pointed to his study with a smile. "One thing follows another. First I bury myself inside myself and whittle away at myself with a dagger forged and tempered by my soul. Then—I let the dagger fall, drag out the old busts again, take the curtain down from in front of my books. And now a little bird comes flitting out of the woods to me, lands right on my foot."

"It wasn't a bird, Friedrich. And not on your foot."

"Do you mean my heart instead? During the war we were on leave from our 'ego.' Is my ego-leave over?"

She pulled the curtains, turned on the light, helped him arrange himself on the sofa.

He laid stretched out on one side and held a book up to his eyes. She knitted at the table.

He surrendered himself to a pleasant feeling that suddenly came over him.

The world is like that, poured out into time and space. It has wrapped itself in time and space as if they were a cape, has pulled up the hood, and now goes its way.

But though it may keep on going for a million years, it never moves away from where it started.

The world is like a boomerang, a ball in a child's hand. The ball is tied to a rubber band, the child throws the ball, it flies off in space, but there it is back in the child's hand again.

But it is not the hand of a child that throws us.

And when he awoke in the night he had dreamed, and the thoughts that he snatched at were the last links in a chain that the dream had taken back to itself.

And he found himself confronted by a phrase: "This is a world of the son"—a sentence to which he looked up as if to a distant snow-capped mountain.

The Roots of Love

Hilda was radiant that morning. Friedrich's mother left her alone with him. At the door his mother's eyes had said, "How sweet she is. What a smile. Gioconda."

He took a long look at Hilda. She is a landscape. Hills, a river, ripe fields of grain, a lake. What words must I find to name her? What avalanches plunge down out of her blond hair toward me?

Someone inside her wanted to lay a hand on his mouth. Another someone let that hand glide onto his neck and left it there. With a deep breath she took in the words that came from his mouth like a queen bee taking in the choice food set before her, the nourishment that is her due.

She listened with many ears, spoke with several voices. He sat on his sofa beside her, held her hand and looked at her. Yes, she had a sweet, gentle expression, some total magic.

And as she edged closer to him and their faces came close together, there was a great resonance within her, and she felt strong and true.

There was that little stolen quarter hour with her cousin in her aunt's garden, it was raining, they had fled in under the arbor, had played and actually should have gone back into the house. How old was I then? Twelve or thirteen, he was fourteen, we kissed, he had loved me for a long time, or I must have already been a bit older than that, and then my aunt called us, and when we didn't appear she came out with an umbrella.

And then later on her drawing teacher, a young substitute; that had been dangerous. He was just as much a beginner as I, although ten years older. On an excursion to Hohkönigsburg we left the path and got lost, and we already knew what it was we wanted, but not exactly, we had both read a lot, and he was an artist and knew the human body. And so while the others went on climbing and didn't even notice we were missing, we could easily, ever so easily, let what we had read about happen. He felt it and so did I, and that's why we ran along as we did, partly in order to do it, partly in order not to. And then all of a sudden we were holding each other's hands tight. It happened so quickly and so naturally, as if each was only the reflection of the other. And then our mouths moved toward each other, the way it is when you lower your head to the surface of the water. And our lips met, but they were other lips and then the arms laid about the neck, and one face as hot as the other, and it was so much and so infinitely much and enough. My knees were trembling beneath me and we ran away from each other, I ahead of him, until we came to the path, where I called out and the others answered from up top and waved.

And then Hilda sank back into the time when she had had to watch over her little brother, who was no longer alive. He had died at age five, and she was eight, and he now showed her his fine, expectant face.

And then she examined Becker, eyes only a hand's breadth away from her own eyes, his expression, his head, his hair, his ears. Because now a time even more distant had made itself known within her and there emerged from her, as if from a woodland cave, the watchful mother, the doe, and she regarded the male animal leaping before her. I want to build upon you, will you assist me in the building of my nest? If you will protect me when the young are born, then I will let you be the father of my children, I will have you.

When she closed her eyes and had absorbed this vision into herself, she saw a lovely rich landscape, she did not know where it was, but the rain had let up, fog lay across the hills, you could see the sky growing bright, and in the beautiful, soft, enveloping mist the colors of a rainbow began to play.

When she said she wanted to go, Becker replied, "Maus is coming to visit me today."

"Do you see each other often, Friedrich?"

"We're friends. He confessed to it on the journey home. How much he loves you."

"What did he tell you?"

"He torments himself so. He longs for you."

"Why does he make grief for himself?"

If she had been another person, the person she had been before, she would have directed her eyes at Becker, anxiously or with a cruel lust. But she was this Hilda now, and it was another creature who had done that, suffered that with Maus, another creature with whom she still lived under one roof.

She laid both hands on his shoulders, shook her head, the corners of her mouth twitching while her eyes gazed into his. "Whatever I had with Maus, Friedrich, must make no difference to you. One has to put an end to many things if one wants to go on living."

As she went down the stairs, he sat at his desk and his own words about "ego-leave" came back to him.

What is this adventure I am entering on? What huge boulder am I supposed to roll aside? The war was really a very easy matter. I hoped for peace, for true peace, and I want it too, and because I am a human being I ought not let anything prevent me from seeking it. And then all this comes over me and wants to throw me off the path. It seems I am to be put to the test. But what is the power that has decided to test me, a good one or an evil one?

He looked about the room. It was a good idea to put the busts back up and take that curtain off the bookcase. There they are: Sophocles, Kant, and the books with all those proud titles. They have not yielded over the centuries in the battle for whatever is human, divine. We have been thrown back again and again. But they have always taken up the battle once more.

Who is this Hilda who has sought me out?

But while he sat there and trembled inside and thought once again of Hilda, the phantom from a dream who had joined him out on the street, he was not yet aware how very true it was that his ego-leave was at its end.

And it would not merely mean an end to peace with that ego, it was to be an end of the ego itself.

She walked slowly down below along the street. This was where she had met him, just as she had expected to. He was walking in front of her.

She caught up with him. But then she took hold of his arm.

She pressed to her face a bouquet his mother had given her.

No More Ego-Leave

Love's burning agony. Consolation is sought at a mass meeting. Speakers drink beer and talk hogwash. When anguish is great, the classics don't help either.

The Rejected Lover in His Lair

Maus appeared before dinner.

He came over to Becker and embraced him. "I talked with her, an hour ago. She was on the street looking for our house. She told me everything. We sat in a big empty café on Bayrischer Platz, all by ourselves. I was happy. I am ecstatic. Becker, please believe me. I understand completely that she loves you."

"My dear fellow," Becker muttered in confusion.

"I cried a little bit, from the excitement and the joy, asked her to forgive me. She doesn't hold anything against me. I'm glad you have her."

And he took a little tin box from his vest pocket and pressed it into Becker's hand. "It's for you. For good luck. I carried it with me during the war."

The little metal box wouldn't open, and they both laughed. Finally, trembling with excitement, Maus used his pocketknife.

"You have to treat it like an oyster," he said, wedging his knife into the crack. He had difficulty prying the two pieces apart, then suddenly there was a stunned look on his face. Then he broke out into youthful laughter. "Nothing in it. I carried it all through the war, and when I was wounded I thought there was a little animal charm inside, an ivory elephant. There's nothing in it. And I was going to give it to you as a present."

They laughed and laughed.

Becker: "Yes, well then why are you still among the living?"

Maus: "You're right, there's no excuse for it whatsoever."

Becker glanced into the empty case. "I'll keep it, if you'll let me have it. The empty box says: 'Thou shalt not pray to strange gods.'"

They sat down.

Maus: "Was she up here?"

"Of course."

"She's magnificent, isn't she? Much too good for me. Even after ten minutes, as she sat there next to me, I realized that what I was thinking was all nonsense. Beside her I'd be only a little boy."

Maus's lower lip trembled. He stood up quickly, went to the window. He stood there silent for a while. Finally he stamped his foot, gritted his teeth and with a snap of his fingers came back to Becker with a firm step. He stood erect beside the desk.

Maus began to talk about the events of December 6th, and about Ding, his comrade, who was lying in the hospital, badly wounded. He had solemnly sworn to stick with the cause, but the oath was completely unnecessary, he would stick with it anyway. He wondered if Becker felt well enough to go hear what was happening out there, at mass meetings or in private conversations.

"Maus, you know how I feel about politics."

"That will get you nowhere, Becker. And even if you're right, your viewpoint isn't worth much. It doesn't work like that. I can't bear it to know that you're just sitting here. If you're ill, that's another matter. But that you simply say no . . ."

"Why does that torment you, Maus?"

"Because they need you. They need every man they can get now, and especially men like you. You shed your blood out there. We owe it to ourselves and the dead—you know, those poor devils who died in the war, and for what? Surely not for the old skulduggery to start up all over again. We are their heirs, the executors of their wills. The deaths of millions must have some result, some consequences. Those of us who got out with our lives are the ones closest at hand to do what needs to be done. And you have to see how the others are working hard to prevent there being any consequences. You would have to see what it's like in our living room with my father. When I see those old ice-cold scoundrels, conspiring away, I could kill them all on the spot. And that would be the best thing, to kill them all. Because until they are all killed, there'll be no peace. Until then they'll go right on with their shenanigans, letting peaceable, unarmed people who only want to protest be mowed down on the streets. Human life is cheap."

"What do you want me to do then?"

Maus patted his hand. "I don't want you to do anything that might hurt you, and if you don't want to go, tell me."

"What do you want me to do?"

"Come with me to a mass meeting. You should see people, ours and theirs, live on the spot. Then it'll be easy for you to make a decision."

324

Mass Meeting at the Bötzow Brewery

"Where are you leading me, my Mephisto?" Becker asked his friend that evening. They got out of their cab in front of the Bötzow brewery.

"To a mass meeting."

Maus helped his friend through the crowd at the entrance. They noticed that the place was thick with guards. They paid the entrance fee, pressed on through a cordon of people handing out flyers, each one bearing a sign with his party's slogan as well.

"County fair," Becker whispered.

"Come, quick."

They sat in the immense, overcrowded room, lighted from the ceiling with arc lamps. Smoke ascended above the heads of the crowd. People sat at tables, the waiters hauled beer, several men with armbands tried to keep the aisles clear. At the front was a small open stage, probably intended for amateur productions. There was a table on it, with a large bell, a carafe of water and several beer glasses. Men stood in a little group at the end of the table beside a younger man, who sat there with papers in front of him.

Now these gentlemen seated themselves. One of them rang the bell. The meeting was launched.

Maus asked Becker, "Should we have brought a pillow for you?"

Becker: "Would've been better, actually. But it won't go on forever."

While people continued to throng in through the wide-open doors at the sides, and while the dense, murky masses sat there, their faces directed toward the little stage, waiting for words that they could obey to enlighten them, one speaker after the other took his place behind the table with the water carafe and the beer glasses. They turned out to be solid citizens or bores or sly dogs. These fellows began to speak, while the one at the end of the table wrote it all down. What they drank was beer; what they said was hogwash.

First the chairman who had swung the bell to open the meeting announced something that remained unintelligible because of his rusty voice. Those assembled took no offense at this. They grubbed about, like chickens in manure, in what was offered them, picked out the phrases they wanted, turned up their noses at the rest.

The chairman wore a long black frock coat and had a hot, red face and bug-eyes. He suffered from asthma. It was hard to say how many quarts of beer ran daily through that vat. That may be how he managed to achieve dignity and prestige, to inspire trust—and to be standing here now.

He yielded the floor to his neighbor, a strapping young man with thick flaxen hair and a sturdy moustache. He was an orator. He talked with his mouth full, but not with a thousand tongues. As the words rolled from his mouth and throat, resounding out to the last corner of the hall, the audience was driven onto that familiar wheel on which guinea pigs run, run, scurry, lunge without ever getting anywhere. Finally the animal gives up, sprawls out and awaits its end.

"From time immemorial," he assured them, blustering and threatening, this strapping blond, before whom someone had shoved the water carafe—probably as a sign of contempt—the neck of which he gripped with his stubby hand as if he were about to throw it into the crowd, "from time immemorial, it has been the will of the German people to govern themselves. But that will was stifled, it was not once allowed to be heard. That will was gagged and muzzled. And especially since the founding of the Reich, since 1870, the monarchist and militarist authorities have made a point of suppressing it."

How that had come about he described with the aid of several note cards, in ever broader strokes. "Following the ignominious collapse of those authorities, the will of the people to govern themselves has asserted itself with elemental force and is now ready to create a people's republic."

They listened to the fellow hawk his salad of words with the same mute resignation of someone at the market who lets his glance sweep across the baskets only to determine that they don't have anything today. There was not a single person in that hall who did not know and who was not reminded by what the blond fellow up there was saying that it had been the American, Wilson, who in his Fourteen Points had demanded that the authoritarian regime be abolished, that without agreement on that point there could be no armistice, no end to the war, and that it was for that reason that the ministers and even the generals had urged the Kaiser to abdicate. The public had been preoccupied with those facts for weeks now, and it had never been a question of some elemental German will for self-government that had now asserted itself.

Now he began to talk about the Kaiser and the authoritarian state and how Wilhelm had provoked the nation and played his role as if he were an actor on a stage.

"Like a monkey," someone shouted up front. That pleased them. They laughed, the orator took the credit as if he had said it.

"Our radiant arms, our Nibelungen loyalty—nothing but show."

The man up front shouted, "The guy should have been an actor." This met with failure, it was a repetition.

"How weak Lehmann showed himself to be in the 'Daily Telegraph' affair." People pricked up their ears, the majority of them did not know what that might be about, but it increased their confidence in the man all the more that he did not go into an explanation.

"Chancellor Bülow, the one with the poodle, though equally to blame, reprimanded the Kaiser, and he took it lying down and went off to pout a while in Potsdam." That was nice to hear. The man wasn't bad.

"Who were the chancellors after Bismarck, from Caprivi to Hertling, Michaelis, Bethmann-Hollweg? Nothing but mediocrities."

From the middle of the hall, where a man with a walking-stick between his legs had been whispering with his neighbor at the table, came a loud shout.

"If they were nothing but mediocrities and the Kaiser was a monkey, why didn't you haul off and let them have it?"

A lot of people turned around. The speaker parried this with a mellow tone in his voice.

"I would like to return the suggestion to the gentleman who asked the question. Why didn't you let them have it? You were alive then, too. Or were you still just an embryo?"

Peals of laughter.

"The man who asked that question should have tried to deal with the Prussian police with that walking-stick of his."

The man in the hall: "That's what we did do. But you middle-class types and socialists stood off in one corner."

The orator: "I will not get involved in the old argument of why we proceeded in one way and not another. Far be it from me, for example, to judge the position of the Social Democrats on the issue of war loans. But that they were simply taking advantage of the circumstances no one will want to challenge." He raised his voice, he sounded angry. "But where do these arguments get us? Shall we not let the old strife among the German people rest? Shall we even now, with the positive task before us of establishing a democratic German republic, continue to tear one another to shreds? Is that constructive? We would soon end up folding our hands in our laps and saying: We Germans cannot manage this all by ourselves. We shall simply have to suffer our fate and, to our shame, have the Allies, who are just waiting for an opportunity to march in, put things in order for us."

Having convinced himself with the roar of his own anger, he pulled back now and picked up a note card. "An authoritarian nation, bright and shiny on the outside and rotten within. The bourgeoisie was healthy and energetic. It rejected experiments before and will continue to do so, experiments that endanger the food supply and the economy of the nation."

He then spoke of this at length until he arrived at the necessity for a constituent assembly and a strong political middle. The masses, the bourgeoisie, the little people, many of them women, listened attentively. The chickens scratched, pecked and looked for a sentence, some hope.

The chairman had to ask that there be no more smoking. One woman who had fretted over this for a long time, shouted into the hall: "The tobacco nowadays is so lousy. Can't you men stop smoking for once when there are other people around?"

Laughter, then numerous no's from inveterate smokers. Someone opened the windows at the rear.

The strapping blond had now ended his lecture. He had to let go of the water carafe, and now a querulous man who suffered from stage fright and had a long nose and glasses took his position behind the carafe that had not yet been thrown into the hall. He did not have much hair. He was tall, and could not look straight at the audience due to some inhibition or other. Sometimes, however, he would convince himself with a stolen glance that the audience was still present. But then he would lower his eyes at once and gaze at his hands lying on the tabletop.

It was difficult to say why the man had been put there. But the crowd was patient and wanted to get its money's worth.

He spoke learnedly, rapidly and through his nose. Soon someone shouted, "Louder!" People began to talk among themselves, so that the chairman bugged his bug-eyes out still further—they seemed to have been made to cast scornful glances—and swung his bell. After which the learned nasalizing continued.

As far as could be determined, his speech dealt with the definition of "the true nature of parliamentary government," and how parliamentarism was related theoretically and practically to monarchism, autocracy, oligarchy and dictatorship, in what nations it had played a role and continued to do so and why, and what role it might, ought and would play in the present, or as the case might be, future German republic—insofar as no obstructions arose, of course.

Certain formulae appeared in his speech and then vanished, like clouds sweeping past and dissolving. Several times one heard that "parliamentary democracy is a historical category."

Maus had prudently placed his friend at a table near an exit. They had been sitting there for an hour now. Then Maus caught the look from Becker he had been expecting. Out in the corridor there were a lot of people milling about. Some had settled in. At the entryway the people handing out flyers stood in a clump, smoking and debating.

Becker and Maus crossed the pavement.

Dialogue in a Café

They sat in the empty front room of a café. On the benches in the back room were pairs of lovers embracing. The two friends drank hot tea.

Maus: "Did it tire you?"

Becker: "My dear Mephisto, where did you take me?"

Maus: "That's how they all are. There are very learned ones as well. The only difference is that some of them tell you what's in the papers and others what's in books!"

"And the audiences? The masses?"

Maus—he sat there gloomily, his cheeks red—took a deep breath and let his shoulders fall. "This evening there are dozens of meetings like that one being held in Berlin, perhaps as many as three right here in this section of town, it's basically the same everywhere, speakers and listeners. They want to hear the latest news, they don't want to do anything. If shots are fired, they run."

"That's what all unarmed people do, my dear Maus. And justifiably so."

"They don't want to arm themselves either. But they're going to have to. They absolutely must. They mustn't put it off. And there they sit and gab."

"Explain to me, Maus, why they mustn't put it off."

Maus pulled his chair up next to Becker. "I am in all kinds of organizations, some shady ones included. Some of them pretend they're guarding buildings—and then there are militias, for home owners and neighborhood residents, and then some play at camaraderie and at lobbying—and some want to shunt people out into the countryside, ostensibly for farm work, and then the troops bound for the East in Zossen and Döberitz. And to cap it all off the Guard regiments will come marching in now."

"But the fact remains that Hindenburg has placed himself at the disposal of the government."

"He's waiting for the troops to arrive and then he'll strike."

"And Ebert?"

"A nothing. Can't depend on him, and probably they're playing him for a fool besides. At any rate, in terms of cunning and resolve, the others are head and shoulders above the workers and citizens you saw there in the hall. At the appropriate moment they'll burst upon the masses like a thunderstorm, and I'd like to know what'll be left then of all the lovely dreams of a constituent assembly and so on. Here in Germany there's always some gang or other running things. Now that the Kaiser's gone, another bunch wants to take over."

"You're pretty ferocious today. Downright vicious."

"I'm still a magician's double-bottomed suitcase. Can't let them believe they have nothing but cattle to deal with. You ought to hear how cynical they can get."

Becker regarded his friend, whom he had never heard speak so bitterly. But within him there stirred a remote uneasiness, a peculiar anxiety, a dizziness.

Maus: "During the war they didn't dare show themselves. There were no parties, only Germans. Now they've let the mask fall. It was all just sand thrown in our eyes so that we would carry their rifles for them."

"Where does all your hate come from, Maus?"

"On Friday we marched along Chausseestrasse, unarmed. They're lying in ambush for us with machine guns; they shoot and then retreat. It was calculated murder. We aren't human beings to them. They're gangsters who have foreclosed our lease on the country. I have nothing in common with them. I have no country. Heiberg says the same thing. We understand each other quite well, even though we've taken different paths. The major took me with him to his office to try and rope me in. He introduced me to Heiberg. We knew each other vaguely from the hospital. They told how he was the one who shot those two soldiers when the colonel was attacked on November 10th. We went for a long walk together. He's the same age as I am. He's at a camp and wants to get out of Germany. He says he's had enough. But don't think it's because he's afraid. He's disgusted by it. The officers and all the rest disgust him. He's not going to ruin his life for them. And not for Wilhelm and Holland either."

A pause. Then Maus: "He just shrugged his shoulders at the workers. He doesn't have the heart for it. I told him he ought to have a look. There was no reason to go running off to Poland right away. But he was determined and said no. It was all one and the same, he said. You could make the proles happy with a few more pennies in pay. What was wrong with them anyway? Now they were letting the troops march on in with their generals, and their soldiers' councils only acted like silly kids. They took bribes from the owners in the factories. And there were never so many grafters and petty crooks as now."

And without looking up from the tabletop Maus went on talking, hammering away at Becker. "I'd like to know where you stand. Give it some clear thought. How are we supposed to have peace when the cynics, who see us as their property, as something they've inherited, are back on top? You know that it'll just end in war and murder again, and then more war and more murder. And if you keep quiet you share the blame."

Maus intended to put a concrete question to Becker. But then he noticed that he had been delivering a monologue the whole time.

Becker sat there ghastly white, the big eyes staring, leaning back in his chair. He appeared to be unconscious.

Maus was terrified. He laid a hand on his friend's arm. This triggered hesitant movement, a twitching around Becker's mouth. His lips pressed together the way a child's do when it is pouting and wants to cry. His glassy eyes moved. Maus spoke to him.

Becker took a breath, looked about the room, recognized his friend and nodded to him. He suggested that they had sat here long enough and got up at once. Maus rode home with him in a taxi. At the door to the apartment they shook hands.

Maus: "I'll come by tomorrow and see how you're doing."

Where to Get Help?

The gas lamp is burning. It is late at night. The house is still.

He sits in his chair. Way off somewhere the meeting is still going on. Up on the podium the speakers stand like animals in a cage and let themselves be gaffed at.

What had happened? He had been more confident. He sensed the good mood coming on again now. He had gone with Maus to that meeting, had wanted to enjoy his newfound health.

But that murky mass of humanity in the hall. That peculiar excitement smelling of war and misfortune.

The blind veterans that were led in. The young lads on crutches. And Maus, so young and yet so completely changed.

And me? What am I doing? I'm playing a role in a prewar play. They're all caught up in it. Not me.

Twice today there was a knock at my door, first Hilda, then Maus. My legs can move now. But now what's inside me won't move.

Becker stands up. The bookcase. He reads the titles, the names. Sophocles, Dante, Kant, somber fear stirs in the background.

Where to get help? Where to get help? The books are mute. The great minds point toward the abyss, who will lead me across the chasm? This uneasiness, confusion, physical fear. This turmoil inside me, as if my breast were a tea kettle, the flames licking up around it. Who can I turn to? My brain is hard, petrified. I don't have a brain anymore. I have a stone inside my skull. It's not human. It must be my demon who has kidnapped me. But I cannot live with him. If he wants me then he should take all of me.

Becker threw himself onto the bed, moaning.

In his mind as he lies there the smoky hall appears, the murky mass of humanity. Now Maus is speaking and his face is horrifying. What mask has he put on? Then other visions appear.

These visions are gray and motionless like photographs at first. Then they are set in motion. And it is as if it were just happening, and it is always the same thing. A street corner, where reservists are standing around an advertising pillar reading the proclamations. They walk off nodding, slowly, loaded down with gear. After a while there they are again, standing on the same street corner around the advertising pillar, reading the proclamations, trotting off.

Then an open square. They march one after the other. Toward the train station.

The visions cannot be erased. The soldiers stand there, read, march off, say nothing.

But as Becker gets up from the bed and suddenly lets out a loud groan, it seems to him as if Hilda has just entered the room, very calm and with flowers in her arms. He wants to lay his heart before her. But he cannot do it. He cannot lift his heart. His heart is a block of granite too.

Becker thinks: I can't live like this. And he hears himself talking to himself. "Peace, sweet peace. You shall reveal your face to me."

But peace is not sweet. Peace is cruelly difficult. War was ten times easier.

A Glance at Other Regions

Following December 6th the people in Munich get some things put down in writing. Kurt Eisner decides to stage a play and to use the occasion to give a speech. Accidents occur at sea. The French socialists have plans for peace. A lady in Paris writes a lengthy letter.

Decisions in Munich

The people of Munich did not hestitate once the reports of the putsch in Berlin began to come in on the night of December 6th.

Four hundred men assembled and forced their way into the offices of the major newspapers. They declared that there was now nothing for it but to establish the dictatorship of the proletariat.

They awakened Kurt Eisner, who was fast asleep. Told the news, he was undecided, as is only proper for an Independent.

Then they marched to the house of the minister of the interior, a Social Democrat named Auer, who was dealing with the masses in the manner prescribed by Berlin.

Auer would not even let the delegates of the four hundred in, so they broke down the door, but did him no harm.

They gave him a complete account of events in Berlin. He replied coolly that this was all news to him. Then they demanded that he resign from office. He wanted to know who they were to make such a demand. They answered that they did not care in the least what he wanted. He was to sit down and write. So he wrote:

"On the night of December 7th I was attacked by four hundred armed men and forced to vacate my office. Yielding to force, I hereby declare that I am resigning as minister of the interior."

One after the other they read the paper and were satisfied. He could write what he liked. Their leader put the paper in his pocket and departed.

The next morning the regimental infantry, which was loyal to the government—that is, they stood behind Eisner, normally they should have been indecisive, but in this case they were resolute—went to the newspapers that had been occupied and threw the radicals out. And wherever gatherings of hostile people formed, they scattered them. As a result of which Auer stayed in office.

Even prior to this, Kurt Eisner found the air in Munich was not agreeing with him. After the call for a general strike and the street demonstrations in Berlin, he found himself involved in some very rough debates with his friends and with the radicals. He appealed to everyone he ran into that all he wanted was the best, the very best. Apparently, however, he could please no one with that.

And suddenly there were students gathered in front of the Residenz, people from the far right, who should have been duty-bound to be grateful to him, and they shouted up at him in chorus: "We don't want a Berliner. We want a Bavarian."

And there he was busy protecting Bavaria from Berlin. He wrung his hands and fled to his friend Landauer.

He returned consoled and with a new idea. His intentions were constantly being misinterpreted. The idea was to appear before the masses himself and tell them what he meant.

His co-workers reported that Auer was still stirring things up, and the people who had earlier belonged to the Center party were inciting the populace on the issue of religious education. Eisner pulled his hair.

"I'm not taking anyone's religion away from him. I'd be the last man to do that. In God's name, every man should go to heaven however he likes. It's only a matter of public education. No, once and for all I must go and explain everything to them in detail, everything."

And he decided to tell them everything.

He picked the next Sunday as the day to do it. At the Grand Theater there was to be an elaborate gala, and he would appear there and put things in the right light. No one would be able to continue to doubt his good intentions. A hymn he had composed himself would also be sung.

Having found the solution, he walked about the Residenz beaming, shaking the hands of all the council members he met and telling them the happy news.

It would be a blow to the reactionaries. He would rehearse the choir himself.

Allied Troops in Aachen

The imperial troops were pressing deeper into the Reich, approaching Berlin.

From the West the great masses of the Allies pushed in behind them.

British regiments entered Cologne in the night of December 6th, that bloody Friday. On the 7th, French regiments under General Degoutte reached the city of Aachen, which had been under Belgian occupation for a week already.

As Degoutte entered, crowds of people stood out on the streets. To the blare of trumpets and the beating of drums, the troops marched in. The bronze monument to the Kaiser, before which the defile took place, had been draped in black on Degoutte's orders. During the parade the Belgian Michel stood next to the general.

They then went to the cathedral. Over the past seven centuries, thirty German kings had been crowned here. Ludwig the Pious, Charlemagne's son, was the first to here assume the German crown.

Charlemagne had made Aachen his base camp, from which he held the pugnacious Teutons in check.

Above the grave slab, gray with age, twenty-seven Belgian and French flags and standards were lowered.

Brief Notices from Around the World

Famous personalities were finding their way to Paris, which was increasingly becoming the political hub of the world. The Peace Conference cast its shadow before it.

On December 6th, even Masaryk came over from London, the indefatigable leader and liberator of the Czechs.

The president of the nation that was more a moral than a geographical concept, Woodrow Wilson, was still sailing on the *George Washington*. But already the masses of the large labor unions were stirring, hoping to show Wilson the French people's unconditional desire for peace, a true, international peace. They wanted the American to realize that he could depend on the French people. There was to be no bullying at the coming Peace Conference and disarmament was to be general.

The Socialists' opponents cursed the workers as utopians and unpatriotic. They complained that the Socialists would make a strong French presence at the Peace Conference impossible.

The flu flared up again. Eighty new cases a day were admitted to Parisian hospitals, mostly pneumonia. And death snatched twenty away each day.

Out at sea, mines floated, left over from the war, staying on for the same reasons as the flu and famine. When on December 5th a light English cruiser named the *Cassandra* approached one of these anachronistic mines in the Baltic, it exploded, the cruiser sank and took a dozen sailors with it.

What should one then say, under such circumstances, to the protest of the widow Prieur in Paris, who instituted legal proceedings against the German Kaiser with Prosecutor General Lescouve? She wanted him prosecuted for the murder of her husband, who had been killed when the ship *Sussex* was torpedoed. The prosecutor general had already asked Avocat Géneral Peletier to write up a report on the matter. The report was in and concluded in favor of the grounds for the suit. Whereupon Lescouve passed the case on to the chancellery.

But English courts demanded priority in the affairs. Two English courts had already debated the issue and sentenced Wilhelm II to death. They called the widow's attention to this decision. An international forum would have to concern itself with the matter.

The widow was not satisfied. In Paris people were of the opinion that Madame Prieur was being given an unprecedented opportunity to learn the meaning of patience.

On December 7th, we see the lady from Strasbourg, Anni Scharrel descend once more on Paris, this time without her two nieces. She plans a more extended visit this time, hoping to regain her mental equilibrium.

And as if to cast off a piece of the past, immediately after her arrival in the room where she had received Hilda's letter telling of her departure, she wrote this same Hilda a letter, telling her what had happened in the meantime. Frau Scharrel gave a detailed report of Bernhard's last days, of his desperate condition and of her vain attempts to calm him.

Concerning his demise, she wrote only what was absolutely necessary, wanting to avoid being confronted with the particulars of it herself.

Sunday, December 8th

It is raining hard in Berlin. There are demonstrations against Bloody Friday, some in halls, some outdoors. An old general speaks what is in his heart and thereby moves a people's deputy.

Day, the Bridge of Light between Two Darknesses

A new day had dawned, December 8th, Sunday, of which it would be said in retrospect the next morning in the lead editorial of the *Berliner Tageblatt:*

"How long yet?

"Liebknecht is no Cataline, no profligate greasy with vice, but his wild fanaticism and his strutting vanity are equally as ruinous as the more murky instincts of that Roman gangster, and that is why we address Cicero's question to him. What is impressive is that under such circumstances the army is returning home without disorder, that the German people . . .

"At that time we argued against the Reichstag's surrendering Karl Liebknecht to be tried by the military authorities. In surrendering him they made a martyr, a people's tribune out of an obstreperous Reichstag deputy. We need not cast blame upon the government. But for it to carry out its honest intentions it must do what is necessary, and soon.

"Let them station resolute troops, quashing the very thought that a disturbance of public order might be possible."

And what did the people of Berlin use this Sunday for, this arc of light between yesterday and tomorrow?

A few of them returned their bodies to the elements. Time had washed about them like waves against a cliff, and ultimately time accomplishes her task with everything.

A number of people were born, rising up out of the waves—buds on the fleshy tree of life.

A good many blossoming girls and women had given themselves to

337

the embraces of men the night before, had conceived and now carried within them the seed of new buds. They had been stung by the ageless wasp. And now time could race by outside them—the seeds grew in preparation for their confrontation with the menace of nothingness.

The living wander through the metropolitan day doing various things. Some sense no desire to wade through the morass of existence and walk across it on the stilts of alcohol, morphine and cocaine.

During the morning a number of airplanes flew over Berlin, machines of the Naval Air Force, part of the revolutionary special forces, whose Committee of Fifty-Three sat in the Reichs naval office. They threw out thousands of leaflets, down upon Unter den Linden, Friedrichstrasse, Humboldthain, the east of the city. The leaflets fell on roofs, on the umbrellas of the few pedestrians, fluttered down into the dirt of the streets. Whoever picked one up could read as follows:

"To all Socialists, to the government of the Reich — Enough is enough. Comrade Scheidemann, Comrade Ebert, Noske, Landsberg, Eichhorn. Do you still love the people? Did you ever love them? Then listen to the voices of those who are no longer satisfied with you. Make way for other men. Do not let your own ambition and willfulness be the guidelines for your actions. The people's blood is more precious than your positions. Let the will of the masses be your highest law. Central Council of the Navy."

Central Council of the Navy

In the course of the morning representatives of the Greater Berlin Soldiers' Council emerged from the Reichstag and went to the Reichs Chancellery. There they demanded that Ebert receive them. They declared to him that they had been delegated by the plenary assembly of the Greater Berlin Soldiers' Council to demand an explanation concerning some seemingly incredible information they had just received:

"At the moment troops are being concentrated between Potsdam and Berlin. The high command has formed a special army command for Berlin under General Lequis, who himself belongs to the high command. This army command recognizes no soldiers' councils. It has enlisted the Guard Cavalry, the Guard Infantry Division and the First Guard Regiment and stationed two thirds of them between Potsdam and Nicolassee."

This news went far beyond what Ebert already knew. He therefore flew into a rage. The men in Kassel were leading him around by the nose. He had to confront them, now.

But in front of the angry men from the Reichstag he acted astonished; he would get in contact with the War Ministry and have the matter cleared up. One ought not believe every wild rumor. After all, they were still here too. At any rate they should do everything within their powers, and above all, as soon as any regiment showed itself on the outskirts of Berlin they should send out members of the soldiers' council to begin briefing the troops.

That seemed plausible to them and they withdrew. Two hours later they received from the Reichs Chancellery a detailed and reassuring report intended for the plenary session. According to the report, the troops in the area between Berlin and Potsdam had nothing to do with counterrevolution, but were quite simply the first contingents of the returning troops for whom even now the Brandenburg Gate and the streets were being decorated. These regiments and battalions had halted, with the full consent of the government, at the gates of Berlin. There were several divisions. They were preparing themselves for the reception ceremonies in which both the municipal and national authorities would officially take part. They had declared their loyalty. Though of course they rejected "Liebknecht's one-sided politics."

The members of the soldiers' council were not displeased with the report.

Hindenburg's Letter

Ebert had received a letter from Hindenburg that every morning, one written in the marshal's own hand. Although its tone was calm, it was obvious from the letter that this was the last word of goodwill from the generals. And so that there might be no doubt about that fact, the generals had appointed Hindenburg to write it.

The field marshal wrote to the head of the government in Berlin as follows: "I am addressing the following lines to you because it has been reported to me that you, as a loyal German, likewise love your fatherland, disregarding all personal opinions and desires, just as I have had to disregard them in order to deal fairly with the emergency in which the fatherland finds itself. On that basis I have allied myself with you, so that we may save our people from the collapse that threatens them."

Ebert sat at his desk and read this opening with deep satisfaction, indeed he was touched by it. It was true. How differently this old general saw things from these crackpots here in Berlin with whom he had to wrangle. How stupid to consider this officer a reactionary. Here spoke a patriot, a German speaking to another German, despite all nuances of party resulting from their different backgrounds.

The Field Marshal spoke very earnestly:

"When on November 9th the officers' corps placed itself at your disposal, it did so in the conviction that loyalty and subordination would bring it both the gratitude of the fatherland and the support of the new government. Instead of which, it finds its authority increasingly shaken from day to day.

"Present events will not be mastered unless the prestige of the officers is restored at all levels and the soldiers' councils are driven from the military."

A difficult, difficult demand, thought the man reading the letter in Berlin. It can hardly be carried out. At least not at the moment.

"It is my conviction that only the following measures can save us in our present predicament:

1. The immediate convocation of a constituent assembly.

2. All official duties are to be carried out exclusively by the bodies legally constituted to do so.

3. Workers' and soldiers' councils are to play only an advisory role."

All of it good, and exactly what I believe myself. Basically what everyone believes to be necessary.

"The fate of the German people lies in your hands. It will depend on your decisions whether there will be a revival of the German nation. I am prepared, and with me the entire army, to support you without reserve in your efforts.

"I felt a most burning need to speak to you about the above-mentioned matters."

Ebert was preoccupied with this letter all day. He could feel it in his pocket when the deputies of the soldiers' council came from the Reichstag with their alarming news, in the cabinet meeting later that morning, and when little Barth dragged out the same alarming news as an indictment of the government (it took him half an hour to do so):

"Guard troops are marching into the city; Ebert, who is sitting right here, must have known about it. I cannot but think that Ebert has suppressed important facts, kept them from us. There must be changes made. Things cannot go on like this. The republic is in danger."

Ebert stood his ground, supported by his friends in the Party. Everything was going as planned. There was no need to make a big thing of these troops marching in. One shouldn't make the people of Berlin crazier than they already were. The Spartacists, by the by, could stand to be taken down a peg or two.

They exchanged home truths. Barth stuck to his guns: It was impossible to see through Ebert, he said different things to Kassel than he said here. Whereupon a Majority Socialist promptly countered: If there was to be talk of double-dealing politics, then let the Independents sweep before their own door. They were secretly supporting the Spartacists.

And a Socialist Democrat allowed himself a scornful question. Who was it actually that the Independents were independent of?

340

"They aren't independent of the Social Democrats. Because they always have to say something different from us. They are certainly not independent of the Spartacists. Because they tremble before them, knowing full well that at the next opportunity their adherents will go over to Liebknecht. The only thing the Independents are independent of is common sense."

Outdoor Rallies

That afternoon the people turned out.

The Majority Socialists had called for thirteen separate meetings. Ebert was received in the Lustgarten with stormy applause.

"We of the SDP," the little fat man with the imperial beard shouted, the obviously indignant representative of common sense, "we want peace, freedom and bread. We want democracy. Without democracy there is no freedom."

The crowd cheered.

"Without democracy there is no freedom. The use of force is always reactionary. Liebknecht's fanatic supporters call daily for force. They distribute weapons. They threaten to attack this government by force of arms. We will counter all such attempts with utmost resolution."

Loud shouts: "Stick to it. Take 'em on."

"We do not doubt that the election of a constituent assembly will show the whole world that the fifty years we have spent educating Social Democrats has shaped the outlook of all German workers. The constituent assembly will be a victory for the SDP. Long live freedom, democracy, the constituent assembly, our old German social democracy."

People shouted: "Liebknecht's deserters will not rule Germany!"

Those standing down below around the basin of the fountain and on over by the museum stairway were careful not to step over the fencing and onto the lawn; they listened to Ebert attentively. They were peaceful men and women, earnest soldiers, they stood here in order to join in the creation of a new, peaceful Germany; many old labor union men, for whom the party and its organization were more important than all else, had complete confidence in those men up front. They had known them for a long time, they were comrades, they had followed them all through the war. Ebert, Scheidemann and Wels would handle things.

The Independents were assembled around the Bismarck monument in front of the Reichstag, also along Friedrichshain and Humboldthain. It poured and poured. The Independents had nothing else to smile about either.

One of the members of the Executive Council, Strobel, protested against the bloodbath on Friday. He threatened Wels, the city commandant. This Wels, Strobel cried, was "not without a role" in Friday's affair.

There was a storm of boos that degenerated into a threefold "Down with him!" and then, since it didn't know what else to do, waited for new fodder.

As far as the Spartacists went, Strobel said, the SDP was now busy trying to turn the tables and claim that they were the real guilty party.

"We know the Spartacists. They shouldn't be taken so seriously. They won't eat anybody. Their ravings simply give Wels and his supporters the pretext for interfering. They as much as hand all the dubious elements in the SDP their legitimation. They disrupt the unity of the working class. It is a pack of lies, sand thrown in people's eyes, to maintain that they are a real danger."

And Strobel went on: "But we must say to the workers that now is not the time to strike. Therefore the demand for a six-hour day must be rejected. We have to create a twenty-five hour day in order to find work for the unemployed. And we will socialize the factories."

A storm of "When?"

"We cannot do it today."

The shouts would not stop. The speaker did not feel at ease.

"Put Liebknecht in charge then if you don't like us. I'll gladly hand in my resignation. There are district chairmen to be replaced too. It is intolerable that the whole military apparatus is still in the hands of Hindenburg."

Who were these men and women at the Bismarck monument, waving the same red flags as those in the Lustgarten? They sang the same Internationale. The band played the same Marseillaise. Many of them came from the older party. They had felt that it lacked élan and had opposed the war policies of the "imperial socialists" for a long time. But they were neither rebels nor revolutionaries. They wanted to take a stronger line, be as radical as the prewar party. They did not believe that their differences with the Majority Socialists seriously divided the two groups or that the division would last forever.

Spartacus was the real hero of the day. They had driven twelve trucks out onto the soggy Treptow Meadow. Around two that afternoon the first contingents arrived, singing and carrying placards that read: "Long live Liebknecht! Down with Scheidemann and his assassins! Get rid of Wels! Long live the Soviet Socialist Republic!"

By about three o'clock they totaled several thousand. They sang without pause and shouted slogans from time to time.

Finally a bareheaded Liebknecht climbed up onto one of the trucks. His stony face was pale and showed he needed sleep.

"On November 9th we had the power in our hands. Today we no longer have a socialist republic. Piece by piece, Ebert and Scheidemann have given that power back to the men who drove the nation to war. The heart of counterrevolution is in Kassel."

The crowd began to seethe. He had to hold back for several minutes until the booing had spent itself. While he stood there on the red-draped truck and waited, the bitterness on his face intensified, it was an expression of pained rage.

"Ebert had himself proclaimed president, just as planned. The infamy of Ebert, Scheidemann and Wels stinks to high heaven. A new army command has been created without soldiers' councils."

He walked up to the edge of the truckbed and flailed his arms.

"The workers must arm themselves. We need a Red Guard. When the counterrevolution strikes they will stand ten thousand workers against the wall.

"We will not stand still here and wait until it comes to that. But neither do we want to create unrest. The others are creating the unrest. If Ebert, Scheidemann and Wels continue to act as they have we'll soon have Wilhelm II back in the palace. Away with these men! Long live the German revolution. Long live world revolution!"

A protest demonstration was formed and began to move toward the city. It was two miles long. At its head marched soldiers with red flags. With the singing of songs, hurrahs and boos it moved along Köpenicker Strasse, Brueckenstrasse, Alexanderstrasse, across Alexanderplatz and past the royal stables, where the sailors saluted them, and over the Schloss Bridge to the commandant's headquarters. There they reassembled.

Liebknecht spoke. From the equestrian statue of Frederick II clear to the Schlossplatz, the call echoed rhythmically: "Assassin — Wels, Assassin — Wels!"

The Infantry Guard in the little guardhouse next to the armory stood with arms at the ready. The throng wallowed its way up Unter den Linden. It was dark now. And it was pouring. Before the closed doors of the Russian embassy three hurrahs boomed out like cannon roars, from every contingent came three hurrahs. And then down Wilhelmstrasse.

Ebert, Scheidemann and the others were in the building when word came that Liebknecht's group was marching toward them in closed ranks. At once the iron grating at the front garden was closed and all the lights extinguished along the street.

In the dark rooms of the chancellery they sat, creeping from time to time to the window and listening to the grumblings of the masses, the jagged fragments of shouts demanding their removal from office, that hoarse voice of Liebknecht that they hated.

The people's deputies looked at one another. They were under siege. It was up to Liebknecht whether the chancellery would be stormed.

Added to their fear were bitterness and anger. They stood silently at the back of the room. Suddenly they heard another voice.

In one of the wings of the building, it seemed, Barth, the Independent, had been waiting. He could not bear staying in his darkened office. He dared to turn on a light and show himself at the window above the roiling street. He began to speak.

He was met with the shriek of "Traitor!"

Little Barth was the man who had organized the strike of metal workers in January. He flew into a rage.

He would not let himself be called a traitor. He would give Liebknecht the opportunity to debate him wherever he liked, in any bar or hall he pleased.

The outraged man, the pioneer of the revolution, thought he could argue with the masses. A wild convulsion of curses boomed up at him. When he opened his mouth again, fists were raised below. He had to give up. Grimly he slammed the window shut, turned off the light and, quoting Goethe's Götz von Berlichingen, told them they could kiss his arse.

The other people's deputies heard all this with satisfaction.

The crowd dispersed. Rain and lack of any definite shouted goal drove them apart. The people's deputies crept with pale faces from their hiding places. Things could not go on like this. They might simply be snapped up and murdered. One must be either a hammer or an anvil.

Barth joined them later on. They did not look at each other.

Sin

In a secular conversation the word "sin" comes up. High authority contents itself with a tactical retreat.

Becker was holding a newspaper in one hand as Maus sat down next to him on the sofa.

Becker said, "We've got people here of late, too, who've got it in for the Jews. Here they're quoting a certain Konrad Alberti who says: 'No one can deny that the Jews are conspicuous by the active role they play in the pollution and corruption of all public affairs. One characteristic of the Jews is their persistent attempt to make money without bothering to do work—which is an impossibility. It means swindles, corruption, an endeavor to create wealth by manipulating the stock market and planting false rumors, then taking this wealth and exchanging it for real wealth earned by hard work, foisting it on others, in whose hands it melts like Helen in Faust's embrace.' Were you listening, Maus?"

Becker took no offence at his visitor's silence, and went on. "This Alberti has a certain literary flair. The Jews, it seems, create illusions which other people are mad to have in exchange for the products of their labor. Afterward they stand there with empty hands and wail. I like the image. Because that is how artists work. They create illusions, magical nothings. And if you are stupid and a bit nasty, like Voltaire, you can also include religion. In point of fact the whole world gladly, fervently hands over everything it has earned by the sweat of its brow for things that have been created without any sweat whatever, but through which work itself only begins to take on meaning and sense. When later on at some point this magical illusion proves to be a chimera, that is a most unfortunate accident, but one for which not the producer is to blame, but merely the purchaser, the owner—that's called disillusionment. It is constantly cropping up in the course of human history, and it's always a sad occasion, but does not detract from the value of the whole process."

Maus shook his head. "I don't know what you're talking about, Becker. The scribblings of this Alberti are propaganda, vicious propaganda. The war criminals are using anti-Semitism now."

Becker would not let himself be led away from the topic.

"I hope that this remark of his is true. In that case the Jews would indeed be the race of the future, as they were once that of the past. Because then they know that ultimately in this world everything is only a matter of ideas that superficial people pass off as worthless. The only question is, which idea? Which idea?"

Maus drummed impatiently on his knee. "You're feeling better, Becker, I can see. You're spinning fantasies again. But please, not right now. You can see there how they're working. They started in early with their anti-Semitism. Someone told me that a Count von der Schulenburg is said to have arrived at General Headquarters before the Kaiser abdicated and said, 'Who then has mutinied actually? The navy that lay in port the whole time, a bunch of lazy good-for-nothings and behind-the-line heroes. And it was they'—I'm quoting Schulenburg—'who stabbed the brave army of the Kaiser in the back, in league with Jewish war profiteers.' That fine general, the Kaiser's intimate, proposed that the army turn around and march back into the Reich under the two slogans: 'Down the Bolshevism' and 'Down with the Jews.' Even then they were prepared to drown all of Germany in the blood of innocent people if only they could avoid their own punishment. Now they want to make good on it."

Becker lay the paper on his desk resignedly. "If only the Jews themselves don't let themselves be herded down the wrong path by these agitators. That would be a shame. Because it's a matter of the idea. And the idea's lacking, lacking. This Alberti, without even wanting to, has put his finger in our wound. What can we do really? Fight wars and make revolutions."

Maus: "I beg you, Becker, enough of this."

"What? I already know what you want. I've already given you the answer. We can fight wars and make revolutions."

Maus propped his head up. Such melancholy glances he threw at Becker.

Maus: "Everything's coming to a head, Becker, with incredible speed. I was at the Reichstag today. It's Sunday, we had a meeting. The Greater Berlin Soldiers' Council. The first division from the front are nearing Berlin, between Berlin and Potsdam, and they're supposed to polish us off."

"Us?"

"Me, if that sounds better to you."

"Then you finally know where you stand?"

Maus: "I'm as sure of it as that I'm alive. They intend to drown all Germany in blood in the attempt to wash themselves clean of their own guilt."

Becker, with half-closed eyes: "They don't feel guilty."

"I don't believe that. I'm in a quandary. They've got their tails caught in the trap, and are biting at whatever they can because they know they'll be killed. Becker, we've seen enough people go to their deaths. You can recognize evil by the fact that it doesn't want to die."

"They'll tear themselves loose and go for your throats."

"That's how I see it too. But we'll defend ourselves."

The younger man regarded his friend lying on the sofa. Something lay in wait between them.

Maus: "You didn't feel well at the meeting at the brewery. Are you doing better now? What do you think about it all now?"

"Is what I think important to you?"

"Incredibly important. I'm paralyzed with the thought of you lying up here and not moving at all."

"Why does that paralyze you?"

"Because with almost everything I do, I think of you, and more and more as each day passes. I'm tormented and compelled to come to you and beg you: join in with us, don't leave me in the lurch. I need you. I'm certain, and I'm uncertain, too. We've been through too much together. I can't let go of you. I'm trying incredibly hard to understand you, but I can't. You laugh too much, you mock, you see everything ironically. But I saw you more clearly on the hospital train. There you pointed out the window into the night and said, 'Watch, now peace is coming, we'll have peace, that will be our life.' And then you literally sang. Becker, what's to become of you? What do you want to do? Do I have to lead you to the window so that you can see what's happening out there? They want to destroy peace."

"I look out there as well."

"And what do you see?"

"Something that upsets me just as it does you."

"And?"

Becker turned his head to the wall. "As you see."

"No, it's not a matter of your getting up, Becker, if you can't do that, or of your going out onto the streets with me. I didn't come up here for that. I only want your approval, your glance, your word."

"I can give you all that, Maus."

Becker stretched out his hand to him.

"I don't want anything more than that from you, Becker."

Becker repeated, "Nothing more than that. I'm satisfied."

He crossed his arms on his chest and looked straight ahead, his expression saying nothing.

Maus bent down to him. "From now on you will always be walking at my side. I'll bear you like a banner. And you will get well again, completely well."

Becker sat up. "And then? What do you think happens then? You must not expect anything of me. That day you met your old school chum, Big Ding, and his fiancée. They spoke with you and you were ripe for what they said even then. People are talking to me from all sides. People hit and shove me. But I'm an obstinate mule. I just kick back."

Maus was hurt. "But I don't understand you now. I thought you agreed with me."

"Agreed, sure. And at the same time something in me doesn't want to, resists. I know what it wants, because it wants something, too." Becker's voice grew harder. "It wants me to get up sometimes, to slam the door and let no one in. No one, do you understand, not even you."

Maus, softly: "What does it want?"

"Maybe to do what I've always done, go for walks, read, listen, warm myself in the sun."

"Then you didn't express yourself correctly when you said you agreed with me."

"I have to be true to myself."

Maus stood up. "What is all this?"

"That's better now, Maus. Better than before when you said I would be your banner. You doubt me—just as I doubt myself."

"For God's sake, what is this?"

"You see, Maus, now you recognize me."

"You're not going to join me then?" Maus took his arm. "Becker, my friend, dear Becker, where are you hiding? I don't know you like this at all. And now I demand, not in my name, but in the name of all our friends and comrades who hoped for something good and lie silent now, rotting away uselessly—in the name of those who still live and who will be awakened tomorrow to murder anew: Becker, I don't need to tell you all this, come, get up. I'll not leave you like this. Come with me."

Becker sat there, his mouth open. He listened attentively. He put his legs on the floor.

"Please, don't begrudge me my peace and quiet. Give me time, Maus. A couple of weeks, please. I can't tell you what it is. Don't force me. I beg you."

But Maus moaned, let go of him and stood up. "Time, time. Everyone you talk to has something he lacks, for one it's time, for another it's health. One fellow's wife holds him down, the other has to put his shop in order, one has just found work. But the other side—they've got time. They always have time. Every one of them has time. They're perfectly free. Tomorrow they'll march in. And they know what they want. And that is why the great slaughter will begin, and because we didn't want to stop them we'll be the victims.

Becker reached for Maus's hand. Maus pulled back. "My head will roll, too. That's for sure."

Becker: "You're going? You despise me, don't you?"

348

Maus: "I'm going." —

Utterly desperate, Becker threw himself onto the sofa.

Ebert Tacks

And finally—Ebert gave in.

The contact with the masses that afternoon and the steady coming and going of delegations had given him and Scheidemann and Landsberg the feeling that they dare not go on with the planned mopping-up operation in Berlin.

As eager as Ebert and his friends were to defeat Spartacus and smother a bad conscience, as touchingly as Hindenburg might write, as savage as the bourgeoisie might raise their hue and cry—one could not risk it. The hint of such an attempt would be sufficient to excite popular rage and they would be swept away.

Ebert was keeping his ears open in the Chancellery; he remarked, "One can't simply let things run their course, it can't go on like this." They had been more or less besieged by Liebknecht; it could happen again tomorrow. Should they in fact break off with Groener and seriously attempt a coalition with the Independents?

Impossible, insufferable, unnatural.

But nothing stirred out there. The hours passed. He lowered his flag and swallowed his pride.

He met for a last consultation with his friends in the Party. Ebert agreed when the others emphasized that under all circumstances the unity of the cabinet must be preserved, in the interest of their own party as well.

A small, ironic calculation made Ebert's decision easier. General Lequis was not very strong. He was definitely not strong enough for the mopping-up operation. The workers of Berlin might win. That could not be Kassel's intention.

Hindenburg's letter still burned in his breast pocket. But it just wouldn't work. The circumstances were too unfavorable. If the workers of Berlin revolt, if the Independents join with Spartacus, then everything is over, that's the end of the old Party, then a reign of terror begins and with it the revenge on the leaders of the SDP that has been threatened so often, and that—and with this he quieted Hindenburg's admonishing voice—also means the end of forebearance with General Headquarters and the officers.

As Ebert left the council chamber with his friends, his face was full of gravity and benevolence. As they sat down to a meeting with the Independents, his glances were melancholy. He asked the Independents to understand the SDP's position. Everything was a result of Liebknecht's agitation. What he would like from the Independents, however, was that they would do all they could to influence the masses if one now said no to some action or other from Lequis's commandos. The democratic middle class would soon understand no longer if one did not call this Liebknecht to a halt once and for all. It was to be hoped that the afternoon had taught a lesson to everyone who had had to sit in the dark here in the Chancellery.

Ebert covered his retreat with a fanfare: Liebknecht's intrigues already bordered on treason. In Kiel, comrade Noske had had to declare a state of siege. Meanwhile one had one's hands full trying to defend the eastern border against the Poles and to extend the armistice. Erzberger would have to make another pilgrimage to Foch. And at a point like this, here in Berlin, a man like Liebknecht dared . . .

Scheidemann finished the sentence for him. "We hear from the provinces that people no longer even risk a trip to Berlin. We are confronted with the dissolution of the Reich."

Late that evening the rumor spread that Liebknecht and Luxemburg had declared Ebert, Scheidemann and Wels to be outlaws. Flyers warned that Spartacus was inciting the masses to panic.

After the meeting, People's Deputy Scheidemann still had to go to a meeting in some luxurious hall in the west end of town. He was exhausted from the struggle, but regained his strength as he spoke.

He mocked the radicals who were making a mountain out of a molehill. Their chimneys only smoked when they used lies for fuel. They screamed their lungs out on account of the alleged arrest of the Executive Council.

"The whole affair was dreadfully blown out of proportion." (A voice: "For purposes of party!") "The vice–sergeant major who undertook the arrest, or was supposed to undertake it, was a young doctor with a downright amazing lack of intelligence." (Laughter.)

Scheidemann spoke about himself. He was being held responsible for everything possible and impossible at the moment.

"Now, my work in the former cabinet,"—he did not say "the imperial cabinet"—"consisted of getting Liebknecht out of prison and dismissing the Kaiser. Ninety out of a hundred Germans stand behind Friedrich Ebert, and meanwhile the government is sitting on a powder keg."

He became more excited. The gentleman was not without a temper, he could be spiteful.

"The result of Liebknecht's strike would only be that for a few weeks we'd have nothing to eat and then finally the French would arrive. The carryings-on of the Internationalists in Munich, Kurt Eisner and so on, is nothing less than the work of unconscionable bandits. But it is me whom they attack, and Solf, Erzberger and Ebert. The accusations," he yelled with a red face, "these people raise against us, in the hope of dissolving the Reich, and they may well yet do it, are completely unjustified.

"For my own person, I declare that I will not work another week under such conditions."

The whole hall was gripped by these powerful emotions.

Gioconda in the Confessional

Maus had left Becker alone. His mother had been gone for hours.

I—am afraid. Don't know what of. These stupid visions that I keep seeing. I'm going crazy.

The doorbell rang. He had waited so long for someone to come, but now he was terrified. He did not open the door. The bell rang again. He was afraid. But it would be his mother.

Hilda extended her hand to him in the corridor. She did not see his face. While she took off her coat he withdrew to his room. He was beside himself. She was the last person he had expected.

While he paced beside his bookcase, his arms crossed on his chest, he heard her come in behind him. The whole situation seemed to him to be fantastic, exasperating. What did a woman want? What could this woman want here?

She sat down innocently. He thought her behavior shameless. He took a position standing at his desk, behind the chair. As she took hold of his hand to ask how he felt, the rage rose up in him. He had to force himself not to draw his hand away from her. But now he was seized with an indecisiveness, trapped in his discomfort, fear and outrage. His hand jerked away from hers, but he did not dare betray himself. To hide the movement, he took hold of the button of his robe and buttoned the top button.

He felt compelled to go through all sorts of play-acting. When she asked him about his doctor and the hospital, it became a signal for him to set himself in motion. And then, unhappily, he had to keep up the pretense to hide his distress by marching a couple of times back and forth in front of her just to show how well he was getting along. He marched in torment and wanted to rebel. But this would probably not last too long. Otherwise he would really have to pull himself together and stand up to her and say to her, to this woman, that she had no business being here, that she was a stranger to him, a pushy one at that, a summer acquaintance. As he came marching by again in that ridiculous way, he turned his distraught face to her.

There—she sat there at the desk, her arms propped on it, her chin in the hollow of her hands, her fingers at her temples, framing her soft face. And beneath her smooth blonde hair, two grave, attentive eyes looked out at him from that face.

He saw a different person from the one he had been fantasizing about, not some pushy passerby who had wandered into his study by mistake, but a human being who looked at him sadly and from a great distance.

He stopped his compulsive marching and stood behind his chair. She shoved her hands further up her head. Her fingers were submerged in her hair, but following his movements with an unaltered melancholy were the eyes of some ancient creature gazing out from the shade of a forest. The corners of her mouth twitched, they seemed to form a smile, a more approachable creature took shape. With a sense of guilt, he laid a hand on the desk and lowered his eyes.

Gioconda asked, "You're not feeling well, are you Friedrich?"

She did not move to go, and he did not rebel. He took his seat across from her at the desk, apparently thinking about something, but in fact simply trying to understand himself enough to do any thinking at all. For she was not disturbing him. He felt, as he pulled his chair to the right spot, that she belonged here in the constellation of his thoughts. She was the continuation of and successor to Maus, someone dunning him as he had done. He put a hand over his eyes and began to speak. Yes, he spoke, he surrendered to these people dunning him. He confronted them with what was inside him. He came out onto the open battlefield. The chariots rolled.

She saw his eyes between his fingers, pale and desperate.

"Hilda, Maus was pressing me hard. You will say he's right. But that doesn't get me any further."

"What would I say he is right about, Friedrich?"

It is good to be asked questions.

"That I sit around here, lie about and stare at these walls. While outside the world is moving, and I do nothing."

"What are you supposed to do, Friedrich?"

"He pleads with me for us to experience all over again what we just put behind us. The powers that caused the war, he says, are already at work again. They are here, and they are paving their way, while we go on believing that they have been defeated, thrown to the ground. And that is supposed to shock me and upset me the way it has upset Maus. It is supposed to set me in motion. It is supposed to be my affair. But—it doesn't set me in motion. It upsets me, but it does nothing to me. It is something inside of me that I don't want. I lie here and stand here and I am a stone that it would take a fire to melt. But when the fire has gone out the stone hasn't melted and it's as cold as it was before."

"What is Maus doing?"

"You would be happy to see how he has grown. But look at this beast here, at this obstinate animal that sits here motionless in front of you, a little flesh and skin and bones. This pitiful beast doesn't want to do anything. What does it want? Ask it, ask it, Hilda, perhaps it will give you an answer. Perhaps it wants to go for a walk, or hear some music, or go dancing. And perhaps someday, if you are still here and haven't run away from me, it will want to kiss you."

"And why would that be so bad, Friedrich?"

He laid his hand on her arm. His hand trembled and was ice-cold.

"Hilda, here I sit next to you and truly feel the desire to pull you to me and beg you to hold me and be happy together with me."

"And why not?"

"I'm lying in some abyss, Hilda. I'm desperate, Hilda. I feel everything Maus feels, ten times, a thousand times over, and I cannot follow him. Listen to me."

And he began to name the terrible things that were pressing in on him.

"Day after day visions appear to me. They creep up on me from behind. The visions are to blame for my not being able to move. They won't leave me alone. They are memories of things that have vanished, of things I thought no longer even had anything to do with me. I was walking, this truly happened, across a square near a train station at the start of the war. And men were being forced along four abreast, each of them with a rucksack or a small suitcase, young men, draftees. The scene is not something I've hallucinated. I know the square, the train station. Men were being mobilized, women were walking along beside them and weeping. That was all. I was waiting for the day I was to be mobilized. And now—my memory hands me this, shoves it at me, and I have to watch it and I cannot do anything else. And it's so real I could touch it. Those young faces are secretive, closed. I know they are dead. All of them walking there are dead. The streets and squares are bathed in bright sunshine. The people on the sidewalk watch them pass. There is the tobacco store they patronized, the movie theater. They are being transported to the freight depot, they are no longer members of the human race."

Hilda listened to him in horror. She watched him, his head buried in his hands, sitting there before her and whispering and whispering and whispering. What was this? What was wrong with him? It all sounded so peculiar, jittery, excited, morbid.

"What's wrong now, Friedrich?"

"The sad way these men looked at me. And why do I see these visions? I thought they had disappeared. But they had only fallen to the ground in order to bounce back up, like rubber balls. Always the same thing. Always the same thing. The look of those men as they drove past in open cattle-wagons. The wagons were even decorated with wreaths, but they are already dead. I see some of them, too, standing beside an advertising pillar, they're reading announcements. They go away and come back again to the same corner, and sometimes one of them turns around, and he has no eyes and says nothing, he simply points at me and demands that I look at him. And doesn't move from the spot, this man without eyes. I saw him back then and did not pay any attention; I was hard inside. And that is why I am being punished now and it all comes back. And now it's no use for me to think. It's too late. Because I cannot awake the dead. They are burning my brains out. They're always standing there, I know all about it, but they won't leave me in peace. Hilda, it's as if someone shoved a telescope in front of me for me to look at a certain star. The telescope is out of focus. I have to turn the focus to find the star. But I can't find it. I turn and turn, and my hand is shaking."

He lifts his eyes to her, a mournful, helpless look.

"How long has this been going on inside you, Friedrich?"

"I was sand and the wind came up and blew now from one direction, now another. I am ashamed, unutterably ashamed."

"I met you in the military hospital. You were badly wounded. You had fought valiantly."

"What does that have to do with it?"

"You had sworn an oath and you did your duty."

"Every word you say is false, Hilda. I accept none of it. Everything depends on whether one realizes things and is in accord with them deep inside. I did not realize it."

"And what have you done, Friedrich?"

"I went along. Which means I was stupid, wicked and evil. Ah, Hilda, when I was in the hospital you stood by me. You gave me your energy. Help me again, Hilda. Help me."

In her arms he murmured, "Don't let me go."

Her eyes wavered. Something had been awakened in her. She laid her face against his. Like a cloud that slides across a mountain top, making it disappear, she let her face down over his.

He began asking again, "Where shall I go?"

She laid both arms out in front of her on the desk, lowered her eyes and said, "You're tormenting yourself, Friedrich. We are all sinners. Don't weigh yourself down so much. If I were all alone, I could not have helped myself either. But the Savior has appeared and shown us mercy. I've experienced his grace and help."

Many things had been said in this room. People had had long discussions here, laughed, cried, kissed and embraced. The busts and books had looked down from their walls and shelves, had preached what they had to say, the wisdom and wit and despair of several thousand years of human existence. But never had these walls heard words like sin, Savior and grace.

That man was sinful had been mentioned casually now and then. But one really has to feel lost before that word strikes him with full seriousness.

But it sobered Becker. He stared at Hilda. Was she joking with him? What were these trite phrases supposed to mean? She was smiling to herself and her eyes were closed. Gioconda.

"I know, Friedrich, that that doesn't help you if I say it. You have to find it out for yourself and you will find it. I'll help you. Believe me, it's not so difficult."

She threw him an affectionate glance.

Then he pulled himself together and began to question her. The busts, the classics, the whole bookcase full of celebrated corpses listened to her.

She told about her pious parents, about her school. She had not been talking long when someone unlocked the apartment door. His mother put away her umbrella. She was happy when she came in. She said she would have been home long ago, but she had been with friends and had not dared to go out on the streets because there was reportedly shooting. But there wasn't anything of the sort, just rain.

She also brought a flyer along with her that someone had tossed into the tram. "Right as we were riding along, a young man in puttees jumped up and tossed a hole bundle of these flyers into the car. The conductor swore at him. The young man wouldn't clean up the mess in the car."

Secret Line 998

That evening, as Scheidemann was speaking in Spichern Hall, Ebert had the telephone conversation with Kassel that he had dreaded.

After several words of thanks directed to Hindenburg for the handwritten letter, Ebert mentioned the misgivings that had been expressed in the Council of People's Deputies. In light of the mood of the population of Berlin, he must urgently request that such actions as the mopping-up plans of General Lequis be held in abeyance.

In reply to Groener's counterquestion, Ebert repeated the sentence. The general thereupon concluded the conversation without the usual small talk.

Groener marched stormily about in his office. The rebuff was a personal blow to him. It compromised him with Hindenburg and his own advisers. It was too late to explain this to the field marshal. Groener could already hear Hindenburg's answer. "This is what I told you would happen. It's a shame I wasted good stationery on it."

Major von Schleicher was called to the phone at the old countess's home and briefly filled in by his commanding officer. He should make preparations to travel to Berlin tomorrow morning, but first he was to report to Groener at the crack of dawn before he left.

The small social gathering at the countess's was just breaking up. The countess was still sitting alone but alert in her easy chair in the living room as Schleicher returned from the telephone. She called to him with a mocking smile.

"And so now he doesn't want to."

She had predicted it two hours before. She had said, "We are waiting for the saddler Friedrich Ebert to condescend to give us his decision."

Now she celebrated her triumph.

Schleicher walked with a comrade through the dark streets of Kassel. The streets were wet, it had been a rainy Sunday today in Kassel as well. Schleicher was a flexible man. Irony and role-playing suited him. But now Groener was demanding a bit too much self-abnegation from him.

A small tailor in a building on the marketplace was still sitting at his table under a lamp, and he watched the two officers from the General Staff walked by below. The way they still marched about at midnight. It was in their blood. They go wherever they want and don't care a bit what other people think. Every day someone arrives with new proclamations, with new slogans that don't make anyone any wiser. But for them everything is cut and dried. It's part of them and they act on it. You can depend on them.

Book Two

From the 9th to the 10th of December

On Board the *George Washington*

President Wilson underway. It must be made clear to the Europeans what has won the victory: that a man is better off using reason and his conscience than a rifle.

The *George Washington,* with President Wilson on board, plowed its furrow across the ocean.

The ship sailed not only under the flag of the United States but under the personal arms of the president as well: on a blue field, a silver eagle holding the red and white shield of the United States in its talons. And this was indeed a very personal voyage for Woodrow Wilson. It was his grand attempt to make reality at last of an idea that had dwelt in the most enlightened minds, to assist reason and moral will to triumph—by means of a political institution.

Wilson bore the plan for such a construct in his pocket. It was the idea of the League of Nations, an idea that had come to him from England. It had been studied out over there, the model of the British Empire lay before them. Lord Cecil submitted the plan to Colonel House, a clever man who had been traveling between America and Europe on Wilson's behalf for seven years now, and who had vainly attempted to prevent the disaster of 1914. The plan was to Wilson's liking. The idea rejuvenated him.

They had sailed from Hoboken on the morning of December 4th, and had looked back for a last glance at the city draped with flags—the city was letting its joy at the armistice flutter above it. The old but powerful ship began to move out toward this small, dark continent, the wicked continent from which their forefathers had come.

They led a quiet life aboard the steamer, recuperating from the rigors of the last weeks. The sea was tranquil. Since it was December, it had every right to storm and toss the ship about. But the sea respected the high commission that it bore. Even the mines floating about left them in peace. Nothing was supposed to disturb this grand experiment.

Guarding the president was a patrol of armed soldiers moving about the ship day and night. The *New Mexico,* connected with the *George Washington* by a special telephone, followed as an escort. A young physician, Doctor Grayson, a man of whom the president was particularly fond, was watching over his health. He had promoted this naval doctor to admiral, over the heads of 117 others waiting in line. And if anyone asked, "What ship does the new admiral command?", the smirking reply was: "Admiral of the Boudoir." Through this Dr. Grayson, Wilson had become acquainted with his second wife, who was traveling with him on this trip. He had met this charming jeweler's widow in social circles to which Grayson had introduced him, and people said it was "love at first sight" for Wilson. Dr. Grayson, then, took care of the health of the president, this physician of mankind, a delicate man, sixty-two years old, who had a weak stomach and neuralgia in his shoulders.

The Hotel Belmont in New York had sent along its best chef to cook for the president. Wilson was annoyed at this, he had little use for such airs, and had been accustomed as a professor to a modest life. But as long as the master chef was there and cooking, they at the most exquisite meals—for better or worse.

The suite of the presidential couple had been transformed into a veritable garden by the flowers sent from all over the country. Wilson was provided with a roomy office. The two telephones on the mahogany desk reminded him that he was not alone, even if sometimes it seemed to him to be the case in these lovely, quiet rooms. His bedroom was kept dark, with heavy green drapes. Mrs. Wilson did not care for this gloomy green.

But he liked it here. Late in the evening, after shining in numerous conversations in society, he could withdraw to this room and dampen, lower the flame of his mind after it had shimmered enough in society. The weary man stretched himself out on his bed, felt the pulse of the engines working through the ship's planks, and gave himself over to their vibration. But before he fell asleep his hand reached out for a small pocket Bible a soldier had given him, one bound in khaki, a Y.M.C.A. edition. The soldier had written in it that he hoped the president would read in it daily, and the president had not forgotten.

Mrs. Wilson had a three-room suite. She had a tasteful dining room, with a table for six, the chairs upholstered in English chintz, the living room was all cretonne, her bedroom a shade of ivory.

With them on the *George Washington* were the French and English ambassadors, also Mr. Davis, the replacement at the English court for Mr. Page, who was ill, plus a host of newspaper reporters, and above all Wilson's advisors, Sidney E. Mezes, president of New York City College, the director of the American Geographical Society, several authorities on colonial territories, a special commission for Alsace-Lorraine, specialists on Russia and Turkey, experts on Italy and the Balkans, numerous financial wizards and economists. Wilson had taken special care in selecting these men. He wanted the best of help for the task ahead.

And if it is important to know who was with him, it is equally important to know who was not—not a single member of the United States Congress. Wilson was content to be the sole representative of the American people. Indeed he was certain he performed that role better than the senators and representatives. He was serving his second term as president, and he did not intend to let politicians meddle with him. A hostile majority had formed against him in Congress shortly before his departure, a fact he acknowledged with only a shake of the head. And in the same way he had merely shrugged when people made scornful remarks about the composition of the party traveling with him. For people out there were laughing at this shipload of bespectacled literati he was dragging around with him.

It is morning on the high seas. The president has slept late and is sitting in the dining room with the first lady over breakfast. Dr. Grayson is announced and he takes a seat at the table. Wilson asks him cheerfully if there is any news; he is wonderfully fresh and hearty, the sea air has been good for him. Grayson knows nothing new, nor is he wildly curious about news. Mrs. Wilson is the same way.

The president: Ah, yes, news, the real news was something he would soon be providing himself. But he was curious to know what America would really hear about that news when it happened. At any rate all sorts of things were already in the works that let him make some good guesses. His opponents were sending their own correspondents over, they might even set up their own special telegraph office.

He rubbed his hands, smiling wistfully. "And all that before I have even begun. If people don't like someone, then they don't like him no matter what he does."

Mrs. Wilson was glad that he took it all so well, and Grayson thought all along that it was an invaluable advantage that for several weeks the Atlantic Ocean would lie between the president and Mr. Lodge and Teddy Roosevelt.

Wilson: "Lodge would not be so bad if only he could tolerate me just a bit more. But he hacks away at me, has to hack at me. He is a very well-read man, though not profound, more a dilettante. But he's got one of the great Federalists for an ancestor, that wise man of Boston, Cabot Lodge, who gave the government trouble because of its vote of thanks to France. He didn't like the French Revolution and so the wording 'to the generous French nation' had to be deleted—and it was done. A glorious achievement. He intends to terrorize me in the same fashion. His secret vexation is that in such different times it is I who is president and not he."

Mrs. Wilson: "Do you think, Woodrow, that he would do things in the same way if he were president?"

Wilson smiled politely. "It's possible. That's a trick question. I'm not sure. I contribute something to it myself perhaps."

He poured himself a second glass of mineral water as he thought, drank it down slowly and let his eyes rest on his wife. He was apparently keeping some thought in reserve, formulating it. He now put his glass back on the table, but kept his hand on it, turning it. "Edith, we are sailing now for Europe. Have you thought it all over thoroughly? Do you really want to go over there? Perhaps it would have been better had you stayed home."

She knew he liked to make jokes. "Why, dear?"

He: "And you, doctor? The question is also meant for you. If I were in your shoes, Edith, I would at least hesitate. And in the doctor's place I would refuse without even hesitating. Just imagine, Edith, you are walking down the street in Princeton or Washington and by chance some man walks up along side you who is a thief, a burglar, and he is arrested right there beside you, and people assume that you know him since you're walking so close together, that he is your friend perhaps—that would be embarrassing, would it not?"

"Woodrow."

"You would be of the same opinion, doctor, and especially if in fact the man were truly your friend."

"It would most certainly be embarrassing, Mr. President, to have a man like that for a friend."

"Well now, imagine the matter in this way. We are sitting, all three of us, in a car in Paris. We are riding through the streets, and on this occasion you discover that I am a swindler, a fraud. The affair becomes even more embarrassing because up to that point you have only known me as a respectable man, but I had apparently been in disguise, leading a kind of double life."

The doctor shook his head; there was no comprehending this.

Mrs. Wilson: "Don't torture us so, Woodrow. What is the matter?"

"Of course I'm only joking, Edith, what else? But they have thought it all out in Europe. We will have our grand reception in Paris, a triumphal procession and words of welcome. And why? Why will they greet me like that? Why will they cheer me? Because I am such a cunning dog, such a successful swindler. I have duped the Germans, with my speeches and my Fourteen Points I pulled it off. Because naturally I have something quite different in mind: the great plunder. The great plundering is to start immediately upon my arrival. They will even be willing to yield some things to us, though of course not too much."

Mrs. Wilson was somewhat frightened. "Where do you come up with such notions? You're speaking so strangely today."

Wilson: "Believe me. They are saying it quite openly in Europe. They are expecting me to be the master swindler. Because in all of Europe no one can imagine that I am really so dumb as to be serious about the Fourteen Points and the League of Nations. They don't think even the President of the United States could be that dumb."

"Woodrow, this is no longer a joke."

"Edith, after the first tumultuous welcome I will whisper in their ears that it is not all some outward show as they had expected. I will say it softly at first and then louder and louder. I mean no offense, gentlemen, and I'm dreadfully sorry, but I really am that dumb. I mean a League of Nations and Fourteen Points. Whereupon they will expedite the whole lot of us back to America by the next post."

Mrs. Wilson shook herself. "Politics are awful."

Wilson: "And you, doctor, what do you say? Are you not just a bit, just a little bit in league with those men over there? You have certainly determined for yourself by now, haven't you, that I am a naive professor, an incurable fantast, a bookworm?"

They left the dining room and sat down in the first lady's bright living room. She wanted to get the president to go out on deck. He should take a little stroll and get some air, but he had pulled a piece of paper from his pocket and was making shorthand notes. They did not disturb him, but whispered together while the doctor smoked a cigarette.

When Wilson was finished, he was more relaxed, seemed ready to chat; they climbed up to the promenade deck. A strong wind was blowing, and the windows on the promenade deck were closed. They ventured to the fore, but the wind whistled and blew the doctor's cigarette away. He had to run after it to stamp out the fire.

They found a place to sit out of the wind. Grayson looked for a while at the president inquiringly. He encouraged him to speak.

Grayson: "Senator Lodge and the others are great ones for eating Germans. Basically, so are the majority of Americans. What caused you to take your position, actually? It is, to be sure, courageous. But—how shall I say it—the Germans have thus far not given much proof of possessing normal human qualities."

Wilson: "In the war. That's true. But to judge them, one must look back over a greater span of time. How long have the Germans been in existence—since the days of Tacitus' Germania? You remember the Holy Roman Empire of the German Nation, I'm sure. In its day that empire included a considerable portion of European civilization. It declined then later. The Germans were outstripped by others, culturally and politically. They specialized more and more in scientific, technical and, unfortunately, military matters. Politically they slipped completely, especially that portion of the Germans who came under the control of the Hohenzollerns. One can't say much for the Hapsburgs either." Wilson was obviously lecturing. "That did not, however, prevent the Germans from developing splendid philosophy, art and music. They excelled in other areas too. Only in matters of social organization, in human and political matters, did they remain backward. You see, doctor, that is the orthopedic task to be tackled after our victory."

Grayson nodded appreciatively. "I'm glad that we have moved into a field where I know my way around. And as far as these patients go, they have, I think, over the course of many centuries, become very used to their way of life and have adapted to it. If I make a faulty splint for a leg fracture and the leg remains in its cast too long, then under certain conditions something dreadful occurs. When you expose the leg, it has grown thin, the muscles have atrophied, and it can happen that the patient never recovers from it."

Wilson listened attentively, replied with several "hm's," before he said, "And that is how the Germans are, you think, now that they've been taken out of the plaster cast of their dynasties."

He fell silent again. Then he gave a gesture of resignation. "Well, doctor, I hope that we have not arrived too late. There are possibilities for recuperation. Nature will prove more powerful than the rule of dynasties, which, ultimately have not lasted so very long. At any rate it will not be our fault. We must not despair. To depart from our medical metaphor, we are all human beings in the end, and if these people over there have sinned, we will not hold their sins against them forever, as the Lord's Prayer says, so that we too may be forgiven. I, at least, will not be led astray by some momentary emotional reaction."

Grayson made a bow. "Mr. President, you are neither a swindler nor subject to emotional outbursts. One must then ask you in all seriousness how you intend to go about your politics."

Wilson clapped his hands. "Bravo. Bravo. That was well put."

But they had grown more earnest, sitting there quietly and letting the wind fan them. Wilson, stretched out in his deck chair, winked at the doctor, who was sitting on a footstool next to him. Mrs. Wilson lay on the president's left.

"In what way, doctor, am I different from Senator Lodge? Let us leave personalities aside. Is it because Lodge, the devourer of Germans, is the greater realist? I think not. In his polemics against me the man has lost all perspective. He suddenly knows nothing now of the power of morality. It was the Germans at war who proposed the creed that physical strength and brutality alone assure superiority and victory. The warring Germans took up their weapons against the conscience of mankind. They presented us with the alternative: weapons or conscience. We at once sided with conscience. And now that the festivities are over, Senator Lodge falls right into the same stupid mistake the Germans made. Because sooner or later, quite apart from all else, the German thesis proves to be a stupid mistake. Morality is not just power, not just the stronger power, but in fact the only creative power."

Wilson looked up at the sky, whistled and said, "The Germans are no different from other people. Marshal Foch declares that he defeated them with armies, ours included. But no, I did my part too, and without even appearing on the field of battle. Generals overestimate the value of arms and underestimate people every time. It was doubtless a necessary first task to show the Germans that they could not be victorious ad libitum. Their crazy arrogance, their war madness had to be broken. That is what Foch accomplished. But it is only half the job. So that now I come along with the second weapon, that of morality. A great nation does not give up its cause just like that. Defeat stimulates, aggravates the energies of battle. That changes when at home things go badly for people and their morale suffers. That was the case with the Germans, doctor, my medicine worked. My method has proven effective thus far. I consider the Germans to be an industrious and decent people. I am glad that they have shaken off the rule of imperialists and militarists. They had corrupted the nation. I plan to continue to apply this method of treatment—but you are correct—cautiously. That the Germans finally came around to shaking off that rule, however, I would like to take credit for that. Now everything depends on leading them correctly. Then they could build a bulwark for peace in Europe."

Grayson was glad to see Wilson's optimism. He did not say what else he thought—that others said the Germans were all a humbug, they were just in hiding and biding their time.

Wilson went on lecturing from his deck chair. "The Germans have brought down their government. We must help them find the right form of government and then stand with them on principle. What is going to happen now? Who knows? What is the greatest battle in the history of the world? That between peoples and their rulers. It begins in the Bible, with Moses. There the ruler did battle for his people. The Jews sat there in Egypt, enslaved and mistreated by their masters. Moses was a true leader among them, was born to be a leader, was chosen for them by God. But he had to employ magic for them even to lend an ear. And as soon as he turned his back they acted like schoolboys when the teacher is out of the room. But his battle is the exception. The rule is just the opposite: a people attempts to resist the tyranny of its master. Thousands of examples! And if I am now traveling to Europe as the representative of a real democracy, I do not do so as blindly as many would seem to think. The cynics of this world have decided among themselves that only cynicism is true reason. They do not know human emotions, they use them for their games. And they run politics. They build a clique. They stand on the side opposite the people. They have learned how to smuggle their way to the top of nations, into their parliaments as well. For them, the people are a business, or at best a means by which to satisfy their private ambitions."

Mrs. Wilson: "I think, Woodrow, that the people have won this time. They fought, they made sacrifices and they know they have a right to speak up. It probably won't be so very difficult for you. They're on your side without a doubt."

"What do you say?" the president said to the doctor with a mischievous smile.

"Why?"

"What do you say to the notion that without a doubt the people will listen to me now. Let me whisper something in your ear, Edith." He thrust his head over to her and said with a tragicomic expression, "They've already voted against me at home."

Mrs. Wilson: "They're demagogues. Ingrates."

Wilson: "An exception to the rule, then?"

He pulled a piece of paper from his pocket. "I jotted this down a while ago. The remarks of a Democrat. What war has been the most difficult one in world history and is not yet over even today? That of the people against their politicians and governments. The greatest rarity: an honest democracy. A democracy is honest when it has a government aware of its responsibilities. That's what I jotted down. Who started the war? Autocratic governments. They oppress the people, acts of violence follow, the Serbs shot the Austrian archduke at Sarajevo, etc. Who can make peace? Similar governments, do you think? What would be the result of such a peace? Another war."

And he patted his wife, who had buried herself under her blanket, on the shoulder. His eyes had their sly look. "Listen to me, Edith. Do you know what the best thing we could do is? The best for everyone— even the best for the general public and for the cause of peace?"

She didn't know. He turned to the doctor. He didn't know either. Wilson laughed like a young man. "Turn around. On a pivot. Sail home. No negotiations for two years. Put together some temporary agreement, continue the armistice, supply the peoples of Europe with food, disarm them, begin reconstruction—and then in two or three years make this trip to a peace conference. But now—every dispatch shows me how raving mad they all are over there. Who can do anything reasonable now?"

Grayson found the plan very clever. He would have been prepared to give the signal for a turnabout right then. He declared the method as the only correct one from a medical point of view.

Mrs. Wilson was frightened. "But, Woodrow, for heaven's sake, what is going to happen if that's how things stand?"

Wilson grinned. "The great prizefight begins. Who is going to knock out whom? I'm standing in the ring with the rest, happy I have

366

my doctor along—and you, Edith. I'm used to boxing matches of this sort from Princeton." He whispered, "Have you spoken already with the Italian, Celleri, and his wife? They are pleased with the victory and keep talking—about Fiume."

"Who is that?"

"Fiume? It's a region, a harbor on the Mediterranean, and its population is most definitely not Italian. They would love to have it so much, Edith. That's what hurts them so."

"And they can't be given it?"

"You see, you're like the rest. But they're Yugoslavs."

"Yugoslavs. Fine, but why shouldn't Yugoslavs live well under Italians?"

Wilson: "Ask the Yugoslavs, Edith. It's a nuisance. Questions of borders can never be answered in that way. We need, I repeat, before we even begin to discuss borders, a League of Nations. Before disarmament, before nations have disarmed themselves emotionally, these questions cannot be answered. We have to show people, now that we have won, not who has won but *what*. They must see that the world will do better using its conscience rather than its arms."

In London

At this time Prime Minister Lloyd George was speaking at a women's conference. He demanded that the whole German nation be held responsible for the war. The conditions for peace should be difficult ones.

"Kaisers, kings and governments"—this was a campaign speech; women had received the vote, and for the first time eighteen-year-olds had the right to vote as well—"must know for all time that if they spread their villainy over the earth, punishment will inevitably fall on their heads. But nations, too, must learn that they cannot go to war and celebrate their victories unpunished."

One woman in the hall stood up and asked whether the Germans would be thrown out of England for once and for all. Lloyd George answered obligingly that they were thinking of doing just that. In any case, these people would not misuse English hospitality a second time.

In Paris

With each new day new kings, princes and statesmen arrived in Paris and were received with ceremony and splendidly treated. Occasionally they and their wives would visit the hospitals and charitable institutions to view the victims of nationalist wrath. They would shake hands embarrassedly with one or another of them. They could not escape a feeling of awkwardness, however, as they confronted the maimed in their splendid clothing and with all their medals. It was better at the cemetaries, there you simply stood in front of a stone monument or wooden crosses.

In the ministries and hotels things moved at a lively pace. Ministers, officials, delegates and negotiators, Balkans and exotics, ran about busy and excited. They were all in a great rush. They had important and pressing interests to represent.

The resident functionarries went about things more calmly, both the upper and lower echelons. They were Parisians, they had their peace now and knew how to value the life they led. They shuffled along down the corridors of their ministries, their coats dangling from their arms (the weather was comfortable), and sat at their desks in their offices. There their faces had the smooth expressions appropriate for a bureaucrat's office. One noontime a man ran through all the rooms and threw a newspaper on each desk, where they could read the massive headline: "Ukrainian Slain by Ukrainian." This time, however, it had nothing to do with politics, but was simply love. The picture of the murderer was exciting, they had photographed him as he was being arrested, with disheveled hair, a vacant look, and a wide bandage over his swollen forehead.

In the corridors people talked with great interest about the American president, Wilson, whom they called with conscious irony the "World Judge." It was hoped he would not make things too difficult. At any rate, to get him into a good mood they were furnishing him with a comfortable apartment in Paris (he was only human after all) in the Hotel Murat on the Parc Monceau—an establishment in most exquisite taste. It did contain, it was true, souvenirs of a horrible warrior, Napoleon I, which perhaps was not the best thing to gladden the heart of this new world judge. But after a time, certainly, whatever is dead is simply dead, and the pain and misery and curses are silent, and only history professors worry about preserving them—and besides, the new world judge was himself a history professor and would have a professional interest in such items.

But what thoughts would occur to this puritan when he viewed the painting that hung over the desk in his study? It was a painting by David, *Amor and Psyche*. Would it shock him? Would it make him more placable, more Parisian? It showed a naked, dark-complexioned young lad, Amor, who represented love. He touches the earth with one foot. But the other leg is raised, the knee bent, and resting against Psyche's body. And Psyche's snow-white arm reaches out toward that ecstatic leg. Her white body is still somewhat turned away from him. She lies stretched out on her couch. Her head rests on her lover's extended forearm. She has one arm tucked enchantingly behind her head. She is not tempting Amor nor is he forcing himself on her. They are simply very close together.

Above the Grave of the Lusitania

Although they are all awaiting him, Wilson has his journey extended so that he can visit that spot in the ocean where on May 7, 1914, a German submarine torpedoed the American passenger steamer *Lusitania.* They pass over the scene of the tragedy.

The American president and his party stand on deck. They hold their hats in their hands.

They are alive, they are sailing on the ocean. Fuzzy memories of the first terrible reports of that cruel torpedoing flicker in their heads. Wilson knows what he wants. There must be an end on earth to the constant recurrence of murder and violence. Once and for all, for Europe and all nations.

They glide across that terrible grave and move on to the subcontinent of Europe, still swimming in blood.

Hunted Game

*The troops are at the gates. An administrator maneuvers, trying in
vain to secure the help of those around him.*

Victory Celebrations in Metz

The Belgians marched on through Neuss. Their forward divisions
had set up camp in the suburbs of Düsseldorf. The British army and
General Plumer marched through the Eifel region and occupied the
banks of the Rhine from Bonn to Düsseldorf. The Rhine sector with its
center at Cologne was apportioned to the American 3rd Army, which
pushed on forward along both sides of the Moselle. The French infantry
had marched across the Palatinate and was approaching Mainz.

Behind this rolling wall of iron, the victory celebrations of the con-
querors proceeded.

In an open coach, soldiers mounted on the four coach horses, gal-
looned footmen in the rear seat, riders brandishing their sabers at the
sides, Poincaré drove through the city of Metz to the Place de la Republic on December 9th. He stood on the platform next to the bald-headed
Clemenceau, whose bushy white moustache fell down over his mouth.
Monsieur Prevel, the new mayor, gave a speech. In front of the platform
the crowd was merry and lively—clubs, delegations, groups of young
girls in the folk costumes of Lorraine including their coquettish bonnets,
all welcomed the liberators of this ancient French province.

Standing next to each other were the massive, jovial Marshal Joffre,
the victor at the Marne, and the generalissimo of the Allies, the small,
iron-willed Foch—right behind him his assistant, General Weygand, the
English Marshal Douglas Haig, the American Pershing, the Belgian Gil-
lian, the Italian Albricci, the Pole Haller.

Poincaré and Clemenceau wore heavy black winter coats and held
their hats in their hands. And when Poincaré had ended his brief address
and stepped back, overcome with emotion, there stood his old adversary
Clemenceau, *le père victoire*. Poincaré laid a hand on his shoulder. Cle-

370

menceau raised his head in surprise. Then the tiger understood. They embraced.

There followed the military parade and the cheering. The girls of Lorraine leaped up onto the tanks, perched on the hoods of the cars, mounted the lancers' horses and took their lances from them. The lancers laughed and led their horses by the reins, the girls waved as they moved past the presidents and field marshals.

The Disbandment of the Army

There was no stopping the German army now.

They left trainloads of cannons and artillery behind as they moved on. Depots full of tractors and automobiles were abandoned. In many companies the soldiers carried two and three rifles on their shoulders, which they sold to civilians in the towns. In the barracks the divisions melted away. Just as things had gone with the 1st Guard Regiment in Berlin, so it went almost everywhere. First the soldiers from the front attack some member of the soldiers' council of the reserve troops they find in the barracks, chase him off, lynch him, and immediately remove all red flags and ribbons. The next day new members of the soldiers' council appear, force the regimental commandant to resign, and the rank and file, which only yesterday had been enraged, behaves peaceably enough today, and tomorrow they'll wear the red cockades and rip the epaulets from their officers' shoulders, demand their revolvers. And where they meet opposition, blood will flow.

Then the soldiers demand immediate discharge. The orders for demobilization read: railroad workers, miners, civil servants in the welfare and food ministries are to be discharged first. Others must wait. But the orders cannot be carried out. Men from the Palatinate and Bavaria want to leave. Troops in Thuringia and Silesia use force to set up a discharge system based on age. The retreat of this army of millions was accomplished in an orderly fashion; the demobilization degenerates into chaos.

This fact is known to the men at General Headquarters. They have all the more reason to be in a hurry. They want to use the remaining solid core of troops for their mopping-up operation in the capital.

When on Sunday evening their confederate, the people's deputy Ebert, compelled by the mood of the populace, declares himself against their plan, they consider transferring headquarters to Berlin in order to take this shaky man under their wings. But afterward they stay with the idea of sending a negotiator, von Schleicher, with instructions to reprimand the cabinet and to present it with the full seriousness of the present situation.

Schleicher Before the Cabinet

The people's deputies, however, had to draw all the consequences of Bloody Friday. The red Executive Council, the hated enemy of Ebert and of Kassel, gave notice to Wilhelmstrasse. The government must sit down at the negotiating table on Monday, December 9th.

The members of the cabinet who are on friendly terms with the officers go into this meeting with pressed lips and leave it not uttering a word. They have signed a verdict against themselves.

The minutes of the meeting report that the Council of People's Deputies is to abide unconditionally by the constitutional guidelines provided by the revolution, with no fundamental changes being made without the consent of the Executive Council. Once again the scope of duties is determined: the Executive Council exercises a control function, the people's deputies an executive one.

The official communiqué of the meeting concludes with the formulation: "Cooperation based on mutual trust shall be exercised to the benefit of all parties concerned."

The Executive Council having said its farewells, the government finds itself alone, and the elegant ambassador from Kassel, the General Staff member von Schleicher, makes his appearance.

He gives the cabinet a detailed report of the situation. He calls their attention to the confusion resulting from the disordered demobilization, the chaotic disbandment of military units that has been accelerated by Spartacist agitators. The mess created by naive soldiers' councils has only magnified the problems of food supplies throughout the nation. What one needed now in particular was strength and unity in order to stand up against the Poles and so as to appear in closed ranks at the armistice negotiations.

The conclusions of the high command, as von Schleicher presents them, are as follows: the introduction of immediate steps to calm the nation, by which is meant disarming the civilian population; this is to be done by the army, although the entire action is not to bear the hallmarks of a one-sided political measure.

The debate that followed, which lasted for hours, concerned itself exclusively with the question of who was to disarm whom, since it was unanimously agreed that disarmament should take place. Major von Schleicher, who at first felt quite pleased to have the initial difficulties behind him, felt quite differently when the Independents interpreted their concurrence as follows: disarmament must take place, but a disarmament of the military to be carried out by civilians. The Independents showed no restraint in expressing their opinion that a good portion of the difficulties to which Schleicher had pointed could be laid at the door of the military, specifically its officers, who were carrying out a systematic sabotage of all governmental decrees and continuing as before to arrogate powers of authority to themselves.

It was part of the tactical finesse of an accomplished politician like Ebert that he was able to lead the ship of discussion across the reefs of debate all in one piece (even in the matter of Bloody Friday). They were all eventually willing to admit that a soothing of tempers and a restoration of order could not occur without a disarmament of the civilian population. The question remained as before, however, who was to carry that out.

Confronted with the warm, approving faces of the Majority Socialists and the icy ones of the Independents, von Schleicher sang Field Marshal von Hindenburg's praises. Moreover, the troops that were marching into the city had received orders, today in fact, to swear a solemn oath of loyalty to the government before entering. That did not soften the hearts of the Independents either.

Finally Ebert proposed a compromise. Since on no account was General Lequis to be trusted with said disarmament, the disarmament of the civilian population would be accepted on principle and the bearing of arms forbidden by decree, made punishable by law, but it should be left to local authorities to carry out the disarmament itself.

To Schleicher's horror, the debate came to a halt at this point. The gentlemen were agreed. That meant: the disarmament would not be carried out by the army command under Lequis, but by the Social-Democratic City Commandant Wels. Schleicher wrung his hands and pulled out all his stops. The local authorities would not have the power to disarm people. They would not want to disarm them, since, at least in part, they themselves were Spartacists. Finally he lost all patience and was ready to bang his fist on the table. He shouted at the assembled gentlemen: "Then let the revolutionaries kill each other." He can change nothing.

The decision is made: the civilian population is to be disarmed, local authorities are to carry out the action.

And Ebert Calms Himself

Afterward Ebert sits alone at his desk and broods. He has Hindenburg's letter in front of him. Danger threatens.

When young secretary Schmidt enters, he lets him wait a while at the window. Then he goes for a walk with him in the Chancellery gardens.

They walk for some minutes in silence until Ebert clears his throat and begins to talk about Hindenburg's letter. Hindenburg has appealed to his sense of patriotism. He considered more forceful action necessary if one hoped to master impending events.

Ebert: "Hindenburg insists that the authority of the officers' corps be restored. In return for their cooperation, he writes, we should have seen to it that the officers were better dealt with."

"Well?" Ebert grumbles, when Schmidt does not reply. Schmidt then asks if it is a private letter or if Kassel does not hope to exert pressure on him by means of the letter. Ebert, annoyed and disappointed, says that basically Hindenburg's intentions are the same as theirs, that is to make the government independent of the Executive Council.

Schmidt was dumbfounded. "We have just released information to the press concerning your conference with the Executive Council. There was agreement between you, more or less."

Ebert, angrily: "He who has ears let him hear, and he who has none can't be helped."

Schmidt bit his lips. "My friends in the Socialist Youth group will be pleased at this development."

"Then what those fellows really want is for social democracy to be defeated, isn't it?"

"They want a unified working class. We would like one, great, unified Socialist party like we had before the war."

"Then they should go see Haase and Liebknecht. They're the ones who destroyed it."

"We think that the rupture can be healed by cooperation on both sides. We think actions must be taken against reactionaries like those behind the events of December 6th."

Ebert's face trembled with rage. "That's how you want to govern. That's how you're going to prevent civil war. Do you know what it means to let a bull loose in a china shop?"

But Schmidt would not let himself be frightened.

"We consider it simply shameful that the things that every Social Democrat of conviction thinks about December 6th are openly and energetically stated exclusively by a man like Emil Barth. We are told that in the interests of our own party we cannot afford such thoughts. But ultimately we have an advantage over the radicals: we honestly want a democracy."

"A valid remark at last."

"As an answer to Kassel's intentions, I could well imagine a call by the government for the formation of a people's army."

At that Ebert knew he had been left in the lurch. He gave up. After a while he tapped Schmidt on the arm and laughed as if in relief, "It might interest you, Schmidt, that we have only recently spoken about just such a call in a cabinet meeting. You will soon have in your hands something in writing about it."

Schmidt's eyes grew large.

"You mean, I take it, a people's army based on volunteers who sign up for it? Tell me, Schmidt, how many would register?"

Schmidt did not notice the mocking expression on Ebert's face, who was recalling Wels's report about the miserable results of an attempt at recruitment.

"Loads," young Schmidt shouted. "Tens of thousands."

"By God's grace."

Ebert cheerfully dragged the young fellow back into the building. Really, one ought to try a call like that. It would have a good effect on all sides. — Icing on the cake for the young members of the party, and a nice cold shower for the fellows in Kassel.

Ebert hurriedly went to look in on Scheidemann, assuming that he might not be feeling so well after the meeting with the Executive Council. And he was right.

Philipp ran toward the little people's deputy in dismay, both hands stretched out to him. "Fritz, what are we going to do? We're on the downhill slide."

He was remembering the great days of the war when his speeches were read from the nation's pulpits. Ebert took hold of both his limp hands and patted them.

Scheidemann whined, "Kassel will simply go ahead and attack."

"I'll arrange things. Just let me handle it. We aren't all that dim-witted after all."

Scheidemann accompanied his friend to the door. "We should have shut those rowdies up right then and there last November."

Ebert nodded and left. That was what the man said who had proclaimed a republic on November 9th. Ebert had already heard enough nonsense for one day.

The Wylinski Academy

*Concerning a man who wanted to become a revolutionary and re-
mained a financier. How he linked social action with an international swindle and was outflanked by his students in the process.*

Wylinski's Revelations

Majestically belting his ample blue robe, Wylinski reached for his
coffee cup before beginning to address his guest of the morning, Brose-
Zenk alias Schröder, from whom he had inherited Toni, the dye-job and
his girlfriend, and Motz, his friend.

"When in his day Julius Caesar sailed to Egypt with ships and soldiers and plundered the countryside, it was thought a heroic deed. No
court would have even considered bringing charges against Julius Caesar
and trying him. It was a first-class piece of work, from which we still
profit today, seeing that Shakespeare wrote a play about it which con-
tains a line that even the uneducated can quote: 'For Brutus is an honorable man.' Now, however, instead of two hundred ships, imagine Caesar
had only three, manned by badly armed soldiers, and that they disembark
in Egypt and start plundering, and what you have is a simple case of
gangsterism, and the deed will be rewarded with the gallows. What is
the difference between the two? Why does history reward the one while
the others end up on the gallows? Because man has an aversion to inade-
quacy. It is a matter of numbers. Small enterprises have to keep within
the bounds of civil order. For great enterprises there are no written rules.
One must therefore always choose to side with great enterprises because,
though dangerous, they guarantee freedom from punishment.

"Just consider it, Brose-Zenk. My suspicion is that you will be undone by some little bungled affair. I can see it already, how your wife or
girlfriend will come to me begging me to say a kind word in the right
places for you because you're in the clink. It will then all depend on how
pretty your girlfriend is and on whether I'm in a good mood. You've got
to get out from under that way of doing things."

376

Brose-Zenk smiled at the flattery. Wylinski tossed such bits of advice his way because he knew that the man would never amount to anything. When Brose was already at the door, Wylinski called to him, "You'll have to look for a way to be a benefactor of mankind. Put your shoulder to the wheel!"

Afterward Wylinski moved on to ham and eggs and did his exercises. When the stomping and snorting had ceased, there was a knock, and Finsterl entered, accompanied by another one of Wylinski's scions named Willi Finger. There is an anecdote about the old Austrian socialist "Doctor" Adler, who is supposed to have said that his two sons were caricatures of himself—the one, the murderer of Prime Minister Stürgk, was a caricature of his virtues, the other of his vices. And these two, Finsterl and Finger, who stood now before Wylinski, were the traits of their master incarnate. Finsterl, a merciless daredevil strategist, but also a neuter, a flunky, an unassuming creature; and Willi Finger, no less an unscrupulous speculator, but otherwise a vulgar Neanderthal, a drinker, skirt-chaser and habitué of race tracks.

Wylinski could not stand Finsterl because of his frugality, and called him Robespierre. He feared and despised him. He preferred to be with Willi Finger, but there again he was put off by the fellow's commonness and provincialism, his average-Joe kindheartedness, his eating and drinking and the indiscriminate way in which he consumed women.

Wylinski did not in general like to compare himself to any of his hangers-on. One can understand that considering his past.

The Development of a Revolutionary

He had risen through the ranks as a revolutionary socialist, having grown up in czarist Russia. Within his cadre he was responsible for flyers and pamphlets, for finding sets of type and for buying and hiding the paper. To disguise these activities he had to have some visible profession—and that was as a man of business. He took over a publishing house that produced market reports and calendars for farmers, everything calculated for a mass market. He did not admit it to his compatriots, but this business that was ostensibly only for appearance's sake began to please him more and more; the publishing house prospered, Wylinski hired traveling salesmen and it was easy as pie to finance the political propaganda and see to its printing out of his receipts. Publicly he paid homage to reactionary causes, secretly he undermined them. His heart, as he said later, had two chambers: one beat for business, the other for the Party.

Then came the war, and Wylinski prospered on a grand scale. His plans grew with the expansion of the arenas of war. He got involved in far-flung transactions. He shifted to supplying raw materials to areas suffering from a lack of them, be it grain, iron or coal, all the while, as a true man of business, maintaining complete neutrality. He would appear now in Turkey, now in Holland, now in Scandinavia. In the old days it was Cagliostro the magician who traveled through Europe visiting the courts of princes and alleging he could turn anything into gold. Now that role was played by a speculator. He caused money and goods to skip across the continent. There was now the telephone and speed could be achieved without witchcraft.

Then suddenly the ground opened up beneath him and swallowed him whole. The year was 1917, the Russian Revolution. Revolution had come, the one for which he had battled as a youth. He left Europe and the telephone behind. He quoted Faust: "The tears well up, and earth receives me back again."

For a long time no one heard anything about Wylinski. A veil lies over his sojourn in Russia. One would assume that there, on his old home ground, he would be brilliantly successful, for now his former friends and protégés were at work everywhere, some of them already in positions of power. Later on he made only occasional references to this period. He played no role whatever in revolutionary Russia, could play none. The days of socialist discussion were over. It is possible for a man of deeds and cash like Wylinski to be scared off by the reality of the very civil war he had so often discussed, indulging himself in elegaic songs of praise from the past?

He attempted to cultivate anew his former image, the easy chitchat, the analysis, but—there was no need for them. He was told that he had to adapt to this new and wonderful state of affairs. He would have to work like everyone else, integrate himself. What was there in that for Wylinski? Take some civil service job? He did not speak about it, but everyone noticed that he could not reconcile himself to the reality of the revolution. At times he would remark, to some extent as a kind of apology, that he was not throwing himself completely into things because this was not what he had meant, but rather "socialism." His revolutionary friends, however, he said gloomily, had suddenly all been transformed into soldiers. He, the most dependable of them all, the man who had grown up as an active combatant for socialism, was a flop when real revolution came and he withdrew into the magic castle of his youthful dreams.

They could not use him in Russia. He was superfluous. He soon came under suspicion, because in order to escape a life of inactivity he had conducted some transactions in the old style, which were now scornfully labeled bourgeois speculations.

And so there he sat, rich in experience, silent and disheartened. Toward the beginning of 1918 he felt the pull to Old Europe. For anyone with eyes and ears could see at this point that there were cracks and creakings in the building inhabited by the Central Powers, by the authoritarian rulers of Europe. Being at that point unemployed, Wylinski wrote several political articles and supplied ideas for essays to a man of letters or two. He showed himself to be a moderate socialist, a man of the opposition, of the same sort as the German Social Democrats, because this old gray bear could only sport in the forest if he were given his freedom. He grew lively again, began to travel, and met (it was wartime after all) the socialist party leaders. He began mixing politics and finance as before.

We are witnesses to the birth of a new Wylinski. This romantic, fresh and indubitably idealistic fellow has become a skeptic with a tendency to cynicism. His old passion to make money, to run riot amid numbers, reemerges. He wants to plug the holes that the Russian revolution has ripped open in him. And without even being clear about it himself he becomes an anti-Bolshevist. He does not announce the fact, and in truth he really is not one anyway. He knows well enough, to his own pain, that his dislike of Bolshevism has its roots in his own failures.

Now we see the great Wylinski at work, busy as never before. For months on end he has no permanent address. When he takes up residence in a capital city he lives in the best hotel, and casts his nets across Europe via telephone, from Constantinople to Oslo, from Paris to Berlin, Zurich and Amsterdam. If at one time men of letters, politicians and revolutionaries gathered around him, now—it was quite another crowd. It would be difficult to call them businessmen. They are a product of war, characters out of the Wild West, men of whom he is the master. They are engaged in enterprise for enterprise's sake, they are "absolute entrepreneurs."

The war had created economic plateaus and valleys that did not balance each other out. It was just the landscape for the coordinating spirits gathered round Wylinski. They organized an economic migration of the barbarians. At one point news came to Wylinski that riots had broken out in Turkey because of famine. It was not for nothing that the rumor came his way. He had good connections with revolutionaries on the Black Sea. He let his telephone begin to play, sent emissaries and organized deliveries of grain. People in Constantinople had something to eat, and immense sums flowed into Wylinski's pockets.

He knew that he was called a profiteer. He answered that he had saved the lives of thousands.

In Berlin he was lured back to the one thing that he could not leave alone and for which he was always prepared to throw away his money: politics. He sacrificed large sums for newspapers, Social Democratic ones. Wylinski became a publisher. He had to invest over a million marks in just one year. For a long time Party leaders felt a deep mistrust for this comrade-in-arms. They warned others about him and called him a political fraud.

Wylinski managed his literary enterprises just as he did the others, like a pasha or sultan, unpredictably. First he would see that they were provided with opulent sums and demand that several people be paid princely salaries. Then he would lose all interest in the matter and insist on economies and come out with a statement of principle most peculiar for a man like him—that a business had to pay its own way. In the last days of the war he put out feelers toward Denmark, creating a political "Research Institute." It was supposed to investigate the causes of the war. This resulted in an opportunity to become acquainted with several Scandinavian Party leaders and to enter into conversations with them about the shortage of coal in Denmark. They noted how this bearded man shook his head in astonishment—the first move in all of his enterprises—and after a few weeks everything was resolved by a wave of the great magician's hand. German coal was delivered in Denmark, and immense sums flowed into Wylinski's pockets.

It is not our intent to speak of all the wonderful activities of the Wylinski Academy. In producing men of this sort, nature seemed to want to compensate for the madness in which war had indulged itself.

Pupils Who Outgrow Their Teacher

Wylinski had gone to his bedroom to dress after his exercises when Finger and Finsterl entered and sat down at the coffee table; he roared a merry greeting to them. They found a bottle of vodka, which they held on to, Finsterl cautiously, Finger resolutely. They reported to Wylinski through the open door the most important news of the day (he read little, was much too much a social creature to give himself over voluntarily to the loneliness of reading).

Armed with a comb and brush, he appeared and curried his bristly hair and beard. Then they all sat down together, smoking and testing out each other's positions. For though they were in this together, each went his own way, and under no circumstances did they compete with each other. To surpass the others, however, was of course the greatest ambition of each of them.

Finger, whom we shall simply call Willi, told about an acquaintance he had struck up in the casino, and that he was toying with a plan that presumably would soon be of concern to the general public. The way Liebknecht's gang was carrying on got worse from day to day. One might, it's true, concede political motives to Liebknecht and Bloody Rosa, but the majority of their followers who called themselves Spartacists were without doubt simply in it for the booty.

Wylinski: "The Spartacists have the right idea there. Every occupation needs an ideology. Willi, do you think this plan of the Spartacists can really be carried out? That's the only question. Are there enough goods in capitalist hands to plunder? If yes, do the Spartacists have sufficient means to get at those goods? We ought to obtain that information."

"Why?" asked Willi in astonishment.

Wylinski: "You, Willi, want either to hold on to what you have or increase it. If you were now to determine that Spartacus is strong and its chances are good, that means there are certain consequences for you. The question becomes for you one of putting yourself at Spartacus's disposal at the right moment."

Willi, dubious: "I'm not convinced that Spartacus can have its way. Tomorrow the troops will start their march into the city. That will mean order will be reestablished in the nation very quickly and that reconstruction will begin on a grand scale."

Having said that, Willi was silent and sullen. For the thought of putting himself at the disposal of Spartacus had taken fire in him, disconcerted him.

"Go on, please," Wylinski encouraged him.

"I would like to know," Willi was still chewing on the notion, "how someone who works with money and securities could possibly manage to cooperate the Spartacus. With people who want to rob him?"

"Don't get theological, Willi. We're specialists, this isn't some public meeting. You want to increase your wealth. Spartacus offers one opportunity. You have to investigate that opportunity."

What Wylinski was doing to kindhearted Willi bordered on torture. He left the silent Finsterl alone. Willi sat there undecided, chewing on his cigar and staring over at his master. Wylinski let up on him and said, "If I understand you correctly, you want to get involved in something that has to do with the Spartacists."

"That's right," Willi said with a sigh of relief. "That's what it was about last night at the casino. People don't know how to protect themselves. Of course I'm not talking about military protection, but about an augmented police force."

"Like the Residents' Militia."

"Something similar. But they're already politicized. That's not what I have in mind as a private citizen. It would mean the end of the whole plan if I were suspected of being involved in politics. I want to protect private property, houses, factories, buildings of every sort, with a private auxiliary force modeled on private security guards. My people would make their rounds, on foot or bicycles, and of course they would be armed."

"Fine. What do your friends in the Party say about it?"

"I haven't asked any of them."

Finsterl, the shadow, piped up, "I could get you the weapons, bicycles too."

"Bicycles, from where?"

"I have several sources."

"Civilian or military?"

Finsterl shook his head. "We'll see."

Wylinski smoked and leaned back. "You probably already know, Willi, how you'll manage the thing, how you'll get the minimum number of home owners together, etc. As far as the guards go, you have unlimited resources. You won't be able to hold back all the discharged soldiers. But first you'll have to invest a lot of money to equip them and to arouse people's interest. You'll have to issue an advertising flyer periodically that makes clear to people what danger they're in in Berlin. And then there might come a day when you'll be sitting out on the street with the whole caboodle, because the troops will have reestablished order. That could happen before you've even begun."

Willi smoked calmly. "I'm not going to be ready with my preparations until tomorrow, so nothing can happen to me there. I'm figuring the disorders will continue for a while."

"I see."

"Yes. Things won't quiet down before there's a constituent assembly. And not even after it, either."

"I could help you out," Wylinski suggested without much interest, "with a little brochure and some propaganda articles. I've got several things just lying around here."

"So you think the idea's worth something?"

"Go to it if you feel like it. You've got people higher up who'll take care of you, don't you?"

Willi scratched his head. "Those fellows turn everything into something political right away. They're not interested in the fact that it's our money and our nerve that's invested."

Finger stood up, unsure of himself. He wanted to think the whole project through once more.

When he was gone, Wylinski laughed out loud. "The man has the best connections in the world, right on up to the highest places in the government, and he's afraid. The idea itself is not bad. The worst thing that could happen after all is if things quieted down or looked like they were going to. But then he would have his watchmen with their rifles, and they would have as little interest in losing their jobs as he has in losing his money. So he could let them shoot things up a bit and you'd have the loveliest disorder right there."

Finsterl, naively: "Why shoot? Shoot at what?"

"Makes no difference. Into the air for all I care, at airplanes—

whether there are any up there or not. You shoot, and your customer knows something is up. My dear friend, if you had ever lived in Turkey you would understand these methods. Wherever you are in this world you always have to be ready to prove you're indispensable."

And Wylinski wandered around the room with amusement, his pipe in his mouth, wearing his brown velvet jacket. It was an elegant room in a pension. He occupied half a floor. On principle he abjured apartments of his own with his own furniture.

The shadow remarked from the chair where he sat: "Willi has done a magnificent job furnishing his apartment in Regentenstrasse. Everyone who is anyone in Berlin—ministers, state secretaries—visit him there."

Wylinski stopped in front of him. "Who for instance?"

The shadow: "Name me a name. You'll be right."

Wylinski: "Ebert."

The shadow: "You're right."

Wylinski pulled the pipe from his mouth and bent down to Finsterl. "I said Ebert."

"That's right."

"You're crazy."

"Who else do you want to know about?"

"Ebert at Willi Finger's? Ebert on Regentenstrasse? But why? What can Willi offer him?"

The shadow smiled gently. "People don't come to see him. They come to sit in his apartment. I have an apartment too, two of them. Other people come to visit me."

"What sort of people?"

"I place my apartment at people's disposal if they want to meet and don't think a restaurant is what they want."

"And what do you serve these people?"

"I treat them to whatever seems appropriate."

"And they provide some tangible show of gratitude for this, do they?"

"For heaven's sake, tangible—it's not a business. The whole thing has purely social dimensions. Willi is wealthy and provides his pleasant quarters for politicians who live some distance out and have business to attend to in town. Naturally they're grateful to him for being able to talk undisturbed. It is important to show hospitality."

Wylinski looked out the window.

"And these ministers, state secretaries and so on—they are not embarrassed at being associated with our Willi? Or be honest, he bribes them, doesn't he?"

The shadow with the dull smile: "Certainly not. Why shouldn't a man frequent the apartment of a rich banker. The Kaiser associated with Krupp after all."

Wylinski rubbed his eyes. His expression was somber as he asked, "And you mean to tell me that Willi's visitors are so blind or so stupid that they don't even notice what is expected from them in return?"

The man who hoped to offend Finsterl would have had to possess supernatural powers.

"There are no demands made of them. Good works are always repaid. And high-placed personages always shed some of their brilliance on their immediate surroundings."

Wylinski spread out his powerful arms and let out a resounding laugh. "That much I know. That much I know."

He pulled his guest into his private office. It was 11:00 A.M. Wylinski was working on an old plan, reviving a project of his youth. He intended to produce popular literature for Russia, print cheap calendars, and flood the country with them to show the Bolsheviks that he was still alive.

All at once he slammed his fist down on the desk, terrifying Finsterl.

"At any rate let me congratulate you on your superb republic."

Their conversation dragged on. Wylinski had suddenly lost all pleasure in his calendars, and the whole battle with the Bolsheviks was no longer any fun.

Just Wait, Soon You Too . . .

The common man retains his faith. The "Council of Intellectuals" searches for definitions and ends with a burst of enthusiasm.

The Proletariat Prepares Itself

Reconciled with the world in a way he had not been for a long time, old man Imker folded up his newspaper as he lay in bed. He called his wife from the kitchen. She came with his coffee. It was broad daylight, late morning, and still he lay in bed, not having returned from a stormy district Party meeting until three o'clock the night before.

"It's all okay," he said to his wife, who wore a coat over her night-gown and put the coffee tray down on the chair beside the bed. "I'll get up now. Today's the day. Am I ever happy! Where's Minna?"

"Why ask about Minna? She's working."

Imker drank his coffee. "Yesterday they said that Ebert would sit down with the Executive Council and they would come to some decisions. We didn't believe it. But here it is in the paper."

"And why does that mean you have to run off first thing this morning even though you didn't get home till three, and you're not so young no more either, and it costs money every time you go."

He sat up, an old working man, with a radiant expression; even in bed he wore a heavy wool jacket and scarf.

"We're working together. Ebert is cooperating with Däumig and Ledebour. When the generals arrive tomorrow are they going to be surprised. Not a sign of unrest or a quarrel among brothers. A unified working class. Isn't that wonderful, Emily?"

He had said it very loud. The door opened. A blue head-scarf pulled low on the brow, knotted under the chin, a stony face—there stood Minna. Her father waved her over to his bed. "Did you hear, Minna?"

The mother: "Lord, Minna, your father always gets so excited when he reads something in the paper."

Imker: "They're moving against the generals. Ebert and the Executive Council are working together."

Minna, the doorknob still in her hand, asked, "And you believe that?"

The old man turned for reassurance to his wife. "I got home at three this morning. It's all agreed, we'll move together against the generals. Not a dog what's going to lay down its rifle. Weapons are being distributed in every district."

Minna closed the door, moved toward the table, and said in her coolest voice, "You've heard that often enough before at your meetings. The speeches are always fiery. You should have come home earlier so Mother could have gone to bed."

Imker: "Here, read the paper, Minna."

She refused it with a wave of her hand. "Father, do you really believe your Ebert is going to sit down and carry out policies that are for the workers? And against the generals? He's simply happy they're here at last."

The old man raised his arms in despair and gazed at his wife, looking for help.

The mother: "Minna, I'll bring you another cup and you two can stop your political discussions. I was so happy that Ed was back from France all in one piece and now he's running around out on the streets and don't even show his face."

Minna, calmly: "We're proletarians and can't hide back in the corner."

Imker: "What's Ed up to?"

Minna: "You'll have to ask him that yourself, Father. I don't think he'll tell you though."

The mother started to cry. "Always fighting."

Imker: "We're not fighting. I'm simply telling Minna something she doesn't want to hear, but it's true anyway. The working class is united and is going to move against the generals. And we're as strong as a stone wall."

Minna stroked her mother's back and gave her father her hand. He smiled at her. "So then, you do believe me and you're happy that things are moving forward now, toward socialism."

Minna winked at him with her small eyes. "See you later. I have to work."

She was disturbed a second time toward noon. Ed came in. She shook his hand. Ed quickly asked, "Father gone?"

Minna: "At his bar. He says there's been unity negotiations."

"I heard that too."

Minna, astonished: "Is it true?"

"They can't avoid them. When's your meeting?"

"After two."

"You'll hear about it then. We're marching with every working man."

"Then it's true. I never would have believed it."

"What they say in Father's paper has nothing to do with us, Minna. When the so-called Executive Council sits down with the bigwigs there's nothing in it for us. The masses will march right on over Ebert and Scheidemann and Däumig and Barth."

Minna with a beaming smile: "We're going with Karl and Rosa, right?"

"With Karl and Rosa. But what are we shooting the breeze here for? Our boys are heading for the barracks, the women are to come along. When will you be ready?"

"I said already, around two."

"Okay, sis."

Morning at the Café on Wittenbergplatz

"Take a look at the girl's face," the writer from Munich whispered to his admirer with the curly black hair, the tall lyric poet, as the two sat in the café on Wittenbergplatz where the lights were already lit on this gloomy afternoon. They were sitting on a sofa against the wall, mirrors behind and in front of them. A couple had taken a seat close by.

"Don't look at her directly. You can see her better in the mirror, next to the gray-haired man who is just folding his hands and laying them on the marble tabletop, now he's looking in the mirror and brushing his hair with his hand. There, he's noticed us. He's turning around. Perhaps he knows us."

The lyric poet: "Probably from photographs."

"Look away. Let's converse about the moon and the stars. — Fine. He's still very young, the gray hair is quite remarkable."

"She's not unattractive."

"Those two young people have such gentle expressions. They look so well-kempt and tidy. The young man's tie—that kind of gray hair comes from certain nervous disorders, perhaps he was under heavy bombardment for a long time—his tie is light gray with blue dots. He is wearing a very decent winter overcoat."

"English cut. Could be a piece of booty."

"Not impossible. One sees all sorts of curiosities these days. People are becoming international. The war has given them some polish. We're nationalists really only at home. They gaze at each other when they talk. We can't understand what they're saying. Don't look over at the two of them, the mirror is more interesting. I imagine us standing in the corridor peeping through the keyhole."

"No!"

"Why not. It's always exciting to overhear people without their knowing."

"Why not imagine you're sitting at a movie?"

"As you please. That's less exciting. Why is he looking at her so seriously? She's making a gesture with her left hand in its black kid glove. She is drinking from a glass, he is having a brandy. He toasts her. They're speaking matter-of-factly, about acquaintances, about what she bought yesterday and is still going to buy today. They're not talking about love and not about each other. The way the woman sits there so erect in her red wooden chair. By the way, tasteless, garish chairs, that's also the result of the war; the screams can't be loud enough, keep on letting out what's left of the tensions of war. We'll find that we have a dreadful hangover afterward."

The lyric poet laughed. "That's the case already."

"The way she sits there in her chair would indicate that the lady is a very decisive person. But she's been walking through town and all sorts of interesting things have floated through that female body of hers, into that female head, and she's taken it all along with her and all that confluence of detail that we notice about her has merged nicely inside her. Look how she talks and serves him some little observation or other. She's practicing an art, a handicraft, when she talks. The gentleman is taking an etui out of his pocket. She opens it. Ah, earrings. She takes them out and holds them in both hands, as in a bowl. There you have Goethe's pious Indian woman rolling the water in her hands into a ball. He's leaned back now and has stretched his hand out to her across the table. The hands of the two embrace and kiss, melt into one another, now creep apart. Now they are two naked hands again, separate from each other. He sticks the etui in her purse.

"She drinks down her glass of light beer, slowly, it feels good in her throat, we can follow it all because we too are human beings, because ultimately we are this man and this woman. That is why every quiet observation is an act of self-observation and self-realization. She happily watches his left arm lying there like a pet animal that has just sniffed at her with its muzzle. The arm is pleasant and almost eerily strange. The sleeve of his overcoat has slipped up, he did not take off his coat because they are in such a hurry—no, because the etui was in his pocket. She examines the soft cuffs of his shirt and the cufflinks. They're concerned again with material things, clothes, jewelry, shop windows.

"They're leaving. The man is actually a soldier, an officer, he is wearing yellow leather gaiters. She has a solid body, very narrow hips, a short, modern suit jacket, powerful calves in bright yellow silk stockings. They're leaving. They have left the mirror. We see ourselves. Our double, triple image has left us. We are by ourselves. Our own face tells us nothing. We know it exactly, like an old familiar apartment."

"And what have you learned? Are there any results to be gained, any conclusions?"

"Conclusions?"

The gentleman from Munich looked skeptically about the room. "I speak my mind. I am a poet. I illuminate the figures of this world and produce images."

The tall lyric poet, eager for battle as always, probably would not have been content with that explanation, but the master was already busy letting his thoughts play again.

The master: "Now the spot where they were is empty, the little marble table. The waiter clears away the glasses and doilies and wipes the table clean. He puts a stand with different cakes on the table. There is nothing more to be seen of the two of them in the room. They remain, hovering about, but only in the air, and in the past, in what has flowed by us, in the incalculable chain of events that includes us, just as they sat across from us a quarter of an hour ago in this café. They have left that behind them, and the big fat fellow setting the chairs to rights, who brought over the stand of cakes, cannot wipe them away if he tries."

Then loud shouts burst in upon them. They turned their heads and saw Morgen beside them, the novelist, the chairman of the "Council of Intellectuals." He was the heavyset, unpleasant man who had settled down on a sofa near them a half hour before and after quickly downing a brandy had just as quickly fallen asleep. He had been snoring loudly. Now he approached the two men, sleepily, but in a cheerful good mood.

"Gentlemen, I must be dreaming. Do you know that I've tried to call you a dozen times this morning and have been sitting here the whole time wondering how I was going to get you here."

"My dear friend," the lyric poet grinned, "telephoning me is out of the question, you cannot have tried to call me."

Morgen, impassive: "Well then not you. Who was it now? At any rate someone I couldn't reach, and here you sit in the café. You'll not object to my joining you."

The man from Munich pulled out his watch and flipped the lid open. "Three minutes of twelve. It may be me that you didn't get hold of me this morning. I had an appointment."

What Shall Be Done to Counter Hindenburg?

Morgen ordered a pilsner, drank it, and it turned out that he had invited several gentlemen from the "Council of Intellectuals" for a meeting at 11:30 in the atelier of a painter on Hardenbergstrasse. He seemed not to be worried about this, told them all sorts of private nonsense, drank another pilsner and dragged them along with him to Hardenbergstrasse where they were expected.

Two young ladies were sitting there, they were introduced as authoresses, but they looked more like the artist's models. Afterward they only opened their mouths to eat cake. It was, they learned, a cake the painter's wife had baked herself for this festive reception. They all, ladies and gentlemen alike, drank an enchanting schnapps provided by a restaurateur whom the artist had paid with a "handpainted picture."

Naturally it was Morgen, quite sober now, who opened the meeting.

He had called them together for this discussion here and not at the Reichstag for two, actually three, reasons. First because of the noise and disruption caused by the soldiers there, who seemed to take pleasure in making disturbances. The Reichstag at that point, if it was anything at all, was a disorderly barracks.

The impatient lyric poet: "Secondly."

"One moment. Secondly there are some discussions one would like to keep secret. We are meeting here today, so to speak, as an ad hoc committee. And thirdly, following our last public meeting, which did not go well as we all know, a number of our members, among them some of the most active ones, were thrown into a fit of depression. We have several new resignations to note on our rolls."

The man from Munich, in amazement: "How can anyone resign from the Council of Intellectuals? Are we a club?"

Morgen agreed. "You can't get through to them. Sometimes one must ask oneself whether one is really dealing with intellectuals, that is with people of special talent, or simply with eccentrics. It is hopeless. At any rate I wanted to avoid having our discussion today used for yet another cataloging of various so-called standpoints, or better put, of varying stupidities. And therefore I took the liberty of inviting you and three others, who presumably did not receive my card."

The lyric poet: "And thirdly?"

"Why thirdly?"

"You said you had three reasons why you had not called this meeting for the Reichstag."

Morgen, annoyed: "You have a doctrinaire personality. This is truly not the time or place for such things. It may well be that a number of us, yourself included, will not be alive tomorrow. Indeed, that is how I regard things. Hannibal *ad portas*. Hindenburg is marching in. And may I offer felicitations to whoever thinks that a joke."

And he implored them, sitting there so fresh and alert, to lay all differences aside and to behave like soldiers prior to an attack. He could only repeat one fatal word: unity—it must be present in such terrible situations. And at that he fell silent.

The artist's wife, who had never before attended such a discussion, was dismayed. She sympathetically pushed the cake plate over toward Morgen. She was soon to rue the deed. After he had thrown the aromatic pastry a hostile glance, he shoved one piece into his mouth, and then another, and was already reaching for a third. His face grew more conciliatory as he did so, and between chews he expressed his approval to his hostess.

In the meantime the man from Munich, the senior member and uncrowned king of the group, had struck a pose and taken the scepter of discussion in hand. He spoke in such a businesslike fashion that the lyric poet, who had just listened to him in the café, was amazed at the hidden resources of this admirable man.

"You are afraid of the soldiers. You overestimate them. I have spoken with hundreds. They all want to go home. Hindenburg has no one behind him. If, nevertheless, he chooses to attempt something tomorrow with a battalion of officers, arrest the people's deputies or the Executive Council, say—it is reported that General Lequis has the orders for such an action in his pocket—then the moment for a popular uprising would be here. You must think historically. The German Revolution requires more time than a mere four weeks."

Morgen, undoubtedly the gravest of the lot today, wiped cake crumbs from his mouth and said, "And what happens now?"

The man from Munich, self-assured: "The existing parties must be brought to the realization that things cannot go on as they have. I say, I plead before the whole world: political parties cannot accomplish anything. Only the intellect can govern, strongly and dictatorially. The intellect will begin to totally crushing these parties, because they are remnants of war. What are we intellectuals here for? To debate in the Lesser Hall of the Reichstag? For what purpose have we moved in the company of Plato, Thomas Aquinas, Kant and the French freedom fighters? Not, I presume, to write books. None of us is interested in the publishing business. To what end are we a "Council of Intellectuals" if we do not place ourselves on the side of power and there exercise our function of giving counsel." He looked at each of them intently, one after the other; they were slightly embarrassed. He sat very erect, the shots his doctor was giving him were working wonders. "We have everything: knowledge, historical experience and a goal—a better humanity. We demand that we be constituted as a political organ to work alongside the people's deputies."

The ingenuous artist was the first to express his delight, and in a South German accent he said, "We should have demanded that first thing."

The man from Munich concurred. "We have let precious time go by. But I hope it is not too late."

He pulled energetically at the creases in his trousers. Only now did the lyric poet erupt in a cry of exultation. "Finally, finally we can see the road ahead. We can breathe again. We'll make our demands. We've found a way out of this dead-end street. Hurrah!"

The young man saw such overwhelming prospects before him that he pursued them about the atelier with great long strides. "A nation that has produced a Goethe, a Herwegh, a Freiligrath—such a nation must be shown what it means to have a living literature, living poets."

The portly Morgen was unusually gloomy, downright morose. "We must ask ourselves whether we shall resist the troops that are to march into the city tomorrow, and by what means, or what other course of action we might like to take."

The cool man from Munich: "No offense, my dear Morgen, but how do you wish to resist these troops that are marching upon us?"

The lyric poet: "Precisely because that will not work and because we have absolutely nothing to fear from these advancing troops, let us agree to present our demand: the Council of Intellectuals must join the government."

Morgen drummed on the table. "Let me think about that."

He looked about him for help. At the back of the room were two younger men, one of whom, a fair-haired fellow, had a permanent look of tense seriousness on his face, while his neighbor, who occasionally whispered something to him, seemed more inclined to good spirits. The tense man turned now to the lyric poet and after clearing his throat said, "Might I ask you to formulate your suggestion once more."

The lyric poet, speaking boldly out into the room: "We offer our services in collaboration with the government."

"They will say thanks, but no thanks."

"Then, recalling that we are in the midst of a revolution, we will form a government by other means."

The man from Munich applauded. The tense man answered vehemently, "We have already made ourselves ridiculous enough in front of people, those at least who pay any attention to us at all. How do you imagine that can be done? Us? With whom?"

The lyric poet: "We have made no headway with our declarations up till now. You won't deny that."

The tense man became more vehement still. "Who is going to give you the legitimation now to found a government, or to set yourself up as a supervisory council alongside the government? Who is going to take you on?" He roared, "Hell and damnation, what are the policies you're going to build or supervise a government with? Who will support you? Where am I? Has everyone gone crazy?"

The portly chairman raised his hands, wrinkled his brow. "I beg you for God's sake not to get so excited. No raw nerves."

The tense man threw himself back into his chair and lit a cigarette. "I have nerves like anyone else. Others are simply losing their minds."

The tall lyric poet, his ams crossed, stood directly opposite him a few paces away. "What do you mean by that?"

The fat man tore at his hair in despair. "So here we are back to this again, how delightful. Well go ahead and slug it out."

There was another somewhat elderly gentleman in the atelier, not a great man, but one whose name was respected, a modest man, a reticent one, a dramatist with a heavy brown moustache. He earned his living as an assistant advisory in a theater. The man from Munich turned to him and begged him to speak up. The dramatist answered politely, "I must ask you to excuse me. I really am only here to listen and to learn."

The man from Munich frowned. "But now is the time to take a position. You have gathered enough intellectual assets in the course of your life. You now have the opportunity to put that capital to work."

The dramatist, whose straightened circumstances were plain to see, pondered the fact that a well-to-do man had spoken to him about capital, and answered simply by explaining who he was, that he worked hard for the money he needed to support himself, his wife and daughter. Until now he had never once thought of any other use for his intellectual capital, to continue using that word.

"What have you thought about then?"

Morgen gave the answer for him. "I presume about how to write good plays."

The dramatist said naively, "To be frank and without wishing to offend anyone, that's right."

The man from Munich pushed back from the table and loudly cleared his throat.

Next to the tense man there was another, smaller, darker fellow who wore a sarcastic smile. He now whistled between his teeth while everyone else was silent, and said in a boyish voice, "And Hindenburg is still at the door."

This young man was a journalist. He frequently attended the Council of Intellectuals. Along the walls of that half of the atelier (it was an attic) facing the barn-like door was a row of broad benches covered with bright cushions. These benches were apparently otherwise used for sleeping. The two young scoffers now made themselves comfortable there, while Morgen glanced worriedly at them. What troubled Morgen, the reason he was so upset, he did not explain—and the others did not ask. He was at heart—a monarchist. On November 9th, fearful that he might miss his opportunity, he had turned full about. And now it looked as if he had bet on the wrong horse. Because lo and behold, at this moment of danger it seemed to him that this new republican freedom had a tighter hold on him than he had thought. Without ever noticing it he had become a republican! And for the first time, here in this attic, he saw what his comrades-in-arms were, these defenders of the republic: rhetoricians. He turned his chair around so that the two young men on the bench at the back could see his strongly flushed face, his broad brow beneath a tousle of dark blond hair. His eyes were bloodshot. He asked the sarcastic fellow, "What do you suggest?"

The flippant reporter: "Me? Nothing whatever."

"I don't understand."

"There's nothing to understand. I was invited to come here, and here I sit and conclude that you're not getting anywhere."

"I still don't understand. You were invited as a member of the council. You come to the comfortable conclusion that today's meeting is not getting anywhere. It even appears to be a source of some amusement to you. Why is that?"

"That you are not getting anywhere is a result of the definition of the group. There can be no Council of Intellectual Workers because there are no intellectuals."

Morgen kept quite cool, while all the others were outraged. "I thought we had moved beyond the stage of definitions."

"One never moves beyond it. You cannot make yourself independent of logic. The most reasonable thing I've heard today came from our colleague the dramatist, who simply said that he wanted to write good plays and found it difficult to earn money for himself and his family. He apparently can't get it into his head that in addition he is supposed to be an intellectual."

Morgen, unmoved: "And where does all your logic lead us?"

"He writes good plays and wants to go on writing them. For my part I would like to develop a certain style of reporting that functions as propaganda at the same time, and to do that in conjunction with a newspaper that I unfortunately have not yet discovered. I am not familiar with those writers of the past whom our famous guest from Munich mentioned a while ago. I only have a high-school education. If one of the prerequisites of being an active intellectual is to have read Kant, Thomas Aquinas and I don't know who else, then I'm sorry to say I can be of no help. My neighbor here, who is actually a musician, has the same problem. And without wishing to offend anyone, I would maintain that there are others as well in this room in the same sad state, and who must therefore be dropped from the register of intellectuals."

"Your conclusions, please. You have not finished."

"Gladly. We have neither the opportunity nor the right to step forward as intellectuals. Firstly, because we're not intellectuals, at least not by the standards that apparently prevail. Secondly, let us assume we are all as learned as learned can be, busying ourselves from morning till night with nothing but Kant and Thomas Aquinas. How does that help us deal with Hindenburg? And now comes the central question: what does a first-class education have to do with politics, with political action? Our guest from Munich proposed that the Intellectual Council make a straightforward demand to be incorporated in the government. I have never heard that serious theologians and professors of philosophy, who know everything about everything, ever came up with a demand like that. What is the nature, then, of our special wisdom? Let us not deceive ourselves. For us to offer to work as a permanent organ of government, to move in alongside the people's deputies, is gruesomely funny. I would like to warn you about making that notion public. We have made ourselves ridiculous enough already."

The portly Morgen let the arm with which he had been propping up his head fall heavily to the table, his breathing was audible. "I see. And now you have spoken."

The young man crossed his arms and nodded.

Morgen resumed, "The situation is clear. We write good things when we can, or bad ones if not. We write newspaper articles, novels, submit them to publishers and feed ourselves and our families. Everything as before and under the motto: cobbler, stick to your last. As far as my own person is concerned—and you know, I take it, that I write novels and am older than you—I envy you your wise circumspection. I am no longer young enough for it. I can no longer hold my peace. And I will not accept the return of the monarchy, and the generals' marching in and occupying Berlin is for me the same thing as if a common criminal were to leap for my throat in the middle of the night. I will defend myself."

But the young man, at whom all this was now aimed, sat there by the wall completely cool and collected, shaking his head vigorously. "And that brings us back to where we started. The events of the last weeks have proven that intellectuals have a need to get involved but cannot. I've given you the reason. It is the result of the definition you detest. But it is not the definition that causes problems, but the failure to heed it. The definition remains unchanged: there are no intellectuals. For there is no such special thing as intellect. There are writers, journalists, artists, musicians, sculptors. And these people have ideas and interests the same as anyone else. And these ideas and interests arise, as with all other people, from their social status and class. Ideas do not become peculiarly intellectual because writers and artists have them. And that is why tomorrow I will do what other people like me, that is those of my status and class, will do. I will put my rifle to my shoulder and march with those others who have the same needs as I—namely those of a working man."

Morgen listened to him with a glazed stare, as if the young man were speaking to him alone.

He answered at once, "That isn't enough. We all could have done that straight off. The fact remains that we have other goals beyond those of mere class, and that those goals make us men of intellect, or whatever you want to call it. We look as if we all belong to the same profession, but we don't. That we have sat here for four weeks now and accomplished nothing, that proves nothing. You can't accomplish anything with a bunch of headstrong, ill-willed people. We only ended up in fact with a debating club, and a debating club cannot get involved in real events. But you and I, each of us individually, you and I—we are not the working class, nor the Intellectual Council. I am merely me—if you like, a poor, desperate man. Yes indeed, that I am, and every man in every class can be that, even a stylite out in the desert. And so don't come to me with your workers and slogans of the moment. Tomorrow the workers may by chance be marching in the same direction that I want to go, but what will they do the day after tomorrow? Who do I march with then? Maybe I shall have to run after them. Maybe they will be my hangmen. It is always fatal, my dear colleague, simply to go along with the others.

"I place no trust in the working class, which has been courted with each enthusiasm of late. Since November 9th, that same celebrated working class has managed to get us into the fix we are in. This working class has not prepared itself for the clearly predictable blow that is about to fall. Neither do I trust the workers' politicians. No one can say that I ever admired them, so there is no need for me to distance myself from them now. Herr Philipp Scheidemann, who joined the imperial cabinet, who swore an oath to the Kaiser and then shortly afterward crowed forth the republic—I do not admire the man. During the days of the empire we would have stuck a politician like that with a name that would have made it difficult for him to appear in public. Besides him, there are others whom I do not admire, who are proud to be manual laborers, who despise all our great learning and have sworn their oath to a certain Karl Marx. I am not surprised that with such figures Germany has come to the point where we stand now. We deserve nothing better if tomorrow the generals knock the tar out of us.

"I know now about German freedom, something I had not experienced before. I have chosen it for myself and will remain true to it. I am its vassal for better and for worse."

The man from Munich, who had stood listening to him, walked over to him, extended a hand and said in his dry way, "And that's that. We need not swear a Rütli Oath. But if this is, as it appears to be, the last meeting of this council, never mind. It was the one that pleased me most."

The sarcastic fellow made several low-voiced comments, for example: "Who are you going to line up with tomorrow then, rifle in hand?" But he had no success now. Morgen's pathetic effusions seemed to have had an effect on him as well. At least he did not prove to be the one-hundred-percent Marxist everyone had expected, nor did he leave when they all stood up and went on chatting in small groups.

It began to grow dark. A kerosene lamp was lit. A mildly enthusiastic, cheerful mood had come over them all. For the first of their number, Morgen, had reached down into his heart and they had felt something that bound them together. They sat there now, as if transfigured by it, around the table with its antediluvian kerosene lamp. They had grown younger. The man from Munich unfolded yet once more his so-called practical suggestions. But it all remained as before a matter of dim generalities, though they were all far too enthusiastic to ask questions, e.g., the question they would whisper later on the stairs and as they were saying their good-byes in the entryway, but not now in the presence of the man from Munich: "Do we have any authority at all, authority legitimated by the public, by the nation?"

But even down on the street they felt ashamed of the question. The afternoon had proved greatly profitable, though it was impossible to define just how.

Naturally, once out on the street, the tall lyric poet called out "Homeland! Homeland!" several times, without the others' finding that absurd.

Soldiers, Old Style and New

Due to the notoriously bad weather, several officers put on rain caps over their helmets. In Steglitz other officers recite an oath for the same reason. But very young officers at a camp in Zossen ball their fists and plot on behalf of the "Holy Reich."

A Curse from Wilhelmshöhe

Several mean and testy gentlemen in Kassel put on their uniforms as usual the day before the troops were to march into Berlin and stuck their legs into sturdy boots with leather gaiters. After which they took their places in comfortable chairs. The rooms were heated. They waited.

Afterward, reports came in about which they could not agree. So some of them went to see others; they stomped around in their offices and talked things over. People stood outside the doors and made sure no one disturbed them.

When the gentlemen had cursed sufficiently and things were getting quite chaotic, one of them arrived and did what he could to calm things down. This was no small task among all these bristling tomcats. But he managed it. They'd be damned if they would, but they yielded. But as soon as they could, they would sure give somebody a dressing down.

Meanwhile the day had passed and they changed the scene of action. One of them stayed behind and telephoned Lequis in Berlin. Hellfire and damnation, there was nothing to be done at the moment. But he was not to give up. Sooner or later they would strike the blow, with or without help, with or without consent, and in a way that would make the buildings of Berlin totter and knock the bejesus out of all concerned.

Comrade Ebert is in a Bad Mood

He was in a foul temper too. Foul-tempered because the day had been much a mess, because of the trick played on him, because people wouldn't believe the enemy was on the left and went by the name of Spartacus, foul-tempered because of the meeting with the Executive Council (the Leftist newspapers printed the communiqué in triumph, with the added comment that Ebert, Scheidemann and Wels had had to knuckle under)—moody because of the disrespectful treatment he had had to show General Hindenburg, the writer of patriotic letters. That was how comrade Ebert—who had risen from humble origins and as a result of the battles of this past year had ended up in the Reichs Chancellery in Berlin—felt that evening as he set out to add the crowning nuisance to the miseries that had filled his day to bursting: to administer the officers' oath of loyalty to the German Republic.

He was preparing his speech in his office. He paced back and forth in front of his desk. No one is really helping me. I am all alone out in open country. It occurred to him how he sometimes had marched around in here rehearsing a dignified style of walking. He cared nothing for that now. When you had to put up with humiliation like the meeting with the Executive Council and to issue a communiqué like that one, then it would be better to be working on Lindenstrasse, supervising Party organization.

His hand touched a black marble paperweight that bore an eagle with wings outspread. Beneath it, under a piece of heavy plate glass, lay a clipping from a newspaper, left there by one of his predecessors, the Declaration of War in 1914. "For the Reich established by our fathers it is a matter of 'to be or not to be.' "

How they had gone off to war, so honest, shoulders straight. On August 4th, Haase, the Independent who now behaved like a madman, then chairman of the Reichstag, had said—and even Liebknecht had agreed with him (the only time the man had ever showed any good sense): "We will not abandon our own Fatherland. We hope that the cruel school of the sufferings of war will awaken a loathing for war in still more millions of hearts and win them to the ideals of socialism and peace among nations."

I have held to that proposition. And then the casualties of the war—even before Verdun 330,000 Germans, 450,000 French and 100,000 English. And now they want to get themselves involved in a civil war over the question of whether we want a republic or a monarchy, and force a dictatorship of the proletariat on the country. It really doesn't pay, just as Bebel said, to bust people's heads open on the issue of what form of government you want. The main thing remains the abolition of capitalism. How right old Bebel was when he said: "The monarchy isn't as bad as people make it out to be, and a republic isn't as good as others like to picture it."

We had gone to Stockholm, in the summer of 1917, with Scheidemann and the Viennese, Doctor Adler, on behalf of the Reich, in hopes of a peace without any annexations. And there in Sweden our comrades, Branting and that Dutchman, bawled at us, made you feel like a prisoner at the bar. Still, in our subsequent report to clumsy old Chancellor Bethmann-Hollweg, we gave him the cold facts: Germany was suffering greatly, had become prey to usurers and the nouveaux riches, the submarine war was not getting us anywhere, we would have to rebuild Germany as a nation of justice and freedom.

Now the war has been lost, the country is exhausted and we have the reins in our hands, but have to beat back our enemies on both sides.

The grim little people's deputy sat down to write. Time was pressing.

The Oath-Taking

The administration of the oath to the troops ordered to march into the city, or in this case, to their representatives, took place in the Steglitz town hall.

Representing the government were Ebert, Scheidemann, Haase, Dittmann. There was no revolutionary Executive Council to be found here; they had not even expressed the desire to be represented. In addition, there were several officers present from the War Ministry, and as the principal figures, General Lequis and the officers and men of the Rifle Division and the Guard Infantry, who were to swear a solemn oath of loyalty to the German Republic for themselves and for the comrades-at-arms whom they represented, all upon the orders of the highest authority in Kassel, which itself had sworn no oath.

Upon entering the festively illuminated hall and in anticipation of the officers, Ebert and Scheidemann assumed a genial expression. They found themselves confronted by a solid front of icy faces. And so they, too, decided to look stern and stubborn.

Ebert delivered only a portion of the speech he had intended. He said: "Soldiers and officers, you returned from the tumult of war and found massive changes before you here at home. The old system had been thrown down." It had to be said, it could not be concealed after all, but he knew enough to add immediately thereafter: "Peace, freedom and order will again be the stars by which we will chart our course."

And the people's deputy, in order to keep things brief, since every word addressed to this front was pointless—the words bounced off it as though from a marble wall—moved on to his conclusion, in which he called upon the assembled representatives of the front-line troops who were to march into the city the next day to swear the following oath:

"We swear, each in the name of the division he represents, to commit ourselves totally to the one German Republic and its provisional government, the Council of Peoples' Deputies."

Those present stood up. General Lequis repeated the formula.

The Arrival of Weary Migratory Birds

Already in the course of that day mixed squadrons of the 1st Guard Dragoons and the 8th Hussars had moved into Tempelhof, in the south of Berlin, with fife and drum, and with black, white and red flags unfurled. Their storm helmets hung from the baggage wagons.

The staff on the Guard Cavalry had quartered itself in Dahlem. The citizens of this fashionable suburb held a small ball for them that evening, and distributed small tokens of their affection.

The Guard Cavalry Rifles were first quartered in Jüterbog. Today they were spending their last night as a field division in Trebbin. They consisted of different Guard Cavalry Rifle regiments, the Garde du Corps, the Guard Cuirassiers, the 2nd Guard Dragoon Regiment, the Guard Hussars.

Thanks to the armistice they all had escaped total annihilation. Pressing forward from west to east, they had marched through dozens of festooned cities. They had been received with music and speeches. But the booming of cannons, the bursting of mines, the rattle of machine guns was still in their ears. It enveloped them like a ghost.

These units had been melted down, jumbled together as a result of the horrible action they had seen. Weary now, they settled into the quarters shown them without ever recovering consciousness, like migratory birds after a deadly flight through a storm.

Poems: "The Eternal Reich"

While these troops were moving in from the West, the first volunteer troops were breaking camp near Berlin and moving toward the Baltic and Poland.

These troops had thrown off the paralysis of war and had exchanged it for something else: a loathing of peace. Many of them had belonged to that human sludge that ebbed and flowed day after day through the streets of Berlin. They had known war. They looked at peace—and drew their conclusions.

It is evening, the evening of the Monday on which comrade Ebert administered the oath to General Lequis. Lieutenant Heiberg is now wearing a uniform again, that of a simple field soldier. He is awaiting the major of his former Alsatian garrison, who has notified him that he would like to say farewell to him personally, in part to inform himself first-hand about the nature of this expedition, which seems a crazy one to him. For he has nothing against a reinforced guard on the eastern frontier, but these troops bother him.

Even at his entrance into the camp surrounded by barbed wire he is at once displeased. Guards approach his car, make him get out, overturn the cushions. He protests, points to his uniform, rubs his identity papers under their noses. He has to put up with the fellows for fifteen minutes. They are brawny lads, however, who do what they think is right, and when they finally let him drive off, he has to halt once more because they want to check his tires—he doesn't know why. Finally he drives on, and notices that one of them gives his car a kick.

The men are sitting in the barracks by the light of kerosene lamps; somewhere along the line there is a strike at the power company.

Three other officers sit next to Heiberg and the major, two younger, one older. The conversation can't seem to get off the ground. The major has the feeling he's in the way.

So he begins talking himself. He asks if Heiberg still remembers the senior officer at their last garrison? Yes? "Well, at age sixty-eight, or maybe he's even seventy by now, he has suddenly become another man. As if someone had been substituted for him. Indian summer. He's fallen in love like a young tomcat."

At this the others grow more lively. "And how old is she, as old as my grandmother?"

"Who is she?"

The major: "That is the key issue. For in fact she's a thoroughly respectable woman, early thirties, beautiful, a Russian, a film actress."

"You don't say."

"A film actress, I tell you, and from an aristocratic family."

"She wants something from him. Does he have money?"

"One thing at a time. He has already fallen out with his family, he cares about no one else, won't return your visit."

"Senile. They should send him for a check-up. If these were normal times, the officers' corps would take the matter in hand."

"At any rate, the old gentleman tells me quite candidly that he feels very good out of uniform. Though I ought to add that last November, when we had to bury those two rascals where we were stationed last, the same gentleman could not be persuaded to come to the cemetery with us. I can still hear him say: I have to wind up the affairs of the garrison here, and then I'm going to take off this uniform jacket. And then later I meet him back home, and he invests his money and falls in love. Of course she wants something from him, probably his name. I can see the newspaper article now, with his picture and hers: "Prussian General and Russian Film Star.""

402

Heiberg: "*In summa,* disgusting."

The major: "What I wanted to say was, her father is quite another story. You'll like this one better. The man is an old cavalry officer, makes a splendid impression. These people found their way to Berlin after the wildest journey half-way round the world by way of Constantinople and the Mediterranean. He showed me on the map, a real geography lesson. He said, however, that that was nothing, that others went across Siberia, always just ahead of the Bolsheviks, and then got stranded in Korea and Shanghai before sliding on over to the other side, to America. When he told me that I began to get some idea of what the Russian Revolution was really like. The count arrives here, then, like most of them, completely broke. He and his family are close to starvation, and as you can imagine, given present conditions, our charity committee doesn't come by money easily, particularly for Russian nobility. So they eat at the same trough with the others—Quaker rations, Salvation Army. But then it turns out that his daughter is very beautiful. And people tell her she should try her luck in films, they might be able to use her, perhaps her father as well, especially since right at that moment they were rehearsing a film about Russian society in the old czarist days.

"So this Russian countess makes a very nice salary doing bit parts, though of course no one knows how long it will last. The daughter gets a little something extra from our old friend the general besides, and he's the kind who does it up right.

"So then now they have to start rehearsing for their film, and the director's eye lands on the count, the former colonel in the Russian cavalry.

"They write a new role for the man to play, some figure at the imperial court, and that's where the trouble begins. I don't know what the film is about actually, no one ever knows anything about these films anyhow. In any case, suddenly the colonel, the Russian count, is supposed to play a fellow who goes over to the side of the Reds."

One of the younger officers: "And he wasn't about to swallow that."

"There you have it. And I can tell by that that you're no actor either. Because an actor takes the role they've assigned him and merely asks how much he's getting paid. The colonel would have pocketed a pretty penny. He took it on in the first place because he didn't even give it a second thought and would immediately get his hands on some cold cash. And then when the real rehearsals start, when they start shooting, he discovers what's up. And he says no. He is supposed to confront his commanding officer, refuse to carry out a battle order and fraternize with the lower ranks instead. And they even expect him to sing the Marseillaise and the Internationale with these people and shout hurrah for the world revolution."

General laughter. Heiberg: "The man isn't like certain other people we know then."

A short, stocky man, who spoke with a Württemberg accent: "No similarity at all with our Groener."

The major: "Right you are. Bravo."

Heiberg: "They fired the fellow, and now he's back in debt?"

The major: "Yes. And the general, our former commanding officer, is having to dig deep into his pockets."

Heiberg: "Why doesn't the Russian come join up with us? He could muster up a Russian volunteer corps."

The major: "These people have lost all heart. They've taken a terrible drubbing."

Heiberg, coldly: "Then there's no use even starting up with him."

Heiberg, to the major: "This is our last hour before we break camp, leaving the old home for a new one. Let's sing a song, with muffled drums."

And first they sang "Oh Germany, Highly Honored," with the refrain of "See it through, see it through, though storm may brew." Then one of them said, "Let's hear what Walter read us yesterday again. As a farewell."

Heiberg explained to the major, "Walter has a friend in Württemberg whose brother was killed in the war. The brothers were very close. The one who survived wrote poems in honor of the one who fell."

The major: "Poems? Don't be offended, but I'm not much for poems."

Heiberg: "They're not poems."

Major: "Oh, so suddenly now they're not poems."

Heiberg to Walter: "I was trying to make you more comfortable. Read us a few of them."

Then the short primary school teacher sat down at the table with a notebook. They pushed the lamps over to him and he said with a warm, hesitant voice: "My friend's name is Paul Schmidt. His brother, the one who was killed, was named Arthur. He was nineteen when he died in 1916. My friend was very fond of his dead brother. That's why he wrote these poems. They're all sonnets." And then, after pondering for a moment, he opened up the notebook, on each page of which was a sonnet printed out by hand.

"There are four cycles of poems, the first is called '1915,' the second 'Brothers,' the third, the main cycle, is titled 'Requiem.' Then the last poems bear the title '1918'."

"They're brand new then?" the major remarked when a pause followed.

"Yes," the teacher nodded, "they're the last."

The major: "Well, fire away."

404

The teacher looked at the others. They were waiting. He said, "One poem from the third cycle, the last part.

> . . . here my wounded hand,
> A servant only to your voice, so light
> That no one but myself could understand.
>
> You sang. I wrote. But in this book I write
> No melody will rustle, all are banned
> But one — I'll not forget you in the night.

He leafed through the notebook.

The major: "Was this man wounded, too? He says 'wounded hand.'"

The teacher, gently: "Probably to be understood as a metaphor."

The major, politely: "Oh, I see."

The major had no taste for literature. But in this case he was paying close attention in order to understand his neighbors, who were listening so devoutly. What did this have to do with these young men who would be marching into the field tomorrow?

Then came:

> One day all German towns will celebrate.
> From every village roof the flags will fly,
> On every road the people stand and wait
> To shout and welcome home the infantry.
>
> I know the sky will turn a deeper blue,
> The peeling plea of bells soar higher still.
> And white and gay, like sloe trees blooming new,
> Trim girls on balconies will wave and thrill.
>
> The season will be spring, when fountains leap
> Like mothers sobbing from the earth's abyss,
> When like warm, happy brides the lilacs peep
>
> And like a sister jonquils smile to kiss,
> With soldiers marching, singing down the street
> And festive day yields to a night of bliss.

The major made a gesture of approval. "Still, he was wrong about one thing, the month. The troops didn't come back in the spring."

Again the teacher nodded politely. He went on turning pages and said, without a change of expression, "Maybe that's to be taken as a metaphor too."

Which only confused the unhappy major the more. Because now he asked himself: spring? To be taken as a metaphor? What's that supposed to mean? While he leaned back in resignation, struggling with his anger, one sonnet followed another. The group sat there at the table as if attending a worship service. The sullen old officer gave another listen once, when the fallen soldier himself was described.

> The dimple still lies hidden in your cheeks,
> That betrayed itself when your laughter rang,
> But almost flees in fright when your bass speaks.
> Awkward your body — half boy, half man.

Then the major woke up, for the simple reason that the teacher's voice grew louder. And these poems interested him more as well.

> The idol perished, a craven beast, and so
> Those reeling round him stole his flaw.
> The banner and the blossoms and the flow
> Of blood welled shamelessly from his maw.
>
> As like a rabid dog he yelped and bayed
> And rasping bit his flank as on he fled,
> And that his torturers might be repaid
> He pulled into his grave the millions dead.
>
> So there he sprawls now, ravished, swollen, fat,
> Robbed of the mask of lies that once he wore,
> His iron body bored with bullets he's spun
>
> Himself, numbed by the lethal apparat.
> Polluted, stiff, inert, the head lies sore
> Beside the perishing leviathan.

Had the major been in another circle of people, he would have banged his fist on the table at this. But now he did not know whether he had understood correctly, maybe it was all to be taken as a metaphor somehow.

> The beast now vomits what vapid rest remains
> Of human stuff out of its maw: compelled.
> And dances, raging at its doom, propelled
> In frenzy out to where death entertains.
>
> The whip goes crack, the mob begins to howl,
> Atune to foaming, manic melody.
> Whore, deserter, coupled, reign, while she
> Has donned a ragged, plundered ermine cowl.

Enemies surround us — revelers all.
Murderous hirelings slink about — we doze.
The ballroom throbs — the thug is burrowing beneath.

Enter the foe. Hail comrade, guest, they bawl
Their greeting. Hand on hilt, he crows.
Our honor aches without the dagger's teeth.

The major recognized this tone of voice as the same he had heard
from Heiberg's mouth. Now he realized why they listened so devoutly.
This was a widespread mood, they even had their poets already.

The reader said, "And now the last one."

He threw Heiberg a glance. Heiberg stood up, the others followed.
The major had to get up, *nolens volens*. Once again his impression was:
crazy, completely crazy, a suicide club.

The reader intoned:

A savage blast of horns, from harp no tone,
The spell's been burst by crooked scowl of hell.
And now no hope awakes, from earth no swell
Of saving blood comes gushing from the stone.

Awaken, Europe. Madness, nothing more.
And not a turning-point. It battered you.
The horror grows to give dark justice due:
That vengeance may perfect itself five score.

Poor nations, slavery is your fate. Beware,
Flushed victors, you too shall plunge in the abyss
If you should break the statute of the dead.

You're breeding still the beast within its lair.
Still sorer penance is required than this —
The Holy Reich, a living race instead.

The major stood there erect next to the young soldiers. The last
words were spoken like a solemn oath. The young soldiers, illuminated
from below by the reddish kerosene light, gazed fixedly at one another.

Heiberg accompanied the major to his car, and they were met by a
surprise—the car was gone. They searched the dark side streets of the
camp with flashlights. Heiberg waved over a comrade, but they could
not find it. The car had apparently been "requisitioned." After half an
hour Heiberg returned with a battered car, barely in running condition.
He promised the major he would investigate. The major, bitingly:
"When you're in Riga, right?"

As he left the desolate camp in this rattletrap he was reminded of the guards who had checked his car so carefully before. They were the ones. What a bunch. Property did not exist for them. Some of them were thieves, the others lunatics.

It was good they were getting out of the country.

Among the soldiers marching out that night was young Lutz, whom we first met on November 23rd, a Saturday, first in his dreary garret room, where a pneumatic postcard asked him to meet his equally indigent friend Konrad at Kemperplatz, then at the rendezvous with that desperado, and finally on Friedrich-Karl Strasse where they robbed and murdered a lottery dealer. The detectives of the Berlin police will not solve the case. Lutz, brutalized by war and now a mercenary, flees his homeland. It will be his fate to remain in the Baltic region, losing his life in the battles around Riga.

The Front-line Troops in Berlin, the First Day

December 10th. When the troops march through the Brandenburg Gate, they seem to be both the present and the future. The farther they move into the city the older they grow, and finally they become completely unreal.

And so the Tuesday had come, the one chosen as the first day for the arrival of the German front-line troops in Berlin.

As the pouring rain let up in the latter part of the morning, the west side of Berlin, the area beween Wilmersdorf and Schmargendorf, came to life. Throngs of children gathered at Heidelberger Platz. Street vendors with black, white and red flags appeared. But the children, who had arrived in organized groups, had brought their black, white and red flags with them, left-overs from the war. The vendors had good success selling souvenir cards with portraits of the former princes.

First a division of the Guard Cavalry Rifles approached. They had been camped at the Düppel estate. They had started to move early that morning. Women and girls polished their saddles for them, helped them clean their rifles with woolen cloths. Young country girls moved back and forth between the formations and distributed bouquets of lilies of the valley. The units attached a black, white and red flag to every wagon. Horses, wagons and machine guns were decorated with evergreens.

Then they set out for Berlin, at their head the military band of the 4th Cuirassiers from Münster, then the regimental standards escorted by officers and ensigns. They moved forward amid fanfares and singing.

From Heidelberger Platz on, the streets were black with people. A great excitement lay over the crowds. The tension grew. People thought they heard a distant beat of drums. A wave of shouts rolled along the streets. The guards formed a chain to hold back the masses. And now trumpets were indeed approaching.

And then began the spectacle that caused many in the crowd to

409

weep. Men as well as women, moved by the emotion of man's common fate, remembering the long war and all the dead.

Did these people see the troops? They were looking at the long war, at victories and defeats. Passing before them was a piece of their own life, with wagons and horses, machine guns and cannons.

An unending hurrah burst about the parade. The children waved their flags. People waved from windows and balconies with handkerchiefs. The officers and the rank and file had attached their lilies of the valley to their chests, many wore the Iron Cross, all had on black, white and red rosettes and ribbons.

Behind the Guard Cavalry Rifles marched the Guard Lancers, Sharpshooters and the combined rifle divisions, decked out in fresh evergreens—each division behind its imperial banner.

Then, to the amusement of the crowd, came the smoking canteens, then medics, paymasters, chaplains.

Higher-ranking officers rode in cars. Bavarians, Saxons and Württembergers combined in one battalion. The division staff with General Hoffmann. The Guard Machine Gun Division, the Guard Cuirassier Regiment, the Life Guard Cuirassier Regiment, the 3rd Dragoons, the 8th and 11th Hussars, the 5th Lancers, the 2nd and 6th Mounted Rifles.

Without the crowd's taking note, the 4th Cuirassier Regiment paraded by, forty-eight men strong. All the others lay on the banks of the Aisne in France.

At last a bicycle company.

They reached the Kaiserallee at 11:30 A.M. Flags fluttered from all the buildings. Children sat up on the horses in front of the riders, laughing—the youth, the future of the nation, everything would be better now. All the trams halted. On the streets a teeming, dense throng of people. The buildings, full of waving men and women, covered with fluttering flags, had lost their inflexibility. The soldiers sang and sang. "We'll meet again, when we come home, when we come home!" The crowd could not contain its excitement and sang along with them. Wagon upon wagon, rider upon rider. The vanguard arrived at the barren Zoological Garden.

Pariser Platz and the Brandenburg Gate had been decorated by the artist Sandkuhl. Evergreen garlands were wound about the columns of the gate. Above the center portal was a banner that read: "Peace and Freedom." A row of tall poles had been set up out in the square, all bearing crowns of wreaths. At the entrance to the central promenade of Unter den Linden stood two immense obelisks with palms of peace covering their fronts and sides. The speakers' platform, since this is where the official reception was to take place, had been erected on the south side of the square.

410

It seemed as if the idea was to make it as unpleasant as possible for the spectators—close to a hundred thousand people stood shoulder to shoulder in the square and massed down Unter den Linden—giving the parading soldiers a foretaste of the disorder of Berlin. There were too few guards. People were dreadfully wedged together. Many of them fought, flailing their arms, trying to get out of the suffocating press. Children were lifted up above adult heads. There were cries for help, shrieking women. The first-aid crews had to use physical force to get through to those who had fainted.

As the music neared, soldiers formed a chain and cleared a path for the troops. The day was still overcast following the rain of the night before, and a gentle fog lay over the city.

Several men climbed up onto the speakers' platform from its rear. And a small, rotund man in a heavy coat could now be seen in front of the winding garlands; he had a black imperial beard and held a piece of paper in his hand. This was People's Deputy Ebert, who gazed in astonishment out at the huge crowd and asked himself how his voice was supposed to carry. But the crowd had other concerns. Just at that moment two injured women were being carried out of the throng along the path that had been opened up for the troops.

Next to the small, portly man stood an elderly high-ranking officer. He wore a spiked helmet covered in field-gray. This was General Lequis, whom the high command had commissioned to be in charge of the special command in Berlin.

Very solemnly and in a foul temper, a gentleman of larger-than-life size climbed up after him onto the platform. He had a mighty moustache and wore a top hat, a real stovepipe. He was said to be the mayor of Berlin, who bore the gloomy name of Wermut, and he did indeed look like he had drunk of wormwood.

The three stood next to each other, the little people's deputy with his goatee, the general in his spiked helmet and the mayor in his stovepipe. They stood there on the platform in front of the surging sea of the crowd and waited.

Great swaths of fog floated from the Zoological Garden over toward the Brandenburg Gate, on top of which the victorious quadriga still pranced into the city, but in bronze, and without moving from the spot.

Music, drums and trumpets, waving handkerchiefs, hurrahs. To the fanfares of the "Hohenfriedberg March" the vanguard of the parade wound its way through the crowd. The effect was disappointing. Despite the numerous banners, the troops were hardly visible in the human sea. Their music was lost amid the cheers. Then the signal was given: "Halt!" And the front rank stopped in front of the speakers' platform, where in addition to a general two gentlemen in civilian clothes evidently had something oratorical in mind.

For the crowd there now came a period of nothing but standing there suffocating while being pushed and shoved. Children and adults screamed. The soldiers stood still, their banners did not move. Word was that some men were making speeches up on the platform.

The journalists and several others near the platform noticed how first the lanky mayor and then the head of state stepped forward and sought mightily to speak so as to be heard, but then gave up and read in normal voices what they found on the papers they were holding.

"Welcome home, brave warriors. Dearest brothers." Then came something about "ineradicable gratitude" and the embarrassed suggestion that "you left an old world and now find yourself in a new." It ended then with "Welcome to Berlin."

The top hat retreated. He had done his duty.

Now the rotund head of state pushed his way to the fore. He began where the top hat had left off.

"Welcome to the German Republic," Ebert shouted. "Welcome home." And as he saw fit, he gave them a mixture of words of welcome, political commentary and admonition.

He flattered the troops. "You could march home with your heads held high. Never have men achieved greater things."

He wooed the soldiers spiritedly, but they, to the extent they heard anything at all, did not think much of the whole affair.

"Your sacrifices have been unparalleled," the brand-new head of state disclosed to them. "No enemy has conquered you. Only when the superiority of the opponent's numbers and matériel became too crushing did you cease to struggle."

Then he rubbed their noses in what had occurred in the meantime.

"The old rulers, who lay like a curse upon our noble deeds, have been shaken off by the German people. The hope of German freedom lies now with you. Our unfortunate nation has grown poor. Our task is to rebuild for the future."

Toward the end he let a few words fall about a "socialist republic" that would be a "homeland of hard work." He then called for a cheer for "the German fatherland, for a free and democratic Germany"; the cheers, however, were restricted to the immediate area around the platform.

After a while the head of the parade began to move again. The pushing and shoving in the crowd grew worse. One could see a few soldiers' heads, the tips of their lances moving next to them down Unter den Linden—apparently mounted. Other helmet spikes moved in pairs in the same direction. Those must be soldiers on wagons and cannons. The parade rolled on down Unter den Linden.

And then the terrible knot of humanity began to unsnarl. People washed in waves behind the soldiers. They left a veritable battlefield behind them. On the asphalt of the square and on the sidewalks around

Pariser Platz lay torn scarves, broken umbrellas, handkerchiefs, crushed apples, briefcases and ladies' purses. There were even single shoes, presumably belonging to the injured who had been carried away.

The little speakers' platform at the south end with its evergreen sprays and rosettes stood empty again. It had been used for only a short time. The guests had fled back to the buildings where they felt secure, the head of the Reich to Wilhelmstrasse, the mayor to his Rathaus, General Lequis to the staff room.

Presumably all three were now eating lunch.

The further the soldiers moved away from their starting point in Schmargendorf and the assembly point at Pariser Platz, however, the fewer the number of people gathered to see them. They halted once again at Opernplatz. Then they disbanded, each unit marching off to its own barracks.

As the troops marched past the palace, red flags were on display. At the gates, armed sailors were on patrol, their rifles slung on straps over their backs, their barrels pointing upward. They took no notice of the regiments as they marched past.

Trams merrily rang their bells in the center of Berlin. On the running boards there were still clusters of curiosity-seekers, but seldom people who waved. People watched the uniformed soldiers with little interest and less joy, all that military spit and polish. The soldiers heard words of mockery. And not a single black, white and red flag in these seemingly endless rows of buildings.

The regiments marched through the fog. Their wagons bore the imperial banner. They still wore the lilies of the valley from Schmargendorf and Wilmersdorf on their chests. Here too there were children standing around, but none of them wanted to climb onto the wagons. Children and adults fell silent at the sight of the black-white-red military dragon.

And so they went to their barracks to the south and north. They had marched for some time without music. It occurred to no one to sing "We'll meet again, when we come home, when we come home!" People watched with hostile eyes as they moved past.

How old one had grown, how unreal, with these rifles, cannons and officers.

Like some fetish from the jungle, with spears and rattles, it wandered through the streets of Berlin. The wind blew dust up around them.

While they were entering the city the Executive Council was meeting in Prinz-Albrecht Strasse, discussing the munitions these troops had in tow. Several formations had brought 80,000 rounds per machine gun with them. It was decided that the ammunition was to be confiscated and this proposal was sent on to the government.

In the Zoological Garden, even before the troops had marched in, some damage had been done to the monuments to the Prussian kings Wilhelm I and Friedrich II. Several bronze crowns were missing. Considering the situation in Berlin, however, they might simply have been stolen for the metal.

Book Three

Around December 11th

The Gate of Dread and Despair

Here a man catches fire and burns brightly.

We are Speaking of Friedrich Becker

The peculiar tension under which Friedrich Becker lived was increasing. He was overly alert. Sometimes, when the excitement—which by the way he showed no one—eased off a little, it seemed to him as if someone (who?) were speaking to him in some strange way, and as if events around him were curiously related to him. Whatever it was that was directly addressing him employed no normal human voice, nor did it contact him in any normal human sense, but rather expressed itself instead in colors and tones, sometimes in figures and numbers, and demanded that he guess at its meaning. And so gradually it had come about that Becker accepted this change, the way a man who is seriously ill finally accustoms himself to his illness, even accepting the pain as something that is a part of him.

Dr. Krug, the science teacher at his school, visited him on Monday afternoon, and he found Becker very much improved. Becker marched about for his easygoing guest like a commandant or army chief of staff. His step revealed considerable vigor. Krug found his manner somewhat provocative. Becker, however, took pains to be courteous.

At first the conversation faltered. That was remarkable for a talkative man like Becker. But the reason lay, as Krug realized at once, in the fact that the man was engaged in an unbroken inner discussion, in a debate that made every other conversation impossible.

Krug mentioned the school several times, spoke of the new curriculum, only to have Becker surprise him after a while with the question "What's new?" Finally Krug pressed him, mildly, with the question whether anything was new with him. But it turned out that although Becker was apparently suffering under an excess of thought, was inundated by images, he knew of nothing he wanted to say. The question did not suit him, he gazed mistrustfully at Krug. Finally he managed a forced smile.

417

He said: "The snail doesn't leave its house. I go to the hospital. They think I'm making progress. Whatever else might be new in my life would have to happen on my way from here to the hospital."

"And what has happened there, for example?"

"Would hardly interest you. Although perhaps it might. But don't make fun of me. Things like a small car that had broken down in Friedenstrasse. It was being towed by a larger one. A rope with a red flag was tied between them."

"Had there been a collision?"

"Possibly. I don't know, I didn't see it. I was impressed by how easily the car in front pulled the other one, the one that had broken down."

Krug did not understand the point of this. Becker brought out another item from the treasure chest of his thoughts.

"It's not important." He paced through the room with the long stride of a hiker. "By the way, I'm glad you came today because I'm preoccupied with matters that are right up your line. I've been thinking about the leaves on trees. You're surprised. You think, there aren't any leaves on trees in December. That's quite true. I was walking through the Friedrichshain, where of course the trees are all bare too. And there, next to a shed that I presume belongs to the parks department, I met two men who were busy with a pile of dirt, or what I took to be dirt. As I got nearer though, I saw it was leaves and dirt, giant piles of leaves that had been raked together the month before and then buried in the ground. They were busy stirring them up with the dirt. It makes very good humus, they said."

"Right. You've probably noticed as well, Becker, how they burn off the stubble in the fields in autumn. That produces ash and other nutrients for the plants."

Becker stood there gravely in front of him. "You see, Krug, that's what I wanted to find out from you, because an old Greek like me knows nothing about this sort of thing of course. Nutrients. Those fellows also mentioned something similar. But now you see,"—and again the commandant's march about the room began, around Krug's armchair, along the bookcase—"those leaves had been hanging on trees. The trees worked hard last spring to produce them. I remember from earlier how leaves first appear as little green buds, the embryo gets larger, opens up and distends, and all of a sudden the whole green fullness is there, the tree, the woods, millions of leaves sprouting from those branches, each leaf with its own special jagged or rounded edge, and as a botanist you can tell from each leaf which tree produced it. That is a tremendous achievement for those trees, a colossal unfolding of energy, to gather up substances out of the earth, to make leaves from it, to use the leaves then during the summer. And then comes autumn and everything drops off. And the gardeners shovel the leaves into the ground once they've dried out, and they say it makes good humus."

Krug: "You mean the natural cycle. It's the way with many things in nature."

"I know the term. It occurred to me right away while I was standing there beside those men and their hole. For dust thou art, and unto dust shalt thou return. That's an idea that is inconceivable, Krug. You can't have comprehended it in all its implications. It simply cannot be accepted. And if you natural scientists say that's how it is, then I say it's not that way. Don't misunderstand me. I'm not saying what you perhaps assume I am—that it can't be so, or that it shouldn't be so. What I'm saying is: it isn't so. Don't misunderstand me. Those trees, just in terms of numbers, have developed incredible energies to form that mass of leaves from the earth, the air, from their own bodies. Then they drop off. Underneath them then, the elements are reassembled, and the trees find themselves in the same situation the next spring. They start in again, like Sisyphus. A new spring arrives, a new autumn—and again it's a failure. All that immense labor wasted. Because what has happened in the meantime? What has been achieved? The tree spent its summer being a tree. You can say no more than that. It developed flowers so that later on other trees could do the same thing it was doing. They all pass the time in the same way. They are simply trees, trees. They work—with no results."

He was standing in front of Krug again. "I repeat, no results. Or have you some reply to give me?"

Krug grinned. "Well, a tree is indeed only a tree. It doesn't speculate about things. It has no brain, for which, perhaps, one ought to simply congratulate it. And as far as that goes, you're completely right. The work that a tree does has no result, as far as I know at least—unless one wants to see a result in the fact that ultimately it will dry out and we'll be able to shove a log on the fire."

Becker raised his arms in excitement. "You'll never be able to make that plausible to me. I mean, what kind of idea is that, what sort of a world do you live in?"

"But my dear Becker, in the first place I did not pick out this world for myself. And secondly, one can make oneself quite comfortable in it, as you know yourself."

"So you pass your time then just like the trees? The trees pump water and elements out of the earth, make leaves, let them fall off, one year is gone, and it's the same the next; and all that energy, Krug, that it takes to form those leaves, has in all seriousness no other purpose than to fill up half a year? To pass the time, to kill time? That would mean that the whole question of the world and of living ends up as: how do I kill time, how do I get through time, how do I get around time?"

Krug exploded in his broadest laugh. "Yes, and why not?" All things considered, we manage to do it tolerably enough, don't we? Listen to me, Becker. When you are finally back on your feet and not just walking up and down between your chairs here, you'll get a taste for it again and find the right answers. Because sometimes it is boring, to be sure, but now and then there are wonderful things strewn for you along the path. And by getting involved with them, and then later in remembering that involvement, time passes almost by itself, for the most part much more quickly than we want, and we don't even have to ask such questions."

"And me?" Becker replied vehemently. "Here I am defending the world and even nature itself against you. Nature is a serious matter. Whatever put that incredible energy into those trees possesses a seriousness and at least as much reason as you or I. It won't let itself get involved in some idiotic natural cycle. The cycle does not exist. A natural cycle is a void. A tree is not simply a tree. It is not just a piece of your botany."

"All right, what is it then?" Krug laughed good-naturedly.

Becker responded violently. "I don't know!" And then while he went on marching around he muttered grimly, "I don't know anything at all. Everything is closed off to me. I'm a man beating his head against a wall."

Krug, still congenial: "Good Lord, man, the things you worry about. Forget that sort of thing. What difference do the trees in Friedrichshain make to you, or how humus is made. Rephrase your question again for me, please."

But he received no answer from Becker, who went on muttering to himself. Krug watched him wander about and suddenly he was alarmed. There was something crazy about the man. He seemed about to topple over the edge. The shrapnel from the grenade had hit him in the spine, but his ordeal was evidently not yet at an end; the spine was healing, but now it was attacking the brain.

Krug asked a cautious question about Becker's mother. Surprisingly, Becker rose to the bait. "I'll bring her in to see you. I've been an inattentive host."

As the three of them talked, Krug observed that Becker had pulled himself together, although from time to time he would begin his general's march about the room. His mother had apparently noticed nothing, for she remarked quite casually, "Sit still for a while, Friedrich. He practices like that half the day. He's overdoing it. It taxes him I'm sure."

"Why don't you play some chess," she suggested.

Krug looked at his friend, who nodded, and they played for two hours just as in their most peaceful days. Becker won three of the four matches. Krug, who usually played better, was not concentrating. At the end he even forgot to exchange a few words with Becker's mother.

This happened on Monday. On Tuesday, the great day of the arrival of the troops, Becker stayed home because of the bad weather. He didn't want his mother to go out either, he had a gloomy premonition of some sort. He did not tell her why, he did not know himself. But she had her little errands; she looked after a few families in the neighborhood as well; he would have to let her do what she must. It was her world, one he heard about often enough, but without really understanding it.

So he sat there alone in the apartment.

Hardly a quarter hour had passed and he was seized with dread.

The room filled with distrust.

The things in the room, the table lamp, the ceiling lamp, the curtains, began to exude something that deprived them of definite contours. Sometimes when he would turn around there was a turbulence around the lamp. But if he focused sharply it stopped.

It was the same with the flowers in the wallpaper pattern. But simply by walking up close he could bring them to reason.

Everything is rising up against me—the thought careened across his mind. I can't control it. Are they demanding I be a sorcerer?

And he went out into the corridor. He wanted to have an umbrella or a cane in his hand to defend himself if need be.

They want to revenge themselves on me, he thought, finding everything calm again when he returned. There's something malicious and underhanded about them. The point is these objects aren't just objects, of course, the way Krug imagines. It would be wonderful, to be sure, if one could get them to be only that. But . . .

He gently laid down the cane he had brought back in with him. Then an unbearable sensation crept up over his body, starting in his legs, spreading to his shoulders and arms. It was not pain, but a queer heaviness that invaded the muscles, a weariness, but not one that invited him to sleep, rather one that made him restless and left him excited, a vibration. Something undefinable, frightening was going on.

Becker sighed worriedly, he began breathing hard to distract it. But it would not go away. And now he sat there imprisoned; this was different from when his "demon" afflicted him, robbing him of his thoughts. He could think perfectly now, felt in full possession of consciousness, could even stand up and take a step. But there was this leaden feeling and a growing apprehension.

What awaits me, he wondered. The walls, the chairs, the curtains are back to normal. Nothing coming from them now. They're just watching. They've assembled against me. They don't know what's coming either.

He groaned—what have I done that I'm being afflicted like this? What is going to happen, what are they going to do to me? This is worse than any pain.

And suddenly it was very bright all around him. And he heard a ghastly scream. There was a shriek, shrill, ear-splitting, then a whimper. A human voice, a male voice. It screeched and rasped. It slid into a hollow moan broken by brief yelps.

When the moaning ceased, a second voice could be heard, a lighter one that let out a volley of crude curses and made disgusting noises. Finally it began to peal with laughter.

This lasted for a long time. Then—it was over.

Becker was sitting erect the whole time. He had tried to pick up the cane laying beside him on the sofa, but his hand had remained lying beside the cane, frozen in an accidental position just like the whole man. Now, hearing no more—but it had not been just something he had heard—he pulled his arm back to his body. The muscles of his face twitched.

The man stroked his forehead mechanically, got up, took two or three steps and looked back at the sofa. There followed a few uncertain steps in the direction of the desk; he held tight to its edge. Now he pulled his chair around and sat down, propping his head up; his face was white and expressionless.

Then he began to moan as well, trying to awaken himself out of a dream. And the moaning went on until coughing and throat-clearing began. Then he gripped the desk, looked for his handkerchief and, as he rubbed his eyes, came to himself completely.

The heaviness still weighed down on his shoulders. He took his cane from the sofa and used it to check the wall, the curtains, the wallpaper. What had happened? There had been screaming and laughing. No one could have been screaming in the apartment.

So that's how it is. I am crazy. I'm going to go completely crazy. I still have my reason at the moment. But it might happen that in the course of the day or at night I'll do something for which I'm not responsible.

His limbs were ice-cold. What's going to happen? What's going to happen?

He began to drag himself about the room to overcome the cold. Now came an attack of shivering and teeth chattering.

And suddenly—everything was totally different. He stood in one corner of the room, his back to the bookcase. A feeling rose up in his breast, climbed into his throat, a sob: have I deserved this, is there nothing to save me? Oh not this, not this.

And he recalled the howling and moaning of the two voices and he wept. Why, what have I done? And that ghastly laughter.

With eyes blinded by tears he looked at the books beside him. No help, none of you. I should have left you lying under the sofa.

I shouldn't have locked myself in like this I suppose. Krug is right. I'm grappling with superfluous ideas. Maus is doing the right thing. I should go out into the street.

And again he sat down at his desk and looked skeptically over at the sofa. An idea was approaching, but he could not grasp it. The weeping again. He laid his head on the desk and sobbed, till the icy feeling stalking him receded. He left the room, washed up and got ready to go out.

He walked along the cold, wet streets. After walking for half an hour, he grew tired. A sudden downpour of no thoughts at all. He could toddle off home now like this, empty, an apparatus.

He could show his mother, who had just returned, a peaceful, serious face there in the corridor.

She was pleased with him and told him that Hilda had been there for a minute, just to ask how he was. She was so open, so affectionate, she had not seen her like that before. She would come back after lunch. His mother told about the troops marching into the city. She had met up with some regimentals in the city. The sight had made her quite sad.

Becker let her go on talking about the soldiers and, for the first time, about the families that she regularly visited and looked after as a member of the Patriotic Women's Circle.

That morning Hilda had received a letter from Paris, via Switzerland. Frau Scharrel writing her about Bernhard's death and briefly describing the particulars.

Hilda sat there terrified, a victim of her own feelings of guilt. She saw Bernhard hanged—and then in his cold grave, saw the man who had come so often to her room, in Strasbourg.

He could not do without her after all. He had not been able to get over it.

She talked to herself. I was good to him, I'm still good to him.

And then, increasingly: I have sinned against him. I beg him for forgiveness, for everything I have done. She prayed. Dear, good friend, forgive me. May you find peace. I will pray for you.

As she stood up and went to the window her thoughts grew more comforting. What had happened was terrible, but Bernhard's soul would find peace. It could not be, she had not dared to stay with him. She had made the right choice. She had to put an end to the wretched past. A new path lay before her. The war was over.

She stood at the window and stretched with the pleasant sensation of her live body. She looked out onto the street. Life. And Becker. Thankfulness for him. With his help I'll slay all the dragons.

With tender eyes she followed the bustle of the street. In her thoughts she caressed Bernhard, telling him she hoped he would find peace and rest.

After lunch Becker's mother walked with him to his room. He pretended that he wanted to stretch out on his sofa for a siesta. She left him alone. She had a busy day yet because in several of the families she was looking after the father was coming home and they needed practically everything.

They're all leaving me alone, he felt. In such a situation there's no one to stand with you. I must fight it out myself. The morning had left him exhausted. He fell asleep before he could yield himself to his thoughts. He slept, only to be awakened by the gruesome moaning.

He sat up with a jerk and suffered agonies. It lasted longer than it had that morning, did not stop so suddenly, and when he finally thought he was free again, the sighing went on for a while yet.

His first impulse was to run to the door, to go out on the street, to be among people. But even as he put his hand to the door, he controlled the urge and went back. Something had to happen. These were attacks, a destruction of his inner self. His ego was being blown apart. Cold terror swept over him again. He sat limply in his chair.

This then was the end of everything, of war and sickness; this was the peace he had yearned for.

And no recovery, no new path.

And as had happened that morning, a hot feeling rose up in him and he wept. To stifle the weeping he pressed his cheek to the divan.

He had to open the door for Hilda. She had come to share her own hopeful joy with him. He had lain back down on the divan. As she touched him—he lay turned away from her—she heard him sob. She did not recognize the red face wet with tears, the blinking eyes and the bitter mouth. She pressed her head to his. He went on sobbing. She thought, it's his wound. But he had never done this in the hospital. It must be the confinement of the apartment. She helped him up. He shivered. His knees were shaky. He was really sick.

"Lie back down, Friedrich. I'll get a blanket."

The trembling slowly receded. She wanted to take his temperature. He shook his head.

"What's going to happen?" he muttered. "I'm going crazy, Hilda."

And now he told her, stammeringly, interrupted frequently by her questions, what had happened to him that morning and again just now—to Hilda's alarm, for she had seen people who were mentally ill. But he was speaking coherently now.

"Something has to happen," Becker muttered. "No one can bear this."

In the meantime he was obviously doing better. He allowed her to help him lie down and cover him, as she had done in the hospital.

"Yes, I'm sick," he said aloud. But he did not believe it. He knew it was something other than illness. He wanted Hilda to confirm that fact.

She said, "You need to rest, also a change of scene. You shouldn't read. I demand that you go out with me. You treat me very badly, Friedrich. I don't know Berlin at all."

He: "I'm not sick. I'm only worse for wear. I told you already on Sunday when we were talking about the war and the oath. The drafted soldiers, the young boys from the reserves; that frightens me, I see it over and over, the way they walk across the square and are driven off in trucks, and now they're dead. I know still more. I've saved things up inside me. Something within me has saved them up without my even knowing it, because it's like letters that were addressed to me but I didn't open. And because I didn't open them I'm now being punished. And in the meantime they've already gone to their deaths. And it's irrevocable. Don't contradict me, Hilda. There is no mercy. Inside me I know that. And inside me I can't bear it. And that's why I'm falling to pieces."

When she did not answer him (a vision of Bernhard, dead), he added with a mournful shake of his head, "I can only notice one bit of progress in comparison to before. I was a stone engulfed in flames, and when the fire went out, the stone was as cold as before. Now the flames have taken hold of me."

Hilda shook him. "Don't talk like that. This brooding doesn't do you any good."

"You'd prefer for me to be sick, wouldn't you?"

"Why?"

"Because I didn't brood then is why I'm in this state now. Had I done my duty, they would not have died and I would not have to look at them every hour. And if I had brooded and done my duty, I would not have ended up in the war."

How can I tear him away from these ghastly notions. He's making wonderful progress physically. If he wanted to, he could be a healthy man again in four weeks—and we could begin a new life.

Becker was smiling now. She kissed both his eyes. He thought, as he felt her lips: but it's gathered up inside me like this, the ongoing revolt inside me, that is grace in itself. Perhaps there is some salvation yet. And this feeling swelled up in him so strong that he moved his arms to pull Hilda to him.

What a wonderful accident, he mused, that this Hilda has appeared to me now. She is a woman—does she want to give me strength or to weaken me? Ah, how happy I am that she is beside me.

"In any case, Friedrich, I am staying here with you, whether you want me as your nurse or as Hilda. I have some things to do this evening, but before that you'll not get rid of me."

Afterward, as the three of them were drinking coffee in the living room, both women were struck by his anxiousness and something unnatural about him. His mother disappeared once into the kitchen. Hilda asked him what was wrong. He said he thought he was in great danger. She should not leave him.

425

"What is preoccupying you now?"

He gave no answer. He did not reveal to her that while they had been sitting there peacefully he had again been visited by the gruesome mocking laughter and the curses.

And then, back in his room, something new appeared: a plunging into hell, down from the ceiling and over the walls and right on over Hilda sitting next to him. Visions rained before his eyes whether opened or closed. When he opened them they lay transparent on top of the furniture. When he closed them they were so close that he was almost swallowed up in them himself. People, naked and clothed, plunging into hell. They clasped one another, fell, sank, spun about, hung from each other like a chain, link to link—the man with his mouth downward, the woman with her lips held up to him, one woman hanging from a man's foot while he vainly tried to bend down to her. They plummeted downward with the thousands of others. No end to it.

Then suddenly there was a tree standing there, beside which workers were shoveling leaves into a pit. The tree caught fire. It had a heart. And flames burst from the heart.

One terror after another.

The War's Over, Go Home

The working class of Berlin was in a state of alarm. Equipped with rifles, the workers and soldiers of all parties stood in their bars and taverns waiting to see how things would develop.

There were tens of thousands of them. They kept their machine guns hidden in cellars and sheds. There was no unified, central command. They were in contact with Party headquarters and the naval divisions. They had set up a system of guards in which women also participated.

Around noon they began explaining the situation in the barracks, storming in on the newly returned front-line soldiers with their black, white and red flags. Flyers, newspapers, speakers, everything was ready. The proud front-line troops under General Lequis, chosen by the high command to deliver a fatal blow to the capital, were put to a terrible test by the inhabitants of Berlin before they could strike that blow. They were not alerted in the name of any particular party. They weren't even called to revolution. The message repeated to them over and over was simple, the same thing they had said and thought themselves: the war's over, go home.

How quickly the imperial ribbons disappeared from their buttonholes. Between morning and evening what a transformation! Even though in fact little had changed, something had only come to the surface.

*   *   *

Standing at ease, the soldiers Imker and Bottrowski were posted at a school in Neukölln that served as a military dispatch center. Old Imker had joined others to set up an emergency first-aid center in Gesundbrunnen, and his wife had helped out. That day there was no dissension in the Imker family. The other members of the family had not known for days where Minna might be. Nor did they find out when all of a sudden she showed up at home again wearing men's clothes, as serious and silent as ever—only to disappear once more.

At the Reichs Chancellery on this first day of the return of the troops they could not shake the feeling that they were sitting on a powder keg. Ebert allowed himself one temper tantrum in the course of the day, when a report came in that the Executive Council had arbitarily had members of the Stinnes and Thyssen families arrested, the well-known industrialists. They were accused of counterrevolutionary activity. They were said to have been involved in Bloody Friday—which Ebert tossed aside as "a fantasy, a farce," and then he immediately had the Executive Council informed that for the thousandth time he forbade all such meddling in executive functions.

The hour for his telephone conversation with Kassel drew near. Ebert collected his thoughts. Was there anything he should reproach himself for? His speech that morning was blameless.

Groener responded with surprising amiability. It took some time before Ebert noticed the forced note in Groener's voice. Finally the general asked straight out whether Ebert had heard anything from the barracks. "Has Spartacus completely got the upper hand there now? I thought there were still some Social Democrats left in Berlin."

Ebert had to pass over the fact that his Party comrades had also participated in this battle for the souls of the front-line soldiers. Groener knew that already. He only wanted to hear whether Ebert admitted it openly. But Ebert did not. With a cold "Until tomorrow," Groener ended the conversation and left the people's deputy sitting there ashamed and annoyed.

Ebert had to don a cloak of trust-inspiring calm for the others. His Party comrades were busy telling one another, gloating, that the army had simply disintegrated like rotten wood. Ebert held his bug-eyes half downcast. He nodded calmly. They rejoiced in his strength.

Regentenstrasse near the Zoological Garden was quiet. Across from the home of Willy Finger, the banker, two civilians walked back and forth. One of these civilians leaned against a streetlamp in front of the house and smoked. These two detectives were watching the house, not because of Finger the banker, but because members of the government frequented the place.

Today, to be sure, no one from Wilhelmstrasse had shown up. But in their place that evening came several high-ranking officers, accompanied by some unknown civilians.

The banker Willy Finger came to meet his guests, moving down the soft carpeted corridor dressed in elegant clothes, a daffodil in his lapel, with a little potbelly despite his youth—really, he was an entirely different sort from his friend from the Wylinski Academy, the shadowy Finsterl. The new guests took in the discrete refinement of the rooms. Soft light from the ceiling illuminated the circular salon where they stood, officers and civilians. A butler and a maid served tea. They grouped themselves around tables. That their host, as everyone knew, stood on the best footing with the government did not prevent a young front-line officer, just returned home, from sitting down with these older gentlemen and saying what was on his mind.

"What was Ebert up to today? The man was really laying it on incredibly thick. Our army has not been defeated, all of you crowned with glory, etc."

The civilian: "Hush. You'll offend our host."

"Farthest thing from my mind. This is the first whipped cream I've seen in years. Well then, does the man mean that seriously or what? All that blarney."

"We shall all find out."

The officer: "At any rate that hit us like a brick, him with his victorious army. Would someone be kind enough to explain to me what all one needs to know in Berlin these days. You're aware, I'm sure"—he set his cup down and put his napkin to his mouth—"that all hell will break loose around here soon enough."

The civilian: "I hope so."

"One can, of course, find a man like Ebert charming, provided his intentions are honest. But then again, if not it makes no difference. The whole way here we got to know the German people. They're magnificent. The army has their utmost trust. They're unshakable."

The civilian: "Easy, my dear Günter. We're not at the casino."

"Well, it's quite pleasant here, too. When we've taken care of things in the next two weeks, I'll suggest our host be given the contract to supply the casinos."

"I'm crossing my fingers that you'll be proved right."

"I say two weeks. Perhaps eight days will suffice. My wife, whom I talked to on the phone this morning, insists on eight days."

The civilian: "And on what does she base her calculations."

"Her impression of the general mood. Now tell me, baron, is it not convincing proof of our chances that at the beginning of December, 1918, not a soul in the country dares speak of a German defeat?"

The civilian: "All in all, why should anyone speak of a German defeat? If you'll pardon the question."

The officer looked at him perplexed and then laughed so loud that his vis-à-vis held his hand to his mouth. The officer hiccupped, his napkin in his hand. "There, you see. Not a soul, just as I said."

The civilian: "All right. And you?"

Again a burst of laughter from the officer, who this time pressed his hand to his mouth.

At last he said, "I don't speak of it either. But nevertheless, as a military man I can't deny my training at the War Academy." He grew more serious. "Baron, how am I to interpret it? You have not all suddenly gone mad, have you? Or are you all so undernourished? Scurvy of the brain? The war has been lost, you know that—and we are still undefeated? How does that fit? The song my wife sang this morning on the phone sounded most peculiar as well."

"Until the end, we were on enemy soil and offered resistance. You know that better than I. Why look at me with such big eyes?"

The officer: "Because this is a new experience for me. Dear baron, when, in your opinion, can one then actually be sure whether one is victorious or has been defeated? How does one recognize it?"

The baron, his face pale, haggard, old, blinked a great deal; his expression was one of suspicion. "What exactly it is you're up to in all of this here on the first day of the return of the troops, I'm not exactly sure. Two months ago I would have made inquiries whether or not you belonged to the defeatists."

"Answer my question, please."

"Seems unimportant to me. I've no use for theory. If you really must know—we did not win, we were not defeated."

The officer: "By which you mean it was a draw. Don't make me laugh, baron. Because, you know, here I am sitting with you, and I ought to know what it was we did on the way home from the front. We ran—ran. It was retreat."

"Absolutely not. The return home of the front-line troops."

The officer: "And why did they return home, these fine lads? My God, simply because they could not stay where they were. And why couldn't they? I am in a position to give you an answer to that question, and with no theory involved. We could not hold out. We had no men anymore. The morale was bad. And on the other side they had everything we didn't have. Fresh troops, weapons, morale. That's why we threw in the towel. Just between the two of us. I can whisper a few more of my ideas, too. To delay is not to abandon. And 'just wait, soon you too . . .' But it could take a little while yet. But how does Ebert, then, get the idea of coming out there to greet us at the Brandenburg Gate, to soft-soap us with his undefeated, crowned-with-glory, etc.? Which in the first place is not true, and which, secondly, we didn't want to hear anyway—and most certainly not from him, and which I'm dead sure is of no

429

consequence to him either anyway. Quite the contrary. You see, that's the sort of thing that angers us. And that's the message he stands up there with now at the Brandenburg Gate in order to sugarcoat his republic for us. I'd ten times rather have Liebknecht than that. He says what he thinks, and we have an equally clear answer at the ready for him."

The baron tapped the officer on the arm and whispered, "Günter, the Socialists aren't all that bad. You would never have thought it possible at one time that you would be sitting in the home of a Socialist. Watch him, the fellow over there beside the floor lamp, the one who shook your hand when we came in. You have the wrong ideas about the Socialists nowadays. They're not revolutionaries. A lot of us are working with them."

The officer, who had just been given more tea and cake, shook his head. "I'll just sit here and drink my tea and eat my cake and not say another word, baron. I'm amazed."

An older officer came up to their table. Bald, sharp-featured, a monocle. They greeted him, he sat down with them.

He asked Günter, "Your men given good quarters? You'll have to make some inquiries. I've been hearing things from the barracks. Who's the Jew who greeted us so charmingly?"

The baron: "Financier. We were just speaking of him. Intimate connections with the government."

The new officer with the cynical face: "Crook? Profiteer? — ? Just my type."

The civilian: "The Socialists have a very healthy view of the current situation. They won't eat anyone. They're agreeable with anyone who will help put the economy back on its feet."

The new officer: "Learned something else new. It looks as if you're one of them. Enough to throw a man into a melancholy funk." He watched his host carefully. "Speaking of which, what do you think of the Jews, Günter?"

The baron: "For heaven's sake."

The bald-headed cynic with the monocle smiled, while their heads moved in closer together. "Seems to me it's time for a pogrom here in Berlin."

The baron gripped the arm of the cynic, who was not to be dissuaded and went on whispering with a smile. "The world has been divided up—we get the retreat, the Jews get the victory. All the way here I kept saying we should do something about the Jews. The times are ripe for it."

The officer who went by the name of Günter winked slyly.

The baron pleaded, "Gentlemen, enough!"

Standing beside the floor lamp, Finger, their host, was defending his view to a full-bearded, elderly gentleman who looked a bit shabby, but scholarly, that politics should employ more ethical methods. He, Finger, understood politics as the attempt to encourage both ethics and progress for the benefit of the state. The learned man found this an admirable view, especially coming from a banker. There was no concealing the great difficulties, however, that stood in the way of such an ethical approach to statecraft. For a government must deal with people, with their selfishness, their avarice, their passions.

One must understand that our good Finger, who was indeed interested in business and horses, had absolutely no interest in philosophy—but what was he supposed to say to this renowned old codger? Cheeky man that he was, he pulled his next comment from up his sleeve: The state must provide the good example, the politicans ought to have an eye for nothing except the general welfare, to be good human beings.

Very noble, the scholar confirmed, who doubtless had been invited only because of his great name and certainly not because of his shabby appearance. Finger was talking with him because he wanted to keep his distance from the officers. Noble, noble, the famous old man repeated, and thought of how his housekeeper tyrannized him and that indeed such a state was necessary to intervene in that instance.

But while his host looked about him uneasily a gentleman with a Napoleonic head (whom we recognize) approached. Motz, Brose-Zenk's friend, now the friend as well of the great Wylinski and therefore of Finger also. Delighted, the ethical banker brought Motz and his famous guest together and hurried off on fluttering wings.

Frivolous Motz did not know with whom he was talking. He immediately learned from the old man what the topic of conversation had been and without further ado he assumed the banker's arguments as his own.

"We need an ethical state. We need it like we need our daily bread. Because we are egotistical and ruled by terrible passions. Someone must be ethical."

The old man, who had no notion of what a rogue this was before him, was uncertain, and thought he had a serious case of Christianity on his hands. He explained the problem, amiably and carefully: world, nature, instinct and eternity.

"If one understands the world as a totality," he explained to Motz, "as a sensual and existential context affecting each individual soul, then one cannot help but view it as a religious concept. The soul remains independent, apart from it, retaining a sense of its own value. But man has long attempted to build bridges across that gulf. And indeed the state as an organized, collective power has found its place at that juncture and is more than a merely negative concept."

Motz pulled the old man, whom he liked tremendously, to one side to sharpen his mind on him. He was getting himself set for a major lark. But as they walked they were surprised by two events. First by a small table that had been placed there especially for them, and second by a pair of gentlemen who at once took them into their midst and with whom they had to sit down at the still wobbling table. Instead of hearing the splendid things the learned man had begun to tell him as they walked— concerning the Roman understanding of imperium, of a world government in which man found himself to be both a responsible and a punishable creature—Motz and the famous man were trapped by an upright Majority Socialist and a morose near-Spartacist who had met one another out on the street and who had not been able to stand each other for years. The Socialist sat on a finance committee. He started talking at once, as if there were nothing else in the world, about the immediate and systematic nationalization of the means of production, which, given Germany's social structures and the advanced state of its organization, could not be done without serious disruption—at least in his opinion. If, however, at this moment, with the war just ended, certain conditions should develop that might hinder this immediate and systematic nationalization . . ."

In contrast, the near-Spartacist, an elderly man with an oversized mouth, inside which he was working away at something with great interest, proved to be more sociable. He at least listened to the topic of conversation Motz and the learned man had brought along with them, but then stared grimly at the professor, in whom he recognized an adversary, and let fly with his own ideas: To enter into politics with ethical categories was a swindle that would no longer work nowadays. There was only one possibility for bringing politics and ethics into harmony, and that could be achieved by those policies that would liquidate the past and put themselves at the service of the historical task of the moment. Our Motz felt sorry for the professor as the sullen man rasped away at him. But he could not intervene. Because the mill of the Majority Socialist had already begun to grind away in the meantime. "Blood-drenched rubble, a new economic order, the end of all culture. A new enslavement of the masses must be prevented now. By all who work with their hands or their heads. In any case, even if the moment has not yet arrived, nonetheless . . ."

Their elegant host was moving off toward his study for a small business conference with the civilian who was addressed as "baron." They made rapid progress with the help of a first-rate cognac. Finger asked the baron about eventualities resulting from the troops' having marched into the city. The baron soothed his nervous host. To express his thanks, Finger, always trying to be helpful, inquired after the baron's family under the current economic circumstances, discreetly offering deliveries of oil and meat—with no fuss, of course—from house to house, from hand to hand so to speak. People must stand by one another after all—in an emergency we're all one big family.

In the bay of his study, by the way, hung a photograph of a young member of the government, with the dedication: "To my dear friend W.F." The financier felt it to be a great honor, but he did not show it to every visitor.

Troops Enter, the Second Day

New troops. Letters from returnees. Two gentlemen are skeptical of an unconditional demand. A specter from the spirit world proves to be quite a sociable fellow.

Troops Enter, the Second Day

It was not raining as on the day before. The new troops marched through the Zoological Garden in a wet fog. In the Kaiserallee there was still a kind of crowd lining the street, but the rows were thin. Here and there one met bands of children waving black, white and red flags.

The trumpeters blew, the drums rolled their old tattoo, the pipers tried to be cheerful. But it would not come to life.

The rows of buildings stood dark and shuttered. If now and then someone waved a handkerchief from a window it looked more like a leave-taking than a greeting.

Those marching in were: the German Rifle Division, the Guard Reserve Infantry, the Guard Reserve Rifles, the old Graf Yorck Rifle Battalion, the 1st Reserve Rifles, the 7th Rifle Battalion, the 24th Field Artillery.

They marched through the Brandenburg Gate to the tune of the Hohenfriedberg March. A fairly large crowd still occupied the Pariser Platz. The soldiers had no difficulty finding their way to the platform.

This time the second string of orators spoke. First a mild-looking man with a very wrinkled face appeared on the platform, small and unassuming, slightly bent, with a droopy moustache. It was People's Deputy Haase, a lawyer. The soldiers close to him heard him say: "We are no longer ruled by a military dictatorship. The senseless mass slaughter is over."

He pointed to the rosettes on the platform. This red was a symbol of human brotherhood. Out of the rubble a world of order and cooperation would arise, without oppression, without exploitation, without mass misery.

The soldiers discovered that these were the usual sugar plums that the simple, overworked man was unpacking and handing out.

434

Then he stepped back and made room for another man, from whom they heard some more words, the vice-mayor of the city of Berlin, Dr. Reike. They were told something about the "flame of gratitude," and that the Rifles had joined "history's host of heroes."

As the troops marched on down Unter den Linden, the boulevard teemed with sailors who grinned tauntingly. And as on the day before, they stood in front of the palace in defiant groups.

Three Letters

The letter of a returnee to his wife:

"We'll be in Berlin on Wednesday. We don't know where we'll be quartered. But I'm not going to try and fool you—I'm not coming home under any circumstances. You've made your decision already. There's no one else. Where was I supposed to find her? If you say I'm crazy with jealousy and you can prove you haven't been playing around, that's just fine, but it makes no difference. I can tell you straight out— you've cheated on me, and that's my honest feeling. You can't buy three new dresses and hats and shoes and smell like a whole perfume counter the way you did on my last leave without money coming from somewhere. And when your mother wrote me that she paid for it all, she did that because you told her to. So I'm telling you, don't expect me home and don't come looking for me.

My best wishes for the new life you've chosen."

A second letter:

"Elsa, you'll finally see me tomorrow evening, or at the latest sometime Thursday. I'm so glad that at last I'm getting back to a solid, orderly life. And I mean that in terms of both job and home life. The chance to have a bath and to see other people besides just soldiers is very enticing. They've all gone crazy and wild here to have a real woman with them again and to be able to do something else with their lives for once. I'm the same way. You know how straightforward I am about things and that I can sound a little crude now and again. Shall I draw you a picture? We're finished here today with the polishing up for tomorrow and they're all like a pack of hounds ready to head home. And I'll say it to you right out now, so that you won't get a shock, because your father and your brother are so patriotic (or were?)—I don't care if it was victory or defeat. We did our damned duty, paid our dues, and that's that. And they won't get me to do it again, and this much I can assure you: ninety-nine out of every hundred of my comrades feel the same.

"Even if we had won, Elsa, you can't imagine what that would have cost. The other side, too, of course. The whole thing is simply a barbaric outrage and a bloody mess, and you can pass on my humble opinion to your patriotic family right off so that they don't start blabbing at me about medals and greeting me like a hero.

"Everything's shot to hell for all of us. It will be a long time before peace comes. There are men here who have got their guns loaded for all sorts of people back home. They won't let people know what they're thinking, though, until they've taken off their uniforms. Does the pastor still visit your parents? Give him my greetings. I've had to dig graves for several dozen corpses with my own hands, and what they looked like I'll save to tell you later. We had to use a spade to scoop some of them up in pieces. Just dumb luck that I wasn't one of them. According to your pastor, God once said, "It's all good.' Dear Elsa, if that's good . . .

"I'll tell you all about everything, tomorrow I hope."

The letter of a girl who has followed her friend from the Rhine:
"And so now you're here. And with me trailing along. I was standing in Pariser Platz but couldn't see anything. I wanted to push my way through to see you, but it was completely impossible. When are you free? When will they discharge you? And what are you going to do then? Have you still not decided? I'm asking for my own sake as well. I don't know what you are to me, don't even know what you may come to mean to me—or could. I only sense that with each week you become more to me and I am starting to really love you. Do you think that's a good thing? Will you jilt me now that you know?

"P.S. I'll just add this. I tried the song you love so much the moment I arrived here at the pension, and I'm just aching to sing it for you, in whatever costume you want me to wear. What I want is to be there, to be there every moment, totally, not just have a piece of you now and then, a little affectionate one time perhaps, a little thoughtless the next, but to vibrate, all of me, totally, and to give myself to you.

"Am I being foolish? Ridiculous and romantic? I can hear you saying so. It doesn't matter. It wasn't you who told me, but I who told you right at the first that I found you "pretty nice." Do you remember what you said in Cologne. *"Tes idées, ma chère, sont un peu ridicules, mais parfois aussi—quoi donc?"* So now I'll be reasonable again. *Bonne nuit."*

Diagnoses

On the morning of the 11th, Becker was sitting in his room—everything having been nicely arranged by Hilda, who had come early—waiting for the doctor. He sat hunched over his desk, his back rounded, his head propped up, his eyes half shut, no energy in them.

"What are you thinking about, Friedrich?"

He: "What's the point of a doctor? Do you really think I'm ill?"

436

"Let the doctor come. Your mother wants him to."

"The doctor hasn't got anything for my sickness. If anyone does, you do, Hilda. How can I bring God to me when I cling to you so?"

She, astonished: "What did you say?"

He did not answer. She saw that there were tears in his eyes. He had been peculiarly gentle and fearful since yesterday.

Hilda briefed the doctor out in the corridor. He was a fat, elderly man who had long had a practice in the neighborhood and knew Becker. In answer to his question about what was the matter, Becker's mother told about Friedrich's visions, his anxiety. He claimed that he was to blame for the war. That put the doctor in a good mood. "Well then, we've finally got him, the archcriminal. Finally someone who admit's he's the one. Kurt Eisner claims we Prussians are guilty. At last a confession. How did he manage it?"

Hilda was not up to this joviality. She told him the little bit that she knew: Becker was seeing visions, the scenes kept repeating themselves, monotonously, they tormented him terribly. Becker said he had not at first known what the visions meant, but that now it had become clear to him he was guilty.

"Strange. That's all? And that is his only complaint?"

And the doctor wanted to involve Hilda in a political conversation, but she had already opened the door to the sick man's room.

Becker, who had had to submit to a great many doctors, behaved politely to the old family doctor as well. He did not let any of his thoughts be drawn out of him.

"Mental exhaustion, nothing serious," said the doctor once outside again. And he disclosed his personal opinion to Becker's mother. "People come back from the front and want to turn everything upside down, but there are others, like your son, who are wiser and probably a bit more sensitive too, they notice that there's not much that can be done and they grieve over it and then there's a collapse. Nervous breakdowns, dear Frau Becker, have become our daily bread."

On the stairs Hilda asked him again what they ought to think about these strange visions Becker was having—whether or not they were hallucinations. The doctor grumbled that they were not; they were obsessions, which explained the monotony, the repetition and the way they tormented him. What Becker thought these scenes meant was another matter entirely. But there were other reasons why these scenes appeared to him.

What Becker got out of this consultation was something to help him sleep and advice to find something to divert his thoughts, to amuse himself, to go out among people.

Krug, who came by to speak with Becker in the course of the morning, went to see his school director afterward.

He reported, "Dr. Becker has suddenly had a collapse. He looks ghastly, cries a lot. He has no thoughts either. The man belongs in a sanatorium. The women around him, his mother and a nurse, are not the right environment. The visit, I must say, has so distressed me that I've decided to devote considerable energy to looking after Becker, since these women continue to be so inexcusably blind."

"What is he like?" the director asked with interest, since he had taken a great liking to Becker.

"His thought processes are absolutely crazy, even though with Becker one always had to be prepared for most anything, as you know. Some of it sounds strange and is probably the result of the influence of the women. Becker, the most cheerful fellow you can imagine, wails and carries on with self-accusations. It used to be that he was more likely to find everything tip-top."

"Definitely the better philosophy."

Krug hesitated. "In any case he sometimes comes up with some striking notions. What would you say, for example, to the following remark? He was moaning and groaning again, and I suggested to him that he shouldn't exaggerate, that one simply should not spend time thinking about what ought to be true, but about what really is as well."

"Very true, very true."

"We scientists are concerned exclusively with what is, and for us it is always astounding, if not to say painful, to watch how people struggle with things they only imagine. So I said that to Becker. And to my surprise he said he agreed with me. His grief at having thoughtlessly taken part in the war (that is, you see, what he castigates himself for), was, for example, something that exists. To which I reply: everything he proposes, including his self-recrimination, is really a result of a certain critique and therefore, ultimately, of an imperative. And then he gave an answer that I still haven't digested really. It was so simple, so elementary. He said: the imperative exists too."

Krug looked at the director, who shook his head appreciatively. "A fine answer. A good remark. But, my dear Krug, then the man is not crazy after all."

"One can't conclude that from a single sentence. I know crazy people who can talk common sense for hours. But you're correct, the statement is remarkable. 'The imperative is a fact, too.' I accepted it, and said to him, fine, then he must go out into life with his imperative, that there was much to do now after the war. That was no news to him, he said, that really was what it was all about. But what position should one take, where did one find the guidelines. I suggested (you understand I don't speak candidly with him, for his mind simply isn't that healthy, after all)—I suggested it appeared that nature had left us in the lurch, but in fact she had left us our freedom, and that we were free to act. He could not see that. He stuck to his demand and went on looking for the higher authority that would show him the way, and of course he couldn't find that authority. I explained over and over: so now you have your imperative, then go to it, shoulder to the wheel, it will work out, you've got to get into the water if you want to swim. But he wouldn't bite. And now he's dug himself into a hole and grubs around in it—and he's gone crazy."

The director listened attentively and stroked both cheeks. "It is the categorical imperative, the absolute."

Krug: "He didn't use the term, but apparently that is what he meant. He once came up with the following proposition: it all depends on one's being completely in harmony with oneself. He criticized a phrase I used when I told him he had to get out of himself. That's precisely what he did not want to do, he said. One ought to go inside oneself. Dreadful to have to listen to things like that."

The director was nodding away, pleased with his own thoughts. "The imperative—how about that? The bare facts have become too much for people now. We men of the arts and philosophy are being given our due again."

Krug: "My dear Herr Director, this is not a joking matter. Explain to me what you mean by that."

The director: "He's splendid. You've brought him here to me as a gift. You wanted to tell me the case history of an illness and then out comes that statement which evidently impressed you a great deal. If Becker is ill, he reminds me of the oyster that produces a pearl from its sickness. That statement means, if one thinks the matter through, the collapse of the natural sciences and at long last the overdue rehabilitation of the arts and of philosophy."

Krug: "If the statement is true. Of course we have something like an imperative within us. But then there are mad notions and illusions inside us as well, you know."

"But that's another topic."

"Oh, have it your way, Herr Director. If you could see our Becker, then you would notice at once that all sorts of pathological factors play a role as well. To say it straight out: there's a Christian odor about his room. Self-recrimination, accusations. It has gone beyond the bounds of normality."

The director: "Christian? I don't believe it."

"The man is sick. He's had a nervous breakdown, but there's a macabre hue to the whole thing."

"It's because of the women, you think."

"Absolutely. Someone must go to him, someone must be concerned about him."

Maus stumbled unsuspecting into the troubled atmosphere of Becker's apartment. He had come to bring news from the war zone called Berlin. And the first thing he was confronted with upstairs—was Hilda. His heart stood still. He had not thought of her for days. She pulled him inside, gave him a sign to be quiet, and hung up his cap for him. She held his hand, looked into his face and whispered, "Aren't you a sight. Are you letting your beard grow?"

"I've been on the move a lot. And you're visiting Becker, Hilda? Is something wrong with him?"

She, tears in her eyes: "He has become very ill. Go to him, but don't let him notice anything."

Maus was shocked despite her warning. Becker was moving about his room bent over like an old man. He collided with Maus at the door. He had Maus take a seat. He himself sat down on his divan. His face revealed disgust, emptiness and bitterness.

As Hilda had directed him, Maus acted as if he noticed nothing, and began to talk. Tomorrow, or the day after, would prove decisive. Decisive in what way?

"In what the troops that have just arrived are going to do. We are working in the barracks."

"Ah, the troops," Becker said, as if he had just awakened. He had Maus tell him all about it once again, but apparently did not listen this time either.

"You've got things good, Maus. You're headed straight down your road, and what you're doing can only turn out well."

"And you?"

"They have placed too great a burden on my shoulders. Being ill in the hospital was the least of it. I was a rich man and now I'm poor. All my hopes have been dashed."

"Oh, come now, Becker."

"I carelessly let myself get caught up in a mad adventure. And it turned out badly for me. I often recall how we rode back in the troop train, the moon was shining, you lay on one bench, I on the other."

Maus: "Peace is never a gift."

"Isn't that the truth."

And Becker's eyes wandered off to one side. "There was someone else who spoke that night in the train."

"What do you mean, Becker."

But now Becker said no more, let his head hang down like a wilted flower. Maus went out on tiptoe. In the corridor he asked Hilda, "He looks like he's starving. Doesn't he eat?"

"What are you talking about? He eats well."

"Well, then you should call in a doctor."

"Maus, believe me, we have one. He says to wait."

"And this is just supposed to go on and on then?"

Meanwhile Becker was carrying on a conversation with that third person from the train. Even while Maus was in the room the other person had stepped out from the wall opposite him. Now he approached.

Becker did not dare raise his head for fear of driving the other man off. Their conversation went on for quite a while before Becker was even aware of it.

Then the other man, who flowed white over an armchair, suggested, "And the flies buzz into your room from the window and after a while you look for them at the mirror and on the ceiling and can't find them. They're lying on the floor. You can sweep them away."

"That's how it is," Becker answered.

"And the housekeeper takes them out with the dust and garbage. But it is the fate of plants and animals, of everything that dwells in the field, the forest, and the meadow. They may grow and they may die. The Lord, who created this world, has called them forth and given them this. You can watch them, observe their kind. The Lord speaks to you from many meadows. That you may know what you are and who you are not. That you may follow the true path, he places many things all about you."

"Which is why I am so desperate, because I see it all and it gives me no answer."

"You are a man of high, proud temper, you will accept no answer but one that makes you higher, prouder still. You have entered through the Gate of Dread and Despair. Your pride has led you along this path. You will not find the truth in any other way. When your body was in pain I said to you: Friedrich, go to your illness, bend down before it and say to it: The greetings of the Lord to you, most bitter of bitternesses, you shall be my sweet sister, you are full of grace."

"Who are you?"

"You see me."

"Johannes Tauler, is it you?"

"Yes, look at me, you are not dreaming. You see me, I am, and I am the bearer of a message to you. You were close to being extinguished, and I held fast to your soul and stood by your bed. You saw me, but you no longer remember that. I blessed you because I heard you wailing. You wailed: Only now do I begin to see, and I must go into the night. That is why I blessed you and saved you. Since then you have not grown weary of working in your vineyard. You have toiled there without help. Your strength wanes, my son."

"I feel it."

441

"But a man should imitate the vintner who labors the whole day in his vineyard. And although he has a great work before him, his custom is to rest for an hour from time to time and to eat something so that he may keep on working that much better. The nourishment enters into his bone and marrow, yes, into all his limbs, and is consumed over and over as he works. And then he eats and drinks something once again, alternating work, eating and rest till the whole task is done. This is the way of the pious man."

"I am not pious. Even when you speak the word God nothing stirs within me."

"I know. And what does that mean? Does God require the approval of your mouth in order to save you? Does he not see what speaks loudly inside you and what must remain silent? You throw great beams across your own path. You do yourself great violence."

"What shall I do? I will withstand all torment to find the right path."

"You have arrived, my son, at the gate that leads man to the high truth of God. You're harassing God. Ease off, my son. Commit no sin. God will not let his grace be torn from Him."

Tauler's hand was cool as it touched Becker's brow. His head sank to his chest.

He could still hear: "Revive, my son. Cast your cares upon the Lord. He will not forget you. He will not leave you in anxiety forever."

And as if struck by some magic blow, the tormented man lay down on his side and slept. Strengthened and calm, he arose a half hour later, saw that it was broad daylight, and knew that Maus had been there before.

He went into the living room and found all three of them together, his mother, Hilda and Maus. They saw at once that he was feeling better. Not that he had abandoned his limp, stooped posture. And there was still anxiety in his gaze. But he greeted Maus warmly, as if he had not spoken with him before. He sat down at the dining table, and they followed the doctor's instructions not to speak about his condition. When Maus said that today was the second day of troops marching into the city and that many people were worried, Becker asked, "Are you afraid, Mother?"

His mother laughed. "Not me. It's Hilda who has to take care. She has a long walk here, and your friend Maus has too."

With difficulty Maus forced himself to describe the troops as they marched in yesterday. But he had felt peculiar ever since he had been in Becker's room. Everything that he said now—although it was the same thing he had just been talking about and was very close to his heart— was thin, dull and empty. It was as though by his mere presence Becker deprived it of its value. Maus exerted himself, exaggerated, but things would not come into focus. He was angry, Becker depressed him. There was an invisible battle going on between them. Finally, at a sign from Becker's mother—Hilda stood up too—he broke off. The improvement that had pleased them so much was not real after all. Becker stared oddly ahead of him. His mother touched his arm, he did not move. Then Maus left the room, and Hilda accompanied him out into the hall as far as the door. There she cried on his shoulder. She did not notice his angry expression.

It had not been five minutes when the doorbell rang again. Maus was standing at the door, wild with rage, his face glowing. He stormed in. Hilda closed the door behind him without a word. Still wearing his hat, he pulled her to one side. "Where is he?"

"In the living room."

Maus pulled her by the arm into Becker's empty study. She grew pale. For God's sake what did he want, he was in a rage.

"You see where all this leads. It's the same with all of them, these intellectuals, they want to go their own way, and then afterward they go over the edge. I hope the whole lot of them goes crazy."

She raised her hands, but he would not let her speak. "Defend him. I know you will defend him. Why should you be on my side?"

He ground his teeth.

Hilda: "He's sick, Maus."

"I don't give a damn. Everything is on our shoulders, while these guys sit home by the fire."

"But he's sick, Maus."

"It disgusts me. I only came back to tell you how much it disgusts me. Today we're fighting against the reactionaries, but tomorrow it will be them"—he pointed toward the living room—"in their ivory towers."

"Go," she said hoarsely.

His face was distorted. He threw her a menacing glance and rushed out.

The Mysterious Brazilian

It was after lunch. Maus had gone, and Hilda could not stay either. Becker's mother was knitting at the window in his room. He had settled on the chaise longue and sat there all hunched up in himself.

He looked over toward his desk. Someone with a smooth, clever face was sitting there looking out the window, an elegant fellow dressed in black. His left hand moved across the green desktop as if he were playing a piano, but otherwise he showed no sign of impatience.

Becker was immersed for a long time in just watching him, and he noticed with increasing amazement how intelligent and attractive the man looked. His mother, there at the window, apparently didn't notice him. Was this perhaps another doctor? No, because in that case his mother would be sitting with him. He was also too refined, too affable for that. Now he made a little movement with his head and looked into Becker's eyes, warm and deep. Would he speak? He showed no sign of doing so. Becker began.

"Whoever you are, sir, I'm happy to see you. You're welcome here."

The man thanked him with a nod. His eyes shone with fire. He had something Latin American about him: his skin had a yellowish tint, his hair was dark black and lay smooth against his skull, and on his upper lip—he had full, pouting lips—there was a small moustache. He spoke with a foreign accent with a guttural sound to it. "My visit to you was delayed. It's not for you to express your good wishes to me, but rather I must apologize that I have not looked in on you before this and introduced myself."

And he gave a lengthy, unintelligible name, at the same time bowing and closing his eyes as if letting a little swallow of something glide down his throat. Becker felt at once that there was a greater sympathy between himself and this gentleman than between the old man named Tauler and himself. He therefore expressed his pleasure once again at meeting the man.

"I was especially interested," the visitor said, "in the position you advanced of late concerning the question of guilt for the war and your own personal responsibility. You have caused something of a sensation in the spirit world. You have probably heard about that."

Becker was surprised that he had now entered into the spirit world, or so it seemed, and that the sort of life found there had something scientific about it. His nods, however, did not favorably impress the man, who asked suspiciously, "Has someone from the other side approached you already perhaps? Well, be that as it may, we'll leave it aside. You are much too independent a man to let yourself be influenced by praise or censure. You let reason and logic speak. That's what drew me to you, like a mouse to the smell of bacon. You insist on being your self. Self with a capital *s*."

Becker: "You said 'mouse.' Did you choose that word intentionally? I have a friend, you see, with almost the same name."

"Mouse? That is interesting. Is he too drawn by the smell of bacon?"

They laughed. Becker: "I know nothing about that, but it's not out of the question. Maus is a friendly fellow and partly to blame that I . . . ."

He got no further. The man tried to help him. "I beg your pardon?"

444

Becker: "By his constant urgings that I do something, he got me so upset that finally I . . ."

He got stuck again. The gentleman: "What is it, please?"

Becker whispered, "That I ended up in this condition. He gave me a light push in this direction. In point of fact, after the war in which I participated I wanted to do something, anything, to make up for what had happened and to see to it that neither I nor others would ever again run so blindly to our doom. Yes, I felt I was guilty, at least partly to blame for the war. That sense of responsibility weighed terribly on me."

The gentleman laughed heartily. "The mood of penitence, one might say. Have I hit the nail on the head?"

"That's it precisely. Only I could not make things as if the war had not happened. But neither could I simply yield myself to the latest slogans they started battering me with right off. I had to test them. And then, and then . . ."

The man waited. "And then? Your report interests me. Thrilling, touching, this path of a human soul."

Becker: "And it just didn't work. Because who was going to give me the orders? So I began to search, to test myself and to look for some fixed point inside me. And that's where I got all tangled up. I couldn't get back out again. I tried. But my ego would not yield anything. It seemed rather unfruitful."

"Well, you can only be grateful to your friend Maus that he got you upset. As a defensive measure, in your struggle against the easy slogans of the present, you drew into your ego. You didn't want to say anything derogatory, I hope, by using the expression 'this condition' for the situation in which you find yourself?"

Becker: "I beg your pardon. I feel rather unsure of myself, I hope I haven't offended you—it has to do with my mother. I feel unsure because—my mother sitting there doesn't see you."

"Your mother! That shouldn't disturb you. Why should she see me? To what end? I have nothing to say to her, except perhaps to greet her. At any rate you see me. I am here, I am really here. And I was here before, too, but you ignored me. But let us not get caught up in incidentals. You are working on your self, on your ego, and I would like to inquire what progress you are making at this work."

Becker: "I am happy to be at your service. But I would not like, if we are going to use the term 'ego,' to earn the reputation of an egoist. I hope that my point of departure, which you know, will protect me from any misinterpretations."

"Definitely. You are a man of responsibility. You are skepticism personified. You let nothing pass that cannot stand your test. Your painful experiences during the war have more than enlightened you. You are busy hermetically sealing up your ego, your inner self. As a result several interesting things are happening, and it is on their account that I would like to flatter you. You not only reject all traditional views, but every bit of traditional wisdom, facts, even the whole of nature. The way you dismiss them with an easy wave of the hand arouses my admiration. It is splendid. You do not, as far as I know, doubt the existence of nature as such—or have you recently come to consider that too an illusion, a specter?"

Becker, uncertainly: "That—no."

The visitor: "I thought not. You merely turn it away, ban it to stay within its own limits. You measure it against the requirements of your ego. Just as when you were in the hospital at war's end you already had the newspapers burned that were lying about your room—by which you actually meant to burn the facts that the newspapers contained."

"You've got things absolutely correct," Becker admitted.

The man smiled affably. "I hope that doesn't surprise you. I also know the story of your second birth, you see. That was, if I may be truthful with you, the moment when I first took notice of you. You would not accept the date on your official birth certificate as your birthday, and with it some accidental genetic heritage, but rather you sought out a point of origin, the beginning of your consciousness, your ego. Whatever lay before that didn't count. And you have progressed down that road with ironclad consistency, without anyone's being able to say that you have already reached the end of that road."

Becker felt that he was confronted by some superior creature. The man began to play on the desktop again as if it were a piano. He is a handsome man, Becker thought, I can't remember ever having met anyone like him, only he's nervous, has something dogmatic about him, he's keeping something from me. I would like to help him.

And so he said, "There are, if I am not mistaken, several points of contact between you and me. It seems to me that you have already preceded me down the road I'm taking. If I might make a request, then it would be for you to tell me about it. It would be truly profitable for me."

Becker had not foreseen what a deep impression this polite remark would have on the man. He grimaced painfully, threw his head back bitterly, his whole being grew darker and Becker feared he would completely vanish before him. But the man sat back up straight again, he grew more distinct. He bent his upper body forward, both hands grasped his left knee, which he had crossed over his right. "We shall disregard private, personal matters. When I have the opportunity to speak with an important personage like yourself, I am not eager to talk about my own small miseries, although something of the sort has indeed touched my life. But then whom has it not? You are developing a special radicalism. And that's your attraction. You would literally climb over dead

446

bodies—and, if it were necessary, you'll forgive me, over your own. I'm not joking. I am preoccupied with two areas of inquiry. First the place of man within nature. I am not doing you an injustice, I hope, when I regard you as a human being. Some explanation from you would in any case make me very happy."

And as he said this, the man, having taken his hands from his knee and with a tender smile on his lips, began to make little enticing gestures as if he wanted to encourage Becker to approach him or to come out of himself. What was Becker supposed to think of this?

"Of course I'm a human being," he answered.

"Indeed you are," the other replied with satisfaction. "Of course it is the proper designation. And with that admission you do credit to your sense of justice. So we will hold to that. You are a human being, you have decided to be one, a human being within nature, within the temporal world. What is your ego going to do now with this human being, what do you plan for him? Do you intend to play the ascetic, mortify the flesh, or just the opposite? Please, please," he cajoled as Becker hesitated, "no need to be coy here. We're both playing open and aboveboard."

"It's not my intention to withhold my opinions from you," said Becker somewhat offended. "My thoughts about a great many things are simply not clear yet. I do not feel my present state to be a good one."

"You don't say. I would hope it is not because you have overtaxed yourself with scientific thinking. Does my conversation tax you?"

"Not at all."

"I think not either. To be clear and decisive, to answer questions, always has a relaxing effect. Would you believe me if I said that many emotional problems are only the result of a lack of clarity, of indecisiveness. People let things take their course, out of indecisiveness they don't grapple with them, and then they get all tangled up and the internal emergency is there. So then, you are not clear yourself what you should do with your human being. Then I have come at precisely the right moment and can lend you a hand. Let us take as our starting point that you refuse to be towed along by the accidental facts of current events. You have declared that under no circumstances would you accommodate yourself to the slogans of the day. You can, you must, seek the basis of your action within yourself. You are in charge of time, not time of you."

"That is precisely my opinion," Becker asserted.

"Excellent, bravo. It is the ticket to our world. You have at once found yourself the right springboard to us. Now the question is: how far do you wish to jump? The first thing to notice is that you are free only in a negative sense, until now. Freedom, however, means power. And what power is at issue here? How do you use the freedom you have achieved?"

Becker was following very attentively. "I would indeed be grateful for any hints."

The man spread his arms in delight. "There we have it. You will sense at once that I come to you like a physician."

"Just a while ago I thought you actually were one."

"You see, your feelings did not deceive you. Now, a secondary question: I was not proceeding too hastily, was I, when I concluded that you are free, but at first only in a negative sense, that you are independent, while real freedom means power? Perhaps our opinions are not quite congruent after all. Perhaps you mean by your freedom, death, obliteration, self-destruction. An end to the ego?"

"No. That is the last thing I want."

The gentleman smiled in agreement. "So then let us move on quickly. It would also be very odd if you've taken such trouble to prepare a clean specimen of your ego, your self, separated it out from the world, only then to destroy it afterward. What I mean then is: an independent life, life lived by your own grace. You direct matters yourself. And now, how shall we proceed? We come at once to a most interesting point. You feel yourself to be a human being among other human beings, in a herd of human beings. You become free when you are not among them, but over them, that is, when you rule over them. You do with them what your ego wants. You let them dance to your tune. You extract from them the things that make you stronger and stronger. That is what is called politics."

Becker was silent.

The man waited. He nodded his head sympathetically. "You're not going to bite. There is no impulse there. Perfectly understandable. A person must be born to that. I only presented the idea to you. One should not, however, reject it out of hand. It has its rewards. One must, I'll grant, watch carefully not to lose one's balance. But there is still another possibility for dealing with one's human being. It ought to be more to your liking."

He pointed to the window. His mother sat there quietly knitting, wrapped in a heavy blue woolen shawl. From time to time she would throw a glance at the sofa where her son was seated, his arms crossed. He wore a thoughtful expression, sometimes a smile played at his lips. His mother was sad, but convinced deep within herself that he was not as sick as Hilda thought.

"Take a look," the man whispered confidentially, "at the lady there at the window. Your dear mother. She is knitting, a feminine activity. You have tender feelings for her. Those feeling come from nature. You recognize yourself as a human being in those feelings, one who comes from nature, from the world of animals and plants. Every monkey knows the same attachment. One can even understand 'attachment' literally—

the monkey hangs onto its mother, at her neck, the mother provides him her protection. If you were to upend the treasure chest of your soul you would stumble across a great many such emotions. Just think, for example, of feelings of love for certain female persons—whereby it is completely immaterial whether you indentify one-hundred percent with such feelings. That would then be another sphere for your human being. Perhaps we can let your ego go for a stroll in these regions, tasting these possibilities."

"I feel I must interrupt," said Becker, "and I beg you not to think me impolite. You appear to be hinting as pleasures, love affairs and so on. That would indeed be a peculiar way to help oneself in one's inmost distress, to cleanse one's ego by throwing oneself into the vortex of pleasure. How can an ego survive that without being sullied and humiliated."

"Humiliated. What strange notions you have. You won't give up. Your ego, when taking its pleasure, is still a part of nature's stew. You are the one who grabs for it, you are your arms and your mouth. And ultimately it is you who senses lust. Sullied—that borders on lèse majesté. Are you dirty, is the world dirty, are your values those of an ascetic? You said no just now. Why then, since you are a human being and nature offers it to you, do you not want to deal with the world like a baker kneading his dough or like a man driving a coach. An incredible number of things go on in this world, and the rewards are great. You can dive into it like a skilled swimmer. What a roiling and flowing, a roiling and tumbling there is there, so that one can hardly decide what one would rather do: hold one's ears tight or sing hymns. Time roars and seethes. Look at this earth, how everything tumbles together, rolls up in itself. The grass grows on the meadow, the cow eats the grass, the human being drinks the cow's milk, and the human being falls and fertilizes the soil. Are you not lured by the thought of throwing yourself into that tumbling world, openly, consciously, without second thoughts, without sadness and melancholy? Yes it is time that roars. Don't forget that you are a human being for only a short time. The dance does not last long. You must accept that tumbling as a bit of eternity granted to you. Who knows what becomes of your ego afterward. You must live so that you can say: the world was mine and I was truly a human being."

Again the man made peculiar, undulating, enticing gestures with his fingers. His lips had now pouted out lustfully. A flush had now mixed in with the yellow of his cheeks. And as his dark, moist eyes shimmered, Becker felt himself deeply moved and excited.

The man stood up and walked along the bookcase.

"You have collected all these minds that thought and sang. Who can speak and sing and not speak and sing of this deep, wonderful and limitless life? For Sophocles it is mourning—but those mourning, weeping and keening human beings are clad in beauty. And when they go to the grave they reach out their hands to us trying to live again, to go on breathing. The gods have set themselves up over man—and what do the gods want? To live, to live forever, this life. You need not fear for your ego. What exists here can only win. It cannot be gnawed upon by time."

Becker was deeply stirred, strangely attracted and yet depressed at the same time. He heard himself speaking.

"You have shown me a splendid, an enchanting path. But you overestimate me. Who am I after all? You forget that the human being, this ego sitting across from you, is a teacher at an academy, Friedrich Becker, doctor of philology, a minor pedagogical civil servant of the city of Berlin, and suffers moreover from a wound he got in the war."

The man suggested offhandedly, "All familiar facts to me. You were hit by an exploding grenade, the lower spine, the healing is almost complete, the paralysis was only temporary. You will shortly be on your feet again. And then you will take whatever actions are necessary as a result of the war, sum it all up for yourself. You will no longer recognize either precept or prohibition. No government will ever again dare send you your mobilization orders. You will be your own possibilities. You have grown hard and unscrupulous. I see you in many shapes. Do not make yourself a smaller man than you are, do not be afraid. One can be much less than a teacher and still achieve power, pleasure, true existence."

Becker stared at him. Whatever it was that the man at the bookcase went on saying, he heard it only in fragments. Then he heard his own rebuttal. "Explain to me once more, please, what my ego wins if it wins power and pleasure. Why does it do that? Who is served by it?"

"Yourself, always yourself. Who else? And who is supposed to be served by it? Why serve? You are free. You are lord. Humble before no one.

"Have you not wandered about lost and served strange gods long enough? Were there not patriotic questions, moral questions, social and political questions enough? You are you—and not the daily news that commands you about. With this brightness you have torn asunder the clouds that engulf you and have gazed into the spirit world. That is why you and not your mother can hear me. You are expecting me to give you advice about what you should do with your ego. My answer to you is: dare, dare, dare. Be cold, clench your teeth. Move ahead through it all."

The gentleman approached him with soft, slow steps. He moved with a hovering, gliding ease, like a boat driven by the wind, and came directly up to Becker, who was afraid and stood up. It seemed as if the man would run right over him. But he stopped, one step in front of him, and there they stood face to face, each face drawing closer to the other as to a mirror.

Becker opened his eyes wide, overcome by the sight of this fresh Latin face with the sparkling eyes, their whites plainly visible, deeply touched by the enigmatic ways of this strange visitor. The man's upper lip twitched, he smiled ironically. "At the moment I can offer you nothing more. Surely you don't demand that I should command your ego. That would be a contradiction. And so what do you say? Quick now."

But at that the gentleman, passing a hand over his temples, had suddenly taken up his gliding motion again. He rolled back to the bookcase and then back again to Becker. At the last moment he realized what it was in this face that had been so enigmatic. It was—his own face.

The stranger glided over him, into him, suffocating him. Becker screamed, overwhelmed by dread, and fell backward onto the sofa.

His mother came over to him. She had great difficulty getting him up again. She felt something moist at the back of his head, and when she looked she saw blood. He had hit his head against the wall as he fell.

Hilda came about half an hour later. Becker was conscious. She dressed the wound and tried in vain to find out what had actually happened.

The Lion

A second conversation with an ambassador from the spirit world.

As Hilda bandaged Becker's head wound—he did not answer her—
she assumed he had suffered a convulsion. She suggested this idea to the
doctor, who came soon after she did. He considered it possible that there
was some inflammation of the brain connected with his war wound.
Perhaps the hallucinations were connected with it as well. The doctor
now ordered complete bed rest, a light diet and frequent taking of his
temperature. Hilda (his mother too) felt very much better now that this
terrible affliction had been placed on a palpable, physical basis. But after
seeing the doctor off with many thanks, as she went back in to Becker
and he stared at her so gloomily and gravely from his sofa, her courage
failed her again. Becker spoke reasonably as if nothing had happened. He
made an effort to joke with her. His mother left him to Hilda.

With complete clarity, with profound alarm, she saw a man before
her who, apart from these strange hallucinations, was in total possession
of his senses. What he now told her about these visions and images in a
calm tone of voice made her shudder. Hilda was a believing Catholic. In
the midst of what he was telling her, she thought of what she had heard
of Satan. A cold shiver ran over her. Becker lay there pale, and apparently
knew nothing of what had happened to him. This was an attempt to
steal his soul. He had been a refined, playful guest—but now he appeared
in a malevolent, cadaverous light.

She had him tell her (he still remained calm, his thoughts collected) about this latest vision once again. He remembered it in precise
detail. As he came to its awful conclusion, he shut his eyes. He did not
speak of an "illusion" but called it "the vision," and once he even said
"the spirit."

"Well," Becker said in his coolest voice, "if you insist on it, Hilda,
I'll admit that I am suffering from simple hallucinations. You will allow
me to add, however, that I carried on a completely serious, businesslike
conversation with my guest. The stranger was my superior in logic and

452

eloquence. He looked like a Latin American, with a touch of Indian blood. I admit that afterward, as he approached me, he reminded me, I can't say in just what way, of myself."

"But for God's sake, Friedrich, he was not here, not at all! Your mother was sitting there beside you in the room. She had let no one in."

"Why certainly, Hilda. He did not come through the door. He has no need of such things. He told me his name, I heard it quite clearly. He is a member of the spirit world."

"Friedrich, what is that supposed to mean? Spirit world? Are you talking about spiritualism?"

"Spiritualism? I hadn't even thought of that. That's true, the spiritualists talk about spirits, but those are usually the dead who give some sign when you call them, aren't they? Do they talk with you the way he did with me? I don't think so."

"It wasn't a spirit, Friedrich. I beg you. You must listen to me."

She took him coaxingly by the shoulders. But he freed himself from her with a jerk and sat up. She was dismayed. He apologized. For a long while they did not speak. There had not been such tension between them prior to this. When they began to speak again he was friendlier, but remained somehow curiously reserved.

She did not refer to the unfortunate topic. She began to coax him again. Something was driving Hilda today to be tender, intimate and, most of all, passionate with him. She felt it as some eerie urge, as a compulsion. It must come from some star. She sat down next to him and he smiled as she did so. He let her embrace him. How easily he changed. She felt happy beside him. She felt the play of his breath on her brow. He put his arms around her and whispered, "Hilda, it will all go away. I'm certain. I'll be well again. It was all nonsense, nonsense." But the minute he uttered that word something he did not understand blared in his ears. He begged Hilda, "Hold my ears closed, tight, both of them, please."

She glowed. Here was the man she loved sitting beside her. The devil wanted to steal him. She was recovering this prize catch from the devil.

She noticed only too quickly what was happening. He lay limp in her arms. When she looked into his face she saw everything. The same as before. In answer to her question of what was wrong, he muttered, "Nothing."

She pulled away from him. He did not move. It was uncanny. And as she saw him like that, pure desperation swept over her and she ran to the window and wept. When she returned, he had sat down at his desk and was brooding. He did not notice her. She took a chair, sat across from him and waited patiently. He said softly, without looking up, "Please, Hilda, turn on the light!"

Why did he want light when it was still bright enough. She

watched him. His hand slid across the desktop to her. He sighed, "How far apart we are."

"That's not true, Friedrich. Why do you say things like that to me?"

But he was no longer looking at her now. She was no longer there. He thought and thought.

So he sat and waited for Hilda to go away. He watched her though his fingers.

Now he laid his head on the desk, for it suddenly seemed to him as if the room were pulsing, growing dark and then bright again. Hilda apparently did not notice this. He heard her stand up. Could she find her way about the room? She moved out of the study and quickly closed the door behind her. Then he raised his head, it was bright again. At that moment his mother came in, got him to lie down on the sofa, and together with Hilda made a large moist compress. He lay there peacefully under the cooling wetpack. When he stated that he wanted to sleep, the women were content and left. He listened. After a few minutes his mother looked in again. Yes, he was sleeping. He heard them whispering in the hall. The women were getting ready to go out. Now the front door was opened softly. He listened, they were descending the stairs.

In a second Becker sat up, tore the compress from his head and threw it on the chair. He went through all the rooms to convince himself that he was alone. Slowly he went back to his study, his "laboratory," and closed the door loudly and tight behind him. He sat down on the divan, a blanket over his knees, and waited.

He sat there tense. He waited for "that man" to come. He wanted to speak to "that man." There were urgent questions pressing upon him. But "that man" did not come.

Then Becker began to walk about the room, whispering and gesticulating, calling "that man" to account.

There has been talk here of science, of a spirit world into which I should enter. I was informed of this. It was said my thoughts were causing a stir. Well then, I must demand that a bit more consideration be shown me and that the lines of communication remain open. One aborted conversation cannot produce results. There is no sense in simply broaching a subject and then ever so preemptorily dispensing with explanations. I have the feeling that I am being toyed with.

Who is it that is confronting me? With whom do I have the pleasure of speaking? I didn't catch the name. What are your thoughts about my situation now that you have heard me, you who are invisible at the moment and pretend to have orders to correspond with me. Those questions you broached continue as before to occupy my thoughts. We must come to some conclusion. For decades I've been traveling paths leading all around my ego, preventing me from doing my duty. Finally, as a result of an officially authorized mass murder lasting four years, the meaninglessness of my previous mode of life has become apparent to me. What now? What now? That is the question. A simple critique is of no use. The path—there's the rub, there's the crux of the matter. I am proud that I have retreated into my ego. But it is fearfully silent, this ego of mine. Is it the veiled statue of Sais? Why doesn't someone help me? The situation is clear after all.

He stood there at the window, arms crossed, and looked back into the room, toward the door. Nothing stirred.

I have a suspicion that I've not broken through to my ego at all yet. I must still do that, and someone wants to use this ambiguous transitional phase for his own dark purposes. Someone wants to throw himself across my path because he's afraid of me. What are you doing, sir, you who are hiding from me? You reach out to me, tantalize me, and you call that a scientific discussion. Why be such a coward, why not come forward? He marched stormily about the room, around his desk, along the bookcase. He picked up the chair the anonymous gentleman had sat in. The chair was easy to lift. Becker examined it from all sides. He isn't there. He let the chair fall hard to the floor. There, please, now come here.

And as Becker moved grimly toward the corner where his library was—the man, the Brazilian, strode softly past him.

Fear crept over Becker because the man was moving so treacherously softly. He had challenged him. Did he have some evil intent or did he just want to slip away? Becker could not say for sure whether it had in fact been the same man, but he observed now that he was moving toward the desk. Becker stood there immobile against the wall, his head lowered. His heart beat, the blood pounded in his ears. Where did this ridiculous anger come from? It took his breath away. He turned his head to the desk with a jerk.

The whole room had grown dark again and was filled with a thin bluish smoke. At certain points, at the window and on the ceiling, the fog balled up into little clouds. But from where the chair stood at the desk came a scatching and a rustling. The chair was pushed to one side and along the carpet runner was stretched a powerful yellow animal that pushed the wastebasket over. And then it lifted its huge head, its mane billowing around it, and revealed the terrifying face of a lion.

Before Becker could let out a scream, the lion had shaken its mane and thrown the man a glance that struck him dumb.

"Why do I frighten you today?" the lion asked. "When I sat in your chair you greeted me with the courtesy befitting an educated man, with a heartiness in fact that made me feel very good. You bade me welcome. We had a rather extended conversation."

"I know," Becker said hoarsely.

"I did most of the talking, it's true, but your interest was obvious. Now you call me, urge me to come, and then you break the simplest rules of etiquette. You act as if you don't know me."

Becker, both hands behind him against the wall, stammered, "On the contrary, I'm glad to see you. I was expecting you. I didn't know it was you. Please forgive me."

The lion laughed. "A philosopher should not say that he doesn't know or recognize a person, you know. You don't expect me always to wear the same coat do you, for I bounce around the world such a lot, gathering information, listening, talking. One has to dress as circumstances demand."

And he stretched himself comfortably and grunted, "I would like to suggest that we use the informal second-person pronoun. It will simplify our relationship. It gets us away from a certain formality."

"Please do!" Becker said in a hoarse whisper.

The lion growled once more. "And you end up gaining something, too, since I'll credit your initial bad manners to the account of friendship."

Then he laid his massive head between his forelegs, closed his eyes and breathed slowly and audibly. Becker waited for what might develop. Perhaps he would fall asleep, perhaps disappear. It took a while, but then he heard the lion speak.

"I have come as a lion, you see, so that you may be in no doubt about two things: first about my power, and second about the fate that awaits you if there should be differences of opinion between us."

And he laughed with a roar, so that Becker feared it might be heard in the apartment upstairs, that people would know about his visitor.

The lion: "I'm very candid, am I not? But why not be when people are friends."

Becker: "Shall we not get down to brass tacks?"

"Please."

But neither of the two began.

Finally the lion said, "Have you made a decision then?"

Becker: "I have not decided."

The lion: "Good things take time. But it cannot go on like this too much longer. I recently warned you about indecisiveness. I advised you to hold on to what you have with both hands. You are on the point of bringing mental illness upon yourself if you remain so unclear about things for much longer."

"You must understand why I hesitate."

The lion shook its head violently. He hit the floor with his tail, sending the wastebasket rolling, spilling its contents. "Don't be a fool. Always this profundity as a pretext. Your reason is good for something besides brooding. It has been generally noted in the spirit world how

456

you have developed. But to be frank—if you call the tune you must pay the piper. If you cancel out your whole hollow existence and, as a reasonable man, draw back into yourself and examine the whole thing in terms of yourself, then you need not fear the consequences. That means advancing with an iron will. It is ultimately the firmest podium a man can stand upon, and what more can a man want. You fling your ego, your will, at the whole caboodle of facts, the inanity of which you've long since recognized. And then when doom bursts upon this so-called world at least there's one man who does not go running after it, at least one man who's not concerned with what that doom may be called, but with what he is called. You're on the right path, my son, of that you can be sure. Look at me. I am a spirit and I move through this world in whatever costume I choose. I move in where I think it might be fun, and in whatever way I like. It's up to you to have the same thing."

"You were a human being too?"

"Yes sir. A human being too. I can be one again, too, if I choose. Who and what could hinder me? Who is above me?"

"There is no one above you, you say?"

"I beg your pardon."

"I merely thought . . ."

"Are you harboring some suspicion or other? Is there a Polly Pious hanging around you hoping to persuade you of something? That would really set you down a splendid path."

He laughed fiercely.

"No one influences me."

"That's the right way. I like my heroes proud. Then you'll follow me and not make difficulties. You're rather slow at being persuaded. You'll hesitate so long you'll go completely mad. And we're not interested in madmen. Kind sir, the coach has pulled up. Climb aboard. It is your very own carriage."

"Where will it take me?"

"Wherever you command, Herr Becker, Friedrich Becker, doctor of philology, doctor of the highest wisdom. *En avant.* Cast your Friedrich and your Becker aside. You are more. You have seen where it got you being Friedrich and Becker. Dare the leap into the spirit world. You are free, there are no laws over you. Who will dare give you orders. Come, join me in learning what existence is."

"What is it?"

The lion fixed him with its yellow, blinking eyes.

"There is a ladder of life. At the bottom are the heaviest things, at the top the lightest. We'll race right up it. We are the lightest and fleetest, we are spirits, we surpass electricity."

"What can we do?"

"We take everything in our hands, we can weigh things and puff them away. You can lie as a lion on the savanna, speed through the brush as an antelope, chirp as a grasshopper, stand as reeds at lake's edge and sigh in the wind. The world stands open to you, there are no limits to your freedom of movement. There is no limit within you, none set over you. Only your self. The existence of the free, the powerful. Our existence burns and glows like fire."

"Are you fire?"

"Mostly fire. For we are power."

The yellow eyes were directed at Becker, who still stood against the wall, but had now let his arms fall.

The voice repeated, "The coach has pulled up, sir."

"Why take the journey?" asked Becker.

"Why take any journey?" the voice answered.

"I beg you not to misunderstand me."

"There is no question here of being misunderstood."

And then the lion stood up on its forelegs, the giant head rose high, the animal sat down. Becker watched terror approach and was afraid. But the fear subsided. He flinched as the animal stood up on all fours in the blue fog, taking the whole desk with him atop his back. It fell off to one side with a loud crash.

Becker thought of his whole life, his mother, of all he suffered in the hospital, how the draftees had stood at the street corner and were then herded into wagons, he thought of Hilda and Maus, and said, "That is not my ego. What you suggest is not what I mean. Not that. I will not be coerced. You can do no more than kill me. You recently employed a nasty method for terminating our conversation. If you are an honest creature, you'll come clean and tell me what game is actually being played there in your spirit world. What were you telling me about flames? You spread your jaws. Are you going to devour me?"

"You have dared to venture out onto this path and must take into the bargain whatever happens to you. I will show you the ego that you seek, the pure, free, unbounded ego."

"You come from a peculiar sort of spirit world. You don't think logically."

"We're up to tricks, is that it?"

"You want to sell me something I don't want. I wanted to get at myself, yes, at my free ego in order not to lapse into guilt again. I sought that precedent, that point, that hard and bright point within me that would let me know what I must do and what I must not. I could not find that point in nature. And in its stead you offer me a coach to climb into and want me to join you in an excursion to some fiery, enchanted land. That's not what we were talking about."

"What were we talking about then?"

"You see how biased you are, that one cannot discuss things with you? Why are you growling so? Why are you coming closer? The room is small enough as it is. I cannot crawl behind the wall and I don't want to open the door."

"That would be of no use to you either. You cannot escape me. What were we talking about, sir?"

Becker hesitated. He did not know how to formulate it all more clearly. But it seemed that he did not want to understand in the least, that he wanted something else. Becker was determined to risk everything.

Then it seemed to him that someone was approaching him from behind. The lion, too, must have noticed it. He had pulled back and was crouching there in the middle of the room. It could be out of fear, or as a preparation for the leap. With a savage, tense stare the beast watched Becker, but at the same time whatever was behind him as well.

This new voice that Becker now heard from behind his head was one he recognized. Now it sang:

"Why do I follow you out of the darkness, good man? You have attained that stage that leads a man to the truth of God. You proud, lonely soul, what is this struggle into which you have now let yourself be dragged?"

And the beast growled once again. "What were we talking about?"

Becker knew the answer. "About the conscience," he said aloud.

Then the beast let out a gruesome growl. But it did not grow into a roar even though the beast had opened its jaws wide, showing its terrible pale red maw. Rather, with great exertion there came from its throat a rattling sound, and then, as the jaws closed again, a wretched howl and whine. And at that, the whole colossal animal collapsed as if it had only been a balloon. Its hide hung and wobbled about it, falling limply aside to the floor, and inside was an animal small as a rabbit. And its whinings grew more and more like human screams and cries, as if a child were bawling. One could see how the yellow animal was struggling there in the smoke, trying to rear up in malice and snap at something. But it could not get up. And then it was no longer visible at all.

And in its place, beside the toppled chair and in front of the desk with its four legs sticking straight up in the air, stood a human being grabbing at its chest as if suffocating.

And although the face was hideously distorted with pain, bitterness and torment while tears ran down over the cheeks and mouth, Becker recognized the handsome, dark-haired man, the stranger, the Latin American from the first conversation.

And the sight of him—of the awful private suffering of this branded man, his venomous, sullen weeping, his whining with icy, impotent rage—so stirred Becker that his sympathy turned to horror, to paralysis, and he lost consciousness.

The Abortive Attack on Berlin

Thursday, December 12, 1918.

The Two Divisions in Berlin

General Lequis wanted to assemble two complete divisions in order to execute the plans of General Headquarters, either with or without the help of the population and the government, and with them to squash the revolution in Berlin.

The citizens waited in silence. In the working class the tension continued. They were armed and ready.

The columns of the Brandenburg Gate were still garlanded with weatherproof wreaths of evergreen. The poles with their crowns, the obelisks designed by the artist Sandkuhl, the speaker's platform—it was all still standing. In the center portal the banner still hung proclaiming "Peace and Freedom."

And once again they marched in from Schmargendorf and moved on across Heidelberger Platz, let their mighty drums boom and played those jaunty marches that recalled the bright days of the past.

Soldiers still wore those black, white and red rosettes and ribbons.

But the present moment was sunk deep within itself, preoccupied with itself like a man at a grave abandoning himself to his grief.

They rattled into town, marched in, trumpets blowing: the 4th Guard Infantry Division, the 1st Guard Regiment, the 5th Guard Infantry Regiment and the Reserve Infantry Regiment No. 93. The tread was sharp as they passed through the Zoological Garden in the winter rain.

The war had left its mark on these men. Their bodies were emaciated, their faces stern and morose. They could still hear the cracking of rifle shots, the barking of machine guns, the boom of the heavy shells. Every man of them was armed with hand grenades. The muzzles of their machine guns glow, the steam hisses from drain pipes, bring water tanks, bring water.

Heavy artillery is stationed over in that village, the red cloud of smoke, a man is screaming, why doesn't he stop? Someone get over there fast, he's gone crazy. Direct hit.

"Home again you'll start anew, live again as you once did, find a wife so fair and true, and Santa Claus will bring a kid."

"See you later in the mass grave."

There, a bloody hunk of flesh on the wall of the trench—and it was a piece of me.

Forward, advance. The new recruits don't want to, they must be driven forward by force. They curse the advancing troops: "Strike-breakers, you're prolonging the war. Watch, Lehmann is already tottering, away with Lehmann, and then all this shit is over."

The lieutenants threaten: "You and your shit-house slogans."

They march along the Charlottenburg highway. That's the Great Star. Watch out, Tommy's coming. In the shelter, misery and despair. The counterattack with flamethrowers, dead, wounded, screams, spasms, death rattles. At the door to the shelter the hole dug by a grenade, we'll toss our dead comrades in there. One of them with a mangled face kneels, "Shoot me, I'm blind." But it is forbidden to shoot him.

Have to retreat, the wounded clutching at you, they want to go back too, but that won't work. Boom, the air pressure, the yellow, sulfurous smoke.

Finally, finally, night, the dusky moonlight. But in the sky the flash of brightly colored flares, the bursting of shrapnel. Home again you'll start anew, live again as you once did.

Brandenburg Gate. The speaker's platform. And some guy is standing up there in a top hat beside a high-ranking officer, and he mumbles, "You have returned undefeated."

And then the march through Berlin. Yes, those are the same old rows of buildings. But it is no longer the Empire. The unemployed stand along the streets, and the discharged soldiers. They cover the sidewalks like sludge. Soon we'll be part of the sludge.

And the barracks haven't changed. Civilians move about, making speeches, no one pays any attention to the officers, a poster about war loans and a picture of Hindenburg are ripped down.

And those whose home is Berlin leave, with or without permission.

And once you're back home and lying in a real bed with no one to order you around and no threat of an attack—you just lie there and sleep.

General Lequis has two divisions in Berlin—on paper. He knows the truth. But he has not yet comprehended it. He wants to execute his plan and that same day he issues a proclamation calling for volunteers. But the government has made its countermove: a call to form a people's army, to be organized in centuries, under the command of the Council of People's Deputies.

Quartermaster General Groener at Wilhelmshöhe received the bad news coming out of Berlin with stoic calm. He remained in contact with General Lequis by telephone. Meanwhile he sat immobile at his desk, both hands flat on the desktop.

At war's close this robust man had worked as a railroad specialist on the eastern front, became Ludendorff's successor, had played a part in the settlement of the affairs of Wilhelm II and was still very much in the thick of things. Now, however, it was truly the end of the war.

When Lequis had nothing new to report, he called in his adjutant von Schleicher. "The army is drifting away like sand. Nothing is left of our two divisions."

They exchanged mute glances.

Groener: "Have you anything to suggest. Do you see any possibility?"

Schleicher, coldly: "Unfortunately, no."

(I'll not be the straw you cling to.)

Groener: "I know of nothing at the moment either. That was an especially clever maneuver on Ebert's part to call out a people's army. One could call it a dirty trick."

Schleicher: "We had spoken of clamping the man in a vice."

Groener: "That won't bring the army back to life. The man is a juggler. He apparently would prefer it if we had our two divisions there. They would have him by the gullet, let me tell you."

Groener cleared his throat when Schleicher did not answer. He shook his shoulders as if tossing off some invisible burden, and remarked, "Someone will have to notify the Field Marshal General."

It sounded like news of someone's death. Schleicher remained silent.

Groener: "I will go to him this afternoon. Please think the whole matter through one more time."

Schleicher left the room, his cap pulled low on his brow. I'll think of nothing. I am the trustee for a bankruptcy.

He telephoned the old countess. The aged woman had her companion place her in her chair by the stove. She was quite fresh. She stroked Schleicher's hand. "I have missed you. I haven't heard from you for a long time now."

"And now I break into your house like a burglar."

"Do it more often, please. I have strong nerves. Your voice sounded changed on the phone. What is wrong, Schleicher?"

He cleared his throat just as Groener had done before. This gave his voice a strange sound. "Serious things have occurred in Berlin."

"Revolts?"

"The army is falling apart. Both our divisions are gone. That, dear

462

countess, is the end of the German army. We have no army anymore."

And Schleicher's voice began to tremble, he could not control himself. The old woman clapped her hands and gave her companion the order to bring some brandy. When the tray had arrived, she pointed to a glass with one finger and commanded Schleicher, "Help yourself."

He poured the glass down. She commanded him to drink another. Her ancient face was stern. "You may smoke a cigar." When he begged her to let him dispense with that, she answered, "As you please."

A half minute later she raised her head again—one might say from its couch on her breast—and said, "Von Schleicher, please have the kindness to explain to me what is happening in Berlin. When an army disintegrates what do you do? Are there no courts-martial? Why aren't the ringleaders shot?"

"It is not a revolt, dear countess. They're all simply running off home."

"By themselves?"

"Yes."

"Then—we're already dead, aren't we."

And she broke into hideous laughter, a giggle unlike anything he had ever heard. He grew afraid, was about to stand up, call her companion. But while still laughing she said, "Stay, do stay, sit down."

And while she laughed—the sound was bestial—while she laughed she managed to say, "But it serves you right, it's just the thing. You see, there is still justice in this world. One needn't wait until the Last Day."

She had had her laugh now, and to recuperate she lowered her head back into its cavity, but then raised it again at once. "And now you're all afraid I suppose? The house is falling down over your heads. Didn't I tell you the house could not stand if you removed its girders? And you still want to complain?"

I just want to go, thought Schleicher.

"You're not feeling well, Schleicher. You did not come up here to tell me this and then run off. What is supposed to happen now?"

"We still see no other possibilities."

"I am old, but you're the one acting like an old lady. Why don't you make a joke of it? You normally love jokes. Laugh at these so-called troops that were none at all. Just don't make such a tragic face. I told you already, an army that is drummed up the way it's done nowadays with universal conscription and no one really wanting to go is not an army. What does a Schmidt or a Müller know about the state? What does he care about the Kaiser and the Reich. He wants to make shoes or plow fields. Of course they all ran home."

Schleicher: "Those men fought courageously, to the last minute."

"They broke off in the midst of battle. The hardest struggle was just beginning. The army has vanished, including its commanders." She giggled again. "Your Ludendorff started it, crying for help. Whoever cries for help doesn't amount to much. Then you came up with your conspiracy against the Kaiser—instead of standing around him with daggers drawn. The whole lot of you could not have found a finer death."

Schleicher sat there before her, bewitched. She said what he was thinking.

The old woman: "Be glad you're rid of these so-called troops. They're all sitting home cozy and warm with the little lady and the kiddies. Now you can move without having to worry about them. The imperial officers, however, know who they are. Hindenburg at their head. What is your Groener up to by the way?"

"He—has been hit hard by this."

"Collapsed? Let him lie. Whoever lacks ideas lacks the deed as well."

While Schleicher listened to her he grew more and more ashamed of the affair with Ebert, of the deals and the begging. That he should have to be sitting here to recognize it! The countess smiled at him. They were united again. He asked to be excused. She nodded, but demanded that he report again tomorrow at the latest.

Out on the street he gazed with a kind of veneration at the simple house where she lived. Now everything depended on what Hindenburg would say. If he made up his mind, then the battle was not yet lost.

He reported to Groener at the appointed time that afternoon. Groener was marching back and forth restlessly, but it did not look as if he were expecting Schleicher. He had him sit down while he went on marching about without speaking. Finally he pulled his own chair around into position.

"How we came up with this plan of using two divisions and depending on Ebert's cooperation—we shall leave that aside for the moment. The way things stand now is that if Ebert is nimble, and he is that, he will oppose us, use some rallying call. If we expose him, however, those still further to the left will come to power."

Groener looked at his adjutant, and noticing something there in his face he interrupted himself and said, "You don't wish to dispute that, do you?"

"On the contrary, I am completely of Your Excellency's opinion."

"It seemed to me that you wanted to make some comment. Whatever else it is that Ebert wants, it is not us—that we know. But he cannot have whatever it is without us either. I'm positive that he's already anxious today about that splendid people's army that he wouldn't tell me anything about yesterday evening. We have no reason to drop the man. What do you think? You have, I think, something else in mind."

Schleicher: "Permit me to submit the results of some very quick reflection. I think we should summon our forces as hastily as possible and strike our blow as hastily as possible, because each new day works for him."

"What forces are you speaking of?"

That is precisely what the old countess had asked before.

"Officers' regiments."

He added that they must be thought of as something like suicide battalions. The idea had a powerfully sobering effect on the quartermaster general. It even gave him—to judge by the easy way he lit his cigar—his poise back again. After he had let the first smoke ring float upward, he said, "Some memories from your youth seem to have flitted across your mind, I'd say. Where do you suddenly come up with the notion of a suicide battalions?"

And as Schleicher spoke of the situation of the officers' corps, of the general despair and disgust and of the officers' desire—though this, he granted, had not been shaped into a unified whole—not to perish ingloriously in the morass of this revolution, Groener was touched in a most agreeable way, and his broad face mirrored honest good cheer.

He declared to Schleicher, "What you say is like a reminiscence from those November days in Spa. We must begin anew then. We shall then ride, as in von Schulenburg's plan, with or without the Kaiser, across the Rhine and into Germany. You are a poet, Schleicher. But unfortunately it is merely the stuff for a ballad. I have not been informed that things have improved in the army since yesterday."

Schleicher battled on: "Of course not. What we have is demobilization and disintegration. But that is what compels us to act now."

"If you can tell me how, I shall turn my command over to you."

Schleicher went on talking, but felt that what he lacked was the voice of the countess. He let her speak, but it was only her words. He summed up. "It is impossible for us simply to accept this blow, bound up as it is with a challenge. It is my opinion that we still amount to something."

"For heaven's sake who, us?"

"The officers, the men who stand with the Kaiser and the Reich."

Groener let a smoke ring ascend and embittered poor Schleicher all the more.

"The Kaiser," Groener said, "is not here. I respect the ideology. But at this very moment, when this Ebert can afford to challenge us openly, to come forward now with ideas of the Reich and the monarchy—my dear von Schleicher, I have no wish to hurt your feelings, I do indeed respect you, but we are sitting here at General Headquarters, as you know, and we have to calculate things. How do we get your officers' regiments together, and as you say very hastily, and how many are there?

And until they can strike their blow where does that leave us, dear friend, you and me, who are after all still authorized agents of this government?" Groener laughed heartily.

Schleicher: "Of course I am talking about an act of desperation. I can give you no numbers, but they are out to exterminate us, and we are going to defend ourselves."

Groener gave him a friendly pat on the knee. "You have belled the cat there. An act of desperation. But old Groener does not lose his nerve that easily. Believe me, certain people in Berlin would love nothing better than for us to follow the Russian example and mobilize regiments of officers and cadets. I'll not be trapped into that."

"If I may be allowed the question: where does Your Excellency see more normal prospects?"

"Prospects is much too grand a word for present conditions. We have to set our sights lower. I like your spirit, Schleicher, it is useful for this period of transition. 'Disciplined, in storm and wind.' But the storm may last for a long time yet."

They were standing on common ground once more. Schleicher took the lead. "And so we remain in contact with Ebert?"

"We maneuver until a situation is reached where something else is possible. This little man, this Ebert, neither will nor can shake us off. Ultimately it is simply a question of whether we control him or he us. To prophesy at the moment is futile."

Schleicher lowered his head. "Storm and wind? It's becoming a chronic agony."

"You ought not to prophesy." Groener crammed some things lying on his chair into his briefcase then placed both hands out flat on the desk. "We have lost the war, that's all. It is five o'clock. I must go to the Field Marshal General."

"Shall I wait for Your Excellency to return?"

"Please do."

One could report to Hindenburg what one wanted—he remained impassive. Without a twitch he heard his colleague's report.

"Then we'll soon have to put on our top hats."

Groener presented him with his plan for a continued, but more elastic connection with Ebert. They must slowly build up their own position. Hindenburg broke in gruffly, "If they let us build it up."

Groener, glibly: "Of that much I'm sure. Ebert needs us."

"You want to sell us out to this man for good and all, am I right?"

Groener described the situation in Berlin. A great Workers' and Soldiers' Congress was to begin within the next few days, the radicals would try to settle their accounts with Ebert, the congress could slip out of Ebert's hands and the Spartacists might under certain conditions be moved to strike their blow prematurely. That would mean it was then their move and they could achieve something with even the few troops remaining to them.

Hindenburg: "With Ebert."

"Yes."

"You'll not have me with you for that part of it. I'll leave that to you. In case it turns out to be true that the army is in dissolution, my task is reduced to settling whatever matters remain to be settled."

There was no warmth of affection between these two, not even the warmth of argument. Hindenburg simply disclaimed his co-worker.

As Schleicher watched his boss, Groener, descend the stairs in slow strides, he grew worried. Because in the final instance he approved of Groener's tactical methods. Groener took him by the arm and, when the orderlies had brought them their caps and coats, they walked out into the wintery park.

"What this means," said Groener with a very grave expression on his face, "is to work on the long range. In the meantime the flags will have to be lowered."

Schleicher could find no words. It was defeat, complete, unimaginable defeat.

They now returned to the building.

In the half hour they spent that dark afternoon in the park of Wilhelmshöhe, Officer von Schleicher underwent a transformation. After their walk, his memories from military school and his affection for the countess no longer assumed the same role. If someone later spoke to him about the affairs of the Reich, touching on them perhaps with a lighter, more playful tone, that random someone could not know—and Schleicher did not let him see—with what reverence and affection those old matters were embedded within him. They had been swept away from the surface only to take on a profound solemnity—so much so that he allowed no one to approach him concerning them.

The old countess saw him seldom from then on. She would have had no reason, however, to complain of his actions.

As Groener and Schleicher approached the portal of the castle on their return the quartermaster general cast a sad glance at the guard who presented arms. He sighed, "What a way for it all to end. The end of the German army."

Book Four

From December 12th to December 13th

The Rat

The third conversation with an ambassador from the spirit world.

A New Guest

As he sat up now on the sofa, where he had fallen in a faint after his ghostly visit, and looked about the room, Becker found that he was alone and nothing was moving in the house. His room, however, looked as if it had been devastated—the desk lay on one side, the legs of his deskchair were stretched into the air, the wastebasket had rolled out into the room, strewing its contents, the carpet was bunched up and shoved to one side. It looked as if a battle had taken place.

Becker stared at it all, he knew at once what had happened: the lion.

He stood up and went to make certain whether or not the stranger was still there. When he came back from the hall he set to work, straightening the carpet, putting desk and chair back in place and stuffing the paper back in the basket. Then everything looked as if nothing had happened.

Now he retreated to his divan. The compress still lay on the chair. He stretched out on the divan as if ordered to do so and laid the moist compress to his brow. He was completely despondent and fell asleep.

That evening Hilda and his mother took turns watching him. He did not speak, his face was tight and secretive. It was possible that he recognized the two women, but he took no notice of them.

He was, given what had now happened (and with no results to show for it), ready to risk everything. He did not know how he would proceed, but he knew that he would come to some conclusion. Hilda watched over him till late that night.

When he opened his eyes the next morning his mother was sitting there. He weighed the situation and pulled himself together. He declared he wanted to get up; he dressed and sat with her, serious but friendly, at the breakfast table. He did not let her notice anything. Hilda had intended to relieve his mother at eight; it was already nine. His mother had to go. He reassured her. He would lie down obediently on his divan, she could lay a compress on his forehead again, too, it had done him such good yesterday. That relieved her. She accompanied her son to his room. He lay there peacefully. Hilda would be there any minute. And then she left.

The coast was clear. He got up in an instant. He sat down at his desk, his right hand balled to a fist and braced against the desktop and said softly, "We shall now proceed from where we left off yesterday. Today we will arrive at some conclusion."

He gave the desk a loud kick.

No one answered. He looked about him, stared at the chairs, the bookcase, the curtains. He felt as if everything here could begin to rotate any second. The ceiling lamp, too; its central rod jerked, apparently in preparation for shooting downward. Everything here seems to be made of rubber. But that's not important. They can't surprise me with things like that.

His own footfall sounded strikingly hollow. Counting, checking his steps, he turned about rapidly to see what was happening behind his back. It was not out of the question that someone would attack him from the rear. For a long time nothing happened. Then a soft but distinct scratching began. He took cover beside the bookcase, his back to the wall, and looked attentively about the room. It seemed to him as if there were folds rising up in the rug under his desk. He was sure of it now, the rug was raised in the middle. Someone was working beneath it. Now the whole carpet started to quiver, and then it fell back smoothly to the floor, and at one corner a small gray animal slipped out, ran back onto the rug and sat down in the middle, its pointed nose directed toward Becker. It crouched on its hind legs and stroked the wiry hairs of its moustache with its front paws. The little black eyes sparkled at Becker.

There were neither mice nor rats in their apartment. They had heard, it was true, that there were some in the next building. But this was no conventional rat, either. This—was he, "that man."

He was twittering now and whistled, but nothing that could be understood. Becker recognized the expression on the animal's face, small as it was and despite the fact that it kept its distance.

"How are you?" twittered the rat.

He answered coolly, "Fine, thanks." (He did not like this feigned politeness.)

"Can't get rid of me, huh? I make myself right at home, don't I?"

He rasped, "Oh, please do. Make yourself comfortable. We have to arrive at some conclusion, you know."

"Very kind of you. Our last conversation, like our first, tumbled quickly out of control. I don't know whether you—but let me use the formal second-person pronoun again if you prefer—had the same impression."

"Definitely. I'm conscious of that fact."

"Why do you use the phrase 'conscious of that fact'?"

"What do you mean?"

"Why didn't you simply say 'yes' or 'certainly'?"

"It's what popped into my mind is all. What bothers you about that?"

"I presumed—I see now unjustly so—that you wanted to allude to a word that entered into our debate at its height yesterday. You know which word I mean."

Becker: "Conscience."

"That's right."

Becker: "But I hadn't even thought of that."

"*Tant mieux.* But you say that very hesitantly. You have apparently been thinking about it."

"Certainly not at the moment. From time to time though."

"When for instance?"

"During the night."

"Aha. Can't sleep. And may I, without desiring to be indiscreet, inquire what the thoughts were that went through your mind in the course of that unpleasant night? I feel myself innocent, by the way, of the insomnia that has upset your nerves. You'll have to lay that at someone else's door. As far as I'm concerned our conversation could have gone on in the most peaceable way in the world, and we could have come to a harmonious conclusion. But we were disturbed. Is that not true?"

"I don't know."

The rat, excited: "I beg your pardon, but who disturbed things yesterday? Me or someone else? Who was the prompter who whispered the word that brought everything to a halt?"

Still sitting on the rug, the rat spoke angrily. Close to a bookcase, at the back of the room, stood a small caned chair normally used only to help order and select books from the highest shelves. Becker now took a seat on it and thus brought himself down more to the level of the rat who continued to bluster beneath him.

Becker said: "Let us deal with one another eye to eye. I must know whether you come to me as a friend or an enemy. If there is to be a battle between us, we want that battle to be fought honestly and resolutely. As sure as I'm sitting here, we will bring this to a conclusion one way or another."

"My view entirely. I betray no secrets in telling you that I appear here today especially for that purpose, both of my own volition and at the request of interested parties."

"In the spirit world?"

"We are always in the spirit world."

"And which parties are especially interested in me? And you, are you here as a reporter or as a representative of their interests?"

"As both. I will report to them objectively. They are interested in proud, energetic, untamable and unbiased minds like yours. Naturally I am concerned that we arrive at a positive result."

"Then we're on the same side. We could have been this far along yesterday. But at the first mention of the word 'conscience' you became alarmed in a way that I still do not understand."

The rat laughed. "Bah, nothing to understand, sir. An idiosyncracy, one person winces when someone scratches glass with a stylus, another not even when lightning strikes right next to him."

"But a clear, unambiguous term used to designate a fact should not frighten a scientist."

The rat, angrily: "What is the point of this attack? You can plainly see that I am here. Or do you want me to go?"

"Not in the least."

"Then you want me to stay. You want it ardently and sincerely, am I right?"

"The struggle between you and me must still be fought out. Either you'll have me, hide, hair and all or . . ."

The rat was placated. "Let us not exaggerate. What's all this about hide and hair. I eat no one. Do I look as if I did? Everything ultimately depends on you. You must decide. You are apparently not to be helped by some grand, unambiguous theory and formulation of the facts, either. Otherwise you would not be waiting for me. Am I not correct? I am at your service.

"Things must be thought through logically and well. I overstated the case somewhat before when I spoke of taking sides for certain interests. For my own part, I would like to phrase it more as a sporting interest. There is nothing in this for me personally."

Doubtless in order to blur the bad impression that this exaggerated assurance of complete neutrality had made on Becker, the rat began at once to lecture merrily away.

"So then—conscience. Let us deal with that. At last, that conscience we're so conscious of. There you have it really: conscience comes from science, that which is absolutely established. If only one knew what that was. Scientific knowledge, nothing shaky there. One must admit, if it existed it would be the crown of creation. One would as a spirit be almost superfluous. Knowledge would be served up on a platter. One need only sit down and tuck in."

"Yes, that's true."

"The prospect delights you does it? Me too. It would be the ideal state—though with reservations, yes indeed, with reservations. Because what would become of freedom then, of human freedom? Man seeks, asks, struggles, and strives, and in a given instance, in the case of some lack of clarity, or of doubt, he would only have to set himself in motion toward that mental safe, and there he would find the answer all nice and ready. Well, how does that strike you? Do you accept that? You would in that case be negating yourself."

The rat waited for the effect of its words on Becker. He had no choice but to admit that there was something frightfully true about that. That made the rat happy. It did not retreat, but pressed forward.

With mocking superiority it now declared, "And so let us proceed with our lesson on conscience, of which so much is made. You see, I for my part have no fear of it. For I can see through it. Let us now analyze the term and examine it precisely. No bluffing allowed. So then, your conscience says, 'thou shalt not steal, thou shalt honor thy father and thy mother.' First, there are people who do not honor their fathers and mothers and secondly, there are certain specimens of fathers and mothers who do not deserve to be honored. But that's just between ourselves. As a teacher you're familiar with such things. There are also people who steal."

"The conscience is weakly developed in certain people," Becker remarked impatiently.

"Doubtlessly. They will soon learn better too, won't they? Where do we have these oracles of conscience from? What lies behind this 'thou shalt not steal, thou shalt honor thy father and thy mother,' etc. etc.? We are of course not interested in the legend, which has a particular purpose and fulfills it, too. But it can hardly be the same purpose that we are pursuing here, namely to ascertain the pure truth. So then, we must ask coolly and precisely, like scientists, like the lawyer, 'cui bono?' Who profits from conscience?"

Becker placed one elbow on a shelf of the bookcase and propped his head against his hand. He gazed distractedly and tormentedly before him. The rat ran up closer. It sat now on the bare floorboards. It did not yield.

"You are, of course, going to pay attention. You have already been the victim of enough orders. You can still recall, I presume, the mobilization orders that have so preoccupied you. There is method to the whole business. You want your ego, your own responsible ego—but the others do not want you to have it. Let us take a look at what you carry around inside you as your conscience and at what is praised as the center of the self, the ego. Let us present it the way a chemist does an element, clean of all by-products, of all impurities. You were raised by adults. You were weaned from certain things, accustomed to others. You consider the result to be your nature. As a teacher you know how that works. Your conscience is nothing more than a sensitivity that you learned, that was drummed into you. Sensitive to what end? So that you may know what things to prefer and what things to avoid. It is true in all nature, of all animals. It is called training. There are prohibitions, precepts, five or ten. They place them inside you, in your ego, so that they can be quite sure of you, the teacher, the governess, the preacher, the judge. You do follow me, do you not, Dr. Becker? We do want to use our reason, do we not? I seem to sense, you see, that I am about to present you with a grand joke. I can already hear you laughing and asking: 'And for that I almost went crazy?' "

"I am curious, I am curious," Becker whispered.

The rat: "You were brought up that way. There was no need to wait long for the results. Your father spoke, your mother warned, your teacher threatened, your pastor thundered, and you now became an obedient boy, and from the obedient boy came an obedient man, and what they said, whispered and threatened is kept within you, and now you fold your hands and believe that it is the voice of your conscience sounding, and that your inmost self is speaking, but that is what they took away from you long ago."

"And where is the joke? What is there to laugh about?"

"Because I still hear you speaking! Still hear you! Is that not clear enough to you? You wanted to be free, wanted to use your own arms, and then, in attempting to be free, what do you do but turn to your conscience, to your teachers, your governess, your pastor, your father, your mother. Do you not see the comedy in that, good sir? Yes, Dr. Becker, that's how they diluted your ego and cheated you out of your self. The deception has succeeded so perfectly that you don't even notice it now, sir. Thus the failure of our first two sessions."

Becker: "I understand, I understand."

The rat: "You mustn't make me responsible for all this. It's simply what your world looks like. Built on a grand scale in six days and declared perfect come the seventh."

Becker: "But I still have my reason and my free will as before."

"Very true, and let us hope you will soon make use of them. Take a look at it: this is what the world looks like, and you're invited then to celebrate it. But it is nothing but mist and vapors, doomed to dissolve of course, not cosmic, only comic. Finally you see it."

Becker groaned, "You're probably right. I have a friend by the name of Krug, a scientist. He tells me much the same."

"How did that conversation run? That interests me."

Becker: "Oh, just that I saw a tree in a park, the leaves had fallen, and I suggested that that couldn't be all there is to the life of a tree, to produce leaves, to cast the leaves off, to produce leaves again."

"And? What did Krug say?"

"He said, why not, why not? One finds one's fun in life one way or another. Time passes."

The rat skipped merrily on its hindlegs. "There you have it! He hit the nail on the head, he'll do all right. Yes, that's how the world is. And now you can laugh about it."

But Becker only groaned, "That would mean that all possibility of ever finding our ego has been taken from us, because—then it wouldn't even exist. But, I can't live like that."

The rat whistled, "But child, that's why I've come, to help you."

"Ah, you, you're only mocking me. What do you actually show me? What do you suggest I do? I am no longer the Friedrich Becker from before, who knew nothing and thought everything was splendid and was reconciled with the whole world. If I don't succeed in finding my ego, if I don't find me, then I'll put an end to myself."

"Who knows if that's an end to you. Perhaps you start all over again somewhere else."

"You want to drive me to extremes. There's nothing good in you."

"What a misunderstanding. If you were reasonable you would already realize, already know that you are what you are and you make of yourself what you can. Just as I do. For how am I any different from a human being like yourself, though now in this state? I have broken through. I already have death behind me. I have overcome my death as a man. I have burst through that wall. I now pass on the message to the living of my species like you. We are ultimately a fraternity. You struggle. I pity you. I bring you help."

"Death?"

"If you like, death. I come from the spirit world. Death is the most foolish word in all language. One should not use it for serious thought. If you will allow me a marginal note—while I still lived I had the same fear of it you have. It is the fear of the unknown. Now that I've opened the door and entered, I can enlighten you: the whole thing is a bluff. It's reminiscent of the chapter on conscience. The whole thing is much simpler. Do you not speak with me as if I were you? And that, whether I come as a dog, a cat, a bird, maybe even a worm—though I don't like that one? Well, that is a feeling of sympathy. It is a dim memory that one doesn't normally allow to surface. Yes, so we are. Spirits exist in many gradations from man to animal, to dog and cat and rat, and when you know that, then you know your ego and you're willing to take the risk. You risk the move, alive or dead, and where is the difference?"

Becker groaned once again, "And that's all, that's all? There's nothing more?" He paced back and forth along the wall, rubbing his hands in dreadful agitation, rubbing his brow.

The rat ran beside him. "Yes, that is really—all."

"I didn't want 'all,' I wanted to find my own path. And you tell me there is no such thing, and I should simply take the risk. Ah, now nothing is left to stand by me, now it's only you, a rat. Yes, you are a rat—you've ripped out my guts with your teeth, devoured my inmost self. You've left me nothing. No, don't contradict me, you've left me nothing. You, you have dug it all out, emptied me, disemboweled me while still alive. You would prefer no recriminations. I hope for your sake you've done the right thing with me. So now behold your handiwork. This is me, a speck of dust, a spark of glowing nature, and a clump of nothing that no longer wants to be a human being, doesn't want to exist at all, and this nothing is filled with disgust and despair."

"You'll soon go into a rage."

"Not against you. There is a raging storm inside me. Ah, won't someone help me. Ah, ah, there must be an end to this. The wretchedness, the wretchedness."

"Don't moan so loud. Someone might come and interrupt our conversation again."

"If only someone would come. Let whoever come who wants to. What does that matter to me. There is a conflagration inside me. That must be the fire, that glorious fire into which you're dragging me. And I cannot bear it. I've been laid on a red-hot grill, I'm being roasted alive, and I cannot bear it, rat, not another minute. It is beyond my strength."

The rat laughed, high and shrill, and danced. "The fire, the fire won't hurt you. It cleanses. You're old childish ego is being burned away, it cannot bear this new knowledge. But now I must really ask one thing of you: prove yourself a man of science. Stick to the facts for just another quarter hour. We must remain absolutely alone, you and I."

"What you ask will be done. I'll bite my tongue."

"And don't run about so wildly."

"Permit me to step over to my desk. I want to look for something. I must hurry. They'll be coming soon."

"I know. Please, go ahead."

Becker went to his desk. He strode with legs held wide apart, cautiously, for the rat slipped in and out between his legs. It circled him and at the sight nausea seized him, adding to those other miseries that were already unbearable. His hands fluttered across the desk as if searching for some soothing medicine. They pulled open one drawer after another. He found nothing. He did not find it, his revolver. His mother must have packed it away somewhere. And when he realized that, he stood back up straight, groaned and looked helplessly about the room. But the rat had already begun to move again, it knew what to do.

He saw it climb up the edge of the bookcase, what did it want, it was way up on top now, where there was an empty shelf holding only a stack of newspapers and some twine. And it had found something. It burrowed and scratched in the pile, throwing newspapers down, and now it had a piece of rope between its teeth, held it in its mouth and dragged it along behind as it sprang down in a single leap. The heavy rope fell down on the rat, throwing it to one side. It was buried beneath a pile of newspapers. Twittering and whistling it worked its way out. It laughed, "Here I am. One doesn't dare lose one's nerve."

It tugged at the rope, leaping now to the right, now to the left. It dragged it backward, laying it before Becker. He bent down and took the rope in his hand. The rat made big eyes up at him and whistled, "Not bad, huh?"

"Will it hold?"

"I think so. It's better than a revolver. That makes such a loud bang."

"I think so too."

The rat: "Now we're walking down the same path together. I'm already so happy for you."

"I'm not happy, can't be. I'm only in despair. Don't bother me now."

"When you have that door behind you, the despair is over."

Becker took a picture down from the wall, then another. He tested the nails. "I'll hang myself at the spot where my most revered teachers used to hang."

"They'll know how to appreciate that."

"Did you think our conversations would conclude this way?"

"You're still not seeing things clearly. This is the normal, the logical conclusion. You're being completely consistent."

Becker looked up at the bust of Sophocles. He took it down and tested the strength of the hook. The rope was hanging over his shoulder. He said bitterly, "I feel sick as a dog."

"You're going to weaken if you're not careful."

"I'm vomiting up my whole self. I refuse to accept this existence. I refuse to accept this gift with its fake ego named Friedrich Becker. The package will simply be returned to the sender."

He went to the kitchen, the rat following him. He came back with a hammer and climbed up on a chair. He had placed the bust of Sophocles on the floor, the rat played merrily about it, doing leaps over its head. From up on the chair Becker began hammering, and the rat laughed as he did so. "Strike hard so it holds." And Becker laughed too and hammered. He quoted Sophocles: "Wonders" — bang — "are many" — bang — "but none" — bang — "is more wonderful" — bang — "than man" — bang — "than man" — bang.

The room rumbled with the blows of the hammer.

Becker thought he was laughing. But it was not laughter, he could hear that himself. What was coming out of him? It was the hideous, ghastly, gruesome screaming of a man. Hammer in hand, he turned around on the chair to see who was screaming so hideously and only then noticed that the sound was coming from himself. And in horror he tugged hard at the hook and stamped impatiently with one foot.

"It'll hold, it'll hold," the rat whistled, afraid that the neighbors would notice something. "Let's finish the job, my time is limited."

So Becker tied the noose and knotted the rope to the hook.

As he opened his robe and tore open the collar of his shirt to lay the noose around his neck, the rat said, "I'll help you kick the chair over."

The Witch's Ride

Hilda awoke late that morning. She looked at the clock and saw it was nine.

She dressed slowly, drunk with sleep, and got ready to go out. But neither the cold water with which she washed nor the coffee carried up to her brought her to herself. Already wearing her coat and nurse's cap, she felt strangely nervous and restive and sat back down at the little table in her room, the coffee things still on it. She gazed out across it and without noticing what she was doing opened the small bag that accompanied her wherever she went.

Suddenly her eyes were wide open. She bent down over the table. She had to look past the little coffee pot and across the tabletop because there was something to see there, something that moved, walked, promenaded. What was it then? Those people, it was her hometown, a bridge. People were out for a walk.

A young man came up behind her, she wanted to get a good look at him. And then came another young man, and another, and he made a grab for her blue nurse's coat and her cap. She was angry, resisted and did not want this. I'm no teenage girl that you can tease, they should leave me in peace. But he blocked her way. They kept coming in streams. What feline creatures they were. When they spoke it was in meows.

Then she said to one of them, "If you're fond of me and leave me alone now I'll give you a kiss." He took her by the arm and leapt up into the air incredibly high, running with her right over the heads of the others in order to carry her out of the throng. But while they flew, she saw his face. It was abominable, so savage and lustful that she pushed against his chest and screamed, "Let me go!"

So he let her fall and it wasn't a cat, but a monkey with a powerful, prehensile tail. He ran off on all fours. And she ran too once she was on the ground. Because there were new ones coming. She ran from them, through crooked and winding streets. She ran in circles, now I'm running in circles, I've so much to do, I have to go. How will this end, how can I find my way out, and they're waiting for me.

And Hilda, sitting there bent over the table, truly wanted to get up.

She pulled one foot out from under the table and let her left arm sink down onto her knee. As she did so the little bag tipped over in her lap, she automatically reached for the fastener. The bag fell open.

But she had already lain her head to one side on her shoulder. She wanted to see the fellow who had just arrived there at the back doing a soft-shoe. What a strange figure, a punchinello, not a real man at all. Is he perhaps a marionette? But as she searched to see if he were dangling from strings, he moved away from her, grew smaller and smaller, soon so tiny and so far away it was like looking through the wrong end of a telescope. Now he attempted to come closer again, bravely stomping toward her, and there he came. What might he be up to? He had a brown, waxed moustache like an army sergeant, and a little pigtail hung behind like a grenadier from the days of Frederick the Great. His knees bent so comically, he must have had artificial joints. But with each jerk of the knee he came closer, incredibly close, leaping, hopping. He had seven-league boots. The hair on his head was totally gray, he had the enamel-red face of a nutcracker. What does he want from me? I'll hide here in this cranny, he intends to do something to me. There, he's hurtling right on by, he's gone.

But where have I got myself now? Who is getting up from the floor there, from the shadows? He must be drunk or something. A bum, a rag-amuffin, he's coming waddling toward me. "Ah, Bernhard, you're here? What are you looking for? What are you standing around for? You're not sick, are you?"

"No, I'm just dead."

"Then let me go."

"You have to help me, you must take pity on me, you'll be my nurse, won't you?"

"Ah, Bernhard, I can't love you."

Then he climbed out of the gunny sack, and only now did Hilda notice that he had been playing tricks on her and was in fact the red nutcracker from before. He was pleased at her surprise. "You see, we caught you there, didn't we. And you can't love me, only others."

"What business is that of yours?"

"For example Lieutenant Maus, from the military hospital, in that empty room. You know."

She was terrified. "What do you know about that? He attacked me. It wasn't my fault."

"You can't get me to buy that. It's our turn now. The party's moving into high gear. Let's shake a leg."

And away they went.

The nutcracker danced off with her, and in no time they had glided down a long set of tracks to the end of the telescope; they had both grown very small and they could go no further. They were stuck there, and this was their dance floor, and away they went.

The nutcracker whirled her about, they were two dolls, he danced with her on her left and right, in front of her and behind, ard above and below her as well. There was nowhere to stand, all around them it was round and black, he reeled her about, making full use of the space. And as he did he became a monkey again, the one who had carried her above people's heads a while ago. And when she saw this she wanted to submit even less than before. But he stupefied her with the spinning and turning. He yelped shrill cries of joy, and she saw too that you had to jump, because you kept hitting against the ceiling, but she wanted to get out, had to get out.

These monkey cries, they cut her to the quick. He mocked and laughed and jeered at her. "Yes, it's just fine that you're in such a hurry, you haven't got time, we've got to rush, it's already a quarter to ten, and Friedrich will be waiting, Friedrich Becker, doctor of philology. He's completely crazy now. Who knows whether he's still alive, or if he hasn't hanged himself by now."

"Let me go!"

Her arms, her legs, she was horrified, filled with dread, for she had monkey arms and legs. "You've betrayed me, you've cast a spell on me."

"Everything is possible, anything can happen. We have to go on, we have to move on from here."

And the brown and white monkey dragged her wildly back and forth, she stumbled and fell against his prickly hair. "I don't want to be here with you in this devil's ballroom, I'm not a witch."

"You want to go to Becker, he's up ahead, he'll wait for you, we'll catch up with him."

He flung her to the ceiling, so that she almost shattered the telescope. They had already come a long way. She gasped, "You're lying, he's not here, let me go, I must go to him, I must go to him."

"We're on our way now. Look at the clock, it will soon be ten. How can you show yourself to him in this condition?"

She had become a monkey, had a monkey's hairy coat like his. This added to her sense of despair. The turns and spins grew even larger, swung out further, the distance between the floor and ceiling increased rapidly, it grew brighter and brighter in the tunnel, they raced along in a zigzag.

He flung her up into the air with his tail. He caught her again by the legs. She screamed as she flew, "We're falling out."

He laughed, he roared, "That doesn't matter. We've got to move on, it has to happen sometime."

She, dismayed: "We'll crash into the lenses, we'll break the lenses and be cut and slashed. We're shooting right on out."

"We have to, we have to, I swear we . . ."

Hilda lay with her chest on the table, her hands hanging down, her face resting beside the coffeepot. As she sat up, she saw that the tablecloth was wet where her mouth had been. Her whole body was trembling. She smoothed her clothes.

Now she stood up and dragged herself to the washstand at the mirror. She saw her face: rigid, distorted, one side was ashen, the other red. And she wasn't wearing her nurse's cap. It had been torn off. It lay crumpled up under the table. Her bag had been hurled at the door and had come open, thermometer and syringe had fallen out.

Tears came to her eyes. She took her handkerchief from her apron pocket, wiped her face and looked at her wristwatch. It was almost ten. She wanted to go to Becker's. I promised I'd be there at eight. And then the great, acrid fear. She snatched up the things from the bag, patted her hair in place—and raced out onto the street, to a cab.

Rescue and Tears

She rang and rang. No one opened the door. She had the key with her. She had fished it out already sitting in the cab. She unlocked the door and ran down the hall. No one in the kitchen. She knocked at the door of the living room, it was empty. She knocked at his study. No answer. She opened the door.

He lay along the wall with a rope around his neck, his face to the floor, next to an overturned chair. The hook had held, but the knot had given.

The room looked dreadful, as if there had been a robbery, the desk drawers were open, newspapers and twine were scattered about the room, the carpet shoved out of place, beside the chair lay the hammer.

Becker was unconscious from strangulation. Hilda dragged him up onto the divan, felt his pulse and in her confusion pumped his arms to help him breathe, which was pointless, he hadn't drowned. When she noted that he was breathing gently, she left him and ran to the neighbors to use the phone. The doctor arrived. Fortunately his mother did not return. Hilda arranged with the doctor that Becker's mother not be told, so as not to frighten her. The doctor painted a heavy stripe of iodine along the bloody welt on Becker's neck and put a dressing on it. While Hilda was setting the room to rights, the doctor sat next to Becker. He had opened his eyes. He stared glassily at Hilda for a long time, suddenly he turned his head to the wall with a jerk and began to moan. The doctor had to leave.

Hilda sat down beside him. What kind of man was this who had lain there, whom she had lifted up? She had not saved him, not she. Had it depended on her, he would not be alive now. She regarded him from above, from one side. His face was no longer bluish, only terribly pale. But that was what was so awful. He was apparently still moving about in another world, in that world . . .

He bared his teeth to the wall. He made faces, threatening some invisible creature, beating at it with his fists. And then he turned his head and his eyes were directed at Hilda. His gaze was rigid. At first there was no life in his eyes. But now he recognized her, and she saw that he recognized her.

And then he let out a ghastly scream and then another. The screams froze the blood within her. They were the screams of an animal whose paw is caught in a trap or of someone being murdered.

And all the while he looked at her, recognized her and clawed at her arm with one finger.

"Why did you cut me down?"

She wept and said nothing. He groaned, "Why did you do it? You had no right."

He breathed heavily, rasping and moaning, his eyes rolled. She could not bring herself to watch.

What should she do? This was how Bernhard had died, this was the second time now, fate was pursuing her, she could bear it no more. She hadn't the strength. She got up and then sat down at the desk. She pressed her lips together to suppress her sobs. But that did not help, she could not do it. She was crushed, broken. No end to it, no end.

She wept to herself. And in weeping she once again became aware of what had happened in her room before coming here, that hideous, devilish scene. The weeping swept her along. She could not control it. The misery devoured her. She was a lost creature, she forgot Becker and everything. She sobbed aloud, stammering words of desperation.

From the sofa he looked over at her. He listened.

He did not say anything to interrupt her sobbing. He listened to her attentively, as if they were having a conversation. He took up into himself each sound, each sob and stammered word.

And suddenly he not only heard her weeping, but it was loosed within him as well. Like rain falling onto dry earth the weeping flowed within him. And his inner world expanded. It was like magic. He felt himself lying on the divan. He felt his arms and legs. He breathed, blood pulsed within him. He could not describe how he felt.

He lay on one side to get a better view. She was sitting in his desk chair, its feet resting on the carpet from under which the rat had crawled. After some time she heard a voice: "What are you doing, Hilda?"

She dried her face and came to him, her knees shaking. Her wrinkled nurse's uniform rustled. She pulled a chair up next to him. Her head lay on her breast.

She spoke, though still shaken by sobs. "Friedrich, is it you?"

He nodded.

Hilda: "What is happening to us, Friedrich? Are you here again?" She took his head in her hands. She looked at him, caressed his face, stroked the bandage. She bent down over him, wept and began to speak again, next to his face—how this had happened, it was an accident for which she was to blame, if only she had come at the right time, but she had not been able to.

She stammered, but could not stop talking, repeating herself. He could not hear enough of her, could not see enough of this face with tears flowing over it, with the bitter, twitching lips.

She said, "I woke up late. I was exhausted from the night, I could not come to. If I had come on time, Friedrich, this wouldn't have happened. But I could not budge. I had already dressed, but then I had to sit back down on a chair, and I couldn't move. I dreamed, or maybe it wasn't a dream, people came and some of them held me back, held on to me, and then came a large man, a cat, a monkey, I can't explain it at all, and when I tried to leave he disguised himself and held on to me tight and wouldn't let me go, and I know it was something evil, a devil. It was an animal and I sat at my table and afterward it was already ten o'clock. Ah, Friedrich, what is happening to us?"

Becker did not move. He stared out into the room. Everything was back in its place. The chair was upright. The bust of Sophocles hung at its accustomed spot. The newspapers lay on a bookcase shelf. "That man" was gone. He had left here and gone to Hilda's. It was the same one. He thought he was being so very clever.

But he had not succeeded.

And for the first time Becker became conscious of the fact that he was alive, was really there. "That man" had not succeeded. Then there was someone who was stronger than "that man." Then it was not a defeat after all.

Draining the German Swamp

Radek the Russian falls into the hands of a Berlin wag who gives his leg several pulls. Afterward Radek realizes the man wasn't so dumb, and it is true enough: the German swamp can be drained only by some outside dictator.

The Wisdom of a Clown

They picked up Liebknecht at the newspaper office, where he had been speaking with Rosa Luxemburg. There were three men, all armed, among them Eduard Imker, the former soldier. They accompanied Liebknecht, a man they worshiped, in the car from the newspaper to the royal stables.

A large crowd jammed the portal of the stables and the wide central hall. They explained to Liebknecht as he got out of the car that these were all people who wanted to sign up. But they could not take them all. Many of them were only interested in pay and rations anyway.

On the second floor, in a small office, Liebknecht met Radek, who was dictating something in Russian and smoking his pipe. The stenographer vanished at once. Radek laughed as she left, "Did you notice, Karl, how glad she was to see you? Her feet were cold and she wanted to leave. We still don't have any heat."

And Radek struck an actor's pose. "This government, my dear comrades, truly does not deserve the confidence placed in it. It must be toppled. It has no supply of coal."

And Radek laughed easily to himself. "Yours is such a learned and well-behaved revolution. How refined you all are. It was different with us. I can remember how the Whites down in the region of Kazakhstan in the south once arrested a member of a soviet just for daring to think for himself, and they wound a hemp rope around his skull. Then they took a toggle and started turning away at the rope until the man's skull burst at the seams."

"Sickening," Liebknecht replied.

Radek: "They probably thought they could press those thoughts out of his head. In Yelets these educated representatives of freedom and culture behaved even more peculiarly. They were led by a man by the name of Manotov. Upon entering the city he ordered that the town's most beautiful girls be brought to him. To start with, he and his cultured officers raped them. Then they were handed over to the Cossacks, who used them for an extra joke of their own. They bound the young ladies, stark naked, to the tails of horses and drowned them all in the Sosna. That's a little river I know well."

"Enough, please."

"At any rate, that's how the—we won't call it the revolution—but the Whites' revolution, that is the counterrevolution, went. The world over, a White is a White, and he'll massacre if he thinks he can get away with it. Reds should know that. And what do the revolutionaries around here have to pit against that? A revolution in kid gloves."

They had wanted to confer about the upcoming Congress and organization in the factories. But very soon they were no longer alone. Someone used something close to physical force to drag Liebknecht out into the court to deliver a speech, and Radek, alone now, pondered what to do with the rest of his morning. He rifled among the papers he pulled out of his breast pocket and found an invitation to a breakfast taking place in the back room of Habel's on Unter den Linden. That wasn't far. The invitation, to be sure, was not directed to Radek personally, but to another Russian, not to a Red one however, but to a White. But the man actually invited was himself not a real White, he simply pretended to be one and was a good friend of Radek's. The breakfast did not sound uninteresting to Radek, who had nothing else to do, after all. He spruced himself up a bit there in the office. As he left the royal stables he looked middle-class, grave and educated. A full brown beard made him look twenty years older.

Once at Habel's, he met a great many people he did not know speaking a hodgepodge of Russian and German. He quickly pulled away from the Russians. The Germans were interested in this clever, patriotic Russian who had arrived only recently, and could explain economic affairs to them particularly well since he was a businessman, despite his rather academic exterior. From a distance Radek saw that renegade, the great Wylinski, whom he knew personally and despised. That usurer and crook was holding court at his own small table, from which mighty laughter rang out every few minutes. But Radek was more interested in the large head table, where he took a seat.

First he made friends with his German neighbor, who subjected him to an almost painful interrogation about the present situation in Russia. Radek explained to him what grand prospects were being passed up, lamenting how Russia could be another America if only the right people could be found. Especially now that the czarists had been toppled, free capital would have had unimagined opportunities, and instead of that, they had this brutal Bolshevism.

They calmed him. Bolshevism would dig its own grave. The hour was nearer than he suspected. And they whispered into his ear the number of troops assembled here in Germany alone—not to speak of the Allied forces. Defeated Germany would march arm in arm with the victors. They would virtually pounce on Russia. The patriotic stranger nodded worriedly: "Like vultures on a carcass."

But they soothed him, providing him with concrete data about these troops. They pointed out to him there in the room this or that respected gentleman directly involved with the matter.

Then, like some doleful know-it-all, Radek began to talk about the atrocities going on at home. They were simply the same stories he had told Liebknecht at the stables but with a change of color. This time the Whites were murdered and raped and the Reds were the criminals. They were only superficially interested in this, but it could do no harm—what he meant to do was legitimize himself. He could now hear more clearly what several of the gentlemen at the head of the table were saying, apparently high-ranking German officers or Junkers. The gentlemen all wore the beloved monocles they didn't dare risk clamping into their eyes out on the street.

One of the men spoke about financial negotiations taking place in Trier. The Allies were trying to prevent German capital from fleeing the country. "The strangulation has begun, they want to shut off our water."

A man with frosty gray hair, tall and gaunt, with bushy eyebrows and a wrinkled face from which sprang a reddened eagle's beak squawked, "That's the same Trier, if I' not mistaken, where a Roman prefect once ordered the massacre of an entire legion."

"Why?"

The man was named Varus, like that other fellow at the Battle of Teutoburg Forest. I don't know why. It shouldn't be forgotten at any rate."

"They'll throw Brest-Litovsk up to us there in Trier."

"Let them, let them. What is that going to get them? God knows that the people we'll be sending had nothing to do with Brest-Litovsk.

They all laughed aloud heartily. "But neither will the right man be among them to give them an answer."

The man with the frosty hair took a look around. For a moment Radek felt the steel-blue eyes rest on him. The old man said, "Only too true, unfortunately. Germany is down at the heels. We're sinking back to the level of some colonized tribe. An empire without a guard."

We know the third gentleman with the great bald head who now joined in the conversation there at the head table. It was the major from the recruiting office on Fasanenstrasse. He spoke with a snappy flourish as always. "We should not shy from dealing with the question head-on: should the soldier, the officer, concern himself with politics? The war has provided us with a clear answer. Without Ludendorff and Hindenburg the civilians would have made an ignominious peace long ago. Germany's fate must not fall into civilian hands at a moment like this. Leadership such as this was impossible under Bismarck, but now . . ."

The frosty-haired man: "A military dictatorship?"

The major whispered something Radek did not catch, because his neighbor asked him for a light for his cigar and then he had to light one for himself too, just as he was about to reach in his breast pocket for his pipe. He heard the bald-headed major say, "The army remains, as before, the backbone of the Reich."

Then the man in the middle, a smooth-shaven fellow of indeterminate age with an oily, sardonic voice added some comments of his own. "Social Democrats—just don't start talking to me about socialism. 'An open road for the qualified man' is what they write up as the latest news in their papers. Who are the qualified men? All I see are asses and people with sharp elbows. People with that kind of qualification were always out front."

The frosty-haired man cursed Berlin and turned to a younger man next to him, a dark blond with a black patch over one eye and a missing left arm. When the man began to speak it became evident that he could move only the left side of his mouth, the right side simply hung there; he spoke in blurred, angry words, and the gentlemen bent toward him in order to hear. Radek pricked up his ears and caught phrases like: "The rich bourgeoisie, nothing but the rich bourgeoisie, who are always out front, grabbing for the leadership, already in cahoots with English and French capitalists. That pack of stock-market wolves always gets along. That's why they tell us we should adopt the English and French model of government."

The frosty-haired man: "And what do we do?"

"You know yourself. We're supposed to go along. It's what's demanded."

The frosty-haired man banged his fist softly on the table. For a long while after that there were only whispers, they spoke about Russia and pointed out several Russians present. Radek also heard the man of indeterminate age asking the maimed man how he was feeling.

He lisped, "They're keeping me busy reading. I'm about to start in on Goethe. He's a strange fellow. That Faust stuff is a story for professors and nothing more."

The frosty-haired man tapped him on the shoulder. "My opinion precisely."

490

Radek looked at his watch and got up. He stood with his back to the table where the hated Wylinski was sitting and things were still quite lively. He heard someone say, "A victory of the red international is out of the question here. Things won't work without free enterprise." "But you can't deny that the Social Democrats, at least thus far, have made a regular cult of denying the human personality."

Radek left in alarm.

At the checkroom a short gentleman with a huge, towering head was just being helped into his coat. Radek seemed to recall that the man had been seated at Wylinski's table. He was afraid he was a Russian. But the man—is our Motz, who of course belonged to Wylinski's coterie. Motz smiled at the learned Radek as if he had many things to say to him, and without invitation walked with him to the door. He said in purest High German, "Impressive, free speech in a democracy, isn't it? Did you see the gentlemen at the head table in the center. They were very big guns during the war. They don't introduce themselves, they simply meet, sit together and talk."

And at that he looked at Radek, who had now assumed the role of a journalist. He made a few kind remarks while they strode together through the empty front room of the restaurant. By the time they arrived at the entry it was understood that they would accompany each other in the direction of the armory.

Motz was feeling neglected by his dye-job girlfriend today. She thought of herself as Wylinski's lady, refused to go out with him of an evening. He predicted she would soon take a great fall, and was now seeking a rival for her on the sly in order to facilitate her return to him. He was looking "all over Berlin," which meant in the various smaller ballrooms.

"During the war," Motz the feckless Napoleon said, "I was forbidden to speak my opinions aloud as a free man. I was a defeatist, they said. They wanted to take from me my right to criticize, to the 'Critique of Common Sense' that Kant did not write. Of course it was all doomed to collapse."

"You would have had better advice for them?" asked Radek, the learned Russian.

"Without a doubt, actually any of us would have. If they had asked us. Now deserters and stragglers form political blocs, and we had the biggest mess just eight days ago because those malingerers hadn't been given the attention they thought their due."

"What sort of interests do you yourself represent, if I may ask? You were on the front of course."

"Absolutely, during the whole war. On the domestic front. I'm a country commissioner, forgive me, a member of a farmers' council."

This did indeed perplex Radek. "How is that?"

"You don't believe it, seeing that I'm here in the city and drinking beer at Habel's. My property lies outside the city gates." (It was still those same garden plots that he had taken a lease on and finally been unable to pay for.) "I keep a few domestic animals. Naturally, I'm neglecting it all at present."

"Why is that?"

"Various reasons. My interests in winter, during the quiet season, are not those of the country."

"But you had yourself elected to the farmers' council."

"The others wanted it. I am fighting to see that the farmers' interests get represented at all. Freedom of speech, that is what I try to promulgate among the people. Present your wishes at the right place and the right time, and with the necessary verve. In contrast to the Bolsheviks, I am for free and open speech at this stage of things."

"We're speaking of peaceful debate then. That eases my mind extraordinarily."

"You've seen what I mean there at Habel's. Wasn't that pleasant? People talk, drink, get to know one another better as individuals, and ultimately that's the important thing."

"And the result? You then avoid moving on to deeds?"

"Who expects results from a pleasant get-together? It's sufficient in itself. We've learned not to act on the basis of our conversations. Russia's example terrifies us, it has been most enlightening. We are in Germany and we'll not let ourselves be swept on to deeds by our words. I, for example, advocate purest, strictist parliamentarianism, an absolute form, parliamentarianism for its own sake. I am reproached for that. But once the dynasty has vanished one should not, I think, immediately fall into the mistake the others are making and start doing everything at once. I express my opinion, I advise others to do the same, that is enough. I even mistrust my own thoughts."

Radek: "And when will you act?"

Motz thought for a while and smirked. (He was thinking of his dye-job.) "When nature urges me to."

Radek hesitated. Is this fellow a fool or are there really people like this in Germany? He slowed his pace so that he could hear more. They were standing in front of the palace of the old Kaiser. Motz pointed up at the window now famous in history.

"Love of country, patriotism—one can say it openly now—have only antiquarian interest. Love of country was let loose on the world by educated fools posing as schoolmasters. The notion originated in Latin and Greek classes; it got stuck in people's brains and so they started applying it to everyday uses. People talk about defensive wars. When the war began in Russia in 1914, did you feel attacked?"

"No," Radek admitted with amusement.

"Me neither. At most by certain restrictions that were supposed to be in the best interests of the fatherland. It was an ugly time. No one was allowed to speak. The tyrants, from the sergeants on up, went berserk."

Radek had trouble following this will-o'-the-wisp. He kept trying to figure out how to classify him. They moved on past the huge monument to Wilhelm I. Radek commented probingly, "They let that stand, too."

Motz, calmly: "It's too big for a museum. And no museum wants it. It doesn't bother anyone here. Dynasties are bearable, after all, when they're in bronze. Old Begas bungled the whole thing of course. Over by the palace fountains are some nymphs of his, nicely developed girls; they're better."

They were already at the square in front of the palace. Radek felt the pull of the royal stables. Motz held him tight by his sleeve. "You're not going over there, are you? It's not worth even looking at. That's the German revolution."

"What do you have against sailors?"

"Go have a look, for all I care. Those are the biggest asses of the century. They think they can create a revolution in Germany."

Radek felt himself losing his temper. "But I don't think you can just reject them like that out of hand."

Motz listened, replied loftily, "Go right on and talk, good sir. It's obvious you're not from here. Rest assured, if you came here fleeing your Russian revolution, seeking peace and security, you made the right move. Nothing can happen here."

Radek: "On the contrary, several things have occurred here already, and more appears to be in preparation. It's awfully dark on the horizon. You'll have to admit that something has to happen now that the troops have marched in. It can't stay like this. Either the generals will use what's left of their troops to strike a blow, or the people will strike it."

Motz replied with a "hm, hm." "You're an intellectual, you can't free yourself from your profession, I can tell. Those are a priori notions. But compare them to reality. Over there you see sailors. They stand around and smoke. Looking at those men, how do you arrive at the conclusion that either the generals or the people will strike a blow? My guess is both will be struck a blow by the German's love of comfy peace and quiet. Just look at those sailors. There they stand, not hurting anyone. They want their rations and their pay, and in their wildest dreams they wouldn't think of laying down their lives. I am convinced a good many of them even visit the dentist. These people are too shrewd and entirely lacking in passion. They are also uneducated, so that in any case the schoolmasters couldn't sell them on classical patriotism. No, good sir, the old adage is still true: there'll be no revolution among the Germans—at best a counterrevolution, and even that only as a police action to restore order. Since, of course, these sailors do get on one's nerves in the end."

Radek shook his head. "Well now, those sailors have some things behind them. They come from Kiel and they started a revolution there last month, a real revolution."

"I know," Motz replied. "I've heard. I've been here in Berlin for a while now. But firstly, these men are hardly the ones from Kiel, and secondly, no matter what, they're completely out of place here."

And just as if he were speaking with Wylinski and Brose-Zenk, he pulled out all the stops. "We just look deeper in order to understand these things. In Russia, if I'm not mistaken, you've had Nihilists, conspirators and terrorists for decades now. Whole batteries of them, your czar was able to populate Siberia with them. They threw bombs and shot pistols and the czar hanged them. But however many he might hang there were always new ones. That was a real movement, and found its capstone and conclusion in the revolution. Our development is just the opposite. We started in 1848. Then came the true red anarchists and socialists. But they got paler and pinker, and now they've ended up with a black, red and gold flag. And who knows what they may yet become. Even old Bebel was not as wild-eyed as he should have been. And when Ed Bernstein came back from England an almost heavenly tranquillity spread over the land, disturbed only by the police."

He placed a hand on Radek's shoulder. "My good sir, my dear friend, as an educated man, as a scientist, you must regard all this from another perspective. We Germans, as I'm sure you heard before you got here, are very businesslike, very serious. If this tribe, of which I am myself a member, is to be forced out of its Buddhistic contemplations, forced to act, then that action must be a consequence of the contemplation. Which means the deed must have a philosophical, a theological core. It is my deep conviction that a revolution can occur in Germany only on theological grounds and to a theological end. All the rest are only peripheral revolutions, in other words, disturbances of the peace. I quite consciously advance my theory as a counter to present-day Marxism, and I prophesy that Marxism will come to a sad end here in Germany, because its theological core is too harmless. The heaven on earth it promises is not enough. Neither hunger nor hate will set us in motion—only God and Satan. And those sailors over there sense that, misled though they are. Someone has stationed them there at the stables and they don't know what they're supposed to do. They'll soon be torn right out of their indecisiveness."

Radek furiously hastened his step. Motz had to cross the palace square with him for better or worse. Motz began to thunder against Russia. "You know, of course, our greatest classical writer is Goethe. But do you know how he behaved at the bombardment of Valmy, when he ran up against the revolutionary army of France? He observed with great clarity: here begins a new epoch in world history. And having said that, he pensively returned to Weimar and went on writing poetry. Later he was enthusiastic about Napoleon, saw him as the great man, which matches perfectly with our schoolmasters' notion of things. I can remember two lines out of all his verses: 'And if you wish to know what's right, then ask the noble ladies, them alone.' If you want to understand Germany, I beg you to visit our beautiful National Gallery as well, where you'll find paintings by Richter and Blechen, wonderful little paintings, miniatures most of them, still lifes, that most authentic genre of German painting. The still life is the German form of existence."

Radek cast a sharp glance at him. "And from that, good sir, will soon come a revolution before you know what's happening."

Motz took the comment with equanimity and a smile. "You're a member of the aesthetics faculty, that's all. Everything seems beautiful to you. You have pipe-dreams and would like to see them realized. But I ask you: who among us is going to revolt and who will lead? I saw Liebknecht in Friedrichshain at the funeral for the victims of the revolution, heard him speak. He is a good man, the salt of the earth. He thinks what he says. He says what he thinks. It is depressing to see that at the head of a revolutionary movement. It's a great pity for him. I truly feel sorry for him."

Motz Finds a Substitute Mistress

Motz continued to stick to Radek as they entered the stables. People were grouped around the speakers in the central hall. The two guests from the breakfast table at Habel's lost one another in one of these human knots. Motz listened to one speech in amazement. The ranting and raving angered him, the whole overheated atmosphere was distasteful. The phrase "loafers and mischief-makers" was on the tip of his tongue. As they were singing the Internationale, Motz left depressed.

He thought to himself: the Internationale is a hymn like "Jesus Christ my Sure Defense"—good for funerals. There are only three things that are international—pigheadedness, stupidity and laziness. And they belonged together since the creation of the world. The Spartacists were fooling themselves imagining they could get by on pigheadedness alone. Stupidity and laziness were sure to battle for a spot and put pigheadedness in its place.

On the Schloss Bridge stood people hoping to sell something, probably stolen goods—army supplies, shoes, new military boots, but Christmas toys too. One frozen young woman without a hat offered Motz a woolen scarf. He bought it because he needed one. He took several steps, then turned around and went back and bought another from the woman in order to get a better look at her. He examined her carefully. He wondered whether he could make something of her. Motz was a great discoverer of women, though generally for other people. But to make something out of a girl was for him one of the most exciting enterprises in the world. His expert eye told him that the young woman was good.

Half an hour later they met again in a little restaurant on Post-strasse, near the Mühlendamm passage, where he sat with his two scarves waiting for her. She had fixed herself up in the meantime, and Motz was at once compelled to forbid her that hairdo, it wasn't for her. He was satisfied with his morning. The educated Russian, that naive dreamer, had not been a bad guide.

The girl has introduced herself as Selma, and says she lives with her mother. That evening Motz will go with her to Resi's, the dance hall on Blumenstrasse in the same building as the lovely old Residenz-Theater, and will dance the fox-trot and the blues-step. He is mistaken, however, in believing he'll have to show her the latest dances—she knows them already.

It is a "widows' ball." They sit beside each other at a little table with a colored lamp. During the dance, with each change of mood in the music, the lighting in the hall changes, moving from a simple reddish-white brightness to a magical dusky violet that gives everyone in the hall a cadaverous pallor as they jiggle to their dance macabre—then to a soft pink when all the widows and widowers float like cherubs, men and women, young and old, smiling sweetly, their faces pressed together. But what happens during the next three minutes when the lights are doused completely (or, if you will, turn to black) cannot, of course, be described. In any case a general and mournful "Aw!" greets the return of illumination.

There at their gaudy table Motz is to learn that his new Selma is married, that her husband is an unemployed musician and is sitting catty-corner from them in the hall at a table in the raised section—with a fat widow. He realizes she wants to make her husband jealous. "She has money, and I have to sell scarves on the Schloss Bridge," Selma says sadly. It is a case for Motz. Right at the table Selma hangs herself around his neck and swears, without his even asking, to follow him to the ends of the earth. At any rate she'll not sell scarves anymore. He figures he has killed two birds with one stone: I'll get my dye-job back and she her musician—if she even wants him afterward.

Motz did not realize what poison he strewed over the stranger with whom he went for a walk.

In his room at the stables, Radek slowly and gloomily took off his beard. Liebknecht was not to be seen, he would have to go off in pursuit of him again. But Radek was not attracted to the hunt. He sat at the typewriter his Russian aide had left standing open, the dictation half taken. It was an optimistic report for friends in Moscow about the mood here. He skimmed the report now, tore it out of the machine, ripped it up, crumpling the pieces into the wastebasket.

He was in a rage. What was this Liebknecht doing now, what did he do all day? He talked and talked. It was parliamentarianism gone berserk. That gasbag from a moment ago, that cynic, was basically correct. They talk, it is enough just to talk, no one thinks about the consequences. It's all a matter of peaceful debate, they are at the stage of free speech. That is what I told Liebknecht before, the liberal revolution with kid gloves, even worse than that. And who acts, who organizes? Liebknecht wouldn't dream of it. He talks, he expatiates, he gushes, a lovely and pure heart letting its feelings run free. I really have to ask myself what these damned Germans have to do with Marxism. Marx gives us Russians a strategic plan, draws up the attack, analyzes the possibilities of the battle, the relative strength on their side and on ours. Marxism is a military academy of the revolutionary proletariat. And what does this pack make of it? That fool, that cynic just now, is ultimately just saying what the others keep to themselves: for the Germans Marxism is apparently a new sort of Middle Ages. Yet another attempt to build St. Augustine's City of God here on earth. And naturally a flimsy one at that.

But they still don't see the main thing, and are so blind they'll probably never see it, that the history of mankind is a morass of such attempts. That's why they can find no Lenin. And that's why there is only one solution for them: somewhere or other, if need be even in Russia, to find them a dictator and assign him to them, a Robespierre who'll drain that swamp and educate them to realism. Heads will have to roll, and no quarter will be shown. A Robespierre, and if I had anything to say in the matter, if I were their dictator now, the first head I would see roll is that of that die-hard pacifist Liebknecht.

What did that cynic, that fool, say just now: God or Satan, that's the only thing that can set the Germans in motion. Perhaps he's right.

Radek brooded there in front of the typewriter. The upshot is that I shall have to act on my own. Time presses. We don't dare depend on Liebknecht. Every day counts. A missed opportunity does not come back. I must see how I can work independently of him. There has to be more than just this endless agitation. When push comes to shove and things start rolling it will carry him along with it. We must shape events.

He stood up and lit his pipe. Then he went through the adjacent room and called a few Russian friends to join him. He locked himself in with them. After a few minutes they left the stables together and went to a small hotel where one of them had a room.

Concerning Black Rays

A physics lesson sets a mystic's mills grandly rolling. Afterward he can still gaze in wonder at his living image in a mirror.

Hilda Says Good-Bye

Becker hung on those dark words: "Then it was not a defeat after all."

The warm, saving melody of weeping—Hilda had again laid her head on the desk, he did not know what was happening inside her—beat without interruption, and yet constantly new, at his ears.

What variety there was in this world. How good her weeping was. Slowly those swatches of mist departed where that brood of hell had moved about, the mocking handsome man, the lion, the disgusting dancing rat.

The world is wide indeed. I dared to crawl along a narrow ledge and I fell—but I'm not dead, not dead.

When his mother unlocked the door, Hilda went out to her and they whispered in the hall for a long time.

Becker saw his mother again now too. Return from a journey around the world.

Hilda and his mother spoke in front of him about the inflammation of the throat he had come down with. His mother considered it a lucky accident. Inflammation is good sometimes when the head is afflicted. Then Hilda gave an evasive account of her long absence that morning. But finally with increasing attention both of them watched their patient, who sat up without difficulty now—they had to hold him down—and looked at them openly and easily. While his mother sat down beside him, Hilda left the room, gathered up her things and crept away.

She had to run. Once again she had to run. It was her fate to run like this, to leave behind the men she was fond of. She had become terribly aware of just how fond she was of Becker—and that she was not good enough to love him. No, she didn't want to do it. She didn't want to ruin this man too.

Dear God, I beg you, be gracious to me and lead me not into temptation. Forgive me for what I intended, and stand by me. If I can not change myself—if you should take your hand from me—then grant that I can separate myself from him.

And as she entered her little room the decision was firm within her. She remembered how just a few hours before she had left this room, how she had wanted to leave but something satanic had held her there until she had subdued it.

She saw his image before her again now, the love and the pain, it overwhelmed her. Again she sat down at the table unable to move.

After a while a voice spoke to her, though not to her earthly ears. It was not even something in her conscious self that heard the voice. But it was like a building moved by an earthquake, swaying to its topmost stories, while inside the people are jostled about without realizing what is shaking them, that was how Hilda experienced it.

The voice said, "You will surely die. Your flesh will melt. The bones that bear you will be broken. But you shall not die with them. Because you suffer, you shall not die. Rise up and go. Leave what you possess so that you do not swell up and then collapse again like a worm, like a fly sucked dry by a spider.

"Do not love the world and what is in the world."

For the rest of the day Hilda did not go out, but her thoughts raced here and there.

That evening she prayed in church for a long time. She had found the solution. First she thought she would return home. But then she sensed that for that she must first be much stronger, although she yearned passionately to see her father.

The next morning she had a long conversation with Friedrich's mother. She did not divulge everything to her, but his mother understood. "I'll stay in the area," Hilda said. She planned to go to Britz, near Berlin, where there was an opening for a nurse in the hospital there. Hilda had in fact already taken the position. Britz was a compromise, not very far and not too close.

She sat down with Becker once more. He lay bedded in the sweetness of Hilda's lament. The feeling had not changed: a weeping human creature. It had left him for several hours and he had sunk back down into the morass. But then his glance had floated up to the hook there on the wall from which he had fallen, and he thought: I have been saved, yes saved, but for what? For what? His mother had not left him for a moment yesterday. It was better today, and finally she was there, his rescuer, Hilda herself.

She saw that he felt better, took the bandage off and rubbed salve on the sore spots.

"Now I'm going to dress it correctly and we'll leave it on then for a few days. Afterward the doctor can decide whether it's still needed."

He gratefully stroked her hand. "Yes, madame doctor."

"And how did things go yesterday afternoon, Friedrich?"

"The visions, you know what I mean, are still there at times, they come and go, but they've grown pale and distant. They don't torment me anymore. No one speaks to me, no one calls out."

He watched her roll up the bandage she had removed. Suddenly, without looking at him, she said in a light tone of voice that it really was time he got better, because otherwise they would have got into difficulty and she wouldn't have known how to arrange things. She had had a call from a hospital, in Britz, and she had gone out there and couldn't turn them down. They needed experienced help, a surgical nurse for men seriously wounded in the war.

"I understand. And you—do you want to go?"

"Friedrich, I must. I have to work. But I'll come see you. I'll keep an eye on you."

He could not get it into his head. He grew anxious. She assured him she wasn't leaving today or tomorrow, wouldn't think of leaving him in the lurch as long as his nerves were still shaky.

But like a child he clasped her to him.

"Hilda, what does that mean? You're going? You saved me. Don't go. I won't let you go."

"Your life, Friedrich, your precious life, do you really believe I'm capable of saving it? I couldn't have done that. But I was able to be here. And that is my greatest happiness."

She covered his face with kisses. Enraptured, she kissed his mouth, his cheeks, his eyes. As she showered him with her fire and passion, he begged her, "Hilda."

She pleaded, "Let me go."

Until at last she could lay her hot head against his and breathe wearily.

"How happy you look, Hilda."

She did not answer. When she stood up and suggested that she had to go, he shook his head. "Britz it is then. And I'm merely a part-time job for you. Britz. It doesn't ring any bell with me. Is that on the tram line or the intercity, Hilda?"

"It's not so far." She tried to smile. "And I'm not taking the job today you know."

And then something happened as she stood there, her coat already on, something that had not ever happened in that room. At the door, she took out her necklace and, holding the little icon of Mary attached to it, she knelt down and whispered a prayer. When she got up again Becker wanted to follow her. But she was already gone and immediately afterward he heard the front door close.

Becker sat there in his study perplexed. His mother came in. Her eyes showed she had been crying.

500

He: "That wasn't good-bye was it? A permanent good-bye?"

"Now Friedrich, Britz isn't that far."

"The house next door can be far away."

His mother noticed that he had begun to tremble again. She had to sit down beside him, and she succeeded in calming him.

He saw Hilda sitting there at the desk, and her long and intense weeping filled the room like organ music—and then her pain just now. She had knelt on the floor, the little icon of Mary in her hand. And now after all the misery of that long, exhausting day that had just passed, now on the morning of Hilda's good-bye, he was granted an hour of deep rest.

It entered him heavily like honey. He felt himself laden with sweet honey. It seemed to him that he could eat it, live from it his whole life long, the rest of his life, this portion of it, this little bit of life.

The Wonders of Nature

Later in the day Dr. Krug appeared at Becker's to ask him whether he would appreciate a visit by the school director. At first Becker's mother did not want to let Krug in under any circumstances, but Becker begged her, "It takes my mind off things."

But when Krug was once seated in his room Becker did not know why he had asked him in. He listened without thinking. So this is the world again. I should receive it as something new. But Krug noticed nothing. And since Becker said nothing he talked about things that interested him. This time he was concerned with "black rays." After a while Becker too paid attention.

" 'Black rays' are invisible to our eyes. What our eyes perceive is only a small band of rays from 400 to 700 microns. It extends from violet to red, that's the zone of visible light. But beyond the violet rays there are the ultraviolet ones, a small band of light that is of interest to biologists and medical experts. They consider it indispensable for life, it creates vitamins; but there are also some highly dangerous rays. There are Roentgen's X-rays, gamma rays with which atoms can be split—the most monstrous thing we can imagine and one with presumably immense unforeseen consequences. But naturally not tomorrow morning—good things need time, and besides, nature sees to it that there are limits to everything. Given what I know of mankind, the first thing he'll do with such a new discovery is build himself motors with which to get up into the stratosphere so he can better bombard his enemies. And then finally—but who can ever say finally—there are cosmic rays. They are five-thousandths of a micron long and can be found only outside our atmosphere. Very refined fellows they are, probably lethal. We're working on that, trying to get them under our control, who knows for what purpose."

Becker: "They're all rays of some sort?"

"Tremendous, isn't it? I'm glad it interests you. Doesn't that sound fine, 'black rays'? The layman is captivated by it every time. But of course the world's full of surprises."

Becker: "And what do you have to say about them?"

Krug smiled. "I simply say, tremendous. I raise a threatening finger and say: 'Be careful, watch out! High tension wire.'"

Becker was fully involved. So there is a spirit world even for scientists. I wonder what conclusions they draw from that. Not just one single world, but countless worlds. What is supernatural, what is natural?

Becker said, "You threaten them, tell them to be careful, high tension wires. But that doesn't accomplish much."

Krug: "By the way, there are still other rays as well. Very curious ones. You never know the ins and outs of nature, and it's better not to have a theory because it won't be valid come tomorrow. There is a man by the name of Wood who is said to have created a filter of nickel oxide that swallows up all visible rays and lets only the ultraviolet ones through. And what do they do? They are invisible and stay that way. But their normally invisible black light causes something remarkable when it falls on certain other substances. The substances on which the black light falls begin to glow. They really give off a form of light that our eyes can perceive, a fleeting light."

"And what substances are those?" asked Becker, filled with amazement.

"All sorts of organic and inorganic ones. They've catalogued some two thousand of them already."

And I am one of them, thought Becker. And if contemporary science never provides me anything more than this glimpse, this metaphor, I shall praise it forevermore.

Krug, happy to see Becker so interested, thought he had to provide more information. "So, you see, there are revolutions not just in governments. Science is in an uproar too. What would Copernicus or Galileo say to our present theory, for example, at least the one that seems simplest and most plausible, that not only does the earth revolve about a fixed star, the sun, but that the fixed stars move as well, that our whole solar system wanders about—so that ultimately one can hardly speak of motion and rest. One must simply see the two in relationship to one another. Because what is fixed, what stands still? We're still seeking the motionless center."

He smiled proudly at Becker, who had cast down his eyes. It is still not the whole of nature, still not the whole world. They exist, and will continue to exist without that fixed point, that is true. Science had brought that to light.

He looked toward the door. In his mind he saw a vision of Hilda, of a human being, suffering. Our existence—a walk along the edge of the abyss. And nevertheless, we are not lost.

Greek Love

When Krug accompanied the director up to see him an hour later —Krug himself then took his leave—another conversation took place.

The director began with the entrance of the troops into the city and how it had all gone quite differently from what many had expected. The whole thing had been blown up in a grandiose way, but had proved a flash in the pan. "It hardly interests the man in the street. People are only interested in what the working class is going to do. They're all talking about this upcoming congress. It looks as if we can expect some new action from Spartacus; I'm afraid this time it could really turn violent. The uneasiness and general discontent are very great."

"The general discontent?"

"Yes, no one is satisfied. Instead of bringing together the energies of the nation for some common effort, they let them disintegrate. What will become of our country? The school is not what it should be either."

After an extended pause, apparently only after struggling long and hard with himself, the well-dressed, clever man spoke of his own troubles. There were intrigues against him. Becker knew that already. He also knew that the director was much too distinguished, too broad-minded, too much the aesthete for him to please these small, mean-spirited teachers. With some torment the director spoke of things that Becker had heard about, but only from a distance, but that startled him now. Pupils from the upper classes often came to the director's apartment. He explained how he loved to show these young people his collections of paintings, sculpture and books, to which Becker could find nothing to object, except that the peculiarly shy way in which the director spoke of it was obvious.

"The things they accuse me of at the school," the man said with a forced smile, "I cannot even mention. The worst thing is that apparently the pupils who felt I was favoring them made other students envious and jealous. And it was from their boasting that this talk of my 'love affairs,' do you hear what I'm saying, 'love affairs,' arose. Yes, that's the term they use. And it has got as far as the parents now. I suspect, by the way, that my apartment is being spied upon of late."

This was a ruined man, Becker sensed, the way he sat there so limply before him. The man pulled himself together, shook his head and changed his tune.

"Let us drop this topic. I really didn't come up to see you on that account. I wanted to congratulate you on the progress you're making with your health. Dr. Krug has told me all about it."

"Krug was sitting here with me just a while ago. He was telling me some amazing things about physics."

"About physics? But what use to us are the natural sciences, my dear friend? You know, they were to blame for a good part of this war. But I believe the war will yet prove a turning point for science as well. The liberal arts, the modern Cinderellas, will be restored to their due honor."

To his amazement Becker did not react to this. And when he asked him directly, Becker said, "I don't understand what you're driving at."

"Well, I mean the reemergence of the arts and all those things in which the human spirit, truth and beauty are implicit. A new brilliance for art, philosophy, literature."

To which Becker responded coldly, "I've heard nothing about it."

"But how is that possible? Dr. Krug was just telling me about your opinions. I'll grant, however, that some wonderful things have been discovered in physics of late."

"And what did Krug describe to you as my opinions?"

"That, as is only proper for a classical philologist, you considered human beings and humanism the most important thing of all. That you spoke of it's 'imperative' upon and in us."

"Of imperative? Ah, yes."

"He came to me quite depressed by that. It had hit him hard, it seemed. Krug is a clever man, and scientists sense the weakness of their own position."

Becker said nothing.

"All right then, my dear Becker, explain your imperative to me."

Becker took some time to answer the man; he had an unpleasant feeling about him, even a slight sense of disgust, though he had at first been so taken by him.

He said, "I cannot recall clearly what I said about that. With an orthodox man of science, a believer in physics like Krug, one ends up on the defensive using all sorts of phrases. Explain to me yourself Herr Director, what intrigues you about the word 'imperative.'"

"I see in it an advance against the contemporary dominance of the natural sciences, and by that I mean an advance on behalf of the arts, belles lettres, all the things we love but have practically dismissed—the splendors of Greek antiquity included. I see you, Dr. Becker, as a true warrior in the vanguard, a man continuing the battle on a new front."

Becker, implacably: "The demand one makes of oneself, responsibility per se, what does that have to do with Greek antiquity, with the arts or belles lettres?"

"The demand one makes of oneself?"

"What demand were you thinking of?"

"Then I did indeed misunderstand our good colleague, Dr. Krug. It seemed to me, of course, that you understood it in the same way. I thought you were speaking in general of an intellectual demand, that someone should rise up in the name of ancient Greece and throw down the gauntlet to this wretched age of reason and expediency. That is how I wrongly construed your meaning. I was mistaken then. But one could go on to discuss the idea."

"I was speaking truly of the demand one makes of oneself."

"One that you, my good Dr. Becker, really need not make of yourself." (That is why he's sick after all.) "As it says in the song: 'after such sacrifices, so great, so noble.' But in such desperate times as these one ought to call mankind to remember the great values of the past and not drag those things that are most sacred through the dirt. And from whom can one receive clearer instruction than from the minds of our old Hellas, which you too love above all else. There stands the bust of the divine Sophocles. Take my advice, Dr. Becker, let no one shake you in your confidence. Here in antiquity live truths that have survived thousands of years and will survive thousands more still."

Becker said calmly, "They—have not brought me any further."

"Such are the times we live in, my dear colleague."

But Becker could not keep silent. "And you yourself, do you get along well using these old truths? Do you have the impression they give you what you need? We are speaking man to man now, but you brought up the subject. Does Hellenic beauty guide you well through life? Did it guide us all well? Does it help us, support us? You were complaining just now about the school, the parents and the students."

"Ah, those intrigues, what have they to do with it?"

The gentleman looked off to one side.

Becker: "And can you battle your way through those intrigues?"

"Easily," said the director, straightening his tie.

Becker glanced up at him: behold my brother, my brother in depravity. He too has come to a dead end.

Becker: "I think if I were to be a Greek once more, with all my heart, I would openly follow my models. I would do it in spite of all the consequences involved. Whether others object or not. Think of Socrates. He did not hide."

The director sat there very erect, and pretended nonchalance. "That would indeed be logical. It would create quite a stir."

"It would be the gauntlet that you would throw down before the modern world in the name of ancient Hellas."

"Certainly, that's true, no doubt of it. But in my position, how could I do that, how could I manage, me of all people, to engage in such an active battle?"

So then he's a coward too. He only drapes himself in aestheticism.

Becker: "As far as the word 'imperative' goes, which interested you so much, I merely mentioned it at one point in order to make a banal point. One should make one's actions congruent with the demands one places upon oneself."

"I understand," said the director with a smile. "It was a matter of moral scruples, like those so many people have nowadays. One might almost speak of a relapse into Christianity. The war generation has a hangover."

He smirked and nodded benevolently. Becker felt he could not bear the man much longer. Then his mother looked in and helped the visitor to bring things to a conclusion.

The Illumination

A unique moment and the reading of a book.

The Sign

For all the rest of that day, Becker was serious and gravely tranquil. For the first time in what seemed an infinity he accompanied his mother for a walk out on the street. His step was superb, and moving as he did on his mother's arm without a cane, no one could notice anything.

Up a side street lived one of the poor families that Frau Becker looked after. They stayed a half hour in the parlor of this war widow and her two small children. "Mother's got a job," the older girl shouted as soon as Frau Becker entered. Then the woman herself came in—it was only occasionally handing out newspapers and flyers.

"Well then, these political arguments are at least good for something," Frau Becker said. He saw his mother slip the woman some money, and they had brought zwieback and apples with them from home. Together the two women examined the four-year-old girl—her adenoids were swollen and she looked very pale. Becker meanwhile sat in the background against the wall. Next to him hung the picture of a soldier, trimmed with a black ribbon. He was an ordinary young man with a heavy moustache. It was impossible to discover anything even the least bit out of the ordinary in that calm, plain face, but he was the man whom this young woman had married, the father of these two little girls, and now a dead member of that giant army sleeping on the fields of Europe. That I can live, that I should be alive.

And he walked over to the two women and began to ask the widow questions. He was simply a dead man like many others he had known. He had left this family behind. Outside, his mother pressed his hand, she was happy for him. "I think, Friedrich, that you are really well again."

But he knew that he was not well "again."

He felt he had to get to his room. Once there he walked about the spot where Hilda had knelt. He gazed at the desktop where she had thrown her head down, where the sound of her weeping had rung out. The wood of suffering.

And suddenly before his eyes he saw the wood of martyrdom, the wood to which that crucified man had been nailed, man and God, a suffering man and God.

And the grand, the precious thought, mankind's king of thoughts pulsed through him: it really happened, it is true. God was here, he did not abandon us. He did not hide away in heaven after creating us human beings the way we are. He came himself, suffered with us and has bound us to heaven once again. Pain and disgust had not deterred him. He shed his blood on earth and ascended into heaven.

The floor, the wood where Hilda had knelt—I have been given the sign.

And a terrible excitement roiled up inside him and overturned everything. His eyes were dry, his body ice-cold. He sank down onto his knees like a sacrificial lamb, his head bowed. Do with me what you will, I am nothing. I do not deserve your grace, destroy this wretched worm of a man.

His brow touched the wood. Destroy me, rip me out by the roots. I have sinned. Let me do penance.

Shaking with cold, not fully conscious, he struggled to his feet and leaned against the wall. It seemed to him as if he must die now. His life would now be taken from him.

But the room grew bright again, grew very clear. He could hear a sound, like the whir and high whistle of a buzz-saw off in the distance. Then a second, hollower sound was added on top of it, and from it now and again emerged something like a spoken word. Sometimes small sentences were linked together.

It asked, it repeated, "Do you understand? Do you understand? Do you understand me?"

He murmured, "Yes." In the first moment mistrust awoke in him. He feared it was once again the Latin American gentleman, but it was not his warm, pliant voice. It was a very deep, evenly modulated voice. Becker collected the words. Why did he hear only tag ends? I would like to listen to this man. But he did not venture out into the middle of the room.

He heard: "Even was now come . . . unto the sea" (the words could be collected better now). "Labour not for the meat which perisheth, but for that meat which endureth unto everlasting life."

And now it all came connected together.

"And Jesus said unto them, I am the bread of life: he that cometh to me shall never hunger; and he that believeth on me shall never thirst."

And as the human being at the wall heard this he felt he had eaten and drunk his fill.

Again the voice could be heard. "I am the bread which came down from heaven. I am the bread of life. Do you understand these words, Friedrich? Do you understand?" He could hear a rustling sound; a long, old-fashioned garment rustled, white and flowing. Behind the tall figure it was bright, the room seemed to vanish, in its place an expanse of cheery, green plain, a river flowing majestically between rows of poplars, and behind that a magnificent cathedral with a steeple. And a memory from the past came to Becker, one that brought pain and yearning, from when the dragon of war still crept across the land.

"And you do recognize me, the old man. And now you speak, saying, 'May God greet you, oh most bitter of bitternesses, you shall be my sweet sister, you are full of grace.' The birds warble their song, he who has ears can understand it and God untiringly sends his messengers and does not cease to call you."

"I know you, Johannes Tauler."

"Now you have arrived at the tree of the Holy Cross. You have entered through the gate of dread and despair. You shall be refreshed, my son."

"Why, why? I have not earned that. No refreshment."

"We humans are struck by the sting of rods. God dusts us off with stinging rods. But he has sent us his son. The sweet wine of heavenly love he has given us to drink."

"Peace, sweet peace," the song broke out in Becker, just as it had in the railroad car as it rolled along. "I greet you, peace, you shall be my friend and brother, I have bound you to me with my blood, you are my blood brother. We have come out of the war, out of a long, hard war. Do not desert me."

Becker sat without stirring at his desk for a whole hour. His body grew warm again.

His mother was rattling about in the kitchen. He stood up and went hastily to the living room where his mother kept the few books she owned in a small bookcase next to the grandfather clock, among them the Bible, a hymnal, a catechism. Becker reached quickly for the Bible and took it to his room. His mother was watching through the window in the door, saw him disappear with a book and knew after a quick look at her bookcase which one he had taken.

He opened the thick, black-bound book on his desk. Postcards he had written from the field had been stuck in as bookmarks. At the front, the table of contents for the books of the New Testament, the Gospels, the Epistles, Revelation. On the first page the Gospel of Matthew began. But the pages opened themselves, and then chapter five lay before his eyes. There were the Beatitudes, the true fulfillment of the law.

He read:

"And seeing the multitudes, he went up into a mountain: and when he was set, his disciples came unto him: And he opened his mouth, and taught them, saying:"

Becker: he sits down and he knows. He opens his mouth and speaks.

"Blessed are the poor in spirit: for theirs is the kingdom of heaven."

It's not probing and tinkering that leads to true life. That is my case. That's why the tempters and seducers, the Latin American, the lion and the rat came to me. He rejects spiritual pride.

"Blessed are they that mourn: for they shall be comforted."

Comforted by Him, by His having lived and walked among us, by the fact that God gave us this sign that we might find Him and cling to Him. And then everything becomes transparent. Like when the wind collides with a black cloud and scatters it with one gust, so He scatters our sorrow and overcomes our despair. The suffering does not yield, but He helps us to bear it.

He read about the meek, about those who hunger and thirst for righteousness, about the merciful and the pure in heart.

I am none of these. But by His naming them, calling them blessed, the longing awakens and grows in me to be those things, to be meek, hungry for righteousness and pure of heart. When I read it I feel as if something in me were rising like grass upon a meadow after cattle had trampled it down.

Now came the sentence:

"Blessed are they which are persecuted for righteousness' sake: for theirs is the kingdom of heaven."

Persecuted for righteousness' sake. To let yourself be persecuted for the sake of righteousness and not yield. That's what He says, nothing lukewarm about that. How could He be lukewarm, though, when with one syllable He could have escaped crucifixion. But He did not speak that syllable. He remained who He was and is. He knew what He knew and would not let the truth be twisted. That means that there are more important things than our day-to-day problems, things you have to remain true to. That's how He acted, and now everyone can know how the Son of God deals with things. There I stood in front of my ego, searching for my self, for my ego, and I shook my ego, told it to give me something, and it could give me nothing because how could there be anything there that could tell me my duties, determine my path, if it were not already planted there by Him. And that's why I had to end up in despair, had already laid a hand upon myself, already hung there from that hook and was about to throw my life away because I thought it an empty shell that could show me no fruit. Then God intervened and saved me, and woke the core of my numbed ego. Ah, it is not an empty shell, this life, there is a seriousness about it. God, how I thank you that you have lifted me up out of that indignity and given me the knowledge that I am not a reed in the wind, that I am from your hand, beneath your eye.

510

You are not the gray terrible fate of the Greeks, an inescapable doom spoken by an oracle. You have come to us in our animal lair. Now—I can look at my ego without dread and despair.

Becker turned back to his book.

It can melt you. It is true, so that you yield up yourself. Yes, we should be burned up within it. Oh, you holy, you true book. That is why generation on generation has warmed itself from you. Men have fought wars for you. But to fight a war for you, that would mean something. What a miserable affair it was for which I almost died.

He directed his eyes to the lines, read the strong words about the fulfillment of the law, and could not read enough.

"And if thy right hand offend thee, cut it off, and cast it from thee: for it is profitable for thee that one of thy members should perish, and not that thy whole body should be cast into hell."

Yes, there is a heaven and earth and hell—justice, punishment and exaltation. Oh what a blessing, what liberation to know that.

And he could not contain himself and stood up. He picked up the book and took it to his mother in the living room. He showed her the passage. She saw how lucid he was. Though his eyes had something peculiarly motionless, his gaze a tendency to fixedness. Friedrich, however, was happy, exultant. She let him explain several things to her.

Then she grew uncertain again, for she did not understand much of what he said. Yes, she became alarmed, afraid this was a relapse. But then she examined his expression, and he was holding the Bible in his hand and speaking calmly and with unusual earnestness. It couldn't be a relapse. But where was the scoffer from before? She remembered a scene here in this room from the days before the war. His friend Krug had been here and with a glance at the little bookcase and at the catechism lying on the table had said (he didn't think she heard him), "Religion is for old people. It's connected with the loss of teeth. Someone ought to call this fact to the attention of dentists." And her son Friedrich had sat there and they had both laughed heartily.

There has been a change in him. All that thinking confused him. Now he has found the Bible, it will help him out of his troubles. With great joy she pulled his head toward her.

"Friedrich, you may be right. You interpret these passages that way because you're clever. I understand them the way I was taught at home along the Rhine."

"And how do you know, Mother, that I am interpreting them correctly?"

"Because you are happy. Whoever correctly understands the words of Jesus is made happy and courageous."

And she looked at him again in amazement, overwhelmed. "Friedrich, is it really true then? You're reading the Bible? You do believe?"

"Do I believe? Is that faith? That there is a heaven and a hell, that there are justice, punishment and grace, that God is not distant. And He is the same God who created the world. Is that faith?"

He went to the window and had to look out. There it is again, Berlin. A great many things are happening here, here and elsewhere in the nation. The war is over. But what I see here is just one small piece. There is also a God and grace and justice. That is what holds the world together, those are its clamps, that is what makes it endure, what pulses without contradiction through the world from heaven to earth to hell. It is the world's fundamental law, its axis.

His mother followed him with her eyes. "Friedrich, why don't you speak? You are better again, aren't you?"

He sat down next to her on the sofa. She waited anxiously for what he would say.

He: "I think so, Mother. I was very weak. It's over now."

She smiled happily. "And you have found help."

It was evening, and she insisted that they go to church together, to the one close by that Becker remembered from his school days. His mother was unutterably happy when he said yes.

The church was ice-cold. A few people sat scattered among the pews. The pastor had just ended his sermon. They sang, Becker's mother held up her hymnal for him.

"Rejoice all ye believers, and let your lights appear; the evening is advancing and darker night is near; the bridegroom is arising and soon he draweth nigh, up, pray, and watch, and wrestle, at midnight comes the cry! The watchers on the mountain proclaim the bridegroom near; go meet him as he cometh with hallelujahs clear; the marriage-feast is waiting, the gates wide open stand; up, up, ye heirs of glory, the bridegroom is at hand! Ye saints who here in patience your cross and sufferings bore shall live and reign for ever when sorrow is no more. Around the throne of glory the Lamb ye shall behold, in triumph cast before him your diadems of gold. Our hope and expectation, O Jesus, now appear; arise, thou sun so longed for, o'er this benighted sphere. With hearts and hands uplifted, we plead, O Lord, to see the day of earth's redemption that brings us unto thee."

They sang the hymn to the melody of St. Theodulf, those few people sitting there in the dimly lit, cold church. Along with the pastor there were the poor, the humble wards of the parish, a few old women, one younger woman leading a wounded soldier. Becker sat next to his mother and paged through the hymnal. She felt that he was growing restless. But the service was soon over.

Out on the street he shrugged and said, "So you see, Mother, mankind knows it all, has long known it, it's all been said, confessed, said as clearly as possible. And here you have the result. Ye mighty rulers on earth, receive your king."

His mother: "Being a Christian is very difficult. Just finding one's way to Him is difficult. People are proud and don't want to submit. But now, Friedrich, let us at least be glad."

Becker was happy for her. This provided a new tie between him and his mother. How strange, how puzzling his behavior toward her during the war had been, he had been ashamed of his illness in front of her, for her he had always wanted to be the cheerful, self-assured Becker.

Warriors and Complaining Physicians

Physicians and mothers complain about deportations carried out during the war.

The Allies in Mainz

The 33rd Corps crosses the bridgehead at the Rhine. General Lecomte installs himself in Wiesbaden.

The belt of punishment is pulled tighter about Germany. The Germans have thus far delivered only 2,000 of the 150,000 train cars demanded. They are allowed to get away with this and are given January 18th as the new date for delivery.

Deportations

The mothers of Lille complain, demanding that the fugitive Kaiser Wilhelm be punished. They say that in April 1916 the commanders of the German army had torn under-age girls from their families and permitted them to be shamefully treated. They had brought the girls into company with loose women and soldiers, introducing them to a life of abomination—which meant that the Imperial High Command and its overlord, Wilhelm II, were guilty of corrupting under-age girls.

Professors Calmette, Witz and Parety address an appeal to the medical academy and accuse the German military authorities of having committed criminal acts during the last four years, acts that violated not only international law, but the most elementary sense of human decency as well. They report the following:

"May it be left to the bar of history to pronounce judgment on the methods by which the factories in northern France were destroyed, our houses plundered, our furniture, clothes and artworks requisitioned by force, and on the imprisonment and deportation of a great many of our fellow citizens for their refusal to work for the German armies.

514

"But it seems to us impossible to excuse or justify the cold and cruel torture to which a totally defenseless civilian population was subjected. Among the most abhorrent instances was a mass deportation of some ten thousand young men and women carried out in Lille during Easter Week, 1916, by the 64th Pomeranian Infantry Regiment. At approximately 2:00 A.M. all the streets of Lille were cordoned off by soldiers armed with machine guns. An officer or noncommissioned officer and several men forced their way into every house, searched each apartment, driving all residents into one room or into the hall, where they selected those who were to be deported. The victims were given one hour to pack a few belongings. Then a soldier with his bayonet fixed came and got them and brought them to the assembly point at the train station. They were shipped off in groups to towns in the departments of Aisne, Ardennes and Meuse, where under constant guard they were treated like cattle, subjected to medical examinations of the most shameless kind and forced to work in the fields for the German army, which at harvest then appropriated almost all of the food for itself.

"Neither the pleas of the families nor later complaints filed with the German authorities could prevent or mitigate the execution of these measures on the order of General Zöllner. This man, whose name must be exposed to public vilification, was the author and instigator of almost all of the cruel persecutions that occurred. He was supported in his infamies in Lille by the police and secret agents under the command of Colonel Himmel, who now resides in Buchheide near Berlin.

"One of our physicians was forced to stand motionless for two hours out in the entry hall while a search was conducted. We physicians were all driven from our laboratories and offices, which were then transformed into military offices.

"Almost all of our children between the ages of fourteen and eighteen were torn from their families, taken from school, and along with old and infirm men above sixty were forced to serve under fire in armored battalions. They were starved, beaten, and forced to haul ammunition and build shelters. A great number of these children and old men were never seen again.

"Under the pretense of being forced to make reprisals on the French government, which was reportedly holding seventy-two German officials from Alsace-Lorraine in France, six hundred men and four hundred women were arrested and taken away as hostages. They were selected from the most distinguished families of our northern provinces. The male hostages were transported in bitter cold weather to Posen on January 6 and 12, 1918, the women sent to a prison at Holzminden in the district of Braunschweig.

"Then in an eight-day train ride these exhausted people were transported to Vilnius. There they lived in two villages, in barns, and for forty days received what was called reprisal rations. They were forced to sleep in their clothes on excelsior mattresses in three-tiered plank bunks. Their daily diet consisted of turnips and barley soup. They were kept at hard physical labor all the while and were refused the right of correspondence. In the very first week twenty-five of them died—among them Professor Buisine, the director of the Institute of Chemistry in the faculty of natural sciences in Lille. He was sixty-two years old and had a weak heart. When at the time of deportation his wife pointed out this fact, the ranking staff physician, Dr. Krug, replied with a sneer, 'He'll not infect the German army with that, my good woman.'

"Perhaps those people who did not suffer such things in the unoccupied portions of France may not comprehend the nature and degree of our grievance. Many will say that the German people are not responsible for the atrocities of their leaders. But if people had seen, as we did, with what readiness and zeal young men from the reserve and officers who were not professional soldiers perpetrated the most shameful outrages without batting an eye, without a word of apology or sympathy, they would then be forced to agree that the German heart in general, with very few exceptions, is incapable of feelings of generosity or even basic humanity.

"For that reason we do not wish in future to cooperate with Germans in any published works or to join them at any international congresses unless they have previously given public expression to their abhorrence and disapproval of the crimes perpetrated by their government and its army."

This petition, written by professors Calmette, Witz and Parety, was issued by the rector of the academy in Lille, to it he appended the following statement: "There are limits beyond which no theoretician of war can justify an escalation of severity. This limit is marked by the inviolability and sancrosanctity of the human personality. The greatest German philosophers have proclaimed this principle in their works; it has come down to us from both Rousseau and Kant."

Reception in Paris

With pomp and ceremony President Wilson is led into the banquet hall and acclaimed. Toasts are made that are intended to be understood.

Wilson

On December 13th the new World Judge, the American president Wilson, neared the coasts of Europe. The sea threw him like a pearl onto the shore. And from all sides people came running to seize and possess him.

He was human like all men, his health not good. Many of those who would confront him there on the continent were older than he, but had nerves of steel. The war was at an end militarily, but that it was only at its military end was underscored by fate—which does nothing superficial—and by the fact that as they set about making peace, in the one camp hard scrappers tugged and pulled, while in the other camp, the camp of hope, there was this delicate man who had to conserve his strength.

December 12th, the last day on board, passed peacefully. They dined with the captain and had photographs taken with the crew, for this was a historic journey, one that none of those who participated in it wanted to forget. Together they stood and sang an old song of farewell: "God Be with You Till We Meet Again." England already lay at their backs, the line of the mainland was not yet visible.

It was the second trip to Europe for Woodrow Wilson. He had made the journey across in the summer of 1904. Those were idyllic times; he was teaching as an ordinary professor of history at Princeton University, living in a comfortable house on Library Place that he had designed himself together with his wife. He had just completed a large volume on the history of the American people, the work was very quickly a success, went through several editions and was translated many times over, but little money was made from it. The work had exhausted

517

the professor. Writer's cramp in his right hand forced him to use his left, but his brain too no longer wanted to work. And he was so confused at that point that something remarkable occurred one evening. He was supposed to go to his room to change for dinner, but in front of the wardrobe he lost consciousness; he took off all his clothes, went to bed and turned out the light. That was how his daughters, who were waiting to go to dinner with him, found him.

An extended rest seemed imperative at the time. But he had had to travel alone. His wife Ellen could not join him, there was not enough money for two. He wrote her long, lovely letters. He did not set foot on the continent itself, making only a long bicycle tour through England and Scotland.

That was a long time ago. Now, fourteen years later, Woodrow Wilson is traveling as president of the United States on one of the ships of his government. He will go to the continent—and not on a bicycle tour. And he finds himself in the company of a charming woman, but not of Ellen Axson, who cannot join him this time, not because of financial problems but because she is dead. And as the representative of life, a younger woman has taken the empty place at Wilson's side as his companion on this triumphal tour. The dead woman would not have begrudged him her company. Wilson had always loved the company of women, he could not exist without women around him; he found women more sociable than men, he lost his shyness around women and children, came out of his shell. Nor did he try to defend himself when his daughters once reproached him for appreciating "sociable women," especially when they were beautiful. Ellen Axson had once said to him, "Since you've gone and married me and I'm such a serious and sober woman, I'll have to find you friends that are merrier."

When on deck or in his cabin, Wilson often reaches into his vest pocket to pull out the buckeye he carries with him. He rolls it between his fingers. And wipes and polishes it with his sleeve and handkerchief. He enjoys its beautiful mirrored surface, its warm brown hue. It is an amulet. Its grain has a light ebb and flow that brings him good thoughts. The buckeye soothes him when bad news unsettles him. Just don't let too many people, too much of the world get too close. He once remarked to his daughter Eleanor, Mrs. MacAdoo, "The public, what is all this about the public? Why must one listen so much to the public? The public is ultimately the most dangerous thing there is. It is always ready to tear you to shreds. Don't bother me with popularity. It is the most transient and finally the most unimportant thing in the world."

The men in his entourage watch respectfully as the tall, gaunt figure of the president climbs up and down the stairways of the ship. His gaze is unquestionably friendly and he has a smile for everyone—but from a distance. There is something of the monk about him, and his face is sometimes strange and frozen. His mouth has a severe, obstinate cut, the gaze comes from somewhere deep inside his head. Yes, he knows and sees through much, but the devil's own pride is also in him. In the ship's salon one evening he boasts, "America will not only be the sole unselfish nation at the upcoming peace conference, but I likewise shall be the sole person who truly derives his authority from the people. The men I shall be dealing with are not representatives of their people."

(He believed he could say that despite the fact that there was a hostile majority against him in both houses of Congress.)

He pulled himself together and waved; Wilson looked through a portal. They were approaching Brest. And the sight of the continent on which such monstrous, inhuman and unnatural things had occurred for four and a half long years staggered him. He was stirred and very grave. He sensed what God had laid upon him. He did not want to have read so much, thought and written so much, without purpose. He must help reason and moral will to their victory. Something must be initiated that extended beyond the horizon of the pitiful politicians on both sides of the ocean. Humanity had a right to demand that.

He looked at the black cloud of smoke coming from the battleship just ahead of them. As he turned back into the salon he said, "We should have no illusions. The world will be unbearable if this time, too, mere compromises are reached. This is meant to be a true conference of peace, and there are to be no more compromises in the old style."

The Allied reporters noted these words and passed them on by radiotelegraph to the American and European newspapers—the words of the American president. These were the words of a Laocoön already in the tangled embrace of the snakes.

On Friday the 13th—the new World Judge was superstitious and noted such dates—Wilson set foot on the mainland beneath the thunder of the batteries in the harbor of Brest. Thirty destroyers and ten cruisers had assembled there to receive him. The *Pennsylvania* bore the flag of Vice Admiral Mayo, the *Wyoming* that of Admiral Sims. The other American warships on hand were the *Utah, Oklahoma, Arizona, New York, Texas, Florida,* and *Arkansas.* The Allies were waiting with a large number of destroyers and with the cruisers *Admiral Aube* and *Montcalm.* At the cliffs where stood Fort Toulbroche, the *George Washington* halted and took aboard the French foreign minister, General Pershing and Miss Margaret Wilson. It became clear she was not feeling quite fit; was that a result of wartime diet or the climate?

On board the *Washington* the president replied to Pichon's greeting, "I deem it a privilege to make a contribution to peace on French soil, a peace that will once again enable the world to march toward progress."

At three o'clock the president and his entourage boarded the steamer *Pas de Calais.* They surveyed the harbor at Brest, which had been greatly expanded to receive American troops landing there. At 3:15 the ship touches the mercantile pier, and Mrs. Wilson, decorated with the colors of France, is the first to disembark. Music plays. The president is wearing a black coat and black felt hat. He receives the welcome of the city of Brest.

In Paris meantime, the CGT, the Federation of Unions, and the SFIO, the Socialist party, have put up posters reading:

"To the workers of France! The workers and farmers of France and the people of Paris wish to express their words of welcome and gratitude to President Wilson during his stay with us. As he begins to carry out his task he should know that the hearts of millions of men and women rejoice with him. Their hearts beat with his. On December 14th all the workers will take to the streets. Call out to the president for international peace, for a League of Nations that will give to all peoples the same rights and the same duties. For permanent peace. President Wilson, we cry out to you: Courage, courage. We are with you, we are counting on you."

And the secretaries of the English Trades' Congress, Mr. Henderson and Mr. Bowerman, publish a message in which five million English workers declare their solidarity with their French comrades, and for their part greet the American president as he sets foot on European soil, bidding him a hearty welcome.

It is Saturday, December 14th. The American guests have a merry and somewhat crazy trip from Brest to Paris. Total confusion reigns in the train, the official train of the president of the French Republic. All the baggage has been mixed up in the compartments. Although telegrams have been sent from Paris asking for the names of the presidential party, which were then provided, they find themselves sitting jumbled in the compartments in total confusion, where they smile at one another, uncertain just how they have ended up in this company. The cars themselves are European, very European, hardly comfortable by American standards, and dirty besides, and the service in the dining car is simply ghastly.

Late that morning, at eleven, the train halts. It is standing at the station at the Bois de Boulogne.

And so this is Paris, and here everything will be decided. The results of the deaths of ten million healthy human beings, of a misfortune without parallel, will be finalized here. If history teaches us nothing— this bit of history stands suffocatingly near, and no one can avoid its lesson.

They leave the train station. Cars are waiting outside. They have entered radiant, gallant, brave Paris, the city of freedom, of freedoms, of humanity, of ideas and upheavals.

Woodrow Wilson and the French president, Poincaré, and Mrs.

Wilson, flowers in her arms, take their places in the first car. Wilson, like Poincaré, wears a top hat. While they drive through the city he doffs his hat continually, waves it, enjoys himself. They drive down the Champs Elysées between two rows of soldiers. Here is the famous Place de la Concorde, how broad, how splendid, how harmoniously laid out. The Rue Royale, the antique temple of the Madeleine, the Boulevard Malesherbes, Avenue de Messine, Rue Monceau, Number 28 is the Hotel Prince Murat, which is to lodge President and Mrs. Wilson.

They gaze at it as they enter, overwhelmed by the splendor. It is magnificent, a veritable museum. Smiling at each other, they are both struck by the same thought, one that the little king of Italy will utter a few weeks later when they receive him here. "My God, they've put you up here? I could not exist in the place." They will give him tit for tat when they visit him at the Quirinal in Rome, and he will answer them, "But what do you mean? I don't live here, you know. I'm only here when you come." And they will all laugh together.

They are picked up in three cars for lunch with the president. The white-bearded Henri Martin is chef de protocole, he stands at the door of the president's car and opens it. He precedes his guests with great dignity. In the court of the Elysée palace they are shown military honors by two rows of the 11th Alpine Rifles. In fact, wherever they go, wherever they halt, soldiers present arms. Are there civilians here in Paris, too?

Henri Martin leads them up the staircase. In the grand hall tables have been set for two hundred people. The tables are decorated with red and white roses. Everywhere there are silver baskets overflowing with red and white roses. Little Poincaré has given his arm to the wife of the American president. She towers over him by a head, and marching into the hall with him she feels as if she were some mighty freighter being pulled out clear of the harbor by a little tug.

They dine. Now Poincaré speaks. The food is sophisticated, French, there are discoveries to be made, the porcelain and silver are exquisite, one does not grow tired of examining them; but one is not sitting here for the pleasure of it, there are to be, there must be, speeches. What will the French say? Certainly whatever they say, they will put it delicately.

Poincaré: "Mr. President, several months ago you telegraphed that the United States would send ever increasing resources to Europe until our united armies would be in a position to overrun the enemy with a flood of divisions.

"France has had to make great sacrifices. But not in order that she may be exposed to new attacks. We wish that those who initiated these criminal acts may not remain unpunished and continue to carry their heads high. Upon the misery and sorrow of yesterday must follow a peace of reparations, and what is more, a guaranteed defense against the dangers of yesterday.

"Without falling victim to the illusion that the future can ever fully preserve us from collective madness, we wish to create a just and lasting peace."

He concluded: "I lift my glass to the health of Madame and Mr. Wilson. I drink to the prosperity of the United States of America, our great friend yesterday, today and always."

Wilson stood up. He had understood all the nuances of the address. "I am deeply indebted to you for your gracious greeting and the words directed to the United States of America, to my wife and myself. I have represented America's ideals and have tried to transform them into deeds. From the first, the thought of the people of the United States turned to something more than the mere winning of this war. It turned to the establishment of the eternal principles of right and justice. It realized that merely to win the war was not enough; that it must be won in such a way, and the questions raised by it settled in such a way, as to insure the future peace of the world and lay the foundations for the freedom and happiness of its many peoples and nations. I know with what ardor and enthusiasm the soldiers and sailors of the United States have given the best that was in them to this war of redemption. They believe their ideals to be acceptable to free peoples everywhere, and rejoice to have played the part they have played in giving reality to those ideals.

"It will daily be a matter of pleasure with me to be brought into consultation with the statesmen of France and her Allies in concerting the measures by which we may secure permanence for these happy relations of friendship and cooperation, and secure for the world at large such safety and freedom in its life as can be secured only by the constant association and cooperation of friends."

Wilson concluded: "I greet you sir, and beg to bring you the greetings of another great people. I raise my glass to the health of the president of the French Republic and to Madame Poincaré and to the prosperity of France."

Marshal Foch Develops His Ideas on Peace

His thesis on peace is: one must make it as difficult as possible for the Germans to wage war. All else is mere rhetoric.

Marshal Foch

And here sits Generalissimo Foch in his office in the Hôtel des Invalides. His adjutant, a colonel, has just brought him the magazine *L'Illustration.* The dramatist Henri Lavedan has written about "armed peace." Foch inquires about the man, and the colonel reads him several passages aloud. He nods at the introductory remark that soon a thousand difficulties will arise.

"Let me hear what his thousand difficulties are," Foch asks.

The colonel reads: "This war was new, and peace will be new as well, and not like the peace we knew before. The main idea behind the previous peace was security. It guaranteed the right and the means to work without a shadow of mistrust. It guaranteed the removal of all the evil that war brings with it, but it did not suppress war itself. It only interrupted it."

Foch growled his approval.

"Peace, true peace, following upon our triumphant victory will now be a peace of struggle, of determination, of permanent vigilance, a peace that, while not militaristic, is militant."

Foch: "The man talks too much for my taste. He's beating around the bush."

"The power of peace will want to secure the greatest good for mankind and the best possible conditions for daily life, but that power must be made fruitful and be organized to set itself in opposition to all culpable acts. This peace will be armed, armed on behalf of human society, armed against the enemies of human society, against the power of evil, against the thirst for plunder, against madness."

"What does that mean? For the thousandth time, that the human spirit does not wish ever again to burden its conscience with the raging plague of war, and that war will be accepted only under the exceptional circumstance of danger to the nation and society."

The reader cast Foch a glance, the marshal sighed. "Go on, go on. I'm waiting. The man needs an enormous running start, let's hope he finally takes the leap. He's afraid I presume."

"In this manner, mercilessly armed and determined to preserve the general peace, we will succeed in placing the brandmark of inhumanity on war between nations, thereby making it impossible. To suppress war, however, one must also think about the causes of domestic war. It is immediately apparent that complete security can only be achieved if civil war is likewise eliminated. The prevention of external war by force of arms and the assurance of domestic peace through cultivation of progress cannot be separated from one another."

The colonel concluded: "So, that is more or less the idea, the principle of the new peace according to M. Lavedan."

Foch looked straight ahead, lost in thought. "Not bad, bits of it, especially the last. War is in fact only one issue, peace after war the second, more difficult one. That's where even Napoleon got in trouble. He brought the art of war to nothing less than dizzying heights; his secret consisted in always running ahead of events, determining the direction to be taken, then letting events catch up with him. But at that point he didn't really know what to do with them. He identified the glory of his country with his own glory, and convinced himself that weapons alone shaped destiny. That, however, is incorrect. A nation can not live on glory, it needs work. In the end the most brilliant tactics of war cannot be a substitute for morality. Above war stands peace."

"Which would mean that this Lavedan is right."

"Absolutely. He's too general for me, too imprecise. If he had presented us with definite plans for domestic progress and for armed peace it would have been better. We have war academies, St. Cyr, etc., one ought to add peace academies to them and teach strategies for peace. But that takes us too far afield, colonel. We have our own worries. Even President Wilson is here now." He smiled at the colonel. "What projects has our general staff worked up to defend us against President Wilson?"

"Against the League of Nations? Yes, that's a dreadfully enticing notion, isn't it?"

Foch: "Oh, why shouldn't there be a League of Nations? You can count me in on any and all plans that hold out the promise of collective security. But I'll permit no plan that wrests France's security from her. Take a look at Germany, keep your eye on it. In terms of its material wealth it is a very great nation. But where did this barbaric war come from, trampling the laws of justice and humanity? Where? From the militarist mentality that the Prussians inoculated their empire with. And as part of that, the axiom of the Germans: morality and justice are not the same for all nations, there are privileged nations who can set themselves above all the rest. They have a kind of moral law of the state, the state is almost a divine entity. An abominable doctrine that infects all of Germany."

The colonel: "The philosophers say it right out. Sorel himself has pointed that out."

Foch: "A nation that imagines it was created to conquer the world will not give up the notion just like that. It will have to be conquered several times. With a maximum of sacrifice we have cast them to the ground this time. But Germany remains an enemy against which one can protect oneself only provisionally. And the need to guard ourselves against Germany is so urgent that until that point has been clarified we cannot allow ourselves to sit down at any table to discuss any other sort of plans. The Germans now have a republic. I do not believe it will last long. It is my fond hope that it may change the German mentality. But one must protect Germany from temptation. And that is what we must tell this American."

The colonel: "Our socialists, workers and trade-union men are all tagging after him. He is their messiah. They visit him to show their devotion, to pay homage. They want to put pressure on the government, they want to make it appear to Wilson that the whole French nation stands behind him."

Foch: "One can well understand that the average man wants peace. But he should not be led to think it can be achieved by everybody shaking hands. All of those fellows have been spoiled by their own negotiations at trade-union congresses."

"They're warming up the old prewar ideas about an International again, but the Socialist International is a bankrupt company too."

Foch had once again sunk deep into thought. He waved the remark aside and did not speak for some time. Then he said, "We are the masters of Europe. We can do what we want. Our misfortune is that we don't know it. This League of Nations that has been served up to us, what can it achieve? Take this war of 1914 to 1918. Compare the French army that Joffre commanded in 1914 and the one I was in charge of in 1918. They are in no way similar. The total number of our soldiers was approximately the same, but instead of 1,634 infantry battalions, by 1918 we had only 1,081. And where in 1914 we had only two machine guns per battalion, we now have twelve, not even counting the thirty-six automatic rifles, one 37 mm cannon and one mortar. Our equipment has increased fourteenfold, and instead of general infantrymen we have nothing but specialists. Moreover, in 1914 we did not have a single automatic weapon, now we have 120,000. And instead of the 5,000 machine guns of 1914 we now have 60,000—twelve times as many. Think of the changes in our artillery, they go even deeper. Instead of 308 heavy pieces we now have 5,000 of all calibers. We possess 3,000 tanks. We began the war with 120 airplanes, now we have 2,000.

"You see, colonel, in both organization and armaments there is almost no resemblance between the armies of 1914 and 1918. Why have I enumerated all this to you? This profound restructuring of our army in the space of four years is food for thought. Assume that we get Mr. Wilson's League of Nations. It will want to reduce armaments. And if certain people have their way, sooner or later they'll get around to the task of disarming us. And what will the League do? It will set up controls and make regulations. But who can determine all the possible regulations that will be necessary, and who can carry them out? Think of some future war. from 1914 to 1918 we saw changes in our army that no one predicted. And what will the future bring? Think of the immense role played by airplanes, by tanks, by developments in chemical warfare, think of gas, of the possibility of totally new kinds of weapons, then of the people's morale during wartime—all factors that no one can calculate ahead of time, that no one can even know about ahead of time. And therefore we could suddenly find ourselves with this League in a situation where we are the ones who will suffer. Because when a nation like Germany throws itself into the fray, only with great difficulty could one prevent them from using every means to avoid controls and employ every conceivable weapon, both those forbidden and those not yet discovered, in order to achieve victory."

The writer Maurice Barrès, a friend of Foch's, was announced and led in. One could see on Barrès's face how happy he was to be able to sit here across from the distinguished marshal. Foch asked him about a lecture tour he had made in Alsace. Barrès chatted away, and with great animation spun out his ideas about the area on the left bank of the Rhine, an ancient region of Romano-Celtic culture that had been subdued by Germanic invaders. Foch did not give much credit to Barrès's arguments, they seemed all too archaeological to him. And he had touched a sore point for Barrès there, too, who after his own observations of the last few weeks had begun to have his doubts as well. And he reported in a low voice what he had himself seen in the occupied Rhineland—the dreadful silence as the Allied troops had marched into Trier, the dangerous, hostile attitude of the population, the closed windows.

"There you have it," said Foch, calmly turning to the colonel, who was sitting at a desk off to one side. "Did you hear that?"

He then submitted his own view of the matter. "My demand to the peace conference remains as ever a firm border for France, and by that I mean the left bank of the Rhine, plus a first-class, up-to-date army. Colonel, please show M. Barrès what this Henri Lavedan has written in *L'Illustration*." Barrès looked at the magazine and declined with thanks. He shrugged that he had read the essay already. In the first part the worthy

Lavedan was relatively clear, but in the second he broke down completely and got lost in rhetoric. There was a great competition going on, by the way, among idealists; elocution was having a field day, and strangely enough Lavedan had felt called upon to enter the lists.

Foch and he, then, were in complete agreement, and so here in the Hôtel des Invalides two sorts of pessimism sat facing one another, saluted one another. Marshal Foch, however, was a robust, practicing Catholic, while the jaundiced, nervous Barrès exuded the sweat of classical despair, transformed now into the terrible and onerous despair of modern man. He had once basked in the sun of Greek mirth, but now only the dark side of Hellenism was left to him, and he was foundering in it.

Foch: "Yes, as far as these Germans go, and unfortunately we aren't finished dealing with them yet, they were infinitely better prepared for the material side of the war. They had thought about a great many things, the role of heavy artillery, trench warfare. We thought morale and élan would suffice. We kept talking about advancing, about offensives, and it is a good idea to encourage that spirit. The ensign had it, and so did the commanding general. But plans worked out by the General Staff have to have another basis than that. Now and then, by the by, the Germans themselves fell into the same mistake, at the Battle of the Ijzer, for instance, which they call the Battle of Langemark. They threw their intellectuals into the line of fire, young fellows from Berlin, the darling sons of good families, simply threw them forward into the battle. And of course such hecatombs were of no avail. Prisoners told us later that they pushed them forward, let them be killed like so many gnats."

Barrès took heart from the calm, from the sense of assurance the marshal displayed. "For heaven's sake, the same misfortune cannot happen to us a second time, can it?"

Foch, the pious Catholic, gazed at his partner silently, gravely.

"As long as man is man, as long as men are afflicted with their faults, my dear friend, everything, absolutely everything will be possible. Since you don't belong to any group of utopians or rhetoricians, you know that. As far as the Germans go, we have to prepare ourselves for any eventuality."

Then Barrès spoke about Wilson and the French cabinet. Foch listened attentively. He replied, "Wilson's participation at the peace conference, America's in general, fills me with a certain amount of anxiety. America is very far away, a huge ocean separates it from Europe, defends it against Germany. It almost did not enter the war. The burden of war was borne by England and, primarily, by France. We sacrificed immense quantities of blood. And now we are suddenly to sit down at the conference as equals. That is not proper, an injustice lies buried there, and our representatives will hardly be in a position to correct this fundamental error. America entered the war terribly late, and hesitantly—would it ever do it a second time, later on, should that prove necessary? Ask yourself. In any case it has a very vague sense of our dangers."

He was not finished yet, but first he stared blankly out the window, where every few minutes the fixed bayonets of a patrol were visible. He continued, "The Americans will leave us to fend for ourselves, and the others too, and we will still remain Germany's closest neighbor. They will deliver us into the hands of a League of Nations that can provide us no security. They will deal mildly with Germany, and Germany will use that mildness to grow strong once more against us. I wish it were not so. But you can't make republicans out of monarchists from one day to the next, and Ebert's statements make it plain to me who is giving him orders and standing behind him."

And Foch turned his face back to Barrès, this time with a smile. "Those are not, however, thoughts appropriate to today's victory celebration, my dear friend. You'll have to pardon me for that; an old soldier can't help being mistrustful, it's a professional disease."

Barrès suggested that the skeptical comments Clemenceau had made concerning Wilson's utopian Fourteen Points boded some good, and that he was still tiger enough to make life difficult for his vis-à-vis.

Foch exchanged glances with the colonel. "He's a civilian. As a soldier I know the soldiers on the other side better. But it's the civilians alone who have the floor now, though the war is still going on. Our experience no longer counts, we are being pushed aside."

Barrès did not want to buy that. He trusted the tiger's hate.

But Foch balled his fist. "He's a civilian, and he won't be able to do anything else. I say the same to them every day: to hell with wars requiring coalitions. The coalition that brought us victory, however, no longer exists today. Just take a look around in Paris. From the largest to the smallest, everybody is running in pursuit of his own advantage, and that means we are losing what the war won for us. What is more important, Fiume or European peace? You can be certain that an Italian will say Fiume. I'll not be able to convince Clemenceau that we are the masters of Europe, and could have our way even against all the others."

Barrès suggested that one needed to have the support of the people. One should explain it all to the people. But now all they wanted was peace. Foch laughed comfortably. "So there you see what sort of a creature man is. And to be sure, what a lovely thing is this universal desire for a League of Nations. The dream of the prophet Isaiah will not leave man in peace. The lamb will lie down by the wolf and the swords will be beaten into plowshares. We Christians consider such plans for eternal peace on earth a sin. It is written: my kingdom is not of this world. Permanent peace—good heavens, I would be satisfied with a couple of generations."

528

As Foch shook hands with him, Barrès had to admit that despite such pessimism he felt refreshed.

Mislaid letters were still arriving in Paris, belated news from the front that no longer existed.

"We have just marched out of camp. I still suffer from the ache of not being able to embrace you. This letter must take the place of our embrace. Forced to be brief, I want to express to you the depth, the intensity of my feelings for you all. My thoughts are with all of you at home, with each of you, and I am so thankful to you for having given me such a happy childhood, the memory of which makes my life easier at this moment. There is yet another reason for tears in case I should vanish. As you know I have tried my hand at painting. I was making progress, though of course, still only a beginner. I shall leave nothing behind, how stupid and disheartening. And finally I beg you, if something should happen to me, find someone to take my place, adopt someone who deserves you. With all my love."

The second letter: "We make the push forward tomorrow morning, with good courage. I embrace you all most fondly. All my thoughts are with you. Think of me. Whatever happens, your memories of me can be clear and fine. Of that you can be certain, even if I have not fulfilled my own wish of having created some lasting work."

The next letter: "We have arrived at our goal. In the infrequent periods of rest we enjoy my thoughts are filled with memories of you. Despite the great distance, I feel how our hearts beat as one, that our thoughts run their course together, that our nerves and blood do as well. I am at the mercy of higher powers, I know that. If they show themselves, I shall submit. But my energies are none the less tensed to confront coming events. I will take the inexorable upon me without flinching. Find someone who deserves you. Henri Remy."

Alexis Vivet, beside him, appends to that letter the following note: "Misfortune was with us. In a bayonet attack my dear friend was shot in the forehead. My heart is broken. We stood side by side. I myself was only slightly wounded and wanted to render him the last service one man can show another, but it was impossible in the machine-gun fire. My poor friend, he fell before the enemy along with many others. It was a terrible encounter. I write to you now since I have only just come into possession of his papers, and I am sending all of his things to you as he wished. We had arranged this in case one of us should fall. I am only a simple workingman, but that did not prevent us from having the deepest respect for each other."

Book Five

Around December 14th

The Divine Mission of the State

A clergyman and a layman are of differing opinions on this topic.

Becker's mother could not hide her joy, and that same day she went to her old parish pastor, with whom she had worked for decades, to tell him what had happened. The pastor did not let it go with a simple warm, congratulatory handshake. As luck would have it, he had as his house guest the former chaplain of the garrison and hospital in that same Alsatian town where Becker had lain. His Berlin colleague told him what Frau Becker had said, of how people in general were once again turning to the church. One doubtless had Frau Becker, an exemplary woman, to thank for her son's abandoning the worldly, even antiecclesiastical position he had formerly taken. The chaplain, a Westphalian by birth, a man constantly on the lookout for souls in the concrete wasteland of Berlin, took this information as a sign, and suggested that his colleague improvise a visit to the Beckers' at once. The case seemed a happy coincidence in every way.

And so we see these two deputies of the church moving down the narrow streets that lead them to the apartment of this fresh convert, First Lieutenant Becker. They are going there partly just to be in attendance and rejoice, partly to find material for a sermon, partly to rekindle old memories.

Becker's mother's eyes open wide when, hardly an hour after her visit with the pastor, he appears, accompanied by another gentleman, in the hallway of her apartment. The other gentleman at once introduces himself as the garrison chaplain—pardon, former garrison chaplain—of the town where Friedrich had lain ill for so long.

At this hour Becker is not occupied with anything in particular. His mother has been sitting with him, has been explaining to him at his wish how she goes about collecting linens and clothes, especially woolens, for the poor, and what different personalities people have—meaning among other things, she laughs, how tightly or loosely they grasp their wallets. Now she asks her son to come to the living room. There is a gentleman there who knows him from the military hospital.

Once inside, Becker greets the pastor clad in gray, whom he had heard at church. Next to him stands a corpulent man with energetic features; however, he is not an officer, as he would seem on first appearance, but a retired garrison chaplain who served at the hospital in Alsace. Becker smiles at his mother—he has her to thank for this visit, of course.

They all take a seat in the living room. The guest from Westphalia, the chaplain, monopolizes the conversation. As he shakes Friedrich's hand, he expresses his happiness at finding him again in such excellent health. The man's rush of words is so vehement because he has at last found someone here in Berlin who knows nothing about him, about the fate of his family and himself, someone to whom he can reveal it all. Ah, this Westphalian is no longer the gruff man who, in peace and war, served as good shepherd to men one could not exactly call gentle sheep. The loss of his official status has broken him. Melancholy and discontent hold sway over him.

The Westphalian speaks of the happy providence that led him to this part of Berlin, to his old friend from student days, where, moreover, he has found a charge from that fine old military hospital. How long has Becker been here then? When was he transported out, how had the town looked in those last hours?

The Westphalian spoke of hospital patients whom Becker had not known. The guest was delighted to learn that Lieutenant Maus, whom he said he remembered—"such a fine man, such a cheerful fellow"—was also in Berlin and frequently visited Becker. ("Can you give me the address? But wait, don't trouble yourself, you can give it to me later.") A few words were said in memory of Richard, the dead pilot who had spent his last days in the room adjoining Becker's—"heroes all."

Becker's mother sat peacefully on the sofa across from the Westphalian. Sitting there in a rocking chair, his arms hanging down so comfortably, he was the picture of natural, though quiescent vitality. She was not sure whether Becker was listening or would go on listening, since apparently the stranger was settling in for an extended visit. But Friedrich was not wearing that impenetrable, polite face he could hold for hours on end when he found visitors uninteresting. He sat bent forward slightly and gazed respectfully at this eloquent pastor who had dropped into his parlor so unexpectedly.

Yes, the fellow interested him. He was intrigued by him: a pastor, a man of God, and at the same time a military man, one who had succeeded in resolving the dreadful conflict between God and war, between

534

God and the state. Becker was suddenly struck with the desire to question, to discuss, to know. How should one behave toward the state, what is this thing called the state? That was suddenly a question for him again. Formerly Becker would have at once recognized the military chaplain in this visitor and dismissed him with indifference.

The Westphalian, noticing Becker's tense excitement and pallor, thought it appropriate to ask whether the conversation was upsetting him. To which Becker replied, "On the contrary, it is a pleasure I've long been waiting for. I consider it a veritable stroke of luck that you have come here to visit me at precisely the moment when I'm feeling better, hungering for spiritual nourishment, so to speak. I must apologize for not having requested you to visit me more often in the hospital. Tha can be laid to my general condition at the time."

And a friendly, understanding smile spread across the Westphalian's face. (And at the same moment was there not a memory, quite distant, quite far back, a memory scurrying across Becker's mind of another visit, another guest, the sinister Latin American, the Brazilian?)

"A stroke of luck," the visitor repeated, flattered. "I feel extraordinarily honored. I realize that all the world is now hungering for spiritual nourishment."

Becker: "It seems to me that a man like you, who has long seen things so clearly, who stands there in the midst of life, that such a man can explain to us what the world looks like now. It is a staggering event for me to see someone before me, here, now, in these first moments when I can move once again, who understands that, and whose profession it is to know what is holy, what is true, and at the same time to bear that knowledge into the everyday world, into the difficult, everyday world."

(The nervous earnestness of his conversations with the three sinister creatures lay upon Becker now.)

"That is my profession precisely, our bitter profession," the Westphalian replied, "to bear the most difficult matters into the everyday world. That is the crux of the matter, and one way or another one must deal with it. It is a hard profession, and one cannot put on kid gloves for it, something I would not recommend generally for anyone who has to deal with other people."

He laughed from his rocking chair, beaming at those assembled.

Becker: "And how do you proceed? How do you find the right way?"

Fervently, proudly, the Westphalian said, "Oh, we muddle through."

Becker would not yield. "I do not include myself in the camp of those who place absurd demands on life. In this world one catastrophe follows another, the most gruesome and ghastly things occur. One might suppose we are living in the Stone Age. But what can one do then? What, for heaven's sake, can be done? We have failed, yesterday and the day before. Will we fail again tomorrow? Must we fail again tomorrow—and so on through all eternity? How do you proceed? How do you find the right way? How do you muddle through?"

The Westphalian received this familiar package of questions with satisfaction. Confident of himself, he winked at Becker. There is nothing lovelier than going through one's paces on such occasions.

He said, "At last a man who understands how we military chaplains stand at a most forward position. Even my friend here, my colleague, has no adequate conception of the matter. Herr Becker, you wish to know our guidelines. You may have them in one sentence: render unto God what is God's, unto Caesar what is Caesar's. That we render to God what is God's, that is axiomatic for us. As chaplains we have our tasks, our official range of duties and special regulations. Things sentimental and humanitarian are not in my line, nor am I a modernist in any other sense. What are decisive for me are the old, defiant Christian hymns, with their earnest penitence and confident faith. For me, tolerance toward an opponent is not Christian love for one's neighbor but solidarity with the enemy. But what should we render unto Caesar? Let me say quite frankly that I'm no tight-wad in the matter. I permit no conflicts to arise. Occasionally I go so far, why deny it, that I consciously let God take a back seat in the assumption that God will be more likely to forgive my sin than will Caesar."

The man to whom he was speaking, Friedrich Becker, did not like the merry, effervescent manner of this gentleman. But Becker wanted, needed to pursue this path, he had to press further into the depths. It was important to make the necessary assessments.

He sighed, "Then it is like this—you consciously assume a partial guilt in order to save the more important whole."

Becker was struggling. That was not put correctly; but he could not find the words he wanted.

The pastor: "You can describe it any way you like. Without God's grace we won't make it in any case. And the main point is that we do not intentionally do evil. As they say, there is no joking with the King of Prussia. My colleague here, you see, has things easier with his civilian sheep."

The old pastor shook his head, considering; he exchanged glances with Frau Becker. Then he said, "Christ lived among civilians."

The Westphalian: "Right you are. And when he happened to run into some non-civilians things didn't work out. But it has to work out for us, every time. That's what we're there for. That is our job. Where would we be—just among us and simply by way of conversation—where would we be if we let ourselves be shot every time we happened to

536

run up against higher authority? What would become of our profession then, what would become of the proclamation of the Word to the soldiers, what would become of the support we always owe them? No, we are part of the team of warriors, and for that reason we can now and again let two and two make three."

Becker's mother nodded gravely. "You have to make sacrifices."

"And we do."

And he let it be understood that quite apart from a very unfortunate private matter (he did not say that he meant the loss of his furniture, he only paused and lowered his eyes, hoping that someone might pursue the question, but they were hardhearted and silent), the general situation in Germany was very depressing. "And we must indeed ask along with our friend Herr Becker here: How do we muddle through? The whole of Austria stands open to the attack of Bolshevism, and here at home that godless pair, Karl Liebknecht and his darling Rosa, are running amok. Well, when these animals have once got what they fancy they want, then adieu dear old Germany, adieu German hearth and German home. Because Bolshevism is serious business. It won't go for a stroll down the street, passing before our windows, it will burst into the house, break down the doors and tear a man away from his wife, children from their parents, forbidding our very tongues to proclaim the truth."

No rebuttal to this came from the audience—none from the civilian pastor, because he knew all this already, his visitor harangued him with it several times a day, and besides the same thing was in the papers and he had trouble enough taking care of the freezing and hungry people in his parish—nor was there a rebuttal from Becker's mother. She was silent, she only thought worriedly: things won't come to such a pass, for then we would all be lost for good.

And since Becker didn't speak up either, the blustering Westphalian found himself confronted with an uncertain front. And he pumped the former first lieutenant Becker to find out how he stood on political issues, whether he had joined any groups, any of those organizations of officers that, thank God, were now forming. People were putting up some defense, after all, and had not been struck so totally blind as to forget their fellow man.

Becker's mother answered for her son, trying to avoid worse complications. Her son had hardly been out of the house till now, he was still under a physician's care, and not much reached him from the world outside.

So that the military chaplain was left no out except to express his wish that Becker get well soon and, with a finger pointed to the newspaper lying open on the table, to ask in a conspiratorial whisper if they knew what was happening at present.

"Our troops from the front have marched into the city. Have you heard? They are not holding firm. They are falling apart. Go to the barracks. It is dreadful. That was our splendid army, our shining armor. Enemy propaganda is devouring it like worms devour a corpse."

He expected no answer; he had something very definite on his mind, he had to get it off his chest. He spoke of the undermining of all notion of morality. And then he let loose on Prince Friedrich Leopold, who permitted red flags to fly from his three castles in Klein-Glienicke. Out of his breast pocket the pastor pulled a newspaper clipping describing how upon the death of Kaiser Friedrich this Red prince had become the patron of all the old Prussian grand lodges, that is, the supreme Freemason. In the pastor's mouth the word Freemason sounded like thief and murderer.

The Westphalian drummed on the table. And that wasn't all. It was now known what sort of a pass things had come to last week as the advancing troops were still outside the city—and it was even more pitiful than one had first believed.

"The Guard Cuirassier Regiment was quartered, you see, in Neubabelsberg. One officer of the regiment, with several noncommissioned officers and enlisted men, went to the prince and requested, in addition to the advertisement of his personal political convictions by the use of red flags, that he also make allowances for the feelings of the troops returning from battle by raising their flag of black, white and red. After lengthy negotiations with the workers' and soldiers' council of Nowawes, the prince declared himself prepared to let the squadron flag be flown, do you hear, the squadron flag. Because he claimed he did not even own a full-fledged German flag."

Instead of a storm of indignation, The Westphalian reaped an icy silence once more. The civilian pastor did not move, the mother gazed straight ahead, Friedrich Becker's brow was furrowed.

"He is a Freemason," the Westphalian whispered, goading them. He did not want to fail now, because someone had stolen his furniture, his goods and chattels, and he was on the lookout for the guilty party. And added to all that he suffered from the fact that nowhere could he discharge his pastoral rage over these earthly grievances from a pulpit. "It is the goal of the Freemasons to topple all thrones, German and non-German alike. Thrones and altars are their enemies. They want their one great League of Humanity, and that means a world republic under the leadership of Jews and Freemasons."

Overcome with the horror of it, he opened his eyes wide. "And do you know that this Red prince, this Freemason from Klein-Glienicke, is as good as a murderer? At one point his wife had to be rescued from the Havel. She had thrown herself into its waters while trying to flee from him. The Kaiser then had to make the duties of matrimony patently clear to the gentleman. This just by the way."

538

Here Becker finally made some movement. His mother looked anxiously over toward him. Becker finally felt he was capable of speech. He did not know, still did not know, if he would say the right thing.

"Permit me, pastor, to inquire further about the Bolsheviks. As you have suggested, it is a large movement that even we cannot bring to a halt. Why can we not bring it to a halt? You describe Bolshevism as an evil power. That means we evidently have nothing with which to oppose it. That means our own power is weak. Even in that case, there is profit in learning that much from Bolshevism. One can then see things more clearly—things about oneself."

The Westphalian sat there stiffly, grasped his knee with one hand and let loose a crude and unambiguous "No!" "No, my friend, I can learn nothing from Bolshevism. It has nothing, absolutely nothing to tell me. It is evil, and evil has been in our bones since the foundation of this world. It dates from the Fall and we do not need to learn that from Russians and Polacks. We can read that elsewhere."

"I hope that we do not then yield to this movement, but rather confront it."

"With an iron fist. The weapons of the whole world will be raised against it, of the whole world."

"Forgive me if I call that yielding. That would mean not wanting to see the hand of God."

"Friedrich," his mother said in alarm.

The Westphalian: "Bolshevism and the hand of God? One might just as well call Satan and hell the gifts of God. No, we must give an answer, beat them back. We must because we have been commanded to march into the world to defend the faith with weapons, drums and pipes. We must wade into it, seeking God at those points in life where things are most earnest. Then God will deal with us. And where he deals with us, everything is at stake. Certainly we must worry about the social issues that Bolshevism thinks it has exclusive rights to. The question of the rich and the poor burns into our very souls. But what Bolshevism has raised up is a cult of property, of ownership, of the desire to possess, of nothing but the desire to possess. Behind that, however, is a cult of individualism. And that was, to be frank, the case with us as well. The individual, whether of humble birth or high, was everything. The highest good of the children of this earth had to be the individual personality—that was our doctrine before. And there you have it. That is what liberalism taught our youth, and out of that came Bolshevism. And besides that there was the haughty idealism of our universities, that knew everything and nothing. They wanted a self-made intellectual salvation. But we can raise ourselves up out of our misery only if we place our distorted and swollen ego before God and humble it, hands folded in prayer. We must lead our ego back to the church and to the state.

Luther recognized the divine commission of the state. That is why I say that authority—and repeat for the second and third time—authority is what is needed."

Becker hunched back over again, breathing audibly, and raised his arms in a weary gesture. "But that is how it always was. We went to war believing that. That is what caused the war, and it was only then that Bolshevism came on the scene. I don't know whether you see the issue"—this was yet another member of the tribe of the three sinister creatures—"whether you see the issue with which we are now confronted. Did we act correctly? Did we render to God what was God's, and to Caesar what was Caesar's? I beg you, chaplain, not to think I would deny the state its right to exist. But where did the administrators of the state, let us say it plainly, the Kaiser and his henchmen, get the right, the legitimation, to sacrifice the lives of millions of people and ravage nations? For what purpose? On whose orders?"

The Westphalian fell silent once and for all. He had raised his eyebrows in indignation and cast piercing glances about the room, at his colleague and at Becker's mother. That they would not even intervene, that they left it all to him! The mother appeared uneasy. The parish pastor kept his small, gray head ducked low and did not look as if he wanted to take sides. And so the Westphalian saw how things stood. He gave a severe, indignant "Hmph!" and sat up militarily straight. He spoke, not without scorn.

"Well, then, my good first lieutenant, I am almost tempted to conclude that you have joined the ranks of the conscientious objectors. Well, given your achievements, I am prepared to overlook the matter."

Becker made a very definite gesture of self-defense. "Please, don't do that. Do not credit me with anything. I don't intend to credit others with anything either. I want to be taken seriously, to be judged severely, and if necessary, to be spurned. To return to the subject. Do you, as a Christian and a pastor, defend the fact that I entered this war?"

The Westphalian reached for Becker's hand and shook it warmly. "To say you were right to do so is not the suitable expression. You did the only right thing there was to do, and at the risk of your own life. And we still need men like you, and can bear it when you are afflicted with scruples of conscience. I am so sincerely glad to hear that you have turned again to our church. Here you will find the answers to all your questions. Do not hold false opinions of yourself and others. Do not be misled. Be the man you were out on the field."

"You admonished the young men out in the field in just the same way, pastor. They should follow their kaiser and as brave soldiers not fear death."

"And what if I did?" the Westphalian urged in dismay.

"What you said is no answer to my question whether I acted correctly. If the whole nation now lies bleeding, I think—it ought to be grateful for that. Perhaps it can still awaken and see with its eyes. Out in the field, pastor, I myself spoke just as you did when addressing my men as their company commander. I did not do the right thing then. I knew nothing. I was a man without knowledge."

The military chaplain leaned back in his chair. This was not the time to speak, but to hear, to listen. He inquired, "What knowledge are you talking about? What knowledge is that, Herr Becker?"

"The knowledge of Jesus. Of his life and teachings. That was hidden from me."

The Westphalian cast yet another piercing glance at his colleague, who sat there like a nobody of a layman, and at the anxious mother. He was helpless. But before he could clarify in his own mind the tactics to be employed for attack, Becker, who was slowly regaining his confidence, spoke again (the sinister trio spoke to me and I held my ground, I'll not fail here).

"Pastor, you know the scriptural passage: 'Whosoever cometh to me, and heareth my sayings, and doeth them, I will shew you to whom he is like: He is like a man which built an house, and digged deep, and laid the foundation on a rock: and when the flood arose, the stream beat vehemently upon that house, and could not shake it: for it was founded upon a rock. But he that heareth, and doeth not, is like a man that without a foundation built an house upon the earth; against which the stream did beat vehemently, and immediately it fell; and the ruin of that house was great.' The same thing happens to those who build upon the state, I think. For the state has no divine mission. It is a creature of nature. And we have failed to do our duty by it. What is left for us now is to say, I repent, I repent. To say, dear crucified Lord, I repent everything I have done and failed to do before this war, in this war and unto the present day."

Only now did it occur to the Westphalian that he was sitting across from a new convert who must be treated indulgently.

"There you have indeed," he said with apparent calm, propping his chin in his hand, "hit the nail on the head. Each of us should and must repent every hour, and we pastors are sincerely glad when this command, which we preach daily, echoes back to us from the congregation itself. For of course we too are only men."

The pastor thought of the crucifix on his desk in the garrison, and how he had gazed at it so frequently in the first days of the revolution, and how he could come to no real prayer. And he recalled his horror at the time, when he discovered that he, the clergyman, could not pray— and yes, since that time nothing has changed with me, at best it's only gotten worse. And what he is blabbing on about is pure nonsense. He is vain about his new Christianity, and the other two seem to support him in his vanity, a frowzy company, no backbone.

He continued, "Of course each of us, clergy and non-clergy alike, struggles for a fuller understanding of the truth of salvation, and we know that we fail to achieve it again and again. No one is an exception there. But neither does anyone need to berate himself for that, assuming that his intentions are good. But we must come to a fullness of life as well, we have been brought into existence. God has not made it easy for us. Feelings, especially those of repentence, are necessary, but they should not serve, forgive me the hard words, as a source of personal pleasure. The world needs us." He was speaking joyfully, energetically again now. "It calls to each of us: you need only trust, do your job. It is our duty to go to work even when everything does not turn out one hundred percent. I would also like to remark as a theologian, Herr Becker, that we ought not forget that the state has been assigned its own legitimacy and sovereign authority within the divine order."

Becker asked softly, "Did I hear correctly? You say as a theologian that within the state their dwells a legitimacy and sovereign authority deriving from the divine order?"

"Yes, indeed. I say that as a theologian, and with all due emphasis. Excuse me for not citing the exact passages, from Paul for instance. You see, Herr Becker, that though we all rejoice that you have again begun to mount the stairs of faith, you still have much to learn, many bitter things with which to wrestle."

But Becker was looking the Westphalian directly in the eye. He had been struck to the core. He was speechless. His visitor had pugnaciously hurled his last sentence at him and was awaiting an answer. The old pastor and his mother sat there anxious and depressed. As Becker saw the two of them sitting mutely beside him he forced himself to reply.

"I stand here on the lowest step of knowledge. I am just beginning even to approach that knowledge. But there is one thing in my personal experience that I cannot keep secret from you. We are clutched by the claws of the state. The state is a natural, a human construction. Under no condition should we attribute sovereign authority to it."

"Indeed not," said the Westphalian, who noticed that his opponent was yielding and pushed his advantage, "we are not speaking of just any natural state, of savages, of Negroes or Indians. We are speaking of our German state."

At which Becker stood up and asked permission to withdraw to his study. He did not hold up well sitting so long. He thought: What was this that had put on such a show here, mere naiveté or impudence? At any rate, every word was superfluous. Should he say, you are my enemy? He endured the man a while longer, in pain and discomfort, as with the complicity of his colleague and undisturbed by Becker, he went on talk-ing, advising Becker, justifying himself. He was talking about the state, the nation and especially about Germany. Again and again, to Becker's horror, the word God and the word Jesus were thrown into the mix. Becker could not force himself to show even one iota of interest. Finally the gentlemen had enough. The old pastor said that Becker was looking weary and that it was time for them to depart.

As they stood beside each other to say good-bye, the Westphalian saw himself as the victor. He jotted down for Becker the address of the major on Fasanenstrasse, where Becker would find everything made very easy for him. There he could meet many a fellow sufferer and comrade. The Westphalian's tone at the end was martially jovial.

And as soon as they were gone—his mother accompanied the guests to the door, the garrison chaplain's merry laughter ringing out for several minutes more in the corridor—Becker had to grope his way as if deaf and blind back to his room, to his sofa to lie down.

His mother found him there. He was trembling slightly. He sighed; she did not understand him. "Why did I have to say anything? Why did I have to do that?"

His mother: "But it was good that you said what you said, Friedrich. Our pastor said the same thing. He thinks the way you do, believe me. He simply didn't want to offend the other man."

"But why ask? Why am I driven to ask? My brain won't let me rest. I cannot make it keep quiet. It is a parasite clinging to me that wants to devour me."

"Friedrich, you've overtaxed yourself, I saw you were doing it."

The True Center of the World

Then he was alone—and at once the terrible words "my laboratory" occurred to him and made him unhappy. He was frightened. It seemed to him as if he had had a relapse and everything was once again questionable, everything lost.

My head and my brain are still the lords of this house, they will not let themselves be dethroned.

He felt ravaged once again. Oh, don't let yourself get caught up in conversations.

And as he lay there pressing his head to the pillow, trying to forget, the hymn he had heard in church echoed in his ear, the thin song of those poor men and women: "Rejoice all ye believers, and let your lights appear; the evening is advancing and darker night is near; the bridegroom is arising and soon he draweth nigh, up, pray, and watch, and wrestle, at midnight comes the cry!"

Becker did not know the hymn by heart, but now every word rang out for him just as it had been sung, just as he had read it. A peace settled in. That was the answer to the question, and the end of all questioning. He could arise. And now came the yearning he had not felt in church, to pray, to cast himself down and plead for peace, for calm.

He looked about the room. In this the place, can I pray here? But as he considered, his knees knew better than he. They gave way beneath him. He knelt down on the bare wooden floor, there where Hilda had knelt. He let his head fall, just as she had and—he could not pray.

He did not dare to pray.

His thoughts yielded up nothing. He had no thoughts.

It is terrible. Nothing has been given to me. It is still denied me. I cannot let go of myself. I cannot approach Him.

I am nothing.

The burning bush. It is too overwhelming. For the first time face to face with the true reality of it. Ah, the brain, the wicked head, the high command. I cannot, I cannot.

Fear ran through him. Let me pray. Let me go, set me free. And his gaze glided across the floor in search of help, gathering up once more the vision of the simple woman who had prayed here. And then his hands imitated her gesture, and involuntarily the words of a hymn he had once learned by heart passed over his lips, he knew every word and every word seized him and pushed his wicked brain off to one side.

"O sacred head now wounded, with grief and shame weighed down, now scornfully surrounded with thorns, thine only crown; o sacred head, what glory, what bliss till now was thine! Yet, though despised and gory, I joy to call thee mine."

He was spellbound, transported. He could speak the Lord's Prayer. It was a complete miracle.

That evening he said to his mother, "When I lay in the hospital and had to endure so much and fight my way through, I thought about something I even told Maus about: now I have served the time of my first life. My first birth has been used up. The Friedrich Becker that my mother bore has gone, has died. Now someone else is here, a new person lives. I thought then that I was a new person, someone who had fought his way through on his own power, and who was standing on his own two feet. I was very proud. I know now that I was not newly born that day. I simply dug deeper into my old self. No, I know now that whoever has still not found God, found himself, is not alive. But I would not have been able to seek and find myself without you and without Hilda."

His mother left the room and came back a few minutes later with a small ivory crucifix that belonged to him, had been given to him at his confirmation. She had kept it for him. He took it and placed it on his desk.

It was nothing dreadful to gaze upon. On the contrary. The world had found its center.

The Sleepless Westphalian

Becker, by the way, had underestimated the military chaplain. When the two men had left Herr Becker's and were moving slowly down the street, the Westphalian said that although he had actually planned to join a patriotic group that evening, he was not in the mood for that now. And so they strolled home. The gray-haired Berlin pastor confessed that he had taken with him a reasonable sense of sweet repose from the conversation. At the apartment door he had asked Becker's mother to express to her son his most heartfelt wishes and his gratitude. The Westphalian agreed now to this, but he could not stop talking, doing battle with his own inner unrest. He sought over and over to justify his position to his colleague, who did not contradict him.

But only when the Westphalian lay there in his hard and narrow bed and could not fall asleep did the meeting with Becker become totally clear in his mind. Yes, this was indeed the first green island in the asphalt sea of Berlin. This young man, the way he had handled himself. Yes, he had been through something. Nothing had been handed to him as a gift. If only he could go through something himself, even if he had to pay for it with a wound.

The Westphalian refreshed himself with Becker and grieved for himself. His old lament—I have already died, my profession has exhausted me, I am a piece of deadwood. What can become of me now? And if I should find a position again—who is going to give me one?—Would I go on preaching and marrying and baptizing and passing on the holy message as I learned it, just as before? But they will not come to me, it is all for others. The sacred words will not transform the bread for me. I dare not eat at that table, I am meant to starve.

And as he mulled over his misery, thinking what a wretched pastor he was, nothing but a pastor, nothing else, his hands folded atop the covers in despair. The gesture registered within him and he whispered the Creed, the Confession of Faith, and a plea for his voice to be heard. He realized that he had prayed out of the need of his heart and that this had been given him once again, and a greater peace came over him. And he thought that he would now be able to enter into the battle for the renewal of the fatherland with still greater energy, with greater decisiveness. God is with us. No thought now of Becker. And as his thoughts grew hazy and he fell asleep, he knew as well that the problem with his furniture would resolve itself, that he would find a position, too.

Poland Is Not Yet Lost

The cat lands on its feet again. Herr Ebert goes for a walk in the Treptow Park. Afterward he offers an orange to his young secretary, who accepts reluctantly—which makes no difference to Ebert.

A Walk in Treptow

Around 9:00 A.M. the telephone clatters in the modest Treptow apartment of First People's Deputy Ebert. The call comes from the Reichs Chancellery. The gray-bearded, taciturn comrade who sits at Ebert's reception desk inquires when his boss will be coming in. Ebert does not ask what is up. He says he'll be there by ten. The secretary wants to know whether it will be exactly at ten. Already certain that it will not be ten, Ebert answers amicably, "You can depend on it."

And he hangs up and looks at the calendar; mid-December, Christmas not far away, there won't be many presents given this year. And then goes to the window and looks out at the street and the sky and sniffs at the air, it is dry and not too cold. Afterward he will go for a short walk, beyond Treptow, along Köpenicker Strasse, but not too far—things are still too uncertain.

At the time there were many people in Germany who said: even if at the moment things aren't so pleasant here and have got a bit out of hand, it will all quiet down in the end and ultimately grass will grow over all of it.

Once downstairs, Friedrich Ebert, from Heidelberg, observes two civilians standing there, his faithful detectives. They greet him, he answers and moves on. He is a short, squat man; his parents came from a village in the Odenwald and had six children. He had sung hymns in Latin as a Catholic choirboy and had been allowed to hold the tassel of the banner in the Corpus Christi procession, always raising his voice in song so loudly that his partner who bore the banner had scolded him. He marches now into a small cigar store and exchanges a few words with the owner while lighting his cigar. Then he walks on further up the quiet, broad Treptow Highway. The trees display their black trunks. Crows sit here and there on the branches or fly above the pavement. Yes, everything wants to go on living. An elderly man walks bent over along the gutter, searching for cigar butts.

Ebert thinks how lovely it all could be if the people in this country would only come to their senses again. They had peace now and could begin their labors anew.

On the corner is an advertising pillar. He walks by without deigning it a glance. The world's gone crazy. I don't need to confirm the fact this early in the morning. Then come more houses and at the next corner a fruit and vegetable shop. He enters and the woman fetches her husband, an older man with many wrinkles, broad shoulders and thin, wispy hair. He is wearing a large blue apron and has a kitchen knife in his hand. He lays it on the table when he sees Ebert, wipes his wet hand on his apron. They shake hands. They are Party comrades. Then the man goes to the rear and returns without his apron, but with cap in hand. Ebert has bought a small bag of oranges. The man carries them for him and accompanies him.

Out on the street Ebert puffs away on his cigar and asks how things are going in the district. The shopkeeper is satisfied; the number of members is growing, although the meetings are often disrupted. "Nothing but political children," he says.

"Let them disrupt things," says Ebert. "They'll learn."

And then the gray-haired greengrocer gets wound up in a long-winded story. The man has lost a son in the war, it was their only child and he has no one to help him, his wife cries a lot. Ebert knows all this already and thinks of his own two sons who fell, a thought that makes him strong, and the memory of the two does not cause feelings of vengeance against the Kaiser and the old Reich to sweep over him, rather he feels: I'll not let them dirty my two lads, nor dirty the cause for which they fell—and concludes with the idea: we want to make peace.

The greengrocer marching next to him with the bag of oranges feels the same way. But his wife is different, she hates the military and wants him to share her scorn. Ebert reassures his comrade. After a pause he says, "Actually it's strange that not a man among us, Party member or whatever, is really happy now that we're masters in our own house. They keep coming around with something new to say and complain about. And now they're talking about how things are shaky at the top."

"At the top," Ebert laughs, "meaning me. Let them talk. Take a look, am I shaky?"

And he turns his vital, flushed face toward the greengrocer.

And then, since they're out for a walk, the man tells about a comrade who lives in the same building with him, on the ground floor on the far side. "They made a pretty mess of him. The way he looked when he came back, you wouldn't recognize him. He only has one leg and he got shot in the stomach, too. Whenever he has to go back in the yard to the outhouse he stays in there for half an hour, and we've only got two outhouses for the whole building and the others all grumble that the outhouse isn't there just for him. But things don't function right for him, and the way he groans in there it must hurt something awful. And then when he comes out he's trembling and white as a sheet and so nasty that if you just look at him it's as if he'd like to take his cane and haul away at you right then and there."

"The man should be in a hospital. Why do you let him go on like that? Give me his name."

"He won't go. He left the hospital without permission. You won't get him in any hospital. Military or otherwise. He's convinced that the doctors botched the job."

"I'll send someone out to him. Write his name and address down for me and send it to my apartment."

Another fellow came along searching the gutter, this one a very young man. Ebert shook his head. "Are there really that many cigar butts?"

"Butts? No. They just do it out of habit. They've got used to walking along the gutter, looking. They already know there's nothing to find here. They're just headed home."

"And look while they walk?"

"I told you, they're not looking anymore. They just stare down purely out of habit."

Again, after a pause: "Do you know what you should do, Comrade Ebert? People are down. They need to be given a little lift. And meetings alone won't do that."

"What then? What should I do?"

"The artists and intellectuals are to blame. They don't care about the people."

"We've known that for a long time."

"Our entertainment committee hasn't got any ideas either. During the French Revolution they had their Marseillaise right off. That was something to sing. And people knew what was up and they marched, everyone with a pair of legs got up and marched."

"Well, Max, we've got the Internationale, you know."

"The Internationale, sure, and we sing it too. But something new has to come along, because people are so half-hearted and down. Something fresh that grabs people. But that's the rub. Nothing turns up. I don't know why not. The artists and intellectuals are washouts. They only compose hits for the bars and that lousy jazz stuff. Well, I guess they can't earn much money with us."

Ebert: "Maybe you'd like a contest for a new song, for a republican hymn perhaps?"

548

"Wouldn't be a bad idea. Otherwise we're going to end up such revisionists that only the middle class will join up with us and no workers at all. They're already running away from us."

And after a pause, he said, "We're losing the faith."

Ebert only half listens. He breathes the fresh air and thinks of his office—but first I'll have this walk.

The greengrocer goes on telling him a great many things, trying to put his views in the right light. "The times really are different from before. We shouldn't overlook that fact. Now we can assemble out here on the meadow and the local police are glad if they can join in. They've been taken down quite a few pegs, and most of them have had their names added to our rolls. Oh, comrade, the way people pester us nowadays with questions about socialism. I sell them all the propaganda materials we're sent, and still they can't get enough. They were more reserved before, had their evening course, the regular meeting and were part of the organization and that was fine and there wasn't much to ask about. Now it's socialism and more socialism. What's there to ask really? That Marx was right is certain. The war proved it. The whole thing was imperialism. That's what I keep telling people. You can't stop socialism. But pushing doesn't help either. It won't come a minute sooner however much you push. But it's like preaching to the deaf." He mutters something to himself. "I can sleep better since the revolution. Before that my boy's death tormented me so. Now I know you're on Wilhelmstrasse and that the whole thing was worth it after all."

Ebert's thoughts were long since in the Reichs Chancellery. He had overcome his fear since yesterday; Scheidemann, too, had calmed down again. The Congress of Councils might turn out to be dreadful, especially after they had had such bad luck with those two divisions. But "Poland is not yet lost." One still had one's common sense, and there were still people in Germany on the side of it.

An empty cab approaches them. Ebert climbs in, sack in hand. The taxi drives under the railroad bridge into the city. The buildings stand there as always, peaceful, immobile, as they were meant to be, always the same number of windows, the same number of stories. The streets follow one another in the proper order. It was a great comfort to be surrounded by such constant creatures. People, too, despite their apparent unrest, were possessed of a great constancy. In the end they all went on doing the same things, you could see it here on the street. The women kept cleaning windows and the windows went on getting dirty again—the street cleaners pushed their carts and swept up paper and peelings, they were constantly busy with gutters. They provided them with their daily bread. If you changed the gutters they could lose their livelihood. But then of course there would be other things to cause the dirt.

The Insel Bridge, beneath it the black Spree. It flows on and on, and is there morning, afternoon and evening, at night as well. The Spree never closes shop. When you ask, it's always there, although you don't always need it, an absolutely trustworthy firm, always open, an example to all.

Rudolf Hertzog on Breite Strasse, that's where, way back when, there would be the great fireworks displays on the Kaiser's birthday. And the royal stables where the sailors wander in and out nowadays. In time there would be others. The Schlossplatz, the Lustgarten, the museum, all still there, good morning, gentlemen.

The chauffeur, the taxi driver, has the same view of things as Ebert, his rider. Naturally they do not express their opinions, but when they exchange a few words at the end about the fare and nod to one another it becomes apparent.

Ebert walks toward the building that stands there with its fence of iron, the Reichs Chancellery. Two soldiers leap up and fling open the gate. The soldiers are still there too, everything in its place just as expected. The taxi driver makes a U-turn on Unter den Linden and begins his retreat through the Brandenburg Gate and out Budapester Strasse.

Ebert's Plan for the Congress of Councils

It is 10:30 A.M. Ebert finds every reception room and corridor full of people thirsting for action. As he strides down the corridor he thinks: the wheels are turning, the chimneys smoking, business booming. And one thing is certain, we'll not let ourselves be chased out of here that easily. The old secretary in his reception room reports that he called earlier because a renowned gentleman, an industrialist, a member of the board of the Federation of Industry, had been there and asked to see him. He made an appointment for 10:30.

Ebert: "It's past that now, fortunately."

Carrying his sack, he enters his handsome office, paneled in white wood, and closes the door behind him. The marble busts of commanders and statesmen look down at him from their pedestals. He sticks the oranges into a drawer and makes himself comfortable in the great presidial chair in which Bismarck had sat; he is content.

We will have our constituent assembly, and I shall be the candidate of all reasonable workers and middle-class people, and of those nationalists, too, who know which way the wind is blowing, and there are more of those than people think. The constituent assembly will come off and I'll be elected, it's as sure as sure can be. They get all excited on account of that soldier named Spiro, because he proclaimed me Reichs President on the 6th. He just was too quick on the trigger, otherwise a very reasonable fellow, one should see that he is taken care of.

And Ebert feels so full of energy and sure of himself that he stands up and marches theatrically through the room with presidential dignity. He takes himself for a walk as president. But now he has enough of that. He sits back down and rings.

Along with the reports comes young Schmidt, very pale, but fresh and lively. He spreads the documents out. They chat a bit first. The news is excellent. Both divisions have as good as fallen apart and otherwise nothing has happened. "I wouldn't care to be in Lequis's shoes."

"You're happy about all this?"

"Sure. Was as good as a belated vote for the revolution."

Ebert: "That's how I see it too."

"I'm glad to hear that. If you're of the same opinion, then we are standing—on the eve of great events."

"My view exactly, Schmidt."

They brought in a folder from the Foreign Office, now under Count von Rantzau. Ebert opened it and shook his head. "Not good. Difficult. Difficult."

Schmidt: "We will now be able to face other countries differently, present ourselves as vigorous representatives of the German people."

"I'm for that."

Schmidt: "We can work more openly now with the Independents, because basically our differences are only in nuances. And," he spoke softly, "we can finally address the issue of our own administration, this Augean stable. The whole place is loaded with reactionary civil servants. It's actually a miracle that with so much lead in our shoes we can even take a single step."

Ebert: "Do you think we can get so many experts together that quickly?"

"Could be difficult. But with these experts against us it makes things more difficult than with none at all. Then, perhaps, the tension will ease with Eisner and Bavaria, too."

Ebert smiled ironically, but said nothing. He was just thinking of his walk through Treptow Park and of the greengrocer and the fellows searching for cigar butts and of the sick man he had been told about. He quickly made a note of that. He leafed through the reports, then looked up.

"We should finally start leaving these superfluous theories and projects at home in the drawer. We're not in school anymore. People aren't that dumb, either. You shouldn't try to sell people something they don't want. But"—he looked firmly at Schmidt—"it all depends on whether we are allowed to live, it does indeed, and not simply shot down or hanged from the streetlamps. Which would you prefer, Schmidt, the one or the other. The question is a timely one, for you as well, Schmidt, since you are my secretary, and what's good for the one . . ."

Schmidt did not understand his boss's joke.

Ebert: "Let's leave the reports aside, they'll not run away. We are thinking about the constituent assembly. The others are thinking of nothing except their Congress of Councils. Why? To settle accounts with us. The congress is next week. We may not even get our constituent assembly at all. They'll have our heads before that."

"But I'm much more confident about that. We now have a whole pile of progressive measures planned that will win general approval. The call for a people's militia, then we'll start to clean up the bureaucracy, and then comes cooperation with the Independents."

Ebert, without letting Schmidt notice anything: "And the settlement with Eisner and Bavaria."

"Yes, and a firm foreign policy. Which reminds me. It's been reported that the French and English labor parties have made direct contact with Wilson in Paris, that Wilson received them and gave them some very good answers, which will be a fine cold shower for nationalists everywhere."

Ebert growled, "Is that right, I hadn't heard that." He smiles mischievously. "If only Wilson hasn't sat down in a bed of nettles in doing so. For my part, I don't think that Clemenceau and Lloyd George are going to be impressed by comrades Henderson and Jouhaux. That's just by the way." He opens the middle drawer and pulls out a sheet of paper. "We sat here for a while yesterday and talked things over, we rolled around some ideas about this congress coming up. Read the proposal we want to submit. Read it aloud."

Schmidt took the sheet of paper, a simple note sheet in Ebert's handwriting. "The following proposal shall be submitted to the Reichs Conference of Workers' and Soldiers' Councils: the executive powers of the government lie exclusively in the hands of the government. The committee to be established by this conference shall be no more than an organ of parliamentary supervision. There must be an end in this nation to the attempt of the workers' and soldiers' councils to meddle in the affairs of the executive."

Ebert observed with pleasure the long face his aide made as he let the paper fall, and said, "You've guessed right; the Independents object. Haase won't bite. It's already happened. But we did not back down an inch from our demands. The doughty Swabian feareth not.—Well, Schmidt? What's on your mind now? What's wrong with it? We want to use this cogent proposal to give the Independents the opportunity to come to a decision. The fellows only have to say yes."

Schmidt, softly: "But they really cannot accept this proposal."

Ebert: "What a shame."

Whereupon he calmly turned to his folders. Schmidt remained at the desk, the paper in his hand again. Ebert turned to him and said, "Oh yes, the proposal, give it to me." He looked up at him. "My dear

Schmidt, has the roof collapsed on you? You're a fine worker in your own area of expertise. But whether you'll ever learn that we're on Wilhelmstrasse now and no longer on Lindenstrasse, that I have begun seriously to doubt."

Schmidt, after a pause: "We *are* on Wilhelmstrasse, comrade Ebert. But in my opinion *we* are the ones on Wilhelmstrasse, the people who came from Lindenstrasse."

"Who are you telling that to? I myself find it difficult to fit in around here. But what must be, must be. Someone has got to put his shoulder to the wheel."

Schmidt, slowly: "Whoever reads this proposal will certainly not get the idea that it has been made with a view to reestablishing the unity of the working class."

"Lindenstrasse, Lindenstrasse, I told you. Just take a look around, is this Lindenstrasse? The Reichs Chancellery, Berlin. Wilhelmstrasse. One of these days I'll hang up a street map in your office and draw a red circle around this building. Tell me, does the chancellor of the German Reich or the Council of People's Deputies have the task of establishing the unity of the working class? Please, a clear answer."

"I would like to repeat . . ."

"A clear answer. Have we been elected to direct the fortunes of the Reich?"

Schmidt let his shoulders fall. "I—cannot answer."

"A sense of place. I, the man most immediately involved, shall answer for you. I am to direct the business of the Reich and it is for that reason that I am sitting here.

"Now," said Ebert, "you look like someone who's lost everything he owns. Put on a friendlier face, Schmidt. Even if you can't bring experience to the job, for which I don't reproach you in the least, you can at least put on a friendly face."

"We'll not have just Spartacus against us on this proposal. The only ones who'll rejoice will be the bourgeoisie and the reactionaries."

Ebert began to wander about. "Indecisiveness will get us nowhere. I want to proceed logically. I don't wish to spill blood. We shall submit the proposal to debate and it will be decided by a majority vote. We shall defer to that decision. We will not take up arms, that is for the others. Perhaps we may be invited to become Spartacists and so avoid the worst. If that suits you, why make use of the invitation. They probably won't even honor me with such an invitation, on the basis of personal sympathy. They'll sweep me right out the door. And because . . ."

Suddenly his face became quite flushed and he stepped up close to Schmidt. "You see, Schmidt, because I know that they want to sweep me right out the door, I am going to steal the march on those gentlemen—and sweep them out the door."

Schmidt: "It's the signal for civil war."

Ebert: "That is just what it isn't. The civil war those gentlemen would like to have is the one they won't get. They want to bar the way to a legitimate constituent assembly. Whoever does that breaks the law. He is a criminal, nothing more. What those gentlemen will do then is to putsch, just as on the 6th on Chausseestrasse. This putsch will come to a bad end—just like the other one."

For a moment his expression was hard, even malicious, then he turned around and withdrew his face from Schmidt's gaze. From the other side of the room he said, "You yammer on endlessly about the unity of the working class. People come to me with the example of Lenin. Please do, I'm at your disposal. Lenin was a reasonable man. Please jot that down, and behind it write 'Hear, hear!' Reason is the same in Russia as it is here. Did Lenin, I ask you, did Lenin create a revolution against the people last year? The Russians wanted peace in 1917. They had had enough of war. Did Lenin answer no? Did he say, 'I can't just now, I must first worry about the unity of the working class'? No, against the will of most of the people immediately around him, he made the peace of Brest-Litovsk, and God knows that was no socialist peace, but a miserable compromise of a peace. But the people wanted peace. That was number one. Next the people demanded land. Russia is an agrarian nation. Lenin had learned as a socialist that one does not divide land up into unprofitable little farms. What did Lenin do? He divided up the land. He didn't care a fig about theories. The people wanted it. What he did was a popular action. And you fellows here? What do you want from me? We need peace and law and order. The people want it. Listen to what they're saying around you. But you won't let me do that. You have your theories. I tell you the people will get their peace and law and order, even if they must roll right on over you to get it."

That was an answer. Schmidt asked uncertainly, at the end of his tether really, "But then how are things to go on from there? Capitalism, robber-baron capitalism, or what?"

Ebert: "Ask Karl Marx. I don't have time for theories right now. I have said what needs to be done and what is popular. And since Marx was a reasonable man that's probably how he would think as a Marxist. That shouldn't cause any headaches. Therefore: the people want to be in charge of things, they shall be in charge, and that is the purpose of this proposal."

Ebert stood behind his desk again, in front of the presidial chair. "Well, sir?"

Schmidt pointed to the paper containing the proposal. "I would only like to ask whether this is the expression of your honest intentions. This paper will perhaps decide the fate of Germany for a long time to come."

"By drawing the line between those who want to work and a band of parasites who set themselves up as councils, we decide the future of Germany. I hope that I will receive support for that. I promise as quickly as possible to run roughshod over that bunch."

He lowered his head again to hide the hard, malicious expression on his face.

Schmidt: "I think, since the Independents won't go along with this and the Spartacists won't either, that we can depend only on ourselves and the bourgeoisie."

"Which means?"

Schmidt was silent. Finally he said very softly, "Excuse me, Comrade Ebert, but it would be a hideous development."

Ebert put his hand to his brow and sat down. "Now you even call it hideous. And if they rip your head off your shoulders, that would be charming?"

"I said hideous because then the whole revolution will have been superfluous. And maybe even . . ."

"Please go on."

"Even the war itself."

Ebert: "Lindenstrasse, this everlasting Lindenstrasse. Because the war doesn't fit your preconceptions, then it was superfluous. They were playing at their war just for us. What a shame they didn't notify us ahead of time and ask our permission. That street map of Berlin with the building where *Vorwärts* is headquartered is yours, my dear Schmidt. You'll have it tacked to your wall by this evening."

Schmidt stood there in dismay. Ebert rummaged about in his papers. Schmidt began again. "And what about Bavaria, Eisner? The Reich?"

"I'm definitely not going to get excited about Herr Kurt Eisner. We can leave him to Comrade Auer."

Schmidt: "What kind of foreign policy can we pursue with a group of followers like these? We'll have the bourgeoisie, the capitalists and the officers. All reactionary forces."

"That's a broad field, my dear friend. Well, what is it now, Schmidt?"

Schmidt sighed and looked at him with large eyes. "I had envisioned things otherwise."

"Never mind that," Ebert consoled his aide. "It's only half as bad as you think, and maybe you'll still get your way and they'll lop off our heads and Karl and Rosa will sit here in this room and Radek will govern as Russia's viceroy. But now go do your work, Schmidt, and keep this matter to yourself and don't go making such a gloomy face, otherwise people will start spreading horror stories."

At the door Schmidt halted once more. "And if push comes to

shove, if the Congress of Councils sides with Liebknecht and they take to the streets, what sort of troops do we have?"

Ebert, outraged: "Schmidt, you really shouldn't ask that. For the maintenance of order and for the defense of this government one can still find troops in a nation like Germany."

Schmidt let his shy gaze fall on the small, heavyset man, who was now sitting up straight in the massive presidial chair; Ebert slowly opened a drawer and pulled out a sack that he placed on top of the desk. He took out a large orange that he turned about in his hand, gazing at it fondly.

"Would you like one, too, Schmidt? Come here, have one, so that you'll look a bit happier."

Schmidt had to walk over to him, he thanked him and smiled.

"These things are from Treptow, from right near my apartment," said Ebert. He pulled out a heavy pocketknife and spread a newspaper on his desk. "We don't have plates. Reichs chancellors have to eat with their hands."

Schmidt regarded his good-humored boss in the huge chair.

And in return Ebert stared at him standing there, then followed his secretary with mocking eyes as he slipped from the sumptuous, handsome room like a ghost, orange in hand.

The iron gates of the Reichs Chancellery on Wilhelmstrasse were locked tight.

More and more troops of men and women appeared now. Civilians mixed with soldiers. They stood out on the pavement and made speeches.

Many of them pressed up against the iron fence, stretched out their hands through it, shouted threats. "Social chauvinists. Traitors. String them up!"

The New Wolf-men

*Two revolutionaries bump into the irritating question: For whom,
then, ought one to create a revolution in Germany? A new sort of
man formed by the war, a kind of wolf-man, shows a lively interest—less in the question than in those who pose it.*

At the royal stables, Liebknecht cast his eyes over the many people
who were reporting in. One had the impression that something was
about to happen. More new people crowded in from the street. Liebknecht stood there in the courtyard, hesitating, and hastily decided that
he wanted to go to Anhalter Station, to the *Rote Fahne* offices to find
Rosa Luxemburg. But at the gate Radek caught up with him, walked
with him a few steps and they stayed in the building. Liebknecht was
happy enough to talk with Radek.

"Well then," said Radek when they arrived at his office, "I've finally
got hold of you. You wanted to take off again. Are you coming to our
meeting with the delegates for the congress or not?"

"How's the general mood?"

"Excellent. If nothing special happens we have victory in our
pocket."

Liebknecht hummed, "On to the Final Fight."

"Given all that I can see and hear, there's no holding our people
back."

Liebknecht nodded absentmindedly. "The flood waters are rising.
We almost don't need to agitate anymore."

"Real revolutionary fever, right into the ranks of the Social Democrats. It will make those nabobs' hair stand on end. Wherever you go
you hear people asking 'When's it going to start?' We have to keep on
the brakes. First we have the congress. We'll watch how that goes.
Maybe there'll be a direct result right there. The Scheidemanns at any
rate will be detonating every mine they have. They're smuggling all sorts
of rabble in under the title of council members. And Haase, the ninny,
he protests. The man is at a loss to save himself from his own cleverness.
But it's all skirmishes in the midst of retreat."

Liebknecht looked at him. "You're in an excellent mood. We can use that. I feel badgered."

He went to the window and looked down into the courtyard. "A mob of people, lots of field gray. Are there any new spies? Have you noticed anything?"

Radek grinned. "You'd have to be blind not to notice something. They send us enough of them. It's an honor. That way you know they're taking us seriously. The nickel-and-dime boys want to earn a little something too."

Liebknecht studied the courtyard. He knew Berlin better than the Russian. He had noticed something.

The troops had ended their march into the city and the army had as good as melted away. They had marched in from Dahlem, crossed Heidelberger Platz with their black, white and red flags waving. But the present had taken no notice of them, had stood there like a man atop a funeral mound sunk deep in his thoughts. They sang: "Home again you'll start anew, live again as you once did, find a wife so fair and true, and Santa Claus will bring a kid." They were marked by war, their bodies emaciated, their faces grim. The volleys of the infantry cracked, the machine guns barked, there were shouts: water here, finish me off, I'm blind, to hell with Lehmann, you bastards with your shithouse slogans. Then you were lying in a bed, you were at home, and you realized that no one was giving you orders now, so you stayed in bed and slept some more.

But then you stood up, and there you were. Act three of the tragedy had begun. The first act, that was the imperial army, with battles and marching and trenches and hospitals—war without end. The second act was the armistice, the retreat, the revolts. The third act: that was now, you were alone, no one could tell you to do anything, but also there was no one to offer you anything either. And now the dragon of the imperial army broke up into its component parts.

And when you looked around, there you were, a discharged soldier. There were already thousands of you standing there on the sidewalks as you marched in. Now you joined them and belonged to that sludge that covered the streets of the city.

But thousands of young men had marched off to war, never thinking about the coming of peace, and most certainly not of this peace. You had killed, and by accident you were still alive. The bourgeoisie couldn't use you, the bourgeoisie didn't have enough to feed itself, and you wanted no part of the musty middle class anyway. You hadn't been out in the field for years to come back and haul their carts around for them. There hung the calls to volunteer for duty, in Döberitz and Zossen, where they were mustering regiments for the Baltic and for a march on Poland, and then there was the revolution—all of it better than this peace, even if it meant thieving, murdering and death.

When Liebknecht kept on looking through the windowpane, studying the throng below, Radek suggested, "If you're looking for someone in particular, we can send somebody down."

"No," Liebknecht muttered, "I'm interested in these people."

Radek: "There are plenty of spies and troublemakers. Our people won't put up with any nonsense."

And he mocked the glorious plans the generals had had to encircle Berlin and throttle the revolution. What a splendid plan had fallen into the water without a sound, without so much as a splash. But the plan had had one direct, unexpected consequence—it had brought people flocking in numbers to Spartacus, vigorous people, transported here at no cost, with first-class equipment, including rifles and hand grenades. Radek swaggered and blustered. But he did not make Liebknecht laugh.

"That rotten Ebert," Liebknecht began, his expression showing his disgust and repulsion, "the man is simply phenomenal. There he sits on Wilhelmstrasse, muddling his way through, sabotaging the revolution. Here we finally have what we always wanted, even more than we ever dreamed possible, no Hohenzollerns and no army. And there sits the man we brought to the top, conspiring with our archenemies, with the nastiest clique of generals in the world. All he cares about is saving his hide. He knows he's lost. But can fear and hate do that much to a man? Make him act like that? What is he waiting for actually? Who does the man think will support him now? Why doesn't he just take to his heels, now, before the congress convenes?"

Radek whistled through his teeth. "The man is a mixture of laziness, stupidity and cunning. And following the laws of laziness and indolence, he'll stay on Wilhelmstrasse for now and wait. Because it is our move. Because he is stupid and can't see that he has no one behind him. But then he is cunning, too, and knows that the revolution needs its antipode and that the bourgeois pack thinks he's their savior. Things wouldn't even be over for him if all the socialists were to desert him. He'd just curse and set himself up with a few loyal followers at the head of the middle class and the officers. We've been through it all in Russia. Every revolution has its Kerenski. For the middle class and the officers it's the lesser of two evils, and they'll let themselves be used. Afterward of course, they would do him in and put one of their own men in his place.

Liebknecht balled his fists. "I am physically disgusted by the man."

An amused Radek stroked his sleeve. "You do him too much honor. But I'll grant your Ebert is even nastier than Kerenski as the destroying angel of the revolution. Kerenski at least was from the bourgeoisie. You raised this man yourselves. Don't be angry with me, but he fits nicely into the pattern of your old Party."

Liebknecht protests. "He was always an opportunist within the Party. He was a tactician—no one gave him much notice, he had no influence—who maneuvered himself into the foreground, the kind, you know, who's always shouting, 'Point of order.' Who says 'order' and means 'treason.' "

"My dear Karl, who likes being betrayed?"

Liebknecht: "I was leafing through my father's speeches yesterday. I was exhausted, already lying in bed. I thought back to those days and allowed myself a little sentimentality. I thought about my father and took down a volume of his speeches. In 1893 he said: 'We have not renounced revolution and will not renounce it. Under the antisocialist law, when deportation hung over each of us like the sword of Damocles, we lifted our heads to proclaim—we are a revolutionary party. We say the same thing today and will go on saying it. We have not changed, and we will not change.' "

Radek: "That was Wilhelm Liebknecht. He was not an Ebert, that's all. You're his son, Karl."

Liebknecht: "Yesterday evening I thought how fine it would be if he were still alive."

Radek started. Why does he wish for that? If he's here himself?

Liebknecht, suddenly: "So how do things stand with the congress?"

Radek: "Everything moving along. The Scheidemanns think they are going to be able to play parliament with us. We'll see to it that the street has its say."

Liebknecht looked at the sheet of paper Radek handed him. Radek noticed that Liebknecht paid no attention while he explained some items. When Radek had finished—it dealt with the delegates for the congress—Liebknecht cleared his throat and said, "You've put a bug in my ear. You said our party developed in such a way that, I hate to say it, Ebert fit right in. You're right, damn it. I see it every day, in the barracks, everywhere. Where are the proletarians? The proles? They're all petit bourgeois, bourgeoisie with no property, who want a parlor. That's their motive. That's why there's supposed to be a revolution."

Radek: "And why not? Let them capture their parlors for themselves. A parlor for every man, just like the slogan of one of the old kings of France: a chicken in the pot every Sunday."

Liebknecht: "You're playing Mephisto. Capitalism promises them a parlor, too. That's no slogan for socialists."

Radek, calmly: "Oh, who knows? In Russia we went ahead and gave our peasants land, you know, because they wanted it and because it fit our plans at that point. So you can go right ahead and give your petite bourgeoisie their parlors, the ones that belong to the others. By the way, it just occurred to me: that would suit you all perfectly, your development as a party, revisionism and so on." He laughed out loud. "We'll make Ed Bernstein's revisionism revolutionary. Glorious. That would make good old Ed tear out his last wisp of hair."

Liebknecht thrust his hands into his pockets. "Which would mean—it really isn't such a fantastic turn of events that this fellow, this Ebert, is sitting in the Reichs Chancellery on Wilhelmstrasse. He promises them the same things we do, but without a revolution. And if I were bourgeois and had to choose between Ebert and me, I'd choose Ebert."

Radek: "Correct. Only our proles aren't so stupid that they believe him. They know he promises and we'll deliver. They can't have a parlor without a revolution. The people know that. My dear Karl, what is the point of this amusing debate. Neither you nor I can issue commands here. Neither you nor I can create a revolution. It is here, and the situation is not that we intend to have a revolution, but rather it intends to have us."

Liebknecht had been sparing his voice because of his hoarseness, but now he rasped, "So that's what our followers look like. A parlor! And those are the people who want to establish socialism."

"I don't understand, I don't understand," muttered Radek. "Let people want whatever amuses them, if only they join the revolution. We'll take care of the rest. Maybe some guy wants to use the revolution to get a pretty girl, what difference is that to me. Maybe one of them has joined up so he can smoke Havana cigars, let him have his fun. We're not all supermen."

And even as Radek spoke, feeling shaky and uneasy, he was suddenly seized with panic. It occurred to him that such endless, painful debates had gone on in Russia, too, but Lenin had been in the thick of the debate, a man of action who wanted something and knew precisely what it was. But in Germany, here stood this man, this—pacifist. That's the way they all are, these Germans, they think and think, talk and talk, and the mills never stop turning until others run right over them.

And sure enough, Liebknecht raised his arms to exclaim, "But what are you talking about! Don't you understand that things are different here with us, even before you can ask the question when the revolution should happen, you must ask whether it should take place at all. Do you want a revolution to happen, would you create it?"

"Me? Yes!" Radek screamed angrily, in a rage. "A thousand times, yes."

He shuddered. Here was the German Fritz, life-size. I'll buy the fellow a stocking cap to complete the picture. Holy Moses, the battle here is lost already."

Liebknecht regarded him affectionately. "Calm down." We're both revolutionaries. It is our duty to analyze the situation.—Let's talk about a date then. You were telling me recently about your discussions. You said that in October of last year, Kamenev and Zinoviev published a call declaring they could not justify an armed insurrection either before history nor the proletariat. And Lenin struck back."

561

Radek thought, yes, but we had a Lenin and not you. Aloud he said, "He was right to strike back. And he was successful. So now you've asked the question as to a date. It's one that must be carefully explored."

"Yes, establishing the boiling point, as a chemist would say."

Patience, Radek said to himself. I looked for him all yesterday, and the day before, to talk with him. But already this is not a conversation, this is the gallows I'm being hanged on. He declared, "The reactionaries' best tool has been broken, their army. The Congress of Councils is upon us. We have to use the congress to unmask Ebert and the current government as the spearhead of reaction, the confederates of the generals, and then deliver them over to the rage of the masses. The Independents are to be separated from the government or split in two. After that the situation is rather simple. That's what I mean when I say it's not we who intend to have a revolution, but it us. It forces us to take the next step. There's no possible way to put it off. And one thing more, something personal, my dear Karl. I hope that it's clear to you that you yourself have no choice. It's now a matter of being either the hammer or the anvil."

Liebknecht made a gesture expressing his indifference. "Thus far I've never learned how to get the jitters. I see you don't want to get to the bottom of the matter, but I do, and I must because it's necessary, it's urgent. I would blame myself if I didn't do it. And others would blame me as well. And I can't avoid it; I can see you're impatient, that you'd like to grab that doorknob and leave. We are in charge of the affairs of the proletariat. I am a socialist and I want socialism, that's what I want, nothing else. I was and am a pacifist. I must think through our present situation independent of any other prior ones. You should not, dare not, keep me from doing that, and you won't, either."

Liebknecht sat there calmly, speaking with a clear, serious voice. "People all over the world, especially the people of Europe, have had war for four and a half years, for fifty-five months. It looks as if between ten and twenty million people died in that war, were killed or starved or died from epidemics. We need a new, a totally new world, a new Europe. Capitalism cannot create it. It cannot find its way out of war. I believe in socialism. We need socialist energies. Let's forget for the moment the philistines and the petite bourgeoisie with their parlors. How do you explain that in this country not even the reasonable men comprehend what needs to be done, neither the intellectuals nor the idealists? Take a look at the intellectuals in Germany. I cannot grasp it. Our intellectuals, among them famous names—many are political children, others are fools, scatterbrains and fantasts, and an awful lot of them are simply reactionaries. All of them idealists when they open their mouths. They don't even want a parlor—they don't want anything at all. They have their dark, totally medieval metaphysics and are content. For that they need intellectual freedom. And those are the helpers you find in this country if you try to tackle the tasks of humanity. Think back to the outbreak of the war when ninety academics, world-famous scientists, issued their declaration, unfolding the banner for the holy war of imperialism."

Radek swore. "Lay into them with your club swinging." His patience was at an end. Liebknecht smiled a friendly smile at him, still the same old Radek. He stretched out a hand to him. "You mustn't despair of me."

Then Liebknecht stood up, and to Radek's surprise he went to the window again, studying the courtyard closely, and now said something new, something that alarmed the Russian. It was apparently what had preoccupied the German all along, formed the core of his reflections. At the window, Liebknecht said, "Radek, you don't fully comprehend what is happening, here below and in the city in general. I realized it in the barracks, out on the street and even at mass meetings. You don't see the same people you saw before. There has been a remarkable change in the last few weeks. It's tied up with the arrival of the troops in the city. Lequis didn't succeed in capturing Berlin with his two divisions, but he did achieve something. Everywhere I go I see strange fellows, I'm literally surrounded by them. They're soldiers, warriors, of a sort I never saw before, or only now and then. How should I describe them for you? Human refuse. Sometimes I can talk myself into believing they've been sent to us by the enemy to disrupt us, to disconcert us. But they can't have been sent. There are too many of them. They come on their own. They are everyday, average Germans, people from that same lower middle class we were just talking about, but some from further up the social ladder too, some of them educated, soldiers and workers. They have an odd way about them. The way they stand there, sit there. They don't honestly listen, they simply stare at you. They have a mean look, the snarling teeth of a wolf. Mostly they just sit there silently, sometimes they laugh with scorn. The war has brutalized people, wrecked them. They leave me with the impression that they are beasts of prey. You can expect most anything from them."

"And certainly not the best."

"I'm sure you don't think I'm a coward, Radek. But when I stand in front of these people I'm almost paralyzed. And they are taking over everything. We ought not take on such people. And even if you should say that one can even use them for the revolution—I'd rather go back to prison than fight beside them. The most profound degeneration. And they hate me because they sense what I think of them and because they themselves know what sort they are."

The Russian: "They're Whites. But let's have no false emotions. They simply want to kill us."

Liebknecht, softly: "So those are Whites, Whites before the revolution. Hmm, that's very German. And with this rabble, with these weeds of war one can of course accomplish most anything. Perhaps Ebert's eyes will fall graciously upon them. They would do a good job for him. I kept hoping you would simply tell me that they are nothing but provocateurs. But there are too many of them."

Radek: "A rotting pack of petits bourgeois. You're not going to let them bully you, are you?"

Liebknecht crossed his arms. "On the contrary, they give me strength, energize me. They bring me to my senses. I feel I have to do something, confront them. Face to face with these creatures, I see clearly; that portion of humanity that is aware must drive the rest of humanity forward, boldly, mercilessly. One should not be ashamed to admit that the proletarian movement cannot succeed without such an aristocratic element."

Radek: "The scum of humanity. You've named yourselves after Spartacus, the liberator of slaves. You must free these people from their own decay. Otherwise it may happen that the generals will round them up and pounce on you with them. And that is what will happen, too, if you don't arrive at a decision. And that not only makes you guilty of crimes against the proletariat, but against Russia as well, which will be invaded by these bands of Whites."

Liebknecht said, "That's probably so. That, too, is an argument."

He stood there for a while yet, his back to the window. Then they left. The conversation was over.

As they descended the stairs, Radek thought: this incurable German obfuscation, scruples and more scruples. I still don't understand how a Karl Marx could happen here.

A somber Liebknecht strode ahead. The conversation wasn't bad. It opened my eyes. We must indeed think of Russia as well. We're risking everything. We have to do something about the decay. The effects of the war are worse than the war. Surgical measures are necessary, and even if that means tying the people down. This is a German revolution.

He began to salivate profusely. He wanted to vomit.

Liebknecht is happy, however, when in the hall below a great many excited and joyful people encircle him, men and women, civilians, soldiers and sailors. A lot of fine faces. His heart grows lighter. It will work with these people. I can move mountains with them.

Among the men we see Eduard Imker, the discharged soldier, and among the women his sister Minna, who is ecstatic to have managed a handshake with Liebknecht. We look around the noisy room searching for Lieutenant Maus. But we can't find him, he is not there.

There are indeed spies among all these excited people. What they see and hear here will be immediately reported to several people who will draw certain conclusions from their reports. Bloody Friday, the 6th, was only a botched job. Next time it will be done better.

But other sorts of men have joined these people too. We accompany three of them out the main portal and walk with them down the quiet Breite Strasse. They are in field gray, two intelligent looking fellows who might be officers, between them a simple looking man whose cap is conspicuously pulled forward on the left side. Beneath the cap he has a mangled, bloody ear. One of the intelligent fellows asks the simple one whether he has seen Liebknecht.

He grins. "The Jew with glasses."

"Right. And well enough that you would recognize him again? Fine. And you're a good shot, too."

The simple fellow says the whole thing is too risky. They'll have to talk about the details again. They then talk about money and assure him that they'll see he is brought to safety. They tell him if he doesn't do it they'll simply give the job to someone else. They have a drink together standing at a bar on Mühlendamm. By evening the simple fellow with the split ear has still not decided.

The next morning he is found in Lichterfelde at the end of a suburban street with two bullets in his back. He has no papers on him and cannot be identified.

Once Upon a Time There Was a 2nd Guard Infantry Regiment

And now it is no more. But in Paderborn plans are afoot for something that will not be inferior to it.

Once upon a time there was a 2nd Guard Infantry Regiment.

Over a hundred years before, in 1813, it had been founded on the orders of the Prussian king Friedrich Wilhelm III, when he promoted a decorated battalion to the status of Guard. The regiment took part in the war against Napoleon in the battle of Pantin and entered Paris. In 1848 it fought against the people in the streets of Berlin, and it was engaged in battle in 1866 at Königgrätz, and again in 1870/71 at St. Privat, Sedan, and once more on the outskirts of Paris.

On its banner it bore two red ribbons commemorating the fact that the second Kaiser Wilhelm had led the brigade; at the tip of the banner was the iron cross. On a silver ring around the banner pole of the fusiliers was engraved: "With this banner in his hand, Sergeant Gursch fell at St. Privat, Aug. 18, '70."

It was the oldest and finest infantry regiment of the garrison of Berlin and was intimately connected with the fugitive German Kaiser. He had paraded the brigade before his father, Kaiser Friedrich, when he lay ill in Charlottenburg. It was a memorable day for the regiment. A few days later they were engaged in a routing spring parade on Tempelhof Field. When the parade had ended, the Kaiser, dressed in regimentals, placed himself for good and all at the head of the troops and rode, preceding all the Guard banners, up the Belle-Alliance Strasse and Friedrichstrasse, back to the palace in the city, while great numbers of people watched, a spectacle of the first order.

This was the regiment that had gone into the Battle of the Marne in France with 41 officers and 1,747 men, and had left it with 13 officers and 610 men.

What remained of the regiment had marched into the metropolis, decorated with evergreens but to no cheers of welcome, and assembled in its barracks, where no reception had been prepared other than that of its replacement battalion, whose men, together with the members of its soldiers' council, received the returnees in the prescribed fashion.

At a farewell dinner they sat in the Atlas near the Weidendamm Bridge, active and reserve officers, all that were still alive. Yes, it was good-bye. They sat at their tables in this middle-class city, in a normal hotel, still engulfed by the horrors and tumult of those last, dreadful months.

And this was the end. Dead, wounded, screams, spasms, gasps. A man kneels there, his face ragged shreds—shoot me; but that is forbidden, back, back, they must retreat, the wounded clinging to them, grenades keep falling, blasts of air. The soldiers sing: "Home again you'll start anew, live again as you once did."

They talked among themselves, mostly in whispers. There was a brief cheer when they heard that a colonel they all knew had been renamed regimental commander. But what was left of the regiment? It would be scattered to the four winds.

They reminisced.

The men near the colonel talked about the Battle of the Marne. One of the staff officers mocked the French and their "miracle of the Marne."

"We shall leave aside what the infamous First Lieutenant Hentsch managed to do. He was, at any rate, supposed to fill the hole between the first and second armies in case of retreat. But where is this miracle of the Marne? I've jotted it down. We had circa 270 battalions, etc.—the French almost twice as many. It seems to me that their success was due more to simple arithmetic than to any miracle."

The colonel appeared not to share this opinion. "Nevertheless, nevertheless. The French had begun a very dangerous retreat. It is a miracle suddenly, without further ado, to have doubled the troop strength we had. In any case we had not presumed it possible."

Again the question, how did it happen and what does it mean.

"Who is this Ebert? What kind of people does he have?"

"He is said to be useful. That doesn't free us of the responsibility of taking a closer look and saying our piece as well."

Questions: How many people were left with other regiments? Gloomy answers. How many officers are being discharged, how many put on half pay?

One of them who had lived through November in Berlin stood up to report; he was full of hate, the colonel had to calm him down.

"We can only speak very softly. We cannot greet you as we would like to. In Kiel, men who broke their oath, sailors guilty of high treason, joined with deserters, criminals and workers who had never been in the field to begin a mutiny, and finally managed to reduce our nation, admired by all the world, to rubble. This cowardly mob ignominiously attacked us from the rear. It is this riff-raff we have to thank for the fact that our enemies can triumph over us today. Although the way to treason was prepared for them, by these Democrats and Socialists led by Prince Max von Baden, Ebert, Scheidemann and company."

They sat there mute, until at last one of them said—a man on crutches, with only one leg—what they all were thinking. "These rebels and that whole democratic, socialist pack will vanish before the vengeance of the German front-line soldiers."

The younger men at other tables knew exactly what they wanted to do. They had heard about the recruiting offices and the war in Poland and the Baltic. They asked around. They had decided to continue the war, wherever it might be.

They listened avidly to what one or the other of them told of subversive activities throughout the nation. One of them was more inclined to blame the Bolsheviks, another the Jews, a third the Freemasons, a fourth the Socialists.

What they were told in the field about a stab in the back was true then. They heard it in every town as they marched back through Germany. There was hatred in them. But they remained somber and sad. They saw no tomorrow ahead of them.

The regiment, the banner, the Kaiser—all lost.

Who could give them new life? To whom could one turn?

General Maercker's Home Rifles

General Maercker, former commander of the 214th Infantry Division, had spoken up at the conference of ranking military officers and representatives of General Headquarters held in Paderborn on December 6th.

"When I was out on the front I knew nothing. When I set foot on my native soil I comprehended the extent of our misfortune. I was bowled over."

On that same day, General Maercker had declared, and had received the approval of all present, that since there was the threat of revolution at home and of Bolsheviks in the East he would organize his division as a volunteer corps with a double assignment, to do battle both at home and abroad. He further indicated that he would offer the services of these volunteers to the government. There were no more detailed discussions of this last point.

December 12th is the third day of the entry of the front-line troops into the city. For the last time, there on the speaker's platform by the Brandenburg Gate a man in a top hat stands next to a high-ranking officer and murmurs, "You return home undefeated."

On December 12th, in the bishop's palace in Paderborn, General Maercker submits to his commanding officer, Lieutenant General Morgen, the commander of the 14th Reserve Corps, a memorandum prepared during those six days with the assistance of passionately committed subordinates. It is a technical explanation of the plan he had suggested on December 6th. He points out that the army is currently in the process of total dissolution, which represents a danger to the Reich both at home and abroad and makes prompt action absolutely necessary. In terms of the plan he had submitted on December 6th, which foresaw the creation of a corps of volunteers from his division, he now realizes that these new units must be completely different from those of the old army, both in structure and spirit. Consideration must be given to both the technical experience of the war as well as to current conditions. The relationship between officer and rank and file must be changed radically. During the retreat it had been proven that reasonable delegates from the ranks could be an effective adjunct to the officers in the areas of administration, discipline, supplies, control of munitions. These delegates are to concern themselves with the canteen, supplies, the library, sporting activities. Complaints, too, should first be registered with these delegates.

As for the spirit of the troops: "The foremost principle is the maintenance of discipline among the men. He who is no gentleman, who follows not our noble laws, should keep his distance from the cause."

Plundering will be punishable by death. Whoever shows himself a coward, steals or destroys property of the state will be cashiered. The mission is: maintaining law and order at home and securing the nation's borders.

Badge: silver oak branch. German Loyalty.

There follows a general plan for the formation of a voluntary Home Rifle Corps. General von Morgen, backed up by an agreement on principle from the recent conference, requests a more detailed plan. The news of the government decree or call for the formation of a people's army has already become known. What that might mean, von Morgen says to Maercker, cannot yet be determined. At any rate, Maercker must accelerate the pace to some extent.

That is exactly what Maercker wants to hear. His officers work day and night. The project lies on the general's desk two days later.

Earth Has a Place in the Order of Justice

How does one best serve the cause of justice on earth? This question is discussed by two friends. But when worse comes to worst and the one renounces his friendship with the other, it has nothing to do with justice but rather with—a woman.

The Archangel Michael

Becker turned on the light in the night—the dim bulb of the small lamp that stood on the table beside his bed—and sat there in the semi-darkness of his room, this one entire room, the scene of his sufferings, of his adventures. The open bookcase with the shadowed bust of Sophocles; at one time he had hung a curtain over the books, put the bust under his sofa, then he had taken the curtain back down and reinstalled the bust.

There stood his desk, the armchair in front of it. That is where the Latin American gentleman had sat and spoken of the interest that Becker's thoughts had aroused in the spirit world.

The lion had lain on the rug, had stretched out into the room from under the armchair. He had upset the wastebasket with his tail. Later on, on that same rug, the repulsive little gray rat had sat.

And there were the door and the naked floorboards. There someone had knelt, someone distant now, had knelt and prayed. And that same person had wept for a long time, her head on the desk.

Becker had to get up now, he slipped on his robe and shoved his feet into slippers. Then he walked through the room. He moved about on his long legs like a stork, approaching all these points as if moving from station to station. As he neared the door the voice of his teacher spoke from the depths, but without words.

"This was all defiance, coldness and sloth. They made of you a wretched creature that dried up and withered. But God did not cease to look upon you with the eyes of His great mercy, and He has offered you knowledge and faith and gracious forgiveness."

"My teacher."

"I followed you in that moving railroad car as it carried you through the night, and you called out from the darkness of your heart, of your desolation. Your conscience called. It wanted more than mere peace. Your soul hungered. Desperation was added to the bitterness of your suffering. You did not resist it. I unbarred the door and God was able to enter."

"I thank you. And what is to happen now? Will you show me a way?"

"Greed is the root of all evil. You shall entrust yourself to the Almighty, your Creator, both body and soul, in living and in dying. Father, not my will, but thine be done."

Then all grew silent. It seemed to Becker, however, as if there were still someone calling, in the depths or from a distance. The call came and sounded urgent.

"Be awake, stay awake. Be vigilant every hour. You have escaped death. Do not rejoice too soon. Ruin is always in pursuit. Death lies in ambush waiting for you as long as you are a human being. Death wants to drag you into corruption."

They're calling me, warning me. And in front of his desk, where the little ivory crucifix stood—it has been there day and night, even when I lie unconscious—he knelt down and directed his gaze at the small base and lower end of the cross. He was unable to lift his eyes to the man hanging there. I must speak words. If I do not direct my thoughts, I shall become a victim of something, but I don't know of what. And he whispered, he wanted to whisper something, but he found no words.

And soon he felt a heaviness, a leadenness in his hands lying on the desktop. He felt himself compelled to shove his arms out over the desktop as far as his elbows, so that they held the crucifix between them. And there his arms lay. But the heaviness extended now to his shoulders. He had to bend down and his breast neared the edge of the desk because the burden pressing down upon him.

The question flitted through his mind: What is this, is this my old demon? But I have my thoughts, my thoughts are clear and free. They're doing something to my arms and legs. It frightens me, yes, it frightens me.

He pulled himself together and tightened his grip. He searched again for words, but none came to him. So he whispered what he saw: ceiling, desk, lamp, curtains. He whispered the words, hoping they would help him endure.

But from second to second the pressure cast upon him grew. He felt himself exposed to a force that kept increasing horribly. It was as if it wanted to rip him away from the desk where he hung at the foot of the cross.

Ah, it is him again. Him again. Can't be chased off. Him. Now he wants to revenge himself on me. He's come with new weapons.

His arms and legs and now even his torso were swathed in heavy smoke. The smoke, the vapors, crept into his limbs. It filtered into his body. And from his head as well, from the back of his head, the heaviness flowed without ceasing. They're letting me have my forehead, my eyes and my mouth free. My mouth can still move, I can think what I like, I am still here.

But it rose up in his throat and weighed down his body. They want to disembowel me, I am to be robbed of my senses.

It was not actually a pain, more of a hollow, deep ebb and flow of an ache and uneasiness, that pounded in him like a pulse, like an onrush of waves.

He clung there to the desk. What they want is to lame me, to confuse me.

It was clear now that some hostile power was attacking him and in one way or another wanted to take possession of him. While his lips moved without a sound an icy horror spread over him. Ah, this is it then, what people used to call evil and the Evil One, and that I thought was a word, a value judgment. It is something else. It has hung itself on me. Why didn't I recognize it. If there is human misery and a God, then there must be evil too, in its own place, in its own garments, with its own means, and it must have its own sort of consciousness, just as I have another sort that attempts to defend me.

This pain. Now it wants to bore into my soul. It rips me open with hook and nails, with claws and talons.

And the horror: he felt his head grow weary. It felt drunk with sleep. Half conscious, his head fell to one side while a warmth flowed over him, and from the distance, from a mirage, sweet images floated over him, and his jaw dropped down and his eyes closed. They flowed toward him, smoke and vapor, now they were flowers, now arms, now faces, glances, eyes, female hair. Music tinkled. His mouth stood open. He panted.

A numbing exhaustion came in a blue wave over his brain. His knees gave way. He slipped down from the desk and lay with his chest and face to the floor, still kneeling, on the rug where the lion and the rat had sat.

He sank down to it, his eyes closed. He could not see what was going on behind and around him.

The room was no longer a room. It had been ripped open wide from top to bottom. There was no apartment, no building, no street.

A bluish gray mountain range rose up. Sharp peaks towered like spikes in the air. The horizon was enveloped in heavy black clouds. A mighty creature flew out of the blackness on violet wings that sparkled in flight. Its expression in flight was joyous and proud. Its eyes shone green.

It flew soundlessly above the people below, and the rush of its flight passed over them. There was a rustle of music. The gentle sweet images spun like rays of light, setting the man in their midst. From the sparkling wings there flowed blissfully beautiful creatures, now humans, now fish, now caterpillars that became human beings.

The bright creature sang surpassingly strangely, a song of enchantment. It opened its muscular arms and with its long steely fingers took the man by the hair of his head while spreading its wings with a whirr. Its song became triumphant.

There was the sound of horses stamping behind him, and before the victorious angel could turn around he was pierced by a lance and thrown down on top of the man lying on the ground. He clutched the man's hair in his claws.

The rider was pure lightning and beams of light. He sat up on a mighty blue-black steed. The angel from whom black rays of light came let out a scream of rage, stood up and swung himself into the air with the speed of an arrow. About him dark clouds eddied. He whirled vertically into the air, toward the mountains.

But the lightning followed him. The black angel hoped to alight in a gorge and hide there. But the angel of lightning pursued him through the valley. The blue-black steed dashed him to the ground with its hooves. Amid groans and cries of pain, the black angel whirled back up and gained the green heights and ragged pinnacles of the mountains.

There he buried himself in the heavy darkness of the clouds that surrounded the peaks and encircled the entire horizon. From there he hurled down his cries of rage.

Only with immense exertion could Becker struggle up from the floor where he had lain hunched over.

He propped himself with one hand on the rug, with the other groped for the edge of the desk. And so he clambered back up, both hands on the desk. And as his hands lay on the desktop, it went through him like lightning. His thoughts were rejoined to where they had been ripped from him. And he whispered, his eyes directed to the base of the cross, his brow furrowed, a few words. They became the Lord's Prayer. And with these words his thoughts grew clear again.

And his soul, which had almost been torn from him, was secured to his body and found its place.

A trembling passed through him. And a wave of warmth and joy poured over him. In the darkness of this ravishment he found himself. His mouth spoke no words. He climbed the ladder of adoration.

Afterward he realized what had been granted him: contact with invisible worlds. He felt as if he had molted his skin. He was not yet back completely among the objects of his room.

Night. The little lamp burned beside his bed. His bookcase, the bust of Sophocles, his bed. He walked through the room, turned the light out from his bed and promptly sank into a deep sleep.

Relief

In the morning he sat down beside his mother at the breakfast table, eating more slowly than usual and less inclined to talk, but his mother was not worried about him. Still, there was a conversation between them later that morning that did frighten her.

Some visitor or other from yesterday, apparently the Westphalian chaplain, had left a newspaper lying in the living room; in it was an article dealing with the refusal of foreign academics to work together with Germans at congresses in the future. The mother showed her son the paper and asked him as if he wanted to take it to his room.

Becker threw a casual glance at the paper, and his eye chanced to fall on precisely that article. It was suggested the foreigners based this boycott on the sinking of ships and deportations.

"I must burn this newspaper," he said to his mother.

"Give it to me," she said.

"No, let me do it."

She opened the door to the stove in his room for him. He flung the ball of paper into it and watched as it caught flame and then disintegrated into ashes. Uneasy, his mother left him to himself.

People are still defending all that. There must be punishment. People must be made to feel that there is justice. If people will not acknowledge God in heaven and pay no heed to the laws of this world, then they have to be dealt with like trained dogs, horses and elephants. If you can't make human beings reasonable and good, you can at least make them bearable. That can be done with individuals, that is what upbringing is about. But what happens when they band together, or when they form power blocs, the state? What can you do with the state? Each one with its pride, its arrogance, each with its border and its greed, what can come of that? Perhaps one ought to take their borders away from them. But how? There is Wilson. But even in antiquity there were the small Greek cities, each of them a state, and they tore one another to pieces—and all the while stood at the height of learning. They founded a league of states. It didn't work. The Macedonians had to come, the barbarians from the north, to subjugate them and take their freedom from them. Then they were unified and there was peace, for a while.

Becker sighed. What am I thinking about now, what kinds of fantasies are these. I dare not even open my eyes to see where you are hanging, hanged man.

You were wretched, like me. You did not fear to enter into a

574

human body. You wanted to show us that you would not leave us to our despair. You chose the most horrible paths of all, none of us could travel such bitter paths.

And then Becker opened his eyes and saw the suffering, dying man. His body gave a shudder. Deep within him he wept with remorse. It was a comfort to him that his mother's Bible was lying there and he came across the words:

"For this commandment which I command thee this day it is not hidden from thee, neither is it far off. It is not in heaven that thou shouldest say: who shall go up for us to heaven and bring it unto us, that we may hear it and do it? Neither is it beyond the sea that thou shouldest say: who shall go over the sea for us and bring it unto us, that we may hear it and do it? But the word is very nigh unto thee, in thy mouth, and in thy heart, that thou mayest do it."

These words were wonderful and transparent, a comfort. And something within him said:

"I submit myself to you, eternal God.

"I know that I can speak to you, that I can reach you, that you are near me, that I need not fall silent and be afraid.

"With all that you have created, you have also created me. I am here only through you, I cannot be without you, I am nothing without you.

"I thank you that I can speak to you, that I can submit my inmost self to you. Crushed, I bemoan the fact that for so many years I did not abide with you. So I beg you, lead me by your grace and accept this your poor servant. What your world is and what you have planned for me goes far beyond my understanding, I cannot know it. For what would I ask you? That it might be possible for me to immerse myself still deeper into your truth and to keep myself far from falsehoods and deceit. Let the emptiness that is inside me be filled, let me find my way to you, who are all fullness and truth. To think only of you, only of you.

"I love you, Father. I cling to you. Let your love engulf me like a flame."

Posters

In the course of the morning Becker went out onto the street. It was the same hour that the train carrying President Wilson, the peacemaker, pulled into Paris at the Bois de Boulogne station. Once outside, Wilson, President Poincaré and Mrs. Wilson, with her flowers, take their seats in a car. They ride between two rows of soldiers, helmet after helmet, rifle after rifle, down the Champs Elysées to the Hotel Prince Murat. Soon Poincaré, the president of the French Republic, will rise from the table decorated with red and white roses and before two hundred people speak of the misery and sorrow of this war that has now ended in victory. Peace must bring with it reparations and guarantees against a recurrence of the dangers of the past. He toasts President Wilson's health, Mrs. Wilson's, and the prosperity of the United States of America. At this, Wilson rises, speaks of the deep impression this reception has made on him. He, too, mentions the new peace that must build the basis for the freedom and happiness of countless peoples.

At this hour in Berlin, Friedrich Ebert has just finished his walk through Treptow Park accompanied by his old comrade, the greengrocer. He let him give him his sack of oranges; an empty taxi comes by and he takes it; they drive down Köpenicker Strasse. They can move peacefully forward between the double row of buildings. For Ebert, as for the taxi driver, it is a relief and a great reassurance to drive through the streets, to be alive amid such steadfast creatures.

Almost simultaneously, Karl Liebknecht enters the royal stables and the Russian, Radek, finally has the opportunity of speaking with the German about imminent events, now that both of Lequis's divisions have fallen apart and left the way free for action. It is a conversation that Liebknecht leaves in a gloomy mood. It has become clearer than ever to him that the Germans do not want a revolution, a minority has to come along and force them into it—but does he want to do that? Should he want to?

Becker permits his mother to accompany him along the street for only a short way. He has taken both canes with him, but he really uses only one for support, the other he carries hung over his left forearm. He says good-bye to his mother; he wants to ride to the military hospital. There they find his condition excellent. The assurance and the energy with which he walks have improved, and by objective measurement the circumference of his leg muscles has increased. They congratulate him and their one wish is that his general physical condition might be stronger. They suggest a winter vacation in a military sanatorium, in the Bavarian Alps perhaps.

Becker is content. The proposal has caught fire within him. He can not hide from himself the fact that other duties call, but that what he would most like would be to withdraw. He has a boundless desire to sink from sight. But the thought frightens him. He fears he will lose himself.

He moves slowly along Friedrichshain, first on the side of the park, then he crosses to the other side, where the houses are. This is a great event, this seeing the earth again.

Posters are pasted to the buildings, and here and there are colorful, circular labels reading: "Spartacus, the stooge of the Entente." One large poster shouts: "Bolshevism, the murderer of Germany. Ruin or Reconstruction?" It was signed by a "League for the Defense of German Culture." I've seen that before, this same poster, so everything is going on just as before.

On an advertising pillar is an illustrated appeal: "Mothers, do you want your children to know a new war, one growing out of an enforced peace?"

As he arrives at the corner, another poster declares: "Shall this misery continue? Our only chance to live will come with a just peace."

At the Königstor the traffic is heavy. Becker feels somewhat unsure; a policeman helps him across and leaves him then standing beside a wall where an immense new poster beams down on him, black on a bloody red background. Its headline: "What is Socialism?"

That is what Becker would like to know now, too, and he reads. "The highest goal of socialism is the total liberation of the German people and of the whole of mankind. It wants to help make a strong, peace-loving League of Nations a reality. Let the banners be lowered in silence, let the drums cease to roll—in the parliament of mankind, in the legislature of the world."

Becker, slightly weary now, stands before it leaning on both canes. He feels like a man stranded for long years on an island and by some strange chance brought back to his native land—but he does not recognize it. Although his crisis has lasted only a short time, most things have diverged from him, and he feels as he had back in the military hospital when he lay in the room next to Maus and wrestled to free himself from physical death. The trumpet in the hospital garden had blown: "God be with you, it would have been so lovely, God be with you, it should never have happened."

Let the banners be lowered in silence, let the drums cease to roll—can drums ever cease to roll? Parliament, a just peace, those are the demands now, the answers to all questions. And what do I answer? What is your answer, Friedrich Becker?

He directs his step into the sunny Neue Königstrasse. What is Friedrich Becker's answer? Even after such labors, such torments, struggles and detours, did he still not have an answer?

I've not become some oracle that receives its answers from a crack in the earth. I'll not let myself be harassed and caught off guard. This question, that question, this imperative, that imperative—I have to know if it is my imperative as well. What is the intention that stands behind all these demands and questions?

They yearn to transcend these times, but then who doesn't. One must do what is possible. There is no dispensation even if some better things remain impossible. The right thing is to steel oneself and go to work. And lot of people have spoken of hell and heaven, and those are not just mere words for children. Because there is justice, earth will have a place in the order of justice.

And nevertheless, just as it is written: "The kingdom of God cometh not with observation. Neither shall they say, Lo here! or, lo there!"

Human Heed and Deliverance from It

There was a surprise waiting for him at home.

Maus, luckless Maus, had come for a visit, and not by chance. Like a shell-shocked man whose mind always runs back to the moment of being buried alive, who dreams of scrambling free, who is constantly reconstructing the disaster in order this time to master it, so Maus was driven to Becker.

For Becker was bound up in Maus's misfortune, and that misfortune continued to bear just one name, Hilda.

He had to talk about her. He wanted to hear about her. He acted as if he only wanted to shift the heavy weight of the guilt he felt toward Hilda, but actually he wanted to hear that it was not all over. And though you might tell him ten times over that Hilda was lost to him, he could not let the matter rest. The humiliation and the pain would leave him no peace.

And politics had been no deliverance either—he had tried everything! And every time he sat there with his own misery. And now he was at Becker's, a fugitive, pursued, in Friedrich Becker's room, with this happy, favored man. What can we poor humans, we miserably equipped humans do about the fact that nature has treated us like this? I don't have Becker's mind. But Becker hasn't had it easy either; he could be living a happy life, but now he's gone off the deep end, a fellow sufferer in this damned world.

Maus was strangely dressed—civvies on top, military below. He wore the yellow leather jacket of an ordinary chauffeur, with a high, white, stiff collar and a necktie, but his legs were stuck into green military trousers, on his calves he wore high yellow leather gaiters.

Maus himself had changed. He no longer hid his suffering. He was not the lively fellow we first saw strolling down the Kurfürstendamm depressed but determined to find work; he had gone then with Big Ding and his fiancée Grete. Two restless, piercing eyes peered now from a gray, puttylike face. Maus wore the expression of a hunted animal that has decided to defend itself.

The doorbell rang. Becker's mother went to meet her son.

Maus saw himself confronted by someone different from the man he knew as Becker, by a man with a peculiarly subdued, quiet, cautious way about him. A friendly brightness suffused Becker's face as he gave Maus his hand. "Well look at you, fellow! A regular field marshal. Back in the war again?"

Maus saluted. "Who knows."

Then Frau Becker helped her son out of his coat. Becker stood against the wall near the stove, warming himself. There was a numbed look about him. (I am not only a citizen of this world, but of the next as well.)

Maus watched him. In the strangely subdued face he found traits that had newly emerged and that he could not connect with the Becker he knew. The face, though no longer the skull from their hospital days, was still long and thin from extended illness, but it had taken on a look of decision. Where did that come from? Maus searched. He noticed that this face was like his own, pinched (only he did not know that while his had drawn together as if reacting to acid, the other was drawn together around a centerpoint). There was a combative line that ran vertically from the top of Becker's nose up across his forehead. And the mouth, too, had small hard lines.

Becker did not notice the gaze with which Maus was examining him. Becker thought: look how the world follows you about. There he stands, my bailiff. He's come to collect debts. But why not? We don't live on the moon.

The mother invited the two friends to go to Becker's study, which was well heated.

Becker sat down on his sofa and shoved a chair over to Maus. Then, since it did not look as if Becker was going to begin to speak in his usual way, Maus sat up (Becker doesn't look as healthy to me as his mother assured me he is) and asked how Becker was feeling after his walk, whether he might not prefer to lie down and be alone.

But Becker said no, and thanked him. Maus should stay.

Then Maus said (still staring at the peculiarly changed face—I'd like to know what's behind that, the eyes are so rigid, as if directed toward a single goal) that Becker's mother had just told him all sorts of things about him, and that he hoped this was not an indiscreet intrusion. What she had told him, however, he had not, to be frank, understood. At any rate she seemed very happy.

Becker answered in a heavy voice, "I would like to tell you myself, Maus. There's not so much to tell. But ultimately what each of us experiences he experiences for the other as well."

He threw his head back and for a moment the preoccupied look on his face disappeared. Maus was dumbfounded at the clear words his friend spoke, an unknown man now, who in a few days had aged by years, his former roommate and comrade-in-arms.

"Maus, you know how I was always a great admirer of the Greeks. But there was a certain point in old Greece that I could never warm to. That was Socrates. In particular, I would stumble over his demand 'Know thyself.' I couldn't bring that into accord with the Greece that I knew—and I certainly didn't know myself at all. To know myself, to worry about myself, to look at myself—I thought all that not just unnecessary, superfluous, but as essentially unworthy of a man. I was who I was and how I was and that was fine. I was given proof of that. There were no apparent problems. How did I live? Like a well-trained creature, a tool turned out by nature's hand. I only needed to be here and do as I pleased. When I compared myself with others I sometimes had the feeling I was fortune's child. I acknowledged my right, my noble right, to live in just that way.

"I got over that in the war, and how; especially when I was wounded and lay there in the hospital. You didn't see it, and the others didn't either. I hid it. I still wore my old face. I knew that it pleased you all, so I kept it. The soul needs time and energy to change a person so much that he takes on a different character. But after I had returned home those questions plagued me terribly, the questions about what sort of man I was, how I had lived, whether my life was really so fine and perfect as I had imagined. Self-assurance and arrogance had been what had determined my character before. I was damned by my whole former personality.

"That bored its way inside me, hammered at me, until everything in me shattered. Whether I wanted to or not I had to wield the hammer, pound away. And a chisel was there too: the questions, and the incessant hammering was my conscience. I either had to answer the questions to my satisfaction or perish. It was a trial, a test, a decree of providence. A decree because we do not, as I had thought, live uncontrolled in this world, but we are led and are given signs. After those long, happy years of blindness I was put to a test, one on which my further existence both here and beyond depended.

"And so that was my fate. It was an operation against which I struggled. Then something unexpected, unthought-of happened. A hand was stretched out to this human being, Friedrich Becker, this spoiled child, and he was given the chance to leave his playground. I had to prove myself the man I had become. And so I was led back to that statement of Socrates that had been incomprehensible to me, 'Know thyself.'

"What happened to me during this test—we'll not talk about that. I found myself in great distress. I went through dread and despair. I was sorely afflicted. I suffered, saw no way out, I lost myself. Things could not go on like that."

Maus murmured, "How awful."

He felt himself flooded with ambivalent feelings, with sympathy and respect, but with anger and a certain indistinct envy as well, for he saw no way out himself, and for him there was only pain and bitterness.

"During one dreadful period," Becker continued, "Hilda visited me. I was already at my wits' end. She wept over me. She could not help me and wanted to go. But before she left, Maus, she knelt down there on the floor by the door. That was the gesture that saved me. It happened with her help, not through her. I became aware of how she was suffering for me. She suffered with me. She suffered too. And that is how God has suffered for us all, because we cannot help ourselves; by reaching down into our suffering, he has taken it to himself, lifted it up, destroyed it and transformed it and there can be no more convulsions of pain, no more desperation, and salvation came."

Becker whispered this. Maus was unable to say anything.

Becker concluded, "At that moment I came to myself. It was the greatest event of my life. Yes, Maus, there is a great deal of truth to what we heard in school and when we were confirmed."

After a pause Maus cleared his throat. He had let himself be carried away. But the word confirmation sobered him. So all it came to was pious cant. He stared hard at Becker. Then it became clear to him: I'll have no part of it. One of us two is crazy, and it most certainly isn't me. He crossed his legs (we're going to be absolutely clear about all this, he slapped the palm of his hand against the leather gaiter, a lovely human sound in this embarassing room, next time I'll bring my hymnal along and we can sing hymns together) and, trying to return as quickly as possible to a normal level of conversation, he said in a businesslike way, "Well, well, my dear Becker. So that's it. And now I know and you've got it all off your chest. I thank you for your trust in me. The whole affair has another side of course. You'll permit me, I'm sure, to respond to your frankness with an equal frankness on my part. For instance, you'll find I've little sympathy, I'm sorry to say, with what you said about confirmation. But let us leave that aside. It's my own private matter. The main thing is the outcome, the result. And that means: what is the upshot of all this? What comes of it? Where does it lead?"

Becker pondered this. "Where does it lead?"

Maus nodded (yes indeed, my lad, you can't just babble on like this with me, you've got to prove who you are). "Where does it lead, of course. To heaven, that we know. But for now we are in fact still living on the old, round and rather steeply tilted earth."

He had adopted a provocative tone that fit his whole anti-middle-class, rebellious appearance.

Becker: "Of course we're on earth. You don't think I'm planning some mystical adventure, do you?" (As Becker said this, he felt as he had just before out on the street: I'm not planning it, but I'm greedy for it, how I yearn for it, to wrap myself up inside it and hear nothing, nothing, of what Maus will say to me now and suggest I do, as he presses me, duns me, plays the bailiff. But am I still capable of paying my debts?) He muttered, "You're quite right, we live on this earth."

Maus slapped his gaiter again and gave a short burst of amused laughter (quite unexpectedly, here he was in a pleasant position over and against Becker—when he had come here more or less as a petitioner, seeking help). "Well then, there's nothing we lack. The whole affair, then, apart from its difficult personal dimension, has had a remarkable result, by which I mean, that for once we can sit down to a practical conversation. What you were talking about just now seemed to me, forgive me, rather puzzling, including that part about confirmation—as if you thought now that we have our God and the Savior too we've got it made, and nothing more can happen to us. Well, that's not quite how things are either. Things are just now beginning of course, and that means we're going to have to roll up our sleeves. By the way, my dear Becker, without wanting to compete with you, I too am a Christian after all, and have my own small, vague conception of what religion is. And I know, for example, that during the war both sides, in their trenches and in ours, both Germans and the Allies, had chaplains and millions of Christians, and they merrily tossed hand grenades at one another and bombed one another and shot each other and happily ran each other's bellies through with bayonets. And do you know what, Becker? Here, shake my hand, I'll bet you—the bullet that hit you was fired by the tender hand of a Christian."

"I'm sure of that, Maus."

"Well, then you also know what Christianity tastes like. And you know too that this sort of thing gets us nowhere, I mean nowhere. Really, Becker, that would make certain parties very happy if we would all stand out in the courtyards like a bunch of orphans, like an itinerant choir and start singing 'Whate'er our God ordains is right.' "

"That won't do any good, Maus. You're completely right there."

For the first time Becker now noticed the mocking tone in Maus's voice. I'm being teased. The way those posters hung there at the Königstor, so nice and peacefully, pasted there, immobile—what is socialism, a just peace, humanity. You could look at them and move on. But now I'm being attacked here in my room.

"Then we're in perfect agreement," Maus said in triumph. "Then we needn't bother with the whole hocus-pocus, all that business about our father in heaven."

Becker bent forward. Maus saw his lips move. I think the man's praying. He really is crazy; I'll simply have to leave him to himself, I only get him excited and he'll have a fit. He's ended up a happy religious nut.

Maus tightened his belt. I'm going to hit the road, and pronto, there's nothing here for me. He felt a certain sense of satisfaction. Our Fräulein Hilda must be pleased as punch.

Then Becker sat up straight, and there was a new, severe look on his face. With a resoluteness that amazed Maus, he said, "You are sitting across from me. We are talking with each other as always in a friendly fashion. I can at least expect that you'll not use offensive expressions. I—cannot tolerate them. I cannot permit them."

Maus, his hand still at his belt, ready to leave (Aha! How touchy we are; I give him a slight rap and he reacts like this). "But of course. Please, I'm sorry. It was not meant nastily."

Becker: "You can't just forget the business about our father in heaven. I would think you could see that much."

"Sure, sure," Maus laughed—I'll give in to him, he knows his own weakness. "Which is why we won't get in each other's hair then. I can be had for anything and everything—even," he laughed "if it really must be, for Christianity. For me the question remains the same for good and all: where does it get us? So then, Becker, instead of our just chatting away here let me describe the long and short of the situation, so that we can see where we are."

Becker, calm and friendly, nodded.

Maus: "So then, here in Berlin there will be a large general congress in the next few days, for soldiers and council members. At that congress the present government, Ebert and his pals, and the Independents and Spartacus will be sitting across from one another, and each will speak his piece. It won't be a simple discussion, but one with consequences. All parties to it know that. It'll come to open conflict. Accounts will be settled. And that's unavoidable now that the front-line troops are no longer together and our erstwhile grand superiors, the generals, can no longer interfere, at least not directly. So what's all this to me, and to you, too, I ask. Why, because the whole shooting match is at stake here. And one way or another we're involved. Let me be quite candid, Becker, this is a hell of a country, this Germany. Just try to find your way around. You can run yourself ragged looking about with your lantern for men who know what they want, or even someone who could point out another way to go. What you'll find is a mess, a pile of broken pieces. I've looked around at the stables and the palace among the sailors. Nothing. Hearts not in it. There's something rotten in the state of Denmark. So then back to our old buddies, or as they say now, to our class, all the fellows who, just like the workers, went through the whole mess and now have lost their jobs and are trying to keep the wolf from the door."

Maus's voice grew softer. "I've had long conversations with them, several times. I've not let on what my own position is of course. But they don't know where to go from here either. A total chaos, a shambles. Don't believe for a minute, Becker, that I'm just sitting here telling you this to hear myself talk, just letting off steam, because after all you know how close we are and what I think of you. But you weren't there. So now I must ask you, and I don't want to offend you, to put religion aside for a moment. Maybe I don't know anything about it, maybe I'm too dumb to understand. At any rate let's talk about everyday concerns, about the things that grab us in the guts. And what's going on in this country, Becker, demands that we take some straightforward position, no ifs, ands or buts. And it's your country, too. We must do our damned duty, even if only as ditchdiggers or hod carriers."

Maus made a violent gesture, he was losing control. "And I won't give anyone a dispensation. And for my sake you've got to participate too. I want to know that I have you behind me, even if you aren't marching beside me. And you aren't to look down your nose at us. I can't bear that. And I'm telling you this flat out, because we are comrades and friends, and because the war is still going on, even if not in the trenches anymore. We both have our wounds behind us, but that's all the more reason not to shirk. Wouldn't that be something, to desert the colors now and let others do the work."

Becker: "I certainly don't want to let others do my work."

Maus: "Well then, show me that you are with us."

What I would like, the sigh rose up in Becker, is to enter a monk's cell, cast myself upon my face and plead with the power of heaven to cleanse my soul.

"Under no condition dare we leave the field to the enemy," Maus's rough voice resounded, the voice of a reckless young man, whose hot eyes bounced about.

Becker stood up and stood there tall and pale beside the end panel of his bookcase. Maus waited. He watched him. Becker's fingers worked nervously. He apparently was searching for an answer, the man felt pressed. Finally the play of fingers ceased.

Becker raised his head, he was frowning, the sharp vertical line on his brow was very clear. "I am not in a position to make a declaration. I must ask your forgiveness, Maus, but I simply cannot let myself be questioned. It is rather for me to put the questions."

"Go ahead, please. I'm at your service."

Becker: "I want to talk with you as if I were talking to myself. I ask you to accept that premise. It will simplify the conversation, and you'll see I don't wish to offend you with any of my remarks or questions. So then, Maus, who is it that forces you to take a position in the way you describe it? To decide among these various programs? Who forces you to find your standpoint between these fronts?"

"My dear Becker, since I'll gratefully accept the kind of intimacy you've suggested, let me answer with corresponding candor. I am forced to take a position because I am a decent man who has a part in the fate of the world about him. I could duck out, but that would be the height of dishonor. It would be a disgrace if I were to sit in a corner and watch while others battled for things that affect me personally, and then to wait and see how it comes out—only then, if it goes badly, to beat my breast perhaps and wail that I should have participated after all but missed the chance."

Becker began to march about the room. "Excellent, my opinion exactly. Neither of us till now has let other people do our bleeding for us. But who tells you where your standpoint lies among all those represented at this congress. Something occurs to me. Six years ago I had a bad case of tonsilitis, high fever, couldn't swallow anything, lay in bed with an ice-cube necktie for eight days. The fever wouldn't go down, I swallowed aspirin by the ounce. Then one day the doctor noticed my temperature curve. He looked in my mouth and said that I must have some hidden abscess. He wanted to wait one more day, and if the fever stayed the same he would have to cut. And sure enough, the next day he made his incision, a pouch of puss came out and I got better, the fever fell, in a week everything was fine."

Maus: "And what is the point?"

"Icebags, bed rest, aspirin are of no use in certain cases. Surgery must be done if there is an abcess."

Maus: "I'm glad to hear you say that. No dabbling about, but a clean cut."

Becker: "To get the abscess out. And what is decisive," Becker stopped in front of Maus and looked him straight in the eyes, "is to know where the abscess is."

Maus (why are you gaping at me like that): "We know who instigated the war. You don't have to look for them long. They almost tell you so themselves. It is imperialism, and behind that it is our whole economy, our economic system, capitalism. That is what got us into war. And it's approximately the same in other countries as it is here with us. We call these fellows junkers and robber barons and generals; in France they have other names, but they're the same people; and in England still other names and it's the same there too. Wherever they are, wherever they exist, they plunge nations into catastrophe, dragging people along behind them into war. There is no one who can stop them. They don't care about human life. The bags of money are in command. The one good thing is that these fellows haven't noticed that the situation at the end of a war is different from that at the beginning. At the end they've expended everything and can no longer stand on their feet. And the people have been bled, it's true, but are enraged as well, and want to slay the beast that has tormented them. That's how things are now. The imperialists don't know what's up or down. Basically they're just waiting, it seems to me, for someone to give them the coup de grace."

Becker stared at him. "You're very courageous and a great optimist. The way you've learned all that. Amazing, I've never heard you sing that song before. Do you really think this way—or are you just trying it out on me?"

"Why do you ask?"

Becker: "Because, for example, it doesn't quite square with your opinion of the sailors."

Maus: "The sailors? Phooey! I already told you, they're just unemployed. Give them a job and they won't be standing around at the stables. We need hard, determined people who go all out for a cause. Warriors to topple capitalism and erect our dictatorship, the dictatorship of the proletariat, making a return to the old state of affairs impossible. Then we'll have peace and quiet."

Becker crossed his arms. "I see."

Maus: "Just because everything is shot now and because the country lies there bleeding doesn't mean we should be shy about being hard and strict. We need a steel ourselves for all events. Punishment and interrogation are necessary. We have to get used to the idea of setting up a kind of inquisition to be sent out to track down every treason like a bloodhound."

Becker: "So those are your ideas and plans for achieving peace."

Maus: "Just as you demanded: going for the abscess with the knife."

Becker raised a hand. "I see the knife—but not the abscess." (Yes, that's how they've thought all through the ages, you cast this out and that out, you clear the decks, set this and that in order, but you always stay in the same house where you were. You think you've got a plan and are convinced that everything will then be different. But it doesn't turn out different, how can it be different?)

Maus: "And so where do you see the abscess?"

Becker: "The institutions of the state, and of the economy too, have most certainly been very rotten, extraordinarily rotten. But when are they ever very good? Yes, when are they good? They've never been good. They can't be good with us as their fathers. What they are, with their brutality, dishonesty, coldness, superficiality and matter-of-factness, with open oppression and with war—what they are, we are: superficial, blind to others, selfish and savage. You can alarm the masses about the economy, you can raise your knife to strike at the state, but if you want the abscess, you must cut into your own breast."

Maus laughed. "Thanks. I'm not interested in suicide. Maybe you're right and we are that rotten—well then, that's how we are. Rascals who give away more than they have. But first let us run the show."

Becker: "Let you—run the show."

Maus: "Of course, us, who else if not us—not kaisers and princes and generals, this time just average guys. And no academics and professors either, but the man on the street who knows where it hurts."

Becker: "How are you going to manage? How are you going to quell the rage, the passion, the miserable envy of one man for another, the inexhaustible hate and wickedness—how, if you put yourselves at the top, you with your bloodhounds, with your inquisition, with revolvers, with compulsion and surveillance? That will just create new fear, and the fury of prisoners, caged in and banging against the bars. And pride will go to your heads sitting up there on top. It's a mystery to me, Maus, how you can fall for that, after this war. To come along now with a dictatorship. We have had enough of that, I would think."

Maus: "I'm still waiting to hear what you suggest. Criticism comes cheap."

Becker (he's right, I have nothing to suggest of the sort he wants): "There was a man here to visit me yesterday whom you know perhaps, at least he says he knows you, the garrison chaplain from the hospital in Alsace."

Maus: "Haven't the vaguest. What was he doing here?"

Becker: "He is a highly patriotic man of the old school. In essence he talks just like you. The state cannot be too strong as far as he is concerned. The old state collapsed because it wasn't strong enough, that was all. There wasn't enough power and authority up top. He demands more."

Maus: "I absolutely do not see what that has to do with me."

Becker: "Well, he's trying to deal with the state, too. But let me ask you—who is going to create this powerful state? I heard you say you want a dictatorship."

Maus: "But ours, yours and mine. We are the dictators. There is no greater security than that."

Becker: "Maus, sixty million people aren't going to form the government. It'll more likely be fifty or a hundred or a thousand."

Maus: "Of course. People from our own ranks, the best of us, the most experienced, our own elected delegates."

Becker: "I'm still asking for security. Who is going to protect me from the delegates? I can't look into any man's soul. If they are good— you give them power and it ruins them. You'll go so far as to give them the right to peer into our thoughts to keep us from planning anything against them in our minds. But that's disgraceful, something we haven't deserved. What you intend—you really cannot have considered it fully— is the maddest sort of outrage anyone could come up with. To take away people's own sense of responsibility and to deny that any other court of appeal might exist in this world, within them for instance, before which they must be held responsible—I hope that this is only an idea and one that stays inside your heads. But perhaps even that must yet be inflicted on us. It would be a continuation of the war."

When Becker fell silent, Maus replied quietly, "Please, I'm listening. You know I'm waiting to see if you have anything better to offer."

Becker: "Just ask yourself how the people you elected yesterday as your delegates will behave as dictators today? Who can still restrain them then? Tell me who topples dictators and how it's done?"

Maus (I see he's peeved that this is a real plan, and that doesn't suit him. Anything past Adam's fall doesn't suit him.): "You're harping on one single word, dictatorship. You have to have discipline, obedience. It all depends on what for. Our dictatorship is unassailable because it stands in service to all men of peace and goodwill who want to build a better world."

Becker: "I'm glad you've told me all this, that I can share in your thoughts. Your intentions are excellent, but the plan is gruesome and you haven't thought clearly about its consequences. This plan destroys everything that makes human beings human, creatures that don't crawl but stand upright and look straight ahead and above them. It casts us down to the level of animals. But that isn't what you want, you want just the opposite. But how will people look afterward? It's really like the story of the man who was lying in his garden and was plagued by a wasp. He asked his friend to pick up a stone and get rid of the insect. So the friend took a stone and killed the wasp—and the man at the same time."

Maus: "Your reply is the obvious one, it's the reply all intellectuals give who don't want to tackle the problem, who refuse to see that they can't handle it and that others will have to be brought in. You could make your sacrifices too, you know, even some of your so-called intellectual freedom, of which you make so little use. Intellectuals don't understand—let me make this clear—that it's simply a matter of the systematic extermination of imperialism and capitalism and that you can't have an omelette without breaking eggs."

Depressed, Becker pulled the small table over to him and propped his head on his hand. "What a shame, Maus, that this is the way our conversation has turned out. What else can I say."

Maus: "I wanted to learn something from you. But you sit locked in your study, and all I can do is tell you what is happening out in the world." (Now he is silent, all wrapped up with his God.)

Becker: "I really do speak very little with people."

He sighed and tried to continue the conversation. "We were speaking before of peace. What we really had intended to do was think about how peace is achieved. That's the main thing, am I right? We don't want to be led back into war again. The slaughter has to stop. Tell me why there should be no more wars after you have conquered capitalism, exterminated one class of people and put dictatorship in the hands of another? The people would then have their own particular doctrine. Would it be such a wonder then, if masses like that were to fling themselves at some other nation precisely out of the feeling that they possessed the truth, the whole truth (because that is what you mean), convinced that the others cannot be allowed to be left with their lies."

Maus: "What you think you have to call a doctrine is nothing more than the observation that it was imperialism that led us into war. Which is correct. Why should we then not help others to eradicate imperialism?"

Becker: "So that you do cling to war. You are even considering war, this time not for colonies or oil fields, true, but . . ."

"To liberate mankind."

"I know. And that's why you want a dictatorship. But you won't liberate mankind that way."

Maus sat there cool and relaxed. What can I do with him? Apparently he was a lamb before and hasn't changed now. The kind who imagines someone is going to give us peace as a present. He stands there and lets out his "baa" and thinks everyone else will go "baa" too.

Maus: "Whoever wants to do away with war, my dear Becker, will ultimately have to go to war himself. Why? Because warriors are armed. And you cannot disarm them without weapons. Talking to them doesn't help. Is that clear?"

At that, Maus stood up, stretched and pulled off his jacket. (He can't accuse me of lacking patience. I don't know how I got the stupid notion actually to get involved in a conversation with this pious sheep. All the same, he was a fine fellow. "I had a buddy in the war, I'll never find a better.")

He smiled down at Becker. "Well, Becker, we don't have much else to say to each other, do we? I take it you have nothing more to add to the topic."

Becker: "Stay, Maus, do, let's not break it off like this. These things have never pressed in on me like this before and I still have to see them more clearly."

Maus just stood there at first, but then he gave in and sat back down. Becker, however, needed time before he could state his case. He spoke with difficulty. "I can't compete with you. You come here with these great issues like capitalism, imperialism, you want to set whole nations in motions, go on fighting the war. You want to start the real world war now, you know, one that will have to go on for decades. You know that that's no way to abolish war, but you hope it will be the last one and that it will lead to a new world order. I have to go back to our very first question: what caused the war, where is that abscess? You tell me capitalism. I won't contradict that. But, Maus, you have to realize that I too am guilty. I beg you, don't leave me out. I beg you, don't exonerate me. Even if you don't feel guilty yourself—and your new comrades don't either—I do feel guilty. Because capitalism is guilty does not diminish my guilt. We human beings, each of us has his own responsibilities. We have our lives, too, and are capable of putting them to proper use. I have permitted grievous crimes. I participated in them. I did not use my reason to recognize them, but that does not exonerate me. If someone were to come along and say he must demand I be held accountable—I'm ready. No one has come to demand that of me, but a higher court has done just that, it has called me to account, set my punishment, and when I recognized my guilt, that court accepted my remorse and forgave me. There will be others, too, many others, who accuse themselves just as I do, now that it is too late for this war. If we had stood up and had acted and spoken out as it was our duty to do, many things would have turned out differently. But now I draw my conclusions. They are valid for me. I have bound my sense of responsibility to a spot no state and no economy can ever touch. I have bound myself to that higher court with chains of steel. And that is my protection—against the state and war."

Maus shrugged. "I can't do anything with that. It's your private affair."

"Please stay, I'm still not finished. Maus, I advise you, I would like to advise you to do the same. Ask yourself, take yourself to task. Go to a cemetery for the war dead if you're unsure. Stand before those crosses, look at them, the rows of them, and ask yourself what you have done, you too, and whether it was enough that you stood row on row with them, whether you were not under another obligation as well. Because *they* did not know. But *we* could have known. And, Maus, if we didn't know it then, we do now."

Maus, flippantly: "That's why I want to enlist in my war."

"Examine yourself. First repent."

"And what's the difference whether I repent or not."

Becker: "You believe capitalism and the state to be the guilty parties. First recognize how things stand with you."

Maus: "Damn it all, what purpose does that serve? I sit here listening to you, but I don't understand you. Who do I help by that? Is each individual, are sixty million individuals, if you like, supposed to stand up and beat their breasts and say, we are guilty? What is accomplished by that? And that would suit the reactionaries just fine. Because, of course, they would be the ones who wouldn't participate, especially not them."

Becker: "We're talking about you and me."

Maus's response was outright rude. "Just leave me out of it. That won't get you anywhere. We're all supposed simply to drop everything, leave it there in the mud and say, 'It's no concern of mine what happens to Germany and what capitalism does from here on out. I might just as well go sit down in a bar and get drunk.' "

Becker's face twitched. He whispered, "What are you talking about? Why do you talk to me like that? How can you talk to me like that? I'm glad you came. But I thought—we wanted to talk things out."

Maus: "It just slipped out. I apologize, but you have to understand that I can't just sit here like you and let it all come to me. I need practical results, the whole world needs them. I told you already that everything is moving toward some crucial decision, the situation is critical, getting worse each day."

Becker: "And you want to strike the blow?"

Maus: "Yes."

Becker: "Then go ahead, Maus, and strike it if you must. It doesn't matter who you hit. I mean that, it doesn't matter. It will do you good. Run home, get your revolver, find a spot where things are happening, like that time you attacked police headquarters."

Maus: "I'm not a lunatic. I'm sitting here trying to talk rationally with you. But what you suggest . . ." He slapped the palm of his hand on his knee, then balled it into a fist. "It's enough to drive a person to despair! What do you want really? You can't create mankind all over again. If people are such wretches, then you just have to take them as they are, and do whatever you can with them."

Becker: "That was fine, what you said about despair. But you're not desperate. When in fact a man must be really, seriously desperate. That is the gate of dread and despair that you have to go through. You can put the blame on everything and everyone, but until you have blamed yourself, the rest is all wrong. You are, and you'll go on being the guilty party."

Maus shifted his chair a bit and held his hand in front of his mouth to hide a yawn (now's the time to take French leave). "I can see where this all gets us. The old story—first you must better the individual before you can do anything with society. Which came first, the chicken or the egg? I can't decide. But I know that before the eggheads agree on the matter, other people will have made history."

Becker: "Let them. If we make *our* history."

Cheerfully, almost overflowing with sympathy, Maus got up and stood across from Becker. He looked directly at him, eyes flashing. "You're a fine fellow. My dear Friedrich Becker, you believe in mankind. But the good Lord missed the boat when it came to man. He had to chase him out of paradise right at the start. And then men perpetrated their tower of Babel, and then they survived the flood, and then they worshiped the golden calf, and then the savior himself came down from heaven—and none of it was any use. Nothing helped. A botched job from the start."

Maus laughed out loud in front of Becker (it was clear all right: Becker, wise old Becker, was barking up the oldest wrong tree there was, a pathetic figure really). "My dear Becker, we are a rotten bunch that God created in his wrath, and that's that."

A silent Becker swallowed hard, controlled himself. Finally he managed to say, "It would be better, Maus, if you didn't rejoice in the fact. I know you're proud of not believing in God. And that you've given yourself a dispensation from believing in mankind and morality."

Maus answered cynically (it's really time to hit the road now—my friend, you've simply turned into a pious biddy), "You've hit the nail on the head. I do not believe. Their morality is all a swindle, too. Have you

591

forgotten how they sold us the goods to go off to war, fresh, free and frisky, and we almost ended up in the mass grave?"

Becker swallowed. "I know that. We've had to atone for that."

Maus, enthusiastically: "They sold me their goods, but I am not some gentle lamb, and I'll give them an appropriate answer. I don't want anyone handing me justice on a platter. We'll fight to get it. We live in a world of wolves, where you have to bite back." Maus was completely relaxed (now I'm the one who's got him by the collar). "I'm sorry we don't see eye to eye. I can only state the facts."

"Don't laugh, Maus, don't laugh. We've had a serious conversation. It stirs me because it also concerns you."

Maus: "Bah, personal stuff. Let's leave that aside."

Becker: "I can't do that. I'll leave everything aside, but not the personal stuff. Why do the things we've talked about torment you so then? I know you, Maus, I really do. You're not so all-fired happy with yourself."

Maus frowned and bit his lips. "Well then, O wizard and solver of puzzles, what is wrong with me? Why aren't I happy with myself?"

Becker: "Because you are in chains. Because you have put yourself in chains and do not let yourself speak. That's why you come up with these wild ideas. You want to drown the voice inside you with them. But it will not be still. You know it. Maus, ask yourself whether a man ought to be living with such confusion inside him as you do, and whether he ought not first find clarity and calm for himself before he worries about the world outside. The fight with the dragon. Ask yourself: are you St. George, the archangel, who can take on a fight with the dragon?"

Maus: "To clean up this pigsty of ours you don't need to be St. George. We aren't angels. We've never said we were."

At that, Becker stood up, walked across the room, stood silently beside his desk and banged—very remarkable for such a calm man—the flat of his hand on the desk. "But you should be angels. To tackle the most immense problems without even stopping to think about how one can first really be a man. Shall I give you a mirror, Maus, so that you can look at yourself?"

Maus (I have to avoid leaving here in a row with this man, it looks like he's getting upset): "But for the thousandth time, we're not talking about me. You make it far too easy for yourself by referring to personal matters. I'm not a good man, I know that." He stoked his unshaven cheek and laughed. "But good men always make bad politicians."

Becker heard a distant, soft voice, the voice of his teacher: "You should know where the true light is, where true love is in man, there where perfect goodness is recognized and loved within him. There must be an end to all egoism, it must be left behind."

Maus marched ponderously across the room, buttoning up his short leather jacket, stood at the window in his high gaiters and leaned against the wall. And from there he looked across to the desk, on which there actually stood a small crucifix—I've never noticed he had that before, he's put it there, and I thought I could talk with this man.

"You should have just one look at yourself, Maus. Why don't you want to do it? Why are you so concerned about everything else, only not yourself? You don't see, you have no notion of what is happening behind your back. Do you think of yourself, your spirit, your soul as a mere figment of imagination, an abstract idea? But there is where you find the whole man, the invisible man, and where a pack of animals is fighting—one cannot be too clear about this—savage and brutal and eerie, all of nature is there and who knows what else. That all goes on behind our backs and wants to seize control of us, and if you are not careful nothing will be left of you."

Maus kept compassionate silence. Then he uttered a few words. "Dear friend, you're wasting your time with me. You've probably already noticed that you're not going to accomplish anything with me."

But Becker could not give up. He waited to see if Maus would add anything. He approached him. He felt anxiety welling up inside. Maus was so hardened. Becker: "What I am saying to you has nothing to do with the church, Maus. You don't need to be afraid of that, I'm not speaking about that. This is something that applies to us all, to you as well as to me. The terrible, dangerous, evil thing inside us constantly breaks loose. But that's no reason to be disheartened. You want to lead your own life, Maus, I'm sure. So don't put yourself in the wrong place. Don't go looking for yourself in the wrong place. I have heard a message: 'The true light and true love in man are where perfect goodness is recognized within him.'"

Maus grinned behind his hand. The true goodness inside me. Wouldn't he love for me to take a look at myself. I'm glad not to get even a peek at this pile of crap named Johannes Maus and his magnificent ego. What is he up to anyhow with his reference to true love? What does he intend with that? That's really a mean thing to allude to. He wants to go burrowing around inside me again. He wants to rub my nose in it. Is it conceivable that he's so nasty?

And suddenly Maus's smart-aleck superiority vanished and bitterness rose up in him. It rose in his throat like stinging lye and he swallowed to force it back down. He couldn't stand this tall, scrawny fellow at the desk at all.

Maus: "Look at myself? What for? And what about yourself, after all? Bah, there you sit chatting away with God. That won't make you any better either."

"Maus, I know that I am sinful and guilty. I almost died of the despair it caused me, with no one to help."

Maus: "Oh, leave me alone, you and your Salvation Army tactics.

Don't come singing hymns of repentance to me, not when everything is at stake. To hell with my private affairs, to hell with what I've had to swallow. We have to do something and we'll get out there and do it, and here you are wailing away, wanting to set yourself up as an example to me, and afterward there'll be a knock at the door and your mother will come in and ask you to come eat, it's on the table. Do you know, by the way, how many people in Berlin haven't got a bite to eat?"

Maus walked toward Becker, the desk was between them. "Do you know, Becker, that you've become my enemy? My enemy. At every point. I don't see you as an individual. You are one of a great many—who have deserted the flag. You hide behind your words."

Some evil power urged him on to talk like this.

"There you stand, Becker, the man I was so attached to, whom I believed in, really believed in."

"I'm still the same man."

"I'd like to shake you. Friedrich Becker, man, come to your senses, wake up. Just look out the window at what's going on, the world is in an uproar. But, no, you don't care one little bit. You don't care about anything. You creep behind God's skirts. They can mow us all down and you'll say: we have not yet scaled the pinnacle of human truth. We still lack the extreme unction of philosophy. We have not get groveled before the cross. Not yet. No, my friend, and never will. Thanks for nothing. For once and for all. We can do without your true light."

"And you are dragged ever deeper into wickedness, devoured by your own passions."

Maus made a brusque gesture. "Becker, I've one straight question for you. What is all this constant harping about wicked passions? Tell me straight out what you mean."

Becker, perplexed: "What you are talking about?"

"Risk it. Shall we not for once really be you and me, have a really personal conversation now, just this once. You're talking about Hilda, aren't you? At the root of it you think you have to preach these sermons to me on account of her."

He bent over the desk and looked into Becker's eyes. "It's not necessary, my friend. I've taken my medicine. And," he raised his voice and stressed the syllables, "I forbid these remonstrations, yes, re-mon-stra-tions, lectures on true and false love and passions. I won't take that from anyone."

"For heaven's sake."

Maus: "So now the light is dawning for you, the old primal light, your own primal light. And now we are finally talking without all the flapdoodle."

He turned toward the door, but came back to Becker once more, and with a face distorted by hate he whispered in his face, "How does it happen that you, you in particular, preach to me about morality, you

594

who deceived me, went behind my back and maliciously stole Hilda from me. Maliciously, that's it. You never said a word to me in the hospital about you two. And afterward you just calmly let me confess my sins, what had happened to me, and were just gloating over the guy who would spill it all to you. And then here in Berlin you let me run around like a silly clown and knew everything about her while I waited for a letter from her. You treated me shabbily. Shabbily. Shame on you, Herr Doktor Friedrich Becker, shame on you."

He was gone. Becker's mother intercepted him in the hall and begged him to stay a while. He left.

Becker was crushed with remorse.

It was good for me to have experienced that. I should realize that. I didn't know. That it was this bad. I didn't know that. —

He sat by himself a long time until his mother came in. She was fearful for him when she saw him sitting there like that. But he looked up as she touched his shoulder and then asked her to open the window.

"But it isn't any too warm in here."

"I'm asking you to do it. Fine. That's fine."

She saw the hopeless look in his eyes. She stopped in front of him. "Maus was in such a hurry. He wouldn't stay for dinner."

Becker sighed. His mother said, "I didn't like what I saw. The way he looks and marches around. That's nothing for you, Friedrich."

He sat up straight. His mother saw the color return to his face and how his calm, earnest look came back. He let his arms hang down limply as if released from a convulsion. "Everyone has bad times. Battles are there—to be lost."

They sat down to dinner. His mother customarily murmured a prayer before she began to eat. Becker respected the pause with silence of his own. Today he put his own hands together, and his mother saw him lower his head.

He was more cheerful during the meal. "Apart from everything else, Maus thinks I've become a kind of monk. He sees me as an Indian fakir—letting himself be buried alive."

Afterward he walked around in the living room. His mother hugged him happily. "Your eyes are so keen. He has made you very courageous. You're not going to quarrel, are you?"

He withdrew to his study, and only when he was alone did it become clear to him what had happened between him and Maus.

He accuses me of doing stupid things; that's bad, but he won't let it rest with that, he'll be back I'm sure. I thought we were having a debate, and that's what he was thinking all the while. That's the way it is, always, this passion or that one, this hate or that unhappiness. And he won't look at himself, he just throws himself into the fray.

It would not leave Becker in peace. He thought back once more over the conversation; worried, he sat down now. Always the same rebuke: I have failed, what can I do? Then the feeling subsided and peace returned. He forgot Maus and the conversation, he breathed easily and felt the urge to go over to the desk and take hold of the little crucifix and to express his love to his savior in jumbled stammerings. Delirious emotion, ecstasy filled him. He stammered, "How you pour out your gifts upon me, how gracious you are to me. I have abandoned myself to you. I am yours entirely."

When the rush, the storm of his fervor had subsided, he moved about the room to calm himself. But something of the heavenly sweetness remained within him, and unintentionally he found himself involved in a secret conversation with a distant, absent friend whom at first he could not name, but gradually the conversation became clearer and it was a dialogue with Hilda.

He heard her complain, saw her hands, how they were stretched out toward him, she was pale and sorrowful, she was wearing her nurse's uniform. She did not have a cap on, her hair was disheveled as he had never seen it before.

"Friedrich, why do you reject me? Don't reject me, that's not how it ought to be. I will do everything you ask of me, I will serve you. Ah, Friedrich, I'm only human after all."

Becker: "I have you to thank that I am alive. I don't reject you; but why did you leave me?"

"I would gladly come to you. The fact that you're there keeps me alive. Tell me, Friedrich, how you are, what you are doing."

"Ah, Hilda, I have to use a great deal of energy just to hold on. Maus was here. He spoke about you. He is suffering. I would like you to help him. You could do it better than I. He hates me now, on account of you."

"I know that. But he shouldn't come to you with such things. I want to talk to him, so leave it to me."

Becker: "You wouldn't believe how much he suffers. He avoids me. I talked with him for a very long time."

"And how are things with you, Friedrich. Tell me about you."

"You have healed me."

"And Sophocles? And your books?"

"More and more I have to apply myself to the secret of heaven, it's there I've been set down."

"What secret are you talking about, Friedrich?"

"Does that frighten you? Hilda, a crucifix stands on my desk. The secret of heaven—is it not our duty to become as gods. Can we stop even there? The world exists not only in the images with which we do battle daily. There are other images besides, I can sense them, I feel the ecstasy even now just thinking about them. It all blossoms as if from a tree, Hilda. Why not heavenly images, in fullest majesty?"

"Ah, I'm afraid, Becker. Don't go too far."

"Can a blossom go too far when it bursts? The world has a place in the order of justice, but it is also bound up with that majesty. Tell me, Hilda, is it wrong for me to feel—that we and this world must die in order to live in God?"

"No, Friedrich, no, don't talk like that. Wake up, Friedrich, wake up. I am just one small person, a woman, but I love you. I'm calling to you, Friedrich, wake up. You're sinking, you sank too far once already, you're sinking again now. I won't stay away for long."

"Why not sink, Hilda? Come, we shall drink at the water brooks like the hart. The hounds will not find us. The world opens up to us."

Becker finds himself in his room.

And as his gaze wanders over the room—the moment subsides. His mind is clear, sober, serene. It has left him. A coolness flows through him. This is his room. What happened here, what was I doing? The rug, the rat, the lion, the Brazilian—what were they?

We see him walk slowly over to his desk. He remembers those events and there is no one standing beside him. No voice sounds.

But it all holds good. Warmth flows through him again. He thinks about it and he can see himself connected to the easy-going, proud Becker, the first lieutenant from the war, lying among the wounded and helpless in the military hospital.

Adsum, here I am. I am a part of reality. This is it.

He goes to the window. Down below, an old woman is pulling a handcart with potatoes in it. Behind her a ragged, half-grown boy is pushing a child's wagon with logs and branches.

It is not difficult to know what one has to do. My mother has known it for a long time now.

Where is the path?

Poor Job says, "The way is hidden from man and is girded with darkness."

Maus Makes an About-Face

Maus marched vigorously through the streets.

Clarity, at last, at least about this one point in his past named Dr. Friedrich Becker.

He had once admired, loved, envied him.

How he had stared bug-eyed. He had not even thought for a moment that someone might tell him off. Such a miserable wretch of a man, just able to stay on his feet.

To hell with Hilda, if she's interested in a piece of trash like that.

What did he look like? Like some of those fine gentlemen in a barbershop who are so grand when the white cloak is spread over them—cut my hair, please, then wash it, then a shave, then a facial massage, then a manicure, perfume, no end to it. They have plenty of time and money and can afford to be pampered. That's just how this Becker pampers his dear, his darling ego. Let's just hope it doesn't get caught in a draft sometime, poor child. That it doesn't get splashed with a bit of mud. Enough to make you vomit.

High science, philosophy, literature—in times like these! In times like these! The house is burning down and he expounds about God. Makes you want to flail away with a club. He doesn't know anything about God or the world, only about himself. He's a coward. Damn it all, and that was my friend.

To hell with him, I say. A rotten fellow, a fraud, a liar.

And by chance Maus happened to see at a street corner that same poster Becker had observed at the Königstor. "What is socialism? The highest goal of socialism is the total liberation of the German people and of the whole of mankind. It wants to help make a strong, peace-loving League of Nations a reality. Let the banners be lowered in silence, let the drums cease to roll—in the parliament of mankind, in the legislature of the world."

No, thought Maus. You won't pull it off. I know you. No, I've had enough. I'm not going to be a part of it any longer. It makes me sick.

And with a jerk, Maus was free of his doubts. The way lay open, the direction was clear.

He knew where he wanted to go. A few days before a comrade had told him about something going on in Westphalia. They were forming a corps of volunteers who loved discipline and the fatherland. You could find out about it at an office on Fasanenstrasse.

That's what I'll do, Maus decided.

"Humanity, parliament of the world." Somewhere in this world there had to be some reason left.

Maus marched. He was sure, wild and vengeful.

Two days after the government had called for the formation of a republican militia, General Maercker, in Salzkotten, Westphalia, presented his "constitutive order" for a volunteer Home Rifle Corps.

Maercker had said: "I have served kaisers for thirty years now. I have shed my blood on three continents in five wars. Emotions that have been formed over the course of thirty-five years cannot be cast away like an old shirt. Whoever acts in such a fashion is a miserable wretch."

"A hundred and twelve years ago, after the defeats at Jena and Austerlitz, Prussia found herself in the same situation as today, equally dishonored and befouled. At that point a corps of volunteer rifles assembled around Major von Lützow in Breslau. Lützow undertook his bold actions with these.

"Such a volunteer corps is what I wish to build."

In Salzkotten, in the office of the division staff, representatives of General Headquarters received General Maercker's "constitutive order" and approved it without a single change.

The order read:

"The corps consists of volunteers.

"It will submit to an iron discipline.

"No soldiers' councils. Deputies between officers and rank and file.

"The more noble the troops, the less reason the deputies will have to become involved.

"Punishment administered by leaders of companies and batteries, and on up the chain of command. A lapse of three hours between the infraction and the execution of punishment.

"No one shall have his honor insulted.

"Looters will be sentenced to death.

"Cowards will be expelled.

"The rank and file may nominate a man who has given heroic account of himself for the rank of officer.

"Every enlisted man must salute. Every officer must respond."

Maercker accepted only older officers. In anticipation of the coming struggle and its peculiar nature and with the untiring assistance of his staff, he formed mixed units, strengthened by both cavalry and batteries.

The question of swearing in the troops was left in abeyance.

And the first volunteers streamed in and were quartered in this country of red soil, in Wever, Nordborchen and Kirchborchen, under the command of Major Anders. The staff of the rifles found quarters in Salzkotten, in the motherhouse of the Franciscans.

Maercker's emissaries swarmed out in search of weapons, equipment and uniforms. The 214th Infantry Division had been last to stand on the front line of battle. They had returned completely exhausted. Their supply depots were plundered. There was talk of weapons and artillery in Münster, of uniforms in Hannover. Maercker's emissaries found ridiculously small quantities of both.

The old army has been crushed, has fallen apart. Maercker himself travels to Geseke, where there are supposed to be supplies from the disbanded 17th Army. He finds a dismal scene. Cannons lying tossed about without anyone guarding them, ammunition wagons, vehicles with bent axles and broken wheels. The depot at Senne looks no better. They start grabbing, working at a feverish pace.

Maercker speaks to his officers. He expresses what they all are thinking.

"The spirit of patriotism, of loyalty unto death, has made it possible for the German army to strike blows before which the whole globe trembled.

"A slow poison has eaten its way through that proud body.

"Above the portals of the new Reich is written large:

" 'Defenseless — honorless.' "

Book Six

Last Echoes, the Sequel

But There Must Be Peace

*In Paris, the American president, Thomas Woodrow Wilson, awaits
his opponents. The battle begins.*

A Month's Vacation

In Paris, however, the gaunt figure with a pallid face had appeared,
the man who had been impelled to cross the ocean to establish the rule
of justice in Europe.

The great man of reason was not one of those who sit in a study,
reading and learning from books. Even at Princeton he had not been satisfied with a studying and teaching, he had had to introduce a democratized curriculum. For a long time the war and suffering in Europe had
barely touched him and his country. Later Clemenceau was to say,
"America needed three years to feel the German invasion of Belgium as a
violation of its sense of justice." But from the moment when America
joined in the war, it was not just one participant among others, thanks
to the great man of reason. At the head of the United States, reelected to
a second term in 1916, stood the amazing schoolmaster from Princeton.
He had studied the history of nations to the point where his health collapsed, almost to the point where his eyes failed him. And in doing so he
had come to a conclusion. What he had read had proved to him that
wars and revolutions are false paths for humanity, that with careful attention and goodwill they can be avoided. They are the costly detours to
settlements that with a bit of calm could have been achieved with ease.

Once before, a hundred years ago, a man had elevated reason to a
goddess, the lawyer Robespierre. She was worshiped only fleetingly in
capricious Paris. Men rushed to demote her and return to man's daily
petty stupidities, to the old "heroic deeds."

And now came Thomas Woodrow Wilson from America, not
nearly as young and fanatic as the Frenchman who transformed himself
from a teacher into a tyrant, but just as severe and sure of himself as he.
He was greeted enthusiastically in that great European capital.

The fairy-tale palace of Prince Murat in a quiet, elegant part of town had been fitted up for him. There he sat and waited. He did not know what lay ahead of him.

The gentlemen whom he hoped to bring to reason had not arrived. They were still preparing the demands they wanted to have endorsed at the upcoming conference. Several of them were needed at their posts at the moment, because things were getting out of hand just then in their own countries, as is common when accounts are being settled after a war.

People asked about Lloyd George, the English chancellor of the exchequer and prime minister. Where was he hiding? For indeed, he was not to be seen the length and breadth of Paris. This was a matter of etiquette. For if the American president was visiting Paris, then he certainly could come to London as well.

When the ship arrived with the president on board, his many helpers had crept from its belly as well, all the smaller men of reason. And with their books, portfolios and charts they ran about the Hotel Crillon in Paris, on the Place de la Concorde, settling in there where gentle, short Colonel House resided, Wilson's friend, the man—a bad omen—whom all European statesmen without exception loved.

On Sunday one could go to church, and so that morning they went to the one where Lafayette lay, a man whose name never fails to be mentioned in speeches jointly celebrating America and France. And in the afternoon they went to worship in the Episcopalian church of the Holy Trinity. And what does the great man of reason do on Monday? We see him driving toward the Paris town hall. There he stands at the center of a frenzied reception. He is made an honorary citizen of Paris.

And at the end someone presents him with a golden pen with the inscription: "The French people present the American president this pen, so that with it he may sign a just, humane and lasting peace."

Back home again, the president pulls the treasured brown buckeye from his vest pocket, rubs it till it is shiny and examines it. Then he holds beside it the pen of peace he has just been given, laying both of them in front of him on the desk. He looks first to the right, then to the left and compares them. The buckeye shines, the gold pen sparkles—but no conversation develops between the two. The lovely buckeye is mute, doesn't feel at home here, doesn't know what to say to the prophecy of the French pen that is supposed to sign a just, humane and lasting peace. The great man of reason stands there full of care. He picks up the buckeye again and tucks it into his warm vest pocket. He locks away the ominous pen. Gifts like that are better left ungiven.

And what does the president do on Tuesday, on Wednesday?

When nothing happens, he comes up with the idea of going to the telephone and calling Colonel House at the Hotel Crillon. He wants to ask what is happening in the world. When will things get started? And good Colonel House answers that they will just have to be patient, it will take a while yet, for various reasons, and that England and Italy also want a visit from the president and it would not be a bad idea if the president were to undertake such a journey.

So he spends more time doing nothing and waits for the conference to come to him. He thinks: every day we give them to calm down is a gain for us.

Old Clemenceau appears and honors Mrs. Wilson with a piece of the white flag the German negotiators had borne with them on the day of armistice. The famous Clemenceau is a squat, gnarled old man with a Mongolian face. The French soldier's "Father Victory," he wears a small black cap and his hands are hidden in gray woolen gloves because of eczema, or so it is said. He is charming and chivalrous. What curious creatures the European continent produces.

Reception after reception, parties. A visit to the French Academy, fat Pappa Joffre, field marshal and victor at the Marne, is received as a member. The innocuous, tiny king of Italy presents himself one day quite informally at the Palais Murat, everything goes smoothly and without ceremony. Things are less smooth when the Italian delegates follow their king—pudgy, soft Orlando and lean Sonino with his small, cunning eyes and eagle's nose. It proves difficult to keep them from talking business at once.

At Neuilly near Paris is the American hospital, spendidly equipped and fully up-to-date. One morning they drive out there, prepared for a normal hospital visit with shaking of hands and cordiality. But in those white beds they find horribly mutilated men, ghastly tattered faces, young men who hardly look human anymore but who still stammer the same English language their visitors speak, the same language spoken out in the fields, in the factories and homes of America, where their parents are waiting for them, parents who raised them so that they—might not look like this. The American guests are so shocked, so frozen by this visit at Neuilly that they cannot eat lunch.

During those four weeks when the great man of reason was left to wait he traveled to both England and Italy. They would have loved to drag him out onto the battlefields of Belgium and northern France to give him a look at German barbarism, but his reaction was sour. They did not get him to do it. He said, "I know what happened. I know the bitterness war causes. But if I were to ride through that area, I'm afraid I would go mad. And I want to be certain that at least one person at this peace conference is not mad." He was a proud man.

In the end he did see the cathedral at Rheims; he had read of its barbaric destruction, and annoyed his companions by remarking that it was not so very dreadful after all.

As Christmas approached they again visited a hospital, this time a French one, the military hospital Val de Grace near the Luxembourg Gardens. Mrs. Wilson came too. There were incredible scenes. This hospital was not so elegant and clean as the one at Neuilly. Babbling away, an old woman clung to the president, she had lost her mind and thought she was a doctor. They were led into a large hall where the only light came from a single light bulb hanging from a cord in the middle of the room. The bulb was decorated with red paper and a small French flag dangled from it. The soldiers all wore blue uniforms. Many of them wore heavy bandages about their heads and eyes. A husky poilu stood at a piano, both eyes bandaged. The "Marseillaise" was played, and the husky blind soldier sang the words.

December 24th. A trip to Chaumont, the American General Headquarters.

Between Langres and Humes ten thousand men had been positioned. The president drove in an armored car, twenty more cars followed. In addition he was accompanied by a squadron of airplanes making bellicose noises above him. Wilson wore his top hat and a brown fur coat. Later he stood bareheaded out in the open in order to speak about the glad tidings of Christmas: peace on earth and goodwill to men. The planes had ceased their noise in the meantime; they had made no impression on the great man of reason.

And in point of fact he was not one of those who simply talked about peace, and these troops, these American men, knew that. They were the men who had fought at Chateau Thierry and in the gruesome Battle of the Argonne Forest. Medals were awarded. They sang "The Star-Spangled Banner," and flyers commemorating the deeds of the 26th, 29th, 77th, 80th and 6th Divisions were put in their hands. They glanced fleetingly at them and said, "Never again."

In London they were guests of the king at Buckingham Palace, and Lloyd George spoke. It was not as bad as they had expected. And in Rome, then, it was splendid, especially at the Quirinal. The year 1919 had already begun. The little Italian king greeted them cheerfully and answered the compliments his American guests made him with a smile.

A huge, excited crowd surged across a square where the monument to King Victor Emmanuel stood. They were waiting for the American president, the man who had proclaimed the Fourteen Points and the League of Nations. Things grew tumultuous. The police intervened, and with the energy typical of their profession, dispersed the crowd. The president exploded later when he heard of this, expressing his displeasure in biting words at the Quirinal. But they calmed him down; they had been thinking of his safety. In these southern climes people were so excitable since the war. He said, hm, hm, and the matter was filed away.

Lloyd George, as was to be expected, won a great victory at the polls from the boys in khaki. Clemenceau as well was triumphant in the French Chamber and praised the "noble zeal" of the American president.

And then things were ready and they could proceed to open the peace conference, to wind up the affairs of the world war that had begun in August, 1914 and ended on November 11, 1918.

Sixty-five million men had been mobilized for that war. Eight million of them had fallen during the war, twenty-one million had been wounded.

The war had cost $186 billion. Property valued at $30 billion had been destroyed, and the warring nations were $340 billion poorer.

The conference.

Illumined by the light of Wilsonian justice, lured by that light, they arrived one after the other, each with his retinue, each in his native costume, and bowed. They were there, they were saved. They were the men, the animals and birds that God had invited to take a berth in Noah's ark, and they had survived the flood and were now about to populate the earth anew with creatures after their own kind.

The light in which they shimmered was that shed by the Fourteen Points, first proclaimed by the great man of reason at the Capitol in Washington in January 1918:

Troops were to be evacuated from Belgium and that nation was to be restored without restriction of its freedom and independence.

France was to be evacuated and restored intact. Satisfaction for the old injustice of 1871 was demanded, and the ceding of Alsace-Lorraine.

Evacuation from Russian territory. The readjustment of Italian frontiers in accordance with the principle of nationality. Evacuation and restoration of Rumania, Serbia, Montenegro. Serbia was to be granted access to the sea.

An independent Poland with access to the sea.

The peoples of Austria-Hungary should be guaranteed the prospect of independent autonomy.

And then the points moved beyond matters of geography, pronouncing upon general guidelines of peace that devolved directly from the mind of the president.

A League of Nations was to be formed, guaranteeing independence to each of its members, a league that guarded over the territorial integrity of all states, both large and small.

Progress in the settlement of colonial questions.

Guarantees for a general reduction of armaments.

The lowering of trade barriers, equal rights of commerce for all nations, freedom of the seas, renunciation of secret diplomacy.

All peace treaties were to be public.

This was the American president's January message that blew over the ocean like a storm, battering the stifling air of war. It was the second great event of the war, the first being the smashing of czarist despotism. This was the proclamation that lifted the odium from so-called "idealistic" demands. And generals, general staffs, slaughterers of men and lascivious politicians lost the smiles on their faces.

On January 12, 1919, they met in Paris at the Quai d'Orsay, in the building on the Seine that housed the French Foreign Office.

When a grim-looking Clemenceau accepted the chairmanship offered to him he made a short speech that immediately demonstrated that he was on top of the situation.

"It is not a mere matter of territory that we wish to decide. We want peace for all the nations of the earth and forever. Those plans speak for themselves."

They assembled daily at the Quai d'Orsay, the Council of Ten; five powers, each with two members: France, England, America, Italy and Japan.

America, represented by its president, made no territorial demands. It wanted a generally accepted implementation of the Fourteen Points.

France wanted security and the Rhineland and the Saar.

For England the war was over.

Italy wanted Fiume and control of the Adriatic.

Japan wanted Shantung.

And now Wilson could do battle. The arena had been cleared. He charged like a bull into the fight.

First Triumph

Things did not go badly at the start. The bloc of "allied and associated nations" voted on January 25th for making the covenant for a League of Nations an essential part of the peace treaty. And they elected a League of Nations Commission, and Wilson, the American president (Clemenceau called him "le Président Sauveur" and "the prophet inspired by the noblest ideology, aflame with the idea of his panacea"), allowed himself to be elected chairman. He retired to the Hotel Crillon with his League of Nations Commission, and there he sat and discussed for hours on end, for days on end, with the others—beside him the other American, the gentle Colonel House, who could cause no one pain, the South African Smuts, the tall, pious Lord Cecil, Bourgeois and the fat, sentimental Orlando.

What emerged was that they each wanted a League of Nations, and each wanted it in a different way.

The French wanted a league that was armed to the teeth and could be achieved as easily as child's play. One only needed to keep together a portion of the Allied armies at hand and grant Marshal Foch the title

"General of the League of Nations." They wanted a general staff made up of the Allies, soldiers from the member states of the League, a strong inter-alliance police force and harsh punishment of aggressors.

The English were back in the North Sea, sitting on the footstool of isolation and dangling their legs. They were satisfied if the continent did not rearm. They themselves had their fleet. One should simply abolish the military draft and nationalize the armaments industry. That was not so difficult.

The American praised those on his right and those on his left. He found it all fine and dandy, was glad they were even sitting down together. But he could not reconcile himself to the proposals of the French, for purely American reasons, quite apart from all the rest: it was against the Constitution of the United States for a foreign power to conscript American soldiers. Quite openly he disclosed to his friends on the commission what he himself thought was the best solution: a "peace without winners or losers."

A plan for a World Court of Justice emerged. Wilson rebounded with: "How do you expect to erect a League of Nations that way? With mistrust, with a court, with penal codes?"

After a day of doing battle, the refined Colonel House, who listened attentively and mollified the others, remarked resignedly, actually more to himself, that perhaps war could not really be abolished just as men had never succeeded in abolishing crime. Apparently all one could accomplish would be to keep war from being profitable. But Wilson, the radical, the man of principle, would hear none of that.

And when negotiations did not really move forward, while famine in Europe was making remarkable progress, the American Bliss, a member of Wilson's main delegation, wrung his hands and cried in weariness, "I wish the war were still going on. Because peace looks like it's going to be worse than war."

But the great man of reason would not let himself be wearied. He removed all obstacles from his path. Because he saw himself confronted by a task with which he identified in a way that was entirely different from all the others. He knew the truth and would not be dissuaded of it: only radicality and reason could heal.

He worked day and night. He went from his League of Nations Commission in the Hotel Crillon to the Grand Commission on the Quai d'Orsay. He received countless visitors and directed the American delegation.

On the opposing side in the main Council of Ten, the old man from the Vendée, Clemenceau, did not lag behind him. He rose at four each morning, often demanded meetings be held at 6:00 A.M. and did not leave the field of battle before nine at night, when all that was left about him were the corpses.

As it became clear that the American who had crossed the ocean was no idealistic professor, but rather a tough fighter and most certainly no blockhead—so that even Clemenceau, at the end of a session that had included a long counterblast from Wilson, sat there stiffly and erupted with the words: "You are a clever man. You are a great man, Mr. President"—they let him have his first triumph. On February 14th he could register a victory at the peace conference: the Grand Commission unanimously accepted the preliminary draft for a League of Nations.

At this point the American interrupted his work. He delegated Hoover, the representative of the United States in the General Economic Council, to use whatever means necessary to check the famine raging in Europe. Then he departed, accompanied by his wife, Dr. Grayson and a small retinue, in order to attend to business in America.

At Brest he climbed back on board the *George Washington,* which was already there waiting for him.

In Germany

By the beginning of January, 1919, troops of genuine soldiers stand once again in closed ranks, recruited by General Maercker, commanded by Lüttwitz, in the camp at Zossen, thirty miles southwest of Berlin.

The "Present Arms March" rings out. The feet pound away at the soil of the Mark Brandenburg, which has known that beat for centuries now.

Wearing helmets, clad in field gray, the soldiers, in sharply dressed ranks, with faces chiseled in stone, march past Friedrich Ebert.

It is the first time ever that Prussian troops have filed past a civilian—they are ashamed and contemptuous.

Ebert holds his top hat in his hand. At last he can breathe more easily.

Beside him stands his friend and Party comrade, a former noncommissioned officer, the lanky Noske.

They both are thinking the same thing: at last.

The Treaty of Versailles

The great man of reason is defeated. He saves what he can.

And Thomas Woodrow Wilson is traveling aboard the *George Washington* once again.

The roomy office with its mahogany desk and two telephones is there, the grand salon—but this time, what a relief, without maps, graphs and diagrams, without learned men and experts. There is the bedroom with its dark green curtains you can close completely behind you. And the small pocket Bible from the YMCA finds its spot beside the bed again.

The president is a totally different man aboard ship. Strangers find him ice-cold and forbidding. But that is only the protective wall he has thrown up around himself in order to be able to exist at all, given how irritable, sensitive and frail he is. Behind his protective wall he continues to be a peaceable, friendly and engaging man who loves art and literature, who charms those in his immediate circle and who always needs some feminine influence on his environment. On board ship, with his wife and the young admiral and Doctor Grayson, he creeps out of his porcupine skin.

"It was difficult there in Paris," he sighed, lying in the deck chair on the promenade deck—the last gulls of the continent had disappeared—"and it will get worse."

They asked him questions, noticing he wanted to speak and unburden himself.

Mrs. Wilson: "Why is that, where does the resistance come from, from a clash of personalities?"

"The personalities involved," he laughed, "are by no means negligible. But one could get by all that. My guess is that they don't enjoy me much either. But for all of them in Europe the reason is to be found in the war. Four years of war, right beside them, on top of them, that's no small matter. It's like suddenly being cast into the wilderness. At home we had no real conception of it. That is one thing, the war. The other is much worse, Europe itself."

Grayson seconded him. How strange Europe was. You didn't really come into contact with the people, except when it's a matter of the most simple things, like a sickbed or whatever.

Wilson: "Yes, that's right. If I were asked to reduce Europe to a simple formula, I mean now the political Europe I have had to deal with, then I would say: it is an old, cynical civilization. They try to refresh themselves with war. And it's really at that level that civilization and barbarism meet. Only that there are two kinds of war. Crude war arises from want and savagery. The other is the perverse war, sought out arbitrarily and indifferently, because you don't get along anymore, because you can't stand putting up with things as they are. Which is the reason why some of these peoples have a cult of death we find so totally incomprehensible, by which I mean something quite different from a simple Spartan contempt for death. It is a cynical indifference to life. Which is why I'm revolted at present by all their fine arts, which I have always admired. It's true—there is a great sense of humanity, harmony and culture to be found in their art. But they imagine that therefore they can dispense with humanity in real life.

"And now, if I ask myself where the actual difference is to be found between the Germans and their European opponents, I find myself in trouble. I cannot find a correct answer."

They were silent. Grayson smiled. "So you would formulate your Fourteen Points differently now, Mr. President?"

Wilson quickly turned his head to give him a sharp look. "The Fourteen Points? What makes you say that? Why? Those are our old, axiomatic principles. At the most you might ask . . ."

He looked up into the sky and said nothing more. The ship sailed on calmly.

Grayson: "If I might complete the thought, one might ask whether, given these facts, we in America would have had any great desire to intervene."

Wilson: "That's just what went through my mind. But it is all idle speculation. We did not seek out our enemies, we had no freedom in the matter, the war came to us. But now as for peace—how are we Americans to cooperate with the Europeans in building peace? When at the very spot where we find a sense of justice embedded in us, a sense of absolute justice, within them there is cynicism?"

He continued, "How can I get the Germans as well to recognize our principles, the power of conscience and morality, and to renounce their faith in brute force if our own friends are unbelievers precisely on these points? The German nation has now been taught a lesson, through military defeat. How does one imprint that in them so that it is not just a defeat, but a lesson? I believe, I am convinced, that you do it by presenting them with a peace treaty that shows them in its articles, in the new arrangements it makes, that a different sort of people have won, a sort of people they have not known before this. It must be a new experience for them. Then they will pay attention, then they can be moved to learn anew."

Grayson wanted to know about old Clemenceau. Wilson gave him extraordinary praise. But it was dreadful to have to fight him, for he was a man of downright Roman patriotism and mistrust. You could only take off your hat to the old man. He was deeply embittered, deeply skeptical, pessimistic. "And that is not how one builds a new world."

Wilson reminded Grayson of the speech he had made before Congress in which he had asked with what governments one could make the peace treaty and under what authority they might present themselves, and that here lay reason for considerable uneasiness. "The greatest uneasiness we can now see, however, comes from another direction. Which governments stand with us? Clemenceau once gave a rather good definition of peace: it is the distribution of power that gives reason to believe a permanent balance has been struck and by which the moral might of justice girds itself against disorder by employing strategic guarantees. But if you now ask Clemenceau what justice is, something very remarkable happens, something that reveals where Clemenceau stands. He says, "Justice is an organization of historical forces, which from time to time call for strengthening." And there you have it. That is Europe: historical forces that from time to time grow weaker and then have to be strengthened. Everything fine and dandy—except that true justice is missing. Everything at the moment depends on the victor's showing that he knows what justice is, what absolute justice is, and acknowledging it. He must begin with trust. Victory has placed that duty upon him. He can only expect bitterness, hate and a thirst for revenge from the defeated."

Mrs. Wilson had been listening with active interest. "Then trust is the main thing? Yes, that's good. I understand. But look here, if someone has robbed you, an employee, a kitchen maid, do you keep him or her on?"

Wilson laughed. "I'll let you decide that. If it happens, I'll call for you to help. But one can also replace personnel. France cannot produce any other Germany. The German is right at its heels. So they have to try to get along. And the moment for it is favorable, France has everything in its hands if it will only risk it. Yes, it must take that risk. I know that is a great problem and that it is asking a lot from a nation that has suffered as France has. But in Germany now, workers and middle-class citizens head the state, a new class of people. I'll place my hopes on them. They will gradually push the generals and junkers out of the way. We will support them in the effort." He punctuated the air with a decisive gesture of his hand. "These European politicians and military men are

613

mistaken if they believe we Americans will let ourselves be yoked into some sort of antiquated victor mentality. Not us. We have been the decisive factor in the war. They are skeptics, but they'll see where that gets them."

Mrs. Wilson: "It will take courage."

Wilson: "We'll make it possible for them. We shall give them the chance for courage, we shall stand by them. That is what the League of Nations is for."

And the great man of reason looked to the right and the left at the two of them, saw how they sat there considering it all. And he felt that they (they at least) believed him and would follow him. That did him a great deal of good.

He lay in his deck chair and leaned his head way back. Let them doubt. Precisely because they doubted he felt strengthened and more certain of himself.

He knew what he knew.

A Brief Glance at America

They arrived in America, the other theater of war.

He was in Washington again now, in the White House. And on February 26th the president gave a dinner for senators and members of the Foreign Affairs Committee, thirty-six were invited. All of them came with the exception of the orthodox isolationists Borah and Fall. The leader of Wilson's enemies, the chairman of the committee, Cabot Lodge, gave Mrs. Wilson his arm and led her to the table. Wilson let himself be cross-examined. He was alert and spoke without the least animosity. Lodge was silent, asked no questions. He did not want any answer to weaken his hatred.

Lodge was, after the death of Teddy Roosevelt the previous month, the undisputed leader of Wilson's opponents. Before, he could not kill enough Germans. In his own way he now mobilized forces against England at the peace conference; since in Massachusetts there were hundreds of thousands of Irishmen, he demanded that a commission be set up in Paris to hear the cause of Irish independence, for everything hinged on the question of national self-determination. He spoke in Boston to the Italians, goading them on in their nationalist greed. Yes, they needed Fiume and should have it—and control of the Adriatic as well. He went so far as to pass on a memorandum to Henry White, the only Republican who went to Paris, asking him to deliver it to Clemenceau, Lloyd George and Orlando. In this way Lodge hoped to interfere in the negotiations and sabotage the efforts of the president.

On March 4th, one day before the president's return to Europe,

Lodge introduced a resolution in the Senate, and Wilson took the words of that resolution with him to Europe:

"It is the opinion of the Senate," Lodge declared, "that nations should unite to conclude a peace and undertake a general disarmament. But the League of Nations in the form proposed cannot be accepted by the United States. The United States should undertake the necessary peace negotiations directly with Germany, and only then should discussions concerning a League of Nations and a permanent peace be considered."

A cheering crowd greeted the president in New York on that same March 4th and accompanied him as he made his way to the Metropolitan Opera.

Before he spoke, the band played the song "We Won't Come Back till It's Over Over There."

After his speech—the president made reference to the lyrics of the song—Enrico Caruso sang the national anthem, "The Star-Spangled Banner." Woodrow Wilson stood arm in arm with his predecessor, William Howard Taft, a Republican, at one time the first civil governor of the Philippines and later chief justice of the Supreme Court. The applause swept about them.

But Wilson did not let himself be deceived. He sensed his opponents behind him like dogs on the trail.

And the country—wanted nothing except peace—oh, a comfortable and thoughtless tranquillity. Out there people were as far from any knowledge of necessary facts as America was from Europe.

The great man of reason remained in America only for a short time. It had been enough to shake him. He looked a grayish yellow. His eyes had a tormented look.

The Battle Is Taken Up Once More

After a nine-day journey the president arrived again in Paris on March 14th.

There was someone else who was ailing in Paris at that point. The French prime minister, George Clemenceau. He had been shot at, struck by two bullets. But immediately after the attempt, the old man stoically observed, "The beast doesn't shoot badly, but it is nothing." And the indestructible old man recovered quickly and appeared at the negotiations as if nothing had happened.

There was little talk now of the League of Nations. The brief period of Wilson's absence had been sufficient to allow the League to disappear from the scene. All that mattered now was national security. There was also talk of forming armies to confront Bolshevism, whose expansion and consolidation in Russia were causing increasing anxiety.

Wilson was indignant with the easy-going representative Colonel House. Now everything must be begun anew. The president's nervous excitability and irritability grew. At the conference he had to pound on the table to make certain that nothing had been changed in the decision of the plenary session of January 25th, which had made the formation of the League of Nations an integral part of the peace treaty. This decision of January 25th had, and retained, binding authority, and there was no reason for casting doubt upon that fact.

At that point they left the Foreign Office on the Quai d'Orsay and moved, in the hope of fraying one another's nerves in peace, to a small palace on the Place des Etats Unis, where no newspaper correspondents or guests were allowed to follow. Sentries patrolled in front of the palace. Inside American soldiers stood guard.

In the salons, however, the peacemakers spread out their maps and plans on the carpets and on the bare floor. And they were often to be seen creeping about on all fours like dogs and cats, their noses to the paper trying to determine where the borders would run that could guarantee peace.

They had violent debates about Bolshevism. It was no joke for old man Clemenceau. In 1871, as mayor of the most revolutionary district in Paris, Montmartre, he had lived through the Commune, and it had been for him a great misfortune. For as a Jacobin, a physician and son of a landowner, he could swing his battle-axe against monarchists, aristocrats and clergy, but beyond that—he was a bourgeois and he hated the Commune. He had already taken flight from his beloved Paris when the men of the Commune began to search for him. They almost shot another man instead of him, a Latin American, by mistake.

With arms crossed, the Americans and English listened quietly to Clemenceau's warnings about Bolshevism. The Anglo-Saxons were not impressed by the theories of the Bolsheviks, it was all cheap propaganda, and they knew their own countries were immune to it.

Clemenceau fought. He could not, dared not yield, because behind him stood Poincaré and Marshal Foch. And though he could restrain the field marshal, the man from Lorraine, Poincaré, had a harder head; he was president of the Republic, the boss. Unwavering, the old man demanded the Rhineland, the Rhine as France's border, the Saar, all for reasons of French security, with a dozen varied arguments. And ever and again Clemenceau let the great man of reason run at him full tilt, only to throw him back with skepticism, sarcasm and fury.

The Germans were the Germans after all. You only had to look their generals and junkers in the face to know that and to know that nothing could be achieved here with goodness and reason. They were krauts. You could not trust them. Just as only yesterday they had torn up the treaty of guarantee with Belgium, tomorrow they would consider any treaty they signed a mere scrap of paper if they so decided. France knew them, after three invasions in the last hundred years.

"What would America say if the exact same enemy were to invade it and plunder it three times within a hundred years? How would America behave? How would it reply to neighbors wanting to give it good advice? Wanting to preach so-called reason to it? Do you really believe that Americans would then speak as you do now, and would not shrug their shoulders and laugh if someone demanded of them that they should embrace these thieves as brothers? And now, now you tell us the fault lay with the Hohenzollerns, and that they have been chased off. True. For how long? You tell us we now have a German republic. For how long? I don't trust their republic. France knows from its own history about republics without republicans. Where are the German republicans? The present leaders of the republic are all well known to us as lackeys of the monarchy who held out in favor of war the whole time. You cannot demand of us that we trust those men and base our security on them. We are strongly inclined to think that these people are letting themselves be used as front men for their old masters, the monarchists. They are taking care of the Hohenzollerns' business for them as long as the Hohenzollerns are inconvenienced. They are probably proud of this worthy task. The only republicans that republic has to show for itself are the Spartacists, who want to destroy the republic! Behind them you'll find Russian Bolshevism lurking. So then, Mr. President, we have no choice but to defend ourselves. We must continue to keep a sharp, attentive eye on what is going on about us not only in our own interest but also in the interest of Europe and America."

The American president: "You demand the left bank of the Rhine and the Saar. What makes you feel protected by that? How will the Rhineland provide you security if the Germans are as you say they are— for all eternity and even without their Hohenzollerns? You correctly point out the three invasions in the last hundred years. But if we begin to speak of history, then I am reminded of Emperor Napoleon I. As you well know, in order to defend himself he took more than just the Rhineland from the Germans. Well the Germans, the Prussians above all, armed themselves for a new war before the very eyes of the emperor, used a system of partially trained reservists, formed their militia and home guard. You know all this better than I. At any rate, you know that the complete subjugation of Germany was of no use to the emperor. As soon as he showed signs of weakness, after the defeat in Russia, he had to begin the struggle all over again, and this time under changed circumstances. He was weaker than the first time and the Germans had joined a fearful coalition. At Waterloo he had Blücher as his opponent and was defeated."

Clemenceau: "To be sure, that may be in store for us as well. We must draw our lesson from Napoleon. We will not allow ourselves signs of weakness. But Germany has twenty million more people than we. That is why we need the Rhine border for our strategic security, and our policy can only be based on strong allies and a strong army. We hope to find these allies. We have been victorious with them—and they with us. The League of Nations is a grand idea. Such a league is useful. But, as things are at the moment, it cannot provide us with absolute security or set our fears completely to rest. We are, you see, simply terrified. It does not release us from the duty to be on our guard."

Wilson: "I understand. Do you believe that I cannot put myself in your place. But the danger is that you may ruin the whole future, you take from it all possibility for a better development. You stand in your own way. Because you cast Germany in the role of the permanent aggressor. It was an aggressor three times over, but you are forcing it to remain an aggressor."

Clemenceau, icily: "Germany considers itself an aggressor and, believe me, it is proud of the fact. It wants to be, will always be the aggressor."

Wilson shrugged his shoulders.

That was the end of all discussion for good. Now one of them shrugged, now the other. Wilson could only say in closing, "But we will not achieve peace in this way."

And if Clemenceau added anything at all, then it was: "You can never achieve peace with the Germans."

And Wilson could only raise his hands in despair.

Lloyd George smiled at the stubborn old man, and Orlando, the Italian, watched the warriors from the background, listening anxiously to how the American reacted. Because he, too, had his demands.

Debates without end. Everyone knew all the arguments of his opponent, they stopped for today, and tomorrow they sat back down again together and spun the same thread—in reality simply waiting until the opponent had had enough and gave in. Once, as they stood trembling across from one another—the American incapable of compromise, the Frenchman in no position to yield—Wilson asked, "If France does not get what it wants, do you want to refuse to deal with us any further? Do you wish me to go?"

Clemenceau answered, already on his way toward the door, "No. But I plan to do so myself."

And the old man left, and—was back again the next morning, freshly armed with the same arguments.

An Ultimatum. The Departure of the Italians

In Germany meanwhile the constituent assembly had been convened at Weimar.

The man who had until now served as First People's Deputy, the Social Democrat Friedrich Ebert (no half-hearted patriot he), spoke of detention of 800,000 German prisoners of war, of the harshness shown by the Allies in enforcing the conditions of the armistice.

"They should not push things too far," he threatened. "It may well be, now that General Winterfeldt has already left the Armistice Commission, that the German government will find itself forced to withdraw from negotiations. We expect the peace Wilson promised and to which we have a right."

The American, however, grew increasingly gaunt, increasingly he had facial tics. Bad news came in from all over the world. A communist republic had been proclaimed in Hungary. Bavaria had its Soviet Republic.

Wilson was taken ill with the flu. On April 7th he decided to give France an ultimatum. He immediately ordered his ship, the *George Washington,* which was docked in Brooklyn, to Brest.

And—France gave in.

The demand for the Rhine frontier was dropped.

But Wilson, too, lost blood. He had to permit a fifteen-year occupation of the Rhineland. And the Saar was to vote after a period of twenty years whether it wished to belong to Germany or France (or to the League of Nations).

And France insisted on Anglo-American guarantees in case of a German attack.

The great man of reason had to concede all that. What was left of his maxim of peace without winners or losers? Granted, as far as the Anglo-American guarantees went, the American president made it clear to the Frenchman that they should be under no illusions about that. In all likelihood no American congress would be prepared to confirm such a guarantee.

Italy came forward. It declared that it could not live without Fiume and the Adriatic.

Wilson was amazed at each new session.

Orlando declared: "A hundred thousand Italians live in Fiume."

Wilson: "Then you apparently also want New York, don't you? We have two million Italians in New York."

The Italian press was set loose. They cursed Wilson, caricatured him. It was all over with the celebrated "religion of internationalism" that had obsessed Europe just a few months before. Demonstrations were held against Wilson in Rome, Naples and Genoa. Wilson declared: "As long as I am here, Italy will not get the Yugoslav city of Fiume."

So—Orlando and Sonino took their hats, left the meeting hall, packed their bags at their hotel, and departed. In Rome they raged and shouted and swore they would not yield.

Japanese Surgery

There now appeared before the already rather exhausted American two noble Japanese, short, thick-set men with cunning faces that did not radiate human kindness. They bowed with Asiatic courtesy and declared they did not wish to disturb the great man of reason in his auspicious task, in his endeavors on behalf of a prostrate Europe. They only wanted, seeing that they were in fact there and would soon have to return home, a little piece called Shantung to be cut from the ribs of China. The Chinese delegate stood there, hopping from one foot to the other.

Wilson felt uneasy at this, physically as well. The flu had settled in his intestines, he still suffered from it. Real peace, he now knew after what had happened here in France, was not to be had. But if one could not have total and genuine peace, then at least half a one would do. For peace might grow from peace. One could at least sow the seeds of peace.

He soothed the Chinese delegate. But the Japanese threatened to leave the conference.

The American could not sleep. And in those long, difficult nights the thought grew firmer in his mind: in wanting to achieve a true and total peace at this conference, with these men, here in this frightfully grim Europe, I wanted the wrong thing, I wanted too much, an impossibility. One can only lay the foundation for peace here. It must be prepared for. These Europeans are still entirely ignorant of the notion of cooperation among nations.

Let me first have the League of Nations, the president dreamed. Just let a little time pass. Then they will begin to get over their wounds. Oh, how difficult it is to create peace on earth. (And he remembered the Christmas message of the angelic hymn, peace on earth and goodwill to men. Yes, heavenly peace.)

And he braced himself, and the next morning the two noble Japanese appeared before him again. The men from Tokyo saw his haggard, worried face, and at the sight a radiant sun of good cheer rose in their hearts, for they understood what this worry meant, and they heard from his own mouth that he would yield for the sake of peace, which was what mankind needed more than all else. One must prepare the groundwork for cooperation among nations.

They bowed, clear down to the carpet. They hid their joy and confessed that they too were here only for the sake of that same peace. They wanted nothing other than cooperation among all nations.

He nodded and put his hand to his face.

They slipped into the adjoining room where the Chinese waited, trusting and unsuspecting. They slipped up behind him and with a bold jujitsu maneuver threw him to the floor. They held his mouth shut. They opened the Chinese's jacket, lifted up his shirt, and cut, slash, slash, Shantung from his ribs—and they were gone.

The great wise man sent a doctor into the adjoining room. He put a bandage over the Chinese's wound and comforted him by saying that it wasn't so very bad, that a man has a good many ribs, sixteen on the right, sixteen on the left, or eighteen or twenty, at any rate an incredible number, some genuine, some false, and who knows whether that one had been genuine or not. He told the same thing to the wise man from America. It was something he was glad to hear.

Not much later there came a mighty sound from some distance away. The Chinese was shaking the dust of Europe from his feet. There was a lot of dust.

And afterward he bathed in the sea, and only then did he climb aboard his ship.

The Germans Do Not Want to Sign

The American, however, still persisted at the conference, even though in the struggles he had had more than one rib broken. He had to swallow what his friend Bliss said to him in rebuke: "It cannot be right to do wrong, even for the sake of peace."

The president thought: we all know that. But it's easy for you to talk, you don't have to decide and arrange things. I am engaged in politics. Politics is the art of the possible. I want a League of Nations. Therefore I must also want the means by which to achieve that league. (What rage and suffering there were inside him.)

When they adjourned, they had managed to write 440 articles on 214 pages. That was the result of the conference, apart from frayed nerves, alienation, anger, disappointment and despair. And when they were all done and not one of them could look the other in the eyes anymore—so little could they forgive one another—then at point the German government refused even to send its negotiators.

They wanted to show the world that they knew what it was they were being offered—a dictated peace. They declared that for such a purpose they need only send an ordinary secretary, a kind of mailman, to Paris. Paris had first to storm and thunder to make clear to them just how things lay: they had been disarmed and had only an armistice agreement.

The German negotiators then set out for Paris, at their head the foreign minister, an aristocrat, Count Brockdorff-Rantzau. They appeared in massive numbers at Versailles, 150 strong and twenty-four hours too early. They were taken to the hotel Des Reservoirs.

On a very lovely May morning, the 7th of the month, twenty-seven allied and confederated nations assembled in the great hall of the Trianon Palace at Versailles and stared at Count Brockdorff-Rantzau as he entered in his black frock coat, pale, distraught, but erect, and took the seat he was shown to. Clemenceau, the tiger who had lived through the bad days of 1870/71, stood up. He had been granted the privilege of addressing him face-to-face. He said to the German, "You have asked for peace. We are ready to give you peace."

The German took a sheet of paper from his portfolio and read the remarks he had prepared. He read them in the harsh German language. He did not stand up.

"We are under no illusions about what awaits us here. We recognize the full scope of our defeat and the extent of our powerlessness. We know what immeasurable hate the world feels toward us. We have heard the frenzied cry that demands that the defeated must pay and that the defeated must be held responsible and punished. We are asked to declare our guilt. Such a confession would be a lie from my mouth. It is to be admitted that the former German government by its attitude at the Hague Peace Conference and by actions both taken and left undone during those twelve tragic days of July, 1914, contributed to the misfortune that descended upon the world. But that Germany and its people, convinced as they were that they were engaged in a defensive war, should confess that they alone are guilty—that we refuse to do."

They saw and heard this German. He was clumsy and defiant. These Germans had learned nothing.

Clemenceau rose when Count Brockdorff-Rantzau had ceased speaking. He turned his head to the right and to the left and peered out from under his bushy white eyebrows.

As the German slipped his sheet of paper into his portfolio (read what you like, we know you for what you are), he growled, "Does anyone wish to make any further remarks? Does anyone wish to speak? If not, I hereby declare the session closed."

That was the shining day in May at Versailles, May 7th.

The Germans Protest

The treaty was 214 pages long, the Germans were given fourteen days to read and discuss it. For fourteen days the German protests rained down upon the peace conference. The Germans now knew what was being demanded of them.

There in the manuscript they could read that the allied and confederate powers accused Wilhelm II von Hohenzollern, the former German kaiser, not of ordinary crimes found in a penal code, but of an assault on international morality and the sanctity of treaties. For which reason, Holland, to which he had fled to escape punishment, was to deliver him over to trial by a court consisting of five judges to be named by the five great powers most directly concerned.

The territorial demands made of them were already known to the Germans more or less. Return of Alsace-Lorraine, areas of Schleswig-Holstein, Upper Silesia and so on.

But they also learned from the treaty that they were to hand over the Koran of Caliph Othman to the King of Hejaz. Moreover the skull of a certain Sultan Okvava was to be given to the English government. And the French government demanded back the flags that had been taken from its army in 1870/71. The Belgians wanted the beautiful tryptich with the scenes "The Adoration of the Lamb" and "The Last Supper."

While they waited, the American walked about looking ashen. The lost battle would give him no rest. But there was nothing more to be done now. They were all at the end of their strength.

The Germans demanded an extension, were given it, demanded yet another extension, were given it. There were some minimal changes made in the draft. Meanwhile the many small nations and states floundered about, especially those that had only just been called into life by the Fourteen Points. With what savagery these homunculi carried on. They did what great powers do, they fought over boundaries, it was a boundless struggle over boundaries. There was the Rumanian Bratianu, the Pole Paderewski, the Czech Beneš, each with his company of historians, economists and strategists. The Czechs did battle with the Poles over the mining areas of Cieszyn. The Yugoslavs and Rumanians both demanded the same region of Banat. Wonderful old Venizelos was enchanted by Constantinople and Asia Minor and wanted to have them, plus Cyprus, Thrace and North Epirus, they all seemed so Greek to him, and after all he was the only Greek at the conference and he ought to know. Belgium believed it would recuperate better still if it had Luxembourg and the left bank of the Schelde. The Armenians wanted to be freed of the Turkish yoke and thought that could best be done if they took over the six ostensibly Armenian provinces of Turkey, which would then be rounded out with the Armenian Republic in the Caucasus and a harbor at Alexandretta.

People could stand it in Paris no longer. The Germans would not stop protesting. Their counterproposals, which they presented on May

29th, covered no less than 434 typed pages. They could be indulged no further. Things must be brought to a conclusion.

On June 20th, Wilson too had had enough and would permit no further petitions and let the others have their way, and Marshal Foch was given authority to march on Berlin if Germany did not sign within three days.

Scapa Flow

A monstrous action by the Germans alarmed the Allies in Paris two days before the deadline.

The great German naval fleet, impounded since the armistice at Scapa Flow near the naval station of Admiral Jellicoe, was sunk by its own German crew on June 21st, apparently at the order of their officers and certainly not without permission from the Germans. Only the destroyer *Baden* and five light cruisers were left. And the French flags from the war of 1870/71, which were to be handed over according to treaty, were burned in Berlin.

The Germans Capitulate

On June 23rd, at 5:00 P.M., the flags on the hotels Crillon, Majestic and Astoria were raised. The Germans had yielded, following a change of cabinet in Berlin that interested no one.

Scheidemann had proclaimed in the constituent assembly in Berlin, "The world has lost one illusion more, the one bound up with the name of Wilson."

Ebert: "It is a dreadful awakening. They lulled us to sleep with promises."

In Paris the German representative had it written into the record that the German Reich yielded to superior force and would sign, but without waiving its own interpretation of the conditions of peace that had been imposed upon it.

The American maintained his calm expression when informed of the capitulation of the Germans and their manner of expressing their submission. He did not know what troubled and tormented him more, the Germans who thought that even after the brutalities of the war they could still speak in such a tone, or his friends who permitted the Germans an apparent right to make such a racket.

When the results were in and the American declared that on the very day of the signing of the treaty he would depart, the French president arranged another gala dinner in his honor at the Elysée Palace.

Times had changed. To think how they had driven then from the Bois de Boulogne down the Champs Elysées and been greeted in the festival hall among those red and white roses! But when the evening of the formal dinner came, people waited at the Elysée Palace for the American presidential couple in vain. White was called in, they sent House to him. He wrung his hands when Wilson refused to come. House said, "What will the public think?"

But the great man of reason had had it. He sat at his desk blowing puffs of air and shook his head. "No, I'm not going. I'll be damned if I'll go."

He sat at his own supper table and said not a word all evening.

The Signing of the Treaty and Departure

On June 28th they convened in the Hall of Mirrors at Versailles.

The long hall had already seen one victor, the king of Prussia who had had himself proclaimed German kaiser here in 1871 after his triumph over France. June 28th had been chosen as the fifth anniversary of Sarajevo, the assassination of the Austrian grand duke.

At three in the afternoon the German representatives were led in, a Herr Müller and a Herr Bell. The treaty with its fifteen parts and 440 articles—of which the first part was the covenant of the League of Nations—lay on the table. The Germans appended their signature.

President Wilson, because his nation's name, America, began with the first letter of the alphabet, was the first to sign after the Germans. In his hand he held the golden pen presented to him at the Paris city hall. On it one could read: "The French people present the American president this pen, so that with it he may sign a just, humane and lasting peace."

Wilson had himself under control. With a smile he bared his strong white teeth as they led him up to the document and showed him the place where his name, as the representative of the United States, was to be set. For a moment he closed his eyes as he stood back up again: may this document, if it does not embody peace, at least represent a major step on the road to peace.

While he sat in his chair again and waited—he saw them each walk up like a file of geese to the document, all of them who yesterday had wrangled over the booty and tomorrow would flay one another again—he was overwhelmed and had to hold his head in his hands. How differently he had imagined this moment from over there in America. So rejoice all of you, you have what you want. You're happy. May God help us all.

So I shall journey back to America. That is the task you've laid upon me. They will pursue me with their cries—I abandoned my principles. I was a traitor.

At 3:40 P.M., the cannons were fired.

A few hours later the president, with his wife and small party, were sitting in the train on the way to Brest.

A farewell to the French authorities. A telegram from King George of England. "In this glorious hour when this long war among nations is crowned by a triumphant peace with justice, law and freedom, I send my greetings to you and to a great America."

The gentle colonel House accompanied the president on board the ship. Bad news from America. The treaty pleased no one. Wilson's opponents had the upper hand. House advised the president to handle his opponents in a conciliatory fashion.

The president (conciliation, mollification—how much conciliation do they still demand of me?) shook his emphatically. "No. We shall gain nothing if we do not fight."

The mild-mannered House heard this with sadness. He had a foreboding of bad things to come.

The great man of reason looked back at the continent from the ship.

He had arrived on a Friday, the 13th.

The Struggle for Peace

Wilson prepares himself for the final battle. He falls clad in full armor.

Wilson Falls Clad in Full Armor

A broken warrior returned home.

He was not talkative aboard ship. There was a raging within him.

Narrow-minded, egotistical and base politicians—the whole lot. Instead of leading their people, they set themselves to defending old, backward notions—boundaries, the dregs of history. I should have appealed to the people directly. But they would not let me near the people. And finally the people themselves, these excited masses, and particularly these peoples of the Balkans, how could they know what they need. As if a physician were to ask the patient how he should be treated.

It did not help Wilson to close those heavy, dark green curtains behind him in his bedroom. Sound sleep would not come.

How peculiar that he had the same dream several times in succession, echoes of a biblical sense he had been confronted with the very first night. Jesus was in the temple, the Pharisees brought a woman to him, an adulteress, set her in their midst and said to Jesus, "According to law she should be stoned. What sayest thou?" They were tempting him. He sat there, stooped down and with his finger wrote in the sand. Then he stood up and answered, "He that is without sin among you, let him first cast a stone at her." And again he stooped down and wrote in the sand. And they went out one by one without saying a word, the eldest leaving first. The woman stood there unmoved in the middle. Jesus was alone with her. He stood up, saw her and asked her, "Where are those thine accusers? Hath no man condemned thee?" She answered, "No." Then Jesus said, "Neither do I condemn thee. Go and sin no more."

The sight of the sinful woman standing there unmoved in the room awaiting sentence—what was there about it that fascinated him? That was the scene, it seemed to be a sign—and yet told him nothing.

627

The scene said: what does it look like inside you, proud man, great man of reason? Judge not, lest ye be judged.

But he did not hear.

America Wants to Be Left in Peace

It was now July. Heat hovered over Washington. The president has been gone from the country for six months. He arrived on July 9th, and already on the 10th he had conveyed the treaty to the Senate, and the Foreign Affairs Committee went to work.

Rich and proud, secure behind its wall of water, America stood off alone to one side. It looked with contempt across to a Europe that could not manage its own affairs.

No one believed that the Germans would obey the treaty. People said the Germans had signed it only to break it, like liars with tongue in cheek and fingers crossed.

Lodge was waiting for the president; in hopes of making his opponent look ridiculous, he would say, "Wilson's erudition, hah! Only once did Professor Wilson wander into the fields of mythology, only to mistake Antaeus for Hercules."

Lodge preached a sermon in the Senate in August of 1918. "No peace which satisfies Germany in any way whatever can please us. There can only be a dictated peace. If we negotiate a peace, then we have lost the war and leave Germany back where we started."

And so now they stormed the treaty with amendments and reservations. The American Senate knew nothing of the untold labor that had been put into the treaty. There was no end to the committee sessions.

In the middle of August the president invited the Foreign Affairs Committee to the White House, and in the blazing heat submitted to a three-hour interrogation. He argued with Harding and Borah. The Republicans Taft, Root and Hughes were in favor of ratifying the treaty, but—they did not want to divide their party.

Wilson's tension and excitement grew. He had escaped the heavy bombardment of the European statesmen and now he had to defend— why lie about it—an imperfect and flawed treaty.

When on August 19th the Senate did not reach the necessary majority in its deliberations, Wilson came to a decision. He declared, "I must go to the people." He wanted now to appeal to a badly informed nation, to make it better informed.

He said (I cannot be stopped, the cause is greater than anything to do with me), "The treaty I have brought back and that we fought for in Paris to the utmost of our powers is the work of men. It has its weaknesses, like everything we do. It is open to improvement. Not, however,

by unilateral action by us, and at the moment not at all. The treaty cannot be written anew. Nor can we simply throw it out and let Europe go its own way. The millions who fell in battle over there would rise up and leave our souls no peace."

Again conference upon conference. Amendments were retracted, and then replaced by others, new reservations were added. Wilson's nervous tension did not abate.

On weekends Mrs. Wilson could sometimes get him to sit calmly in an armchair, not even allowing him to read. They looked at pictures, souvenirs of France. Then he would relax. They talked and laughed, about the odd French countess, for example, who lived on Boulevard St. Germain and who would have loved to receive the first lady but was bothered by the fact that Mrs. Wilson was after all a commoner—until it was ascertained that among Mrs. Wilson's ancestors there was a real princess, an Indian one, from a family of Indian princes. They talked about the funny, excitable chef du protocole. Despite their arguments, Wilson had a liking for Clemenceau and that black cap of his. His wife suggested that he had become an even worse pessimist than he already was on account of his eczema—always having to walk around like that with those gray cotton gloves on.

Once Wilson sighed, "I am worried about the French. I hope the Germans can deal with their militarists. But if not, if not. We must have a League of Nations. That's why I pray for it. We must have it. We must stand by one another."

Another time he said, "I have a different view of Europe now than before, not such a lovely, idealistic one as before, but a more human one. Europe is a terribly human continent. Maybe I should have taken some reasonable senator or other along after all."

"You were afraid they would get in the way."

"And interfere. But I learned things over there. The desperate fear of the French—yes, if only we had the Rhine between us and these Germans. Lloyd George is unruffled. England is not afraid, and that is easy to understand. Ever since Lincoln freed us from our own little national difficulties—and they can be so dreadful—it is hard for us to put ourselves in their shoes. I can't forget what Clemenceau recounted about 1870/71, and it was phenomenal how he handled himself during the war. Even the generals admitted it. A country is fortunate to have a man like that. But where will they find another when things get difficult? They can't depend on the miracle of the Battle of the Marne. When good fortune comes, you have to hold fast to it. Otherwise it becomes mere accident and brings no results. Just look at art. An artist like Michelangelo is a rarity in this world, one among the millions born in a generation—and how many generations must pass before that particular one? What he created, however, remains. It can remain because it is made of stone or painted. The centuries preserve it. They know how he was an unbelievable stroke of luck and that mankind must profit from it. But what happens with the moments of genius in history? How do we hold fast to them? How can we make use of them? Such a moment is here now."

The Senate did not alter its position. The president, just as he had battled against passions and short-sightedness in Paris, took up the battle against the egoism and indifference of the American people. The point was, now that the Senate had failed, to bring the facts to the American people. There, when no longer opposed by the maliciousness of Lodge and his confederates, he would be understood.

Dr. Grayson and Mrs. Wilson wanted to stop him. They knew how things stood with him—every hour of the day they saw that gaunt yellow-gray face with its deeply engraved lines. How the man had aged in the last year. His tired eyes quivered and twitched. Grayson spoke of the awful heat. It was out of the question for the president to take off now on a journey of several weeks, wearying himself with daily speeches. He was demanding superhuman things of himself, and all that after the nerve-shattering conferences in Europe.

But the great man of reason felt especially good. His new plan revitalized him. Yes, that was the thing: to speak directly to the people. This time no one would obstruct him. The League of Nations can only be understood and created by the people of a nation. It was not an idea for parliamentarians, but for the great, simple masses. It was a crusade, against the corrupt governments who were responsible for all backwardness.

The president clapped his doctor on the shoulder. "You want to stop me, do you doctor? Who are you talking to? Would you want to stop a doctor from going to his patients? Really, my own health is of no importance when it comes to the security of the world as a whole. You must understand that. If this treaty that I went to Europe for is not ratified by the Senate, then you must understand that the entire war was fought in vain. And the consequences are immense. A whole series of wars will follow. But I promised our soldiers when I called them to arms that this would be a war to end all wars. If I do not succeed with this treaty, I'll no longer be able to look them in the face. And your advice is, spare yourself, Mr. President. Why me? Why just me?"

And meanwhile there were times when his pulse was weak and he had to have camphor injections. But he stuck to his guns. "I shall present my cause to the American people."

He said, "My cause."

The Mayflower

A train was equipped for the president, the *Mayflower*.

A journey of four weeks was planned. They set out on September 3rd. The president was accompanied by his wife, his doctor and his secretary, Tumulty. Over a hundred reporters and photographers were dragged along. They moved out across the blazing hot country.

The president had proved himself with a great many documents. He spoke for the League in Indiana and in St. Louis. He forged on through the Dakotas, Montana, Oregon.

No one could ever say that this nation was nothing but a wilderness of greed, indifference and egoism, if only on account of this one man, who, though unsteady on his legs, would not lay aside his armor. He refused to speak in Chicago. Because the city had elected a man named William Hale Thompson as mayor for a second time, something the president declared might have been a mistake the first time, but the second time was simply proof of political decadence.

He spoke in Pueblo.

"Again and again, my fellow citizens, mothers who lost their sons in France have come to me and, taking my hand, shed tears upon it, not only, but they have added 'God Bless you, Mr. President!' Why, my fellow citizens, should they pray God to bless me? I advised the Congress of the United States to create the situation that led to the death of their sons. I ordered their sons overseas. I consented to their sons' being put in the most difficult parts of the battle line, where death was certain, as in the impenetrable difficulties of the forest of Argonne. Why should they weep upon my hand and call down the blessings of God upon me? Because they believe that their boys died for something that vastly transcends any of the immediate and palpable objects of the war."

The president warned of the danger of new wars. Wars would become even bloodier. All the wars from 1793 until 1914 taken together had cost the lives of six million people. This last war had killed eight million.

The hope of these eight million was: no more war. Their last will and testament was: a League of Nations.

Was Wilson seated on the famous horse Rocinante and wandering aimlessly as a new Don Quixote through the American countryside, among its mountains, across its plains and deserts of cactus, riding his nag to do battle with windmills that would toss him into the air? That is how the critics of his nation saw it, the professionals, the old hands.

That is how the godforsaken always view the nobler men they cannot endure.

He had been in Europe and had seen what they all had not seen: the icy, taciturn German, Count Brockdorff-Rantzau at Versailles, the philistines Müller and Bell, nurturing vengeance in their hearts and yielding only to force, signing, but all the while determined to go back on their word. He had seen the fervent hatred of old Clemenceau, whose land had been ravaged by the Germans three times in one century. He had learned of France's fear of a new invasion. He had seen the English who swore by their island and their navy. And the nationalism of the Balkan peoples. And America stood between them and had to remain there because there were now only world wars. And they thought, the Americans, his countrymen, that they only had to slam the door behind them as if it had nothing to do with them. As if their own house could never be blown sky high. But they did not want to believe that. After their victory of yesterday, such a fear could not even arise today.

A League of Nations, a League of Nations, how could you fire people with that idea! They are children, easily moved, easily inspired by agitators for this, that and everything. They will go to war for most any reason. Why could one not also inspire them for a good cause, for their own salvation?

It was not easy. In many cities no hands stirred to clap after his speech. And sometimes he would become aware—and the awareness was still more painful than the reception—how very much everything he said sounded as if it were from the past, had been outlived, when only a year ago the cannons had thundered in France and Americans had fallen by the thousands.

What did the masses think of this wandering preacher from Washington with his propaganda about a League of Nations? He wanted to bind their fate to that of unknown, distant and deranged nations. But people here were glad that they hardly knew the names of those nations.

They asked questions. He had to make it clear to people that there was truly nothing in the treaty about annexations and reparations. (He had to keep silent about the blank check for debts that the treaty did contain. But that did not bother him now.)

He understood, and it did not please him, what the frenzied applause meant when at one point he cried, "If this treaty is ratified and becomes operative, never again will American boys in khaki be sent across the ocean."

He held up well. He felt surer of himself as the journey went on. How necessary this educational trip had been. Even if the treaty was a botch, the League would make up for all that. His headaches grew grimmer. Grayson could not help him. He had to tax his voice terribly. Bad news came from Washington; his aide, Lansing, had let it be known that he was in no way a supporter of the idea of a League of Nations. That almost brought Wilson to a collapse. The man had stood next to him in Paris. He had apparently been frustrating the work in Paris as well. There was indeed no one to help.

In the colosseum in St. Louis, in Des Moines, in Montana, in the states of Washington, Utah, California, in Los Angeles his message aroused a storm of enthusiasm. The masses began to welcome him more and more. His success alarmed his opponents. He was intending to go to New England as well, to defeat Lodge on his own ground.

In Denver he was at his height. He made a speech in the morning and talked about France and how he had visited a military cemetery and of the forest of crosses he had seen. He extolled the French people who had been liberated again by America. "There is an ideal for which the American people will ever rise and stretch out its hands—for the imperishable truths of justice, of freedom and of peace. We have acknowledged these truths and let ourselves be led by them. And so we will lead other nations out onto the meadows and pastures of peace, of a peace such as the world has never dreamed before."

Then they came to Kansas. During the afternoon Dr. Grayson had the train stop along the way because the president wanted to take a walk. They walked for an hour in the fields, it was autumn, perfect peace, a wonderful soft breeze was blowing. When they climbed back into the car the president felt refreshed, and he was cheerful and relaxed during supper.

But during the night he knocked on the door of Mrs. Wilson's compartment and then sat on his bed for hours, looking exhausted, holding his head and groaning softly. He was suffering from an unbearable headache. Nothing could be done to help him. He tried to stand up. He couldn't, he was too weak.

The president's secretary was notified and counsel was taken. They rode on to Wichita. He made a last effort, shaved, but then he simply could not stand on his feet any longer.

The journalists buzzed the news by telephone. The president had collapsed.

The train traveled the 700 miles back to Washington in forty-eight hours. On September 28th the *Mayflower* halted in Washington. Wilson could still walk erect to the car waiting for him at Union Station.

Only after several days did the illness become clear. A weakness on the left side became evident, he lost feeling in his left hand, it hung there motionless.

And then on the morning of October 20th he lay unconscious in the bathroom. He was paralyzed on one side.

From his sickbed he fought for the League of Nations, for his treaty. On Jackson's birthday he dictated a speech for the Democratic party; he had not yet given up all hope.

He was informed about the reservations attached to the treaty. They expected him to approve them. He said, "No. It were a thousand times better to fall in battle than to defile the flag with dishonorable compromises." He shoved the paper aside. "Changes in the treaty are not possible. Otherwise any of the other signatories could claim the same right."

The reservations were rejected by the Senate. On March 9, 1920, the treaty itself, just as he had presented it, was sent back to the president by the Senate. It had not found a two-thirds majority.

That was the end.

The great man of reason hid his agony. His condition had improved. He was told he would recover. In Paris, Pasteur, the great serologist, had suffered from the same illness, but he had recovered completely. It was not bad to hear all that. It was good. But his pain was not centered there.

Because one way or the other it was all over.

He had fought bravely. He was lying on the ground and still he fought. He had not followed some chimera. His idea of peace was a useful one, a reasonable, a logical one.

It was the first great attempt to bring peace to the nations without subjugating them.

That the old governments had resisted—was no wonder. But that his own country had refused to follow him.

He had got mired down halfway home.

The paralyzed man said from his sickbed in Washington, "I was not able to do it. But the course of history will show that I was right and my country wrong."

Edith Bolling Wilson, his wife, who cared for him and was at his side, expressed his bitterness even more clearly, "The hope of mankind lies broken at the door of Mr. Lodge."

2300 S Street, Washington

The end of Thomas Woodrow Wilson.

The German Counterrevolution

Meanwhile in central Germany, in the former grand duchy of Saxe-Weimar, the German constituent assembly had completed its work.

On August 11, 1919, it published the constitution of the new German Republic, a faultless constitution, formed according to the best western models. Like a textbook, it gave its pupils goals and principles and guidelines and instructions. Friedrich Ebert, the Social Democrat from Heidelberg, was indeed elected the first president of the Reich, just as predicted there on Wilhelmstrasse by the soldier named Spiro on December 6th of the previous year. But at that time Ebert had suspected a trap and declared that it was too important a matter, that he would first have to discuss it with his colleagues. Now, however, he had been elected, they had accepted him as a model of moderation and calm, and because he seemed predestined to lead his people down the path that was prescribed by the constitution.

Slowly the prisoners of war returned to Germany. Allied troops occupied the Rhineland.

But within two years the same Friedrich Ebert, still the head of government, issued a call to the German workers as he fled in the direction of Stuttgart:

"Workers, comrades. This is a military putsch.

"The Ehrhardt Naval Division is marching on Berlin.

"We did not create a revolution so that we would now have to accept government by a band of mercenaries. We would be ashamed to act otherwise."

The Great Man of Reason Leaves Office

On July 15, 1920, the ailing American president sent out the invitations to the first session of the League of Nations in Geneva. The meeting took place on November 15th.

That morning all the church bells of Geneva rang out. A procession moved from the city hall to the Hall of the Reformation, where men were gathered for the first time to establish peace for the world.

President Wilson was awarded the Nobel Peace Prize for 1919/20, along with Leon Bourgeois, the French member of the League of Nations Committee at the peace conference.

And then it was time for Wilson to take leave of his office. On the morning of March 4, 1921, they called for him at the White House. He sat there haggard, gray and hunched over in the car next to a new gentleman, Warren Gamaliel Harding, a healthy, robust man who took pleasure in the cheers of the crowd. Wilson stared straight ahead. (I know the people. They are rid of me now.)

Her sat in the president's room of the Capitol with his wife, Dr. Grayson and his secretary, Tumulty, and waited. At about 11:30 A.M., the door opened and an erect, self-confident man entered at the head of a delegation. He had gray hair and spoke in a cold, hard voice. He reported to the man who would still be president for a few minutes more, "Mr. President, we have come to you as a delegation of the Senate to inform you that the Senate and the House have convened. We are at your disposal."

It is Henry Cabot Lodge, who has emerged as the victor in battle. Only for a second does wrath flicker in the face of the defeated man. Then he answers with a slight, obliging smile, "Senator Lodge, I thank you. I have no messsage to give them. Good morning."

The delegation withdraws. The clock strikes twelve.

Thomas Woodrow Wilson is once again a private citizen.

The Private Citizen in Washington

He lived at 2300 S Street in Washington. He chose Washington so as to be near the great libraries there, because he wanted to write a work dealing with his administration. But instead, the man who had always found it so easy to write did not get beyond the dedication, which read: "To E.B.W.—dedicated to Edith Bolling Wilson. I dedicate this book to her, because it is a book in which I have tried to interpret life, the life of a nation, and she has shown me the full meaning of life. Her heart is true and wise. She teaches and directs me by being who she is."

He did not get beyond the dedication. He had chosen government as his topic, government and the people—and he did not want to go on.

And who should appear in Washington to visit former president Wilson—like a ghost from the past—but his former companion and adversary, Georges Clemenceau, now no longer the French prime minister, also the Greek Venizelos.

Old Clemenceau looked younger than at the peace conference. He came up to Wilson and literally embraced him. It was a more honest embrace than the notorious one he had exchanged with Poincaré on the esplanade in Metz.

They chatted. Clemenceau had been there fifty-three years before as a teacher in a girls' school. It was wonderful here in America, he said, a great deal had changed since then and he wanted to come again in another fifty-three years.

He was on a lecture tour here, basically following Wilson's footsteps. He wanted—he too in vain—to convince Americans of Europe's desire for peace and of the danger of Germany. And perhaps the old man with his great bald head was here for another reason as well at the close of his life.

Because fifty-three years before, in a school in Connecticut, he had taught a girl named Mary Plummer (he was 26, she 18), and had become engaged to her. They had broken the engagement (because as an orthodox atheist he did not want a church wedding) and he had returned to France; but he came back and married her.

She accepted a simple civil ceremony at City Hall in New York. They had led a happy life for seven years, on his father's farm in the Vendée and in Paris. Yes, a happy life for Georges Clemenceau. The happiness fell apart. She bore him three children; but after seven years she left him. And that was all, and nothing stood in the way of his becoming the "tiger." And now life's close was here, and Clemenceau wandered aimlessly among the old places, gorging himself on new bitterness.

During these long months the ailing Wilson was often visited by the pastor of a neighboring church. They spoke of Wilson's parents. His father and grandfather had been preachers.

In his invalid's chair Wilson said, "My father and grandfather had the task of bringing Holy Scripture to people. That was the way, the office they employed, to educate people. It fell to me to study, to learn—and to get involved in politics. I could not keep my knowledge to myself. I admit that there is always a certain impatience and need to dominate that drive people into politics. Where, however, does the real difference lie between my way of doing things and that of my father and grandfather? They went at things from the inside, from the center. They had a smelter for melting the ancient holy truths by which they could make people fluid and mobile. We politicians don't have it so easy. We work from the outside. We break people more than we form them."

The pastor: "They awarded you the Nobel Peace Prize. That must be a great satisfaction. People have recognized what you have achieved in the cause of peace. But you are quite right—there are many others who could be awarded such a prize. It is an institution that has no end. For to tell the truth, nations do not want peace. When they are tired, they want peace for a while. Then they can't keep away from it and have to attack one another again."

Wilson: "I know. But that does not get us anywhere. We know other things about human beings, too. We have a state, laws, justice. We strive to be masters of evil. Certainly people will always want war somewhere, one way or another. They also want a great many other kinds of wickedness. They want to cheat, want to get drunk, to drug themselves. But we make laws against opium and imprison the smugglers. They want war, but it is not a matter of what they want, others have the right to speak up too. A nation must be led. It needs leadership.

"And the great misfortune is that the person who leads has the reins of power in his hands. Or worse still: he immediately possesses power. The problem of every government is the problem of responsible leadership. But in the European states government was simply the private property of a few families, or a few groups. They had taken control of 'the government' by theft or conquest. We have had the good fortune to abolish these familes of thieves who go by the name of dynasties, the Hapsburgs, Hohenzollerns, Romanovs and Osmanlis. What are the concerns of such hereditary thieves and tyrants? Do they feel themselves responsible? To whom then? Even the churches are at their service. No, they want to hold onto their power and if possible accumulate more. In those nations all that happens historically concerns these dynasties. The people are merely subsidiary. They provide soldiers, pay taxes, write poems, paint and compose music. Beneath the surface a certain civilization develops, but a lamed, deformed and distorted one, for it cannot develop its potential. It can be as peaceable as it likes, but it must go to war because at its head are the thieves and their gangs."

The pastor: "But now things have changed in Europe, at least in the major nations. People can develop in freedom now."

Wilson sighed: "The devil has been chased off, the devilry remains. Who knows what heritage the tyrants have left behind? How do you burn out what remains?" He stared ahead, thinking. "Do you know that I have often indicted myself for advocating national self-determination."

The pastor: "For that? But why?"

Wilson: "I should have lived in Europe for a few years in order to see things more clearly. What do they understand by self-determination? More nations, and still more—and the new ones have the same delusions of grandeur, are just as warlike as the old. I wanted to set them free, but so that they could unite that much the better. Because they belong together: freedom and a union of nations. But they took the one and cast away the other. Oh, I have my cares, dear friend. People will curse me for that."

"It was not your fault, Mr. Wilson. You wanted to do the right thing. You sacrificed yourself for it."

Wilson stared straight ahead, playing with the cane he held in his right hand.

"They mutilated what I did. But one way or another, I think the generations who follow us will learn from my example. For what I hoped to do cannot ultimately be stopped. They will go about it differently. The functioning of a League of Nations cannot depend on the wishes or moods or incivility of one of its members. Even a teacher in a school has a right to demand discipline. You cannot expect immediate discipline and insight, but you must not let the whole enterprise be destroyed simply because all nations are not alike.

"That is why the democracies that have created the League must not for a moment let victory slip from their hands. They have to know that a democracy without responsible leadership creates nothing but chaos. Othewise they might just as well have done without their victory.

"As president of the United States, I never allowed the rights given me by the Constitution to be taken away. And in the same way the democracies, as victors, should assume their position of responsible leadership. A discussion about mutual cooperation is no longer permissible. That is the result of the war. Because they are in possession of the valid principle that respects the dignity of man, that is of democracy, they are permitted to incorporate all nations into a natural organism. There will be no more votes as to whether one belongs to this nation or to that. The nation of tomorrow, the only one that will exist, is the global league of all peoples. There must be an end to these artificially created and perpetuated nationalities. They no longer correspond to the real world. The world has grown larger, more interconnected. Technology and science have changed everything. Politics must follow where it cannot lead. The democratic victors will have to supervise the education of the old nations and their adjustment to one another within the new framework, which is the only natural and timely one. Ah, they will have to be the victors yet again."

The pastor: "For God's sake, do you believe there will be a new war? That America will have to fight once again?"

Wilson groped for the hand of the white-haired man next to him and looked into his eyes. "We two will probably not live to see it. The nations have not yet suffered enough to want real peace. But let us speak of something else. I know that your goal, your thoughts and methods are better, higher than ours. I envy you. I remember how nobly and peacefully my father died in my house in Princeton. But do not despise our work. What we politicians do must be done, within the state, in a government, and it is unutterably laborious. We work in the cold, in mud and in rain, and everything keeps running through our fingers. We have to erect the dam against human savagery, stupid egoism and wickedness."

The pastor: "We know, dear professor, how you've worked at that since your earliest years. But how is it possible? Look at the Bible. Look at what was tried out on human beings even in ancient times. That's how man is. Only faith, humility, yes humility, will bring him any further."

The End

Wilson was still living on S Street in Washington when on August 2, 1923, the newspaperboys cried out "Extra, extra!" from the street below. And there in his room the ailing man learned that the robust man bursting with good health who had ridden next to him in the car on the way from the White House to the Capitol was no longer alive, had suddenly fallen ill in San Francisco and lay dead in Washington. He was still alive, his successor no longer lived. And the 30th president of the United States, Calvin Coolidge, was moving into the White House.

On the evening of the fifth anniversary of the armistice, Wilson has himself led down the steps, small and bent, to speak to a small group that has gathered on the street below. He holds his head on his chest, his left arm trembles. He is thin and withered, his clothes hang on him.

He speaks very softly, "I am not one of those who have the least anxiety about the triumph of the principles I have stood for. That we shall prevail is as sure as that God reigns."

Not long afterward, on Sunday, February 3, 1924, a small band of people kneel at 11:00 A.M. on S Street in Washington in front of number 2300 and pray. The church bells toll.

For the soul of the 28th president of the United States of America has departed from the battlefield of this earth.

His body is buried at Mt. St. Albans, Washington.

The Old Grim Cry for War

They have done it.

The Old Grim Cry for War

The League of Nations was formed. Soviet Russia was excluded. America excluded itself, Germany was not on hand.

Clemenceau later declared:

"I admit we did not enter this war with a plan of liberation. The czar was on our side, after all. But with the collapse of Russia, and after Brest-Litovsk, our war was transformed into a war of liberation. We were victorious.

"But piece by piece the scaffolding of peace fell apart.

"The military solidarity of the three powers, America, England and France, was rejected by America, silently abandoned by England, and both facts silently accepted by France.

"The victory had been transformed into defeat."

Lloyd George declared in 1922 that France was maintaining too many troops considering that Germany had only a small army of 100,000 men. In reality Germany offered no reasonable pretext for armament on that scale. Lloyd George bewailed a Germany that had a population as large as that of Poland, Rumania and Yugoslavia combined and possessed an army only one-seventh as strong as theirs.

On October 4, 1925, delegates from France, Belgium, Poland, Czechoslovakia and Germany met together in Locarno, Switzerland, and ratified a treaty that guaranteed the inviolability of their borders, and they swore never to attack one another.

In September 1926 Germany was admitted to the League of Nations, marking the end of military control over the Reich.

Several months later France spent seven billion francs for its defense, for the building of a steel wall that was to extend from the North Sea to the Mediterranean.

And already in February 1927 the Belgian foreign minister, Van der

Velde, raised a public outcry at the alarming rate at which Germany had begun to arm itself, stating that they were planning a rapid invasion of Belgium.

But the German minister of defense, Gessler, answered, "The intention of the nations along our borders is to attack us rapidly and to penetrate deeply within the first few days of a war."

And more and more the dagger in an iron fist rips away at the thin wall of paper, the wall of parchment that the world of peace has wrapped around itself.

The hard, strong arm is already pushing its way through the jagged hole.

And the hairy chest, the flat, sloping shoulders and the throat become visible. And this creature, half animal, half man, this gorilla with its flattened black face, with its deep-set devilish eyes beneath massive ledges of bone and its low receding brow, with teeth bared, this human animal rises up to full height.

Its eyes glitter.

A grim, bloodcurdling cry emerges from its throat, floating out over mankind, the cry of war—the raging death rattle, the triumphant howl of the unredeemed creature.